Loving Aretta

Loving Aretta

R.W. Mathis

To order additional copies of this book, contact:
Xlibris Corporation
1-888-795-4274
www.Xlibris.com
Orders@Xlibris.com
74567

Contents

This first and great work is dedicated to all the people in my life who inspired it, helped me through it and supported me while I wrote it. I love you all and will never forget you. God bless you and keep you.

Sincerely

Matt.

Fadana Presley
Aretta L. Davis
Georg A. Williams
Lisa A. Wolverton Johnson
Tonya Rodgers

Authors Note

All my life I have secretly searched for my "Retta" and never found her. During my teen years when I did and we were in school and in love, I felt indestructible. I learned a great many things about myself and the true power of that love I had for her and would carry until now as a man. My life up until I met her was a sluggish mish-mash of wasted living. I didn't care much about anything or anyone, as I was almost always alone. Sure I would try to mix and to blend like other teenage boys by going to school dances and to the skating rink, but it only ended in heart break with me usually standing alone in the dark as I watched the many couples holding each other dancing or kissing and wishing it to god that it were me. I am much older now and as I have said have learned a lot about myself as well as others and the great mystery of love. I was married twice since this book was started in may of 1995 and have four wonderful sons. I won't go into any dialogue about my former wives accept to say that they were good women in some ways and not so good in others. I was looking for the love I had with Aretta in each of them and was disappointed to find it wasn't there. I should have been surprised to find this out because a woman is an individual and singular creature all unto herself. Yes they have similarities as most things go but you have to understand that you won't find a peach orchard in a pecan patch (apples and oranges) don't go looking for something old and familiar in something new and undiscovered you'll get your feelings hurt every time. Take a woman as you find them and go from there. Or like my mom used to say (god rest her soul) don't go trying to love the one you want but love the one who loves you . . . the one you love may not love you back.

Chapter 1

Passionate Beginnings

"Hurry up! and get inside" she said closing the door quickly. "Did you hide your moped under the stairs?"

"Yeah" said Matt all excited and glad to be there.

"Mama said she'll be getting home at 10 o'clock so we'll have some time together before you have to go" said Aretta leading him into the living room and onto the couch. Matt followed her, hardly listening to a thing she said but instead was overjoyed to be there. He could only hear the beating of his heart in his ears as he looked at her. He loved her deeply and she knew it.

Matt breathed in deep as she curled up on his lap. The scent of her was intoxicating and made his pulse race. She snuggled closer to him and looked up at him. Matt felt as if he was daydreaming as he relished and took in her beauty. Her deep auburn eyes, that semi crooked smile and the neat and protective way she braided her hair to the crown of her head. Her creamy soft skin and caramel complexion was like a drug to him. She looked so angelic and sweet cradled in his arms this way.

She had the body and shape of a figure skater. She was somewhat slim but with subtle yet noticeable graceful curves. Aretta had modest breasts, somewhat small in comparison to other girls but yet satisfactory as far as Matt was concerned. She was quite a few inches shorter than Matt but was still in his opinion just the right height.

"Lori, what are you doing in there?" yelled Retta, startled by the clamor of a plastic cup bouncing all over the kitchen floor.

"I'm getting something to drink!" she yelled back.

"Well don't drink all the "kool-aid" because you know how momma gets when she doesn't have anything to drink with her dinner."

"Okay."

"Man she can be such a hog at times! She just got finished eating before you got here" fussed Aretta getting comfortable once again.

Matt just sat there smiling down at her.

"What?" she asked looking at him curiously.

"What do you mean . . . what?"

"I mean why are you staring at me like that?"

"Don't you know?" he said drawing her closer and tightening his arms around her.

"No . . . Not really" said Retta meeting his advance.

"I love you baby!"

"Oh, I knew that already" she said nuzzling his cheek with hers and gently kissing his neck. "Then how come you said you didn't know?"

"I just love to hear you say it" she said looking up and smiling at him sweetly.

"And I love you too Puddin" she said squeezing him tighter.

They sat quietly kissing, caressing and holding each other in the darkened living room. The only light was from the moon and it was glowing bright and full tonight. The iridescent glow it cast through the window gave the room an enchanting and sultry atmosphere. A small oscillating fan on the television in front of them brought in the crisp night air as it hummed quietly to and fro. "Retta when are you gonna tell your mother about us?" "It's been almost a year and a half now."

"I know" sighed Retta, leaning closer to him as if she were afraid of him slipping away.

Anxiety began to course through her as she thought of all the amount of time that she had let pass and had not told her mother about her and Matt's relationship. It was no big thing in the large scheme of things as relationships go when you stop to think about it. Retta was 15 and a half and Matt was 17, which is thought to be a proper age split between girls and boys dating in the early 1980's.

Unfortunately, the thing that made Retta and Matt's situation so vicarious and somewhat difficult was her mother was a jealous woman and did not want anybody pawing all over her girls.

"Are you ashamed of me?" he asked with a slight croak in his voice, thinking maybe he shouldn't have said that.

"No! How could you ever think that when you know how much you mean to me!" she said sitting up almost shouting. "Matt I've never loved anyone the way I love you" (come to think of it, I haven't loved anybody at all) she thought in passing almost about to smile in spite of herself but thought better of it.

Matt thought he saw something in her eyes but just dismissed it as paranoia and nodded in agreement with her platitude.

For a minute or so, he just sat quietly and picked at the lint on her sweater as if it was the most important thing on his mind but it wasn't. Matt started to say something but she touched a delicate finger to his lips and shook her head slowly then embraced him and kissed him deeply with total abandon as if knowing what he would say and gave him the answer.

"Ooh! I'm tellin!" sang Lori from just around the corner. This was Retta's 8 year old little sister. Lori stood there half way between the kitchen and the living room holding her cup to her cherry stained lips snickering and grinning from ear to ear.

"So, I don't care!" "Why don't you just go on in the room and play with your dolls or something!" hissed Retta.

"I don't have to, this is my house too!" she protested pouting and stomping off into her mother's room in a dignified and defiant posture as if to say, "I can go anywhere I want to."

"Come on Matt, let's go in my room, then we can have some privacy from little miss busy body!" she said springing from the couch and pulling a surprised Matt with her.

Matt was all for it and in fact was just about to suggest that very same thing but held off not wanting to appear too eager or one-track minded. Retta led him hurriedly into her room with a flourish bred of pure defiance and the justification that comes of being an older sister. Matt glanced back one last time before closing the door and saw Lori peering devilishly around the corner at him and grinning. She looked somewhat like a little woodland elf with her blue and pink footy pajamas and her round and rotund little tummy that always seemed to be hungry.

As they sat on her bed, Retta casually reached over to her nightstand and lightly flipped on her little boom box. The song that was playing just happened to be their favorite song, "Open Arms." From the moment it began to play something sweet, familiar began to fill them both, and they just stared at each other with slow building passion and anticipation. Matt stood up taking her hands and pulled her to him. His hands were shaky and trembling with anxious anticipation as he held her close. The sweet smell of her hair and the unbelievable softness of her body were getting to him and he began to tremble in spite of himself. Retta noticed and smiled to herself and felt secure within that she could still make her man fall apart at the touch of her hand or the closeness of her warm body.

Matt was in rapture and felt ecstatic.

"Retta?"

"Yes Matt?"

"Do you think it will always be like this?" she raised her head from his chest and looked up at him with confident love swept eyes and just stared into his for a moment. She didn't say anything but then again she didn't have to because at that moment Matt knew all he needed to know. Retta would be his and he would be hers forever. As the song began to fade away, they just stood and relished the closeness and warmth of each other's embrace.

Random thoughts and feelings of desire and lovemaking began to flood Matt's mind. He could see the two of them in his mind eye standing there nude and inter-twined as electric highlights danced around their bodies. This stimulated Matt even more. Retta's breathing was getting shallow and faint as her own mind and body caught fire as well. She didn't look at Matt but just slowly parted from him and led him back to the bed again.

Matt was excited now and the thoughts of what were about to happen scorched him like hot steam. He wanted her, needed her every fiber and muscle strained against him to be inside of her. "Come to me lover" she said in a whisper as she eased herself further onto the bed.

Matt followed her like a bull led by a nose ring and never took his eyes off her for a second. Retta lay sensuously with her arms behind her head like a Greek goddess. Nothing more was said, instead they became acutely aware of each other and the room as it spun and expanded further away the closer they drew to each other. He could see the passion building in her eyes as her breathing came harder and slower making her breasts rise and fall much deeper now. Retta's silk blouse was threatening to burst open as the pressure from her firm and full breasts pushed against it. She slowly began unbuttoning it, taking her time, and watching Matt's response to the slow process.

Retta undid each button painstakingly slow as Matt squirmed and hovered in painful silence not wanting to break the spell but wishing she would get to the last one so he could feast on what she'd been hiding there.

"Do you want me Matt?" she asked coyly once she'd undid the last button.

Matt's only thought before tearing off his own shirt was, "Are you kidding me or what?" He was glad he'd worn a pullover as he tossed it on the floor, and then began clumsily working off his pants and totally forgetting his shoes. Retta just grinned at how his eagerness had made him so clumsy and forgetful. But then again she quickly became animated herself when she saw the bulge of his penis in his shorts.

"Oh Shit!" she thought then quickly unbuttoned and scooted out of her pants but not as haphazardly as Matt. Retta slid them down quickly, revealing to Matt's unwavering eyes, her radiant flesh. Matt moved in quickly to help her take them off being the gentleman that he was. After accomplishing this, he reached back again to help her remove her lacy panties.

"DAAAMN!" his mind screamed as he could finally see what he had been hoping to get closer to than just grinding for the majority of the time they had been together. He was still a little tender from their last interlude and could swear he'd left the imprint of the zipper of his jeans on his member. He still couldn't believe that she was actually going to finally make love with him!

Retta notice his hesitance and sudden shock at finally gaining access to her most prized possession, her virtue. She felt a little guilty about making him wait for so long knowing how much he truly did love her but she had to be sure. She didn't want to wind up like so many of the girls she knew or heard about at school. Now recalling the reason for her perceived ill treatment of Matt for so long it reinforced her resolve and made what she was about to do all the more profound and right. Not to mention her own hormones were at their wits end to and she had an itch she was definitely going to scratch this night.

Matt, now just about naked couldn't take his eyes off of her long enough to complete the task. The sight and fullness of her sensual pubic mound was such a shock to his system it immediately filled him with such unbridled lust that he could swear that his penis had grown another two inches beyond max. His hands were a little shaky as he moved to touch her. The excitement he felt was almost too much to bear as he beheld Retta's beauty and vibrancy. He was so caught up in his own emotions and what he was feeling that he almost didn't hear her calling to him.

"Make love to me Matt" she whispered seeing how much he truly wanted her.

Retta positioned herself so she could receive him completely. Matt got into bed beside her after shedding his last piece of clothing. Instead of mounting her directly, for some reason he himself couldn't figure except to say he was taking his time and wasn't about to rush this special moment. As bad as he wanted her he still had to put on a jimmy and began rifling through his pants to find one he'd placed there earlier in the hopes that tonight would be the night.

"Damn!" he muttered to himself when he couldn't find it.

"What's the matter baby?" asked Retta feeling a little concerned and annoyed that he might not have a condom.

"I don't have a condom baby" he said in the most distraught way.

"I thought I did but I guess I left it at home" he said in a defeated but hopeful tone, hopeful that she would still let him play without one, but the look in her eye told him different and sent an involuntary chill down his spine and made him quiver.

Retta sat with her legs and arms folded in a most forbidding way like a checkpoint on the East Berlin wall. She was getting anxious and feeling a little embarrassed at the same time. Anxious because she wanted what he wanted . . . probably even more but at the same time she felt embarrassed at the thought that she too had prepared for this night and thought it un-lady-like to have done so.

So there they were two sexually frustrated teenagers with a problem and Retta was getting all the more anxious with every moment and the thought of Matt forgetting his condom was downright criminal!. Matt felt like a chest x-ray, as Retta just silently sat and burned his soul with those intense auburn eyes. He sighed deep, shrugged in resignation and mentally prepared to retrieve his clothes.

Retta scowled at him a moment longer, flashing him with those eyes he'd come to love and fear when she was angry. Suddenly they began to soften, she gave him a most pleasing smile then reached into the headboard of her bed and produced a little round compact filled with little white, and pink pills, Matt raised an eyebrow at the funny looking things but said nothing.

"You're lucky I prepare for other peoples failures lover" she said wiggling the packet in front of his face then quickly putting them away. Matt felt a little embarrassed that his girl had to cover his bets and on a night that was most important. Matt figured that the odds in getting laid now was slim because she didn't appear to be too turned on anymore but instead just kind of lounged with her hands behind her head and her legs crossed most languidly.

"Damn! How am I gonna get her fired up again?" he thought. He didn't want her to lose any of the fire she had been recently smoldering him. He finally thought of a way, he leaned over placing a leg between hers slightly bent so he could feel the rich warmth of the body against him and to give himself a minute to calm down. Matt then began lightly kissing his way down her tummy going lower and lower until he reached her pubic mound.

"You're not gonna get me that easy "Mr. Man" in fact you better not stop if you know what's "SSSS!" good for you." She thought to herself as she began to swoon at his new maneuver and just looked at him and spread her legs a little to accommodate him and wondering just how far he would go being he'd never done this before.

Matt looked up briefly without disengaging to see how much his attempt to jump start her was affecting her. He saw that her face was awash with an exquisite pleasure he's never seen on her face. She bit her lip and began to suck her index finger. Matt raised an eyebrow and would have grinned if his mouth weren't currently tied up into other things. He let the tip of his tongue glide ever so slowly down the inside of her thigh and up to the very tip of her vaginal lips then waited as he could feel her tremble beneath him. Retta's mind was set ablaze with flashes of light, color and feelings that threatened to wrench her body like a washcloth.

"God what is this man doing to me!" SSSS . . . MMM . . . sigh! Oh shoot! She whispered as Matt's tongue penetrated her and teased her from top to bottom. Retta couldn't decide whether to hold his head to stop him or the bed, to keep from coming off it; as wave after wave of pleasure laced lightning shot through her entire body threatening to tear her apart. Retta decided to just give up on resistance and spread herself wide open to give him maximum access to her. She could feel herself twitching with desire as her juices ran free while Matt's tongue slowly, expertly, yet viciously parted her, entered her and traveled up and down her clitoris and then deeper.

"MATT! MATT!" she whispered, almost yelled. Retta was bucking like a horse and calling, begging, pleading for him to stop but not to stop all at the same time. For a minute, he thought she was going to pass out. Matt decided to raise the temperature one last degree and began to suckle her clitoris, the response was instantaneous, and Retta grabbed his head by the ears and pulled like she was in a tug-o-war and thrust her hips into his face at the same time as if she was trying to recycle him. At that moment, she let go, grabbed her pillow, and screamed into it like a banshee as her legs locked around Matt's head and she just convulsed and convulsed again and again, her back arched like a bow to the point of breaking. She gave into the feeling totally with a harlots abandon and zero shame.

She had never felt anything so powerful and erotic in her life and it drove her wild. She could feel it from the deepest place in her body all the way to her toes and back. The whole episode all 5 minutes of it made for a really neurotic and surrealistic scene and threatened to consume the both of them. Matt releasing her and withdrawing slowly, was feeling hornier than he ever had. He kissed his way to her dry and hungry mouth and kissed her. They kissed slowly at first then it grew feverish and they groped, felt and caressed each other from head to toe not leaving any areas unmolested or unexplored on each other's body. Matt could see how much he had drained her with his new trick and as much as he wanted to explore her depths, he felt it only right to give her a chance to catch her breath.

Retta still on fire rolled over putting Matt on his back. As she did this her crotch brushed passed his thigh and came to rest atop his swollen member as she straddled him. Matt sucked in hard as his penis rose to the occasion to meet her. He was so eager not wanting to take her too fast and then blow it without satisfying her or himself properly. He decided to try talking to her and whispered endearments to her. She grabbed Matt kissing him even hungrier and harder than before.

"Oh! Hell, she wants it as bad as I do, so maybe it won't be too bad if I blow it sooner than later" he thought. Matt could feel her lust for him in her movements as she sucked his neck and probed his ears with her tongue driving him nuts. For added effect she glided up and down the length of his shaft not letting him penetrate her just yet wanting to maximize the moment and also return the favor for what he'd done to her only moments ago. Retta's movements became even more urgent and demanding as she ground her crotch into his and enticed Matt to enter her.

"Now! Matt!" "Please, now baby! Sss yes . . . now!" Matt could smell her musky dampness and feel his own desires building beyond his control at the scent of her. His penis begged and yearned to be inside of her so bad it hurt. Matt rolled her over on her back once more. She parted her legs willingly inviting him to take full control of her. She reached for him and guided him into the center of her wetness. Matt felt himself jerk viciously when he slipped into the center of the silky fluids and creamy soft flesh deeper still.

"Damn!" he muttered to himself at climaxed too soon.

"Oh well, so I won't get a full blast but what she don't know won't hurt" and with that he plunged deeper into her.

"Oh Matt!" she moaned breathlessly with pleasure at his command of her. Retta, being a virgin, the pain was sharp and unexpected but lasted only a moment as wave after wave of rapture took its place.

"Yes, baby, take me now!" she begged and urged as the two of them churned and gyrated into each other viciously. Retta begged for more as he held her hips and controlled her with each pelvic thrust. She just held on tight and marveled at how expertly and rhythmically he drove into her again and again.

"I love you Matt" she breathed then joined him in his drive to ecstasy.

Matt tried hard to slow his actions so he wouldn't come again too quickly and really mess things up. Matt surmised from her momentum she still had some mileage to go before she got hers. He pulled out slowly and worked the tip of his penis up and down between her swollen vaginal lips teasing her and preparing to lunge long and deep once more . . .

"Retta! Its 9:30" yelled Lori through the door. The shock of her voice was so sudden that it made Matt miss his mark and inadvertently deflected upwards ejecting his load all over Retta's tummy as it recoiled again and again. Matt grabbed the wayward thing and tried to strangle it but that only made it worse and he found himself helping it along to the shock and amazement of Retta who just kind of bridged on her elbows and stared humorously at the strained but dedicated look on Matt's face while he emptied himself all over her.

"Lori go away!" she yelled, now angry and disheartened at Matt's premature explosion. It felt all warm and silky on her skin but only served to make her angrier as she'd wanted to feel it inside of her not on her.

"But momma will be home soon!" she protested outside the door.

"And what are y'all doing in there anyway? It's too quiet" She said with muffled lips to the door.

"None of your business!" yelled Retta.

"Damn! She makes me sick sometimes, I can't stand her little butt. Matt, I'm sorry baby" she said cradling his face in her hands.

"Maybe next time, okay?" Matt just nodded half-heartedly and smiled as the words rang in his ears like a school bell. He could feel himself deflating mentally and physically from the loss of sexual pressure that now covered them both.

"Damn baby!" he pleaded.

"Can't we do it just a little longer? I mean . . . we hardly got started" "Are you sure about that lover?" said Retta arching an eyebrow and smiling sweetly at him with a hand held up that clearly showed the glistening evidence of their efforts and his poor aim.

"Sigh! I guess your right on that point" he said feeling more stupid than he could remember.

"But can't we still get in a little quickie anyway?" he urged further. Retta just looked at him sideways and gave him a most peculiar expression. This told him her answer in a New York minute.

"No, I guess not" he relented with a sheepish grin then shied away from her uncomfortable stare as he got out of bed.

"Matt, I love you honey with all my heart, and I don't ever want it to be that way with us . . . ever. I want you all to myself and alone the way we want it to be, not in a hurried up meaningless hump fest!"

"I know Retta, but" . . . he started to say but never finished. She gently put a finger over his lips and shook her head.

"Another time my love, another time" Soon they had gotten dressed and left the room. It was now 9:45 and he had precious little time before her mother would get home.

"Lori I'll be right back, I'm going to walk Matt down to the corner." Lori just flashed a cold stare at them from the table and shoved another bite of pie into her upturned little mouth.

"Shh! We have to be quiet leaving cause the old lady down stairs always tells on everything we do around here" said Retta taking Matt's hand and leading him out the back door and down the metal staircase.

The night air was cool and balmy thought Matt. It was spring and it hadn't quite gotten warm yet but was still a little chilly with a light breeze. They crept down the stairs trying hard not to upset any of the many flower pots and dog dish that covered the lower three steps. As they reached the bottom, Matt turned her around and kissed her deeply. Their tongues played a sensual game of tag in each other's mouths as hands blindly searched out and found already enflamed body parts all over again. They did this selfishly coveting and wanting what they each could not have. Slowly Retta parted from him.

"Matt, you better go puddin before we get started again and really get into trouble."

"Okay baby" he said not really wanting to stop or understand.

It took a little effort to get his moped off the old woman's porch without being heard. They ducked down and ran between the apartment buildings trying to avoid the drainage ditch that separated the upper side of the complex on the hill from the lower.

"When can I come over again?"

"I don't know Matt, Mamma's work schedule just got changed and I'm not sure how it goes yet, but I'll see you this weekend okay?"

Matt wasn't crazy about having to wait so long to see her again but said okay anyway. He reached to take her in his arms once more and kiss her one last time then started his bike. He stayed a bit longer to see her safely back to her door as she ran quickly into the night. All the while brooding and fantasizing over the moments they had shared a short time ago.

"Man! I feel so warm all over and so alive!" he thought to himself.

For the first time in his life he had the woman he had always wanted and she was all his. She broke his revelry by whispering loudly, "I love you Matt!"

"I love you too Retta!" he half whispered half shouted in return then waved at her until she was gone inside.

The ride home was quiet except for the light putter of his mopeds engine. He gunned it more to get up the hill past the entrance to Crystal Lake. Once he'd past that point the rest of the ride was smooth sailing till he got home.

"Boy! What a night!"

It's Friday morning and time to get up. Matt's dad was up already and getting set to leave for work. Matt yawned, stretched, and crawled out of bed. As he was heading to the bathroom, his dad called to him.

"Rodney!"

"Yes sir?"

"You up?"

"Yes sir"!

"Well when you get home from school today, do me a favor and clean up the yard a bit and wash up the truck a little OK?"

"A little?" he thought mumbling to himself remembering the recent trip to the land fill and how nasty and smelly it left the truck while driving through all those filthy mounds of smelly garbage and construction waste.

"Alright" he answered finally.

Matt thought about heading into the bathroom at that point but thought better of it knowing his dad would have more to say.

"And tell your brother to keep his friends outside while I'm not at home!"

"Yes sir"

"Do you have any lunch money?"

"No sir"

"Well here's a ten, bring me back my change wouldja"

"Yes sir" said Matt standing in the doorway to the kitchen in his underwear, arms folded and watching his dad pour coffee from the pot into his thermos.

"You stayed out pretty late last night didn't you?" he said with a bit of a grin. It actually looked more like a smirk than anything else.

"No sir, not too late" said Matt shuffling his feet a little. "I was at Aretta's house".

"That's your new girlfriend isn't it?"

"Yes sir."

"So when do I get to meet her?"

"Umm, probably this weekend" he blurted out not really knowing, seeing as how Retta wasn't quite sure herself.

"Where does she live?"

"On the West side in Bloomfield"

"Oh" he said not looking up from what he was doing.

"Well I'll see you this evening. Have a good day in school, okay?"

"Yes sir" he said to the retreating back of his father as he went down the steps out the back door.

"Well there he goes" Matt said to no one in particular then scratched his head and breathed, feeling as if a weight had fallen from him he didn't know he was carrying. Matt's dad was a tall stately man of about six feet with a distinguished and dignified appearance. It was just him, Matt, and Matt's oldest brother Jr. His other brothers were Kevin and Tony who lived with his mother in another state.

As Matt returned to his room he flung himself on his bed and lay there belaboring the obvious of why he stayed out so long last night. He was feeling a little too tired to get up for school but knew he had to anyway. Just about then, his friend George or "Ant" as he was called came dashing into the room and pounced on him. He landed on top of him hard, firmly planting his butt on Matt's face. With great disgust and surprise, Matt shoved him off and onto the floor then regrouped for his own attack.

"Wake up butt head!" yelled Ant from the floor laughing.

"Okay ass wipe, you got me, but you know what they say about "payback".

"Yeah, but you won't get the chance chump" he said getting up again.

"Alright scare crow" said Matt pointing at him and nodding as if to say "it's on now sucka."

Matt started getting dressed. he put on his ROTC uniform pants and shirt.

"Hey stupid, what are you doing?" asked Ant in a curious tone.

"Getting dressed, what's it look like I'm doing Moron?" he retorted.

"Take a good look at what you have on and think about what day it is then, let's see who's the moron." Matt looked at his clothes and looked up with a surprised look and felt embarrassed when be remembered that ROTC was on Monday's. Now feeling a warm flush go through him he tried to save face.

"Oh, I forgot NUMBSKULL."

"Are you going to the game tonight?" asked Ant changing the subject.

"I don't know, I might what about you?"

"Yeah I'm going; I'm supposed to be taking Michele."

"I thought you stopped seeing her when you got busted in her bedroom by her dad?" Ant just laughed and fell on the bed hysterically.

"Man let me tell you . . . when he came in the room I was trying to get my pants on. He saw me and just reached over and grabbed a hand full of my chest and threw me against the wall. Michele was just sitting on the bed with a terrified look on her face. For a minute I thought I was gonna have to fight his big ass but then he just yelled at me".

"Get the hell out of my house now before I kill your ass".

"Man I stumbled across the bed pants still hanging around my ankles and got up and hauled ass outta there!"

By then Matt was rolling around on the floor laughing at what he imagined was a hell of an episode. Ant finished and just shook his head and grinned, thinking to himself, *"Yeah you laugh now, but my ass was lucky to get away with just a bruised ego instead of worse."*

Matt got up shaking his head and grinning but in full agreement it could have been much worse.

Ant was a tall skinny guy with mocha skin, soft eyes and a smooth way about him. He was the kind of guy who could make you laugh at yourself even if you didn't want to. He was a good basketball player too and sometimes they would shoot some hoops during R.O.T.C class before formation.

"What about Aretta, what are you two gonna do tonight?"

"I don't know, I was over there last night". Ant shot him that sinister grin he sometimes offers up when there are games a foot or somebody is doing the nasty, and then started chanting his favorite cynicism, which never really made sense. Ant chanted, pointed, and danced around the room in a goofy singsong manner then started laughing at Matt as if he should be ashamed of himself.

"I was nice man, we got busy for awhile but her little sister Lori was in the way and her mother was coming home soon, so we didn't get to spend much time".

"Too bad" he said in mock sympathy.

"Oh, well no matter, we are gonna get together this weekend."

"Has she told her mother about you yet?"

"No" said Matt feeling uneasy again.

"Well don't worry about it, she will".

"I guess so" said Matt not really believing it himself being that so much time had passed already. "Well we better hurry up and go man or we'll be late and you know you don't want to get detention on Friday!"

"Shit no!" said Matt stripping out of his uniform and quickly jumping into some jeans and a shirt.

Soon he and Ant were on their way. It didn't take long to get to school because he lived just over the railroad tracks and across a large field next to the cotton mill which is right behind the schools parking lot, soon they were in the building and down the hall through the pockets of students clustered together in small groups by their lockers.

"Oh by the way Ant, did you do your English homework?"

"Yeah, I finished it yesterday when I went to my grandmother's house, how about you?"

"Naw, man I got side tracked doing something for dad and only finished half of it".

"Well you'll have sometime in home room to do it" well I'll see ya later man in the wind my friend" he said shouting over the noise in the hallway, turning to dash to his own class.

"Alright man" said Matt as he ducked and shot by people who seemed to come out of nowhere.

Soon He made it to his homeroom just before the bell rang.

"Whew! I just made it" he thought to himself as he eyed the teachers turned back and headed for his seat.

"One more late slip and I get a free tour of detention!"

"Alright class, let's get our seats" said Mrs. Pratt his home room teacher. She began giving out the days announcements but Matt wasn't really listening, he was busy trying to finish his already late homework assignment. But even that was becoming difficult as thoughts of Aretta kept drifting into his mind. He stopped writing and looked out the window remembering when he and Retta first met.

He had no idea he'd ever grow to love anyone so much. It was in the spring when he had been transferred from Central Jr. High to Southwest Ballard Hudson. He was totally against the move but the new zoning change had found him to be in their district and not Central's. This didn't make much sense to him at all. Central was just down the road and Southwest was clear across town. That's when his dad bought him a moped so he could get to school being he was outside the bus route and he could not take him to school because he left much earlier than Matt.

Matt thought that was cool riding himself to school. His first day was a little strange and precarious, he wore his colors and didn't care what anyone thought however, the indignant stares of contempt he got from just about everyone he passed showed him that there were no Mends to be made here.

Central and Southwest had always been harsh rivals thought Matt, but until he got on their turf, he had no idea that it was that bad. Yeah he'd heard stories of school buses getting stoned or shaken up a bit on days their teams played on their side of town and vice versa, but these kids that were looking at him now literally had blood in their eyes.

Matt was glad when he finally got to the office to check in. As he sat down in the administrator's office, several people entered and left, most of them students looking for late passes or getting something for their teachers. Others just looked his way with surprise and dismay that he was there in the first place and had the balls to wear his colors too! Matt began to sink into himself much like a rock sinking into a mud puddle. He could feel his face wax warm as the desk clerk an elderly black lady in her late 50's who looked as though her false teeth were in backwards and her underwear didn't fit right, stared at his letterman's jacket with all his achievements emblazoned on it for all the world to see.

Usually Matt would be proud to have someone look upon him that way but not today, right now all he could think of was peeling it off and putting it as far from him as possible before it caught fire due to so many laser like stares. Finally the tension broke.

"Rodney Mathis?" some unseen voice called out of nowhere. He stood up quickly looking for the voice. It was the principal.

"Would you come this way please?" Matt followed her amused by the irony of the situation (to be saved by the very person he spent most of his time dodging) and at the same time glad to be out of the lime light. As they sat down in her office, she smiled.

"So . . . how are you this morning?"

"Fine" he said lying.

"I understand that you're from Central Jr. High".

"Yes ma'am" he said thinking, "how'd you guess!" she went on telling him about the school and its policies, soon after he was given his class assignments.

Matt walked down the hall admiring the murals and plaques. A girl passed by carrying a load of papers and books.

"Hi" he said surprised at his boldness so soon.

"Hello yourself!" she said smiling at him.

"Are you new here?" she asked smiling guardedly at him.

"Yes, I just got here today from Central" he said a little prouder than before.

"Oh really" she commented with mock sarcasm allowing her eyes to roam over his jacket, driving home the point that she already knew that.

"What's your name?" she asked.

"Rodney, but my friends call me Mathis or Matt for short."

She was stunning he thought and had the most alluring eyes he's ever seen! She also had a confident and firm yet pleasant demeanor about herself he'd found a little intimidating but not to the point he was ready to run yet. The girl noticed that he'd assessed her body and persona as quickly as she'd done him and was a little amazed that he wasn't intimidated by her like most boys were.

"My name is Aretta, Aretta Davis" she said adjusting the pile to shake hands with him.

"Nice to meet you" she said.

"It's good to meet you too" said Matt admiring her strong yet subtle grip. He began to feel easier about the relocation each minute he stood there with her.

"Well I gotta go, I have to get this stuff to the office for my homeroom teacher" she said withdrawing her hand slowly.

"Maybe I'll see you later" Matt said eagerly, maybe a little more eagerly than he had wanted to appear on their first meeting.

"That would be nice" she said turning and shuffling away.

It took Matt a few seconds to recover from her presence, he did a mental tally on what he'd seen and noticed that she was about 5'6 inches tall, about one hundred and ten or fifteen pounds, light brown or bronze naturally curly hair and light brown or caramel colored buttery soft skin to match. Her hair was braided around the sides of her head in a crown, she sported the most beautiful smile, and her eyes were a warm burgundy color almost auburn by the way, light danced about them. She wore a red I-zod button-down collar shirt and a pair of Lee jeans that fit her quite well and showed off her well-shaped athletic legs. She looked athletic and firm but Matt wasn't quite sure if she was a jock or not. Either way he couldn't wait to see her again and find out.

"Young man!" barked a bowel chilling voice behind him breaking his revelry.

He turned to see it was a sour looking, old black lady who looked to be in her late fifties with an upturned little nose and a large chest. It was too large in fact for her small frame. Matt thought that she might topple over any minute but her big feet that she incessantly kept taping the toe of told him she would stay put with no problem.

"Do you know where you're supposed to be?" she snapped noticing how the young man had so brazenly perused her body with his eyes before acknowledging her authority, in a way it amused and somewhat elated her that she had this affect on younger men and was even more pleased when they were intimidated by it later.

"No ma'am!" chirped Matt when he'd come to his senses.

"Do you have a hall pass?"

"No ma'am, I just got here" he offered quickly then rummaged through his jacket to find his schedule.

The teacher took the paper from him in a most unsavory manner then tipped her half lens glasses to scrutinize the document.

"You have Mrs. Spivey's class right now and that's down this hall, third door on your left, I suggest you get there!" she said putting emphasis on the word GET.

"Yes ma'am!" he said and quickly reclaiming his schedule, thanking her and leaving quick, fast and in a hurry.

"Man this is going to be a real blast I can see that right now . . . thanks! "Zoning Board."

Soon class was over and it was first half lunch period. Matt thought this was a real strange concept, one that definitely was not part of the curriculum or management process at Central. However, he was glad to be in a section that was first to go. The morning abuses had weighed heavily on him and his appetite was just about to get the best of him. Now he just had to find the lunchroom.

"Hey dude?" he said calling to a little white kid.

"Where's the lunchroom?" The kid pointed down the hall.

"Take a left at the corner then follow your nose." He said grinning disarmingly not wanting to send the wrong message to the much larger and powerfully built upper classman who had stopped him.

Matt chuckled lightly and smirked at the kid accepting his attempt at diplomacy.

"You're a funny kid, is everybody here as amusing as you?" asked Matt turning and walking in the direction, he was given not waiting for a reply.

Matt made a stop by his locker to put away his jacket since it was on the way he didn't earlier do to being sent to classes all over the building. Besides the looks he'd got from his fellow classmates, didn't reassure him of his safety this day should a fight break out.

Finally, he headed down the hall to the chow hall. His stomach was growling by now and needed a rest. He'd run out of jelly beans an hour ago and the taste of them had long ago passed away. As he got to the main hall, he could see a long line of people to his left and right. He decided to take the left side of the hall, it seemed shorter, and after a short wait, he was inside and through the line with his lunch in hand. He sat down at a table that was near the outside wall near the exit. He dove into his lunch without fanfare. The food was good he noticed, a little better than that swill he sometimes got at Central. He noticed that the lunchroom was enormous with salad bars, several dessert counters, and even an ice cream churn. "They sure know how to live in this place" he thought to himself as he looked around. There were several tables of kids around him and for the most part, he sat alone. Matt thought it best until he knew his way around better and could determine who was and was not his enemy.

"Hello! Again" chirped a happy and encouragingly familiar voice. Matt looked up from his tray and saw that it was Aretta, the girl he'd met in the hall earlier this morning.

"Hi" he mumbled through a too full mouth.

"So how do you like it here so far?" she asked going on without encouragement.

"It's okay, if you don't mind being a specimen" said Matt rolling his eyes.

"You don't know about it then do you?"

"Know about what?"

"That you're a celebrity around here, word got out the day before you got here that you were coming".

"Really?" he said swallowing a gob of burger in disbelief.

"How could I be so well known so soon, I'm nobody special".

(Oh I wouldn't say that handsome, I think your very special), thought Aretta.

"The grapevine sweetie" she said notably pleased with her knowledge of current affairs.

"All of us office runners got a look at the transfer list last week and your name was at the top of the list. Of course we didn't know it was going to be you per se' but we knew someone was coming today and when you came prancing up sporting your colors, well that just blew the whistle on you."

"I see" said Matt feeling quite bare and exposed.

"Look around you" said Aretta pointing over her shoulder. Matt looked about sheepishly and saw that just about every other eye in the joint was trained on them or at least on him.

"You said celebrity, are you sure you didn't mean sacrificial lamb instead?"

Aretta laughed easily and the sound of it was light and sweet like the melody of a love song.

"Do you mind if I join you?" she said finally, standing there holding her tray.

"Sure, but are you sure you should be seen with me under the circumstances?" he said casually tipping his head referencing the crowd around them. Aretta just snorted lightly and smiled waving them off.

"Don't worry about me, I'm nobody special so they don't really care about me sitting with you" she said with her voice dying off notably and her head drooping slightly.

"I'll be damned if that's so, you could have fooled me" thought Matt as he silently marveled at how a girl that looked and acted like her could feel she didn't matter.

"So what's it like at Central?" she said breaking the awkward silence as well as reminding herself of her own peculiar existence.

"Not bad I guess" he said thinking how far away it seemed right now.

"Do you live near here?" she asked suddenly wishing she hadn't asked that and wishing she could retract it. (What kind of girl asks a total stranger where do you live?) Matt noticed her bite her lip in sudden distress and smiled to himself at her clumsy revelation of unintended interest in him.

"No, I live on the West side of town on Vineville Avenue".

"That's a long way from here, did you ride the school bus?"

"No, the school board doesn't have anything that comes from there to here so I rode my moped". "You have a moped?"

"Yeah, it's the only way I could get here" said Matt taking another bite of his lunch, but not really tasting it.

"Do you know how to find your classes yet?" asked Aretta trying to keep the conversation going, seeing how Matt wouldn't be there much longer the way he was devouring his lunch.

"No, not really, these last two somebody had to help me".

"Here let me see your schedule" she said reaching for it as he fished it out of his shirt pocket. "Here you go" he said passing it to her.

As he did this, her hand lightly touched his. She was very soft he noticed and soon found himself day dreaming about her while sitting there. Retta was or appeared to be something of an organizer of sorts by the way she took charge of things and yet still remained a quiet beauty much like the maidens of the old English countryside.

"I can help you find the rest of these if you like" she offered eagerly.

"That'd be nice, are you sure you can spare the time?" said Matt returning his schedule to his pocket.

"Yeah, it's no problem; I have a free period this hour anyway".

"A free period?" said Matt taken back by this new term.

"Sure! I'm an honor student, and during this period I can study, tutor someone, or help the teachers . . ."

"Like this morning?" he cut in.

"Yeah like that."

"Are you done eating?" she asked looking at his mostly empty tray.

"Yeah I'm through".

"Good then, we can go now if you like"?

"Sure" said Matt not really feeling sure of himself yet and whether or not he should wait on the bell to ring.

Retta sensed his thoughts in his reluctance to get up.

"Don't worry, people come and go as they please and nobody says anything about it".

"Damn! Central was never like this" thought Matt.

"This place has got it going on!"

They dumped their trays and left winding their way pass the tables and chairs. On the way they picked up a few stares from the other students, some were guys but most of them were nosey females.

"We can go this way" she said pointing to a side door exit.

"It's quicker than going around to the main hall" or translated, she meant it was quicker and less painful than running the gauntlet of vicious looks she was getting from the elite of the bunch and the fact that she was breaking in the new guy instead of them.

She led Matt outdoors and past the dumpsters near the lunchroom. The smell of old milk and ice cream had a sickening aroma and was being raided by a million of hungry flies. The sun was warm this afternoon and gave a good feeling after having been cooped up in a windowless icebox all morning long. They walked by several students on a nearby wall. Some were smoking and talking while others were off to themselves hugging and kissing.

"You guys have a lot of freedoms here don't you?" asked Matt pointing over his shoulder at the couple kissing themselves into a coma.

"Oh that" she said looking then quickly turning away.

"People do pretty much whatever they want around here".

"Even smoking dope?"

"Yeah that too" she said leading him away from the area that had just become uninhabitable when someone struck up a marijuana joint.

"The white kids do it on the sly behind the gym and the black kids hang out on the bleachers on the track field to do their thing".

What about you?" asked Matt slowing and looking at her with an emotionless stare.

Retta squared off on him slowly as if in a ring and setting up her prey for a haymaker, but instead just looking at him and feeling a little hurt that he would ask such a question feeling that the answer should be as obvious as the pounding of her heart for what she was beginning to feel for him.

"No" she said flat and toneless.

"Heck no!" she said now motivated by some unseen power that urged her to attack.

"Do I look stupid?" she said getting in Matt's face so close he could smell her essence in her breath and it was like that of a puppy's breath or in terms of pheromones, quite intoxicating and alluring.

"No, I'm sorry" Matt said backing slowly from her an arms reach now seeing the fire in those hypnotic eyes.

"I'm sorry Aretta . . . I didn't mean to imply that you did. I just thought that since you knew so much . . . I Figured . . . well" he said stammering.

"Well, no I don't!" she said relaxing a little but not entirely.

"And how about you?" she stabbed at him closing the space once again and folding her arms across her chest and propping on one foot.

Matt looked her over appraising her posture before he spoke again. He looked her up and down slowly, then backed up a step and replied evenly,

"No, I never found a good reason to start either" he finished.

Retta thought of how the two of them looked standing there ready to strike and a small grin crossed her luscious lips and she just giggled at the awkwardness of it all. Matt caught wind of the visual and joined her no less. As they laughed at their mutual misunderstanding of each other, Retta began to develop a liking for Matt, maybe even a mild kindred ship of sorts. Soon they were back in the building and heading down one of the many long corridors. There was much silence about the hall and not much to indicate that there was ever a student body at all much less the 1,500 students he'd heard populated the complex of Southwest High.

"Man! if a guy didn't know better he'd swear he was in a cemetery".

"Oh yeah? Well just you wait and see till school gets out, you won't feel that way for long!" said Retta grinning at him still.

Matt was glad to have her company, as was the case, it had been a long time since he'd been with or had a decent conversation with a girl and he found Retta's gentle nature and quiet confidence most reassuring and inviting.

"I wonder does she have a boy friend?" he pondered to himself far too afraid and bashful to ask her much less think about it. "Oh this is stupid; I just met the girl and hardly know her. And here I am playing "Devil's Advocate" with her already! Hell I'm sure she wouldn't want anything to do with the likes of me anyway".

"Penny for your thoughts" said Retta most sweetly looking up at him with hope filled gentle eyes.

"Oh! I'm sorry" he stammered surprised and a little embarrassed for having been silent for so long. "I hadn't noticed I was being so quiet". (That's okay I'm used to people not noticing me) she thought to herself as she walked beside him hands folded behind her.

"What were you thinking about?" she ventured just to keep him there.

"Oh just stuff" he lied trying to sidetrack her from his true feelings and thoughts.

"All good I hope?" she said.

Soon the tour was over and Matt knew how to find his remaining classes and none too soon because just as they past the last room on the schedule, the bell rang and second lunch was about to begin, this also meant classes for Matt . . .

"Well here you are" said Retta, her tone a little dampened at having the quasi date interrupted.

"I better go or I'll be late for art class".

"Oh really? You draw too?" asked Matt interested.

"A little".

"So do I" he said warming to her again and enjoying the fact that they had something else in common.

"For real" she said getting the gist of the game and following suit.

"Yeah, just a little" they both laughed at this.

"Well maybe I'll see you later" said Matt turning to leave but not wanting to go yet. Retta sighed heavily and smiled shrugging her shoulders.

"Maybe you will" she said looking at him for a moment longer as if not sure she should let him leave or leave herself. Then just as abruptly as she had come she turned and strode off in the opposite direction, her hands in her back pockets and head slightly tilted forward.

For some strange reason Matt had the impression that she had said or let him see something she had not wanted to reveal. He pondered it a moment then dismissed it as hopeful thinking. "RING!!" and there it was in all its clamorousness . . . . the bell for first period. Matt had been lost in rapture of his thoughts and daydreaming during the entire homeroom period and hadn't done the first page of work on his English assignment.

"Damn" he said pissed at his lack of concentration and inefficiency.

"Now I'll never get it done, this period I have Science and next is English!" he spat angrily at himself.

"Oh well maybe I can run a copy and say I left the original at home or something, man I hate Fridays".

As the hustle to make it to the next class began, Matt started looking up and down the hall for Ant. He'd hoped to catch Ant before he left the building so he could get him to run copies of his notes before going across the road. Now Matt was caught up in the soup and knew he'd better catch him or all would be lost. He ran through the crowd in the opposite direction ducking and dodging as he went.

"Oops! sorry, scuse me, pardon me, pardon me."

Right about then he slammed into something and bounced off. It turned out to be Sammy Thomas the school bruiser.

"Watch where you going FOOL!" he shouted going from "0" to asshole in just under 60 seconds. Matt picked up his book bag and stood up to face him, he hadn't seen him coming in the rush and now wished he had, cause Sammy stood a good six feet three inches tall, had a bouncers physique and weighed in at about 200 pounds, most of which Matt was sure was muscle.

"Hey man I'm sorry, I didn't mean to run you down or nothing" he said attempting to ease tensions. Nevertheless, Sammy had long since established the fact that he couldn't be negotiated with once pissed off. He put a stiff arm into Matt's chest shoving him backwards a few feet and causing the crowd to scatter somewhat and surround them. Fights on Fridays were almost a normal occurrence and just about, everyone loved to see them.

"What's your problem man?" shouted Matt once he'd gotten his balance back.

"You! Mutha fucka!" blasted Sammy throwing his book bag to the floor to punctuate his point and intent as he stepped closer to Matt.

"Hey man, I think you better step off before you get bum rushed!" said Matt tossing his own bag aside and squaring off on the larger kid seeing now that there was no way to avoid this. His body was a rush with emotion and excitement and his pulse was raging and rushed all through him making his breathing hard and his chest pound.

"This fool must be crazy" he said to himself, not taking his eyes off Sammy for a minute. Sammy never got enough of harassing Matt every chance he could. He did this especially when he was with his friend Ernest Miller. He pushed Matt again.

"If you don't like it then make a move SUCKA" and Matt did just that and the fight was on.

Matt swung and caught him in the face with a right cross but being that he was a little out of his effective reach the punch didn't pack as much as he'd intended but however was enough to get Sammy's attention.

The crowd had gotten loud and drew in closer to give the fighters as little running or maneuvering room as possible and maximize the contact. There were oohs and ahh's coming all around at Matt's attempt, but no sooner than his punch recoiled he felt a shattering blow in his chest. Matt felt like his lungs had exploded. He doubled over gasping for air and was on the rise when Sammy pumped another shot into his gut sending him to the floor in a crumpled heap. "KICK HIS ASS SAMMY!" yelled someone.

"YEAH, FUCK HIS SHIT UP MAN, HE AINT SHIT" yelled another.

Pain was all over Matt's body and the cheering crowd made it hurt even more. The hall was a crescendo of yelling, rooting, bloodthirsty students. Just who it was for him or against him he wasn't sure.

He was beginning to recover some now and started to rise again cautiously and as he did Sammy was setting up to put his size thirteen's in Matt's face to take him out once and for all. Matt saw it coming and rolled out of the way as quickly as he could but still caught it on the shoulder instead. Now feeling a little strength return he rolled upright onto his knees and tried to get in a gut shot but his punch was low and weak as his head was still a little fuzzy. He wound up connecting on Sammy's crotch instead. Sammy was stunned and going down, Matt seeing this acted quickly and got to his feet, he was in a blood lust now and more than vengeful as he drove a solid knee into the side of Sammy's huge head and felt it rebound off the floor.

"WHOOM!" shouted the crowd as he repeated this again and again raising even louder and louder cheers. But no matter how many times or how much force Matt put into it Sammy still would not go out and kept trying to get up! Aware now that he was becoming tired, as well as concerned that Sammy would recover and get up and beat the shit out of him; Matt looked around quickly for a weapon or something to finish him off.

The crowd seeing this offered him large books or book bags and one girl even offered him a high heel shoe! The crowd was in total bedlam now and the teachers were doing their best to get through to the two fighters but was deliberately blocked out until it was finished, meaning when somebody didn't get back up or was dead. Matt spied a fire extinguisher on the wall and quickly snatched the huge bottle from its hook! This really drove the crowd wild now thinking that they may actually see some blood and somebody was going to get dealt with! Matt turned and charged back towards Sammy who was now on one knee and getting up. Matt brought the bottle down with a murderous thrust towards Sammy's exposed head. As the bottle came down Sammy saw the gleam of the shiny metal and immediately coward again in a weak attempt to ward off the impending blow.

As Matt's mouth was sour sweet and he could no longer hear the chants of the crowd but just a constant buzz. His skin was icy hot and cool salty sweat ran down his face and stung his eyes. He for a moment felt a pang of remorse for Sammy but it was a short one. The bottle was inches from contact when a dark shape came into view and was followed by a shattering blow to his mid-section. Something had tackled him and sent the bottle flying. Someone had blind-sided him.

"Oh shit!" he thought frantically. It must be Ernest his buddy.

"I'm sure to get fucked up now, how can I fight them both when I'm too tired to finish this asshole."

Confusion and despair gripped Matt's soul as the tall dark figure arose, quickly getting off him.

Matt was expecting to be stomped to death and got up with equal speed preparing to fight on both fronts. Then he saw that the person he was about to punch the shit out of wasn't Ernest after all but instead his own best friend Ant. He'd gotten wind of the fight and knew it was one of Matt's two enemies who had to be at him because he didn't have any enemies he knew of other than Sammy and Ernest.

Ant seeing that Matt had gotten hold of a weapon and where he was going to place it. Not to mention him being too far away to take it from him, Ant did the only thing he could do and that was to launch his six foot four inch frame at him and hope he could at least spoil his aim some. He didn't want him to hurt the fool or maybe even kill the son of a bitch!

"Don't do it Matt!" he said quickly, seeing his friend coming at him with death in his eyes.

"He ain't worth it man don't throw your life away on a piece of shit!" pleaded Ant winded from the effort.

"You got him back Matt, let it go man . . . let it go" he urged softly getting between Matt who was still standing with fists ready as he glared at Sammy who was staring back at him but still on one knee.

The crowd was more than upset at Ants interference and wanted to do him harm but didn't because Ant was not one in which to fuck with. His reputation as a brawler was long since established in his Freshman year when he kicked the crap out of the Rainy twins, another reason that Sammy didn't push the fight any further. Matt slowly dropped his fists and came back to his senses, his legs a little shaky and quite jittery from the spent and unspent adrenaline still coursing through his body. The bloodlust was slowly beginning to lose its grip on him as he looked at Ant and saw the broken spirit and concern in his eyes. He turned away briefly to see Sammy getting up.

Blood traced down his face from the corner of his right eye and lip where Matt had recently put his knee to him. Finally, breaking through the crowd, the BOE (Board of Education) police made it to the center of the problem.

"Okay break it up! Break it up now or I'm taking all your butts to jail!"

"Now what's going on here" he demanded as he looked over to Matt and Sammy and what remained of the crowd. Some shuffled and looked away blankly as most people do in this kind of situation. A few others began to give their side of what happened. When the short investigation was completed, Matt, Ant, and Sammy were taken to the principal's office to see Mrs. Hard Castle.

"You sit over here and you sit over there, and I don't want any talking out of either of you . . . understand me?" said Officer Grant.

The boys nodded as they took the seats directed to them. A minute or two later Mrs. Hard Castle came into the office and was clearly surprised to see three Board of Education Policemen in her front office and three of her students. She was over at the boy's school when the fight had occurred and only just got wind of it after it ended and quickly headed across the street. Officer Grant gave her his report and she was not pleased, she looked at Matt and Sammy as if she would jump on them herself once the officers left. Once the reports and other formalities were done she nodded and told them thank you and to wait outside while she investigated further before giving them any more instructions on what to do with the trio.

Matt was getting nervous and a little anxious as he wrung his hands over and over while trying to avoid eye contact with Sammy who was rubbing his bruised temple and doing much the same as he.

"Let's go you three!" said Mrs. Hard Castle as she pushed back the swinging gate at the counter to let Matt and Sammy pass through with Ant in tow. Mrs. Hard Castle was a short black woman of about forty years old. She had short curly bronze colored hair, a nice figure and the most intense pair of green eyes you ever saw, you would swear she could see through lead! All this would have been a nice package if she didn't have that mean grandmotherly attitude. She sat on the edge of her desk and eyed the three of them placidly while drumming her french manicured nails on the desk. "The clickety-clack of her tapping was becoming as annoying as hell!" thought Ant but he sat quietly and endured it as best he could.

"Mathis, what's the problem?" she said zeroing in on him first.

Matt didn't speak right away all be could do is glare at Sammy and hate him. "Mathis" she snapped getting louder.

"You can either start talking or start walking and I mean towards the officers who brought you here and into expulsion for disruptive behavior because I don't have the time or the patience for this CRAP!" she said pounding her fist on her desk for emphasis.

"Do you understand me young man?"

"Yes ma'am" he said clearing his throat.

"Well you see it's like this Mrs. Hard Castle, I was coming out of home room heading for my first class when all of a sudden THIS FOOL!" he said thumbing harshly at Sammy.

"Watch your mouth young man!" she warned cutting him off.

"Sorry, anyway I accidentally bumped into him in the hall. I didn't see him coming . . ."

"You shoulda looked where you was going you BLIND FOOL!"

"Sammy Thomas, that's enough out of you too young man!" shouted Mrs. Hard Castle.

"You can walk just as fast as Mr. Mathis here so keep it up, now go on with what you were saying Mathis".

"Well like I was saying, I bumped into him and then he called me out and pushed me so I asked him what was his problem and he said "You! Muther-F'er" then pushed me again".

"So what did you do then?"

"Well I told him that if he didn't step off me he was gonna get bum rushed". Mrs. Hard Castle just shook her head and clicked her nails together. Matt took that as a sign that he was sunk because she seemed to be weighing the matter before he was through.

"Then what?"

"Well he pushed me again and then I cold cocked him across the face!"

"And started a fight in my school!"

"No ma'am! I was just defending myself, he started it!" protested Matt as he began to feel a trip home was imminent every second.

Sammy just grinned and relished at the reaming that Matt was getting. He knew he wasn't going home . . . at least not yet . . . not that way.

"You lower your voice Mr. Mathis; you're already in enough trouble without raising your voice to me as well".

Matt just sunk down in his seat further and shook his head.

"Man this still ain't right" he mumbled to himself.

"And you, Mr. Thomas, what do you have to say about this?"

"Well like he said Mrs. Hard Castle, he came running down the hall like some fool!"

"Young man you either lower your voice and watch your tongue or you are out of here and I mean it!" she said getting up, snapping her fingers at the office door window to get the attention of the officers that were awaiting her next move.

They stood and approached the door looking in but did not enter, but instead just glared at the two boys letting them know they were just outside the door and waiting for them. Sammy quickly got the hint, changed his tone and sunk back into his seat, and looked at his shoes.

"Anyway he bumped into me and almost knocked me down and then didn't say excuse me or nothing! and when I told him to watch out he said kiss his "A–" "THOMAS!"

"Scuse me, I mean his butt".

"That's a damn lie!" shouted Matt and getting to his feet.

"Sit down Mathis or I'll have you restrained!" she said pointing to the huge black officer who was just about to enter the office when she waved him off.

"He's lying Mrs. Hard Castle!"

"Mathis, you have had your say now let Thomas have his!"

"Yeah! and then he took a swing on me and we started fighting".

Sammy said finishing his statement.

"Okay Williams, you've been sitting there all quiet, just what do you have to do with all of this mess? I've never had any trouble with you before".

Ant, up until now was just slouching in his seat biting at the quick on his thumbnail and watching the may lay.

"Well it's like this Mrs. Hard Castle; I was on my way to the boy's school for first period when I heard there was a fight between Matt and Sammy. So naturally I ran back to see because Ernest Holloway and Sammy are always together and trying to start something with him by the time I got there he had grabbed a fire bottle off."

"The wall and was about to bust Sammy in the head with it."

Remembering this, Sammy adjusted in his seat nervously and looked at Matt pensively like he couldn't believe he'd gotten the best of him or would actually hit him with it.

"When I jumped on him and tackled him to the floor because I didn't want him to hurt him and maybe go to jail, and that's why I'm involved?" he said finishing.

"Why didn't you just keep on going on your way to where you were supposed to be?"

"Taking care of other people's problems is not your business or why you come to school Williams." she chided.

Ant just nodded and bowed his head slightly. "And what if you had found Ernest there, then it would have been the four of you and God only knows what kind of a fracas I would be having to deal with."

There was a long silence after that and it was a long time before Mrs. Hard Castle spoke again, she just shook her head and walked her eyes over the three of them then sat down behind her desk looking blankly out the window. When she finally did speak, it came out slow and flat but with a firm strength to it.

"Mathis, it seems to me I've heard something of this private little war you Sammy and Ernest have going before, and I'm sure I've warned you both countless times about it but it hasn't seemed to sink in any!"

By now Matt was beginning to feel ill and each word she spoke filled him further with dread.

"Oh hell, here it comes; I just know I'm going to be suspended now".

"Williams, you may go" she said waving him off.

"Thomas, you wait outside for a minute I will call you back in shortly".

"That's it, I know I'm history now" thought Matt as his best friend and Sammy walked out. "You'd think if she was gonna let us off the hook with an ass chewing, she'd have gone right to it, not separate us like this".

"Mathis, I just don't know what you expect me to do about this! This is way out of line and boarders on expulsion! Why is it you just can't behave for any long period of time young man? Why?" Matt just shrugged.

"And to make matters worse you're really not a bad student, in fact some of your teachers say you have your moments of inspiration and creative genius that seems to help motivate others around you to do better and that's good!"

"But then you get into things like this and that's something I can't tolerate!" she paused for a moment readjusting in her seat.

"Mathis, were you really going to hit Thomas with that fire extinguisher?" she said softly almost sadly.

Matt scanned her face to see if it was a question that required an answer.

Matt swallowed hard trying to remember and assess how he really felt at that time and whether or not to tell her.

"To tell you the truth Mrs. Hard Castle, I really don't know, when you're in the thick of a fight, things get distorted and move around real fast and go from lick to lick." "You suddenly become a two dimensional character on a page until it's over and then you feel the weight of what just happened and are unable to do anything about it."

Mrs. Hard Castle was on the edge of her seat hands folded on her desk and staring at Matt incredulously.

"How could this little upstart only moments ago who wanted to bash in another kids skull, give such an authoritative overview of the esoteric and psychological aspects of a fight!"

"Mathis, go to your next class" she said shaking her head.

"I'll let you know what I'm going to do later okay?"

"Yes ma'am" he said grateful for the short stay of execution.

"And try to stay out of trouble the rest of the day till then, will you?" she said almost pleading but at the same time much too over worked and tired mentally to pursue it further just now.

"Yes ma'am" he said then shuffled out the door.

Aretta was sitting in her desk in art class drawing, doodling and making formless shapeless squiggles on her paper, daydreaming.

"He is so sweet and I just love the way he smells and makes me feel so light headed when he kisses me. I love the firmness of his chest and gentle way he holds me in his arms, I could gaze into those dark limpid pools forever! I wonder is he thinking of me just now?"

Last night was so wonderful even though we didn't get to finish what we started. But just the feel of his hands touching me and caressing my breasts made my skin burn and tingle! I could feel myself grow weak in his eyes and my body melting at his hot passionate kisses. It was all I could do to keep from screaming when his hand touched me between my legs! I wanted him inside me so badly and to feel the strength of his body all hot and sweaty against mine that I could just BURST! Not to mention the hardness of his penis pressing into me just made me crazy all over! Gosh! How I wanted to scream for him to take me, tear into me! Possess me completely forever never to stop!"

Aretta hadn't noticed that the bell had rung and the class was slipping away from around her. She didn't hear it because she was totally oblivious to all sight and sound.

"Retta!"

"Huh?"

"Wake up girl, where you been?" asked her best friend Alfreida.

"Ohh . . . no place" she said weekly.

"Girl you should see your FACE! You're glowing and you don't even know it."

Oh, she knew all right and she smiled somewhat ashamed and bashful for having been observed so closely. She had an idea long ago that she was probably radiating something by the steamed moistness she felt between her thighs.

"Come on girl let's go! The bell rang a few minutes ago!"

"Oh hell" she muttered hustling out of her seat angry with herself for allowing her mind to wander so callously.

"What period is it, Fifth?"

"No girl its sixth period, where is your mind at today?" said Frieda re-evaluating her friends fuzzy state of mind.

"You've been thinking about Rodney again haven't you?" she said curtly.

"Yes . . . a little" said Retta blushing more.

"I love him Frieda, I've never been with anyone like him before; he makes me feel warm all over when he looks at me and when he kisses me . . . GIRRL! let me tell you! Sometimes it's all I can do to keep from falling down!"

"Yeah he's fine alright. Do ya'll get busy much" she asked smiling capriciously.

Retta blushed and turned away suddenly more embarrassed than she had ever remembered at Frieda's question.

"No, not much".

"Girl what are you saving it for! you don't let a hottie like him go to waste, you better get off the ball and get on the STICK!" she said eyeballing her up and down.

"And you know which way I mean that too!"

Retta just shaded more and didn't comment but only nodded her head in agreement.

"Frieda you know how it is with mom, she's so strict on me all the time and then there's ole busy body Lori to worry about. I hate living there sometimes. It feels like I'm a prisoner in my own house!"

"Yeah I know what you mean".

"And when I'm finally alone with him everything is okay".

"Yeah I can believe that" said Frieda consoling her.

"Aww! what could you know! you're an only child!"

"SO, I still get horny sometimes! and my mom gets in my way too".

"Aw girl your horny ALL! the time" shot Retta smiling at her.

Frieda just shrugged and smiled in acquiescence to her truth.

"So tell me, does Rodney have any cute friends?"

"I don't know, I can ask him".

"Okay that'll work; if he does then we can get together this weekend and . . ."

"Oh shoot!, I almost forgot we was supposed to be going to my grandma's house this weekend. Mom came home last night and told us and Matt wanted us to get together then too!"

"Now what are you gonna do?"

"I don't know, I don't want to go but I don't have any choice and I just know Matt's gonna be upset with me".

"He might not get mad at you, you said so yourself that he was understanding".

"Yeah!"

"Then it will be alright!"

"No it won't!" she said howling.

"I keep putting off telling mom about him and he thinks I'm ashamed of him and now this has come up, oh! Frieda he's gonna quit me! I just know It".

"Come on girl, get a grip, don't carry on so, it'll be fine. If you like I'll tell him for you".

"Naw, that's okay, I'll do it."

"Okay, if you say so".

"Yeah I'll do it."

"Well you better fix your face so we can go, you still have one class to go".

Retta tried to smile but felt worse than she looked. They ran on to their class trying to beat the bell. Retta's class was just down the hall around the corner. Frieda had a little further to go and hustled on the way. Retta ran in to the gym just as the bell sounded and went over to drop onto the bleachers. After awhile and a tiring workout, the bell rang again ending the class and the school week.

"Let's go Retta! the bus will be here soon" said Frieda running past her in the hall. Retta was busy adjusting her book bag on her back and redoing her hair because it was a mess from working out.

"I'm coming! where are my hair barrettes? Darn! I can never find anything in this purse" she grumbled impatiently.

Soon the bus had arrived and kids were running all over the place glad to be out of school for the weekend. Aretta got on her bus and went to the rear to sit by Frieda.

"So, how are you feeling?" asked Frieda moving over so she could sit down.

"Any better?"

"I'm alright I guess, but not much better".

"Well when we get home we'll call him and see what he says, okay?" Retta just sighed long and nodded settling into her seat.

The bus trip was long and noisy and Aretta lived on the farthest end of the Bloomfield area, which just happened to be the last drop off of the ride. Soon they had reached their neighborhood and Retta got off. Frieda was slacking behind talking and smiling at the bus driver. He was a young man of about nineteen or twenty, with short curly hair and a nice muscular body. Retta found herself comparing him to Matt, and smiled devilishly to herself when the stranger didn't match up to the one she loved.

"Come on Frieda, let's go!"

"Oh! okay, wait just a minute!" she said asking for a piece of paper from the bus driver.

"See you later" she said smiling then jumping off the bus, her over-sized breasts bouncing and undulating up and down as she went. Retta noticed and grinned to herself as the shock from the landing shook her whole frame.

Frieda was a large girl of about five foot eleven inches tall. She was tall and big boned or as a country boy might say, "One corn fed heifer!" Frieda had long black hair that she wore half loose and half braided. She also sported a massive pair or breasts that were at least a "D" cup and those added to her generous shapely hips and that apple bottom, behind. Even at the tender age of sixteen, she was just about every boys and some men's wet dream. She topped off her assets with a dazzling pair of dark brown eyes that always seemed to have a smile in them. Frieda was a nice enough person and had a quick wit. She lived just across the parking lot from Retta's building in the same complex. They had met many summers ago when she, her little sister and mother had first moved in, and had been friends ever since.

"Girl you need to curb your hormones" chirped Retta with a defiant grin.

"Listen who's talking *Ms. Hot Box!* herself!" She retorted unscathed.

"Well at least I kept my virginity longer than you could" said Retta proudly.

"Yeah, but you wouldn't know it the way you've been carrying on with *"Rooddney"* said Frieda in a sing song.

"Uh oh, I almost forgot, I still have to call him before mom gets home".

"Well you better get on it then, I'll just see you later" said Frieda waving goodbye as she hurried to her own flat. Retta said bye and broke into a sprint as she ran through the parking lot, she ducked into the entrance and dashed up the stairs. As she got to her door, she stopped and rummaged through her purse for her key. Just as she was about to insert it into the lock the door suddenly flew open. It was Lori her eight year old little sister. She stood there pigging out on a glazed doughnut and smiled.

"Rodney called" she managed to say between bites.

"He did?"

"When?"

"Awhile ago"

"What time?" she pressed eagerly.

Lori just shrugged. "Momma called too"

"How long ago?"

"Before he did"

Retta just sighed and waved her little sister off in exasperation and proceeded to take off her heavy backpack.

"We might not be going out of town today"

"Oh really?"

"Why"

"Who said"

"Mamma".

Hearing this, Retta ran to the phone totally ecstatic and renewed at the possibility of not going away for the weekend.

"Hello?"

"Hello" "May I speak to Rodney please?"

"Who's calling?" said a male voice.

"Aretta"

"Well hello Aretta, I'm Rodney's father".

"Oh hi Mr. Mathis, how are you?"

"Oh, fine and how are you doing these days?"

"Oh I'm okay sir, just getting in from school".

"Is that right?". "It's kind of late to be getting home from school isn't it?"

"Yes sir, it's the bus ride that takes so long."

"I see, well I'm sorry to say that Rodney isn't home yet, he's still at school working off a debt on the track field".

"Working off a debt you say?"

"Yes, I assume he's gotten into something today in school and is getting his reward for it".

"Oh I see". Retta deflated considerably. "Well could you please tell him to call me as soon as he gets home Mr. Mathis? "It's important".

"Is everything alright Aretta?"

"Oh, yes sir! I just wanted to tell him I may be able to see him this weekend after all".

"Okay, I'll tell him."

"Thank you Mr. Mathis . . . bye now".

"Bye bye hon."

(click)

This was a real drag she thought, and would only hold up her communicating with him sooner, but still her hope was renewed and she found it hard to contain herself.

"Lori! I'll be back I'm going over to Frieda's house for a minute okay?" Lori just nodded and sucked the filling out of another doughnut . . . *SLUURRRP!*

Frieda was just coming out of the shower when she heard a loud knocking at the door.

"Who is it?"

"It's me, Frieda, let me in".

Frieda opened the door and Retta pushed by her quickly not waiting for her to fully open the door.

"Durn! girl, what's up with you?"

Retta was smiling from ear to ear.

"Lori said Mama may not go to the country today!"

"Ooh! Girl that's good, so what are you gonna do tonight?"

"I don't know yet".

"Have you talked to Matt yet?"

"No" she said pacing like an expectant father.

"Rodney wasn't home yet, his dad said he was at school working off a debt or something".

"A debt, what kind of mess is that?"

"Girl I don't know, that's what I said too!"

"Well at least you got some good news for him."

"Yeah, that I do" she said beaming.

"So what about you Frieda, what are you gonna do tonight?"

She just looked at Retta with a smirk on her face as she picked up a small slip of paper from the table.

"Do you remember the bus driver?"

"Yeah, what about him?"

"Well, while you were home I called him and he said that we could get together tonight if I wanted to."

"Girl! are you nuts? he's too old for you".

"No, he isn't, he's only 20 years old."

"And YOUR only 16!" Retta finished.

"So . . . Rodney's 17 isn't he?"

"Yeah"

"And your 15 right?"

"So . . . What's the big deal?"

"The Big Deal" is "I'm 16 and a half!"

"Oh, sure, a really big difference" said Retta flaying her arms in indifference. Frieda just folded her arms and looked at her precariously.

"So where are you two gonna go?" asked Retta changing the subject.

"He's gonna stop by at 7:30 and pick me up to go to the movies".

"That's a good idea, me and Matt may go ourselves, I don't know for sure."

"So why don't you call him back?" "He may be there by now".

"Naw, I'll wait, that'll give me some time to get cleaned up in case we do go someplace". Frieda just nodded.

"So I'll see you later girlfriend, and don't do anything I wouldn't do".

"Oh, you don't have to worry about that" she said letting Retta out.

She leaned against the closed door looking quite smug.

"You mean don't do anything you! *Can't* do, then she went in her room to take a nap. "Retta, momma said she'll be home soon" said Lori as Retta came in the door.

"Is she still going out of town?"

"No, she said it was too late in the day to travel and she's too tired to do it anyway".

"*YESSS!*" said Retta pumping her fist triumphantly and dancing about. Lori just stood by staring at her in amazement and curiosity.

"What's gotten into you?" she asked.

"Love! Little sister . . . just love."

"Ooh! I'm telling" she crooned giggling wildly.

"You wouldn't understand "Mrs. Piggy" but one day you will."

"You really like Rodney don't you?"

"Nope!, I LOVE HIM!" she corrected loud and astutely.

"Well *excuuusse me!*" said Lori craning her head from side to side, hands on her little hips then walked off indignantly leaving her big sister to her thoughts.

Retta was still prancing and humming to herself when her mother came in about ten minutes later.

"Hi girls" she said sounding tired. "I'm home".

Retta poked her head out of her bedroom door "Hi Mom."

"Where's Lori Retta?"

"I'm here!" said a food clogged voice from the kitchen.

"Hi Ma".

"Is that child eating again?" asked Retta in mock surprise.

"She just had a sandwich and doughnuts a half hour ago!"

Lori appeared around the corner, her "Not-So-Little" tummy showing first.

"Girrrl your gonna turn into a hog!" teased Retta.

"Nuh Uh!" she protested and pouted with what looked to be Peanut butter and mayonnaise on the corners of her mouth.

"Lori Davis!, if you don't stop eating so much your gonna sit down one day and not get up!" said her mother.

Aretta made pig faces and giggled, Lori just pouted all the more.

"So what are we gonna do tonight Ma?" asked Retta heading to the bathroom.

"Well I don't know about you guys, but I'm going to relax and watch TV, I may even drink some wine and dance around with no cloths on in the nude!".

"OOH, I'm tellin" said Retta and Lori simultaneously then all broke up laughing. Soon after the noise and craziness had died down, Retta thought about talking to her mother about Matt.

"Uhh, Momma when I finish my bath, can I talk to you about something?"

"Sure, honey is it important?" she yelled back.

"It is to me!"

"Then why wait?"

"Well it's kinda private" she said, her voice trailing off.

Retta sat covered in bubbles – her knee's in her chest and a somewhat glum look on her face, her mother walked in but she didn't look up but just sat with her chin on her knees.

"What's the problem baby?" she said with concern in her voice.

Retta wasn't quite sure how to answer now that she had her attention and this only served to alienate her more and make her nervous, so she choked up and started crying in spite of herself. "OH! baby what's wrong!" said her mother now kneeling beside her and holding her gently. "Oh Mamma!, I'm afraid that if I tell you you'll reject how I feel and refuse me what I want" She said crying warm tears of despair.

"Retta you know that there is nothing you can't tell me or ask that I would refuse you or get for you . . . within reason". Retta still cried softly.

"Momma I love him and I want him and he loves me TOO!" she blurted out.

"Love who? baby, what are you talking about? start from the beginning".

"Well some time ago last year I met this boy in school named Rodney, he's really a nice guy and you would just love him!" she offered enthusiastically.

"He transferred from Central to our school last semester because of the zone change by the school board and then we met."

"OH! Mamma I love him so much!" she gushed again still unsure and equally bereft that what she was leading up to may cost her – her love.

"Retta! calm down honey" soothed her mother holding her close. "It's alright! *Shhh* you can talk to me."

"Oh, my Lord!" thought Audrey. "Just what did this kid do to my baby!"

Slowly Retta released her wet grip on her mother and relaxed.

"Let me see if I understand you correctly. You met someone in school last year and you two fell in love and now you want me to give my blessing and consent to you seeing each other, is that right?".

"Yes ma'am" she nodded.

"Okay" she said staring off into space now sitting on the commode.

"Is this the same boy that has been coming around here from time to time on a yellow motor scooter?"

Aretta was rigid with shock and remained silent.

"How did she know! who could have told her? I thought we were so careful!, it must have been Lori!

"I'll fix! her little butt! just wait!" She couldn't figure it out so she just bowed her head and fumed about it.

"Aretta" said her mother her tone slightly raised.

"That WITCH!, she's always meddling in other people's business!" she thought.

"I knew it for some time but I just wanted to see if you'd lie to me."

"So tell me . . . what has been happening between you two while I wasn't home?"

"Nothing Ma!"

"Aretta, don't lie to me!"

"Mom we didn't do anything, you can even take me to the doctor and see for yourself!" she said standing up and revealing her youthful nakedness.

"Sit Down! girl! and don't get cute with me or I'll bust your little backside!" Retta eased back into the tub feeling slightly proud of herself for challenging her mother to a body cavity search, a challenge that could have clearly blown up in her face had her mother decided to call her hand on it.

"Look baby, I'm not really mad with you not anymore, I mean how could I when I did some of the same things when was I your age myself!"

"So you *do*! understand! how I feel!"

"Yes, but that doesn't mean I condone or appreciate you bringing boys into my house when I'm away *either*!"

"Now Retta, be truly honest with me you know you can trust me – have you two had sex yet?" "No mamma" she said lying her naked ass off.

"Has he pushed the idea on you?"

"No Mama".

"You know how men can be, so are you sure he didn't – maybe try it a little?"

"Yes Ma'am!" she protested, tired of this question.

"Well what about you?" "How do you feel honestly?"

"Well, Mamma like I said I truly do love him" she said looking deeply into her mother's eyes unflinching.

"I want to be with him in every way". Her mother blanched at this and drew back slightly now looking at Aretta in a new light.

She just sighed heavily and shook her head.

"Yes, I do believe you do and would baby, I guess I waited too long to talk to you about these things. I'm sorry sweet heart".

"It's okay mom, I'm still your little girl, I mean it's not the end of the world or anything like that I've just fallen in love that's all."

"Well it's still no excuse. I guess I was just so busy trying to raise you girls right all by myself that I forgot to look at the young woman you've become. I'm sorry I failed you baby, can you ever forgive me?"

Retta quickly reached for her mother and hugged her close.

"You didn't fail me momma you couldn't possibly watch everything and yes I'm still your baby. I mean we haven't done anything yet, just kiss and maybe a little touching here and there" she said lying further, her voice dropping lower as if not wanting her mother to hear her. Her mother drew her away slowly looking at her oddly.

"Then you've done far more than I thought or expected." Retta just blushed and eased back into the warmth of the tub.

"You go ahead and bathe, we'll talk about this more when you get out".

"Yes Ma'am" she murmured.

Just then they could hear the scampering of little feet retreating away from the door, they looked at each other and smiled shaking their heads.

"I guess Lori will be next" said her mother then left.

"Okay, Mathis, that's it for today, time to go son".

"Alright coach" said Matt stacking up the last of the football tackle dummies in the storage shed.

"Man I'm buttermilk tired!" he sighed thoroughly spent for the day. The coach signed off on a checklist and detention time sheet on his clipboard and just laughed to himself at Matt's statement.

"You know something Mathis you're a good kid . . . I mean that!"

"So they tell me" he grunted as he closed the huge steel doors to the shed.

"No really! I mean it, your other brothers were too!"

"All of you guys are great athletes and could really go a long way with training and the right motivation". Matt leaned against the wall somewhat curious but indifferent.

"Do you remember those ten laps you ran on the track today?"

"Shoot! how can I forget! My feet still feel like lead".

"Well that'll pass, you're just soft from lack of training that's all, but did you know I was also clocking you on the first four laps?"

"No I didn't."

"Son, you ran a mile in under five minutes . . . five minutes!" He emphasized gleaming now. "That's good enough for varsity! son!"

"Oh really?" said Matt suddenly interested.

"Hell yeah! and with that build of yours and some training I'm sure you could do better and be one hell of a discus thrower too! I mean it!"

"No kiddin?, hmm I never thought of myself as an athlete."

"Maybe you ought to think about it and joining the track team cause it's starting up soon and you can end the year with a few trophies under your belt and maybe another letter too".

Matt scratched his head, he'd never thought too much about sports, even though he played several years of baseball for the city and Jr. High football, but after seeing he could add to his collection of trophies, it didn't sound too bad!.

"Okay coach, I'll think about it."

"Good, now get the heck! outta here before I have you re-chalking the football field".

"I'm outta here!" he said grabbing up his books and jacket.

"What's up Matt" said a voice behind him, it was his buddy Ant.

"What's up snake bite?"

"How long you been there?"

"Not too long, I just left the house a minute ago."

"So whatcha got planned for tonight?"

"Man I don't know, a shower, maybe stay up watch TV, then bed, I'm BEAT!".

"Yeah, I'll bet you are" said Ant.

"Coach give you a real workout didn't he?"

"MAN! HECK YEAH!" "He ran my butt into the ground and then had me do a bunch of other stuff for him too."

"But that's okay, I guess I could use the work out and besides, compared to suspension this wasn't nuthin!"

"Yeah, I guess your right when you put it that way, but still it's a shame you had to do it because of Sammy".

"What happened to that fool anyway?"

"You mean you didn't know?" said Ant.

"Naw! man, you know I left shortly after you did".

"Well Sammy got ten days suspension".

"Ten days! damn that's fucked up! but then again he did start that shit."

"Yeah, I figured that he did; shoot every since school started those two have been out to get you, what did you do to get them so mad at you?"

"Nothing! I just came to school one morning and they were all sitting on the steps cracking jokes, him, Ernest, Dabba Doo, CED and John Cotton, when they saw me coming he tried to be funny and said something about my momma, so I just said, that's okay, how's your mother and the rest of my worthless ass kids!"

"Oh, no you didn't Matt?"

"I sure as hell did! and his buddies tripped out on him and he got mad and said he was gonna get me one day, so I just told him shootcha best shot ASSHOLE! then left".

"Now I can see why they want you DEAD – you beat him crackin! and nobody does that to him or Ernest."

"You know they think they're as good as Richard Pryor."

"Well they can go set themselves on fire like him too! for all I care, I ain't backing down for shit! and while I think about it, do you know you scared the HELL out of me! today?".

"How?"

"When you dived on me and knocked me down, I thought it was Ernest!" Ant just laughed hysterically.

"No man! I'm serious! I really did!".

"Yeah I know, I saw the look in your eyes when you turned around; you were scared SHITLESS!"

"For real!"

"Yeah but when I saw it was you I relaxed a little."

They walked on in silence for the next few minutes each pondering the day's events and their mutual feelings. "Ant?"

"Yeah Matt?"

"Thanks for saving my bacon man, I really appreciate it."

"That's okay man, you know I always gotcha back."

Then he put his hand on Matt's shoulder and squeezed him confidently.

Chapter 2

The Meeting

Aretta was busy sitting on the couch drying her hair when her mother came back from taking Lori over to her friend's house to stay the night. "You're out of the tub I see" she said coming over to sit down next to her. "Yes Ma'am." "Ohh boy!" she yawned. "What a day! Sometimes I wish I was your age so I wouldn't have to work." Retta didn't speak but just smiled lightly and looked at her.

"Retta, let me explain some things to you I've been thinking about on the way home, and I want you to understand that I only have your best interest at heart so don't take this the wrong way, Okay?" "Yes Ma'am". She said then stopped drying her hair. She sat up Indian style in front of her, fully alert to whatever was to come. "Now Retta, most men ain't worth JACK! and they wouldn't piss on you if you was on fire; all they want is to take you to bed and that's ALL!"

"Now I'm not saying your friend is that way" "You mean Rodney?" . . . she interrupted. "Yes, Rodney, he may be the best of them all but until you've had a chance to see them all or at least a few of them, What do you really know?! Retta, I love you, you're my first borne! and I expect good things from you! yeah, true enough you have been a real good girl and no trouble at all and really smart in school too! I'm real proud of you, but there are a few things I don't think your quite ready for."

Anticipating her mother's chain of thought, tears began to warm her eyes and slowly break through. "Momma!, you can't mean what I think you're trying to say are you?" "NO! baby just listen for a minute" she said brushing back the damp tresses that fell into her face. "I just want you to be sure about this boy and not restrict yourself so soon before you have a chance to live a little and experience other people baby, do you see what I'm saying?" "Yes Momma, I know and I'm sure he's the one I want, I've never been surer about anything or anyone in my life!"

"Okay Retta, I just want you to be happy and safe, that's all". "I am" she said smiling and wiping back tears. "Alright honey, now that we've gotten this much out of the way, I want to talk to you some about "sex".

Retta felt a warm flush go through her as she heard this and bashfully shied away not really wanting to reveal just how much she knew already, but at the same time afraid her mother would catch on anyway. "Retta, you alright? you don't look so good." "Oh, I'm fine mom, it's just such a new thing to me". She lied evasively. "I see . . . well don't worry I won't make you ill with any of the gory details you've probably heard already in the bath rooms at school, and since I've already told you about a woman's body, "How and Why" it works the way it does I'll just tell you about men."

"Oh, this is gonna be good!" she thought readjusting her position. There was still so much Retta didn't know and couldn't wait to find out about because deep in her heart she so wanted to please Matt as a woman and not appear ignorant about the ways of love and love making, as is normally the case with virgins. "Retta, when a man and a woman prepare to make love, all the things they do to and for each other are expressions of that love for each other." "It can be a very beautiful thing if kept in the proper context".

Retta was aflame with attentiveness as she leaned toward her mother, her head resting on her hands as if listening to the juiciest gossip! "When a man becomes excited or hot for a woman as they say, his penis gets rigid and hard as well as quite long depending on the man." Retta flushed red and thought of how Matt must have felt the other night when they made love. The thought brought a smile to her face and made her pulse quicken. She had seen him naked but didn't get much of a look at his penis but imagined it was quite large from the way it felt against her and inside of her.

Retta's mother silently took in her responses and subtle changes as she spoke and described the male anatomy and condition. She also noticed the tiny beads of perspiration beginning to form on her upper lip and temples. "The Penis, she went on, is the man's sex organ, and is very, very sensitive." "It not only responds to a woman's vagina, but also the hand or what he sees." "Now after it has been stimulated by either one for a certain period of time he gets even more excited and aggressive as his orgasm draws nearer".

"How will you know when that's gonna happen?" asked Retta now ecstatic with curiosity. Judging from her daughters rapid evolution before her eyes she wasn't sure she should tell her more, but decided it was better to know now as it could save her later on. "Well what I remember happens, is his penis will start to swell and grow just before he's about to ejaculate."

"What's that?" chirped Retta, "Uh . . . that's what they call "Cumming" dear." Retta closed her legs with a resounding "SMACK!" as her bare legs slapped together, she could remember the feel of Matt's warm juices on her tummy from the other night and could no longer hide her emotions or what affects this conversation was having on her mind and body.

Her body was a kaleidoscope of warm and tingling feelings that her brain had long since processed into a living-breathing – sultry man by the name of "Rodney!" "Retta!" "I'm sorry mom, it just got the best of me and I couldn't help myself!" Her mother looked at her, slightly pensive with more than enough evidence now that Retta was no "prude" and just how chaste or virginal remained to be seen.

"Mmm . . . maybe I better stop now" she said raising an eyebrow. Retta blushed all she was worth and tried to appear less excited and imbued by it all. "Well anyway once that happens he will inject a milky white substance called sperm, and this is what makes babies and this is also why they make birth control pills." She said over emphasizing the word "Birth". "It's for responsible people who aren't ready to have children yet".

Retta couldn't help thinking her mother was aiming this particular missile at her, but didn't let on she knew. "Now! for us women, we have lots of things we can use for birth control." "Oh really?" "Yes, you mean to say you didn't know or hear about this in the locker-room yet?" "No ma'am" she said shaking her head. "Well my stars!, finally there's something I can teach you that you don't already Know!" said her mother gleaning at her. "We have foams, diaphragms, I.U.D.'s that's Internal Uterine Device or another name for a diaphragm".
"It's really nothing more than a rubber hood you place inside the vagina to cover the cervix so if a man's condom breaks "and by gosh they do" or if he isn't using one he won't get you pregnant by accident". "Oh".

"Now for the men, they have only one thing and that's a condom, have you ever seen one before Retta?" she asked cautiously trying to gage her expression. "No ma'am". "Well I'll show you one." Retta sat up ramrod straight when she saw her mother get up to go get it. Her mouth fell open like a trap door when she thought of her mother having such a thing around. She was modestly surprised and wondered why she had it! Her father had been gone for some years now and her mother's last boyfriend was long gone too!

Soon her mother returned with a small flat square packet-red in color with the name Trojans written on the side. "This is what it looks like in the package she said sitting down again and then she opened it and took it out. Retta looked at the odd-looking rubber object with curiosity and mild interest as she decided it was silly looking and didn't seem like much.

"It . . . It's kind of small isn't it? I mean is that all there is to it?" she asked bashfully. Her mother looked her over reappraising her as if to say, "How would you know! how *LONG* it's supposed to be?" but then decided instead that it was a good question. She took the slippery device out and placed it atop two of her fingers popping up a small nipple that Retta hadn't seen before and it made her jump, she then slid it down the length of her fingers rolling it down as she went.

"Now do you get it?" she said with finality, Retta now seeing the full potential of the transparent device appreciated it more and understood. "Yes, I get it" she said smiling. "Good, do you see this shiny fluid on it?" Retta nodded, "Well it's for an easy fit around the man's penis and also for an easy entry into the woman's body.
The thought of this strange and alien device entering her body make Retta feel squeamish and clutch at her stomach. She shook it off like a sudden chill and thought it repulsive and would avoid it being used on her if possible. Retta's mother was suddenly pleased at her new reaction to this training aid and felt relieved that Retta felt that way. "Now maybe she'll wait a little longer before involving herself with sex". She got up and threw it away then washed her hands and returned to sit down beside Retta who by now was sporting a perplexed look on her face.

"So you see baby making love and sex are the same but also different. It's *why* you do it that more or less determines what it is. If you don't want any unplanned pregnancies you or the man will use one of these types of birth control, "questions?" Retta shook her head slowly. "No ma'am. "Good! now when do I get to meet your new boyfriend?".

The words hit Aretta like a bus and her joy exploded all over her face! She just threw herself at her mother and hugged her. "Do you mean it momma?" "Yes baby, I'm sure your intelligent and responsible enough for you first boyfriend and by the way how old is he anyway?" *"Oh hel!"* she thought, "I didn't even think about that part."

Retta looked at her mother sheepishly "seventeen." "*SEVENTEEN!* Retta? don't you think that's pushing it just a bit? I mean couldn't you find someone closer to your own age?" Retta just sank away from her looking bereft and crest fallen, she knew convincing her mother of this whole thing would be a challenge and up until now, she was at least optimistic about winning her freedom to court. But now that the stakes had been raised so to speak she was sure her mother would reconsider her approval and cancel the whole affair.

Seeing Retta's broken spirit, she swallowed her concerns and conceded to it anyway. "Oh, I guess it's alright, your Fifteen and a half and you've been doing pretty good . . . so go ahead she sighed in submission." "Oh, thank you! Momma" she said overjoyed and hugging her again, "Can your friend come over tonight? I'd like to meet him." "I guess so if he doesn't mind or have anything to do, I'll go call him now" she said springing from the couch in a flash. "Oh well, she had to grow up sometime . . . I can't keep her young forever".

Soon Matt and Ant made it to his house, it was 6:00 o'clock, and the sun was down. Just as they stepped in the front door the phone rang. "I'll get it!" he said running for it. "Is that you, Rodney?" asked his dad "Yes sir!" "Aretta called you awhile ago". "Okay, thanks dad" he said then picked up the phone. "Hello". "Hello Matt, is that you?" "Yeah, sweet pea." "Hi! baby! where have you been all day? I called and you weren't there." "I had to stay after school and work off some detention with Coach Jones." "I see, so what are you doing right now?" "Well, me and Ant just got in." "So do you feel like doing anything tonight?" "I don't know babe I'm kinda tired and I need a bath big time." "MOMMA! WANTS TO MEET YOU!" she gushed at him.

Matt was suddenly renewed. "When do I need to be there?" Retta giggled at his sudden change of heart but knew he wanted to break the ice as much as she did. "How about say . . . an hour, hour and a half?" "Okay, let me check it out with dad first – hold on a minute" he said putting the phone down. Ant was already there talking with his dad when he darted in.

"So what's up "Hot Shot?" he said leaning back in his chair. He had always called him this since he was a kid and Ant had always laughed because he knew the story behind how he had gotten the name. "Nothing much just hanging around." "Do you boys have any plans for tonight?"

"Well Ant was talking about going to the ball game at Henderson Stadium." "And what about you . . . you planning on going?" he asked. "Well, not really, Retta just told me on the phone that her mom wants to meet me." "You haven't met her yet?" "No sir, it's my first time, I've been waiting on Retta to tell her about me so I could." "Well that's nice." "So I came to ask could I go over there for awhile." "I don't know son, you never did do those chores you were supposed to do and from what your principle told me today I'm not sure if I should let you" he said, his face expressionless.

Matt felt deflated inside and began to sand his shoe on the edge of the doorframe. "I'm a fair man son, and I'm sure you know this, so why don't you tell me what *you* think I should do?" "It wasn't my fault dad!" he blurted out. "I was gonna tell you but I just got home!" by now he was giving Matt the "*aw boy I'm just kidding*" look. "Alright son" he said grinning, "go on out for awhile, I know how much you think of your girl so go on and spend some time out, but tomorrow your gonna have twice as much to do . . . okay?" "Yes sir" he said then ran back to the phone.

"Red you still there?" "Yeah, what took you so long?" "I had to explain to Dad that the fight I got into today wasn't my fault cause he wasn't gonna let me come, so I'll be there in about an hour okay?" "Okay Matt, I'll be waiting . . . I love you". Matt looked around bashfully to see if anyone was in earshot. "I love you too Red" then he hung up. As he turned the corner to go down the hall to the den, he passed his dads room. He poked his head in to summon and then headed to his room to get ready.

"So you going to Retta's house?" He asked catching up. "Yep" "Well, I'm going to the game, I'm supposed to meet Tamika Worthy there". "Tamika Worthy!" how did you get her to go out with you "SNOT FACE!? I thought you were taking Michele?" Ant just polished his nails on his shirt smugly. "Just the Williams charm." "Naw, you probably paid her to go out with you" said Matt walking into his room and beginning to undress.

With that being said Ant lunged at him while he was taking his pants off. They both hit the floor hard and Matt quickly rolled away from him his pants still around his ankles. Matt got up quickly and with one great leap, he landed on Ant's chest and scooted his butt onto his face and head while pinning his arms in reverse position. "Eat BUTT CAKE ass wipe!" he said grinding his rear onto his face. "Ow! you son of a bitch!!" he spat then hopped off of him rubbing his backside. Ant was grinning devilishly from ear to ear – completely happy with himself for his quickness of attack. "You said eat butt cake so I did."

Now they were both laughing and rolling around on the floor. The noise must have made his dad curious because he appeared in the door and saw them rolling around on the floor laughing with Matt's pants around his ankles. He just shook his head and went back to his room to finish his paperwork. "Let me go shower man" said Matt stripping off his pants and getting up, "I gotta get across town." "Yeah, you better go see your little sweetie face before she changes her mind and buys a goat to keep her company" he snickered.

Matt just struck a seductive pose with his hands on his hips, "WATCH IT SUCKER! you don't know me that well!" He said imitating Aunt Ester from Sanford and Son, then walked off swinging his hips to take a shower. "I'll see you in a few minutes Ant!" "Alright!" he said then kicked in the stereo.

Matt thought the shower felt great as he stepped into the spray and let the stream drench him. The soothing warmth of it helped to relax all the tension and stresses of the day. Everything seemed to melt away leaving him renewed with strength and new life. "Boy! am I glad this day is over" he thought. "The next time I have a run in with Sammy, I think I'll just bust him upside the head with something and be done with his crazy ass. Ain't no need playing around with him cause the shit ain't gonna end but one way! and that's either him gone or me, and I don't plan on getting kicked out because of that fool."

Soon the rapture was over and Matt got out and dried himself then headed for his room to dress, once there he noticed Ant had taken the liberty of picking out some clothes for him to wear. He thought that was a nice and considerate gesture and reached over to give him an affectionate – brotherly punch in the arm to show his gratitude.

Once he'd gotten dressed they shut off everything and headed for his dads room to let him know they were leaving. His dad motioned him to come over to him, and then reached for his wallet to give him his allowance. "Don't spend it all in one place" he teased. "I won't" he said stuffing the bills in his wallet. "I'll see you at about 11:00 o'clock dad, okay?" "Okay son, you boy's be careful and have a good time". "Yes sir, we will" they said then turned to leave.

The ride to the stadium was rough, and being on a moped in all that Friday night traffic didn't help much. The streets were packed full of "Sunday" drivers and people who didn't seem to know the difference between a green light and a red one. "Man, this traffic "Sucks!" complained Ant, holding on tightly to Matt and grimacing at each turn and close call they encountered. "We'll never get there on time like this!" Matt looked at his watch and noticed the time was beginning to run late and they were nowhere near the stadium yet. Just about then, as they headed up between the two schools Matt got a devilish idea. He pulled back hard on the throttle "VRROOMM! went the little scooter as he darted in and out of traffic like a federal express truck gone mad, and much to the dislike of the others too! "Hey fool watch where you're driving that thing!" "BEEP BEEP!" "Damn Matt!" you gotta death wish or what?" Matt wasn't listening, he just headed for the side walk at the intersection to jump it. He had no intention of waiting out this endless convoy of Friday night cruisers.

"Bump Bam!" went the moped over the curb and up the hill beside the girl's school, they were in the clear now and nothing but open grassy fields stood in their way. "How ya like me now?" he said smiling back at Ant who was quite sure he was gonna have the worst case of hemorrhoids ever recorded. "Man, what the hell were you thinking about?" he said half laughing and half complaining. "You wanted to get there on time didn't you?" "Yeah" with his voice vibrating as Matt drove over a series of knobs and knolls "BBBut in one piece! Though." Matt just laughed at him because it felt good to cut loose and be wild for a change and to get away from the normal routine of school all week.

It was Friday night. As far as the two best friends were concerned, no laws would be recognized tonight, especially traffic, at least not right now anyway. "We'll be there soon!" Matt yelled over his shoulder. "The game starts at 8:00 o'clock and its only 7:15". "That's good, but now your gonna be late for your date with Aretta!" "No sweat, I'll just call her at the stadium and let her know what's up. Besides she doesn't live far from there anyway!" "Okay if you say so."

Soon they were pulling into Henderson Stadium's parking lot, it was huge and completely filled with cars and trucks for as far as you could see. The stadium was lit up like a super bowl game! and the new scoreboard with its digital display and sponsors all over it looked great in the distance. People were everywhere and kids were yelling at their parents to buy them some popcorn or a banner or something to pacify their little hands. Once Matt had navigated his way through the parking lot, carefully picking his way through the cars. He made it to the front gate.

"Whew!" we made it" he said pulling up to the fence and stopping. He was glad to be getting off his bike for a few minutes to sooth his sore butt. "Hey! check this out!, Southwest's cheerleaders!" said Matt appraisingly. "And look at those gams!" "Aw you wouldn't know what to do with that if you did have the chance." "Oh yeah? well what about you "WORMSNOT!" one bounce from the rump roast on that girl and your skinny ass is out for the count!" said Matt triumphantly.

Ant just laughed fiendishly and rubbed his hands together. "Well my friend, there's only one way to find out!" Then he strode off like a drill sergeant on his way to chastise some recruits. "Hey KNUCKLE HEAD! I'll be back through here at 10:30 to pick you up!" "Naw, that's okay, I'll get a ride with my cousin Peanut, I see her van over there on the end". "Okay dude, I'll catch you tomorrow alright." "Alright Matt, tell Retta I said hello." "Will do."

With that Matt rode off moving much faster than before due to the lack of an extra one hundred and eighty pounds of weight. People were still flooding in the parking lot, which was already full with both exits blocked. "Here we go again" he thought to himself then nosed the bike down the hill between the two lane road. "BEEP BEEP!" Damn! I just missed that truck back there.

"If I'm not careful I won't be visiting Retta *she'll!* be visiting me! . . . in the Medical Center!" Matt got his bike back under control and headed through Macon Homes, projects, then rode across town. The city was alive and buzzing he noticed as he passed several car loads of people, mostly high school students some he knew, some were from other schools and other places clear across town and from Warner Robins judging from there many high school bumper stickers.

Soon he reached Aretta's apartment building. The neighborhood was as quiet as a grave yard on Halloween, but this was normal seeing as how they lived on the farthest point west out in the Bloomfield area close to the motel chains. Anyone who wanted some excitement had to come into town for any fun or amusement. Matt felt like an intruder in a strange town, he had never ridden down the drive way when going to her place in the past and it made him feel strange and self aware at the sound his moped was making.

He killed the engine and coasted down the parking lot not wanting to defile this tranquil set and draw attention to himself, that's the way he always was, he was always thinking of others no matter the situation. Matt noticed that the night air was calm and a little cool but that was mostly because of the highway just north of him, and Crystal Lake to the East. He was beginning to perspire as he drew closer to her unit. His legs felt heavy as he hopped off to walk his bike the rest of the way. Matt's mouth became dry as an autumn day as he anticipated his meeting with Retta's mother for the first time.

"Will she be nice or not? Is she old or young? . . . will she like me or not? . . . damn! I hate this shit!" The moon was out full tonight and hovering over the area like a grim ominous specter on guard. It cast a grotesque and ghostly shadow on the buildings and cars giving them a bleak and stark appearance much like the way things appear on Halloween. There was small sand and grass blotted playground at the end and to the left and a swimming pool with a small deckhouse across from it surrounded by a chain link fence. The moon made it all seem eerie like something out of a werewolf movie. It was only just a simple meeting but for some reason as it always happens, Matt's mind tended to over analyze and implicate things that didn't exist, further magnifying his potential dread like an execution.

"Aw man, this is nuts! I'm standing here scared shitless for nothing and why . . . because I'm afraid of a woman I haven't even met yet! and don't even know! let me stop" he said trying to boost his courage to move himself from the spot he was standing and up the stairs. He paused a moment longer to decide and practice his introduction and what he would say – all the while staring blithely in the direction of the pool which swished and gurgled quietly in the slight breeze as though there were something living in it and moving ever so slowly like it was lying in wait for some unsuspecting midnight swimmer. Matt had never came this way and was used to the back yard's dark seclusion and the many red tip bushes that he was sure hid his comings and goings with great secrecy.

Matt pulled his thoughts together and stubbornly jerked his bike up the stairs to the main entrance. A sick feeling of abandonment and being utterly alone washed over him as he looked back at his moped, somewhat afraid to leave his old friend for fear something sinister may come along and devour it in his absence. Matt looked at his watch, "Oh Dam! I forgot to call her at the game to let her know when I'd be here!." "Oh well, it's too late now" he said to himself in the main foyer of the eight unit cubicle. The units were setup in quads, four on the bottom facing each other and the others on top. Matt felt much like a burglar as he climbed each step. He tested his footing not wanting to make any noise or draw any attention to himself, soon he reached Aretta's door and there was a faint noise coming from the inside so he was sure there was someone at home.

He began methodically adjusting and rearranging his cloths and hair in an attempt to look as presentable as possible. He was unbuckling his belt and adjusting his shirttail when all of a sudden! the door sprang open!. "OH FUCK!"

he screamed in his mind. It was her mother or some woman he wasn't sure which, but knew one thing it sure as hell wasn't Retta!

Their eyes met and caught fire as they looked and pierced each other with question upon question. Her eyes were a blazing sunset red with thick eyelashes. Her hair hung at shoulder length and was a honey brown in color. "She must be Aretta's mother!" thought Matt, as he stared blankly back at her unaware that he was still slightly undressed before her. A slight smirk began to cross her lips and the movement of this stoic woman brought him back to life, he quickly realized his disposition and immediately turned his back to her out of respect. "Damn! caught with my pants down again!" he muttered to himself angrily. "This ain't good at all!" Retta's mother was now somewhat amused and taken back by this strange and handsome young man outside her door, and to be caught in such a compromising position.

"Oh my, may I help you?" She asked quizzically. Matt recovered himself and turned around, "is this the Davis residence?" "Yes, and who might you be young man?" "Uh, my name is Rodney and I'm here to . . ." his words never came. No sooner than he mentioned his name, Aretta came bursting into the opening – eyes wide with joy and excitement.

"Hi! Matt, Mom this is Matt, the boy I told you about". "So I see" she said half smiling not completely immune to her daughter's enthusiasm. "Won't you come in?" she said opening the door wider to let him in. "Thank you." "Please have a seat" she said motioning towards a chair, but Retta quickly guided him to the couch to sit beside her. Her mother sat down opposite them and crossed her legs. Matt didn't sit back but instead upright and quite rigid. "Well, I finally get to meet you" she said most officially. "My name is Audrey, you may call me that or Mrs. Davis, if you wish but I prefer Audrey". "Thank you, I will" he said but mentally ignoring the offer as he had no intention of equating himself to her level by calling her by her first name.

Matt just sat still and played with his hands and smiled trying to be at ease but his heart raced. He never did like being in close proximity of women for very long and particularly two at the same time. She was a handsome woman though, about average height but slightly taller than Aretta who was all of 5ft 4in tall. She had a very sexy figure and well defined hips and a small waist, her breasts were well rounded in shape and stood erect as though they didn't wish to be ignored. The cleavage that showed through was very distracting and made Matt blanch as she had surely been watching him as well as he had been watching her!

Audrey wore a form fitting rust colored dress that looked as though she was poured in it and it complimented her apricot yellow pumps. Her hair was much like Aretta's but she wore it in a conservative yet teasing mushroom style that crowned her face. The intense auburn eyes and cute little astute nose made up quite an ensemble to mark her as a very good looking and sexually arousing woman. Clearly, Matt could see where Retta got her good looks. "Rodney, would you like something to drink?" "Yes ma'am, if it isn't too much trouble" he said still locked in her gaze. "Oh, it's no problem, I've made some tea already." Suddenly he felt a sharp jab in his ribs as Audrey left the room.

"Ow! what'd you do that for?" he whispered fiercely as he turned to see Retta sporting a more than menacing look. "I'm right here Matt!" she said between clenched teeth. He hadn't noticed that he'd become so engrossed in her mother and had blatantly forgotten her, but she didn't! "What took you so long? you were supposed to be here a long time ago!" "Well, I'm sorry I had to drop Ant off at the stadium, he was with me when I got home." "Oh, well you could have called and let me know something! I thought you had changed your mind so I called and your dad said that you had already left" "I'm sorry" he said softly squeezing her hand. "I didn't mean to make you worry, I was going to call you from the stadium but I got side tracked and caught up in traffic."

Just then, her mother reappeared with a pitcher of tea, Matt stood to help her. "Thank you Rodney, that's very thoughtful of you" "Your welcome" he said smiling as he began to feel a little better about her and not quite so tense anymore.

"So tell me about yourself Rodney" she asked as she adjusted herself in her seat. "Well ma'am, I live across town on Vineville Avenue. "That's a nice area" she interrupted. "Yes ma'am it is I'm a sophomore at Central High School" he went on. Then he told her about his family and all the other things he thought she wanted to know. She appeared to be genuinely interested and smiled and nodded every so often. "So . . . how did you two meet?"

Retta gave me a small brief on it but I want to hear what you have to say. Matt looked at Retta bashfully, she sat much closer to him now, and didn't look the least bit inhibited about showing her love for him and so worshipped him with her eyes. "Me and Retta met in my freshman year after I got transferred to her school. Shortly after I got there and registered I saw her, he said looking at her again. "Despite the reception they gave me when I got there, she was very nice to me and friendly. Not that I expected any special treatment you know and I really didn't expect her to say anything to me either when I passed her in the hall. I just braced myself for more nasty looks or worse, but she was really nice and helpful – making me feel a little less rejected and out of place".

"Aww, Matt stop" said Retta laying her head against his arm affectionately. "I was just being helpful that's all – there's nothing special about that." "Now wait Red, don't sell yourself short, you didn't have to do anything for me at all or even acknowledge me but you did and that was real important to me – being that I was the new kid on the block". She didn't argue the point further but just lost herself for a minute in his acknowledgement and consideration of her humanitarian efforts. She eased up to kiss his cheek but quickly remembered that her mother was sitting right in front of her watching her every move. "Oops!" she thought and quickly recovered herself blushing righteously from the incident.

"Anyway, we began to see each other from time to time between classes and talk and hang out together which everybody around let us know that our association didn't go unnoticed by their evil eyes". "Probably jealous" muttered Audrey who was sitting legs crossed and hand under her chin in a resolute but relaxed posture, eyeing him speculatively. "I was a little off balance but Retta didn't seem to care about them at all and that made me feel good". "I was glad to have her for a friend although I don't know why she chose to hang out with a school house outcast like me when she could have had her pick of any boy there!"

Retta slunked lower in the seat and turned a deep shade of red at hearing this new adulation of her, she smiled bashfully at the both of them. "Matt stop!" Matt just grinned at her, flashing her a look that said *"Ohh NO! Sweet pea, you've left me in the dark for too long so now I'm gonna expose you for who you are! and how much you mean to me."*

Audrey just watched the exchange with mild temperament and replayed thoughts of her own glory days as she reached for her glass of tea. She knew how Retta felt about the young man next to her and had she been her age she would definitely be out to coral herself one just like him. "So after a while, one thing led to another and we fell in love with each other and that's what brought us to where we are now" he said finishing.

Matt now aware of having said these things felt very strange, a really tingly and nervous feeling gripped him all over but a proud one too at having said what he felt. This affected Aretta also and she gripped his arm tenderly and laid her head amorously against his shoulder in spite of her mother looking on, and this really made Matt nervous but he didn't dare move to correct her or entice her to straighten herself.

Audrey didn't say anything, but gave instead a most intense stare as though she were seriously scrutinizing his merits in regard to her love stricken daughter as well as the relaxed posture she was in against him. Matt began to feel raw inside at the prolonged silence and tried not to fidget and give away his discomfort at her gaze.

Finally, she spoke "Well that all sounds good and pretty interesting but . . . Rodney let me try an explain myself to you, she said choosing her words carefully. "I'm a stern woman when it comes to things that concern me or anything I care about and I'm sure you can see that Aretta falls into both of those categories." She didn't even blink – Matt noticed and kept his posture stock still.

"I'm not so old that I can't see that when a young man and young woman spend more than a normal amount of time around each other, things like this happen" she said pointing at them lazily. Matt felt a nervous twitch in his spine, as he wasn't quite sure where she was going with this. "I have always taught my daughters to do the "right thing" and to know right from wrong, I also realize her feelings for you are real and genuine no! I have no doubt about that". "But are you aware that I have never allowed her to date and that you are her first boyfriend?"

Now Aretta felt a little chagrined at her mother's line of questioning, she hadn't told Matt the reason she was single for so very long and for this very reason, and no matter how much he pressed the issue. Oh she had tried hard not to fall in love with him because of the dilemma it would and currently was causing at present, she also didn't tell him for fear that he would pick up with someone else and leave her flat which was something she could not accept or see happening. "No Ma'am" said Matt looking sheepish. "Well you are, and what I want to know is what are your intensions and true feelings for my daughter." Her eyes auburn like Retta's became as red as coals as she wore a look that threatened total hellfire and damnation if his answer wasn't completely to her liking.

Without breaking his eye contact, Matt took a second or two to fully grasp his feelings for Retta and recover from his uneasiness that had unbalanced him somewhat during her "Malay." As clear as a bell and as sure as the blow of a wrecking ball it came to him, "Mrs. Davis" he said without tone. "I've met a few girls in my time and haven't dated any of them; they all either found me not masculine or cool enough one way or lacking something in another." "Either way they turned out to be superficial and cheap."

"When I met Aretta, my life wasn't in the best shape – I missed my school, my friends, and everything that meant anything to me and I felt as though I was being hijacked! or something. Aretta showed me a new way to feel, she gave me inspiration and showed me charity when everyone else showed me their disgust at who or what I represented coming into their school . . . I was truly alone. As sweet and gentle as Retta was she surly didn't need anyone to mess up her life, not me not the other guys and sure as heck not me! For some reason or another she found something in me she could like and respect and maybe even love. For me it was already that way but I couldn't bring myself to tell her for fear of rejection and coming off like a dog, like most jocks or some other guys do."

Aretta sat up and stared at him totally amazed as she had never heard him say these things before. The courage in which he said them to her mother, a woman she thought should be feared and respected by all!. "This is a man! . . . my man!" She thought to herself proudly. "Mrs. Davis, I simply and without reservations *love* Aretta with all my heart. I don't have any ulterior motives or ill designs on her. I don't think of her as a plaything or a sex object or anything like that." This statement definitely caused movement in Audrey's pristine form and her eyebrows shot up as if to say "Oh! yeah!" well you'd damn sure be the first who didn't!.

I'm sorry I haven't had the opportunity or was made known to you before now and I want to apologize for any bad ideas I've given you about me as this wasn't my intention, but Aretta thought it best to wait until we knew each other longer. I am sorry if you feel deceived Mrs. Davis or put out by all this – but I love Aretta and no matter what happens and from this day on I will always love her.

For a while there was a long pause and no one said anything. The silence in the room was deafening and the only sound was the faint tinkle of a melting ice cube as they repositioned themselves in Audrey's glass. She reached for it taking a few short sips and sat back in her seat.

"Audrey. What was that Mrs. Davis?" He asked eager to have her say anything. "I said my name is Audrey if you are going to be coming over here and seeing Aretta, you'd better get used to saying it. I'm only 32 so I am not that old yet and Ma'am strikes me as something a child says which is also something you clearly are not." Aretta giggled quietly, feeling better about the situation.

She'd known before her mother had consented to their relationship but for a moment was unsure as if she had quietly changed her mind. "Rodney, I've heard and seen a great many things in my time involving boys and men and their mutual frame of mind, but you seem to me to be the exception to those rules. I believe what you say about how you feel for Retta and I think you would be good for each other, but let's get something straight, I don't condone or allow anyone in my home while I'm away understand?"

"Yes Ma'am." she said turning her head towards Retta slowly and narrowing her eyes into slits. She knew full well her daughter had been deflowered sometime ago and wasn't fooled one bit by her act of innocence.

"I also don't go along with the idea of you two getting involved sexually either!" This made Retta sit up straight and Matt cleared his throat in embarrassment. "I know you two are at that age of curiosity and desires and I'm sure if it hasn't happened already, there have been times you wished it had!"

"Man! did this shit hit close to home, she couldn't be any closer to the truth than if she was in the bedroom with us the other night!" thought Matt as he tried to avoid any direct eye contact. Matt was beginning to think she knew more about their late night escapades than she let on. "I'm not telling you to abstain even though I would like you to. I was once Aretta's age and in love too so I know what it's like. All I'm saying is "avoid it!" if possible and if not, be responsible enough to do the right thing! and protect yourselves."

Now feeling thoroughly laid bare and somewhat unclean they agreed to her terms. "Now that we've had this little talk I feel better and have confidence in you two. Rodney?" "Yes ma'am?" he said quickly as if waiting to be addressed, she just glared at him half smiling and frowning at his answer. "I mean Audrey!" he said quickly changing it. "Come here, please" she requested. Matt got up slowly, kind of curious as to what she wanted of him that he needed to approach her any closer than he was. She stood and held out her arms motioning him into them smiling encouragingly.

Matt was a little confused and afraid to come into her embrace and concerned he just might like it giving away his thoughts of her youthful and voluptuous body. She felt wonderful! he thought as they pressed together, he tried to restrain himself but couldn't and just allowed himself to melt into her completely all the while giving the impression it was her doing. She smelled great! and he could feel her soft full breasts burn into him through her dress.

She then called to Aretta who by now was so happy of her mother's acceptance of him that she couldn't get mad about their overzealous contact. "Because you love my daughter Rodney, I love you, can you understand this?" "Yes ma'am" he nodded not really relating but believing it anyway. Soon she released them, "Now you two I'm sure have some kind of plans for tonight don't you?"

Retta and Matt looked at each other perplexed and unsure as to what to do. "Uh . . . sure! we can go grab a movie and some dinner" he offered looking at Retta not quite sure if it was to her liking or not. She agreed quickly. "Yeah that's a good idea Matt, we can do that!" "That's good then" said Audrey. "Unless of course you guys want to hang around here and watch a naked lady get drunk!"

"OOH Momma!" Audrey just smiled and ignored Retta's righteous indignation then started undoing the belt on her dress. She headed towards the bedroom and dropped the zipper in back, as she went. Matt found the light strip tease amusing and felicitous as he watched the soft material come off her shoulders. "Whack!" "Ow! What was that for?" Retta just eye balled him pensively then opened the door to push him out into the hall. "We'll see you later Ma! . . . okay! . . ." "Okay . . . have a good time and don't stay out too late!" "Yes ma'am!" she shouted back closing the door.

Soon her and Matt were putting their way blissfully along and happy beyond belief. She held him tightly around the waist snuggling her head against his back. The closeness felt great and Matt couldn't have been happier with the way things were going. Retta was fifteen and a half and he was seventeen. They were young and in love and nothing else mattered.

"So what movie do you want to see Red?" "Oh . . . I don't know . . . you decide." "Okay that'll work." "So Matt, what did you think of momma?" "She's a lot more different than I expected, at first she seemed like a woman who wasn't about to let her daughter out of her sight with anybody and that she wouldn't trust me as far as she could spit!" This made Retta laugh cause she knew the encounter wouldn't be totally smooth and had no idea Matt would get such a solid feel for her mother's true nature so soon which made it all the better that they got along so well.

"Well now you see her in a different way don't you?" "OH yeah" (snicker), I can definitely see that and I feel a little different too." "Oh? How's that?" "Well . . . you see I got this burning sensation on my right cheek and a pain in my eye an . . ." Retta just poked him in the ribs playfully. "Serves you right! You pervert! you should have had the respectable sense to turn around, then I wouldn't have had to pop you one!"

"Hey, I didn't tell her to start stripping in front of me!" "Well you still could have turned around Matt" she said sounding a little sorry about hitting him so hard. "Well I'm sorry okay baby? I didn't mean to gawk at your mom." "You know there's only one woman I want to see naked and stare at!" With that, she squeezed him a little tighter and kissed his neck. "I love you Matt." "I love you too Retta."

Soon they reached town and decided they would go to the Mall Theater. It was now 8:30pm and they were too late for the early show so they decided to walk around in the mall for a while and catch the next movie. They rounded the parking lot and found a spot for the moped near the entrance. "Ow! My butt is sore" said Retta rubbing it tenderly. "Do you want me to rub it for awhile?" said Matt coming after her with a devilish grin.

Retta just squealed happily and backed away quickly. "No! way hosea . . . at least not here silly!" "Alright we'll wait then" he said smirking and rubbing his hands together briskly.

The mall was a little crowded and Matt didn't think it would be on a Friday night but it was. Most of the people were middle aged to elderly, some with children some in couples. The majority of them was trying to get something to eat or rest from having been shopping for most of their visit and wanted a break. Retta and Matt walked along for awhile looking here and there into different shops and browsing.

"Matt?" "Yeah babe?" "I didn't know you felt that strongly about me" she said looking up at him with her arm hooked into his leaning on his shoulder. "What do you mean?" he said not quite paying attention to her. "You know? when you said all that stuff to momma about me . . . us" her gentle eyes were like dark shimmering gems as she looked into his looking for solidification of a truth she felt but wasn't sure of.

"Well it was true even if it was difficult to say" he murmured slowly as he slowed then stopped walking to face her. "Why was it difficult baby?" "Sometimes it's hard for me to say what's on my mind and in my heart, expressing my true feelings to someone I don't really know is hard but since it was about you it just came out because I truly love you and care about you baby" he said cradling her face gently.

They walked on and she stopped him at a nearby bench and sat down. "You see baby when we started hanging out in school together I felt it was just too good to be true and wouldn't last. I could never tell you these feelings because I was scared that you would be skittish and think I was like all the other guys and run from me." "Why would you think that Matt?" "Hell, look at you!" he said emotionally hissing under his breath. "Your smart, beautiful and your fun to be around, a guy would have to be nuts! not to go for you and I was sure you wouldn't want me and that's why I could never tell you until now" he said lowering his eyes.

Retta gently raised his chin and their eyes met. Her hand was so very soft and gently on his face he noticed and the tears that began to well in her eyes. She spoke so softly that he could barely hear her. "Matt, don't you know anything?" He just shrugged slowly. "Don't you realize that all you see in me is there only because you alone see it!" A silvery tear gently rolled down her angelic face. "Nobody has ever paid me any attention and the girls at school would always talk about me and call me a tomboy or stuck-up!" "The boys didn't notice me at all and when they did it would only be to pick at me and call me old maid! or iron box!, because nobody has ever seen me with my hair down or in a dress or a skirt until that one time when you saw me your first day there." "I didn't wear them because I didn't like to and related more to pants because I didn't feel like a woman or feminine."

"But when I saw you that day in the hall and you spoke to me after I said hello I was surprised and you made me feel good inside that day, but then again I thought "he won't want to talk to me or like me when people start talking about me to him."

She was crying softly now and Matt held her and wiped away her tears, fighting to hold back his own. "Then after you kept coming around me I started feeling better and I truly began to think that you might like me for real! for myself but then one day I heard a girl tell another girl that you was probably only doing it so you could get me into bed."

Hearing this Matt was shocked and let go of a tear. He was about to speak but a croak was his only response to come. Retta placed two delicate fingers upon his lips and slowly shook her head. "Matt when I heard that I was crushed and felt so dirty and stupid for letting myself like you. Soon after I got to thinking that . . . if this is what boys . . . men want then I'll just have to resign myself to it and give myself to them if I'd ever hoped to get one for my own."

Now Matt's mind was really in a tailspin as he took all this in. Revelations of last week came back to him like an evil ghost to haunt him. "The other night when I was at your house with you, was that what you wanted? Or you just did it because you thought I wanted it and wouldn't be with you otherwise?" She just nodded painfully and sighed. "Oh Retta! baby how could you?" he said. His voice trailing off as silently as a spring breeze.

In spite of the crowded mall and himself he buried his face in his hands totally distraught from this realization and cried openly. "NO, NO, NO! Matt, don't feel that way!" He just shook her off and would not be consoled. "Look at me, you don't understand baby . . . yes! It's true I was gonna do that to please you so you would love me and never leave me!" "But when I heard what you said to momma tonight knowing how shy you were, I just knew! you truly did love me and I just didn't know how much!" I almost ran you away from me and lost you for good! she said tears flowing and trembling in her voice now.

Matt could stand no more, he arose quickly, his heart afire, felt like it had exploded in his chest. His love for her was insatiable and like the force of a super nova. He seized her by the her arms and pulled Retta into a suffocating embrace. He did this so powerfully that she could feel her breath being forced out of her like a squeezed balloon. But she didn't care she met his embrace with equal force and he kissed her feverishly with total abandon. Their bodies were fused together and their mouths locked into a tortured and passionate kiss. His hands were all over her reaching, feeling, searching for her and wanting more.

Retta was warm clay in his hands and gave into his quest completely, matching him equally in her own hunger to find and possess him as well. Matt didn't care who saw them or what anyone walking by was saying about them. She was the love he'd always searched for. A woman who could make him feel whole and give him solace and desire, a woman whose very existence strengthened his fortitude and will.

Before her there was none and after her there will be none. Retta could no longer hear the murmurings of the bystanders, but instead the rhythmic crash of her heart and Matt's in her ears as well as the pulse in her body racing through her like a raging river. Over and over he thought and screamed in his mind "I love you, I love you . . . OH GOD! I love you" all the while hoping and praying that she could feel what he felt and somehow hear in her mind his desperate commitment and everlasting endearment for her. "Rodney, Oh sweet Rodney" she called his name in her mind. "Can you feel me? Can you possibly know the desire you fill me with, my love? Scorch me with your kiss my lover, my man, my all I've ever wanted!" "You touch my soul with eyes and bring me to flight at the caress of your hand. I lay bare before you my everlasting love, don't ever stop loving me Rodney . . . never, for we are one! . . . ."

"Hey! you guys!, your gonna pass out if you keep on like that" taunted a familiar girls voice. Slowly they parted and came back to reality still holding each other and gazing sleepily into each other's eyes. A flame still smoldered between them and threatened to engulf them again in its rapture were it not for their intruders still being there. "Okay you two . . . it's time you had some air."

Retta and Matt looked around them slowly and sheepishly and saw the many faces that had stopped to look and admire or ogle at their over indulgent display of affection. Just then Retta's friend Alfreida popped in between them sporting a satisfied grin. "It's a good thing we came along when we did or else you guys might have been picked up for inciting lust in public"! Retta just blushed and smiled then leaned against Matt's chest and looked at her.

"So what are you doing here besides sucking face?" Frieda chimed further. "Well we were going to the movies but we got here a little too late for the first show so we're going to wait and catch the next one" said Retta. "Oh okay" "So how about you . . . what are you up to?" "Oh, I'm just window shopping with a friend of mine" said Frieda with a sneaky grin. "Where is he?" "He's over there by the cookie factory" she said pointing.

Retta grabbed her arm and hustled away quickly as if she had a juicy piece of gossip that just couldn't wait! Matt just stood there with his hands in his pockets and watched them go. Soon Alfreida's friend was back and had two small drinks and a large cookie. He looked around curiously and glanced over at Matt since he was the only person standing there. Matt nodded, "What's up my man?" "Nothing much, he said half smiling at him. "Hi, my names Rodney." "Hi, I'm Curt" he said still smiling. "So what's so funny?" said Matt. "You two" he pointed at Matt and Aretta. "Oh, how so?" "If you guys could have seen what you looked like and the crowd you drew awhile ago, you would blush like a beet."

Now thinking back to the last few minutes Matt felt a little self-conscious and started sanding his foot on a spot in the carpet. "Hey, but don't be embarrassed my man, you love the girl!" "Anyone can see that and she feels the same about you so GO FOR IT!" "I only wished I could have someone to love like that."

Right about then Matt became aware that Curt looked a little older than he by a couple of years at least 21 he thought. "So are you and Frieda hanging out together?"
"Yeah, we met Friday on the school bus."
"Oh, so you're a senior then?"
"Nah man, I graduated two years ago, I just drive the bus."
"Oh, that's cool, so how do you like it?"
"It's a job at least until I finish college and go in the military."
"What branch?"
"I was thinking of the Air Force but I might go into the Army instead."
"Those Air Force guys are weird."
"Are you going to be in the flight side if you go?"

"I don't know I'm not much up on the flying stuff."

"How about you?"

"Me? I'm just a sophomore, I've got a year and a half to go!"

About then Aretta and Frieda rejoined them and both had a suspicious cat that ate the canary grin on their faces. "Are you ready Matt?" "For what?" "I thought we were going to window shop awhile?" she reminded him. "Oh yeah! I almost forgot that." "I'll bet you did" mumbled Alfreida as she and Curt walked on ahead. "Hey you two! Take care and we'll see ya later okay?" "Okay Curt, we'll catch you later" said Matt waving him off. "So where do you want to go first Red?" "How about to eat? I'm starved." "Yeah me too." So they headed down towards the food court and saw a nice restaurant on the side.

They went inside and waited to be seated. The place was called Annabelle's and it was very nice. The lighting was subdued and there were plants and flowers placed all around the room, each of the tables had a small candle in a vase, which gave the table an intimate glow. They managed to get a table in a corner near a stained glass window. The dark wood, the candles and the stained glass windows all came together to create a beautiful setting thought Retta. The table cloth was a rich burgundy color and Matt noticed how the light from the candle shimmered and made a glorious reflection in Aretta's eyes as the flame bathed her face in an angelic halo. She must have known what he was thinking because she just smiled and motioned him closer to her with her finger and gave him a kiss. "Thanks!" "For what?" "For letting me see myself through your eyes." "Aww!"

Soon a waitress returned. "Are you guys ready to order now?" she said with a smile. "Oh! I'm sorry, we hadn't even looked at the menu yet" said Matt a little embarrassed that they had spent so much time ogling at each other and had totally ignored the menus in front of them. Matt grabbed his and skimmed it quickly not wanting to have the waitress come back as he figured it would be a while before she did. "Fish or Steak?" he asked Aretta, "Umm, Fish." "Okay, fish it is, she will have the broiled swordfish steak and I'll have the Talapia." "And to drink?" "Sweet tea." "Sounds great, I'll have it for you in a jiffy" she said gathering up the menus and leaving.

Retta just leaned forward resting her chin on the back of her hand and eyed him curiously with a sweet grin on her face. "By the way where did you get the money to pay for all this? did you rob a bank this week?" she asked flashing her gorgeous amber eyes at him. "Why do you say that?" he asked slowly folding his arms and sitting back lazily. "Well for one thing, this ain't "McDonalds" and "Two" we didn't order "HAPPY MEALS" either." Matt grinned smugly. "I've got a little stashed away." "Oh I see!" she said looking at him with mock surprise.

Soon the drinks arrived followed by their dinner. The food smelled great and the drinks looked pretty inviting too. "Do you think they noticed that we're kinda under aged to be here alone?" asked Matt. Aretta thought a minute, "If they do, they ain't talkin much, maybe it's because of the way we're dressed and carry ourselves." "Yeah, I think your right" he agreed. "So, you gonna say grace or should I" said Retta reaching for his hand. "Nooo! it's MY job to do that part sweetie face." Retta just grinned.

Soon they were digging in and the food was great. Matt never had Talapia before but always wanted to try it. Since he was having something special he figured, ordinary fish would be too tacky so he got the biggest they had to offer. "How's your fish?" He asked between bites. "Good! I've never had a fish steak before . . . much less SWORD FISH!"

As they ate they heard a familiar song playing, it was "their" song. They stopped eating a minute to stare at each other and smile. "Do you want to dance?" he asked her. "Maybe later puddin" she said squeezing his hand lightly. This was her pet name for him. Soon they were done eating and sat together on the bench side of the table and slowly sipped their drinks, it felt good and everything was right. Matt's only real concern was how much the heavy meal was going to affect him later when they tried to leave.

"Do you think we'll always have good times like this Matt?" "Only as long as were together babe . . . only as long as were together." At that moment she reached up and kissed him on the cheek. Just then the thought hit him "OH damn!" Matt grimaced and looked at his watch and saw it was getting late and others were starting to leave. "What Matt? What's wrong?" "Our movie, were missing it again." She just waved it off, "Aww screw it . . . Why don't we just go someplace else?" she suggested. "Okay Red, you're in charge."

It was now 9:50. "We still have some time to kill or do we?" Matt thought not really knowing when he was supposed to take her home. "Red, I forgot to ask your mother when to have you home?" "She said about 11:00 o'clock so we still got some `time". "Okay then" he said relaxing and motioning to the waitress to bring their check." "Can I get you anything else?" she asked. "No thank you, just the check please." She scribbled something on a pad, set it on the table and left, they both reached for it but Matt got to it first. He made a funny Google-eyed face at Retta which caused some light hearted giggling.

"How much do you think it is?" he asked. "I don't know? how much?" He took a peek at the check as if he were playing poker and didn't trust his opponent. "Fifty dollars" "FIFTY DOLLARS!" "OOH Matt, I didn't know we spent so much, can we cover it?" She asked now turning a little pale. "What do you mean "We?" he said with mock seriousness. "I've only got twenty five bucks . . . where's YOUR HALF?"

Retta was completely stricken now. "Rodney I don't have any money!" "Well I guess we better get some aprons and start bussing some suds then." Retta looked most devastated now and Matt just sat and smiled tightly trying hard not to burst out laughing. Oops! Too late she noticed his weak attempt and started laughing. "OOH Matt, you're a "RAT!" how dare you trick me like that." Matt was almost under the table from laughing so hard. Retta just pounced on him straddling his lap and started lightly punching his arm while swearing in some strange language.

She suddenly stopped and drew him up close then kissed him deeply. They broke up when they heard the distinctive Eh hmm! by the waitress. Aretta quickly recovered herself and returned to her seat completely embarrassed, Matt reached for his wallet and brought out a hundred dollar bill and laid it on the tray.

The waitress left and returned shortly with his change. Matt tipped her nicely and they left. "Come again" said the small group of waitresses as they walked out. The night air was just great. It was cool enough to smell but not enough to feel. They held each other and kissed as they walked to the area he parked his bike, "Your chariot awaits my princess" he said while bowing royally. Retta just laughed, then got on.

Soon they were on their way. It was getting late now and the streets were quite empty except for a few people who were either going home or continuing on to other things. The night was still young by weekend standards, and Matt and Aretta were in no real hurry for it to end. "So where to my love?" he said over his shoulder. "You pick" she said squeezing him so tight he began to taste his dinner again. "Alrighty then" he said pulling off.

The trip to her area didn't take long, as the mall was only two miles from there. "We're not going home now are we?" she said looking up and seeing the way he was going. "Nah babe, I thought we would go over to Crystal Lake and sit awhile – you know chill a little bit." "Oh, that would be nice."

Crystal lake was a very *'chic'* high rise community near where she lived, the whole area was densely forested with roads going through it and small town houses strewn throughout the property. The main attraction was a man made lake that was centered in the middle of this horse shoe community. It was beautifully landscaped with all types of trees and water birds. On a night like tonight Matt was sure it would be especially beautiful because the moon was full and all the stars were out.

As they got to the lake he cut his engine and coasted to the parking lot trying hard not to alert anyone or the security guards to there presence. Matt parked between two cars then got off and headed for the paved trail that bordered the lake. Oak and pine trees formed a living awning over the trail and the moon showed through the branches just enough to light their way without giving them away. All that could be heard was the faint chirp of a cricket and the gentle surge of the lake against the shore; the moon reflected off the water with and enchanting glow making them clutch each other closer and closer.

They walked in silence for a bit just listening to their own footsteps and the sounds of the night. As they walked on they began to hear the faint sounds of music in the distance, they weren't sure of where it came from but kept walking anyway and soon found it was coming from the clubhouse further down the trail. It had Japanese paper lamps hanging all around giving it a soft festive appearance; there were couples all around dancing to tunes of the old greats (Cab Calloway, Count Bassey and others of that era). Most were in their golden years but there were a few middle aged couples and some in their twenties.

Matt and Retta thought about whether or not they should join them because the music was sweet and inviting but they hadn't been invited or were residence of the community so they just hovered and listened in silence. Just then a middle aged couple walked behind them on their way to the dance. "Hi kids" the man said holding his wife close to him. "Are you guys going to the social?" Matt and Retta looked at each other not sure how to answer. "Well sir, we just happened to notice this while walking so we haven't been formally invited" said Matt. The man, whom Matt found out later that his name was John and his wife Maggie, made a gesture with his hand as though he were impatiently waving off the notion as being trifling said, "now you're invited, so let's go everyone – the music's hopping and so are my feet".

What could they say? They went with them and everyone greeted them with approving nods and smiles, even though they were one of the only two black couples and certainly the youngest. Everyone treated them the same and with no bias.

Soon the band played a song by the Platters and boy, they were good! The lead singer sang "SMOKE GETS IN YOUR EYES" and it got to all who were there. Matt drew Aretta to him enveloping her in his arms and falling deeper in love with each passing minute. Before he allowed himself to go further he decided to check the tempo of the other guests, they were equally enraptured with each other so he and Aretta went virtually unnoticed.

"I love you" she said looking deeply into his eyes as if he were far away. "Rodney" "Yes love?" "do you think this night could possibly get any better?" "No, I don't think so, but it sure would be interesting to find out." With that she laid her head on his shoulder – arms tightly around his neck as their bodies moved in a slow fluid motion keeping time with the music. "THEY ASKED ME HOW I KNEW . . . THIS TRUE LOVE WAS TRUE . . . OHH-OH-OHH-OH-OH, THEY DON'T REALIZE THE MOMENTS THAT IT TIES WHEN SMOKE GETS IN YOUR EYES" on and on the leader sang, pushing the lovers deeper into a sweet oblivion of love. "Aretta, would you ever leave me? for anything I mean?" She slowly raised her head from his chest and placed her hand on the side of his cheek. "Rodney" she said softly, her eyes burning into him with the fire of true love brimming over and over in them. "For the rest of my life I will love only you" then they kissed sweetly and deeply, this time not caring about anything or anyone who cared to stare.

Her tongue searched and probed his mouth. The sweet smell of her was a drug – intoxicating him further – making him yearn for her more and more. She let out a whimper as their movements became more pronounced and Matt felt a tear touch his cheek and it wasn't his. This only made him swoon for her more as her eagerness to behold him grew with intensity. He could feel her heart beating stronger and stronger – keeping time with his own. Finally, he could stand no more Matt broke from her and the all too consuming desire that threatened to devour them both;. still holding her hand he ran from the dance hall into the night, and up the trail.

No one had noticed their quick and sudden departure and if so, they weren't showing it. "Matt where are we going?" she said totally confused and disoriented. "We gotta go Aretta." "But why?" "Baby, I love you so much it hurts, and being with you back there like that was just too much for me, awhile longer baby and we may have gotten beside ourselves . . . know what I mean?" "Yes I do Matt, but baby, I wanted it to happen, RIGHT THERE AND THEN!, I was caught up as much as you and I'm not afraid of it."

With that being said Matt grabbed her and they just held each other not speaking – not kissing just holding as if their lives were about to end. "We better go, it's 10:30 Red." She just nodded sleepily and allowed him to walk her back down the trail.

Soon they were on the road again and the trip to her house didn't take but a minute, they only had to go down the street a little ways. Once there, they walked upstairs holding each other not wanting to reach her door but knowing fully that it had to end sometime. Matt knocked on her door and her mother opened it. She wasn't quite asleep yet and was wearing a close fitting peach robe.

"Well" she said semi-surprised with a yawn. "I see you two made it back alright." They said yes and walked in. "How was your evening?" said Retta. "Just fine, I was just relaxing and flipping channels." "YAWN, well you guys I'm going back to bed; Rodney it was good meeting you, I hope I see you again." "Yes ma'am, it was nice meeting you too." With that she walked away yawning and scratching her head.

Now all alone and no distractions – Retta and Matt sat down on the couch and she quickly positioned him without a word into a modified laying position then lay on top of him, her head on his chest. The feel of her was great and he just loved being there that way. "Matt" she said quietly. "Yes Red?" "Are you afraid of me? I mean when you feel that way about me are you afraid to love me?"

This was strange and he couldn't really answer her. He had always envisioned that-when the time came they would know what to do. But now seeing how he had been fighting her and himself he could see how she would arrive at this conclusion. "No" he said. "I just want it to be right when it happens, I don't want you to ever think that our love is only what it is because of sex." "I want you as much as you want me – but I won't make a quick decision based on how my body feels and the convenience of time and location." "Baby, you mean more to me than that and you always will." She just held him tighter not speaking.

Soon she was fast asleep and Matt along with her. Matt awoke much later with a startle; he hadn't been aware of how long he'd slept and was now a little worried. "Aretta" he whispered, "Wake up" "Wha what's the matter Matt?" "I'm the matter, that's what!" it's 12:30 and I'm still here." She sprang to her feet. "Oh! My goodness, your really late now." "I know, it must have been all that dancing and being out late after dinner." "Yes it was" she agreed. "Look babe, I gotta go, would you please call dad and let him know I'm on my way?" "Okay" she said concerned about the time and his long ride home. She walked him to the door and he silently let himself out. "I'll call you tomorrow baby." "Okay, you be careful now?" "I will, sweet dreams Red" he said then gave her a quick kiss and left.

As he got out of the building he saw her wave at him from the living room window, he waved back and tried to ease his bike off the kickstand noiselessly. Soon he was on his way, by now the streets were empty and not a car in sight. Matt was really pushing it because he had a long way to go before he reached home. To try and make his travel time quicker, he reached down beside his left leg and adjusted the throttle control, this really boosted his speed and soon he was doing about 35 mph – his tie flapping in the breeze like a squirrel's tail on a car's antennae. Traffic lights meant nothing cause he wasn't stopping for JACK! "You stupid fool" he said to himself. "I told dad 11:00 o'clock and here it is 12:30, that's my ass now, "SHIT!" I'm through dealing now, just wait 'til tomorrow – I'll be lucky if he lets me take out the TRASH, Oh well no use bitchin about it now, I just hope I got enough gas to get there."

Matt began taking all the short cuts he knew, he went down Mercer University Blvd up Pionono Ave to Vineville, 5 or 6 miles at the least. He got to the house and cut the engine just up the street then coasted the bike down the driveway all the while praying that the neighbor's dog was asleep. "Good" he was, that dog could wake the dead".

He walked back to the front and slipped onto the porch remembering not to let the screen door slam, he passed through the second entrance door to the outside. "Boy Am I glad I chose this room instead of the other one, I can slip in and out of the house virtually undetected without waking anyone, plus it was also good for nights when it was hot. You could leave the door open and allow the wind to blow through."

Soon he let himself in, it felt good to be back because he was beat and only wanted to sleep. In no time at all Matt was undressed and in bed asleep. "What a day" he thought then passed gratefully into oblivion.

It was about ten in the morning when he finally woke up and the sun was shining brightly through his window. Matt could see the trees moving as well as feel the light breeze that was blowing today. "Great now I have to deal with the wind today too!, I hate raking leaves." Soon he dragged himself out of bed and stood in front of the mirror on his dresser. "God what is that! ?" he thought aloud disgusted by his reflection. "Man, what a difference a night makes." He poised his hand to his mouth to breath onto it but stopped and thought better of it fearing it would be just as bad.

Slowly he managed to drag himself into the bathroom to pee. "AHHH!!! must have been holding that forever!" Once finished he stripped and hit the shower. "OH! Damn,'" he screamed tumbling out of the stall onto the floor. "DAMN, THAT'S COLD!" He accidentally turned on the cold water instead of the hot, and the rush of cold water struck him like lightning.

He was fully awake now and highly pissed at himself for not paying closer attention to what he was doing. After getting his senses back he tried again but this time around the outside. He reached in and hit the hot then mixed in some cold to get it just right, then stepped under it.

"AHH! this feels better than sex . . . at least for a moment anyway." Matt just languished there until the water threatened to turn cold. "Oh well, enough of this" he thought feeling so much better now. As he walked through the den heading for his room he spied a piece of paper taped to the fire place mantle. When he got closer he saw it was a note from his dad. "Uh oh, here it comes" he thought thinking the worst case possible. "Dear Rodney, I see you got home all right, here is the list of things I want you to do today. Don't worry about the last two if you can't complete them, as I know it takes two people to do it. Fix me a lunch and I'll stop by at about eleven to pick it up okay? Take care, love dad."

"11 :00 o'clock?" thought Matt. "Hell, that's only 30 minutes from now, better get crackin, damn I'm always getting caught by the clock." So off he ran to get dressed. "BAM BAM BAM!" "Who the hell is that?" Matt looked out the window but saw no car in the drive. "Who is it?" "It's Milton, Rod" "Oh, Milton! come on in man." "What's up YO?" "Not much, I just got out the shower and am trying to hurry up and get my dad's lunch ready before he gets home." "I thought he takes a lunch or eats on the road?"

"Yeah sometimes he does, but if he's on a route that may bring him near home he'll take a minute or two and eat a hot lunch. So let me get busy." "Alright man" said Milton. "Hey you can come an help me if you want to" Matt said thinking it would go a lot quicker with the both of them doing it. "Yeah, that'll work" he agreed. Now dressed in a pair of sweat pants and a tee shirt, Matt and Milton ran for the kitchen. "I'll tell you what, you get the bread and bologna, I'll get the eggs, cheese and mayonnaise." They moved quickly and Matt started breaking eggs on the griddle and laying slices of bologna on the side. While this was going on, they started on the bread with the Mayo.

Just then the phone rang, "Get that Milt my hands are full." "Hello?" "Yo! What's up man?" he said happily. "Who is it?" It's Ant!" "Oh . . . Ask him how the game was." "Hey Ant, who won the game? Southwest? By how much? Oh that's not too bad, what did you do after the game? Oh yeah? How was it?

Who did you go with? You bull shittin!" By now Matt had gathered Milton was talking about George's date with Tamika by the surprise in his voice.

"So tell me, did y'all do the *wild thang?* he asked grinning then bursting into a wild laughing fit." "What's up? What happened? Alright Ant, we'll see you later." Click "What happened?" "Ant said he and Tamika had gone to the dance after the game and while they were there, they ran into her old boyfriend with his old girlfriend." "Tamika got mad and wanted to fight so Ant grabbed her and split."

"Yeah? What else happened?" "Well, awhile later they got ready to leave and some people were standing around a car with Smokey and Gant." "He said when he peeked in through the crowd he could see her boyfriend in the backseat half-naked with old fat Barbara Walker." "HA not that elephant!"\ "Yep!" "What happened to the girl he was with?" "Well, she got mad and went with some friends after the fight." "So what did George do with Tamika? did he get busy or what?" "Nah man, she was just playing him to get into the game." "That's too bad" said Matt not sounding too disappointed, then just looked at Milton and burst out laughing.

They had warned him she was no good. "He said he was gonna come over in a few minutes" said Milton. "I'll tell you what, why don't you go get him on my bike while I finish this." "Then we can get something going later." "Alright man." "My keys are on the fire place." "Okay" he said walking away. "Hey, CHECK THE GAS, IT MIGHT BE LOW!" "WILL DO!"

Soon Matt had finished the sandwiches and started on the juice. He found one of his dad's igloo canteens and began washing the old stuff out "YUCK!" It was a strange orange and purple colored mess and it smelled AWFUL! "Dad, you gotta start dumping these things out when you're done."

About then, he heard his bike start up and Jr. on his way up the driveway. "Jr." was Milton's nickname or short for Milton Jr. after his father. Jr. was an only child and a kind of funny guy with one of those devilish grins that made him resemble "The Joker" on Batman. He had light brown skin and a slim to medium build, brown eyes and a crew cut hairstyle. For some reason or other, women just loved him to death! You never saw him with the same girl twice in the same week, plus all were very good looking Matt thought to himself. It was probably because of the smooth – devil – may care attitude he always sported and because he was also a good dancer. It was really something to watch when he did his routine with all those waving motions he made with his arms, legs and an occasional head movement to accompany the others. He was good. He also had a step he called "ticking" it is a series of short robotic movements he made with his hands and legs. He did this while constantly touching himself in various places as if to tell a story of what he WAS or what he was trying to do.

Matt could do some of this himself but was nowhere near Jr.'s skill level. He was basically a good guy but he had a bad habit of not remembering what he was told to do in process of doing it. If something drew his attention or he got an occasional wild Hair up his butt he was gone and you might as well forget seeing him for awhile; to which made Matt cringe when he remembered that he had sent him off on his bike to get Ant.

"Oh hell, I've screwed up now" he thought; now feeling the weight of his decision. "He'll be back soon, cause George knows his bad habits too and would keep a tight leash on him where my moped is concerned." Matt's dad had bought him this yellow Suzuki moped while he was in Florida on business, which was just the ticket when he got transferred to Southwest Jr. High last year and later back to Central when he became a Sophmore.

Soon Matt could hear the sound of a mail jeep coming down the drive. It was his dad. "Oh hell" he thought. "Am I done?" He checked the set up – 2 sandwiches-a snack-2 sodas, oh yeah, and his canteen, I need to put some ice water in it. As he did, his dad came up the back steps in a hurry. He looked like an Englishman on safari in Africa, with his blue shorts, socks, matching shirt, and a huge white safari hat. "You up and at it?" he said. "Yes sir, I was just putting your thermos together." "That's good" he said fishing around in the fridge for a cold drink. "Did you get my note?" "Yes sir" he said then stood in wait of an order like the good soldier he had always tried to be. "You came in late last night didn't you?" "Yes sir." "How was your evening?" "It was great" he told him then proceeded to tell him about the highlights. "Sounds like you had a real nice evening." "Did you meet her mother?" "Yes sir" "How was she?" "She was pretty nice, maybe you could meet her sometime?" "Maybe, is she married?" "No sir; divorced, and from what Aretta says, she used to date a guy named Butler not too long ago but not anymore." "Butler, you say?" "Yes sir." "I used to know a guy named Butler, he was working at Delta Life Insurance with me some time ago." "Oh, do you think they're the same person?" "Not likely, maybe I will meet Retta's mom."

"She's really nice looking." "What's her name?" "Audrey I think, Yeah, that's it Audrey." "Where do they live?" "They live on Chambers road; you know where it dead ends and turns right and left at a light?" "Yes." "They live straight ahead at the bottom, not far from Crystal Lake." "Oh, I know where that is, that's Avalon Gardens, I've been there on another route from time to time" he noted. "What's their apartment number?" "D-6" "Now I know who you're talking about, she's about 5'6" inches tall, brown complexion – brown hair and looks kind of nice around the hips right?" "She's the one" said Matt somewhat amazed at his dad's powers of recollection. "Not bad, maybe I'll give her a buzz sometime." "Uh, Oh" he said looking at his watch. "I better go, I only had a few minutes, you got my stuff ready?" Matt quickly reached behind himself for the bag and thermos. "Good" he said inspecting its contents quickly. "I'll see you later on today son, and take out something to cook and I'll do it up this evening." "Okay dad" he said watching him go as quickly as he had come. Now fully relieved that all had went well, Matt started cleaning up the kitchen so he could prepare a little lunch for the fella's when they got back. "Hmm . . . what do I want to eat?" he thought then whipped up a big stack of hot cakes, sausage, some eggs, and milk. He barely got it on the table before he could hear the faint sound of his moped coming up the street. "Their here" he thought then headed to the bathroom to wash up right quick.

"BAM BAM BAM! Sounded the front door. "Hold up" he yelled. "BAM BAM!" They sounded once again. "I'll fix you MONKEYS" he mumbled then grabbed his dad's shaving cream, smearing some on his face then headed for the door. "BAM BAM BAM!" Matt opened it fast, growled, and hissed at them. "ARRGGHH!" then sprayed them both with the shaving cream. They screamed and stumbled to the floor and scrambled to get out side. Matt chased them completely off the porch, now happy with himself. Matt watched them roll around on the ground laughing and pointing wildly at him and each other's new paint job. "Man, you're a MONSTER" yelled Ant. "That fool is crazy" said Jr. "OOH, look at I'am" they said to Matt's satisfaction. He just started stalking back and forth on the porch like some rabid troll or something.

After a minute or two, the shaving cream started to get into his mouth and eyes. He stopped and tried to wipe it clear but the cream in his mouth caused him to choke and gag making a strange sounding noise that brought on even more hysterics from those two knuckleheads in the yard. Matt spat out the goo on the ground and ran semi-blindly to the bathroom to wash it off. It was a good trick he mused to himself. Soon he heard the slap of the screen door closing. Ant and Jr. had just come in – both a little tired from laughing so hard.

"You guys hungry?" "Heck yeah!" "Okay" said Matt heading through the den, "Let's eat." He never made it through the door, both Ant and Jr. grabbed an arm and PULLED him back into the room, they looked like the three stooges trying to get to the table. "Man you cooked a lot" said Jr. "Hell, YOU ASSHOLES EAT A LOT" said Matt sitting down. "Dig in" he said. They moved like professional swordsman as they each stabbed their forks into the pile of pancakes wiping it out totally. Now looking at the empty plate, Matt just shook his head dejectedly. "FUCKING VULTURES" do you think I could partake of just one of those pancakes?" "I mean after all, I DID MAKE EM!" Both Ant and Jr. were grinning now both with their mouths full. "NO! GET'CHOR OWN DAMN PANCAKES!" they shouted then started laughing.

They did this to each other on occasion when they ate together or shared anything. Whoever was the slowest of the group usually didn't get much if ANY, but they were just kidding and they each gave him two and some eggs. "Thank you, you been helpful." "So what's going on?" George asked. "Not much, dad gave me a list of things to do today, it's not a lot; just some raking and a little clean up in the house and he wants that dead log in back moved to the front." "We'll help you" Milton said now belching and wiping his mouth. "Then we can go to the mall or something" Ant added. "All right then, if you two are done we can get started; first I'll do the dishes." "I'll do the yard" said Milton. "That leaves the bathrooms and the den Ant." "No sweat!" "Jr., you'll find the rake in the shed under the stairs out back and George the cleaning stuff is in the pantry, I'm gonna turn on some music okay?" "Alright go ahead."

Soon they were done and it had only taken about an hour with their combined efforts, the hardest thing was the log out in back. They all had to help to move it. "Whew, I'm glad that's over" said Matt. "But we did a good job and now we can split" said Jr. "Give me a minute to shower and change." "Okay, go ahead" they said dusting themselves off. They all headed for the house when the phone rang and Matt ran up the stairs only to be caught by the foot on the third step. "BUMPITY-BUMPITY – BUMP!" "Ow" Damn someone had stepped in his butt and was heading up. Matt heard laughing, it was Ant. However, he didn't make it either cause Jr. had him by the trouser leg and was threatening to pull him back down too.

The phone rang incessantly and Matt managed to get up and climb over the two sprawling bodies and into the kitchen. He pounced on the phone just about out of breath. "Hello?" "Hello, Matt?" "Oh, hi sweetie face." It was Aretta. "What's up?" "Oh, nothing much, the guys and me just got done with some housework and stuff." "What are you doing?" "Nothing, I just got up and am now eating breakfast." "You sleep late don't you?"

By now, Ant and Jr. had made it into the house after so much wrestling. "HI Aretta" they yelled as they walked by. "Tell them I said hi Matt" she said. "Hi fella's!" "So did you enjoy yourself last night?" she asked. "Oh yes, very much!" "How about you?" "You have to ask?" "Naw, I guess not." "So what are you planning to do today?" "Well I thought me and the fella's might hang out and maybe go to the mall." "What about you?" "Momma said we're going to visit some relatives in Gray, Georgia." "That's a long way to go." "Not really, only about a half hour." "So when will you be back?" "About five o'clock I guess, I'm not sure."

"Hi Rodney Honey Pie." "Girl, get your pie face off the phone." "Who was that?" "That was Lori, she's so crazy, she just got home from spending the night at her friend's house." "Oh yeah, I almost forgot, did your dad say anything to you about coming home late?" "Naw, he just asked some questions about your

mother." "Oh, what did you tell him?" "I just described her and said she was nice that's all, did your mom say anything about you being late?" "Ha! are you kidding me or what, that woman passed out the minute she hit the bed and she still ain't up yet!"

"I saw an empty wine bottle so I guess she got tanked up an fell out, she does it every Friday, so it's okay." "That's good." "Rodney?" "Yeah babe?" "I really had fun last night, it was really special to me, I dreamed about you last night." "What about?" "You know, me and you together, it was beautiful." "Yeah, it was!" "How do you know?" she shot back at him. "Oh, I'm sorry, I was day dreaming about last night." "Oh, I thought you had the same dream I had." "Naw, I don't think I did any of that, I was too zonked out." "I'll bet you were, you fell asleep on the couch before I did." "No, I didn't!" "Yes, you did!" "You thought I was asleep but I was just laying there listening to your heart beat, I was talking to you and you didn't answer then I looked up at you and you looked so sweet lying there like that." "I gave you a kiss and you didn't even feel it." "Oh really?" "I couldn't have been that out of it I know." "Yeah you were, I wasn't too heavy for you was I?" "No baby, you felt good and warm like a teddy bear." She giggled at this. "I think that's why I fell asleep as quickly as you say." "I say!" "Rodney, don't you wish we could have stayed together all night like that?" "Yes, that would have been nice, maybe one day Red." "You really think so?" "Hey, you never know."

"Hey man let's go!" "Who was that?" "Aww, that's Milton." "Well, better let you go then, besides momma's up now and I need to do some house work myself." "Okay babe, give me a call when you get back okay?" "Okay Matt, I love you." "You too sweet pea." As Aretta hung up, she could see her mother lounging behind her on the couch with a cup of coffee. "Hey sleepy!" "Hey yourself" mumbled her mother. "You really tacked one on last night mamma!" "Not really, I was mostly just tired, the wine only carried the symptom." "Was that Rodney?" "Yes ma'am." "How'd you guys do last night?" "Oh, we did alright, everything was great!" "What movie did you see?" "Oh, we didn't get to see one, we hung out in the mall too late to see it, so we just had dinner instead." "Oh, where?" "Some place in the mall called Annabelle's." "Annabelle's, you say?" "Yeah, that's it." "That's a nice place, kind of expensive too!" "Yeah, I know but Rodney didn't care, and we had a great dinner anyway." "We ate swordfish and Something called Talapia."

Retta's mother's eyes were completely open now. "Swordfish you say?" "Just how much did he spend?" she asked completely surprised that a young man his age could afford to dine out so well. "I'm not really sure, I think it was $50.00 dollars cause he gave the lady a hundred dollar bill." "I see."

"Who is his father?" "Mr. Buford." "Have you seen him?" "No ma'am." "What does he do?" "I don't know." "Is he single?" "I don't know" she said curious and a little surprised at her mother's line of questioning. "What else did you guys do?"

"Well, after that we left and came here to Crystal Lake." "They had a really nice dance going on." "A dance?" "Yes ma'am, and they played some old time music too by the Platters and a bunch of other groups; it was a live band with brass and everything." "That place is exclusive, how did you two get in?" "Well, we were just walking along the trail looking for a spot to sit to watch the moon and the lake, when we heard some music playing."

"When we went to see where it came from, this middle aged couple came up behind us and asked us to join them so we did, and Mamma it was wonderful!" "You should have been there" she said excited. Her mother looked at her appraisingly and sized her up in a sort of older woman-younger woman type stare. "You mean "HE" was wonderful don't you?" Aretta smiled wide. "Yes, he was, he really swept me of my feet Momma, and I've never known such passion could exist in one night . . . in one man!" "Oh really?" She said changing her position on the couch. "Did he kiss you?" "Mamma!" "Well, did he?" she said half smiling. "Yes, and how he kissed me, I could feel him down to my feet Momma!" "And the way he held me on the dance floor – the music, it felt so wonderful that I was completely swept away!" "All I could do was squeeze him tighter and tighter, 1 wanted so badly to pull him inside me and melt with him into just one body!"

Aretta now noticing her own extravagant and highly suggestive body language during her detailed explanation to her mother, quickly sat down feeling somewhat ashamed at her display. "Don't stop now" her mother urged. "You've got me going now kiddo!" "Ooh, I'm telling" sang from around the corner and startled the two confidants. They both looked over towards the kitchen and Lori was standing in the hall munching bacon with the most devilish grin on her Kool-Aid reddened lips. "Oh, you get lost!" hissed Aretta.

"I'm surprised you guys made it home at all" said her mother. "Now do you see why I told you about watching out for men and their charms." "Yes ma'am." "I'm only glad I told you about sex before hand and by the way" she said lowering her voice conspiratorially. "You two didn't get involved in anything did you?" "No! Ma'am" said Retta quickly. "You stopped HIM then?" "No ma'am." "I don't understand, didn't you say that nothing happened?" "Yes ma'am, I did but it was HIM who stopped me, not the other way around" she said now a little embarrassed at her own admission. She looked away from her mother and started playing with her nails. "Oh! I see" said Audrey almost shouting. "Now this IS! News, I haven't heard of anything like this before, not to be funny, but is he gay?" "NO! She blasted, eyes now aflame and her small frame mildly agitated, "HE'S NOT GAY!"

"Hey, Hey relax Retta, don't pop a vein, I was just asking cause usually when a man or boy has such an opportunity he usually takes full advantage of it unless he's either sick, gay, or impotent."

"And I'll let you in on another secret" she said looking deadly serious. "He's not impotent and that's for damn sure." "How would you know?" challenged Retta now completely pissed off at what her mother's statement implied.

"Remember when he hugged me last night?" "Yes!" "Well it must have done something to him because unless that was a branch in his pocket, he was excited! know what I mean?" she said with and odd expression on her face. "Momma, he's MINE! how could you?" She shouted and stood with fists clenched and mouth drawn and twisted. "Now wait a damn minute dear heart, he's a nice young man alright but understand that, that's ALL he is, "A YOUNG MAN'" do you understand?" Retta just turned her head and looked out the window. "Listen baby, I know how you feel" she soothed then held her lightly about the shoulders. "But your Momma doesn't need any young man, especially yours okay?" Right about then Aretta's hurt pride gave her an idea.

"Did you know his father isn't married anymore?" she said almost questioningly without turning around. "NOW, wait a minute CUPID, I'm the last person in the world to play matchmaker, I don't expect YOU to do it either especially in my case." "I'm doing fine without Butler or anyone else for that matter and when I think I need a man in my bed I will get one myself and certainly without the help of a love sick-starry eyed pup like YOU!" she blasted relentlessly at Aretta's tuned back. Aretta caved in on herself and cried softly, her face in her hands. Her mother sighed, "Baby why are we fighting, there isn't anything in this world we can't work out together is there?" Retta just shook her head. "Well then, let's forget about men for today shall we?" "I feel like doing some girl things today." Aretta just sniffed and turned around. "Girl things?" "Oh, come on now, you mean to say that on your way to becoming a young woman you've forgotten how to be girlish?" Aretta said nothing but just smiled a crooked I-don't-know-the-type smile. "Well girls, you're in for a treat today."

By now Lori had joined them and was elated to be a part of anything that remotely resembled grown up stuff. "We are going to have some FUN!" "Yeah how?" said Lori. Audrey left quickly and stole away to her room. "You'll see! she yelled. They could hear her digging in her purse for something then she reappeared with a most sinister and toothy grin. "This is how" then she produced a Visa Gold Card. The girls sang out, *TA DA DA DAT TA DA! CHARGE IT!*" Then they all fell on the couch laughing and totally pleased with themselves. "Now you girls get cleaned up and get some clothes on and we'll clean this place up and go have the time of our lives." Just then, Aretta remembered something, "but don't we have to pay it back?" "Aretta, don't be such a prude, live a little child. Just stick with me kid and I'll show you how to really get Rodney's goat." With that, they were up and gone, each to her own tasks.

Chapter 3

School Daze

It was pretty warm today, at least 85 degrees as Ant, Matt, and Jr. walked to the basketball court behind Winship school. There were a few guys there already but not too much of a crowd. "Hey, you guys wanna get a game going?" asked Ant. "Yeah, we can shoot a few" said Matt. The ball court was a medium sized concrete and gravel strip with four hoops. Not really regulation size length, but was wide enough to run full court. There were about eight guys already there when they walked up. Matt knew one of them and Ant knew the rest. "Wuss up Fella's?" said Jr. "You got it my man!" "You got a game already?" asked Matt. "Naw, man" said the tallest of the group whom Matt knew to be Cedric. "We're just playing twenty-one." "Hey, well let's get something going then!" said Ant, full and boisterous with the joy of competition. Cedric got up in his face and smiled.

They both were 6' 3" and played a mean game. "Well, make me know it!" said Cedric palming the ball with one hand trying to intimidate Ant. "You take out first then" said Ant. "Alright, "Mash Tater!" Now it was on and the air had become thick with the heat of competition. The "Gauntlet" as they say had been tossed and accepted. These two giants would square off for a one on one, neither giving any slack, neither expecting any as the rest of us just sat back to watch.

Ced' took the ball out first. "Check!" he said passing George the ball that quickly passed it back. Cedric slowly dribbled twice, keeping Ant to his left away from the ball, then suddenly he broke like a race horse coming out the gates as he headed for the hoop, Ant countered and stepped in front swinging and countering his movements. Cedric pulled a fake to the left and was dribbling fast!

The sun reflected off the ball giving it a shimmering effect as it moved. Cedric quickly came to a stop at the top of the key-set then threw up a long jump shot, the ball moved in slow motion as it hit the back board and bounced in, SWISH! "That's two points" he taunted bouncing and hopping backwards to reset at the half court line. "That's okay" said Ant defiantly. "That's your last one, so you better enjoy it!" "What's the game going to?" asked Jr. "Ten" "Okay"

Now it was Ants turn to take out. "Check!" said Ant passing the ball. "Check yourself!" shot back Cedric. Ant didn't give him a second, he bolted from the line in blinding speed and Cedric tried to keep up by coming around wide to set up, but Ant was too fast, he took two big steps and went airborne from the foul line. He floated forever then SLAM! SWOOSH, went the ball through the hoop. "Ooh WEE! did you see that shit?" "Damn big "C!" "Oh it hurts! it hurts!" Came the roots and jeers from the sidelines, Ant most happy with himself pointed at him and said "Meditate on that SUCKA!"

After about ten minutes, the combat was over. Ant had won 10 to 6, and the others finally got a chance to play. It was Matt, Ant, and Jr. on one side and Cedric, Carlos, and Jon Cotton on the other. The game went quick with Matt's team winning 20 to 16. "Hey guys, good game" said Matt and they all shook hands and left.

"Hey Ant, let's go to your house and chill awhile before we go to the mall, okay?" "Okay." "Hey, Ant, that was some cold shit you did to Cedric" said Jr. "That game point was just too damn hype!" he laughed. "Yeah man, you took him to the hoop-past it – back to me then I set you up for the ALLEY OOP!" he was still looking around when the ball fell." "Yeah, he thought he could hang with me" said Ant. "I think he needs to buy a clue" they just laughed and walked on chiding each other playfully about each other's performance on the court.

The cool breeze that blew by felt good on their hot parched necks and sweaty backs, oh how a dip in a swimming pool would be great right now. "Hey man, you think your grandmother would mind if we washed up some in her bathroom?" "Cause I don't want to go to the mall musty and stankin" said Jr. Matt and Ant just looked at each other, "NO, USE YOUR OWN DAMN BATHROOM" then started laughing and ran off. "Hey man, that's cold, wait up."

They ran down the street and to the house, as it wasn't very far. They got there fairly quick. Ant knocked on the door and an elderly lady with smoke gray hair and reading glasses came to the door. "Hi grandma, these are my friends Rodney and Milton, we're going to the mall in awhile so we just stopped in to rest and wash up." "Well, you know you don't have to ask me BOY, get on in here and do it."

She was a large woman not fat, just big. She wore a gray taffeta dress with a high collar. She would have looked regal if not for that gob of snuff in her lip. "You boys been playing ball?" she said, her voice kind and soft and a little unclear. "Yes ma'am." "Cause you don't have on any shirts on your backsides!"

Remembering this, Matt and Jr. scrambled to put them on. "Don't worry yourselves boys, come on in and wash up, I'm used to Antney coming in like this from time to time" she said with her voice hissing on every other word. They shuffled in slowly taking in all the sights and smells of this huge entranceway. The house was well over 50 years old but still very sturdy and solid. There was roman sculptured trim around the doorframes of the adjacent rooms and a huge Persian carpet in the area they stood. The furniture was done in early American with lots of solid oak and mahogany combinations. High on the wall there was a large three mirrored dais in front of them and one of those roll top desks. It looked as old as the house but very well preserved. There were some very soft and fragile looking chairs placed in each corner of this large entry way near each of the doors to other rooms giving it a waiting room appearance. The walls were painted in a soft peach color and accented in mauve around the baseboards and ceiling trim. They were led to the right and this room must have been a parlor at one time or another because it displayed a beautiful collection of furniture all around. There was a love seat in the middle that looked like Henry the 8th owned it. It was red with crush velvet buttoned padding and very delicately crafted wood framing all around done in gold. There were other chairs and serving trays all enhanced by the old player piano up against the wall.

Matt felt as though he was in a museum of some sort. She must have caught him staring around because she said, "Thank you, I like it too" breaking him out of his wonderment and deep interest in her home. Finally they reached what Matt assumed was Ant's room because it sported more modem furnishings and several posters of his basketball hero's. "You guys can chill in here" he said heading on to the next room.

"Would you boys like something to drink and maybe a snack?" "Yes ma'am, thank you." Soon they heard the sound of running water. "George must be washing up." "Man this place is nice" said Matt. "Yeah, it does have an antique look don't it" said Jr. "Where does his moms stay?" "I'm not sure, he doesn't speak of her much." "Oh, do you suppose there are a lot of girls at the mall today?" asked Jr. "I don't know if there was a day for them to be out there in numbers it would have to be this one."

"So, Jr. who's your latest flame?" "Nobody right now, I'm just hanging around playing the field, you know how it is." "Yeah, I guess" said Matt thinking of how his life was before Aretta. "But still there's nothing like the one you love and that feeling of confident security." "Izzat so?" said Jr. looking like he had a secret that Matt knew nothing about. "Yeah, that's so!" "Do you know something I don't or should be aware of?" He just looked and grinned at Jr.

"No, not really, but in my experience, all women one way or another begin to grow tired of the same man day in day out and sometimes they want a little variety every now and then." "For instance look at me, you never see me without a girl for very long and I keep an active list of phone numbers all the time." "So" said Matt now getting irritated by his arrogance. "So, who do you think some of these girls are anyway?" "Do you think they just sit and wait for me?" "Hell no, they all got boyfriends or had e'm awhile ago until they got a load of me." "Man look, I don't mean to sound rough or shake your faith in Red."

"That's ARETTA!" growled Matt with clenched teeth, his whole demeanor now taking on a hostile appearance. "Any way" said Jr. unshaken by his hard stare. "Your girl is no different than any other girl, she just hasn't come across it yet and there is one thing you better accept if nothing else homeboy" he said pointing at him with a glare of his own. "There are guys like me all over just waiting for the chance to get at some sweet young naive little virgin to come along with a problem just so we can fill in the gap and you KNOW which way I mean that!"

Now completely pissed off at this asshole's nonchalant and sadistic evaluation of women especially HIS! Matt reached for him with the quickness of a light switch. He had, had enough and wanted to take his fucking head off! But just before he could get a solid grip on Jr.'s throat, Ant's grandmother walked in.

"I'm back, hope I didn't take too long." Matt quickly retreated to his seat, not wanting to be caught brawling in her very nice and very fragile home. Jr. just sat back and looked at him grinning completely satisfied with himself that he'd gotten Matt's goat again so quickly. Matt just mouthed his silent threats to him not wanting Mrs. Williams to catch on. "I brought you boys some tea and some doughnuts, enjoy" she said turning on her heels to leave. Matt spoke first, "Thank you ma'am." "Yeah, thanks Mrs. Williams" added Jr. As she cleared the door Matt got up and stood over him. Jr. was drawn back in his seat still grinning and munching a doughnut. "This ain't over asshole, not by a long shot, so just you stand by!" he threatened in a low voice wishing Jr. would stand so he could knock his ass back down.

"Hey what's up?" said Ant just coming back from washing up. He stood there toweling himself off and looked at the two of them somewhat perplexed by the silence of the room. "Nothing" said Matt retrieving his glass and plopping down in his chair once again. Ant quickly assessed their expressions and deduced that something has hit the fan in the short time that he'd been gone. Knowing that Matt was never the type to start or instigate anything he knew right away who started it.

"You need to quit fucking around man, one of these days Matt's gonna tear you a new asshole!" "I doubt it" he said waving him off. Ant quickly changed the subject. "Well there's the bath room, I put a towel in there for each of you." Matt took a big swig of tea and headed to the bathroom. After awhile they had all been washed up and were ready to go. "Hey mom, were going now." "Okay, you boys have a nice day now okay?" "Okay"

"Come on Lori, your taking too long" said Retta. "Well these shorts don't fit and I can't get em on!" "Guess why?" said Retta pointing at her little sister's tummy and lower half. "I'm not fat!" "No, your clothes are just shrinking." "Girls come on now, no fighting alright?" "Lori just put on something else honey, okay?" She was fuming now and not too willing to do anything anyone said but just stood there pants half on and open and pouting. "Retta, don't tease her so, you're bigger than that okay?" "Alright mom, I'll chill out." The house was ready and all that was needed was to leave. "Don't forget your bathing suits!" "Bathing suits?" they said together. "What do we need those for Momma?" "I thought we were going shopping." Audrey poked her head in the door grinning, "don't worry about it, trust me" then she disappeared again.

Soon they were on their way, the sun high in the sky and a gentle breeze blowing just strong enough to tickle the daisies on the lawn. All three threw their gym bags into the rear of the car and climbed in. "OUCH" said Lori quickly jumping from her seat, and rubbing her scorched bottom. "These seats are HOT!" "I thought I smelled bacon cooking" commented Aretta giggling. "OOO-HOO-HOO I'M TELLIN Maa!" shouted Lori angry and butt sore. "Aretta!" "Okay, okay I'm sorry, here sit on this" she said passing her a towel. Lori just snatched the towel and said thank you between gritted teeth.

The car took its time starting as the starter ground mercilessly. "Oh come on you old fart! it's too nice out to act like this." She tried again pumping the gas pedal a few times and finally with a sputter the engine came to life. "Hallelujah! I'll be glad when I can get this car fixed!" "What's wrong with it?" asked Aretta. "It's the starter or something, plus it needs a tune up real bad but I can't afford all that right now." Then why are we going on an outing if we can't afford to get the car fixed?" she wondered. She dismissed the thought and rolled down her window to let in some air. It was hot, at least 90 degrees.

"Where to first mom?" asked Retta. "First ladies, we are going to the beauty parlor to get a perm and a nail job and maybe a facial too" she said devilishly. "Then I've got something really special planned after that, but that's a surprise!" The girls were starting to rip at the seams with anxious curiosity of their mother's plans, but decided not to pry and just savor the anticipation. They pulled away from the curb and were on their way. "Turn on the radio" said Lori. "I want to hear some music." Aretta turned it on and a song by Michele Jackson was playing. "OOH! leave it there" she cooed. "I just love him . . . don't you Retta?" she said gyrating and wiggling in time with the music. "He's alright, but I like Prince better." "Prince?" her mother said curiously. "Isn't he supposed to be gay?" "No ma, he just looks that way and dresses that way for effect, besides he likes to wear high heels." "OH, I see."

Once they'd gotten to the end of Bloomfield Road, they could see the Mall. The town was really buzzing today with traffic and seemed as though anyone who had ever thought of doing anything this weekend was doing so! They managed to wind their way through all the traffic without too much trouble and drove down Eisenhower Parkway past the mall then into the Bloomfield Shopping Center.

"What is the name of this place were going to?" asked Aretta. "It's called "The Hair Affair." "A girlfriend at work told me about it." "Don't we have to have appointments?" "Naw, they have a pretty liberal walk-in policy, so you don't have to make one if you don't want to." "That's good!"

They found a spot and parked, the lot was almost full and they wondered would they be able to get in and out quickly enough to do the other things they had planned. They shuffled in, looked around, and saw that the shop was big and had 12 chairs all along the walls, they could see shampoos-conditioners and other various beauty aids for hair. Along another wall sat a display of wigs of every color, size, and shape. Soft pop music was playing and the air was tainted with the acrid smell of ammonia, Lori made a face and held her nose.

"This place smells funny!" "You'll get used to it" said a young pristine looking white girl. "Hello, my name is Margery, how are you today?" "Oh fine" said Audrey. "So what can we do for you ladies today?" "Well, we would like to get a perm and a facial." "Okay, let me see" she thought. "Oh yes, we have a special going on this week." "You can get a cut and style, a makeover, and a manicure all for only 35.00 dollars." "That sounds good" what goes with the makeover?" said Retta.

"Well, what we do is; we clean out all your pores with a special mud we use." "Then we massage the entire area and apply an aloe based mask to soften and bring out all those tiny wrinkle lines making you look years younger." Hearing this, Lori looked in a full-length mirror she happened to be standing near and curiously poked and prodded her young face and tummy.

"If it does all that I'll be back in diapers before you're through!" They all let out an uproarious laugh and drew looks from the other customers and beauticians. "Well, what do you know?" said Retta looking at her little sister. "The little butterball made a funny!" "Aretta!" warned her mother cupping her arm. "If you ladies will wait a minute I'll see if I can get you all at once." "Oh, that would be so nice" said Audrey, knowing full well that getting your hair done alone could take half the day.

Soon the woman reappeared. "Good news, I have three seats open now because one of my appointments canceled at the last minute." "So if you'll follow me to the rear we'll get you set up." As they went Lori was looking around amazed at all the strange machines and gadgets with surprise and bewilderment. She spied a woman getting her hair put in rollers of the strangest colors and sizes, she subconsciously twisted her own pigtail around her little finger. Soon they were seated and the torture was about to begin.

"Man I feel good" said Ant. "That wash up really did the trick." "Yeah, it's too hot to be walking around musty and sticky" said Matt. "It's too bad I don't have my license yet, I could probably get the truck." "Yeah, that would be cool said Jr." "So how we gonna get to the mall?" "I don't have any money for the bus" said Ant. "My mom's not home either" said Jr. Matt didn't say anything but just reached into his pocket and pulled out a bankroll and waved it over his shoulder at them, "This is how" he said smugly. He didn't have to see their faces to know that they were smirking at each other and secretly planning to bum rush him for it.

"Get em!" was all he heard before he broke and ran. Ant and Jr. were in hot pursuit like two hounds on a rabbit. He purposefully led them through the hedges at the end of the house because he knew that the small spot of fence between the hedges in the back yard would more than facilitate his escape. Once it had been at least four feet high, but after so many trips over it throughout the years by any and everybody who wanted a short cut, it was now just a foot high, booby-trap hidden by a nearby shrub. "CLANK" "Oh fuck!" they found the trap, Matt just laughed to himself as he ran through the bank's parking lot. "Gotcha!" he said then turned to see if they had recovered. They hadn't, both still lay in a twisted heap with bushes and fence all tangled about their feet. George had all sorts of trash in his hair where he nose-dived and Milton wound up buried in the nearby shrub upside down. Matt just stood there and laughed his ass off! "Man that was really fucked up,'" said Ant spitting out bits of straw and grass. "Yeah man, you set us up" whined Jr. "Fella's" said Matt in a tone almost reverent "I cannot tell a lie, I purposefully hooked ya'll assess up and that's what you get for trying to pilfer a man's bankroll!"

"Here, let me help you guys up, are you alright?" "Yeah we cool" they said dusting themselves off. "Come on lets break, we got a ways to go to get to the bus stop." They started walking through the bank parking lot heading towards the corner, once they got to the street a car passed and blew it's horn a few times.

"Hey Ant, ain't that you're pop?" said Matt. "Yeah, that's him alright." "Hot damn!" chimed Milton "we got a ride now" he said starting to walk down the side walk in that direction. They cut through the neighbor's yard and could see him getting out of his car. "Hey what's up pops?" said Ant running up to him. "Hey, what's up Anthony, how's it going fella's?" "Fine." "Well that's good, I was just coming to get you Anthony" he said. "Oh yeah, what for?" "Well, I'm getting ready to move some furniture for your step mom and I need a hand." "Aww dad" he protested. "We were just getting ready to go to the mall for awhile." "I'll make it worth your while" he coaxed.

"How much?" Ant said immediately. "How much, Oh, it's like that huh?" he said folding his arms. "You'd charge your old man?" "No! not really, I just need some dough to spend, I'm broke this week." "Oh, I see okay, I'll tell you what, how about ten bucks a piece, how's that sound?" he said checking their expressions. "That'll work" said Matt. "Sure, we can hang with that" added Milton.

"Okay good, give me a minute to check on Momma and I'll be right back." "Okay pop." "Now we got some spending money" said Milton. "How long do you think it will take to get done?" said Matt. "I don't know, my step mom has a lot of stuff, mostly odds and ends, no real big furniture so it shouldn't be too bad." "Well, we don't want to spend too much time on this, otherwise our whole day will be shot to hell and I'm not looking forward to getting sweaty again either!" "Yeah, I know what you mean, I didn't think about that side of it."

Soon his father came back. Matt hadn't seen him but one other time and that wasn't very long. His name was George also but everybody called him "Big George" because he was a big man at least 6'8" and weighed anywhere from 200 to 250 pounds. Although he sported a small beer gut, it didn't take away from his huge stature. He was very dark in complexion and had two golf ball-sized brown eyes that didn't look as though they missed much. He wore a short wavy hairstyle and sported a nugget bracelet on his right wrist and what looked to be a class ring of some sort on his left hand. He had thick full lips and a stark white cheerful smile. You could clearly see the resemblance in him and Ant. The only real difference was Ant hadn't quite filled out yet, but given the time he surely would.

"Let's go fella's" he said and got into the car. They all scrambled for the front seat or "shotgun" as it's called but Ant won out the privilege. "I know you didn't think you was gonna get my seat did you?" he said looking over his shoulder grinning at them in the back seat.

The car was nice and well kept considering its age and all, in fact it was so clean and preserved Matt had to ask Mr. Williams was it new or not. He just chuckled, no son, I've had this car for a couple of years now." "I'm planning to get a new one someday and let this one go." "Then this one will be mine" said Ant proudly with a broad grin on his face. His dad casually looked at him sideways. "Oh you're sure about that are you?" Ant sported a dejected look. "But pop! you said I could have It when you got another one!"

Matt and Milton were laughing and rooting at him now for his show of heartbreak at this new Information. "I don't know, your step mom said something about getting it, so I may give it to her instead." "But she's got one already, what do she need with two?" "Well she has a son too Jr. and he's in college and needs some transportation to get around too." "LET HIM WALK! I was here FIRST! dad!."

Ant was beside himself now and was about to get hotter. "Aww, man . . . see I knew you was lying, you say one thing and then do another, but that's okay I'll get my own one day." "You'll see, SHOOT!" His father was looking at Matt an Jr. in the rear view mirror grinning and winking as if to say; "See how big of a baby he is?" Matt and Jr. just shook their heads and grinned at the two of them. "Aww, boy quit whining, I was just pulling your leg – you know I been told you I was gonna give it to you when I got another one!" Now aware of the joke that had been played on him, Ant began to blush and feel somewhat foolish for selling out the way he had in front of his hommies. "Aw, dad that was cold G"!

Soon they had reached his father's house, it was a one-story cement block and brick house; one of many like it in this subdivision called "Kings Park." It was nice enough though, and was painted maroon with cream accents on the shutters and trim. There was a rose bush near the front door that was growing up a white lattice frame that ran from the roofline to the ground and gave it a nice effect. "Is Anita home?" asked Ant as they pulled into the driveway. "No she went out to shop for some curtains and stuff." As they walked into the house, they could see that Mr. Williams had already moved some of the furniture around in the living room.

"What are we doing first dad?" "Well she wanted to take the furniture from the living room and put it in the den and put the den furniture in the garage so we can make room for the new living room suit we're getting." "Oh, okay" he said nodding in agreement of the proposed plan. "So why don't we split up into two teams; you and Matt break down the den and me and Milton will do the living room, Okay?" "That'll work" they all agreed then set about the work.

"OH! look at you now Lori" squealed Aretta. "Your hair looks good!" Lori stared into a mirror at her new hair style which was a smaller version of her mother's previous hair style but with the addition of curls that crowned her little face in a soft innocence, making her look quite sophisticated for her age. She grinned at herself and decided she liked it. Aretta and her mother both decided on a style that was more provocative. It cascaded long and shiny around their shoulders with a rich body and shine that gave both of them a more sexier disposition.

This was a more prominent change on Retta's behalf because she had always worn her hair up and braided to the sides somewhat like Lori's but with the pigtails braided to the rear. The change made her especially beautiful and more mature. Retta couldn't believe the miracle these ladies had worked on her in such a short time, it had taken only an hour and a half for the three of them to get done and they all looked like three gorgeous sisters more than mother and daughters.

"So how about it ladies?" said the leading beautician. "You like?" "WE LIKE" they all sang with great satisfaction. "Now to keep it looking that good longer, I'm going to give you these products to use on it" she said handing Audrey a large bottle of shampoo and conditioner.

"Thank you very much, you've all done such a wonderful job on us, thank you." They walked to the front, paid their bill and left; feeling and looking like a million bucks. As they walked out, they each noticed that the sun was beaming down and felt wonderful on their tired and cramped bodies. They had stiffened quite a bit after having sat there for so long.

"Now for part two" said Audrey now smiling and thinking of her surprise as they headed for the car. Some older teens walked by and whistled their approval at the women's appearance.

"Hey baby" one of them said speaking to Audrey. "How's about we get together and do something fun?" She looked at the girls in surprise. "I don't think you could stand the heat" she said then walked away, all of them laughing.

Soon they got loaded in the car and headed off to their next destination. "So mom, where is this place?" "You'll see" she said. "It's over near the mall by Kentucky Fried Chicken she thought. Aretta couldn't figure out what it could be even though she had a pretty good idea of everything that was in the area, she just gave up and figured the place had to be new. Aretta looked into the rear view mirror and admired herself.

She really liked the new look and couldn't wait to show Matt to see what he thought. "Matt's eyes are gonna pop!" she said aloud. Audrey just looked and smiled. The trip took only ten minutes from the beauty shop.

They parked in front of a place called 'Hands on Training.' "This is it girls" said Audrey. "WHAT is it?" said Lori not sure of what 'IT' was supposed to be. "This place" she said pointing at the sign. "What's this place supposed to be?" said Aretta. "This ladies, is the land of good feelings and soft hands!" "Oh, I get it now!" said Retta. "It's a massage parlor!" "You got it!" "Let's go in!"

The girls were a little apprehensive and unsure about this because neither of them had ever been to a place like this much less the thought of some stranger massaging and putting their hands all over them. "Don't worry, you guys will love it" said their mother. As they walked in, the smell of rich oils and exotic scents attacked their senses. All were accented by a subtle hint of steam and this added had an intoxicating affect.

"Mmm" said Retta. "It smells good in here." "It smells like baby oil" cried Lori. "No Lori, those are body fragrances and oils used to bring out the best results when the masseuse rubs them on you." "What's a mass use?" she said. "You'll see soon enough."

They went to a desk in the back of the room. There were all kinds of wonderful and strange plants all around and the decor was done in an oriental setting with Bonzi plants and dragons. The calming sound of oriental music could be heard coming from a room to their left and classical to their right.

"Hello" said Audrey to the girl behind the desk. "Hi! Yourself" she said sweetly. She was a short oriental woman, a little shorter than Aretta, with long flowing black hair that she had worked into a French braid. She was very well defined for her size noticed Retta, and she displayed the most alluring and intense pair of smoke gray eyes that she had ever seen.

"What can we do for you today?" she said politely. "Well I and my girls would like to see what kind of services you have here." "We've never been to a place like this and only know of the masseuse part of your business." "Well, you've come to the right place, my name is Annabelle" she said extending her hand warmly. "Pleased to meet you, my name is Audrey and these are my girls Aretta and Lori." They both nodded and shook her small dainty hand.

Aretta mused that it felt softer than a baby's Butt and was also firm. "Well let me start by explaining what we do here at 'Hands On Training.' "We are a total body care center." "Our services range from facials to complete mud baths." Lori laughed at the thought of this because her mother didn't like for her to get dirty. "We have several well trained masseuses on staff who are trained in all forms of body wellness." "Body wellness?" said Audrey not quite getting what she meant by the term. "Yes! Body wellness." "This is the oriental art of relaxing the body's muscles and restoring strength and vitality while at the same time treating the sensitive nerves and mind through various massage techniques and music." "It's quite an experience and it leaves you completely calmed and relaxed with a great feeling of satisfaction and contentment."

"We are very discreet and have male and female technicians to suit all preferences." "That sounds great" said Audrey, now tingling all over with the thought and anticipation of some handsome stranger touching her all over her body.

"When do we start?" "Right now if you like" said the woman amused at Audrey's eagerness. "First let's get you changed." "Did you bring a bathing suit or anything?" "Yes" they said. "That's good, most people do but you won't need it." Lori gasped and covered her mouth in utter surprise. "Ooh, I'm telling" she said in a low voice almost whispering.

Aretta also reflected a perplexed look of shock at the prospect of being butt naked in a place full of strangers. Seeing this, Annabelle smiled sweetly and said, "Not to worry girls, your first stop is the sauna where you will all be together secluded and completely alone." This sounded okay but still left them a little raw in spirit at the thought of being naked in any place other than their own home.

"Come this way please" she said leading them through a set of double doors to a dressing room. Everything was done meticulously well.

They noticed the wallpaper was a beautiful red and gold oriental pattern with a dark clover green accent around the room. The carpet was plush green like the wall and smelled new. "After you ladies get undressed, just step through this door and the sauna will be there to your right" she said then turned on her heels and left.

Aretta and Lori looked at their mother. She was unshaken and quite ecstatic by this new experience. "What's the matter girls?" she said getting undressed. "We have to get naked?" asked Aretta. "Yes, but don't worry, the only one who will see you is us, and it won't be like this the whole time, plus you'll have a woman as your masseuse." "Come on let's have some fun!" Seeing their mother's confidence, they relaxed and got into the swing of things.

Once they were all undressed, they opened the door the lady had told them to. As they did, the sight was a spectacular and breathtaking scene! The room was like a rain forest; there was a huge hot tub in the center of the room and mirrors lining every wall! To the right and just above the sauna, a beautiful waterfall emptied itself into the sauna. Plants were everywhere of all sizes and shapes. It gave the room a rain forest like appearance. The sun could just barely be seen thorough the tinted ceiling window giving the room a soft eldritch glow. "My goodness!" sighed Audrey. "I never expected anything like this!" "Holy smokes!" said Retta. "This ain't the YWCA either, It's pretty" crooned Lori touching the bloom of a nearby plant.

"Well let's go girls! we didn't come to stand in the nude and gawk all day." They tiptoed their way to the hot tub, which was bubbling and steaming its sweet enchantment to their senses. "It's all so inviting" thought Aretta.

First Audrey got in to test the water and to find a suitable place not too deep for Lori. "You sit here, Lori" she said pointing to the right. Lori let out little squeaks and squeals of delight and excitement, as she stood poised at the edge waiting her turn to get into the bubbling pool.

Aretta stepped in and seemed to dissolve as she relished the warm softness of the sweet smelling water. "AHHH, this is the life" she said and lightly flicked the suds away.

Just then, the slow and faint sounds of music could be heard. It began with a soft exotic bass beat and was replaced with the sweet whine of a violin accompanied by a piano. They couldn't identify the music but thought it was a mixture of a Latin and classical tune with romantic overtones.

"So how do you guys like my surprise so far?" "It's great" said Lori, splashing and playing with the bubbles. "You've outdone yourself this time momma" Breathed Aretta. She lay back with her arms spread wide and closed her eyes letting her mind wander and just losing herself in the luxurious warmth of the tub. She began to feel a tingle run down her spine as she thought about how wonderful it all felt. The water churned and rushed all over and around her body, her nipples were starting to blossom, a sweet and engrossing feeling that made her breathe in deeply. This was soon accompanied by the sinfully sweet girding of her legs. She soon became strangely aware of the friction between her soft and sultry legs.

Retta soon began to feel an ache, a yearning as the pulsating waters rushed between her legs. She allowed the feeling to posses her further hoping her mother couldn't see the ecstasy she was feeling. "OH! how I wish Rodney was here" she thought, now boosting her desire more and more electricity danced about her skin as she thought about this. It made her gasp aloud but it was lost in the gurgling of the water. She began churning and rubbing her legs together more fervently now, uncaring of what she was exposing to her mother's periodic observations or what she thought.

"I want it! "she whispered softly. "NOW! Please!" She gasped still envisioning her invisible lover atop her with his manhood fully erect and yearning for her, threatening to explode if it's hunger to taste her wasn't satisfied. Suddenly when she thought she couldn't take anymore, a strange and wonderful feeling overtook her entire body, causing her to arch and vibrate. She threw her legs wide apart causing the churning waters to abruptly change course and channel with great force between her aching thighs! she gasped aloud staring blindly into space as this new feeling made her shudder and quake! Splashing water back and forth.

"Aretta!" her mother said softly. "Are you alright honey?" Aretta didn't answer right away, she couldn't answer she just gave herself up to wave after wave of pleasure and warmth. The shock now slowly and deliciously ebbing away, still washed her with subtle tremors of pleasure.

Soon the wave was over, her head was still thrown back and chest heaving from exhaustion against the side of the Jacuzzi. Her breathing was slowing to normal now and she could hear the faint sounds of someone calling her.

"Aretta!" her mother called, speaking more deliberate and with concern. She quieted from her calling when she saw. Aretta slowly right herself without speaking but just looked at her with a soft faraway glassy-eyed-stare. From the comer of her mouth, a smile began etching it's way onto Aretta's mouth. Her face was now aglow, her eyes had taken on the appearance of someone who had just had a miraculous revelation.

All of a sudden, Audrey knew what had been going on, she didn't speak in words but from the eye contact and facial expressions her mother was giving her, Aretta was sure her mother knew what had happened to her. "Momma?" said Lori now interested and a little excited by all the silence and stares her mother and sister were passing between them. "What's wrong with Retta, why is she wiggling and moving like that, is she sick?" Lori went on for a minute or two more unanswered and growing irritable fast. "No honey, she's not sick or anything like that, nope this *young woman* is just fine."

Audrey gave her oldest daughter a sanguine smile and just nodded as if to say, now you know what it's like to be a woman. Aretta just returned the smile silently and remained quiet. A few minutes later Annabelle poked her head into the sanctuary. "How are you ladies doing in there?" "Oh just fine" they said.

"That's good, we have your tables ready for you, so if you'll just step into this room over here there are towels to dry off and robes to put on." "I'll come back for you shortly" she said nodding and giving a generous smile and left.

"Okay girls, let's go, part two is about to begin!" With that, they pulled themselves from the pool, Aretta still flashing an unbreakable smile. Her mother looked at her as she passed into the room. "God, she's literally glowing!" she thought to herself. "I don't think I had anywhere near that much fun when it happened to me at her age." "Oh well, sweet youthfulness!"

"Momma, I feel all soft and mushy" said Lori toweling herself off. "I know what you mean sweetheart, my skin feels all soft an mushy too." "That is from the oils and the warm water we just came out of." "Oh, it feels so good" she commented rubbing her arms and testing it's elasticity.

Soon there was a tap on the door. "It's me, Annabelle! are you ladies ready?" "Yes" they said. "You each should find a bath robe in your sizes behind the door."

Aretta reached behind the door and there on hanging hooks that looked like hands, she found three thick terry towel bathrobes. They smelled and felt great! "If you will come this way we'll get you set up for part two and three." They all hustled into a large room and there were three gurney type beds like what you find on an ambulance but only nicer, set side by side and a small partition between them.

They each sat down on a bed. "Here you are" said Annabelle giving Aretta and Audrey two moderate sized photo albums. "These are our masseuses, you may choose anyone you like male or female. "Lori" she said bending down a little so they were eye to eye. "I'll be your masseuse if you like, is that okay?" Lori sat grinning and bobbing her foot over the edge of the bed. She did like the small and pretty lady because she was about her height and size anyway. Lori just nodded her approval and smiled.

"When you have decided, just push the button on that wall and punch in that persons code number okay?" "Okay" they agreed. "I'm going to get set up for Lori here while you look through the listings" she looked back and said she'd be back then left.

"These people are good" said Audrey. "Yes they are" agreed Aretta. "Have you decided on one yet momma?" "No, not yet, but I will" she said turning a page and looking at the other technicians.

She found two that she liked but could not decide between them so she just showed the page to Retta. "Which one do you like?" "him" she said quickly. "Yeah I thought so too!" "Who did you decide on Retta?" "Carrie" she said then showed her mother the picture of a pristine looking young woman of a Spanish nationality.

"You don't want a guy to do it?" said Audrey. "Nope" she said blankly. "The only man I want touching me is Rodney, if he can't relax me and make me feel good "NO" man can." Audrey's face was the picture of surprise that her daughter was so adamant about one man that she wouldn't allow any other to cater to her female base needs or desires even when she had the choice of so many handsome men and total privacy to boot.

"I guess that settles that" said her mother lying back on the bed with her arms folded behind her head and just stared at the mosaic patterns in the ceiling. "Do you want me to punch in your code?" said Audrey. "Yes please." Shortly there masseuses came in.

"Hey Ant, where do you want this piece to go?" "Oh uh, just set it near the table, Anita will just change everything around anyway" "Okay" said Matt easing the chair to the floor. "What's left?" "Just the couch and a few chairs." "Good, I'm just about beat." "Yeah me too!" "How much do your dad and Milton have left to do?" "I don't know, let's go see." "Hey Pop, where are you guys?" "In the kitchen!" he said yelling around the corner. Ant came in and sat down with a plop. "Whew" are you done yet?" "Yeah, we finished a little while ago" he said wiping his for head. "What do you two have left?" "Just a couch and two chairs."

"What time is it?" said Milton. "It's 3:00 o'clock" said Mr. Williams. "Man it's getting late, we'll be lucky if anybody is out there when we get there." "Oh! that's right, you guys were supposed to be going to the Mall right?" "Yes sir" they said eager to get going. "Well why don't you boys go ahead and set those few items in the den and I'll run you out there right quick." "Let's move it fella's" said Ant.

Soon they had the furniture in place and were ready to go. "Don't forget to lock the door Anthony." "I won't" he said closing the door. Matt and Milton were already in the car. "Okay, let's go" said Ant jumping in the car.

Big George was backing out slowly and watching over his shoulder at the multitude of children that were running around in back of him up and down the street. Soon they were on their way and glad to be going.

"You guys hungry?" he asked. "Yeah, but we can wait" said Ant not wanting to stop and get tied up in traffic. "So who are you boys going to meet at the Mall?" "Oh nobody special" said Matt. "We're just gonna go an hang out, maybe play some video games and check out a movie or something." "That's good" he said. "You guys gonna need a ride back?" "Naw, we'll just catch a bus or walk." "Alright then" he said speeding up a little.

The trip back through town took less time than the trip up. It was 3:30 now and most of the downtown traffic had made its way to where it had been struggling all day to get to. Milton was leaning against his door snoozing. Matt noticed his door wasn't quite closed so he lightly reached over him without waking him and pushed in the lock, not wanting him to fall out should his door decide to open by accident.

"So how have you boys been doing in school?" "Oh fine" said Ant. "Have you been staying out of trouble Anthony?" "Yeah Dad" he said shooting Matt a subdued grin in his sun visor mirror. "Rodney I hear you been fighting lately" "Oh?" he said completely shocked at how he knew this. "Yeah a good friend of mine said that you and Sammy Thomas, got to fighting Friday and you did a real job on him."

Ant looked at Matt with pleading eyes as if to say "I DIDN'T TELL HIM!" "Uh, yes sir" he said reluctantly. He didn't really want to talk about it but felt ill at ease not to. "He started it when he pushed me in the hall and then punched me" "That must have felt good" he said grinning. "Sammy is a big boy!" "I know" said Mat still wondering how he managed to take him.

"If you don't mind my asking, how'd you find out about this?" said Ant looking just as surprised as Matt was. "You know your principle Mrs. Espy?" "Yeah" "We used to go together in high school."

Their mouths fell open like the hatch on a dump truck. "No shit?" said Milton now up and fully interested. "OOPS, I didn't mean to say that!" Big George was quite pleased with himself now for having upset their false sense of security they thought they had within their little group. "Yeah Milton, NO SHIT!" "So now I think you boys will pay CLOSER attention to what you do in school now that you know I have inside information on you."

Ant looked away and started to blush. "I wonder does he know about me an Pricilla in the locker room." Coach said he wouldn't snitch.

"And YOU, Anthony" he boomed flatly. "How's Pricilla doing these days?" "Damn! he knows!"

Soon they were pulling into the mall, it was still quite crowded which was a good sign. Mr. Williams pulled to the front entrance on the JC Penny's side of the building.

"Here you go fella's" he said reaching for his wallet. He gave them each ten dollars. "I'll see ya later Pop." "Okay, give me a call this evening okay?" "All right dad" he said then slammed the door and walked away.

"ALRIGHT, we finally made it!" said Matt. "With ten bucks to boot as well" said Milton. "Let's go get some grub first" said Matt. "I'm starved, then we can go check out the arcade for awhile, I hear they got this new game that you control the character instead of having a preset moving pattern to run him through."

"Oh, that's called Dragons Lair" said Milton. "And it's dope too, I've played it, you have to make the movements for the knight as he comes to different scenes." "That's not new" said Ant. "The trick of the game, "BUTTHEAD!" is to make the move before you get to the point that you have to so the computer can tell your character what to do." "It's a lot of fun, you guys should try it."

"So I see" said Matt pointing at the cluster of kids standing around that particular game. "We'll come back" said Ant.

Just then two girls walked by looking their way and smiling. "Hi Milton" one of them said. Her voice was dripping with flirtation and enticement. "Yo baby, wass up?" said Milton giving a wild hand and arm display. "Nothing we're just hanging around, how about you?" she said standing closer. "Oh I just got here, me and the fella's" he pointed in the opposite direction. The girls gave them a polite smile and nod and returned to Milton.

"Hey dude" Ant said. "We're going, we'll check you out later." "Alright home boys I'll get whitcha" he said then walked into an alcove near the entrance by the arcade for more privacy.

"Nothing but a cock hound" said Matt as he and George headed for "Mickey D's" or McDonalds. "Yeah, one day he's gonna catch something bleach wont take off" said George.

There were four lines at the counter when they got there; each one represented at least a 10-minute wait. There was one other cashier station but it was closed so they settled themselves in the line that seemed to move the fastest. "Man, I'm so hungry my stomach thinks my throat is cut!"

George burst out laughing as it was a habit or Matt's to say strange and metaphorically cryptic things like that in certain situations. "Boy your crazy, where do you come up with shit like that?" "I don't know, I just say how I feel at the time" he said looking sheepish because he wasn't the only one who had heard the remark.

Soon the line moved again but not fast enough for them. "Man! let's bug out" said Matt feeling more irritable by the minute. "Where else you wanna eat at?" "Let's get some pizza or something else . . . anything I'm hongry!" "You know I don't have much cash on me" said Ant.

Matt held up his hand in front of his mouth indicating, "NOT ANOTHER WORD" then produced his money clip and flipped the edge of the bills for effect making a flapping sound.

"Remember these guys?" "Oh yeah" he said making a useless grab for the bankroll. "AH AH AH, behave yourself "ANTNEY" he said pronouncing his name like his grandmother had earlier, this really cracked him up.

That's one of the things he loved about his best friend, he was always happy and easy going and quick to crack up. He also loved the strange half-crying' half moaning sound he made while laughing. His eyes would begin to tear and a large vein would strain itself to the surface on his forehead giving him an even more hilarious appearance. "Man cut it out" he whined holding his stomach. "You know you trip me out when you talk like that." "So come on, let's break!" said Matt pulling him along.

"What about Jr.?" said Ant. "Aw, he'll find us, besides have you ever known him to spend any money on any girl?" "Now that you mention it, No" he said with a peculiar smile. "So let him be" said Matt. "Bet!"

"So ladies how do you feel?" said Annabelle. "Was it everything I said it would be?" "OH, YES!" they said. "I feel so good, I don't know whether to lay down and sleep or run a marathon" said Audrey. "How about you Retta?" "I'm speechless! my body is still tingling."

"Carrie has very good hands, I never knew anybody could make me feel so good, let alone another woman." "Retta" said Audrey in a slightly embarrassed tone as she signaled to Retta's rear with her eyes. "Oh! I'm sorry" she said blushing. "Did I say something wrong?" "No sweetheart" said Annabelle. "I know how you feel, I felt the same way when I first did it."

Lori was just now coming out of the dressing room. "Hiya cutie" said the lady as if they were old friends. "How's the "Bod?" "The what?" she said twisting her head in funny way.

"The Body" said Retta. "Oh, it feels all mushy-gushy but I like it." "Mushy, gushy?" "Now that's one I haven't heard before" said the lady laughing. "If you guys are through dressing we can go to the front."

All of them had smiles because it was an experience they wouldn't soon forget. As they went through the door they saw a couple sitting in the spot they had been only hours ago, their eyes met and each acknowledge the other. "So how was it?" said the woman. "You'll love it!"

With that she went up to the counter and paid the bill. "Here you are" said Annabelle handing them each a small complementary package.

"What's this?" said Lori. "Oh, it's some of our oils and bath fragrances, it helps relax you and remove tension as well as softens the skin." "It also helps you to remember your visit here so you will want to return." "Thank you" said Aretta. "You guys come see us again okay." "Oh we will" said Audrey. "We will!"

They were back out in the sun now and the sun was still high and bright in the sky. "I feel so good momma that I can't stand having clothes on!"

"Now just hold on a minute MS SQUISHY!, at least wait until I get you home okay?" she said smiling and getting into the car. "Now for the grand finale" said Audrey.

"What's that?" said Aretta and Lori. "Shopping!" "Where?" "The Mall silly, where else?" So off they went all smiles and completely satisfied with their day so far. Aretta was thinking how much she couldn't wait to tell Rodney what they did today, then thought, 'Naa, I'm gonna let him see for himself.'"

"I only wish he could have been there with me in that hot tub, "ooh" that felt so deliciously wonderful!" she thought. "I wonder is it going to be like that with Rodney when we Do finally get the time and opportunity to be together like we want.

Audrey was looking at her but she didn't notice it, "I swear, this girl never ceases to amaze Me! She's becoming more self aware faster than I thought, it's almost scary the way she thinks so much more mature than I gave her credit for." "I wonder if I should let her continue to see that friend of hers, he's a little older than what I had in mind for her and he's no fool either from what I can see and especially the way she goes on about him."

"You'd think he was the best man in the world not to mention the most exciting lover too if that's become a fact yet. She's just so full of him I really wish

I knew him better, then I could be more sure of him. Then again, maybe I can! Didn't she say that it was just him and his father? hmm I wonder . . . but how would I get to meet him without seeming forward or presumptuous?"

"I've got it!, I'll let Aretta invite them to dinner tomorrow, that'll do it!"

"Audrey, your a sneaky little minx but your cute though . . . Verrry cute!"

"Mamma, watch out" screamed Aretta. Her mother hadn't noticed the car coming on her left side and had drove out into it's path. It was because she was too busy daydreaming. She quickly slammed on the brakes and the force threw them all hard against their seat belts. "Are you alright!" she said checking both girls. "Yes ma'am were okay, didn't you see that car momma?" asked Lori. "No baby, momma's mind was some place else" she said now hugging both girls tightly.

"That's okay, we're alright" said Retta. "No harm done!" "Oh, okay so long as nobody is hurt." With more caution this time, Audrey pulled out into the mainstream once again and went looking for a place to park. She pulled the car into a spot on the other side of the mall near the door. She saw a wagon to her left pulling out then whipped the little import into it quickly to avoid losing it to an approaching truck.

"Whew!" she sighed. "That was close, we almost missed that one." "Well you guys ready to go?" she said giving her best effort to ease the tension seeing that the girls were still a little shaken up from the close call they'd had.

"Yeah lets go" said Aretta. "I'm starved!" "Yeah me too!" said Lori. So they locked up the car and went inside.

"This is the way me and Rodney came Friday night" said Retta. Her good mood returning as she thought about him. The three of them went through the double doors and the acrid synthetic smell of the place rushed out to greet them.

"Yuk, what is that weird smell? it smells like plastic or something" said Retta. "That's where we ate dinner." Her mother looked and nodded her acknowledgement. "It's nice, very nice but we won't be eating there today dear heart" she said with a staunch expression on her face, the girls just laughed. "Aw momma, you're a mess!" chided Retta.

"How about Chicken Fil-a?" said Audrey. "Yeah, that's a good spot" they agreed.

"What can I get for you gentleman today?" "I'll have a Monte Christo and an ice tea, how bout you Ant?" "I don't know man, I can't decide, everything looks expensive." "Oh, quitcher bitchin, I got the tab." "I'll tell you what, if it makes you feel better give me your ten and I'll take care of us today okay?" "I don't know man, it sounds good, but I can't let you do that" he said shaking his head.

Just then the waitress, a young pretty brunette smiled sweetly and said, "We can always use an extra hand in the kitchen doing dishes." Having said that, Ant reached into his pocket and quickly withdrew a crumpled ten-dollar bill.

"Here take it, I get the message." "So what will you have?" said the waitress with a satisfied smile on her face. "I'll have two of what he's having." Matt and the waitress just looked at each other amazed that someone as skinny as Ant could eat so much.

Sensing their surprise, he spoke up. "What? why ya'll looking at me like that?"

"Obviously you've never had one of these before have you?" "No I haven't." "I thought so, excuse me waitress" called Matt. "Give him some horse radish sauce to go with that too and bring a pitcher of tea instead of a glass." Ant was a little puzzled. "Why do we need a pitcher, won't that be too much to drink for just a samich?" he said looking back and forth from the waitress and Matt.

"You won't think so in a minute" she said sweetly collecting their menus and leaving. "Matt what did you order me?" "Just chill homeboy, you'll see in a minute." "Okay" he said sitting back and relaxing. "So where do you think Jr. is right now?" asked Ant. "I don't know, knowing him he's probably down near the bathrooms knocking boots on one of those girls he's with, either way he's doing his own thang."

"I heard that." "So when did you start coming to this place?" "I never have prior to me and Aretta coming here Friday night." "So how do you like it so far?" asked Matt. "It's real nice-kind of sophisticated and romantic." "Yeah, I thought so too." "You want to dance?" joked Matt giving him a sinister grin.

Matt was well known for being a little livid and wild at times. Ant just laughed. "Boy you're a nut." "I know, I can't help it I just like to have fun!" "I see that" said Ant. "You know something Matt, we always have fun together." "Did you ever think about that?"

All of a sudden Matt started to feel a strangeness wash over him like a chill or something. He had had many thoughts about his best friend but he'd never given voice to them or acknowledged what he was to him.

Matt lowered his eyes and nervously started playing with his silverware. "You know Ant" he said speaking softly. "For as long as I can remember it's been me an you." "We've shared a lot of good times together, even while we was in Jr. High."

"Yeah, I know" he agreed. "We've always been close like brothers, we've gone on dates together and we cruise together." "Hey! do you remember that time when we had Kim and Michele in your pops car on 7th street that night?" said Matt breaking in.

Ant started laughing. "Yeah we did have fun that night!" "Ant, do you remember how your date couldn't get enough, it's a wonder you didn't pass out!" "I thought I did" he said remembering that sexually demanding night.

"You know Ant" said Matt getting serious again. "Did you ever wonder why we know what each other is thinking and feeling most of the time?" "Yeah, I guess" he said slowly. "But then again I kinda always knew." "You did?" said Matt believing that he did know how he felt. Suddenly he looked up at Matt, his eyes more intense and softer than he could ever remember seeing them. Then he spoke, his voice was low and almost undecernable. "Your my brother Matt, I've always thought of you that way. And throughout the years you became more special , more closer than any friend i've ever had" he paused for a moment weighing his words. "It guess i love ya man" Matt knew this was true because his heart and the gut wrenching feeling he was now experiencing told him so. Matt reached out and cupped his hand in a familiar handshake know only to them both. "Ant i love you to man" it was a powerful feeling that had just passed between them. They had shared their most private feelings and emotions about each other to each other in complete frankness and honesty. Matt could never see himself telling him openly but would let him know he was more than his best friend with the many hugs and looks they shared. This wasn't supposed to happen, they were boys-men. Their gender forbade this form of male bonding but it was out now and they had committed the ultimate heterosexual sin . . . they spoke their heart felt endearments to each other and had meant it. Matt felt warm all over and still a chill managed to wash through him. It made him acutely aware of himself and gave him strength and pride in himself because he had never told any other male that not even his own brothers. Still he was glad he'd said it because now he knew they had a bond nothing and nobody could ever break. They loved each other as soul mates and friends and that was that. "Matt" he said weakly, still locked in thier handshake. "Yeah Ant?" "Does this mean we're gay?" "Matt smiled wide at him and burst out laughing then punched his arm. "Naw man! it just means we know what each other means to the other and we're happy about it and accept it. Matt didn't know where the wisdom and maturity came from to give him this new revelation but the feeling! that had overcome him left him elated and heady like that of an out of body experience. His perspective was changed and all his perceptions of his old classic male self seemed to fall away as he began to feel himself rise from within. His body felt like it was floating . . . hovering and yet still be sitting. "My god! this feels wonderful!" he thought to himself amazed. "Am i supposed to feel this way at this age? my mind and awareness is totally scorched and wide open! even my eyes see differently" Matt hadn't know it but he had reached the first real milestone of manhood and to becoming the compassionate, altruistic, perceptive caring person he was destined to be. Just then the waitress came back, breaking into his revelry and breaking his psyche. "Hi guys, I'm back and here is your orders" she said setting down the dishes before them. Instantly Matt began to see the young woman, a girl about his age in a new light.

His order in front of him.

He found himself appraising her features and scanning her body from head to toe, all the while luxuriating in his newfound awareness and retrospect. "Why am I doing this?" he thought to himself. "I got a girl, so why am I scoping this one out so hard?"

Finally he said something to her, at first he didn't think it was his voice that was speaking. His tone and voice seemed different somehow; more direct and sure almost like a surgeon speaking to a class full of interns.

"Excuse me miss, may I ask your name please?" She smiled and stood up from her task. "Sure my name is Melanie; Melanie Colfax" she said staring at him with mild surprise and a slight hint of pleasure that he'd asked. Matt reached out his hand to make her acquaintance.

"How do you do" he said. Ant was watching closely now and with curious interest and awareness, for he too had noticed something different about Matt. A certain boldness – a sternness as well as something compelling in his tone.

"Hi my name is Rodney and this here is my best friend George." She smiled and shook his hand. "Melanie" he continued, not quite knowing what he had stopped her for or intended to say. "I've been watching you since we got here and I think you are a very attractive and beautiful young woman."

"Listen at ME!" he thought to himself. "She's as old as I am and I'm speaking to her as if she were much younger." Now she was blushing deep red and stood erect with her arms to her sides. "Are you seeing anyone right now?"

Matt was shocked at his own question as was she and George who displayed the most stricken look he'd ever seen.

"Nno" she stammered still locked in his gaze, her face seemed only inches from his. "I like you Melanie, and what's more I think my friend here likes you too."

She was looking at George now in an embarrassed but approving manner then smiled her approval of his unspoken opinion of her. George of course never looked away from Matt, his face still aghast with shock at what Matt was doing and the professional way at which he was doing it.

"LOOK AT HIM!" he thought. "So cool and calm, this can't be Matt, he NEVER had the guts to do anything even close to this, and he's so smooth with it too!"

"I think that you and him would make a nice couple, what do you think?" he said still holding her attention. "I don't know, he's very handsome and all but I would have to get to know him better" she said in a weakened voice almost too afraid to speak.

"Well then sit down" he said almost commanding her while taking her hand. His aggressiveness and authority mesmerized her; she'd never had a man control her so thoroughly and completely. Melanie tingled all over and was totally enslaved by his will.

"She smells wonderful" thought Matt and so fine!" Melanie was about 5' 8" tall with sea green eyes and a sensual mouth, her hair was as black as onyx and flowed lovingly down her back. She had high cheek bones and full breasts and her figure flowed in a fluid hourglass shape. She radiated with a dark golden tan, that was even and smooth looking. As she sat next to Matt, he could feel her warmth. It was penetrating and absorbing to be near, he purposely and without hesitation raised his hand to remove a lock of hair that had fallen over her shoulder onto her face.

She was beautiful but Matt wasn't interested in her, he was just spellbound and committed to bringing her into Ant's horizons. Matt allowed himself to gently caress her silky cheek with the back of his hand, Ant just sat and stared at her.

"Melanie how old are you princess?" he asked still caressing her cheek. "I'm eighteen" she said still locked into his gaze. Matt felt as though he might kiss her but thought better of it and just smiled.

"I really would like to see you with him Mel, he's a real good guy and I'm sure you would like him as well" she just nodded. "I'm not going to pressure you Melanie because I know that this is all so sudden and new to you." "Have you ever dated a black guy before?" he asked now close enough to smell the sweet aroma of her breath as she breathed ever so lightly. "Would you object to it?" "No."

"Then you're in for twice the thrill and surprise you've only heard about, still interested?" She just nodded. "Good, then I don't want to keep you any longer because I know you have work to do, so I'll just give you his number and you can give him yours okay?" he said holding up his free hand signaling Ant for one of his business cards he had made in school.

Matt placed it in her hand then gave her a pen he always kept in his wallet. She scribbled and handed the paper to Ant without looking at him. Matt then made a motion to rise still holding her hand and now taking the other, helping her from the double bench seat.

"Give him a call this evening if you can" said Matt standing very near her. So near that her breasts brushed lightly against his chest. "Okay" she whispered.

Matt slowly let her go as if prolonging his controlling affect on her. She seemed reluctant to go then she dropped her gaze and walked away, her gait was not as confident as it had once been but more cautious and reserved as if she didn't trust herself.

Matt sat back down and Ant was staring at him as if he never saw him before today. Matt was suddenly aware of what just took place and the thought left him kinda cold and bewildered.

"Ant? what just happened here?" "You mean you don't know?" he said disbelieving him. "No! I mean I'm not sure, was that me?" Ant shook his head up and down. "Why did I Do that?" "HOW! is more to the point! Never in my life have I ever seen anybody do that to a woman except maybe Dracula. Here . . . let me see your teeth" he said reaching for Matt's lips. "OW!" Matt bit at him nipping his finger, Ant just laughed and so did he.

Now Matt was feeling like his old self again. "So . . . did you like her?" said Matt sipping his tea. "Yeah!, Hell yeah, she's dope." "I'm sorry man, I didn't mean to do that to you, I mean it just came outta me and I couldn't stop myself."

"Well I'll tell you what Matt, if that's the kind of women you have in mind for me I'll gladly accept anything you bring but to be honest with you, I think she's locked into you" he said taking a huge bite of his sandwich.

"Why do you say that?" asked Matt, not having witnessed what he did from his perspective. "You shitting me right, man the look that girl had on her face when you was talking to her, I thought for sure she was either gonna kiss you or collapse."

"Either way you had her in the palm of your hand dude! And what's more, if I live to be a hundred I know I'll never see again what I saw here today!" "It was that strong huh?" "That strong? man you had her body and soul, if you had told her to strip naked she probably would have without too much hesitation." "She was hypnotized by you man, and the way you was touching her and she let you."

"Just how was I touching her?" he said not quite sure he didn't do something he wasn't supposed to do in his clouded state of mind. "You was touching her hair and face like she was yours already, and the part I can't believe the most is that she actually let you do it! What came over you Matt?"

"I don't know, hell, I was just suddenly aware of myself after we talked and she just happened to be near by when the spell came over me. Damn, that's some feeling! I wish I could get it" said Ant. "Believe me Ant, you might not want it." "Well maybe not, but it would be nice to see what it felt like anyway" he said munching his sandwich.

"So how do you like the sandwich?" said Matt. "It's good, but what is this yellow mustard like stuff?" "Oh, you haven't tried it yet?" "Well go ahead an try it, it's really shit hot" said Matt smiling to himself. Ant grabbed the sauce and poured a healthy portion on his sandwich. "Smells good and kinda hot" he said then bit down big on it.

"AHHH!!!!" His eyes grew as big as silver dollars and just as shinny. You could almost smell the smoke coming off him. "It's called "Horse Radish" sauce, you like it?" said Matt grinning openly now and trying hard not to burst out laughing at Ant an giving away the fact that he knew it was hot as hell and had deliberately set him up.

Ant was frantic and trying to drink anything he could find, ice cubes and all, whatever it took to cool the inferno in his mouth. "Want some more?" said Matt handing him the dish of liquid hell. Ant said nothing but glared at him in pain burning a warning to him that he was gonna kill his ass when he finally got though this.

"HAAA haa haa hoo ha" Matt laughed long and loud, so loud that the few people that were in the restaurant began to turn their way and stare. They displayed puzzled looks at Ant in his discomfort and frantic movements about the table for anything wet.

Matt just laughed on noticing that Ant began to resemble a blow fish with his cheeks all puffed up with half a sandwich sticking out of his mouth and still trying to pour tea into it. It was a fiasco and Ant was quickly becoming a mess. Finally he just spit out his mangled – half eaten meal on his plate, "SPLAT!" it landed with a disgusting sound.

"OOH!" said Matt flinching away from him still hooting at his Malay. "Is everything okay?" said a young white guy in a tie and white short sleeve shirt. "Oh yes" said Matt. "He just loves your Monte Christo, especially with LOT'S of horse radish sauce on it."

The man looked at the upturned empty container of sauce and knew what was wrong now. He just shook his head and mouthed, "Oh my god, this man is gonna need a tongue and mouth replacement when he gets done."

"Aretta are these the one's you want?" said Audrey. "No mom I want the flesh tone stockings not the tan ones." "Well I don't see any difference, so just take these for now." They were well into their shopping routine now, and Aretta was trying on different dresses and accessories. "How do you like this one?" asked Lori turning around for her mother to see. "It's nice but isn't it a little bit too big?" she said.

Lori had put on a warm up suit that hung off her quite loosely around the ankles and on the sleeves. "Why don't you try on something else okay?" "Alrighty" she said running off to change.

Soon Aretta stepped out of the dressing booth. "How do you like it?" she said smiling from ear to ear. "Ooh! Retta" her mother crooned. "You look GORGEOUS! Baby!" "Thank you" she said. It was an evening gown she had picked out, the sleeves were long and ruffled at the shoulders had a deep-revealing neck and back line which more than showed off her womanly figure.

It was ruby red with diamond and gold sequence all over it. The dress was form fitting with ruffled pleats around the hips giving it a French look. The split that gently spread from just beneath her crotch and expanded into an upside down 'V' at her feet, more than excited the imagination. Even though she stood bare foot, she still looked quite elegant.

"Can I have it mom?" she asked about to bust with excitement. "Oh, I don't know Retta" she said examining the garment closer and speculating on the price. "Oh please, I know I'll never see another dress like this ever again." "Oh, now I don't believe that" she said with her hands on her hips. "But you do look real nice though" she said agreeing with her own thoughts.

"Well, I guess you can have it." "YESS!" shouted Aretta jumping up and down happily and kissing her mother's cheek.

"Okay okay, don't kill me already!" she let her mother go and stood there looking at herself in a full-length mirror. "Oh Rodney, Rodney" she thought to herself turning from side to side. "Boy are you in for a surprise!"

A man who was walking by with his daughters noticed her and stopped a second for a closer inspection. She saw him in the mirror, and there was a lusty smirk on his face as he raised an eyebrow showing his interest in her young and luscious body.

Just then her mother caught the reflection of the man's face and quickly turned on him giving him a frigid stare, "PERVERT!" she hissed at him angrily. The man turned red with embarrassment then made a quick retreat dragging with him his confused and protesting daughters. "But daddy I'm not finished looking" one cried as he quickly cleared the area.

Aretta hadn't given him a second thought but inwardly felt a warm flush as she stood basking in the man's suggestive gaze. "Maybe you better get something else Retta" said her mother rethinking her daughters choice and the potential problems wearing it would cause.

"Uh, baby this one might be just a little bit TOO provocative for you at this time." "Oh, come on mom, you said I could have it, your not going to back out now are you?" "Don't worry, the only time I'll wear it is when I'm out with Rodney, and I'm sure he can protect me if anyone gets beside themselves."

"Oh, girl come on let's go" said Audrey sounding quite impatient and tired. "Get changed before I change my mind." Retta didn't stick around to hear more but just scampered into the booth as quickly as the dress would allow.

"Mom I couldn't find anything" said Lori coming back very discouraged from her search for a better fitting suit. "We still have more places to look before we leave and by the way I almost forgot I need to go call your grandmother to let her know were not coming this week so she won't expect us."

"Aretta" "Yes ma'am?" she said peeking over the door. "I'm going to the lobby to make a phone call, meet me out there when your done okay?" she said pointing towards the circular sitting area around a huge planted tree and walking away. "Okay mom." "Are you done yet?" asked Lori fidgeting with the door handle. "Almost, I still need to take off these stockings."

"Is momma gonna let you keep the dress?" "Yeah, but for a while I wasn't sure, get me that hanger over there Lori." Retta hastily put the dress on the hanger and got dressed in her own things.

Soon she stepped out of the booth and headed toward the cashiers desk. There was a middle-aged woman behind the counter. "Hi!" she said looking over her reading glasses with a grandmotherly smile. "You must be Aretta and Lori." "How do you know that?" asked Retta curiously. "Your mother said you would be coming so she paid for the dress on her way out." "Oh" she said nodding, "but how do you know which one I got, I could have put it back and gotten a more expensive one?" she said doubtfully. "I saw you trying it on sweetie" said the woman smiling at her as if she were an infant asking the simplest of all questions. "That's how!" "Oh, I see" she said feeling a little hot about the face.

"It is a lovely dress said the lady, attempting to diffuse any shame Retta might feel due to her uppityness. "Is it for a special event your going to?" "No, not yet, but there will be" she said feeling light hearted again at the question and what it implied.

"Well he must be a special young man to be getting to see such a beautiful young lady like you in such a beautiful gown" she added. "Oh, yes ma'am" said Retta blushing. "He is and I can't wait for him to see me in it either." "Well you have a nice time and a nice day." "We will" they said now walking to the door.

"Lori, which way did momma go?" "! don't know, she just went." "Well, did you see the direction she went when she left the store?" "Yes, she went that way" she said pointing to the right. "Well let's go then!"

The Mall was huge. It was two stories tall and had a green transparent ceiling, the area they were in looked like a courtyard. It was set up in a circular arrangement with a combination of stores and food shops intermixed as you went. There was two large passageways that intersected the circle, one led to the outside and the other was the main artery through the Mall. There was also an escalator in the center of the courtyard with many fountains and plants set up in little islands of stone and brick. "I don't see her Lori!" are you sure she went this way? "Yes" she said almost whining. "Well let's go the other way, she's got to be some where near here."

"Hey man! that was a dirty trick you played on me" said Ant. "You could have told me that that stuff was hot!" "I'm sorry dude, you know I couldn't resist getting you on the sly" he said still chuckling at the scene they had just left in Annabelle's Café."

"Just look at my shirt man, it's all messed up, now I'll look bummy and shit." "Don't sweat it, I'll get you another one while were here okay?" "Alright" he agreed and starting to relax a little. "Come on, let's go this way" said Matt heading left. "Hey, I know a store near here that has some good sport shirts."

"Hey, isn't that Aretta?" "Where?" "Right over there! walking with some kid." Matt soon saw where he was pointing to and all he could see was a young woman with long flowing black hair and dressed in a jean skirt and a red polo shirt. She was very sexy thought Matt as he watched her some more and smiled when he marveled at the way the sun had shown so brightly in her direction. It reflected off her rich head of hair and accented her tan skin. "Naw, that ain't her." "Aretta has her hair braided all the time and I know that ain't her sister Lori because there's no food sticking out of her face."

Ha ha ha, they both laughed thinking of the little piglet they both knew so well. But still Ant persisted, "Man I tell you it's her, I saw her face." Matt looked at him wrinkling his eyebrows. "Alright Sherlock, lets go an see if it's her." "Now when you see you done made a fool of us in front of a perfect stranger, I want you to explain it to her okay?" "Okay" said Ant feeling confident and doubtful at the same time because he was remembering that Aretta's mother had long ago established a set and unbreakable dress and appearance code that would not be altered under any circumstances.

They followed them down the breeze way and in an out between the venders that dot the main floor throughout the Mall. They were trying to keep their interval and pretending to be looking for someone but at the same time trying to catch up without being noticed.

Matt tried to get an angle on her from the side hoping to get a better look at her before he committed himself to embarrassment, but her collar was up and the sun defused the shop windows so he couldn't see her reflection to well either. "Damn!" he thought to himself at his bad luck. Matt noticed that she was very nice looking and she had nice shapely legs that were lightly tanned and a heart shaped bottom that made Matt readjust his crotch.

"Come on!" said Ant pulling him along. "Quit stalling!" "I'm not stalling!" he whispered loudly. They were very close now and almost to the next courtyard on the other end. They caught up to her and got her attention.

"Excuse me, miss, miss!" She stopped and turned around quickly. "Yes?" she said pensively then quickly softened her stare when she saw who it was.

Matt was shocked and could not speak. He wanted to say who he thought his eyes were seeing but his tongue would have no part of it. She was breathtaking! Her eyes shown with intense satisfaction and joy, Matt marveled as he gazed over her entire body. She had a soft tan that gave her an iridescent glow in the sunlight. Her luscious body was an hourglass shape and the way her hair hung slightly across her shoulders and crowned her face, made Matt tingle.

Before he knew what he was doing, he grabbed her arms quickly, pulled her to himself, and planted a hot kiss on her surprised and waiting lips. His mind reeled as the taste of her sweetness flooded his senses, their tongues played about each others mouths in a gentle ballet of searching and desire, her essence filled his nostrils making him weak and giddy.

Matt heard himself moan and this made her more aggressive than Retta had already become! He held her tighter and tighter, coming bonding even closer as her hot breast threatened to penetrate his shirt.

All this physical contact made Matt sweat and he began to get aroused as her bare leg between his own and threatening to climb his body and ravish him! By now, they were picking up quite a few stares as they held this position for what seemed an eternity.

Matt heard Ant laughing wildly behind him with the nervous tone of someone not quite sure of what to do. "OOH! I'm tellin" sang Lori. She had been much in the same awkward state as Ant but less embarrassed.

Suddenly a familiar voice broke in, it wasn't loud but still very firm and authoritative, "Excuse me" she said. "Do you mind if I watch?" They broke up with a sudden startle and their lips made a smacking sound from the quick separation. Matt could feel a silky trace of saliva on his lip and he subconsciously wiped it away.

It was her mother and she stood looking at them in a most unsettling way, her face was angry and twisted and she stood with her feet slightly apart with her hands folded behind her back much like a drill sergeant. "Ohh, shit! we've done it now" thought Retta. "We're busted now" thought Matt as he sheepishly looked at Aretta, she must have felt the same because when their eyes met all they could do was smile nervously at each other.

All of a sudden and with great speed, her mother reached out an seized an ear from each of them, "Come with Me! you two "Heart throbs" she said in a most abrasive yet controlled tone. "Ow! Ow" they protested in vain. They didn't resist her but just felt incredibly embarrassed at being dragged off like naughty children. The crowd that had gathered to gawk at them was now laughing and smiling at them as if to say, "Now your gonna get it!" Audrey didn't speak but just led them to an alcove between two stores.

Lori and Ant followed them and keeping a respectful distance away. Once she had them where she wanted them, she placed them against the wall as if to execute them then turned quickly on Lori and Ant causing them to stop short. "YOU TWO, SIT!" she said pointing at a nearby bench.

Thank God, there was a bench just behind them because they would have surely sat on the floor. They sat with a plop and didn't move or speak, "Now you two" she hissed turning her full attention on the two love birds. "Just what the HELL! were you trying to prove back there?" "Just WHO! do you think you are."

"Damn, I hate these kind of questions" thought Matt, "Because you never know if you should answer or not." "Aretta, you know better" she growled pointing her finger into the soft center between her breasts that Matt not to long ago felt burning into him. "Do you know what you two looked like?" "You looked like a DAMN SOAP OPERA OUT THERE!!" "You didn't even have the decency to at least move out of sight."

"Do you know what one of those people said out there? they said, Look at that little tramp, she's well on her way to being another unwed teen mother on welfare." Aretta just hung her head in shame, Matt could see a tear land on her shoe and it tore him up inside.

That did it, now he was 38 hot, he didn't know quite what to do and felt guilty for having gotten her into this mess and the turbulent emotions that thundered through him didn't help either. He didn't like this but felt ill at ease to let her take the rap for it! Finally, it came to him, quickly and firm. "ENOUGH!" he shouted loud enough to stop traffic on 1-75. He didn't recognize his own voice at this point and even more he was afraid he would be doing more harm than good.

Audrey stopped her attack on Retta and was suddenly taken back that a young whelp like Matt would dare and confront her on any issue particularly about her daughter! "She's innocent" he said now feeling surer of himself.

"She had no idea I was going to approach her, this is my fault." Audrey just stared at him blankly as if seeing him and not seeing him at the same time. "I didn't know it was her when I saw her, but when I was sure I couldn't believe my eyes." "She wasn't the same person, she was beautiful the way she was, but seeing her now like THIS! she's unbelievable, I couldn't resist her so I grabbed her before she knew what was going on an kissed her."

"Please don't blame her, she only went along and was just as surprised as I was." Audrey stepped back a little folding her arms and readjusting herself as she tolerated his plea.

"Please Mrs. Davis, don't be angry with her, I'm to blame not her'" he said, his voice becoming lower and more relaxed. "I love her, I just didn't think."

Now being at a loss for words he just bowed his head breaking her piercing stare. She just stood there tapping her foot; he could feel her eyes looked from him to Aretta even though he couldn't see them. Finally, she let out a long sigh, "Sigh."

"Rodney" she said reaching up to raise his chin so, she could see his face. "Look honey, I know how you feel about Aretta, I'm not so blind as I can't see that, but your older than she is and must know better." Matt nodded. "I'm not telling you two NOT to be affectionate, hell I couldn't if I tried."

"But, I don't like it when you expose yourselves so openly and without regard for discretion." "There are times and places for such expression and I'm sure you will agree that this isn't one of them." "Come on you guys, use your heads and don't let what you feel for one another sway your better judgment." "It's hard enough for me as it is to accept your relationship because of your age, Rodney, you're 17 and Aretta is only 15 and a half technically, too young but I trust her and know she's a responsible girl or so I thought she was" she said looking at Aretta.

Her head was still bowed. "Don't give me reason to renounce my decision okay?" "I want good things for you two, and I'm glad she found you to love Rodney but you must be more responsible!" "Don't let her rile you, or make you lose control and don't say she can't, because she's my daughter, and if she has an ounce of my blood in her, you better watch out!"

A light smile creased her lips and Matt was smiling inside thinking that Aretta already has made him lose control. "So let's work on this okay?" she said pleadingly. "And try not to let this happen again, alrighty."

"Yes ma'am" said Matt nodding his head like a child who had been thoroughly chastised. "Now, you young lady" she snapped as Retta's head popped up like a cork from a champagne bottle. "We've had our little talk already haven't we?" "Yes ma'am" she said slowly. "What is it about you that you can't control yourself?" "Is Rodney really that overwhelming" she said turning her head slowly towards Matt staring into his eyes, filled with all the love and undying devotion in the world.

"Yes ma'am" she said reaching for his hand. "Aretta" said her mother grabbing her chin to face her. "THIS MUST STOP . . . UNDERSTAND?" "Yes ma'am" she said softly. "Okay you two love birds, now that we are clear on this matter let's go do some shopping." She led them out of the area, Lori and Ant was still sitting but Ant had dozed off a little.

"Hey you" she said kicking his foot and shocking him awake. He jumped to his feet with a start. "Yes ma'am" he said with eyes blinking and disoriented. "What's your name?" "Ant ma'am, I mean George" he stammered.

"Well George, I'm Audrey, how do you do?" she said sternly shooting out her hand. "I'm fine" he managed to say still shaken. "Well guess what, cutie pie . . . your my date for the day" she said then quickly hooked her arms around his. "Let's go you guys" she said leading the way.

They all just stared and smiled at him, he looked so helpless.

"Momma" said Lori whining. "Can we get something to drink, I'm thirsty." "Alright, we can get something over there at the Cookie Factory." "So Rodney, what are you guys doing here?" said Audrey still clinging to Ant. "Uh, we were just hanging out and thought we would do a little window shopping and maybe play some video games before going to the movies."

Aretta shot Matt a hurt look as if to say, "You didn't ask me to go." "Well that sounds good, tell you what, if you guys don't mind waiting we can all go." "How's about that?"

Ant looked at Matt for support. "That sounds good to me D" said Matt. "What's in the bag Retta?" he asked reaching for it. "OH NO YOU DON'T" she said pulling it away quickly. "You don't see this until I say so!" "When's that gonna be?" "You'll know when I tell you, that's when." "Meanwhile, no peaking!" "Alright" said Matt not wanting to pry further.

"Tell you what Rodney, I need to get Aretta a few things and Lori too and I'm sure guys don't want to hang around, so if you have some shopping you need to do you can do that and meet us at the entrance of J.C. Penny's at five o'clock okay?"

Matt looked at his watch and saw it was four fifteen. "That'll work" he said. "Come on Retta, let's get busy" said her mother. Retta looked back at Matt with displeasure and hurt at leaving him so soon. She wanted them all to stay together.

Matt quickly kissed her and let her go, her mother didn't see. "Let's go Matt" said Ant pulling him along. They didn't speak for a minute or so then Ant asked "What was that all about?" "What was what?" "Her mom, that's what" said Ant. "The way she was all over me like we was dating or something!" "I don't know, my ears are still ringing from the tongue lashing I got!"

Ant was laughing now. "Man you should have seen the look on your face, you looked like you was having a "shit fit" and didn't have any paper!" "Aw, forgetchu man" said Matt pushing him away.

"But I gotta give it to you though man" he went on" you stood up to her like a champ, I couldn't have done it myself." "What can I say man, I love her and it was my fault, so I couldn't just let her take the rap for that could I?"

"No, I guess not" he said placing a hand on Matt's shoulder in support. "So what do you think about her mother?" said Matt. "She's cute but harsh!" "Well get used to her because she's your date today old man." "Well that's okay, I don't mind, at least I've got one luxury you don't". "OH yeah, and what's that?" "I don't need her mother's permission to stay out past midnight!" HE HEEE! "Aww, damn that's cold."

"Hey, but don't get me wrong though, Aretta is a KNOCKOUT, I couldn't believe that that was her man." "Me either, she looks like she spent the week on an island somewhere in the Pacific and her hair, didn't know she had hair that long!" "YOU didn't?" "Hell she's my girl and I've seen just about everything you could expect and I didn't know it either."

"I see why you went after her like you did, I'm just surprised that you didn't go even further than that!" "Yeah, well maybe later" said Matt smiling at him. "Come on let's go get your shirt." "I want to stop by Victoria's Secret before we meet up with them again." "Alright, let's break."

They headed to a store called the "Gap." Matt knew they weren't too expensive and they would be able find something fashionable for Ant to wear. When they got there, the place was crawling with High School kids bustling about trying on this and trying to see the latest styles. It didn't take long once they muscled through them. "Hey Ant, what about this one?" said Matt holding up a nice peach colored Oxford shirt with a button down collar.

"It's nice but it's too warm for long sleeves." "Oh yeah, I almost forgot." "Hey this one's cool" he said producing a black Izod short sleeve shirt. "Black?" said Matt. "It can't be that bad outside" he said in a guarded tone. "Besides I've got all the other colors but this one." "Okay" said Matt seeing he couldn't change his mind. "How much is it?" asked Matt reaching for his wallet. "Umm, it's twenty dollars." "Damn, they've gone up!" "You didn't know" he said grinning. "You should see what Davidson's wants for them!"

"Naw that's okay, let's get it here, is this your size, or do you have to try it on?" Ant was looking in the collar. "Naw this is it." "Okay, Super chicken, let's go." "We better get going" said Ant pulling Matt out the door. "Didn't you say something about going to Victoria's Secret?" "Yeah, I wanna check on a teddy I saw last week."

"Well they're not far from here and we still got a little time left." They started moving a little faster heading towards the other end near Penny's. Soon they glided into the store and saw that it was as crowded as the last one. There were a few men, mostly middle aged with their wives. Others were mother-daughter combinations.

Matt saw the counter he wanted and headed straight for it. "Excuse me" he said brushing by a small group of men who decided to clog up the main path through the store. He picked up a nice peach and black teddy and it had paisleys all over it and was trimmed in black lace. "Is this the one you was talking about Matt?" asked Ant. "Yeah, this is it." "It's nice, do you think it will fit her?" "I guess, I'm not sure, the lady up front told me last time I was here how to determine a girls size by using her breast size and waist measurements."

"So I remembered to check out Aretta's bra and panties last time I was over there." "That was good thinking" said Ant.

Matt folded the nighty and headed back to the front, as they waited in line they started getting strange looks from the older women around them. They seemed to be saying by their expressions, "What are YOU doing here, you're too young to be buying ladies under garments for ANYBODY!"

Matt just smiled and brushed by them without looking at them a second time. "The hell you say" he thought to himself. "That will be thirty dollars" said the cashier who was now giving him and the garment he gave her a scrutinizing look over her reading glasses. Matt gave her a fifty-dollar bill just to let her know what he thought of her unspoken opinion about him and his purchase.

"It's about that time Matt" said Ant pointing to a clock near the door. "Alright" he said putting away his change then walked out. As soon as they cleared the doors, they broke into a light trot and headed back, the way they had come toward Penny's. They looked like they were trying to catch a plane or something and was dodging in an out of crowds and slow moving couples.

"There they are" said Matt slowing to a quick walk. "I hope we didn't keep you guys waiting too long" said Matt. "No we just got here ourselves" said Audrey.

Retta was giving Matt one of her I miss you stares and slowly glided to his side to hold his hand. "Hi stranger" she said sweetly. "Wanna go to the movies?" "Naw, I got a date already" he said jokingly then reached out to take Lori's little hand. She just giggled and an blushed.

Aretta was less amused and punched his arm. "That's not funny Matt" she hissed. Now he was laughing. "Okay you two" said Audrey, "Lets go before we miss the opening" she said holding Ants arm again.

"Do you want to walk or ride" she said. "It really doesn't matter, because it's nice outside" they said. But when they got outside there was a cloud burst in the area. "OOh! Pretty" said Lori looking at the bright and sunny blue sky amazed that it could rain while there were no rain clouds. "I guess we'll ride after all" she said covering her hair with her bag.

Then they ran to the parking lot and the smell of the rain on the hot cement had a thick dusty aroma while little puffs of steam could be seen rising from the pavement. The rain evaporatcd upon impact and everything was stark shinny and bright. "I should have brought my shades" said Matt weakly.

Soon they reached the security of the little car, Audrey fumbled with the keys trying to find the right one. "Damn it!, I hate these keys." Finally she got it and opened the door and they all piled in. "You didn't get too wet did you babe?" said Matt noticing the light dewy droplets on Aretta's hair. She pulled up a towel and pat her self dry still glaring at him somewhat angry for teasing her.

Matt leaned over and kissed her cheek. "I'm sorry Red, I was just kidding okay?" She pulled away lightly, folded her arms, and gave Matt a disbelieving "HRRUMPH!" "Okay, be that way" he said now reaching to the floor for the small gold and brown bag that held her nighty. "I wonder what this is?" he said softly dangling the bag and swinging it to and fro all the while grinning at her turned face.

She cut an eye at the little bag and gave it a dismissing wave of her hand. "Whatever it is, you keep it!" she mumbled. "Okay then" he whispered unfazed at her stubbornness. "Hey Ant" he said reaching in the bag. "Do you think that girl you met in Annabelle's might like this?" He was now holding it out far enough for her to see what it was without giving away it's true nature.

"Yeah she would!" he said giving him a sly grin as if to say, "You sly dog, how could you burn her ego like that."

He knew what Matt was up to and went along. Suddenly her hand shot out grabbing for it, but Matt was quicker an pulled the bag into himself so all she got was a hand full of chest. "Oww, let go of my chest!" "Serves you right you lizard" she said withdrawing her hand. "You shouldn't have teased me" she said giving him a look that said, "You thought I wasn't watching you didn't you smart ass!"

Matt just smiled innocently an gave her the bag she had been groping for. She didn't lift it out but just randomly moved it around in the bag glimpsing at it's color and general shape. A wide smile softened her face. "Oh! Matt it's beautiful!" she whispered then gave him a hug. "I hope I get to wear it sometime for you!" "Me too my love, me too."

Soon they were at the theater on the outermost parking area to the mall. "So which one do you guys wanna see?" asked Audrey. "Let's see" said Matt looking out the window. "How about "Blade Runner, that sounds good?" "What about "Robo Cop?" said Lori. "We have that at home on tape honey" said her mother. "We could see "Back to the Future?" Retta offered.

"Okay" they all agreed. "We'll do that" said Audrey looking for a parking spot.

She parked and they all got out, they all noticed that it had stopped sprinkling and only the hot sun and blue sky remained. "You know this would be a great day for a picnic somewhere" said Matt looking up. "Yes it would, why don't we do that when we leave here?" said Retta. "Shouldn't you check with your mother first?" said Audrey who was now looking their way. "Can I mom?" "Where at?" "How about Lake Tobasofkee?" "That's quite a ways isn't it, and how will you get there?"

"My bike Mrs. Davis." "Your bike?" "Yes ma'am, I have a motor scooter." "Isn't that kind of small Rodney?" "No ma'am, we used it when we went out Friday night." "Oh yeah, I had forgotten that, I thought you drove." "Yes ma'am, I do but I don't have a car yet and dad doesn't let me use his car." "Why not, do you drive safely?" "Oh yes ma'am, it's just that dad don't let anyone drive his Mercedes."

"Oh I see" she said a little impressed. "Well let me think about it while were in the movie and I'll let you know okay?" "Okay" they said.

Soon they bought their tickets, got their snacks, and went to get seated. The credits were beginning and they got in just in time.

"Where do you guys want to sit?" said Matt. Audrey was heading toward the middle rows halfway down. "Anywhere you want to" she said.

"Lori you sit with me and Anthony" announced Audrey grabbing his arm an placing him in a seat. He gave Matt that awkward "OH hell" look.

Matt just shrugged and let Aretta pull him to the far right near the wall and up from them a few isles. It was dark, and all that could be seen were the tops of people's heads. Matt noticed something sticky and disgusting under his shoe. "Ooh yuck, what the hell is that?" he said looking down.

"Oh never mind that Rodney, come here!" she said pulling him around. She had positioned herself to where she was half turned side ways an leaning on her arm rest. Her eyes sparkled in the half darkness as the light of the screen reflected off them.

She was so beautiful! thought Matt as he turned to get closer to her. His eyes were locked with hers and time seemed to stand still, and he could feel himself floating. He reached for her placing his hands just behind her neck to cradle her angelic face in his hands. Her hair smelled and felt glorious as he rubbed his cheek against hers an heading for the softness of her neck. She craned her head back and sighed giving him full access to her lovely throat.

He kissed her and lightly suckled on her neck. "OH Matt" she sighed deeply now griping him tighter. Matt let his tongue play lightly about her neck from side to side and gently working his way to her cleavage. She moaned wantonly guiding his head down to where he was dying to go. "OH" he shifted with eagerness trying to give her more access to his firm stomach.

Retta prodded and groped blindly-feeling her way to his blossoming manhood. The heat grew as her fingers got closer to the object of her desire, she could feel his pubic hairs now and they were curly and soft. This new feeling made her gasp and swoon and she dug deeper and with more force wanting to feel his hardness in her hand.

"Oh my gosh, it's so huge" she thought as her hand found the tip of his penis. It felt hot and soft in her hands, while at the same time it was rigid and erect. Retta let her finger tips caress and tease it, amazed at its sensitivity. It grew each time she touched it getting fatter and more swollen. She began to feel the exquisite force of her own juices working their way through her, causing her to close her legs and churn-them together.

"I got him now" she thought as she had his full shaft in her hand. She couldn't close her hand around it because it had grown to enormous size. "Oh how I want to feel him burning inside me and driving me insane with pleasure" she thought as she squeezed his member to the rhythm of her fantasy.

Matt was moaning now and some how he managed to get his hand under her skirt and into her panties. His fingers were probing and caressing her pubic hairs making her sweat. Retta opened her legs further to allow him more access to her already sopping wet vagina. Matt moved with the fever and desire of a panther on the hunt, Retta felt him penetrate her with his fingers in one smooth and deep thrust.

"OH gosh!" she whispered in ecstasy. She gyrated her hips in time with his probing hand. Matt, wanting to maximize her desire so she wouldn't be able to resist when he tried to really put it to her. He brought his thumb into play professionally working on her clitoris to the point she could scream.

"OH my God, he's so good" she thought with every thrust of his hand she was boosted higher and higher. She was no longer concerned or very aware of anything but her own passion and wanting. Retta was now stroking his penis with strong determined effort, keeping in time with his fingers, which now grew from two at the beginning to three.

'OH! Sss OH sss" she moaned at this new addition to her already tortured hot spot. She was so hot, so very hot that she couldn't stand it and her body began to gyrate wildly and with more effort. Her loins strained to be satisfied.

"Deeper" she whispered now covering Matt's face and neck with hot wet kisses. "OH Retta" he breathed biting and sucking her neck. "Oh shit, I can't stand it baby, I want to fuck you now baby!" Just the thought of what he had said and the sound of it caused her to erupt.

Tidal waves of pleasure gushed and flowed through her making her tremble. Retta couldn't speak and the warm juices that flowed from between her legs felt glorious. Just then, she felt a new and even more exciting feeling; hot liquid began to blast from Matt into her cupped hand.

Three, four, five times or more she felt him give all of his love juices generously and unfailingly. His body was stiff as he moaned and this made Retta come again as she imagined what it would feel like to have his swollen shaft explode it's warm silky treasure inside of her. Finally, they could go no further and was totally spent and exhausted. They just lay there in their seats or at least she did, seeing how she had his hand still buried within her and her hand still wrapped around his now shrinking penis.

It was an effort to hold his juices in her hand as it was so much and was gently-oozing away through her cupped fingers. They looked at each other smiling, completely satisfied. Matt then looked over his seat craning his neck to see if they had unconsciously drawn any attention to their wild and ardent fondling. They hadn't.

"Whew, baby I love you" said Matt, his eyes showing with a flame she could still feel. "I love you too!" Matt looked at where her hand was and sheepishly shook his head. "I think we made a mess of ourselves" he added. "Yes, I guess we did" said Aretta looking under her skirt and seeing her somewhat soiled panties.

"How are we gonna get out of here to the rest room without being noticed?" said Matt. "I'm not sure, I'll tell you what, I'll go first and you follow me in a few seconds okay?" "Okay" said Retta adjusting her skirt with her free hand. "Uh Matt, if I let go of you, you'll be a mess baby." "Yeah, I guess so, but don't sweat it I'll fix it in the bathroom." "Don't you think you need to remove your hand before you try to get up?" said Retta pointing at his hand still embedded deep inside her.

Matt was blushing now and slowly began to remove his more than wet hand. She sighed with pleasure as he did this and the feel was exquisite and the sight deliciously tempting thought Matt. He allowed himself one more plunge. She sucked in deeply, throwing back her head with pleasure. "Oh baby, you gonna make me explode again doing that."

"Okay baby, I'm gone" he said finally clearing her, she moaned as she felt his presence leave her. He then leaned over and kissed her lightly. Now it was her turn to let go of him so he opened his pants enough for her to remove her hand without too much effort.

"Matt what I do with this stuff?" she said looking at her full hand. Matt quickly gave her a hand fun of napkins he had picked up at the snack bar.

"I'll be waiting outside, okay Retta?" "Okay" she said cleaning her hand. As Matt cleared the door at the top he looked back through the window in the door and motioned Retta to follow. She scooted out of her seat and headed up the aisle, looking back to see if Lori or her mother was looking. Matt held the door for her as she came to the top. "I'll see you in a little bit" he said kissing her lightly. "Okay Matt."

"So Anthony, how long have you known Rodney?" "Oh . . . about three years or so."

"I've only just met him this week and I understand that he and Aretta have been seeing each other for over almost a year." "Yeah, that's about right I guess." "Tell me, what kind of person is he?" this made Ant a little uneasy because he'd never discussed his best friend in any detail to anyone. It wasn't thier business as far as he could see.

"Anthony" "Well you see Mrs. Davis, it's like this." "Call me Audrey" she said placing her hand on his shoulder to relax him. This only made him more nervous and apprehensive. "Okay Mrs . . . . I mean Audrey, Matt is a complex person." "He's a kind, light hearted guy." "He enjoys a good joke, has a very good sense of humor and he's patient and generous and passionate." "So I've seen" she commented.

"He's the kind of guy who you can depend on and he'll go out of his way to please you and make you feel good." "He's very trustworthy and determined, he never quits on something once he has started and is always ready for anything."

"You make him sound like a saint." "Well not necessarily a saint, but real close." "What about his bad points?" she asked watching him closely. "Hmm bad points . . . . well I wouldn't piss him off, he's not a hot head by any means but if you go to all the trouble to push all his buttons he'll hurt you!" "And don't ever try to get in the way of something he cares about or loves" he said sounding more solemn. "He's got a temper but it's a slow if burn, you know what I mean?" "Yes I think I do, so as his best friend what do you think about him and Aretta being together?" "Doesn't that cut time out for you two to be together?"

"No ma'am it don't get us tangled at all, in fact I think it's great that they are together." "He talks about her all the time, she means the world to him." "Is that right?" "Yeah, it sounds like you know your friend quite well." "Yeah I do, just as he knows me."

Audrey got quiet for a minute biting her lip lightly in thought. "Does he sleep around?" she asked inquisitively. Ant at the sound of this exploded and went right to the defensive. "Hell! No!" he blasted almost coming out of his seat. "I'm sorry" he said catching himself and easing back into his seat feeling somewhat ashamed at sounding off and cursing at her, much less an older person. Some of the people around them looked on perplexed and annoyed as sounds of shushing could be heard.

"Don't be Anthony, I'm sorry I upset you but I had to ask you that, you understand don't you?" she said looking at him with kind and pleading eyes. She seemed to have regressed in years.

"You don't fault me for asking do you?" she said, raising his lowered chin to look into his eyes. "Naw I guess I don't . . . I understand." "You really care about him don't you?" she asked, quite sure this was the case judging from his emotions. "Yes I do. and in a way you wouldn't understand" he said with a calm firmness to his voice that made Audrey blanch.

She pulled his chin towards her and lightly kissed his cheek. "Thank you Anthony, I think you're a very fine young man and friend. An asset to any young girl who should find you. Too bad I'm not your age or I'd give you a run for your money" said Ant smirking and shifting his eyebrows at her.

Audrey's eyes grew wide and the hairs on the back of her neck rose slightly as the concept of having such a viral and handsome young man make a pass at her assaulted her body and mind.

She adjusted her legs uncrossing and crossing them again, secretly letting some of the steam escape from between them.

"You don't say?" she offered in her own defense. Ant just grinned in his own devilish way and raised his eyebrows yet again while letting his eyes roam up her curvaceous legs, around her sultry bottom, up and over her generous breasts and back to her waiting stare.

Audrey felt him touching every part of her body even though he never raised a hand. It made her tingle all over and hold her breath. Ant having made his wordless statement and acknowledge that she had received it, the two of them just smiled at each other for a second or two imagining the implications then turned to watch the movie.

Matt was done now and had taken off his underwear in a stall and quickly washed them in the sink. The hand dryer on the wall dried them in record time. "I wonder how Aretta is getting along?" he thought as he put them back on.

Just then he heard a light tap on the door. "Matt are you done yet?" she whispered. "Yeah babe, I'm coming out now." Retta was standing there in the hall looking stunning.

Matt just grabbed her up in his arms and planted a hot kiss on her soft waiting lips. They held it for a long time before breaking. "I love you Retta."

"I love you too Matt." "You make me feel like a woman and I want to be everything you are to me." "You are and more" he whispered. "I will love you forever baby" she whispered.

They held each other for awhile longer then went back inside the theater. They decided not to sit in the same spot as before because it made them feel a little strange and they didn't want to tempt fate by getting started again. They sat and held hands with her head on his shoulder.

It felt so perfect that Matt didn't know how it could possibly get any better. "Hey! look at your mom and Ant!" said Matt pointing at the row of seats in front of them. She was resting her head on Ant's shoulder like they were lovers or something. "What's up with that?" Retta just shrugged her shoulders and smiled then proceeded to copy her mother.

Soon the movie was over and they all headed out of the theater. "Do you see mom and George yet?" "No, I thought they would have met us in the lobby by now, maybe they went out the side door" said Retta. "I hope not otherwise we wouldn't know until this place was empty!" Just then a hand snatched Matt's shoulder jerking him away from Retta. "Hey!, what the hell . . ."

Matt then saw that it was Ant. "Come on man, we been waiting for ten minutes!" "Well you could have let us know you were going out the back door BUTT HEAD!" Matt said thumping him on the forehead. "Come on let's go" he said turning to leave. "So where do you guys want to go?" asked Audrey as they got in. "I don't know, what time is it?" asked Matt. "It's 7:30" said Audrey pulling out of the lot before traffic got tight.

"So much for the picnic" said Retta slumping in the seat. "Yeah it's too dark now" said Matt looking at the sun dropping out of sight. "We could always go back to the house and have some cocktails or something" said Audrey semi-joking and speaking more to Ant than anyone else.

"Um . . . I gotta go!" he said quickly with nervousness in his voice at her unspoken intentions.

"I just remembered dad wanted me to help him finish the remodeling at his house!" he said winking at Matt for support.

"OH yeah! he did say that when we got out of his car earlier." "Well . . . maybe next time then" she said sounding a little depressed. "So where can I drop you guys?" "Home will be fine" said Ant. "And you Rodney, are you going by Anthony's house too?" "Naw . . . I'll just head on home, I need to check in myself." "Okay then."

"You don't want to come over to my house for awhile Matt?" whispered Retta. "I'm sure momma would take you home afterwards." "Naw I don't think so, maybe tomorrow babe, I'm kinda worn out if you know what I mean" he said smiling. "Yeah I guess I do" she said snuggling closer and placing her head on his chest.

Soon they arrived at Ant's house. "I'll see ya later Ant." "Alright man give me a call when you get home okay?" "Alright "B." "It was nice meeting you Anthony, maybe I'll see you again sometime when Rodney comes over again." "Yes ma'am . . . that'll work. "See you later! Anthony!" yelled Lori. Ant closed the door and waved as he headed up the stairs.

Matt and Retta noticed that her mother had the strangest expression on her face as she said goodbye to him. Retta and Matt just shrugged it off and sat back as she sped away from the curb.

Chapter 4

Girl Talk

"So how did you guys enjoy the movie?" she asked breaking the silence. "OH it was fine" said Matt answering first. "Especially that part when Marty was playing for the band at the dance." "Yeah that was pretty cool wasn't it?" said Audrey now lighting a cigarette. "Your friend is nice Rodney" she said blowing a long stream of smoke out her window. "How old is he?"

"Umm . . . he'll be 18 next month." "That's too bad, he has nice eyes" she commented taking another long draw on her cigarette. "Sooo what's your father doing tonight?" "Oh, I don't really know . . . probably relaxing or doing some paperwork of some kind."

"Hmm . . . where's your mother . . . if you don't mind my asking?" "Oh she doesn't live with us anymore, they've been divorced for ten years now."

"Oh that's too bad" she commented not really sounding too remorseful but instead catty. "Which way is it to your house?" she said turning off Pio Nono Avenue to English Avenue.

"Just keep going straight until the stop sign then go left." "This is a nice quiet neighborhood you live in." "How long have you lived here?" "I guess about three years or so." "Is your father renting or buying?" "I'm not sure . . . I never asked" Matt said getting curious of her line of questioning.

"I wonder what she has on her mind?" he whispered to Aretta. "I don't know, she just likes to ask questions I guess." "That's my house over there!" he said pointing to the right side or the street. She pulled in the driveway and stopped. "I'd like to meet him if you don't mind Rodney" she said putting the car in park and killing the engine. "This is nice!" she said looking around at the house and landscape.

The house was somewhat early American in design and had a modest front yard that was split in half by a cement walkway that ran from the sidewalk to the steps of the house. There were large rows of Red Tips bushes on the left and small green bushes on the right side near the driveway. Two other large bushes sat in front of the house on each side of the walkway blocking any direct sight to the porch. The porch was large and had a grey wooden deck. There were four large screened windows that overlooked the front yard and both sides of the house giving it a quiet coolness of privacy. There was also four sets of windows on the front of the house divided by an entrance door that was the main foyer into the house. Those on the left were the living room and the windows to the right were my bedroom. As we stepped in to the hall you could see a staircase that went up to an attic apartment where a German lady was living.

As we entered through the living room door Audrey asked, "what's that door to?" "Oh, that's my bedroom". "Oh that's nice" she said her voice betraying a little admiration.

As we went into the living room I noticed that the lights in the dining room were on. "Ooh! pretty! said Lori looking around the room. It had high sculpted ceilings and a huge stone fire place up against the wall parallel to the front door. A large comfortable looking brown couch sat under the window on the left with a love seat to the right near a small window. There was a brown recliner just behind the door next to the coffee table and tan carpet all over the room.

"You sure there's no woman living here Rodney?" she said again taken in by the neatness and cleanliness of what she saw and that a man could keep it so well. "I'm sure" I said closing the door. "Is that you Rodney?" yelled dad from somewhere in the house.

"Yes sir!, I have someone here who would like to meet you if you have a minute."

"Oh. who could that be?" he said now coming our way from the sound of his footsteps.

"Please sit down" I said motioning to the couch and chair. I quickly hit the light switch that turned on the soft lights in the huge Turkish lamps that sat on each end of the couch. Dad strode in and was surprised to see us.

"Hi there!" he said giving his best warm smile. "Dad this is Mrs. Davis and her daughters Aretta an Lori." "Hello, I'm Audrey" she said rising to shake his hand. "I'm Rodney's father Buford it's nice to meet you." They all smiled and said hello as he reached to shake their hands. "You guys kinda caught me by surprise, I wasn't expecting anyone to stop by so I'm not dressed too appropriately for guests."

He wore a rust colored short sleeved sport shirt and a pair of white tennis shorts and a pair of slippers. His hairy muscular legs Audrey noticed, appeared to be very strong and virile and gave him the look of an athlete, but only more sophisticated.

"OH! I don't mind!" she said more than satisfied with his appearance. "Can I get you ladies something to drink?" I offered. "Yes thank you" they all said. I left and went into the kitchen. "This is a very lovely home you have here Buford". "Oh thank you, we like." "Is it only you and Rodney who live here?" "Yes, my other two son's are living with their mother in South Carolina and my oldest is in the Navy." "Oh that's nice." "So what have you guys been up to today?" he asked now getting comfortable an crossing his legs.

Aretta spoke first. "We went on a female Trist today! and ended up at the Mall where we ran into Rodney." "A female "Tryst?" he repeated.

"What Aretta means, is we all went to the beauty parlor and a few other shops today doing girlish things." "Oh I see, and you all look very nice too!" "Thank you" they all said blushing.

"So Lori what grade are you in school?" "The third" she said bashfully and teasing her hair that the older cute stranger would notice her at all much less inquire anything about her personal life. "And you Aretta?" "I'm in the tenth this year" she said proudly. "Oh that's good" he said nodding.

"Rodney has spoken of you from time to time, but he never said you were such an enchanting young lady." She bowed her head slightly and blushed a crimson red color "Thank you Mr. Mathis." "And I can see where it comes from too" he said now looking at Audrey.

She too began to redden a little. "Oh, Mr. Mathis you're much too kind."

"Oh yes, dad was definitely that and more, as I'm sure you she would find out." I soon returned with a tray and a small dish of cookies. "Here you are" I said smiling at Aretta but placing the dish closest to Lori whom I knew would be the chief partaker of it's contents. True to nature, Lori quickly seized the cookies I put before her as I knew she would.

"So Mr. Mathis." "Just call me Buford please" he interrupted. "Buford, I seem to remember you from someplace, but I can't place you!" He was grinning to himself smugly now and thinking the same thing. "Is that so . . . tell me, do you live in Avalon Gardens Apartments?" "Yes . . . yes I do!" she said a little surprised. "Then that's where you've seen me . . . I'm your Mailman."

"What?!" she said then burst out laughing at the revelation and the irony of it. "So what about you, where you working these days?" "Oh, I'm out at YKK." "That's the zipper factory isn't it?" "Yes it is." "So how do you like it?" "It's okay" she said now wringing her hands somewhat nervously.

Just then Dad shot me "The Look." One I knew too well as a signal to divide and conquer or what ever the situation called for. He and I had a form of secret unspoken or military language that we developed over the years. It made me feel somewhat militaristic and prideful that we could relate to each other in this manner. He was my Captain and I was his Soldier.

"Hey guys, can I show you around?" I asked looking from Lori to Aretta. "Mom" she said in a tone that seemed to ask permission. "Yes go ahead if you like". "Come with me" I said heading out of the room. "And Lori you can bring "Your" dish of cookies if you like". She was happy at this prospect for she'd made them hers from the outset anyway.

"Anyway, this is the dining room" I went on. It was adjoining to the living room and it had an antique candle like chandelier which hung over a table that seated six people. It was a rich brown mahogany finish with gold padded velour chairs with bamboo braided backs. There was also a piano on the right and a china cabinet in the comer by the entry way to the living room. A large half moon four deck bookshelf sat at the end of the table, it was a part of the wall which divided the hall from this room. On the other side of the table was a row of windows that ran from one end of the wall to the other and was positioned too high to see out of. Just beneath this was a long bench with a built in storage area, all of which was attached to the wall. Two doors accessed the dining room, one on the left and one on the right. The left side had a swinging door that led to the kitchen and through the rear of the house to a small office in the back.

Actually it was a sun room, but dad made it his combination office and den. It had windows all around it and a set of provincial doors that opened to his bedroom. "Wow! now that's what I call a bed!" said Aretta pointing at my dads huge lumberjack bed. He also had a fireplace in his room which he never used but was a nice effect anyway.

We passed through and ended up in the hall, from there we went to the left down a short hall or corridor as it were. There was a closet on the right and two doors. One separated the hall from the den on one side of the door and the other closed off the den from the hall on the other side. The den was a good size room about 25x18, three windows dominated the rear wall and ran the length of room across from the entrance door. There was a small bathroom on the left adjacent to another fireplace and my room to its right after you passed through a kitchenette. There was a large comfortable couch in the middle of the room with a television in front of it against the wall between it and the door. A coffee table and other chairs sat around the room finishing off the ensemble.

"Can I watch TV?" said Lori plopping down on the couch. "Sure" I said switching it on and giving her the remote control. Aretta gave me an "I CAN'T BELIEVE THE LUCK WERE HAVING!" look. I just smiled and said, "Now if you will come this way . . . this is my room." "Lead the way mister" she said grabbing a generous amount of my butt and squeezing it devilishly to get me going.

The room was dark and the only light was from the TV and the bathroom. I opened the door to my room and walked in. It was nice and comfortable inside since I'd left my windows open all day. "Here, let me cut on the lights so you can see". "OOH! this is a nice, BIG room!" she said. "You think so?" "Yes, I like it".

My room had high ceilings and a fire place much like the rest of the house only it had two windows on each side of it as you entered from the den plus the outer windows facing the porch. I had a large mirrored dresser in front of them and a chest of drawers near the outer door. My bed was a smaller scale of my dads and on it I had my stereo and records.

"Like father like son eh, Matt?" she said smiling at me. I just shrugged in an oh well fashion. "Do you want to hear some music?" I asked her. "You have to ask!?" she said almost sarcastically. I reached behind her and switched it on and put on a tape I had made sometime ago. It was nothing but love songs mostly our favorites.

"Hold on a minute" I said opening the outer door and going into the living room. "Excuse me" I said as I entered, dad and Audrey were on the couch now sitting together with their own brand of refreshment. "Can I get you anything from the kitchen while I'm in there?" "Yes, how about some more ice" said dad. "Okay, you got it" I said passing through and into the kitchen.

Soon I was back with more ice and another dish of cookies and a soda for Lori. "What are you guys doing?" he said.

"Oh just hanging out, Lori is watching TV and me an Retta are listening to some music". "Oh, that's good" they said content to be left alone to themselves. "How about flipping on the stereo on you way out" he said behind me. "Stereo, what stereo?" said Audrey. I lifted the lid to the consol by the door and cut it on. Dad always kept it set on his kinda music and the volume pre adjusted. "I didn't now that was a stereo, I thought it was a book shelf or something".

Dad just chuckled. "Naw, I've had that for years" he said refreshing their drinks. I slipped out closing the door behind me. As I passed into my room I saw that Aretta had taken off her shoes and was looking through my records. "Oh you're back." "Not quite" I said heading for the other door with the cookies and soda.

Soon I was back and the lights were out. Only the moon light could be seen through the side window. "Retta?" "I'm over here dear heart" she said. I reached out my hand to feel my way to my bed. "Here I am lover" she breathed as I slid onto my bed and was quickly drawn close to her by a pair of hungry arms.

I adjusted myself so she was lying on my chest and we began to kiss, slowly at first taking in the dark silence and the sweet music. We just lay there her head on my chest and my arms about her, gently stroking her long and silken hair. "Rodney?" "Yeah babe?" "Do you think it will always be this way with us?" "Yeah baby, why do you ask?" "Oh I don't know . . . I guess sometimes I get scared." "Of what?" "That you will some day get tired of me and want someone else." "Aww baby" I said rubbing her more passionately and hugging her closer. "That will never happen!" "How do you know?" "I just know, that's all!" "Look at it this way, do you love me?" her head quickly came off my chest to hover over mine. Her eyes shown like ebony pools with the moonlight reflecting off them.

"Rodney how could you dare! ask me that?" "I know my love and you must know I feel the same!" "Retta you are my life, your all I live for and I've never loved a woman as I love you!" "Sometimes I wonder would you ever tire of me?" "I mean your younger than I am and there are always much nicer, younger guys around."

"OH! Rodney, how could you?!" I could feel her body trembling as she sobbed on my chest. Heartfelt despair racked her small body. "Rodney" she muttered between sobs. "I wouldn't want to live if I couldn't have you dummy." She was staring into my eyes now. "I would just die before I let another man touch me, or another 'girl come near you!"

"Don't be afraid Retta, we were meant for each other, you know that!" "Yes I do, from the moment I first met you when you came to our school I knew you would be the only man I would ever love!" I seized her lips fiercely kissing her and trying to give her all the love I had and felt for.

Her body came to life on top of me kissing me with an undying fever. She moaned and whimpered as our passion grew. I quickly rolled her over an she automatically adjusted herself and positioned me between her legs. I began kissing an nibbling her neck.

"Oh Rodney! . . . oh baby" she cried breathing even harder than before. I could feel her hips grinding into mine pushing churning longing for me. I returned her movements stroke for stroke, we moved like a well oiled machine grinding hard and lustfully. I could feel the moistness and warmth of her sexuality and this made my desire grow as my penis grew!

I felt as though I would explode if I didn't take her now. She felt it and quickly struggled out of her panties. Her jean skirt lay bunched up around her waist and I was madly groping around in my shorts trying to free my severely enflamed tool which was now beyond control. I felt a fire glowing at it's head and a strain in my groin that pulled at me as if my penis were trying to launch itself from my crotch. I couldn't stand it! I finally got it out of my shorts.

"Hurry! Rodney . . . do it now!" She begged in a lusty voice her legs now wide apart and waiting for me. I could see the silvery juices starting to flow from her love hole as the moonlight briefly shown between us. Quickly I was on her! she threw her legs high and wide around me viciously grabbing my dick to guide it into her.

I felt her wetness and it's sweet encouragement. It was too much! I didn't wait! . . . I forced myself into her up to the roots! She gasped loud and half screamed my name "SSS! . . . Rodney!. She was tight and burning hot!

It was like a slippery inferno all molten and consuming inside. Her nails dug deep into me and her legs locked around my back like an octopus with cramps. I put my hands around her ass an held on for support and control, then began stroking.

"Oh! YES! . . . YES! she moaned as I pulled out to the tip and drove until our bodies slapped together again making a slippery wet sound. It was WONDERFUL! and the more I thrusted the tighter she squeezed and the deeper her nails dug into my ass now beginning to sting from the sweat.

Finally she began meeting my strokes halfway, her hips grinding hard against me making our bodies squish and fart with each stroke. "Fuck me! Rodney . . . oh YES! fuck me!" her breathing was hot and heavy on my neck and lips as she hungrily sought them again and again. "SSS! . . . OH! Matt! . . . OH Matt damn you feel good!"

I don't know why I wasn't screaming from the start, when he first drove that long monster of his into me. I wanted to die! gosh it's so big! And juicy! I want it all! . . . "Stick it all in baby" I moaned shamesely. "Take me now Matt!"

Can he possibly know how good he feels inside me? I'm so wet I can't stand it, I can feel him deeper and deeper with every thrust! Oh how long I've waited for this, he's mine, all MINE!

"Oh baby don't stop yet" she said noticing that I had slowed my rhythm and stopped for a second. "Oh no! . . . OH! NO! not yet please don't let me cum yet! SSS OOOO!"

"Damn" I came. Soon after I felt her lock down on my softening tool like a vice as she led her own mix to the primal ooze I had started. "OOh Mat!" she said still panting, her vagina still contracting wildly.

We just lay there breathing completely spent and worn out from the effort, I let her legs down and rolled off. The air was heavy with the odor of sex and sweaty bodies, a gentle breeze cooled us and made us shiver for a second, we held each other and kissed softly not wanting it to end.

"Matt" she whispered. "Yeah Red?" "I love you." "I love you too baby." She kissed me again and squeezed me close to her. "Are you alright?" I asked. "Yes baby" she said with love showing in her eyes as she looked at me. "How about you, Matt?" "Oh yeah baby, I feel REAL GOOD!" "Did you enjoy yourself . . . I mean was I okay?" she stammered. "Are you kidding me or what!?" I said getting to my elbows. "Girl, you was like a Panther! you was GREAT!" She smiled at this, "So were you Tiger . . . so were you." We held each other awhile longer. "Matt?" "Yeah baby?" "I think we better get up . . . Momma could call us anytime now cause it's getting late" she said looking at her watch.

"Yeah, I guess your right" I said getting ready to crawl out of bed but not quite sure how without making a mess on my covers. "Matt we need something for uh . . . this um stuff" she said bashfully looking down at herself and the mess

I'd made between her gentle thighs. I started groping around in the dark for the towel I had shed earlier today. "Here you go" I said handing it to her. "Thanks."

Soon we got ourselves straight enough to get to the bathroom and clean up. Lori hadn't moved an inch and was engrossed in a movie on HBO. Retta soon came out of the bathroom and I dashed in for a quick clean up. I heard someone say, "Yes! Ma'm?" "Are you ready to go girls?" "Yes ma'm" said Lori.

"Matt are you done yet?" she whispered through the door. "Yeah babe, I'm on my way out now." I dropped my towel in the hamper and went out. "Come on, we better go." "That was close" I said holding her around the waist. We entered the living room and could see that dad and Audrey had gotten better acquainted.

She was now sitting with his arm around her and both had their shoes off propped up on the table. "You girls ready to go?" "Yes ma'am." "Okay, you two go on out to the car and I'll meet you in a minute." I walked them out and into the balmy night air.

"Didja ever notice how the air smells different right after you've just got laid?"

Oh well any way, Lori jumped into the car while me and Retta stood in the driveway holding each other, kissing and exchanging long satisfied looks. "You made me feel like a woman tonight Rodney . . . did you know that?" I didn't speak but just stared. "I can't describe it" she went on. "But it makes me feel so full and alive and beautiful inside!" "Me too baby" I said holding her closer.

"I'm so happy Rodney, I could just float away!" Her happiness made her glow in the moonlight and so was I. "I'm sorry I didn't get to wear your gift." "You mean the Teddy . . . . , for get about it, its no sweat you can wear it next time" I said patting her soft behind.

She cut me a sly smile and said, "you can bet on it . . . Lover!"

Just then her mother and "dad" appeared at the door. "You all have a safe drive home" he said as he walked her to the car. "I really enjoyed meeting you Aretta and Lori." "Us too!" they both chimed as I helped Retta into the front seat. "Now don't forget, dinner is at 6:00 o'clock okay?" said Audrey. "Okay we'll be there" he said smiling like he knew already what color underwear she had on.

"Looks like we got another date for tomorrow night love" she said squeezing my hand. "Looks that way don't it" she winked then gave me a quick kiss goodnight. "Sweet dreams Red!" "You can bet on it Matt, and you too!" All having been said Audrey started the car and waved one last as she drove away. I stood in the drive way and watched till the car was out of sight, dad was staring at me in a funny – sort of, "Sooo! . . . what have you been up to all this time."

"O DAMN!" I thought, suddenly remembering that I had left my bedroom door open to air and cool it off. "Did dad notice anything?" I wondered. "Naww, he couldn't have, maybe the alcohol has dulled his senses a little."

I turned to see if he was still watching me, nope he'd gone inside. I quickly followed suit and was curious to find out how his evening went. "Hey dad!" I called stepping into the living room. "Yes." "Oh, there you are" he was collecting his little cocktail glasses and was straightening up the living room. "So what do you think of her?" "Oh, she's not bad . . . maybe a bit over zealous but none the less a nice girl." "You guys really caught me by surprise and I really hadn't intended to entertain any company tonight because I had some paperwork to finish".

"Oh I'm sorry . . . I didn't know . . . I guess I should have called first". "That's okay I appreciate your concern for your old dads well being." "Oh, it was nothing . . . really, actually it was her idea to get out and meet you." "Is that right?" "Yes sir." "Well we have a double date tomorrow." "I know" "Does this bother you?" "No sir, why should it?" "Well seeing as how you and Aretta are an item it wouldn't be to wise or gainly for me to start seeing her mother . . . know what I mean?" "You mean on a regular basis?" "Yep, and what's so bad about that?" he said putting down his glasses and turning to face me. "Nothing I guess" I said under my breath, not too sure of all the ramifications something like this would entail.

"Son let me try to explain something to you, or better yet let me give you an idea of what I mean." "Suppose you had a ranch full of cows and right after the calves were born I came and took all the cows away, what do you think would happen to your calves?" I had to think a second because dad always made loaded statements like that when he wanted to drive a point home or get me to see what was obvious to him. "I guess I would be out of business cause my calves would die without their mothers milk."

He then looked at me over the rim of his glasses in a funny way. "OH! now I get it" I said semi-elated. "What your trying to say is that if you and Audrey get together and see more and more of each other it could turn serious and if that happens you and her could be . . . " I never finished my sentence. As I rationalized the entire evolution, the real end result slammed into my mind and gut like a punch from Larry Holmes. "OH I GET IT, I SEE WHAT YOU MEAN NOW!" I said reeling on this revelation.

"I thought you would" he said grinning and turning to recover his glasses then left the room. "Well I guess I'll turn in" he said yawning from the kitchen. "What are you gonna do son?" "Oh, I'll probably watch some TV or go to bed myself . . . I'm not sure which" I said weakly still stunned by what he implied just seconds ago. After a minute I shook it off as fantasy.

"It won't happen, he was just showing me some foresight." Soon I dismissed the thoughts and headed for my room to clean it up some. "Boy did we destroy this place or what!" I said looking at the knarred bed covers and shifted mattress. "BUT OH, HOW WONDERFUL SHE WAS!" I said aloud to no one in particular as I dived into the mess. "Man don't I feel good!"

It didn't take long to redo the bed and stuff and it was now midnight and I wasn't sleepy at all, so I decided to get a shower and then maybe settle down for some ice cream, cookies and television.

My mind was flooded with thoughts of Aretta. I noticed as I undressed and turned on the shower, "I really love her . . . I really DO love her!" I said grinning to myself. The sound of my own voice and having said this caused a strange and eerie feeling of revelation to wash over me as I began to see what I supposedly always knew. "SS-OW SHIT damn that's hot." It's funny how hot water can bring you back to reality real quick-like. After awhile I'd gotten showered and set up for my all nighter.

My bowl of ice cream on my right, cookies on my left and the TV in front of me. "Well let's see what's on the boob tube tonight, ah yes, a classic monster movie, "Gooey gets Gotcha." Sometime during the movie I dozed off to sleep, I was totally out of it and having a beautiful dream as well. It was me and Aretta and we were having a picnic on a huge grassy hill some place, there were daisies and other pretty flowers all around us and we were relaxing under a tall oak tree with large green branches that seemed to house every kind of bird known to man.

Aretta wore a soft white sun dress with a halter top and a crown of flowers on her head, I was laying with my head on her lap feeling the breeze and just enjoying myself in general. Just as I was about to reach up to kiss her I heard the annoying sound of what seemed to be a large fly or something buzzing near by, at first I didn't pay it any attention but then as I looked passed Aretta's face I saw it!

There it was, perched on the first branch just above us, it was a huge nasty looking house fly with big enormous eyes and oddly enough had my buddy George's face!. He was gorging his face and making a general ass of himself with a rotten looking jelly doughnut he'd found. This monstrosity in one bite gulped down the rest of that mass of messy pastry he was eating using his forelegs to stuff it in at arms deep into it's mouth!

He then proceeded to clean himself, wildly licking and servicing each leg meticlsey. All of a sudden the little bastard looked down and spied us underneath him, he gave a sinister snicker, scratched his huge butt and then nose-dived right at me! I swatted at him but missed, finally the little cretin alighted on my ear and stuck out his long proboscises to take a large slurp of ear wax for dessert.

"SLAP!" I'd crushed the little asshole upside my head or so I thought. I quickly awoke to the sight and sounds of my buddy Ant rolling around on the floor with a can of shaving cream in his hand laughing himself into a fit. Only then did I notice the huge gob of white foam on my hand and the even bigger explosion of it upside my head. "You asshole!" I hissed at him not wanting dad to hear.

"You rotten, stinking, slime soaked, flea bitten, dog shit eating "HOUSE FLY!" You set me up! He was near tears now and laughing so hard he stopped breathing, he recovered for a second to look at his carnage then went into a relapse all over again. I jumped from the couch where I'd unintentionally spent the night and grabbed the can from him and gave him a head full as well as decorate his ugly face. He looked like a mad dog and the sight we'd made of each other had us both laughing uncontrollably.

Bush-whacking each other was like a customary thing with us and we never passed up a chance to discombobulate each other if caught off guard. Just then dad came weaving down the hall towards use while we were still on the floor fighting for the shaving cream can and another chance to blast the other worse. As he came into the room we froze, shaving cream was all over and we were a mess. He strode passed us with groggy eyes that seemed to be fixed on some unseen object on the wall in front of him.

"Morning boys" he mumbled not looking directly at us but obviously not missing us either. We just stared at each other amazed and laughed cause we expected to get busted for screwing around and messing up the house. We quickly got up and began cleaning the mess we'd made. "So where did you come from, you old snot rag?" "Home." "I know that worm dirt, but how did you get in?" "Oh, your bedroom door . . . you didn't lock it, coochie face."

"What time is it anyway?" I said still a little sleepy and stiff from having slept the wrong way. "11:00 am." "So how come you didn't call last night?" "Aw man, Aretta and her mother stayed over awhile and I got busy and forgot."

Soon dad reappeared in the room looking a little better than he went in. "You boys hungry?" I looked at Ant to see what he wanted to do. "No thank you sir, I already ate." "Yeah, and I'm not hungry yet either dad, but if your hungry I can fix you something." "Well that would be nice if you really don't mind." "No sir it's no problem" I said honestly, and it really wasn't.

You see I loved my dad, he was an enigma to me that I would always look up to and be glad to serve even if he was hard to figure out some times. We never really said it to each other or at least none to often but he knew it.

One of the best things I liked about him was his quiet and cool disposition. He had a soft strength that always let you know that no matter what happens in life it will be alright. I respected his patience too, although I never could seem to develop much of it myself, but for him I would try. I always sought ways to please him, to make him happy with me and smile. I could remember as a child when he would come home from work in his army fatigues, he was all crisp and sharp and the epitome of power, grace, and control. I would patiently wait for him to get home much like a dog would a child coming in from school.

"Hello hot shot" he would say to me as he saw me coming to the car to meet him. I glowed with appreciation and admiration, for he was my world and everything in it and I wanted to grow up to be just like him in every way.

Most kids would complain when their father or mother told them what to do or gave them a job or something, but not me because he was "SGT MAJOR BUFORD MATHIS" and he could do no wrong in my eyes. "I love you dad."

"Hey Mat!" "Huh?" "Where were you man?" "I was calling you and you didn't answer, you just sat there lifeless with a stupid grin on your face and a far away look in your eyes." "Are you okay?" "Yeah I'm okay, thanks for coming over today Ant." "No problem man, you know me." "Yeah I know you!" "Come on, let's go fix your pops some breakfast."

The sun slowly peeked into Aretta's window and bathed her room in a warm glow, the birds in the trees outside her window were chirping and singing her sweetly awake. There was a gentle breeze blowing too and it moved just enough to plant a small kiss on her cheek and awaken her. Her eyes slowly fluttered open and she just lay there feeling completely rested and content. She raised up and stretched herself breaking from her long nights rest.

"I wonder where everybody is?" she thought because Lori wasn't in her bed and she couldn't hear anything in the apartment that sounded alive. A deep smile had embedded itself on her face and refused to leave. Slowly she stretched, then got out of bed and went to the window. She drew in a long deep breath and held it savoring the sunny sweet smell of spring. Everything felt wonderful, the world was a better place and she was in love.

Retta began to notice that her awareness had changed some . . . maybe even intensified a little leaving her with a greater sense of self. She looked slowly around the room, amazed and en-lightened by her new found feeling. She began to see things as a new woman . . . Yes! a woman she thought to herself as she danced and spun around her room happily like a child at Christmas. "I've never felt so free and alive before!" she thought as she frolicked and leapt in the air like a ballerina. She was so full of life and happiness. Finally she'd spun herself onto the bed exhausted and just lay there panting, smiling and laughing. "I can't wait till school starts so everyone can see the new me!"

Just outside the door a tear hit the carpet at her feet. Audrey stood peeking through the door watching her daughter in silence. Right before her eyes Aretta was transformed from the mild and timid little girl into this glistening crystal of light. She smiled to herself "My little girl is growing up!"

Audrey knew deep down that it would happen sooner or later and was very fearful of something happening to Aretta at the hands of some thoughtless-black hearted youth bent on sexual conquest instead of the love and admiration she knew Aretta would return to him. But now she was glad, not because it had happened, but because she had planned for it and tried to bring Aretta up the best she could, fully aware of all the things her life as a young girl and eventually a young woman would experience.

She was also glad it was Rodney who had been her first, for she knew from the first time that they met that there was something special about him, and for him to love Aretta as he does it would only have been a matter of time before it manifested itself into something more physical. Rodney would be gentle and caring with her and hopefully responsible as well. It is for this reason she allowed or accepted what was to happen proceed and blossom without any interference from her.

Yes the tears were freely flowing now and she had peace. "Now Audrey" she scolded herself. You've still got work to do cause it ain't over yet, this is only the beginning and you must see to it that respectability and restraint is maintained. She quickly went into the bathroom and washed her face not wanting Retta or Lori to find her like this.

Meanwhile, Lori was outside splashing in the pool with her best friend Margareta and her dog Cocoa. "Lori!, throw the ball." "I can't!, your stupid dog won't let me, he keeps trying to take it!" The girls screamed and splashed about, and the small dog; a French Terrier, was wildly swimming about and going back and forth between them trying to take the ball from them. Lori threw the ball high and it landed on the deck. "Get it Lori!" Lori's excess weight worked against her in the chest high water, but Cocoa on the other hand had no such restrictions and quickly beat her to the side and got to the ball first. Off he ran yapping and barking, ducking and dodging Lori to the point of frustration.

"Get him Marquette!" she shouted out of breath, as she reached dry land. The dog made short work of her as well in no time at all. "I'm tired" said Lori leaning with hands on her knees and breathing hard. "Me too." "Tell you what, why don't you go around the right side of the pool and I'll go around to the left and that way we can catch him in the middle and trap him." "Okay" said Marquette easing her way around the pool, trying not to be noticed. The dog wasn't the least intimidated by the pair and further showed his contempt of their potential to catch him by laying flat out and legs wide much like a teenager on the floor talking on the phone.

As the girls approached he just wagged his tail much like a cat about to pounce. "Okay Marquette, were almost on him, don't let him know your after him." "I won't, you just be ready!" They were mere feet from him now and about to jump him. Cocoa sensed there plan and gathered his ball and lower half up in readiness for them and gave a warning yap and a growl. "Get him!" yelled Lori as she rushed him full speed with her head down and arms poised to grab.

Cocoa was much better suited for short bursts of speed and just bolted straight out from where he was lying at the pools edge, right into the pool "SPLASH!". Suddenly there were screams and two more splashes, but these weren't intended. Lori and Marquette, due to bad coordination had collided with each other head first, bounced off each other and fallen into the pool with two terrible and unintended headaches.

By now the dog was out on the other side of the pool and sitting pertly on a lawn couch barking his approval of their ill planned attack. Lori surfaced first sputtering and rubbing her head, and more than irritated at their mishap. Soon Marquette joined her on the edge of the pool. "Ole stupid dog" she said pouting and rubbing her head some more.

"Mom is that you?" said Retta suddenly aware she wasn't alone anymore and hoping she wasn't seen dancing about. "Yes it's me." "Oh, when I woke up there wasn't anyone here or so I thought." "I was just outside with Lori, so sleepy head, are you hungry?" "Yes ma'am, what time is it anyway?" "Noon" she said looking at her watch. "Noon, you mean I've been asleep all that time?" "Well don't worry yourself dear heart, it's not a week day so don't get yourself in a tizzy." "I'm not, I wasn't aware that it was so late." "So what would you like for breakfast?" "Umm . . . some scrambled eggs and sausage." "Okay, I'll be done in a jiffy." "She's awfully happy today" thought Retta. "I wonder what she's been up to?"

"So . . . what did you and Rodney's dad do last night?" "Oh just sit and talk and have a few drinks." "That's nice" she said reclining in a chair. "So mama, what do you think of him?" She turned to give Retta a smile then returned to beating her eggs. "He's nice, quite a gentleman." "And" she coaxed. "He has a nice body too, now I can see one of the things you love about Rodney so much!" "And" "Just What do you mean, Retta?" she said turning her full attention to her and folding her arms suddenly perturbed by Retta's implications and tone.

"To be perfectly honest with you, it's really none of your business!" "Oops!, went too far this time" thought Retta wincing from the reprimand. "But!, since you asked" she said getting friendly again. "He was something else!" she boasted plopping down in a chair beside her like two girls running the latest gossip.

"Girl, he smelled so sweet, and those strong arms and that sexy smile of his, I wasn't sure I could keep myself respectable!" "What else?!" said Retta leaning into her, completely absorbed. "We talked about our pasts and the people we knew and had been seeing." "We talked about you and Rodney too!"

"Retta, you know, those two are spit from the same mold!" "They talk alike, sound alike, act alike." "But do they kiss alike?" blurted Retta, thinking about some of the finer attributes of her man. "Now how would I know that?" aid Audrey sitting back, hands on her hips.

Retta was enjoying this fact finding immensely. She had already known about their likenesses and thought it funny her mother noticed it to. "What a crazy thing to say, I ain't never kissed Rodney before . . . but I could if you'd like me too" she said giving Retta her most seductive smile and feminine gesture.

"NO!, that's okay, we'll just have to compare notes or something!" Audrey was beside herself with laughter at how fast Aretta would jump to the defense or more or less protection of her man at the slightest hint of a female threat. Soon the laughter faded and there was a long silence.

"So Aretta, how was your evening?" she said with a soft voice and looking in her eyes, teasing the hem of her apron. Retta was moved by this sudden and all to quick change and wondered what she was digging at.

"I wonder what she's getting at, she couldn't possibly know anything about last night, could she?" thought Retta. "It was just fine mom, we just chilled out and listened to some tapes he made and talked some." "Is that all?" Retta was on guard now and figured her mother did know something but what and just how much she really knew and how much more she should tell her was the question. Finally she decided that her mother was no fool and knew a whole lot more than she originally let on.

"No, that's not all, we also made love" she said lowering her voice to almost a whisper and expecting to be hit any minute. Audrey didn't speak, she just sat there looking at her with a forward look on her face. She wasn't angry with her because she already had a feeling that this was so. But to hear it from her honestly where as she kind of expected a lie, well this had unbalanced her some.

"Mom, are you okay?" she asked risking imminent destruction. "What?" "I said are you okay?" "Uh, sure, . . . sure I'm okay, I was just lost in thought for a second, how did it happen? (A dumb question at best but she needed to say something to keep herself talking!) "It just did mom, we didn't plan any thing, one thing just led to another and there we were." "How do you feel?" "I'm not sure." "I know what you mean." "Hmm, neither do I" she said throwing her hands up in frustration at not quite being in control of the situation, particularly since she wasn't caught blindsided by any of this.

"I hadn't planned to be giving this talk for quite some time, but now that it's upon me I'm not sure quite how to deal with it." "Are you angry with me momma?" "No!" "Are you ashamed of me?" "No!, Retta!" "Then I guess I feel okay then, I mean my body feels really different and I see things differently than before, but that's about it." "Oh yeah, my butt hurts a little too, but that's about it!"

Audrey allowed herself a small chuckle to relieve the tension. "Well sweetheart, that's to be expected when you make love for the first time . . . . that was the first time wasn't it?" she said looking at her with questioning eyes. Retta just rolled her eyes and frowned. "I'm sorry sweetheart, I just thought I'd ask, but not to worry I've got something for that discomfort." "Thanks mom." (more silence) "So . . . was it what you expected it to be?" Aretta thought for a moment trying to remember if she'd ever given any thought to sex and the way she thought it would be by the way other girls described it.

"No, it was better than I expected it to be, or maybe it was because of the way he was so gentle with me and patient, I can't say for sure I just know it was more than my imagination ever came up with."

Audrey sighed long from relief, she had thought this was the case, but was glad to find out it was true. "I think you'll find that your body is going to change even more because of this, but don't worry, you'll enjoy the subtle changes and then again there maybe some you won't, depends on how you see it." "Great, I can't wait" she said almost sarcastically and rising to get up. "Mom I'm going to take a shower." "You go ahead sweetheart, I'll finish getting your breakfast ready okay?" "Okay mom!" she yelled from the bathroom.

"Well that wasn't so bad" she thought turning on the shower. "I expected to get beaten beyond all recognition when she found out, and she didn't even ask if he wore a condom or not, now that really surprised me!" I wonder if her and Mr. Mathis will get together, it's been awhile since she's been with someone and even though she doesn't show it, I know she's lonely. They would make a nice couple and me and Rodney could see each other even more!

This thought gave her a warm flush of delight as she stepped into the shower. The warmth of it felt luxurious on her soft golden skin. She stood there allowing the water to cascade over her head and down her back and shoulders giving her a gentle massage.

"How many sausages do you want, Retta?" Retta didn't hear her because the shower had drowned her out. She began soaping herself all over using just the bar itself. She stroked herself all over, letting the soap tease her lightly about her neck and breasts, all the while reliving last nights journey through passion. She imagined it was Rodney's hands caressing her.

"Oh God!" she whispered. "Will I ever get enough of him, his touch, his sweet smile and the way he holds me so close." I'm like a moth to a flame when I'm near him and can't wait to be scorched by his burning kisses! Oh! How he loved me last night, I can still feel him inside me so full and hot and "Aretta you gotta stop this shit" she told herself; as she halted her hand from placing the soap she was lathering with in a place best reserved for other things!

You are so full of that man! Moreover, you don't really know where this may lead. You could get pregnant stupid! He may get bored with me after awhile or worse, mom and Mr. Buford could really get to liking each other. And if that happens where will you and Matt be?

"Aretta!" her mother called pulling back the shower curtain quickly. "What!" "I've been calling you for five minutes, didn't you hear me?" "No ma'am, I'm sorry." "I was calling you to find out what else you wanted with your breakfast." "Nothing, I don't want anything I'm not hungry anymore" she said rinsing herself.

"I'll just have a piece of toast if you don't mind." "Are you all right honey?" "I didn't mean to startle you." "Naa, I'm okay" she mumbled stepping out to dry off, but she wasn't.

It was always her way to analyze everything closely and to check and re-check to see how it would affect her. But not this time, this was something she couldn't possibly see the out come of because it involved people she had not considered would factor in her life. Her worst fears were slowly becoming possibilities and she found this hard to deal with or understand. Retta went back to her room to finish drying off; as she got there, the phone rang.

"I got it mom!" she said picking it up. "Hello?" "Hey! Girlfriend" "Oh, hey Frieda." "So what's been up?" she asked sounding enthusiastic about something. "Oh nothing, I just got out of the shower, how about you?" "Girl it's been great! Curt and me had a good time! We went to the Red Lobster then we drove to Atlanta." "Atlanta, why did y'all go way up there?" "Well he told me about this club called the Purple Onion, and said it was a cool place to jam." "So I said okay let's go!" "So how was it?" "Girlfriend let me tell ya THAT PLACE WAS BAD! I mean BAD!" "Soon as you walk in they got this guy standing at the door to let you in." "A bouncer?" "Yeah that's what they called him, he stamps your wrist with some kind of invisible stuff so you can come and go without paying twice." "From there you have to walk down these stairs to get to the main floor, but when you look out over the whole place it's got mirrors everywhere!" "In addition, there were all kinds of flashing lights and two DJ's, the floor was transparent Girl, it had FISH! In it!" "Fish?"

"Hell yeah, fish! and in between the mirrors was black leather walls with little mirror dots that reflected when the lights hit them." "You go girl!" chimed Retta impressed with the place. What else did they have in there?" "Well just as you come down the stairs on the left, is a huge long bar, it was white and black marble with a mirrored top and leather armchairs." "Over to the left of the bar was a private lounge with couches and love seats and chairs to sit if you didn't want to drink in the main area or at the bar." "Oh and guess what else they had?" "What?" "Girl they had half naked dancing girls in there!" "Naw they didn't!" "They had on them bikini drawers that go up your butt crack and little tassels on their titties!"

"Ooh Frieda! You went to a place like that?" "Shoot yeah, it was fun honey child and we danced a lot and had some drinks, aw, girl we had a good time in that place." "They let you drink?" "Child please, with all that darkness and light shows an shit, they could have sold beer to Lori and wouldn't have noticed it."

Retta was laughing her ass off now picturing Lori with her plump little belly up to a bar chugging beer. "So what else happened with you an Curt?" "After awhile we left and went to the Marriott to stay the night and get something to eat." "Ooh! Frieda, you didn't wait very long did you?" "Now just wait a minute Betty Crocker, before you go cooking up some shit . . . you best let me finish!" she said putting Retta in check. "We only went there because it was so late and we had been drinking." "MMHMM, go on." "When we got there to our room he didn't even try anything, in fact he was the perfect gentleman, all we did was order some food and watch a little TV before going to bed."

In fact he even offered to sleep on the couch." "What couch?" "Oh didn't I tell you, we had a really nice suite on the tenth floor, it had a tub with water jets in it." "A Jacuzzi?" "Yeah one of those, it also had a stereo in the wall and everything girl!" "So did he sleep on the couch?" "Naw, I told him we could sleep in the bed together and that it would be okay."

"Did you have some night clothes?" "Heck no! I told you I didn't have any idea that we were going any where but to dinner and a movie in Macon." "So you slept in your clothes then?" "Nope, what do you think I am, a wino?" "You didn't get under the covers with him in your underwear did you?" "You damn Skippy I did" she said proudly. "And we didn't do anything, Okay! Mrs. Nosy!"

"Okay, if you say so" said Aretta giggling. "Why don't you believe me?" "You act like I'm a whore or something." "Oh, I believe you Frieda, but I also know you too, and you have the modesty of a politician on campaign and the virtues of a housefly." "OOH! Retta! How could you say that about me?" "I thought I was your best friend!" she said sounding a little hurt but amused. "Oh, come off it Frieda! You know how hot you get around men sometimes."

"Do you remember that day in gym class last year when you and Derrick Jackson snuck in the equipment room and got busy?" "That was different!" "Oh yeah how?" "Well for one we knew each other for at least a week before we got into anything and . . ." "I rest my case" said Retta cutting her off. "Okay MISS Prissy!" "What about you and Michael Foster, in the book room?" "What about that!"

"You're fulla shit, I didn't go in there with him!" Retta shouted. "I was walking by there and his friends pushed him on me and we stumbled into the room and I slapped him for it too!" "Now if you don't believe me you can go and ask him Monday!" "Okay, okay, don't get your panties in a wad." There was a long silence after this as both girls were getting steamed up and trying to decide whether or not to accept this stalemate or go on bickering. "Sigh! well anyway, once we had showered and settled in, he fell asleep dead away."

"Retta he was so fine girl, you should have seen him in that bikini underwear he had on and he has some nice muscles too!" "Girl them thangs looked like speed bumps on his stomach and I wanted to touch em so bad!" Retta could hear her drooling over the phone and just shook her head laughing at her. "And his legs, Girl, them thangs was so fine and hairy, and he had hair on his chest too!

Oh man, how I just wanted to take off all my clothes and slide up and down all over him!" Retta completely lost it at this point and guffawed herself right to the floor in a butt-naked heap. "To be honest with you girlfriend, I did want him and if he woulda just touched me a little bit I would have raped him!"

"Girl your sick!" "Maybe, but I know what I like!" "We got up early, had a nice breakfast, did some looking around, and went shopping in the Peachtree Mall." "Damn! Frieda, are you sure you didn't give up some booty anyway?" "Yeah I'm sure, he's just a really nice guy that's all, we came home soon after that about 2:30, he asked me when we could go out again, I told him anytime was fine with me, so he said he would give me a call sometime and we'd work it out then." "Sounds like you got him girl!" "You think so?" "If you didn't I'd be real surprised!" "Oh, and do you know what else Retta?" "I can't imagine." "He didn't even try to kiss me or nothing when I got out, he just said he would see me later." "Oh yeah?" "Humph, and what did you do?"

"What do you think I did?" "I didn't fuss if that's what your thinking, I just acted like a respectable lady, I was polite and sweet and just told him "okay Curt I'll see ya later." "You did it didn't you?" said Retta, her voice flat and toneless. "You damn right! I did" she yelled with pride. "You would of thought I was trying to suck his eyeballs out through his mouth I kissed him so hard!" Retta was hooting again and this time didn't try to keep it quiet from her mother. "Girl your nuts!" "Yeah I know, but It was fun and he liked it too!" "So your gonna keep on seeing him then?" "Yeah, why not?" "I don't see anybody else trying to go out with me." "You got that right." "So how was your date with Rodney?" "Oh no! Sweet pea, you're not getting a word out of me, you think just because you sold yourself out I'm supposed to follow?"

"Your gonna have to work a little harder than that." "I'll be right there!" said Frieda hanging up and dashing for the door. She knew full well that Retta had some juicy gossip to talk about and would make her earn the right to hear it. "What was that all about Retta?" asked her mother.

"Oh that was Frieda talking about her date Friday with the school bus driver, a guy named Curt." "The bus driver, isn't that pushing the age gap a little?" "Not really, he's only 19 from what she tells me." "Well, that's still three years her senior." Retta just shrugged and closed the door to get dressed. "Lord these girls are trying to grow up to fast."

So dad, what are you going to do today?" asked Matt handing Ant another dish to dry. "Well let's see, I'm supposed to help my buddy Whitherspoone get his truck going." "He's been having some problems with the carburetor."

"Oh that doesn't sound too bad, what time will you be back?" "I don't know, maybe a couple of hours or so, why? You need something?" "No sir, I was just thinking that I could take out something for you to cook for dinner or maybe cook myself." Matt's dad just chuckled-and-shook his head. "What's so funny?" "Boy you just don't pay attention to anything do you, have you forgotten already that we have a dinner date with Aretta and her mother at 6:00 o'clock today?"

"OH YEAH! I forgot." Matt's dad just shook his head again and went on out the back door and down the stairs. "I'll see you after while" he said waving to them. "Well that's that" said Ant closing the cabinets. "What kind of date you guys got going Matt?" "Me and dad been invited over to Retta's house for dinner with her and her mother." "Oh hell" he said laughing. "What's so funny about that?" "I knew you and your pops were a lot alike but for you two to be hanging out together, now that's too much!" "Well it wasn't our idea, when they was over here last night, Retta's momma told us to come over there for dinner today." "How long did they stay over?" "About two hours I guess." "What do you think Fart Face, and what were you doing all that time?" he said cutting a sly smile. "Oh, it's like that huh?" "Damn Skippy" said Matt then smacked him upside the head with the dishcloth and hauled ass out of the kitchen and down the hall.

"Mat! you know I'm gone stomp a mud hole in your butt when I catch you!" he shouted running after him. But too late Matt was already out the door and heading around the back. He had a good lead on Ant and it was his intention to double back around the house, come in from the rear and get him again.

"Yo, Matt, come on out man, I ain't gonna hurtcha!" he said standing in the front yard with a hand full of evil looking switches he'd torn off some bushes nearby. Matt was laughing to himself at his quickness of foot and even quicker thinking as he'd gotten not only the jump on Ant and was staring down at him from the roof but also had managed to grab two eggs from the refrigerator before climbing up. Ant was now sitting on the stoop and Matt could see his feet. He was talking to someone he couldn't see but figured from the accent that it was Mrs. Latenburger their neighbor who lives in the loft apartment upstairs. "Damn, just my luck, now I have to wait till she goes in before I can bust him up" thought Ant to himself. Soon she left and he got up and stepped into full view. "Hot Damn! That's your ass now "Sucka!" Matt shouted while aiming at the back of Ants head and throwing as hard and straight as he could. "Bishl Plosh!" Both eggs connected within seconds of each other and exploded like they had firecrackers in them. But as fate would have it his own handy work was quickly turned against him and he lost his balance from the force of the throw and fell sliding to the end of the roof. "Oh fuck!" SMASH!, CRUNCH!, "OH DAMN!" FWOOSH!, "OW!" Matt had fallen through the big bush just beneath the roof and ended up flat on his face, pure ass holes and elbows in position. He was in pain now and had scraped his butt on the gutter and caught a good-sized branch in the balls and was sure he'd loosened his brain bucket when his face hit the hard packed earth.

Meanwhile, Ant was busy laughing his ass off – rolling around on the ground like his guts hurt. Matt was just about to get up and go fix his ass but stopped short when he heard someone else laughing. It was Ivory Cummings or "Frog" as they called him. Matt wanted to hit him in the face with an egg too but was a little short on those just now. "Man come on" said Ant "Let's go get cleaned up he said laughing." "Hey Matt, I'm gonna make a sandwich okay?" said Frog. "Go ahead." "So what's been going down Frog?" "Same ole same ole, I just got back from church a little while ago." "How bout Nana, she's still in church?"

"Damn! Your sister stays in church a long time!" "She always stays late." "Man, it must be rough being a preachers kid!" "It's not as bad as people like to think, your folks are the same as anybody else's, no matter what and their job don't make em any harder on you either, they just do what they gotta do and that's it." "What about church?" "If I want to go I go, if I don't I don't, it don't mean it's a bad reflection on him if don't!" "Okay." "So what you and Matt got going on for today?" "I don't know man, I just got here awhile ago myself." "Any ball games going on anywhere?" asked Frog.

"I saw some dudes at Clisby on my way over here but not much else." "Okay man, I'll catch you later." "Later Ant" he said scampering out the door. "Well I guess its you and me Ant." "Ain't it always like that anyway?" "Yep, you got that right, so what are you gonna do?" "I don't know, probably go home and call Brenda or Melanie." "Melanie! you talking already?" "Naw man, you must think I'm Jr." "Hey, you tell me?" "Naw, I just haven't gotten around to calling her yet." "Oh, and what about Brenda?" "I thought you was supposed to be through." "Well you know how it is with her, she gets mad then blows up just to come back whining for forgiveness." "Yeah that's her all right, are you gonna take her back?"

"I don't know, we been going together for a couple of months and she still don't wanna gimmie no play." "You mean to tell me you ain't got them drawers yet?" "Nope." "Why not?" "She won't let me, she says she's scared she might get pregnant or something." "Aw man, what a prude, has she ever heard of birth control or condoms?" "She won't let me use a condom and I don't know if she is on the pill or not."

"It sounds to me like you have a real problem on you hands brother man!" "No, not really" he said smiling and waving the phone number he got from Melanie the other day. "So are you gonna call her?" "Yep, what do I have to lose?" "Not much I guess, all she can say is get lost." "Why don't you give her a call now?" "You got time."

"That's my plan man" he said heading for the phone. Ring ring . . . "Hello" said a female voice. "Hello, may I speak to Melanie please?" "This is she, who's calling?" "Well you may not remember me, but we met at Annabelle's Saturday." "You was working and I was sitting with a friend."

"Rodney!?" she blurted out happily surprised. "Oh no, this is George his friend." "Oh" she said sounding let down a little. "So how are you?" said Ant attempting to squash his blossoming embarrassment. "Fine, I'm fine thank you, and you?" "I'm fine too" he said glad she had asked because he would have been at a loss if she hadn't responded back. A long silence passed before either said anything more and it was beginning to feel uneasy, especially Ant cause he didn't know quite what to say right about now anyway.

"Oh Melanie?" "Yes?" "I know this is kind of awkward and strange that we met under these circumstances but I would like to get to know you better if I could." "Well, George, I'm not sure, this is all so sudden and to be honest with you I was really expecting Rodney to call me." "Oh-I see, well he's seeing someone already, that's why he thought we could get together and be friends."

"Well it's a nice idea and I'm not totally against it but I must tell you that I'm kind of skeptical about it." "Okay, I understand but tell me this, is it because I'm black?" "NO!" she said almost yelling.

"I'm not prejudice, I just thought it was Rodney who was interested in me that's all!" "Well I can understand that, and I'm sorry for putting you on the spot like that seeing as how he did approach you first and all, tell you what, why don't we just forget the whole thing and I'll just apologize for calling you and not call again okay?" he said poising to hang up.

"No George . . . wait!" she said feeling she may have hurt his feelings. "I didn't mean to hurt you and I really do think you're kinda cute." "But" he said kind of cool. "But I need more time to get to know you okay?"

"Okay, that's fair enough, when and where?" "Well I'm not doing anything at the moment, so why don't we meet say . . . at the Westgate Theater out front in an hour okay?" "Okay . . . that'll work" he said feeling a little pumped. "Are we going to the movies or are we just going to meet there and do something else?" "We can if you want to." "Sure, anything you like." "Good, then it's a date." "So let me get out of here and go home so I can change, then I'll meet you there." "Your not home?" "Nah, I'm at Matt's house." "Who's that?" "Rodney" "Oh really?" she said sounding excited. "Do you mind if I say hello to him?" "Naw, I'll go get him" he said coming to get him.

He sat the phone down and as he turned to leave, came face to face with Matt who was standing there with a "Cat who ate the canary" look on his face. "Damn!" said Ant caught by surprise. "How long you been standing there?" "Oh long enough." "Melanie wants to talk to you." "Hello?" he said picking up the phone. "Hello Rodney?" "Yeah babe, it's me." She got a warm flush from hearing him call her babe. "How are you?" "I'm fine, and you?" "I'm okay, I was hoping you would call me when I gave you my number, I didn't know you were planning to give it to George instead."

"Is that a problem?" "Well No, not really, I just thought that it was you that was interested in me." "Well Melanie, I'm sorry if I led you on or misguided you in any way babe because that wasn't my intention at all." She began to feel a lump in her stomach and wanted to just fall into a hole. "Yes, I thought you were very beautiful and I did feel you, but what I was really trying to do was get you and my friend together." "Oh, I see" she said folding her arms slight disgust and feeling like she had been orphaned. "You know something Rodney, all that day all I could think about was you and how you made me feel."

"Melanie." "No wait, please, you must let me finish." "Okay" "Like I was saying, you made me feel wonderful and nervous inside at the same time and I never thought anyone could give me that feeling! And I really couldn't believe it when you just reached out to me and sat me down beside you . . . and the way you caressed my cheek so softly and . . . well I thought I might just melt!"

"I mean don't get me wrong, I'm not an easy woman by no means and it takes more than just a few words and a handsome face to get me interested, but the way you handled me, and I can think of no better way to describe it . . . so carefully and patiently, I was enslaved by you Rodney."

Matt shifted his weight uneasily and toyed with the phone cord at hearing this. He was at a loss for words and didn't quite no what to say to her at that point because he had never had an experience like that in his life either. "Not to mention when you stepped out to help me up again, I was in such a fog at your control over me that I was indisposed to do anything about it except to be led!" "Mel" "And those deep brown eyes of yours!" She said getting more excited. "Rodney" she said in a whisper before he could speak. "You know, when you drew me up close to you I felt a hot flush come over me and for a brief moment I really thought you were going to kiss me, and even though I didn't know you and was a little afraid . . . I wanted you to" she said finishing with a long pause that Matt failed to take advantage of due to the fact that he was dumbstruck.

It completely surprised him that this girl or anyone else could be so quickly enamored or taken with him and in such a short time with such a profound affect on them! This made Matt sweat and it didn't help matters much that Ant was standing there the whole time listening either. "Melanie, I'm sorry I made you feel all those things because we can never see them through, had circumstances been different I would have been completely engrossed in you as well and you must believe me when I say, I felt something too!" "I was not totally immune to you babe (there was that flush again) or how you made me feel, but Melanie It can never be angel, cause I love someone else and could never go against her for anyone."

"I see" she said feeling dead inside and numb. "Is . . . is she black also?" "Should it matter?" "No, I'm sure you would say the same to anyone else if it had been me you were in love with." "This is true Mel, I love only one woman and with only one heart, do you understand angel?" he said feeling himself slip like before in the restaurant but some how controlling it this time. Melanie sighed long and low. "Well I guess that's it then." "I'm afraid so Mel." "Can we still be friends?" she asked half-heartedly. "Yes, I would love to have a person as special as you as my friend Mel."

"I like it when you say my name like that Rodney, it's like a kiss only not close enough to taste but enough to feel." "Thanks I think" he said blushing. "So when do you think we can see each other again?" she asked quite pertly. Something in her tone and quickness to agree to a limited friendship caused Matt to be on guard. "Melanie" he said stressing her name just enough to let her know he was on to her. "I'm just kidding Rodney, honest, I understand our relationship perfectly and I plan to adhere to my end with the utmost strictness." "Okay, so long as we understand the ground rules."

"Ohh, I understand them alright" she said rather saucily with a smirk. "You must be nuts if you think I'm gonna let some girl have you all to herself for one minute mister" she said under her breath with the most sinisterly sweet bum swelling inside her. "Can I speak back to George? We have a date this evening" she said faking ambivalence. "Okay, I'll talk to you later Mel." "Okay, bye Rod."

"Here you go Ant, she's all yours" he said handing him the phone and leaving the kitchen and a stupefied Ant holding the phone. Matt hadn't known it just then but he'd given his best friend a time bomb and gift-wrapped it with a bow. "Hi George!" she boomed at him. Ant just looked at the phone as if he'd been offered a trip to a Klan rally.

"What's up Melanie, are you okay?" "Oh I'm fine, just fine, so why are you still there, we still have a date don't we?" she teased. Ant didn't waste anymore time . . . history had taught him that when a woman switches out that fast it's best not to bandy words but instead beat feet! "I'm just leaving . . . Bye." "Hey Matt!" "Yeah" "What did you say to her man?" he asked turning the comer into dad's room.

"I just gave it to her straight man, you heard what I said to her." "Yeah, that's what's so fucked up about it, I was there" he just folded his arms and looked at Matt with a strange look on his face. "Now how come when I do that they never want to speak to me again, but when you do it they still like you!" "Hell I don't know, maybe It's not what you say but how you say it." "Well I'll have to take your word for it cause you still shock me every time I see you handle a woman like that, have you been taking lesson's from Milton?"

"HELL NO!" Matt shot back feeling completely hostile for the first time today. He couldn't stand being compared with that ass hole in any way, shape, or form. The look on his face only made Ant laugh because he thought it was all too funny that Matt had such a venomous attitude towards Milton or Jr. as they sometimes called him, but yet would still hang out with him. "Man that vulture just uses them and throws them away like toilet paper!"

"And what do you do Matt?" "I love em!" "Yeah, I guess you do at that." Just then a car ran down the driveway and into the back yard. "Oh fuck! that's dad and I'm not even finished with his clothes yet!" "Well you better get on with it and have something done before he walks in." "What time is it anyway?" It's 5:15" "Hell, I'm not even done getting my own self ready." "Hey Ant." "I know-I know, you want me to get your stuff ready while you finish his right?" "Yeah homey, would you do that for me please?" "Yeah, I gotcha covered" he said leaving.

Quick as a flash he'd finished his dad's shirt and could hear him coming up the stairs in back. Matt quickly put it on a hanger and went to check the machine to see if it had finished. "Good! It had." "Hidey ho son, what's going on?" he asked coming into the kitchen. "Oh nothing much, just getting done with your clothes." "There not done yet?" "No sir, there was a stain on your pants so I had to wash them." "That's good, are they done?" "Not yet I still need to dry them." "Well go ahead and do that, I'm gonna go and shower right quick." "Okay dad" he said throwing them in the dryer and putting it on it's highest setting so they would dry quicker.

Then he dashed to his room to check on Ant. "Hey Ant, you done yet?" he said coming into the room. "Yeah man, I been done, what do you think?" he asked pointing to the clothes on the bed. He had chosen a pair of blue Duck Head shorts, a pink short sleeve button down collar shirt, pink socks and a pair of blue Docksider shoes.

"Good job man, that's just fine, sometimes I think you dress me better than I do myself." "Well I couldn't do it if you didn't have the clothes in the first place, Preppie" he said but he was as much deserving of the title as Matt was with his combo of either two button down collars of different colors or two Izods. "So what's the plan with you and Melanie?" "She said to meet her at the Westgate Cinema later and we'd figure out something from there." "Oh yeah?" "It was her idea."

"So you have a 6:00 o'clock date too?" "You know it" he said happy with himself. "Hey man I really hope things go well for you two today" said Matt slapping him on the shoulder. "Well thanks man, I really appreciate you looking out for me." "So how you gonna get there?" "I don't know, I thought I might catch the bus from here."

Matt quickly looked at his clock on the nightstand. "You just missed it, its 5:30 ole buddy." "Damn! I guess I'll be late so let me go an call her to let her know I'll be late." Matt just smiled at him shaking his head. "What?" "You never learn do you?" he said reaching up on the mantle piece for his moped keys and dangled them in front of him. "Oh I forgot, I didn't think about that, I thought your pop didn't like anyone to ride it but you." "That's true, but your an exception to that rule!" "You sure about that?" he asked taking the keys. "Go ask him yourself then."

"Nah I'll take your word for it, what time do you want me to bring it back?" "No special time, just put it in a safe place okay?" "Alright Matt, you have a good time at Retta's and bring me a doggie bag" he said grinning as he walked out the door. Soon Matt's dad was out of the shower and he was in.

Since Matt hadn't really gotten what you'd call dirty, he only needed a quick rinse off. "Rodney are you ready yet?" his dad yelled from his room. "Yes sir, I'm just putting on my shoes." "Okay, when your done just meet me in front alright?" "Yes sir!" Matt hustled to get finished and damn near tied a knot in one shoelace. You know how hard it is to get a knot out of a leather string?

Soon Matt heard the roar of his dad's Mercedes starting up. he made one last quick check around the room to see if he had forgotten anything, once he was satisfied he grabbed his little ditty bag and sport coat, locked up the door then bolted out of the house into the front yard. His dad was waiting in the driveway. "Did you lock up everything?" "Yes sir, all is secure." "Good, what's that?" he asked pointing at his gym bag.

"Oh, it's just some stuff I brought along for later." "Like what?" "You know, tapes, my radio, a blanket, it's such a nice day out I thought me and Retta might take a walk up to Coleman Hill after dinner." "Coleman Hill, what's that?" "Oh, it's a small grassy spot up on the ridge past her house beyond the woods." "Oh I know where that is, that's a nice area how did you guys manage to get up there?" "Oh, we know a trail that leads up and over to one side, it's really nice up there too!"

"I'll bet it is, so you guys don't plan to stick around after dinner then?" "Nope, not this time, I thought it would be better for you guys to have some quality time together." "Well that's mighty white of you" he said chuckling with a funny expression. "But did it occur to you that we may go for a ride later and get some ice cream or something?" "No sir it didn't." "Now we can pass on it if you would rather hang out with your girl." "Let me check with her first then we'll see."

"Aretta are you ready yet?" asked her mother. "Just about mom, I just need to put on my stocking." "Well, hurry up! they'll be her soon okay." "Retta my tighties don't fit!" whined Lori.

"Well put on another pair then." "But I don't have anymore!" "Well then, don't wear any!" "But I have to, I'm wearing a dress!" she whined further. "Oh Lord, no you don't Lori, you can wear socks with lace on them." "But mine are dirty" "Here! take em" she hissed thrusting them into her eager little hands. "Just hurry up, okay." "Okay" said Lori sitting down with a plop and working the her foot into the sock.

"Mom how are you coming along, do you have everything you need?" "Yes, I'm fine dear" she said coming around the corner putting in an earring. "Wow! You look great" beamed Retta. "Mr. Buford is gonna love you in that dress." "Why thank you sweetheart you look scrumptious yourself."

Retta blushed and reassessed herself in the mirror with new appreciation. Soon all was in readiness. Audrey went into the kitchen and rechecked the table settings for the hundredth time. It was a beautiful table. It had a red table cloth with a rosy pink coverlet exposing the corners. The table glistened with china, flatware and crystal glasses. She had little place setting cards on each plate and a beautiful bouquet with two red candles for a center piece. Aretta was tending to the stereo trying to find some good easy listening dinner music. Just then there was a knock on the door.

Retta looked at the clock, "Mom its 6:00 o'clock!" "Oh my lord, that must be them then" she said hurrying from the kitchen. "Wait Retta!" she whispered. "Don't open it yet . . . how do I look?" "Fine mom just relax okay?" "Go ahead and open it!" "Hi!" "Hello gorgeous" said Matt looking Retta up and down like a flag pole, giving an approving nod as he stepped into the room and handing her some flowers.

"OH! Matt they are beautiful!" she gushed taking them and inhaling deeply. "So are you" said Matt giving her a wink and a smile. "Aw Matt that's so sweet" she said waving them in. "Hi Buford" said Audrey.

"Hello sexy" he said and gave her a dozen roses. "Oh! You shouldn't have" she crooned as she took the flowers into her arms and led everyone into the living room. "Please sit down, I'll be right back with some refreshment."

"Aretta" she said nodding towards the stereo. "Okay mom" she acknowledged them and moved to turn it on. "I have some music but nothing you guys may like, so do you have any preference?" "No, not really, anything is fine" said Matt's dad. "Hear try this" said Matt handing her a tape. "What's that?" asked Retta. "Oh, just some music" he said giving her sly grin. She put the tape in the machine and turned on adjusting the volume so it didn't blow out anyone's ears. A soft slow melody began to play and the a familiar voice began to sing. "I . . . . I'm so in love with you . . . whatever you want me to . . . . is alright with me . . . ee . . ." "That's Al Green isn't it?" "Yeah"

Al Green was one of Matt's dad's favorite artists. He knew he would enjoy listening to him. It was a mixed tape Matt had made from his dads many reels of tapes. His own stereo was too big to bring along and he was sure he would like the surprise. "So when did you start listening to the old greats?" asked Matt's dad. "Now dad you ought to know how that came to be with you always playing those old tunes all the time when I was little."

"Do you remember the time you picked me up out of my crib and started dancing around the room singing and making Google eyes at me?" "You remember that?" "Yes sir!" "But you were just two years old, how could you have?" Matt just pointed at the stereo. "The music dad . . . I remembered the music." "Well I'll be" his dad said shaking his head smiling and tousling Matt's hair.

Soon Audrey was back with a tray of glasses and hor'dvores. "This looks good" said Buford. "It's shrimp and crab salad said Audrey giving him a big smile of appreciation at his comment. Matt grabbed a cracker and dug in deep not trying to hide his hunger. "This is good" he commented reaching for another cracker. "Thank you Rodney" she sat the tray down and sat next to Buford on the couch.

"You guys are looking fine today!" "Well thank you" said Buford readjusting in his seat. Matt and Retta were sitting close on the love seat feeding each other and giggling. They had forgotten all about their parents and just sat eating and staring into each others eyes, falling in love over and over again. Retta was breath taking Matt noticed. Her thick rich ebony hair was styled in a simple fashion with a gold hair clamp in the top. Her bangs came over her forehead just above her eyes. The sides flowed gracefully to crown her face. It gave an intoxicating affect.

Retta's dress was a burgundy satin oriental "B" girl dress like you see in those war movies. It had tiny golden dragons and gold trim around the high collar. The way it fit her, you could see every curve on her body. Those full and petite breasts pushed teasingly against it giving full definition to her athletic frame.

"I love you" he mouthed silently. Matt reached out and placed her hand on his chest to feel his heart beat. Retta understood and smiled.

"Hello everybody" said Lori walking into the room finally. "Hi Lori" said Buford. "Hey pretty girl" said Matt reaching into his coat pocket. "I've got something for you." Everyone sat up and looked on curious at what Matt had brought her. "For me! . . . really?" chirped Lori with eyes happy and fully of glee. "Yes . . . it's for you" he said motioning for her to come to him. Matt opened up a little black satin jewelry box. "OOH! That's nice" said everyone in unison. Matt brought out the little gold heart shaped locket then opened it. Inside was a tiny little ballerina on one side and a rose on the other. Lori was flabbergasted. "Ooh! Pretty" she cooed getting closer.

Matt opened the clasp and placed the chain around her neck. She looked at and delicately ran a tiny finger around the edges of the locket feeling the tiny roses. "Oh! Thank you Rodney nobody ever gave me a present like this before" she said throwing her arms around his neck and squeezing till Matt coughed from being choked. (wheeze) "No problem Lori, I was happy to do it, I figured that since your mom and your sister were getting something you should too!" Aretta and her mother just sat smiling at him with gratitude and love in there eyes for the gesture. "Thank you" mouthed Audrey silently.

Matt's dad was smiling too but didn't speak cause he knew his son had a heart for people and was proud of him for it. "So are you guys hungry?" said Audrey. "Yes ma'am" was the reply as they all began to rise and head to the kitchen. Lori and Retta began putting their glasses on the tray and walked into the kitchen. "Wow!" said Matt looking at all the great looking food on the table.

"Man . . . Annabelle's ain't got nothing on this spread" said Matt surprised. "Who is Annabelle's?" asked his dad. "It's a restaurant in the mall dad, me and Retta ate there last time we went out." "Oh, I see." "Aretta, could you get the juice and wine from the refrigerator." "Yes ma'am" she said moving to get it. "As you guys can see there is a place setting for each of you."

Matt looked for his and saw it was next to Retta's and across from Lori's. His dad's was at one end and Audrey's was at the other. Once they were all seated Matt's dad started to say grace. "Let's bow our heads . . . Okay." "Rodney grace the place boy." "Aw dad." Soon the meal was done and over, all Matt could do was sit back and moan. "Mrs. Davis that was the best roast I ever ate!" said Matt patting his stomach. "That pie was great too!" "Why, thank you Rodney, would you like some more Buford?" she asked reaching for the platter of meat. "Oh thank you Audrey, but I couldn't eat another bite myself, in fact one more meal like that and you might have trouble getting me to leave."

"Oh, is that so?" she said sipping her wine slowly and looking at him over the rim of her glass. "Well then let's see what I can dig up for next time" she said, her eyes still glued to his and a subtle lilt in her voice. Just then there was a knock at the door. "I'll get it" said Retta getting up. "Who is it?" "It's me Felicia." "Oh . . . Felicia I didn't recognize your voice" she said opening the door. "How are you sweetie?" "Fine" she said giving her mom's old friend a hug. "Mom! Felicia is here."

"Okay, Buford will you excuse me for a minute?" "Sure take your time." "Come on Lori your ride is here." "Okay" she said gulping down the last of her dessert. "I've made arrangements for Lori to spend some time over at my girlfriends house with her daughter." "Oh . . . Okay" said Buford non-chalantly. "Bye Mr. Buford" she said getting out of her seat. She looked at Matt, smiled real big and gave him a big hug. "Bye Rodney."

"Ugh! . . . bye bye sweetie." Soon she was gone and the two couples sat relaxing in the living room listening to the soothing voice of Al Green on the stereo. "Rodney would you like to go for a little walk?" asked Retta squeezing his hand in a signaling manner. "Uh . . . yeah, sure Red." "Hey dad, me and Aretta are gonna go walk off this meal awhile, we'll be back after while." "Okay son . . . you two have a good time" he said relaxing further and putting his feet up on the coffee table. Retta's mom just cuddled under his arm with her head on his chest.

They looked completely content and satisfied with each other like they weren't planning on going anywhere. Matt took off his jacket and hung it on the coat rack at the door as they went out. "I think we better knock first when we come back" said Retta smiling and thumbing back at the door. "Yeah, you may be right . . . there's no telling what those two will get into."

Soon they were down the stairs and out the door. "Hold on a minute babe, I need to get my stuff from the car." "What stuff?" "Oh, just my tape player and a blanket." "Oh, I see" she said giving Matt a sly grin. "Where are we going?" "I thought we might go to our favorite spot on Coleman Hill." "That would be nice." They started walking down towards the pool and behind the pool house.

Their trail was still there but partially covered by underbrush. "Matt what about the small ditch I can't cross it in this dress?" "You could take it off!" he said smiling deviously. "Yeah right Matt, keep on dreaming." "Naw babe I was just kidding, here hold my bag will you?" "What are you gonna do?" "Just watch and see" he said quickly scooping her up in his arms and jumped across the ditch. "Matt!" she cried squeezing his neck harder. "You could have fallen in or something!"

"No I wouldn't, you don't weigh a Buck-05, wet with a brick in your hand." "Ooh Matt, you're making fun of me?" "No, I'm not my love, you know you're just right for me!" "Am I?" she asked looking into his eyes. He could see only pain and anguish in her eyes. "Baby why do you worry so much, haven't we pledged ourselves to one another?" "Yes" "And haven't we kept that promise?" "Yes" "Then why do you still doubt me?" Retta didn't speak. She just eased herself from his arms and quietly led him the rest of the way to their favorite spot. It was a beautiful area. It was a large round grassy knoll with an oak tree in the center. All around them were tall pine trees and other smaller bushes and shrubs. Behind them was a lake in the distance. Oh what a sight it was to see! You could see everything from that vantage but in their little spot you could hide and not be seen by anyone . . . including the upper apartment windows.

Once they had gotten there Matt began laying out his blanket and setting up his stereo and tapes. Finally Retta spoke, her voice was hoarse as if she were a little choked up. "Matt sit down baby" she said guiding him to the oak tree. Matt sat down and leaned against the tree. "Do you remember when I told you I had something to talk to you about earlier?"

"Yes" "Well I've been thinking about your dad and my mom spending time with each other." "Yeah, what about it?" "Well has it ever occurred to you that their involvement could cause us trouble?" "Yeah . . . that question has crossed my mind once or twice." "So what do you think?" "To tell you the truth I really don't know what to think, I mean what's the worse that could happen if they did get together? . . . marriage? . . . and if they did which is out of the question it won't affect us anyway." "How! can you say that? . . . if my mom marries you dad we will be brother and sister!" she shouted upset now.

"Wait a minute Red, just chill out a minute, now look . . . you must understand something." "They are older and supposedly wiser, I'm not sure they are thinking the same as we are." "Hell, they only just met yesterday, so why are you sweating the load about it . . . we're safe." "I guess" she said still not secure in her feelings and wanting to believe Matt was right. "Hey pretty girl, I thought this was supposed to be our day together?" "Yes it was" she said holding herself and feeling an unnatural chill go through her. "Then how come the sad face then . . . come on let me see that smile I love so much" coaxed Matt turning her around to face him. Retta's gentle auburn eyes shimmered with love and great gladness at the man she called hers.

She fell into his arms and held onto him as if she were drowning and he was the only thing to cling to. "Okay, I'll be good Matt." "That's my girl . . . now how about some music?" said Matt wanting so badly to free her from her dismal thoughts.

He reached for the radio and a tape. "What would you like to hear?" "Oh, anything soft and sweet." "Soft and sweet, huh . . . how about me then?" he said teasing her and shifting his eyebrows as he said it. Retta's mood changed from that of a person just told they were dying of cancer to one of a person possessed. Her disposition was now one of bold and sultry intent.

For a brief second Matt could swear he saw the reflection of a she-wolf in her eyes and was pleasantly shaken. Retta slowly eclipsed him, crawling over him causing Matt to lower himself slowly onto his back. "You know Matt, you shouldn't tease like that . . . you never know what a girl like me has on her mind" she said in an even but committed tone. She straddled him with her legs and hovered over him like a panther over its prey about to rip into its exposed throat.

Matt just laid back and put his hands behind his head. He gave a little smirk of confidence. Retta noted this, responded by narrowing her gaze on him to a lasers edge, and drew closer still. Her eyes were like crimson Matt noted and he could feel the heat of her intent on his face with every breath she took. Retta didn't blink once but relished in her ability to shake him up at will . . . god it was delicious. She darted her face closer but not to close kind of like a boxer getting his range before he struck. Matt was amused at her attempt to goose him further but at the same time beginning to rage within himself. Retta drew down painstakingly slow as if she were a spider descending its web. Matt blinked . . . she had him. Retta crashed upon Matt's lips like a rogue wave and assaulted his mind and body like a hurricane.

Matt heard himself sigh and exhale involuntarily as she took him and took him and took him. With each torched kiss, he could feel how much she loved him and wanted him. Matt wrapped her in his powerful embrace and squeezed her until she whimpered . . . but not from pain but an untapped desired to be over powered and absorbed into his embrace like water into a sponge.

Their mouths hungered and ate of each other over and over again . . . tasting and teasing each other then crashing together again with lustful force. Matt fought to enslave her tongue with his own but only managed to enflame her as she deftly stole it back from him and took his in return. Matt altered his embrace from her back to her bottom and squeezed it savagely as he pulled her onto him. Retta broke from her attack and screamed with delight at the sweet and naughty harshness of his grip on her butt. The suddenness made her explode with perspiration between her thighs.

Matt took full advantage of her weakness when he saw how she responded. Matt held her hips like a vice and pulled her down hard onto his crotch and drove upwards at the same time. The move made Retta suck in her breath hard and go weak in his control. The rough feel of his pants against her inner thighs made her swoon. She licked her lips and relished at his professional handling of her body and just where and how she like to be molested. Retta threw back her head and bucked as wave upon wave of sweet hot pleasure washed over her.

Matt just knew he was gonna break through his pants if he got much harder. Retta heard music in her ears and her body at the same time. She moaned and sucked in hard each time he ground and drove himself into her. She bucked once more then attacked his mouth again. Slowly she worked her feet under his calves and locked in her heels forcing him to straighten out his legs.

Matt wasn't sure what she was up to and it kind of limited his amount of control of her hips. Retta eased from his lips, staring into his eyes, "You know Matt . . . up here no one can hear you scream" she said in an even lusty tone. She raised an eyebrow and smirked at him for punctuation then quickly without warning rolled him over onto her.

Matt was shocked at how she was able to do that but then he thought about it and remembered how she had snaked her legs behind his in a classic wrestlers move. Once Retta had him on top of her she clamped down on his neck and bit down on his neck and sucked him like an orange. "SSS . . . Oh! shit!" he thought as her teeth bit deep into the base of his neck.

While Matt was distracted with her working on his neck she took the opportunity to unzip his fly. She moved with determined movements. Once she'd found what she was after Retta didn't wait to put it to use. She just pushed her panties aside instead of wasting time to remove them.

Matt took her lead and just took the plunge. "Oh Matt!" she breathed as he literally knocked the wind out of her. The pair moved together like a well oiled machine fueled by flames. Retta and Matt made love with total abandon like it was the last time either would ever see the other. Retta clawed and pushed herself into Matt so hard he had to brace himself just to stay with her.

Retta was insatiable and seemed to have come unglued, Matt thought, but he wasn't complaining it was unbelievable. Every fantasy Retta had dreamed that week had all come home to roost at one time and she couldn't believe it. "SSS . . . Matt . . . Matt . . . SSS ooh yes . . . yes!" went on again and again.

It must have been the sun and the breeze that did it for them. Matt couldn't remember another time to date that compared to what he and Retta were experiencing this moment. Retta rolled Matt back onto his back like he was a rag doll. Matt couldn't believe the strength she had when she wanted something. He didn't try to control her but instead just let her do her thing. "Damn baby!" "Oh, I'm sorry baby" she said as Matt hit with a thud as she rolled him over.

Matt just smiled and got back to business. She straddled him and remounted him quickly before he could cool off one degree. As she rode him she breathed and moaned faster and louder as she bore down on him. She ground herself against him harder and harder. Matt just squeezed her hips and pushed back stroke for stroke, finally it came, that familiar feeling as before. Matt felt his toes begin to draw up inside his shoes as if they were being drawn in like a mini blind! His thighs burned and vibrated. He began to lock up and freeze from the bottom up as if the life were being literally sucked from him.

"AHH . . . AHH! He yelled with each orgasmic blast that jetted from him. Retta shouted as well when she felt him exploding within her. She held onto his belt and pulled to stay with him as her own convulsions began. "Ooh a Matt . . . ooh Matt! She moaned. Her voice so strained you could hardly hear it. "I love you" she gasped almost out of breath. Every time Matt felt her contract, he blasted another crotch rocket into her until finally they were both spent.

Matt slowly released his grip on her and let his hands fall to his side. Retta still sat atop him with her head back swaying like a rag doll in the wind. She was still coming down from the heights of her own rapture. Matt reached up to caress her face but grazed her breast instead causing her to suck in hard in recoil.

"SSS . . . Matt" she moaned weakly almost a whimper as she convulsed again. The reaction was so strong that Matt was sure she was gonna snap him off inside her for sure.

"Please don't Matt . . . I can't take it . . . I'll faint if you do that again" too late Matt's hands were already in motion. Retta sighed deeply, clamped down on Matt's ribs like a vice and screamed into her cupped hands before collapsing onto Matt's chest.

The two lovers just lay there basking in pleasure and the glow of the evening sun breathless and completely satisfied. Retta felt as light as a sheet on him he noticed as he held her and caressed her hair and back slowly.

"Baby . . . are you alright?" Matt asked her. Retta didn't answer but just placed a finger on his lips without raising her head, "Shh . . . don't speak" she whispered then eased herself up to give him a weak smile and a light kiss before returning to her state of exhausted rapture. After awhile the sun had set and it was getting dark.

Matt and Retta got themselves together, collected their things and headed for the apartment. They did not speak on the way down but just held each other close and kissed every few feet. "I love you Retta" she pulled him closer and placed her head on his chest. "Rodney I'll love you forever" she whispered.

Matt knew then that he would someday marry her. She was his soul mate and they both knew and felt the same way. Matt was equally glad that he had gone to the jewelry store while him and his dad stopped in the mall for flowers. Once they reached the steps of the apartment building, Matt stopped and threw his gym bag into the car.

"Aretta" he said turning to her. I know I'll never find another woman like you and I don't want to. I've been thinking about you a lot these past few months and every time I do the same thought comes to mind. "What baby?" she said with concern showing in her eyes as she held onto him. "You may reject this but I have to try . . ." "Matt, your scaring me . . . what is it?"

Matt reached into his pocket and gave her a little black box much like the one he had given Lori. She looked at it then back to him almost afraid to touch it much less open it. Retta took it slowly and opened it.

Her eyes told Matt all he needed to hear. "OH Matt! . . . wh-what does this mean?" she stammered looking at the diamond engagement ring. "Baby, will you marry me and be mine forever?" he said feeling a warmth and strength he'd never felt before. Retta just collapsed against him and sobbed uncontrollably.

"You big dummy" she whispered between sobs as she pounded his chest. "See what you've done?" "What baby . . . I thought you would be happy with the idea" he said shocked and beginning to feel a little stupid.

Retta looked up with tear stained eyes. "I am silly, can't you tell?" "I wasn't sure." "Yes, I'll marry you, yes I want you!" she croaked. "But Matt, we aren't old enough yet sweet heart . . . isn't this a little early?" "I know baby, I was just getting ahead of the competition" he said smiling bashfully. "Oh Matt" she said placing her hand tenderly aside his cheek. "You always had me . . . there was never anyone else, nor could there ever be, truth-be-told, I was afraid that after awhile you wouldn't want me." "Not want you?" he said feeling a little misty himself and a lump in his throat.

Matt quickly took the ring from her and grabbed her hand. He then placed the ring on her finger with finality as if to say, "your mine now sister!" "Aretta, I love you and want you with all my heart for all my life, I ask you now in the sight of God that when we graduate from high school, will you marry me?"

"Yes, yes yes!" she shouted over and over again as she threw herself into his arms and kissing him madly. "I'm yours as long as you want me Matt!" "And that's forever" he added returning her kisses but more passionately. They were so into each other at that point that they didn't hear the foot steps of their parents coming towards them.

"Hrrumph!" chided a his dad as he snuck up on them. They broke apart quickly startled and embarrassed. This time they had been caught by both parents. "That's a strange way to teach CPR" commented his dad with a grin.

Matt noticed that he was standing with his arm around Retta's mom. Audrey just twisted an eyebrow at them as if to say "told ya it would get you into hot soup one day!" Matt and Retta just bowed their heads shame faced, looked at each other and just shrugged. "It seems to me I spoke to a certain pair just the other day about using discretion and public displays of affection" chided Audrey. "I'm sorry" said Matt attempting to tip the blame.

"Ah! ah!" said Audrey cutting him off. "Don't even speak, you two know I spoke to you about this already so just zip it" she said closing Matt's mouth like the tail gate of a pickup truck. "Aww man." "At least you two were discrete this time." "Has it been that bad?" asked Matt's dad. "Oh yess . . . ,you should have seen them Buford." "Yesterday I got the surprise of walking through a large crowd of people at the mall only to find that the main attraction was these two, they were so wrapped around each other it looked like two snakes trying to eat each other!" Matt's dad just nodded with a blank look on his face. "Yeah, let me tell you . . . they were HOT!" "I didn't know whether to go and get some popcorn and a chair or sell tickets."

Matt began to shrink into his shoes wishing he could disappear. A million thoughts and feelings ran through his mind like sturgeon on a migration but nothing seemed to fit so he just hung his head and bit his lip. Seeing that her retort had done its job, Audrey elbowed Buford in the rib and cut him a smile as if to say; "You think I've dragged them enough?" Retta not having anything much to say either just retreated further into Matt's embrace and squeezed his hand like a vice.

"Ha! Gotcha" chirped Audrey poking Matt in the gut. "Don't sweat it, "Hot Rod" . . . we were just hacking on you guys." "We know how it is with you two!" When Matt exhaled it sounded like the air coming out of a compressor. "Whew! For a minute there I thought you were gonna shoot us out into outer space" said Retta smiling now at the joke and stealthily hiding her hand so as not to give away her rings existence before she was ready.

"No Retta, I'm not the bad guy here . . . not tonight anyway" she said looking warmly at Matt's dad and snuggling up to him like they were old friends. "Just keep it down to a slow burn will you?" "We wouldn't want the rest of this town to get jealous, besides we just came out to look for you." "Is it that late already?" asked Retta surprised. "Yes dear heart it's 7:30 and me and Buford must prepare for work tomorrow and you two for school."

"Oh yeah, I forgot about that" said Matt stretching and yawning. "Yes Rodney, it's time to get back to the land of the living, the weekend is over but don't worry I'm sure you'll be back here before too long" she said grinning. "So why don't you escort Retta upstairs and I'll say goodbye to your father." "Yes ma'am" he said taking Retta's hand and heading upstairs. "Those two are something else" muttered Audrey under her breath as she watched them steal a kiss before ascending the stairs.

"They're young . . . you know how it is" said Matt's dad snuggling with her now that they were alone. "I know Rodney is a responsible young man and has a great deal of passion for Aretta." "I believe you" said Audrey putting her arms around his waist and looking up at him. "I can see where he gets it too" she said then kissed him deeply.

Not to be outdone, Matt and Retta were busy in the doorway themselves trying hard not to consume each other. Matt had in a gesture of gallantry carried her up the stairs to the apartment like they had just been married. He stood holding her in his arms and cradling her like a child. They stood this way for what seemed forever.

Retta kissed him one last time then painstakingly pulled herself from his strong grip and eased to the floor. "You better go Matt." "I know babe, but it's so hard to leave you, I just want to hold you like this all night!" "Are you sure I'm not heavy?" "Well lets see" he grabbed her up in his arms again and tossed her effortlessly into the air like she was a bag of oranges. "Matt! Don't do that" she screamed in delight. "You scared me." "Aw, I'm sorry boo boo" he said cuddling her and giving her baby kisses on her eye lids and fore head." "Okay?" "Okay" she said smiling with a pouty little mouth and kissing him one last time before getting to her feet. "Remember not a word to your mother about our engagement." "You mean, Pre-engagement?" "Okay, have it your way, just don't tell her yet, she might flip."

"Then tell me professor, . . . why did you give me the ring so early?" she said sticking out her hand proudly to flash her jewel at him." "Because I wanted too and I wanted you to know as well as to prove that I was serious about marrying you." "You didn't have to . . . I would have believed you Matt" she said getting serious. "OH! So you don't want it then? I can take it back" he said coming closer, reaching for her ring hand as if he was stalking her. Retta quickly folded her arms and propped on her hip giving him a most disdainful look. She looked him up and down without moving her head . . . "Over my dead body, you will, you're mine amigo, got me?" she said grabbing a hand full of his collar and throat and pulling him into a hard kiss. "Yes ma'am . . . I'm yours" he said resigning.

"So how are you going to hide it?" "Who said I was?" "But you have to, or she'll ask questions." "Don't worry, I'll keep it hidden, but I am wearing it though" she stabbed back at him proudly with a smirk. "Okay babe you do that . . . well I better go, I'll call you tomorrow okay Red?" "Okay Matt, kiss me good night" she said holding out her arms and puckering. "Ugh! You want me to kiss those lips?" said Matt blanching away and heading for the stairs. Retta looked stunned, "Rodney Mathis, you better get your butt over here and kiss me!" She said fuming.

"Okay babe, just messing with ya." They for the hundredth time that day kissed but instead of fervently as they were used to it was tender and soft. "Your some piece of work you know that Ms. Davis" "That's Mrs. Mathis to you she gleaned." "BEEP BEEP!" "Uh oh! Gotta go babe I'll see ya soon okay?"

"Okay Matt . . . I love you!" "Love you too" he said as he bounded down the stairs passing her mother on the way. "Bye Rodney." "Goodnight Audrey, thanks for dinner it was great!" "Anytime honey." "Ready to go?" asked Matt's dad as he got into the car. "Yeah dad, let's break"

Matt had forgotten to set the alarm clock last night before he went to bed. The warm warmth and snugness of his bed was like a cocoon and he didn't want to leave it. His mind slowly began replaying yesterdays events when all of a sudden he began to feel a penetrating warmth on his face. Matt creaked open one eye to get a fix on where it was coming from but the stab of sunlight that flooded in was more than enough to make him close it again. Now aware that it was morning and the sun was up he groaned and retreated deeper within his covers confident he had time for one more snooze.

Just then his mind repeated itself "THE SUN IS UP" "Oh fuck!" Matt bolted straight up and jumped out of bed. Despite the morning sun's heat, the hard wood floor still had a coldness about it. Paying his frigid feet no mind he hauled tail into the bathroom like a mad man to shower quickly. This time he remembered to hit the cold water first. "Damn! I'm late" he said looking at the clock on the wall in the den.

"I know Miss Pratt is gonna have my butt in a sling now." Soon Matt was out of the bathroom and back to his room to dress. "Matt wasn't paying much attention to what he was putting on but just trying not to clash the colors too much. Matt didn't bother with breakfast he just grabbed a pop tart and ran out the back door into the yard and looked for his moped. Ant had placed it under the steps. "Good! I hope he gassed it up for me." The keys were under the seat. Matt quickly pulled it from the stall and slammed down on the kick start and was on his way. Just as he got to the end of the drive he noticed he didn't have his book bag "Damn!' Matt did a doughnut and drove on the front lawn.

"It's a good thing my head is screwed on or id leave that too" he muttered to himself. Matt's door wasn't locked "Good!" he said relieved that something worked in his favor this morning. Besides he didn't want to take the key from the bike. Now he had everything and the house was secure. Matt shot from the porch like a scalded cat and landed on the seat of his bike. "Yee Haa!" he yelled pulling back on the throttle full and pushing the bike off it's kick stand. Matt left a two inch wide two foot long skid mark on the sidewalk as he left.

"Come on Seed Biscuit" he yelled to his bike like it was a horse. He slapped it brusquely on the seat and bounced up and down like a jockey. "It's a good thing I'm not too far away or may ass would be doing detention until graduation." There wasn't much traffic on the way and he took a short cut past Ivory's house so he would come up on the back side of the school. This way he would be closer to his home room. A quick glance at his watch told him he had just two minutes before the bell rang.

He quickly reached beneath the seat to turn up the fuel and air mixture to make it richer . . . "VROOOM!" went the little moped. Matt was running at 45mph now and really moving. Most bikes like this could only go about 30 mph but Matt had a buddy do some work on it to enhance the engine to give it just a bit more boost. It was worth the fifty bucks he paid him because many a time it had saved his bacon from the fire. Soon Matt was in the rear of the building with a minute to go.

Matt bore down on the throttle even harder to get every ounce of horse power the little engine would give him. It whined in protest but gave it up anyway. Matt drove right up to the door and in one fluid motion slammed on the brakes, killed the engine and skidded to a stop. Matt jumped from the bike and parked it against the wall, "30 seconds to go!" Matt bolted through the double doors and down the hall. His class room was 20 yards away and he was kicking it to get there.

Somehow he over sped and was about to miss the door. Matt started breaking like a diesel on a hill but to his surprise someone had waxed the hall floors over the weekend. "OH SSHITT!" Screee! Matt had slipped and fell on his butt. However, that wasn't the end of it. Down the hall he slid on the highly polished floor, past the entrance to his classroom and into the storage locker at the end of the hall. BAM! SLAM! CRASH!. He had managed to tip over a cart full of books and brought them down on his head in a shower of literary pain. "Ringgggg" "Aww shit!" he muttered as he pulled himself from the pile of carnage. As he walked to the room he saw that the whole class was standing in the door laughing at him.

"Didn't know you were such a heavy reader Matt" chimed one kid which brought on a torrent of laughs. Mrs. Pratt just leaned casually against the door frame with her arms folded and a smile of complete content on her lips. She methodically and triumphantly scribbled on a yellow detention pad she was holding and tore off a sheet handing it to Matt as he came into the room. "Finally caught you didn't I Mr. Mathis" she said grinning and trying hard not to laugh out loud. Matt didn't speak but just gave her a strained smile and schlepped to his seat. As he undid his book bag he noticed several girls looking at him and smiling at him. "Damn . . . I was just about to break my record too!" he mumbled under his breath.

"Too bad Matt" chirped another kid from behind him. It was Charles, a guy he knew and sometimes chatted with from time to time. "You almost made it man, did you know she had you on the stop watch this time?" "Naw, when did she start doing that?" "Sometime ago . . . I think it was after you made that comment that it would take a greased monkey on a rocket sled to catch you."

"She heard that?" "Up until now you been dusting her heels and she couldn't catch you late before the bell, hell when she got in this morning the first thing she did was look for you." "When she didn't' see you at ten minutes to eight she broke out her stop watch and sat at her desk facing the door." "Damn . . . she had a warm fuzzy for me didn't she?" "Yeah, but she got you now slick!" "Yeah, I guess you gotta die sometime" he said looking up at Mrs. Pratt who was also watching him with a cat that ate that canary look on her face. She smiled a little smile, head tilted forward slightly with her arms folded and legs crossed. She sat bobbing her foot to an unheard rhythm.

She had hung the stop watch around her neck and let it hang there with pride like a trophy of sorts. In a strange sort of way she was beginning to take on some sexy and elusive changes right before Matt's eyes. Was he hallucinating from being over heated or was he just now seeing her for the first time as a woman and not a teacher. Matt took a second to really look at her, he sat back in his seat and gave her a kind of chin up defiant smile of acknowledgement. Kind of like he was saying, "Hey cutie . . . you got me alright but I made you work for it . . . damn! your sexy."

To be perfectly honest Mrs. Pratt really wasn't a bad looking woman. She was in her early thirties about 5 foot 4 inches and one hundred and ten pounds. She looked like she could have been a cheerleader or a tennis player back in the day. She always dressed conservatively with either a modest pant suit or a comfortable loose fitting dress. Today she wore a lime green terry cloth dress that wrapped around her with a sash. It was cut just above the knee and molded to her body well. She was white and had a nice mocha tan that she must have worked on daily. Her hair was shoulder length and honey blond with highlights.

She also had an intense but soft pair of ocean blue eyes that accented her dress and punctuate well her current attitude and state of mind. She had soft and demure lips that seemed to be a contradiction at best. They looked as though they begged to be kissed but at the same time could bust your bubble with a word. She didn't appear to lonely to Matt but then again what could you really tell from just looking at a person . . . look at how he came by Retta.

Either way he was feeling a little proud that he had brought some life into this middle age woman's eyes. A woman who seemed to be immune to all and tolerant of nothing . . . still she was a nice lady at heart he thought to himself and not bad looking either. "Okay class" she said without breaking her stare from him. "We are starting to collect for the yearbook so all of you who wish to order early may do so here in homeroom, the fee is $10.00 and that final day for ordering is April 20th, two weeks from now, so don't wait till the last minute to order said Ms. Pratt.

Just then a small White girl raised her hand. "Yes Tiffany?" said Ms. Pratt. "How long before we get them?" "You'll get them a week before the end of the school semester." There were several moans and comments at the prospect of a long wait. "Well class it is not up to me, the books have to be printed and pictures have to be taken a right?." No one said anything but just shuffled in their seats.

"Now the next thing on the schedule is the track team, if anyone wants to sign up go see coach Jones at the boy's school during lunch, but get a pass unless you have a class over there!" "Okay class have a nice day" she said as the mob rushed out the door.

"Retta wait up" said Frieda running to catch her. "What's your hurry?" "No hurry, I'm just trying to get to first period class that's all." "Okay, so how was the dinner date?"

"Oh it was great!" "How about your talk with Rodney?" "Oh, that went okay too." "That's nice, so now I won't be seeing anymore sad faces will I?" "No at least not for awhile." The girls had a time getting to class as hundreds of students ran in and out of doors and hidden spaces to add to the human traffic jam.

Everyone was either going to or coming from somewhere. Most never made it to class on time nor did they seem to care very much. This was Monday morning and everyone was buzzing with stories of their short two day vacation. "Okay people!" yelled a loud female voice over the crowd. "Let's clear the hall now . . . please get to your classes and clear the hall." "We can always talk about the weekend during lunch, so let's clear the area." "I'll see you after class Frieda" said Retta ducking into her classroom.

She grabbed her seat just as the bell sounded. "Good morning everybody, I hope you all had an enjoyable weekend, but now today is another work day." "If you will all turn in your text books to chapter six we'll start off where we finished on Friday." "Aw man! . . . Shoot . . . Man I hate rocks." "Ooh . . . she is so mean" taunted the teacher clinching her fists and putting them up to her face much like a child in a horror film. "Ms. Murchison could you please tell us what is one form of sedimentary rock?" "Umm . . . granite?" "Nope! Close but no cigar . . . Ms. Davis?" "Yes ma'am?" "What's the answer?" "I don't know . . . what's the question?" the teacher sighed and shook her head. "Shh! Settle down" she said as the classroom began to buzz with giggling and chatter. "I said what is one form of sedimentary rock?" "Sandstone." "Very good Ms. Davis, at least one of you studied, now who can tell me a form of volcanic rock?" "PSST . . . this subject leaves me stone cold" whispered a girl behind Retta.

"Ms. Jefferson you seem to have a lot to say this morning . . . why don't you tell us one." "Oh! Hell" she said sinking down in her seat. "Uhh . . . Pahowee-howee?" "Marvelous! I just may go home early today and forget about giving out homework . . . how would that be class?" "Yay! . . . Alright!" "But for now I'm going to give you a pop quiz, so everybody put your books and papers under your desk's."

Aretta wondered about how well she would do being she didn't study much either. The teacher scribbled furiously on the black board, only stopping momentarily to think up another question. "Okay people lets go to it" she said tossing the chalk into the tray and dusting off her hands. "This ain't too bad, I should be able to lick this easy enough. It didn't take too long and soon everyone had finished and passed their papers up front. The rest of the class period was spent doing self study and a brief intro into the next subject.

Chapter 5

Sporting Chances

After awhile the bell rang signaling the end of the period. The entire class split for the door at the same time. Aretta didn't wait for Freida but instead headed for her locker to get her gym bag for her next class. The hall was a beehive of student's and everyone was haphazardly running about trying to get somewhere. It was a nightmare to get through if you were short. "I wish they would get out of my way" grumbled Retta pushing pass the mob. She soon made it to her locker but to her dismay found some older boys or thugs as she had come to know this particular bunch, leaning against it. They didn't appear to be in any real hurry to move or get anywhere but just stood around and took up space trying to perpetrate as it were. "Could you please move?" asked Retta with a hint of aggravation in her voice.

"Sure, MISS THANG!" said a tall boy who seemed to be the center of all their attention. Retta brushed by him and went to work opening her lock. She soon had the combination lock off and opened the door quickly letting it slam open with a clang. She did this on purpose because the boy was still hovering over her not really getting out of the way but just being a nuisance. She'd hoped he would get the message and haul ass and leave her alone . . . no such luck. As the door slammed open it almost hit the tall boy. His crew was animated and began hooting and chiding her to instigate something. "UH oh! . . . she's hot now" said one boy pushing the taller boy and trying to goose him.

"She can get hot all she want too, I don't care about her skinny ass getting mad!" said the tall boy standing up-right and squaring off on her. Retta still had her back to him and was trying hard to ignore them and get her stuff so she could get away from them. "God I hate Mondays" she grumbled under her breath. Just then the boy reached into her open locker and tried to grab a picture of Matt that was on the door. "Hey, who's this?" he said pulling at the corner of it to remove it. Retta smacked his hand away with lightning speed, "POW!" "Oh, shit man she slapped you dog!"

"Keep your damn hands off and out of my locker and my stuff!" she snapped at him and flashed fire red eyes. "Whatchu gonna do if I don't bitch!" he said pushing her up against her locker and holding her there with his hand on her chest just under her throat. The other boys were getting loud now. "Yeah dude buss her ass up, she ain't shit!" "Kick that little bitch ass homey!" "Let her know who in charge, you!"

"You better chill out before you get fucked up Ho!" spat the tall boy now being supported by his entire crew. Retta just kept cool and stared at him with venom in her eyes. "You mean before you get hurt" she hissed back through clenched teeth. The boy not wanting to be upstaged by a small girl like Aretta in front of his crew reached out and slapped her book bag to the floor in response to her defiance of his so called authority.

The mob in the hall all of a sudden stopped what they were doing and changed flow much like a school of fish when a net hits the water. Everyone was beginning to crowd around the small group because there was blood in the water and they wanted to see it. Retta on the other hand didn't wait for an invitation and acted on the attack like a bolt of lightning. She brought her right arm across her chest and the boys arm, smashing it down with her elbow. The boy didn't expect this and was caught completely off guard. The next move she made really fucked him up. Retta came back in a reverse motion the planted her fist right in his mouth knocking him back into his crew and on the floor.

"Damn! did you see that shit man?" shouted one of the boys in the crew. Retta didn't wait for the much bigger boy to regain himself and stomped him in the groin while he was trying to get up. "Shit!" yelled another voice from the crowd at Retta's speed and control of the situation. After she did this, she reset herself with hands pointing like knives and taking a Karate stance. Two of the other boys that were standing by rushed her not really sure what they were gonna do but after seeing their leader put down so easily they felt they had to do something. One reached for her with both hands trying to get a hold on her arms. Retta caught his hand and raised it over her head and rotated through him pulling it up behind him.

With one viscous jerk she flipped him over and into the lockers she had been standing in front of. "Daaammmn! Did you see that shit?" said a bystander. "Man that bitch know some shit!" jeered another. With a loud bang the boy hit the locker and slid down like a wet rag thrown against a wall.

Retta was a little slow recovering from that move as she didn't have much room to maneuver and the boy was a little heavy. The third boy took advantage of this and grabbed a hold of her pony tail and gave her a savage jerk backwards. The air had temporarily left her as the pain of being violently snatched backwards took hold of her mind and body. As she sat sprawled on the floor she looked up to see that the assailant clearly had the upper hand now as his foot came down on her stomach with force.

"UHN!" she grunted and rolled onto her side. She felt the pain all the way to her feet and began to see stars. "YEAH! FUCK THAT BITCH UP MAN . . . GET HER ASS, SHE THOUGHT SHE WAS BRUCE LEE!" shouted supporters of the three boys who attacked her. Retta could only see feet and floor around her with little splinters of light as the crowed shifted and people jockeyed for a better viewing position. Retta was now suddenly aware that she wasn't wearing pants but instead a jean skirt.

She didn't know why that mattered to her just now seeing as how she was getting her guts stomped out by three boys she didn't know. Retta tried to put the pain away from her and get to her feet before the three of them took turns turning her into a floor mat. She rolled over just in time to see the first boy getting up and setting himself to return the favor she had given him only minutes ago. As she saw him hold back his friends and raise his foot to stomp her again she quickly rolled the opposite way and swept her leg at his planted foot.

Once again shock was written on the boys face as his leg came up to join his other one and it was, "Assholes and Elbows!" Wham! He hit the floor again taking one of the others with him. Now the three of them were on the floor like tumbled chess pieces. The crowed was beside itself and bedlam and bloodlust were in the air. They couldn't believe the efforts of this one lone female against these much bigger and supposedly stronger boys. Retta feeling better, quickly got to her feet.

The one she toppled wasn't aware yet and it would serve to his downfall. The boy sat there a little too long nursing his sore Achilles heal and momentarily forgetting the she-devil who had put him there. Retta on the other hand wasn't so deluded and took full advantage of the confused attacker. She stepped to the far side of the circle which really wasn't more than two or three feet cause the crowd wasn't allowing any breathing room. She set herself like a field goal kicker and charged the boy delivering a bone jarring kick to the boys already sore crotch. "WHOOOM!" "OH! SHIT! SHE FUCKED HIS ASS UP!" . . . "YOU GET EM GIRL, DON'T LET THEM MUTHA FUCKERS GET YOU!" shouted the crowd as she landed her foot on target. The blow was so hard the boy screamed and just rolled over into the fetal position.

He coughed and spat a little blood onto the floor. Seeing this the other two boys just stood there not sure if they wanted to try their luck with her or join their friend on the floor. Retta stood near the boy like a hunter just falling a deer. She clenched her fist and set for her next move as she glared unblinking at the other two. "And I ain't no Bitch!" . . . . assholes" she hissed at them seeing they had had enough.

She slowly turned to pick up her things and leave but just then male teachers and other staff rushed the mob and burst into the circle. "Clear the way . . . move out the way! . . . move on now!. Retta's homeroom teacher Mr. Simpkins and two other male teachers came though the crowd.

The carnage that they saw made them draw up short and come to an abrupt halt. He looked over to his left and saw two boys he recognized as Troy Mitz and Ernest Dillard. The larger boy still rolling around holding himself and coughing blood was Terry Hollings. The fight for that most part only lasted a few minutes but had the look of a war zone that was in progress for a lot longer. "What the hell is going on here?" he boomed over the crowd. Everyone just pointed at the small tattered and bruised form of Aretta.

She stood with her head down rubbing her arm and fighting the warm tears that were trying so desperately to come forth. Her shirt was half pulled out of her skirt, one sock slid down to her ankle and her hair a mess with her pig tail being partially unbraided. She looked quite pathetic Mr. Simpkins noticed. He assessed her for a moment silently, trying to figure how in the hell she could have had anything to do with this mess! "Aretta?" he said reemphasizing his original query.

She didn't speak at first but just stood erect as a soldier having regained her composure. She stood with her feet together like a ballerina, one hand holding her gym bag and the other rubbing the other. "I happened . . . that's what" she said quietly staring at the teacher for a moment then turning slowly towards her locker. She shut the door quietly, gave him and the crowd one last look then walked off through the crowd towards the gym. Nobody said anything to her or tried to stop her not even Mr. Simpkins who figured he would get to the bottom of it sooner or later and would just let her go and recover herself some. "You two come here . . . get him off the floor Mr. Brooks and take him to the nurse." The halls were cleared and order was restored once again.

There were a few OOH'S and AHH'S as Retta walked down the hall. As she got to the corner of the hall to turn she could hear a boy make the last she would hear of the matter. "I'll bet they won't fuck with her no more . . . she' s bad!" Aretta allowed herself a little smile and thought to herself, "You damn right they won't!" Then a warm tear was released. This was Southwest High. Over 10,000 students in six buildings in this complex. The student body was made up of 8th graders to seniors. They were in different buildings and staged all over the west side of town. Being that the school's were located in that neck of the woods you automatically grew up knowing you either kicked ass or got your ass kicked.

Aretta of course knew this long ago and long since had taken up Karate when she was just a kid of 8 years old. Her dad was in the army and had taught her how to defend herself and put her in the classes at her mother's dismay. Never-the-less there have been quite a few times that the teachings have paid off like now. Now Retta was a freshman in high school. She had no past and wouldn't have much of a future either if she couldn't stand her ground and take care of herself amongst her peers.

She was now in the gym locker room and most of the girls were already dressed out for class and standing around chattering about the fight she had just been in. When she walked in everyone grew silent and turned to look at her as she went to her locker. Retta lamely glanced over her shoulder at them not really caring what they thought or were talking about. They all slowly walked their collective stares all over her from head to toe, noting that her clothes were in an upset torrent.

Her hair was a mess with multi-colored rubber bands lending an awful twist to her pig tail. It looked like a pissed off question mark. She didn't care one way or another though, and just ignored their stares and began to undress. Camille Murcheson was the first to speak. "So . . . Aretta" she called, her voice dripping with contempt. "I see you've been out playing "tag" with the boys?" "Not now "Camille" she said in a soft but warning tone not wanting another confrontation just now.

But this was Camille, she was always quick to irritate and patronize others when the opportunity presented itself, which was most of the time. Camille simply thought she was better than anyone else. She was a little taller than Retta with much lighter skin. She had Buckwheat-honey brown hair and grey-green eyes that had minx written all over them. She was gorgeous and knew it!

Camille had a sexy-seductive shape or was built like a slut as most of the boys described her. She had medium breast that made her hour glass shape even more sensuous. Her family was financially well off. Her father was the president of a large defense aircraft company. She had three older brothers who were in college and she was the only girl in the family which meant she got spoiled a lot. Camille never passed up the opportunity to belittle someone else. She was always boosting her already oversized ego by flaunting her new clothes or the fact that her brothers were in college.

Some of the girls thought of her as a queen bee and was very aristocratic. She never failed to show off her many expensive gifts and trinkets on a daily basis and then brag about her upper class friends. And the fact they lived in Crystal Lake didn't hurt her rep either. "What's the matter Retta?" she said pouting and talking at her sanctimoniously. "Boys play too rough hmmm, or is it that they wanted something you can't give?" "I said get lost Camille!" she said turning around with her hands on her hips and giving her a most fierce stare. Aretta's auburn eyes began to glow hot like coals in a fire place. "I've had enough shit for one day and I certainly don't need you in my face too!"

"Ha! Listen to the little prude, you should have enjoyed your little play time because that's as close to a man as you'll ever get." "I mean look at you . . . you're scrawny, you barely have a curve on your entire body . . . hell if you didn't have joints to bend at you wouldn't have a curve at all!" Aretta was getting hotter with every second. "You take that back!" Camille just gave her a smile. "You must be kidding me, the only way you could get a man is if you sell yourself and I'm sure no one would buy you and oh my stars, what do we have here?" she said clasping her hands and feigning mock surprise. "It looks like a pair of breasts!" she said reaching to poke Aretta in her right breast.

Aretta quickly slapped it away. "Don't touch me slut!" Camille just laughed wickedly unfazed by the rebuke. "You ought to be glad I touched them, as tiny as they are no one else would look at you!" she yelled getting closer to her, nose to nose. "Retta you're a carpenters dream . . . flat as a board and needing a screw!" That did it. Retta's hand lashed out like lightning and connected hard with Camille's face knocking her into a locker.

Camille never saw it coming and the force of the slap was so hard it spun her around and she bounced off them landing on the floor. Camille just sat there with her mouth open wide like a gold fish out of water. She raised a shaky hand to her face and stared at Retta blankly as the pain began to come forth. "You bitch! . . . you hit me!" "Come on Camille" said Retta flexing her arms and stretching her legs like she was setting up for log cutting competition. "I've just had lunch and I'm still hungry" this infuriated Camille and she quickly got to her feet and charged Retta who was calmly waiting for her.

"I'm gonna kick your ass you whore!" she spat, then swung at her head wildly with uncoordinated fists. Aretta was ready now after having been warmed up on the last episode only a few minutes ago. Camille was no challenge at all and Retta secretly laughed within herself as Camille swung at her. Retta easily ducked the girls haphazard swings and connected with a fist of her own right in the gut and completely knocked the wind out of her. "UHN!" she grunted as she doubled over in pain. Camille had the look of utter shock on her face as she looked up to see Retta smiling at her.

Retta leaning over getting in her face. "Kinda hurts don't it?" she patronized folding her arms in utter contempt for her. Camille tried to recover with her own insult but it came out like a croak instead "You bit . . ." was all she could manage before curling up again. Retta looked at the other girls who were standing by waiting silently for her to finish her off. They to had suffered at her hands at one time or another and enjoyed seeing Camille getting her ass busted. Retta all of a sudden got a devious idea and motioned the other girls to come to her as she grinned to herself. "Girls would you please help Ms. Murchison to the bench and hold her down for me?" she said pointing to the bench behind her.

The girls did as they were told partly out of fear and respect for Aretta's proven ability to whip their ass, but mostly because they wanted to anyway and couldn't wait to see what she would do to her next. Retta took a minute to get changed while a protesting Camille wiggled and tried to get loose.

"Let me go you bitches, I'll have my brothers get all you your asses!" she complained. Another girl who Camille had abused on a regular basis was familiar with the over used trump card of her brothers and took this opportunity to get even. "Not today they won't" she said quickly reaching into her open locker for a large feminine pad and her towel. She stuffed the pad into a shocked Camille's mouth and tied it there with her towel. "How's it feel now . . . Coochie face!"

Camille was beside herself and screamed behind the gag and wiggled to beat all but she couldn't get loose from the five girls that were holding and sitting on her. Retta turned to see the ruckus and almost choked with laughter at the scene. "How's that Louisiana White fish taste Camille?" she commented to the hilarity of the other girls.

"Ladies were going to have some fun" she said folding her arms and smiling big. "Yay!" shouted one of them. "What are we gonna do with her Retta?" asked another girl. Retta gave Camille a sinister grin then looked at the girls. "Just hold her for a minute . . . I'll be right back." The girls looked at each other perplexed but too charged with excitement and curiosity to do anything else so they waited. Retta quickly returned with a pair of long black handled scissors. "Click Click!" went the scissors.

Camille's eyes got huge and she couldn't imagine what Retta would do with them but didn't like the ideas she herself was getting. She whined shaking her head and pleading with her captors to let her go. "Girls, it seems to me that we all have been mistreated and unfairly laid bare at the hands of this creep, I think it's time we return the favor don't you?" All the girls nodded with wild grins crossing their faces. "First lets start with this mess she calls hair" said Retta approaching Camille and grabbing a good hand full of her bronze locks. "Why Camille, this just won't do darling . . . you have way too much hair on your head sweetie" she said in a patronizing motherly sort of way. "SNIXT!" went the large scissors and Camille watched in horror as her once lovely hair came cascading down her face and onto the floor.

"Oh my lord! I have cut the wrong thing" said Retta mockingly. The other girls just laughed wildly like Indians after scalping a cowboy. "This just won't do . . . here let me try again" she said as Camille protested to no avail. "SNIXT!" and down her face again went more golden locks. Retta had her looking like an English monk with hair missing in the top and only hair around the boarders. "Now girls for the grand finale!" she said passing the scissors to one girl who was standing by. "Now Camille it's been said that you have such a great body and a nice ass too I might add" she said getting next to her ear. "I think we ought to share that with the world don't you?"

Camille was beyond resisting and just lay limp and whimpered. "Girls lets say we help Ms. Murchison out of those cumbersome clothes." "A girl has got to be free to express herself . . . STRIP HER ASS!" Chirped Retta and the girls moved like well oiled piranhas. They tore and ripped at Camille's one piece gym suit like they were at a free for all red tag sale at Macy's.

"Get her on her feet ladies, I think she want's to strut around for us a little!" The girls did as they were ordered and stood Camille up. All she had on was her bra and panties. She shook her head violently and begged through a muffled mouth for them not to do this. Too late, they were way past that intersection of judgement and she was finally getting what she had for so many years dished out to all of them at one time or another. Retta walked around her like a drill sergeant inspecting a troop.

"Not bad Camille, you do have a sexy little bod don't you?" she said smacking her soundly on the ass. "Whack!" "Move her to the doors" said Retta recovering her scissors again. "Well Ms. Murchison are you ready for your big public debut?" Camille just cried through angry tears. "Okay girls on the count of 3 sling her ass out the door okay?" they got her ready. Two of them were standing by to open the double doors as the others threw her through them. "One . . . Two" said Retta counting down. "Oh wait . . . I almost forgot, we can't have any obstructions such as these to hide your true worth darling" she said reaching down and grabbing the cuff of Camille's underwear and in one snip cut them off of her, snatching the thin cloth from her and repeating the same for her bra.

"Three!" she shouted and the five girls threw her out of the locker room and into an already full and active gymnasium. All she had on was her sneakers. One of the girls remembered to take off her gag just before they tossed her. Camille screamed like a banshee as she skidded onto the well polished wooden basket ball court. Retta tossed out one last insult before running to the opposite end of the locker room to come out on the far side to avoid implication.

"Why Camille . . . your as bald as an infant!" the other raiders laughed uncontrollably and ran behind her. Everyone had stopped short and turned to see the shocked and naked Camille standing trying to cover herself. The thought had occurred to run back into the locker room but she thought she would face them again so she didn't.

Retta had the foresight to have one of the others lock it before they dipped. "Oh shit, look at that!" yelled one boy shooting hoops. "DAAMMN!" commented another. Most of the girls who could see her were awe struck and covered their mouths and gasped in horror. Others just laughed and fell on the floor. Camille absorbed all the looks and comments buzzing around her and having lost all rational thought long ago, she broke and ran wildly for any door that was open.

Unfortunately there were none on that side of the gym and she wasn't trying to go to the other because that's where everyone was.

"Come here girl" shouted two of the boys who where nearby. "Come here and let me suck on ya BUUUTT!" he said in a lustful guttural voice then ran after her. Camille screamed and ran wildly through the gym as several boys chased her like ravenous wolves lumbering and shuffling along behind her. They weren't really trying to catch her but was instead egged on by the crowd and just went with the "Naked little red riding hood" scene.

Retta smiled to herself immensely at her handy work and just lay back on the bleachers and watched the carnage unfold. Camille for a long time had been asking to have her ass handed to her in a basket and now the time was here. She would never forget this day or the fact that the little girl with the braided hair she loved so much to torment was the cause of it. Yes it was sweet and Aretta was going to enjoy every minute of it until she was either caught by the boys chasing her or some teacher stopped it. "Sweet!"

On the other side of town, Ant was standing by the door of the bus taking names as students got on. "Hi Anthony!" said a tall skinny girl named Brenda as she walked up. He looked up and just nodded to her without speaking. The coldness of his attitude made her flush warm with embarrassment. She just looked down and got on the bus. The class was going on a natural science field trip to the park and it would take most of the day and would be a lot of fun if you didn't mind getting your feet wet once in a while.

"Anthony is everyone onboard yet?" asked his teacher. "No, not yet Mr. Burke, there's still two people missing." "Where are they . . . didn't they hear the call out over the PA?" "I don't know but I heard it." "Great! Just great" he said shaking his head in frustration. "This trip won't even get started if they don't hurry up and get here." "Who are they anyway Anthony?" "Umm . . . lets see Mathis and Johnson." "Where are they now?" "Well, Cheryl had home economics last period and Rodney had industrial arts so they shouldn't be far away." "Well we can't wait much longer, how about going to get them for me okay?" he said thumbing over his shoulder to the building behind them.

"Okay, Mr. Burke." Just then the two missing misfits came running around the corner of the gym like two tourists about to miss their plane. Matt was carrying two bags and a medium size box and Cheryl had her purse and a gym bag. "What took you two so long?" "We were about to leave you." "We're sorry Mr. Burke, but I had to go by the lab supply room to get those specimen cups, jars and formaldehyde that you asked me to remember to bring on Friday and Cheryl was finishing a batch of cookies she had made for us."

"OH! I'm sorry, I guess I forgot I asked you to be in charge of the supplies, and thank you too Cheryl" he said slapping his forehead. "Thank you very much, I'm sure everyone will enjoy the nice treat you've brought." "No problem" she said with a big country girl smile. "Okay people let's motivate!" he said climbing aboard the huge yellow school bus. Matt took a window seat in the rear and stretched out across the long seat. "Ahh, it's good to get away from this joint for awhile!" He reached up and adjusted the window for some air.

Soon Cheryl came behind him after storing her things up front. "Is this seat taken?" she asked smiling at him sweetly. "Aw Cher, I was just getting comfortable, now why you wanna go bustin up my peace huh?" The tall blonde was not affected by his rudeness one bit. "Peace huh?" she repeated to him then just plopped down on top of his legs anyway.

"Quitcher bitchin Mathis, you know you want me to sit here." Matt just sighed long and struggled out from under her ample country girls ass. He didn't like her boldness but did have to admit that she was hot and a sexy little peace of eye candy. She was cute and had a fine body for a white girl. She was a about six feet tall with hazel eyes and a few freckles. Cheryl had a cute little turned up nose that made you think she had just picked up on something that just didn't smell quite right. She also sported a pair of dimples that Matt found a little alluring at times when she would smile at him from a distance when she would see him in the hall way.

Her shape was nice too with full and generous hips and a heart shaped ass that put you in mind of Tony Braxton or J-lo. She wore Jordache Jeans like most girls but Lee's really made that ass stand out, BOOYA!

Matt swore he would smack dat ass if he got the chance but gave up on the idea when images of Retta over lapped her face. Any man would've wanted her, and it just so happens she was single and looking. "Okay Cheryl, take my seat why don't you!" he said slightly annoyed. "Aw Matt, you know you like me, so why don't you stop playing around, I'm down with it, so why you keep putting on this act like you don't want me?" Cheryl readjusted in her seat and sat with her arm on the seat back, one foot under her, greatly exposing that sensuous triangle between those healthy thighs and greatly stressing the jeans she was wearing to an obscene tension.

She dropped her head only slightly, just enough for that long sexy blonde hair to drop softly across her face. She then took a deep breath expanding those world class breasts, leaned back against the window and motioned him to her with her finger and flashing him with a look that clearly implied; "come over here Matt and . . . . FUCK THE SHIT OUT OF ME SEXY BASTARD!"

Cheryl was from Texas; the land of the super size, hard tough men and bold sexy women. She knew what she wanted when she saw it and didn't have any understanding of the word submissive when it came to getting it. Matt saw the intent in her game and relaxed against the adjacent side across from her. He let his eyes roam slowly and freely all over her. He knew she was trying to fuck with his mind and push any buttons she could reach including the ones on her blouse that she suddenly began to play with when she saw he wasn't going to run away.

Matt gave her a smile half raising his eyebrow in appreciation for what she was teasing to show him.

She wore a sunshine yellow blouse that even though was made of a sturdy cotton blend, looked more like polyester the way those double "D's" were pushing through. Cheryl started getting a little warm and decided to push yet another button on Matt's mind. She slowly put a finger to her mouth and teased the corner of her mouth as she let her legs fall open a little more exposing a well made monkey that Matt would have whipped all the gorillas in wild kingdom just to see!

Matt let his eyes and his guard drop to what she was hoping he would not fail to see. "I got him!" she said to herself smiling even wider and with even more mischief now that she had his full attention. She could feel the tiny bead of sweat trickle slowly down her back. Her breath caught quickly when the drop of liquid stimulation hit her spine just above her bikini line. Matt was trying to be cool and not give away too much but could clearly see that Cheryl was beginning to get off on her self as her nipples that looked more like large olives were making themselves known against her blouse.

Matt allowed his mind to wonder just a bit more before he pulled the plug on his imagination and came back to Aretta and reality. Besides, what could he accomplish on that crowded bus anyway except personal aggravation at his own inability to not satisfy himself properly. "Cheryl" he said leaning closer to her and motioning for her to come to him. She moved like she'd been attached to a rope. "Yes Matt?" she breathed rather than spoke. He hovered a bit closer and let her strain against the leash she was keeping herself on. Matt looked her over thoroughly from head to toe and in between, not letting anything go unmolested by his eyes and to make sure she was about to bust with lust. Cheryl was beginning to sweat openly now and didn't care that her breast's where perspiring and leaving a moist trail down the middle of her blouse.

"You know baby" he said drawing it out slowly. "I like ice cream too, but you don't see me jumping in bed with it do you?" Cheryl's mind did a double take and she wasn't sure at first what she had heard was what he had intended. But now seeing the grin slowly crossing his lips and the quick action of his eyebrows going up and down as if to drive the point home. Matt quickly leaned back in his seat and watched the show as Cheryl suddenly transformed from that sexy minx of a minute ago into a fair haired demonists.

Her eyes that were soft and sultry only moments ago took on the gleam of a serial killer stalking his next victim, and her full and ample breasts that were full and ready to be caressed now stood erect and hard like loaded cannon balls ready to fire.

Cheryl didn't speak right away but instead just absorbed the knowledge that she had been had and Matt although putting out all the right signals had only been leading her on and was just walking her down the primrose path of desire and deception. He had changed gears so fast before her eyes that it left her breathless. "Oh, so it's like that is it Matt?" she hissed at him so silently that he almost didn't hear her. She started slowly moving back against the window when Matt let his grin go flat and he got serious. "No Cher, it's like this" he said then reached out for her with the speed of a cobra and seized both her arms and snatched her to him.

"Matt, what are you doing?" she whispered sucking in her breath hard and sudden. Matt had pulled her so hard and quickly that he had plastered her right up against his chest. For a brief moment she had enjoyed the exquisite pleasure of having her breast pressed hard against his even hard chest. She found herself reeling at the mixed emotions she was having. Sudden shock mixed with extreme pleasure at being handled so roughly and familiarly. She'd had many dreams about her and Matt; about him doing just that before taking her and ripping her clothes off before taking advantage of her.

It was a challenge not to let her pleasure show and what she was thinking while being in his powerful embrace. He was close enough to kiss but instead she just relished the feel and scent of him, thinking he might be further upset with her and maybe push her away from him for trying or worse. Just then she subconsciously thought to look around to see if they had drawn any unwanted attention from the front of the bus. They hadn't, the only person appearing to be aware or notice was Anthony, but he was modestly looking away and feigning he was interested in something else.

Cheryl felt a little better about things knowing no-one was looking. But just as she had begun to get comfortable with the concept, Matt had spun her around from the position of sitting on the edge of her seat in the isle into his seat and laying down flat on her back in his. A move he'd learned in wrestling practice long ago. He was laying partially on top of her with one leg between hers and one between that seat and the one in front of them. He was well braced as he put his face extremely close to hers.

Cheryl was completely shocked and no previous fantasy could ever match what she was experiencing this very moment. Her legs were partially bent at the knees but in the isle. The big girl was shocked because she had never been handled so completely by anyone since she was a little girl in Texas and use to wrestle with her brothers.

She found herself not moving or resisting but instead just looking into the piercing dark eyes above her. Cheryl felt warmth and excitement rush through her. It was all so new and wonderful. Matt slowly raised her head seductively holding her by the back of her neck. "Oh my gosh, he's gonna kiss me!" she thought to herself with anticipation; mind reeling and spinning out of control. Her breath coming irregular and slow. "Is this how it is, is this what love feels like?" "I never knew he wanted me this much before, I had always liked him and wanted him to like me but I was to afraid to ask him and now all in one second he's going to kiss me." "OH! How good this is gonna feel."

"Will I be able to handle it, and then what?" "Oh lord! How weak I feel!" Matt smiled sweetly at her knowing completely what she was thinking and feeling because he'd seen the same look on Retta's face many times. He almost felt like a rat for what he was thinking about doing but not so much that he was gonna betray Retta to make Cheryl's fantasy come true.

He drew closer to her still, keeping her gaze in his not letting her close her eyes until the last second. Now poising her lips to take his full on to hers, Cheryl could feel her body tingling all over and tensing at the same time as she could feel Matt all over her and taste him even before his lips touched hers. Closer and closer they came, she could feel his pulsing muscles all over her breast and wanted to scream it felt so damn good, but she wasn't going to blow it especially after she had waited so long for this moment. Matt got closer still and was just about to touch his lips to hers when suddenly he pulled back at the last second and lightly grabbed her nose between his thumb and forefinger.

"Honk Honk!" he said playfully then quickly got up from her and went towards the front of the bus near Ant who had been watching the whole scene quietly and now was working feverishly not to let her see him laughing himself into a fit under his shirt tail. Cheryl was pissed . . . no she was LIVID! as she got up quickly and looked up to see him giggling at her. She was so mad she couldn't believe it. Her emotion was sporadic as it swung between sexual excitement and enflamed anger at being used and cheated. Cheryl quietly straightened herself and adjusted her blouse that had come open some and out of her pants during the short wrestle mania they had just had.

She wanted to cry but her Texas heritage wouldn't allow her too. "Ranch girls don't cry" she told herself then looked up at him and said evenly with her head high, "Matt . . . that was wrong, it was rude and crude and I nev . . . !" "And you probably never will" said Matt evenly completing her statement and soundly shutting her down. She shook her head in disbelief that the boy she had had such strong feelings for was such a rat. "Mathis you're . . . you're despicable!" she yelled finally not caring who heard their drama now.

Several girls looked back not having been aware of what had been going on since they were into their own little world of gossip and boys of mutual interest. "Why did you do that to me?" she said, sadness clearly in her voice and lowering her voice again. Matt looked at her and could see that his little joke didn't go off well. He could see the hurt and shame in the big girls eyes. She had assumed and given herself in mere seconds to the man she had wanted most and who she thought had finally wanted her. But it was all a joke, a sick little joke that left her burned and rebuked.

Matt just sat and smiled weakly unspeaking. "Rodney, I asked you for an answer" she said evenly not accepting his cavalier mannerism and silence. The sound of his first name coming from her lips shocked Matt back to reality. Not many people ever called him that or even knew his first name except Ant and a very short few others. Matt straightened up and got serious again.

"Okay Cheryl" he said getting up and walking back to where she was and sitting beside her. The abrupt feel of him sitting down beside her made her feel squeamish and she wished he'd stayed where he was, but it was too late now.

"I think you're beautiful Cher and more desirable than any woman I have ever laid my eyes on, you're intelligent, sexy and fun to be around." "Hell, a man would be a fool not to want you . . . !" "Any man but you right?" she said completing his sentence. "No! that's not true!" She looked up from working the quick in her nails and stared right through him as if he'd said he was gay. "NO?" "I do want you!" "Then why Matt . . . why don't you want to be with me . . . why treat me so coldly?" "All I wanted to do was show you how much I like you and wanted you to like me!" she said, her voice getting strained and cracked from warm tears beginning to work their way into her dry throat.

Matt looked deeply into her eyes and for a moment allowed himself to be overcome by how really beautiful they were and drawing him in like a fish on a line. He took a chance on his strength that was beginning to wane and drew her closer to him and placed his hand upon hers. Love and confusion showing in her eyes. "Why Matt?" her voice rasped. "Why don't you want to be with me . . . is it?" she paused and swallowed hard then looked away still holding his hand. "Is it our color difference . . . is me?" "No, Cher, its' none of those things" he said feeling her pain and slowly turning her chin to face him. He tried to smile and make her smile, but it just wasn't there.

Matt cleared his throat and just went for the truth. "The thing is Cher that I'm already seeing someone angel . . . that's all." Cheryl looked at him incredulously for a second then shook her head. "I don't believe you Matt" she said bringing a shaky hand to wipe a bit of snot that was trying to come down as she sniffled. "I think you're just saying that because you don't want to tell me the truth, that you can't see me because were so different and you think people will talk." Matt looked her in the eye and shook his head. Oh how much hurt had he brought on her. This girl, that had only wanted him for himself. Now he did feel like a rat. "What can I tell you that you will believe Cher, what will make you understand that there is no such thing as color with me?" he thought to himself as she let a tear fall.

Matt slowly reached up and cupped her gently behind her neck. He could feel the warmth and softness of her vanilla skin and the silkiness of her hair as it touched his hand. Matt drew her slowly to him. Cheryl saw or at least sensed what he was or wanted to do and was afraid. She didn't know if this was a trick or not and if it wasn't' then she was really afraid because she wanted him, but if he really did have someone else she couldn't see herself ever sharing him with another girl. She would fight! She would win she would.

Matt seized her lips with his and sighed a sigh of mixed sadness and sheer bliss at the touch and taste of Cheryl's sweet and tender lips on his. For a moment she was numb and just trembled in his light embrace then slowly and ever so steadily she gave into him . . . melted to him and reached up and possessed him as the once light an gentle kiss grew into a strong and passion filled quest for each others acknowledgement of love. "Retta forgive me" he cried within himself as he felt a part of himself begin to die. Matt slowly and regrettably pulled himself from her oh so comforting kiss and embrace.

Cheryl not yet aware that the kiss had come to an end was still poised for more as her mind was awash with ecstasy. She held on to him awhile longer then let her head fall to his shoulder as if being released by some unseen power or force that held her in its exquisite magnetic pull then let her fall to earth much as a comet coming from space. "OH Matt I love you" she heard herself whisper while clinging to him. Why was it that only Ant and a few others (mostly girls) were aware of the serene drama that had unfolded only a few seats down the isle. Mr. Burke was up front sitting just behind the bus driver appearing to be going over some notes or documents as most teachers did when they got a free moment. But then again Mr. Burke was nobody's fool either. He had learned long ago that although it was his job to keep control and decorum amongst his students when in or out of school, he himself remembered what it was like to be in love and in high school.

In fact he wasn't really that old as teachers go. He was in his late twenties so was not to far from the memories of high school. He'd looked up in the rear view mirror and seen the multiple act play that had unfolded behind him sometime ago. Yes, he could have said something but why . . . what would really have been accomplished by interfering? Sometimes you just have to let kids work out their own little drama's. "Sometimes you just gotta let em be" he said to himself as he rubbed his finger lovingly over the face of a small picture of himself and a very striking bronze colored woman in a white sun dress as they stood on a beach somewhere, some place in time.

Cheryl not wanting to prolong the fantasy any longer than need be raised up and released herself from Matt's embrace. She reached up and cupped his cheek and smiled weakly knowing she could have him and he was really to good of a guy to push her away. All of the games of earlier was really him trying to be nice and let her down as easily as he could without actually telling her that there was another woman which would have hurt her more. "Is she pretty?" she asked motherly wiping her lipstick from his lips even though she really didn't wear any. She was just trying to erase any evidence of her having been there.

"Yeah . . . she is" Matt answered weakly, feeling completely drained and lost at the same time. "Do you love her?" asked Cheryl wishing she hadn't asked that the minute it came out of her mouth. "Oh! I'm sorry I shouldn't have asked that Matt . . . forget I . . ." Matt didn't answer but just reached out again and gently cupped her cheek.

Their eyes sought each other once more for the thousandth life time that day. Cheryl could feel the waves of love and the power of that love every second he held her in his loving gaze. "Oh how I wish he would look at me that way, love me that way, oh god I can't let him go, I can't" she whispered in her heart as she reached out to hold his face in hers for what would probably be the last time. Matt let their heads touch and they sat that way for a minute then released and sat beside each other feeling it would be safer. "I guess you do huh" said Cheryl finally. "Does she go to school here?" "No, she goes to Southwest." "What grade?" "The tenth." "How long have you been seeing each other?" This was beginning to feel as if Cheryl was his wife and was questioning him about an affair he'd been having.

Matt didn't want to be rude to her and felt that the questions may help her to come to grips with the fact that they could never be. Maybe some time ago but not now . . . not since Retta and not ever more. He was very much in love and devoted to one woman . . . the only woman he would ever love. "We've been going together for awhile, I don't remember exactly, but it's been for quite some time, maybe four or five months." "Sounds like you guys have been together for awhile, how are you able to keep up a relationship like that being that she lives on the other side of town . . . you probably don't see each other much do you?" she ventured, hoping that there was a kink in the chain somewhere that she could get in edgewise and exploit.

Matt saw through her question and tried not to grin. "No, no we see each other enough." Cheryl just bowed her head feeling defeat was the soup of the day and just started fumbling with a hole in the seat between them. "You know . . . we could still be close friends and stuff . . . I mean . . . you know, call each other sometimes and . . ." "No Cher" said Matt cutting her off clean and with a defiant shake of his head. "We can't, and I think you know why" he said raising her chin to look at his piercing brown eyes.

As their eyes met Cheryl felt a rush go through her and she felt the urge to reach out and pull Matt into her full breasts and awaiting arms. But after thinking better of it held her own hands to keep from doing just that. "We can be friends Cher but that's about it . . . nothing more okay?" Cheryl's mind was in despair but her heart was doing flips at just the thought of still having a part of him at all. She had never met anyone who made her feel like he did . . . black or white.

Cheryl and Matt had met over a year ago and since then had grown into casual acquaintances. She had begun to like Matt and just about the time she felt confident enough to tell him . . . he got shipped off to Southwest. She hated him for leaving her but then thought better of it and realized that it wasn't his fault but instead the lottery and the school board. The same program had caused her parents to move into the area closer to Central when it threatened to relocate her to the east side of town where she would have been going to either Northeast High or some other school in the county.

Yes, she really liked Matt and now that he'd come back to Central since his father moved to a part of town closer to Central's zone he didn't have to stay at Southwest and quickly put in for a transfer after his freshman school year. But by then it was too late, he in the time he was gone, met and fell in love with Aretta and they were inseparable as far as he was concerned. Their stare lasted a bit longer than Matt would have liked and began to feel a little uncomfortable. Cheryl was still micromanaging ideas and concepts in her head as to how she could make this thing work and she have more access to him than he was allowing. "But Matt!" she protested squeezing his hands, her eyes beginning to wax over with tears. She never got to finish her thought.

Matt couldn't help himself nor the feeling of compassion for this girl or anyone who felt as strongly about him as she seem to. He gave in and drew her into himself fiercely in a sudden embrace that pushed that wind out of her. The look of utter shock and surprise mixed with the sublime as her full lips met his in a torched kiss. Cheryl swooned and melted into him and her eyes rolled over as she couldn't keep them open. The softness and warmth of Matt's lips covered hers and she heard herself squeal as he hungrily sought her lips over and over again. Matt knew that what he was doing wasn't right but was predisposed to do anything about it. He didn't mean or want to be kissing her and holding her the way he was. His intent was to just give her a final kiss off and hope it would suffice her not to come after him anymore. Unfortunately that's not what was happening and he couldn't separate from her.

The girls in the front of the bus began giggling and high-fiving each other as they watched what they considered the best soap opera they have ever seen and they had front row seats!. Ant just shook his head and laughed to himself and went back to his papers. He for a minute thought the drama was at an end and that Matt had made it known to Cheryl that he loved Retta and couldn't see being with her on any level other than as a casual friend. He sighed long and tried to convince himself that Matt would fix this and explain what was going on to him soon enough. On the other hand though, Cheryl was having the time of her teenage life! She didn't understand or really like the way he was bending her emotions back and forth like a wire clothes hanger but she loved what he was doing to her body. Cheryl's body was on fire now and her nipples were getting as hard as unripened olives on a tree. She held Matt so tight her arms began to ache a little but she wasn't about to let go of him and began to grind her chest into him more.

"Sigh!" Matt could feel the big girls eagerness to be all over him and god help him, he wanted to slam her onto the bench seat and beat the brakes off dat ass! She wanted him to do more! Touch her! Feel her! Put his hands on her and squeeze her! Cheryl could feel the heat between her legs rage and wanted to feel Matt between her legs and inside of her like nothing else. She jerked Matt to her attempting to square his body with hers but it resulted in a sweet mistake. The bench seat would not allow but so much in the way of squaring yourself with another person and you would actually have to stop, take a leg and put it in the seat to allow that person to lay upon you or you on them.

Matt lost his balance and his hand reflexively left her waist to right himself or keep himself from falling off the bench and wound up jamming it in between her already parted legs. "SSS . . . Matt!" she swooned sucking in hard and shouting his name in a strained whisper. The feel of Matt's hard hand pushing abruptly against her crotch was all the motivation she needed to get where she was dying to go. She felt herself lock up and muscles between her legs that she didn't know she had began to convulse wildly and squeeze again and again!.

Matt could feel the deep warmth between her legs and how soft and giving her crotch was. Oh, it felt nice, even though he had the barrier of her jeans to contend with, he still could feel a good bit of the woman that was Cheryl between those generous inviting thighs of hers. Matt allowed himself one probing and caress of her just to satisfy his own curiosity. He felt himself grow rock hard when he did, and the effect on Cheryl was no less overpowering.

"SSS . . . Matt . . . Matt . . . Oh God that felt good!" she whispered loudly into his ear as she held onto him like a drowning man to a life preserver. Wave after wave of excitement went through her and she through her head back as she orgasmed over and over again. Her long back-length blonde hair gleamed as it danced in and out of the rays of sunlight coming through the windows of the bus. Matt could see this was not going to end well so he had better end this now and cool both their heals before they got busted by the teacher.

The bus driver was no problem. He was enjoying the show anyway, Matt noticed when he looked up minutes ago to see him wildly twisting the tooth pick in his mouth to the point it was shreds. Cheryl, while enjoying the ecstasy of the moment had another thought that sent a cold shiver down her spine. She knew that there was no way to discretely do what she was so dying to do to Matt on a semi-crowed school bus in broad daylight. She let out a little whimper of mixed pleasure and sadness as Matt began to slow his movements and eventually break from her. "Damn! I knew this wouldn't last for long" she said to herself and just as the soundless words left her mind Matt suddenly broke from her pulling away with his hand over his mouth as if it burned.

"I'm sorry Cher . . . I shouldn't have done that" he said looking around and seeing the many faces that were zeroed into their position like radar on a fighter plane. "Please forgive me, that was wrong of me, I only wanted to . . . to . . . "

he didn't finish. At this point so much had passed between them in such a short time that he didn't know what to say or if it would be believed so he just sat still and looked at his hands and inspected his nails.

This came as a surprise to Cheryl. She was fully aware that he knew what he was doing and took masterful control of it too. She didn't see any wrong in what he did or was probably wanting to do, cause she wanted it as much or more than he did! OH! Snap! She thought to herself as she became aware of exactly what all this had done to him. Cheryl in all her lustiness didn't think about his girlfriend or how much he really loved her and felt bad about betraying her with what they were just doing. But then again why would she, she was where she wanted to be doing almost what she wanted to be doing and with whom she wanted to do it with. So why would she think about another girl and her loss! "If he was my man I would hate him for what he was doing and feel just as bad as he does right now" she surmised to herself having come out of her lust filled stupor.

"Matt I'm sorry, I didn't mean to pressure you that way, I just wanted you and only wanted you to feel the same." "I know you didn't Cher, and don't blame yourself, I was as responsible as you were, can you forgive me?" "Yes Matt, if you can forgive me and not hold my caring for you against me?" Matt smiled at her, put a playful hand atop her golden head and jostled it playfully. "Yeah we alright Cher." Cheryl smiled brightly as she felt she'd been vindicated. The pair sat quietly for a moment.

Matt content that he had finally reached an understanding with Cher and there would be no more contact or shenanigans from her. Cher sat still facing Matt and dreamily drawing circle and squiggles in his hand. "You know Matt . . . I'm gonna be honest with you, I've always liked you and wanted you to feel the same about me since I met you last year, I can't deny my feelings for you Matt . . . I'm falling in love with you!" The sound of her voice was soft and gentle but her words were as deafening as the sound of a bomb going in a china shop. For a while there was a long silence and Cheryl began to wonder if she should have told him that given all the drama they had endured this morning. She looked at him as he raised his head.

Matt just couldn't figure women and shook his head as a small grin crossed his face. He knew that the drama would never end and she was going to be a ever present and constant nuisance to him for as long as he went to Central. "Sigh . . . ah me" he said shaking his head and patting her hand. Cheryl accepted this as his way of saying,

"Okay Cher do with me what you want to . . . I'm not gonna fight you about it." The two of them sat back finally and stared straight ahead not speaking. Cheryl with a smile of contentment and Matt with the reticent look of a Monk. He allowed her to hold his hand and believe that she had won the day but secretly he knew she had not. Just then Cheryl announced to him just loud enough for him to hear. "And I always will no matter what you say or do!" "Gat dammit Cher!" As the trip grew near it's end and they were getting close to the park. Matt looked out the window and watched as they passed road side shops, strip malls and side walk vendors as they passed through downtown.

Matt looked towards the front of the bus and noticed that Ant was sitting two rows up and across from him with his back to the window staring at him. Ant was looking at Matt in the most peculiar way as if to say "How do you manage my friend? . . . how do you manage?" then shook his head smothering a giggle and turned around to face the front. After awhile the bus rolled across the railroad tracks to the entrance way to the park and there were a few old civil war era trains on both sides of them and a huge black locomotive with it's coal car behind it. On the side was painted "Southern Railroad #6."

The park was huge and was divided into three large areas with access roads dividing them. There were Dogwood, Oak and Cherry Blossom trees all over that were in full bloom. The site and smell of the pink and white blossoms made Matt feel good and he smiled in spite of himself. On the far right side was a parking area with a small building that belong to the DMV. On the far left was a sea food restaurant with nautical themes and sea going memorabilia hanging from the front of the building. Behind that building was where the class would be collecting aquatic and samples for the science class's "Life Tank." The bus driver swung the bus in a wide left turn and pulled into a spot at the end of the restaurant parking lot. "Okay class let's get all the stuff we need and leave the rest on the bus" said Mr. Burke. "I'll give you some time to stretch and relax awhile because it's a nice day, but remember we only have an hour or so before we have to leave okay?" "Okay" everyone agreed.

"Mathis, I want you to pass out the specimen cups and log sheets to everybody and Anthony you start filling the jars we brought with formaldehyde, okay?" "Okay Mr. Burke" they said getting up and getting off the bus. Matt had forgotten for a second that he was still holding Cheryl's hand. She got up and stepped into the isle letting him get out but still held onto his hand. Matt stopped, looked at his hand in hers then looked into her big blue eyes. They bored a football size hole in Matt's heart and he couldn't shake her.

Cheryl smiled timidly when she noticed that he was no more eager to let go of her hand than she was his. Matt stepped to her and gave her a light kiss on the forehead. "Just friends okay Cher?" She just nodded and dropped her head releasing his hand. Matt quickly retreated to the head of the bus to get his supplies and other stuff before he once again did something he would regret. He was already sweating a load wondering how he was gonna tell Retta about this little escapade. He knew she would flip and probably go postal then go into a crying fit. "Damn I'm so stupid" he said punching his leg as he got off the bus.

Ant fell in behind him and was laughing at him cause he knew what had been going on in the back of the bus and knew that Matt would have a lot to answer for to Retta and him but also to himself. Matt looked back and saw him grinning at him shaking his head. "Boy you stupid!" Off the two of them went to get set up and to hand out supplies and other stuff. Matt put his gear on the ground and began to tear open the box he had brought. "Okay people let's get it and go" he said waving them pass like a traffic cop as each person got what they needed then went on their way. They all headed over the hill behind the restaurant and over the hill to the river. The area was partially empty with only a few people around.

"Hey! Let's go over to the end of the dock area class" said Mr. Burke pointing down the shoreline and away from the patrons who sat nearby. He didn't want to make anyone sick being exposed to the slime and frogs the class would be pulling out of the river. Once there they laid out all their gear. "Listen up people, the object of this little scavenger hunt is to identify, locate and collect samples ranging from frogs, tadpoles, lizards, newts and any other odd aquatic animals you see." "We are also going to collect algae samples, water plants and fungi if you see any, so I want you to pair off and spread out cause there is a lot of area to cover." "Some of you on this side, some on that side."

Matt quickly grabbed Ants arm and snatched him to his side so as to deter Cheryl from even thinking about being his partner. She saw the move and folded her arms in frustration giving him a little pout. Matt just smiled and headed off with Ant. "Be careful people, it is warm enough for snakes, so watch where you step, there are moccasins in the Ocmulgee." Cheryl quickly forgot about Matt and thought about the possibility of snakes. She cringed and went looking for a partner a little nearer to the dock where there were no bushes.

Matt and Ant headed down river away from the crowd. They had hoped to get more samples than anyone else because it would give them a better grade and more points for the activity. "You catch em Ant and I'll slam dunk em in the juice" said Matt referring to the chemical in the jar he was carrying. "Oh no you don't slick, you catch em and I'll drown em!" said Ant pushing him towards the water. "Why should I do it? . . . you got them long frog catching arms and that goofy face that any lizard would love to come to" said Matt tossing it back to him. "Yeah, but you have a face that only a frog would love!"

Ant shot back not to be outdone at hurling insults. Matt and Ant did this all the time and would go as far as booby-trapping each other and many other antics just to have fun. It just wasn't a complete day if they didn't jibe each other about something.

"So how was your date with Retta?" "Man, let me tell you that girl's mother can cook!" "We had seafood dip and some wine and we had a roast that was so tender it fell off the fork!" "How come you didn't invite me?" "Because I'm greedy . . . dummy" he said giving Ant a larger than life grin to drive home his point as well as show as many teeth as he could. "All right . . . that's okay . . . I'll get you back!" "So what did you and Melanie get into or did you just sit around looking stupid?" "I think it went okay, we talked a lot and held hands some." "Oh yeah? . . . what else?" "Then we got a pizza after the movie and went riding around." "Uh huh . . . oh bye the way where did you park my bike while ya'll were doing all this running around?" "Oh, we put it in the back of her truck"

"She's got a truck!?" "Yeah, a Ford Ranger I think, but it's not really hers yet, it's her dad's and he's letting her use it." "So did you kiss her?" "Man no! . . . not on the first date, you cave man!" Matt brushed off the comment and just looked at him with a smirk on his face and lightly scratched his chin with his fore finger. "Did you try?" "What did I just tell you?" "Okay, okay! I was just checking!"

"We held hands a little though." "So who started it?" "Man! You so nosey . . . why don't you go find Cher and ask her who started it first" he said grinning at Matt with an even bigger toothier grin and raising his eyebrows high for affect. "Oh shit, that's cold" said Matt smiling back. "Don't worry about little miss Texas . . . I got her under control." "Yeah, I could tell by the way she was trying to suck your eyeballs out of your mouth!" "You saw that, huh?" "Hell, damn near the whole bus saw that!" "Nosey bitches, what about Mr. Burke . . . did he see us?" "Yeah, but he wasn't sweating you though, he's cool, he know what time it is."

"That's why most people like his class, because when you go on field trips he don't sweat you unless you back there trying to really get busy." "Oh okay, but hey, I still wanna know!" said Matt punching Ant in the arm. "Ow! Faggot!" "Faggot . . . well come on get some of this juicy booty" said Matt bending over and waggling his butt at him and making kissy faces like he was a sissy or something.

Ant was on the ground laughing his guts out at Matt's antics. He could always count on his friend going off the deep end no matter what. Matt took the opportunity to jump on him and punch him in the chest and stomach. Ant just laughed all the more. "Tell me, come on tell me" he said punching him everywhere there was a free spot to hit. "Okay! Okay just stop punching me" Ant said pushing Matt off him and rolling to get up. "Okay fella's we need to cut the horse play and get to the business at hand alright?" "Alright Mr. Burke we was just goofing off." Mr. Burke just nodded and waved them off as if to say "yeah, yeah, okay let's get with it." "Look Matt there's not much to say, we just rode around talking about me, her school and some other junk." "Did she ask about me?" "Yeah, you know she did ass-wipe" said Ant cocking his eyes at him. "Well out with it . . . what did she say?"

"She just asked how you were, what kind of person you were, your birthday . . . you know the usual stuff." "She asked about my birthday?" "Yeah what about it?" "Well nothing really." "It just don't happen is all." "How do you know what a girl is supposed to ask and not ask about somebody?" "Listen man, a girl don't ask those kinda question unless you've been together awhile or she's trying to scope you out." "Oh yeah?" "Yeah!" "But I thought you made it clear to her about Retta and you?" "So did I, but some women are head strong and don't stop for nothing when they see something they want." "Yeah, I guess your right, just look at how Cheryl was trying to rape you in the back of the bus or get you to rape her" he said chuckling. "So tell me what was all that about between you and Cheryl Walker?"

"Just how much did you see anyway?" "Everything!" "So what's the deal?" "There is no deal, I was just chillin out when she came over and plopped down next to me." "So what's that got to do with you kissing her like that?" "Man I don't even know, she was all over me at first and I was just fooling around with her . . . you know just joking, then I found out she's been nuts about me for a long time and wanted to get with me!" "You told her no, didn't you?" "Hell yeah! but by then she'd lost it." "Well that ain't your fault." "I know that, but still it made me feel kinda bad for her and before I knew it I kissed her to try and make her feel better."

"You always was soft hearted" Ant commented as they got down close to the water's edge to at least look like they were working so as not to get busted for goofing off the project by Mr. Burke. "I couldn't help it man, she was so close and so so . . . you know what I mean?" "So irresistible?" Ant finished for him. "Yeah! You know, but still I got may point across and she understands now." "Are you sure about that?" "Yeah I'm sure!" "Well I guess we'll see then won't we" said

Ant giving Matt a funny look. "What do you mean, we'll see?" Ant just pointed over his shoulder in the direction they had come from. "Oh hell!" said Matt impatiently shoving his jar into the muddy bank.

It was Cheryl and Brenda coming towards them. "Maybe they're looking for lizards" offered Matt not really believing it when he saw the look in Cheryl's eyes. "Yeah maybe, so let's act like were looking and maybe they'll pas us by." "Yeah they might, and maybe I'm a squid looking for a pizza in a hen house" shot Ant looking at Matt from the corner of his eye. They both started pulling back large stones and bushes looking for anything that crawled or hopped. "Hi guys" said Brenda leaning over to see what they were doing. "Have you found anything yet?" "Naw, not yet" said Ant turning to look at the tall skinny girl. "Hi Matt" said Cheryl not wanting to be left out.

"Hi Cher" he mumbled not wanting to look at her and faking like he was really into the search as he moved grass and rocks from left to right to unearth something. "I brought you guys a little something" she said holding out an object wrapped in plastic wrap. "Oh thanks" said Matt reaching out to accept the cookies he'd forgotten she baked for everyone. "Can I help?" she asked hopefully with an eager smile on her face and wringing her hands together. "I thought Brenda was your research partner?" "Not anymore" she said pointing at the backs of Ant and Brenda as they walked away chatting and eating cookies.

"Thanks a lot Ant!" he muttered venomously under his breath. Cheryl must have caught Matt's expression because she drew back with a hurt and stricken look on her face, turned around and began walking away. "Never mind! I'll just look around on my own Matt, you don't have to be with me since I bother you so much." Matt could hear the obvious hurt in her voice and it made him feel like a shit. "Damn! how the hell did I get into this" he muttered to himself then got up leaving his things on the bank. "Cheryl wait!" he said running to catch up to her.

Cheryl slowed some but kept walking, her feelings clearly laid bare. Finally she stopped and turned to face him. "Baby please don't do this to me" Matt heard himself say as he caught up to her. Cheryl was equally stunned that he had used such a familiar term to relate to her when he clearly didn't feel that. "Cher don't you see how vulnerable I am around you?" "It's not fair for you to come at me this way."

Her mouth fell wide open and her eyes grew wide as the words began to sink in. "How can you say that to me Matt? when it was you who selfishly led me on then threw my feelings to the rocks like a useless toy! . . . no it's me who is vulnerable" she said stabbing a finger into his chest. "Matt can't you see I've fallen for you? God I can't believe what I'm saying" she said turning away from him shaking her head in disbelief that any of this was going on but couldn't stop herself. "Listen Matt" she said turning around to face him. I've never felt like this before and didn't think I cared for you so much until just this moment and its more than I ever expected, can't you see that?"

"Cher . . . please don't" said Matt trying to collect his thoughts and respond to this emotional attack at the same time. "I don't . . ." he said trying to find the right words but nothing was coming just convoluted thoughts of her and Retta passing through his mind and heart. "You don't what, Matt?" "Let me speak Cher" he said grabbing her arms. Cheryl involuntarily turned her head towards his hands as the feel of him touching her and being so familiar with her was still fresh in her mind and warm to her body. She was angry and hurt but could not deny she reveled each time he touched her. It was like a warm bath or a spring rain shower that left her body tingling all over.

"Look baby, I am very much in love with my girl and I don't want to jeopardize that in anyway, I've already committed too many crimes against her with you that I'm gonna have to tell her about, I thought that we had covered this . . . didn't we agree that we would be just friends?" "Don't you see that it would be wrong for me and for you to get involved with each other?" "By all rights, we shouldn't even be having this conversation, I should have moved away from you when you sat next to me on the bus, but I'm not a cruel and insensitive person, in fact I fall in love to easily and too hard!"

"Then how can you say you love her if your with me now?" she said cornering him, staring him silent with piercing blue eyes. "All I want is for you to love me, is that so wrong Matt?" she said grabbing his arms now. The pair looked quite involved noticed some of the other kids and they wondered how long the two had been going together as it tended to look as though they did. Unfortunately, for Cheryl it wasn't so. "No . . . I mean Yes! it is" he caught himself. "Aw hell I don't know what I mean, all I do know is the longer I stay around you the more it makes me compromise myself even more Cher."

"The truth is I'm just not that strong Cher when it comes to my own stupid heart, I know I love my girl but I can't deny that you do, and have gotten to me." "Then you do! care for me Matt . . . don't you?" she said half questioning half stating it as a fact and all too afraid to hear the answer. Her eyes were turning into a tempest of blue and gray hues of the most intense effect and I was fucking with Matt's mind something terrible.

"Yes, Cher, I have feelings for you, but they can never be fulfilled." His words made her swoon and a giddy feeling ran through her stomach just to hear him say that he cared for her and to end it by suggesting she was his baby . . . oh how exquisite! "But why Matt, why can't you love me?" "I can accept sharing you so long as I have you!" "No! Cher, I thought we went through all of this before." "No, we haven't! . . . it will never be through!" she whispered through a dry and cracked voice.

She was in tears now and they flowed freely down her soft beautiful face. Matt's heart began to break a little more with every tear that fell. "Cher" "NO! Matt don't touch me" she said as she jerked away from him and ran down the shore towards a picnic area in the tree line. "Cheryl wait!" he yelled then sheepishly looked around to see if anyone had noticed or heard them. No-one appeared to have if they did and just kept on with their work. Brenda and Ant were just returning and caught most of the drama.

She gave Matt a harsh glare then ran off to see about her heart broken friend. Ant didn't say anything but just came over to put an arm around his confused and distraught friends neck.

"Come on Matt, let's go take a walk man." Matt felt kind of numb all over and just let Ant lead him away like a horse on a leash. "Why me Ant?" "You can't help it Matt, it's not totally your fault, somewhere between the 8th and 10th grade you just grew into something some women can't resist."

"Hey man, I ain't no damn cock hound!" said Matt pulling away from his best friend and squaring on him. "No your not, that's what Jr. is, what you are or have from what I've been seeing is a person with a shit load of compassion and love for people . . . women in particular and they see that! Hell they can smell it." "What you need to do is be more careful about how and what you say and do around certain women." "Now how am I supposed to know when to do that?" Matt snorted at his friend.

"Hell, I don't know, I ain't never been in your spot before!" "Well no shit Sherlock!" "Hey don't blame me, I never told you to leave yourself open to all these bleeding heart chicks." "Hell if you had it your way, you would have a shelter for battered and rejected women built and then run it your damn self!"

said Ant half joking but serious. "Okay Ant, I get the picture, I'll be cool." "You better be, because if you don't one day and one way as sure as shit stinks Aretta is gonna get wind of this and then where will you be?" The thought of any of this getting back to Retta even though Matt said he was gonna tell her, still sent chills down his spine. "I think I would rather face castration than to hurt and lose her Ant because of my stupidity." "So what are you gonna do then?"

Matt thought quickly about what had transpired between himself and Cher in the last hour and he had come to grips with the fact that he didn't lie to her or betray her and wasn't completely responsible for everything that had happened that day. He did in fact tell her what she had wanted to hear just not on the same set of terms as she wanted. "Naw, I ain't going out like that" he said to himself thinking of Retta and how she was his world. Matt looked at Ant and nodded with resignation about what he needed to do. He grabbed Ants specimen jar and walked off towards the spot they had started in. "I'm going to find some frogs . . . that's what I'm going to do!" then he tramped off through the underbrush. Matt didn't have to walk far before he found Brenda and Cheryl. Brenda had her arm around her consoling her. She must have heard him because she looked up suddenly and gave him a nasty "keep away from her look."

"What do you want? Haven't you caused trouble for one day?" Matt paid her no attention but just squared off on her and put his hands on his hips. "Brenda, I can understand and appreciate what you're trying to do for your friend, but right now this doesn't concern you, so if you would please leave so I can talk to Cher I would appreciate it." "She don't want to talk to you! Why don't you leave and let her alone." Matt just bit his lip and let out a long sigh. This wasn't going to be easy. Cheryl slowly brought her head off Brenda's shoulder and looked at Matt with red tear stained eyes then back to Brenda. "It's okay Brenda, I'll be okay." "You sure girl? . . . cause I can stay as long as you like" she said looking at Matt defiantly. "Yeah, it's okay, you go on ahead and work on our stuff I'll catch up in a minute."

"Well okay then . . . you be strong girl and don't be fooled honey . . . all men are dogs!" Cheryl cracked a slight smile at this truth and Brenda got up and left but not before looking back and giving Matt one last warning stare. "What is it you want Matt? have you come back to see your handy work? or do you just want to add more to it?" "No Cher, I don't want to do either" he said sitting down beside her. "I just want to apologize and try to talk to you." "About what? . . . you've already made yourself clear about what you want and don't want." "No, I don't think so." "What do you mean? What else is there to say Matt?" "Well for one thing, I was wrong for not having told you anything about me or my life sooner, if I had, we would be good friends instead of two upset individuals."

"Cher, I never wanted to hurt you or cause you any pain baby, but I must be honest with you, I'm the kind of guy who wears his heart on his sleeve and has compassion for people especially when they are hurting or needing." "The problem with that is it tends to cloud my judgment and get me into trouble instead like now." "Matt, I'm not sure I understand . . . what does this have to do with the way you have been treating me today?" "It has a lot Cher, just let me finish." "Okay I'm listening" she said turning to him and giving him her full attention. "Like I was saying, I care too much and when I'm with someone I love long and deeply, you know I love my girl cause I told you but not in so many words."

"Cher, when you started in on me letting me know that you were interested in me I was flattered and in another life I would have gone after you in a big way, I'm also the kind of guy who looks deeper into a woman and not just between her shoulders or her legs." "I'm more complex than that and once I see what I want I go after it with a vengeance."

"So your saying that you didn't see much in me you liked or wanted is that it?" she said wide eyed and searching his face for any confirmation of any kind. Matt just shook his head in frustration. He was getting a little angry that she didn't understand what he was trying to say and that he couldn't quite get it out better in order for her to understand him. "Cher, would I have kissed you if I didn't?" he said grabbing her arms and squeezing them.

Matt looked around realizing that he'd raised his voice a little louder than was intended. No-one was looking their way so he relaxed a little. "Matt! please don't yell at me, I'm confused enough as it is" she said gently pulling from his grasp. "I'm sorry Cher, I didn't mean to scare you, its just hard to say what I want to say . . . especially with all these people around . . . let's go someplace else." "Okay but where?" she asked looking around. "We'll go back to the bus . . . come on" he said taking her hand and running over the hill just in front of the building on the driver's side of the bus.

They crept around the back of the bus heading for the door side and could see Mr. Burke and the Bus driver sitting at a picnic table just over the hill. The two men where engaged in a deep conversation about something and didn't see Matt and Cher slip onto the bus. "Let's sit in the back so nobody will see us okay?" said Matt. "Okay"

"Whew! What a day" Matt said as they plopped down on the bench seat in the rear of the bus. Cheryl just nodded and smiled a little and was just glad she could have this time with him dangerous or not. They sat in silence a minute to catch their breath. "Okay Cher it's like this, I'm a passionate guy and once I love a woman I love only that woman you understand?" she nodded slowly. "Cher, when I first saw you months ago in gym class I thought you were the sexiest thing I'd ever seen on two legs, you really moved me baby." Hearing this made Cheryl blush and perk up some. "Did I really Matt?" "Hell yeah girl! You was hot! wearing that one piece spandex gym suit, the one with short legs and V-neck top . . . I wanted to run down there and get a good seat right across from you so I could look at your sexy ass all period."

Cheryl was really blushing now and couldn't help but smile even though she didn't want to just now. "And I thought you didn't notice me." "Oh yeah, I noticed you alright and when you started coming to some of my classes and sitting next to me each time, I just knew you were gonna be trouble!" She pouted and began to feel chase again, "why do you say that Matt?" "You didn't know did you?" "Know what?" "That when you would come in and sit down next to me, all I could do was stare at you, smell your sweet perfume and fantasize about you, I had to shake it quick though because I was already seeing somebody."

"I see." "But hey, that still didn't change what you made me feel over time about you . . . like I said you moved me." Cheryl felt a warmth begin to stir in her stomach and in spite of herself she smiled at him for saying so. Matt could see that what he was telling her had a bitter-sweet affect on her and she looked like a starving person who had just been given a death sentence but still glad for the plate of food that was their last meal. Matt was really considering should he just let her hover like that or show some compassion and reach out to her. Problem is, every time he did that it went bad and she got the wrong idea or took advantage of it.

But then again Matt was as guilty as she was cause he liked it himself when she did. "Oh, what the hell" he told himself. "I'm probably gonna burn in hell for all of this shit anyway so whatever." Matt slowly opened his arms and Cher without further coaxing came into them laying her head on his shoulder and sighed deep and long as if coming into a warm house out of the cold.

Matt sighed too but for a totally different set of reasons. He knew he shouldn't be allowing this or encouraging this but "God! this big girl felt good! and he loved every second of it." "You know Matt . . . you could still have me if you wanted" she whispered to him. "I mean we don't have to date or go out and stuff like that, but just do things . . . you know be close and stuff." Matt wasn't sure she was saying what he thought he was hearing and did a double take raising her from him.

"Do you mean to say the you would be happy with just a physical relationship?" Cheryl nodded yes. Matt didn't speak but just chewed this over in his mind while his eyes glided all over her full and generous breast, torso and down deep into the cleavage between her healthy sexy legs. Matt's penis grew hard . . . real hard . . . real fast! "WAIT! A minute, hold up" he said shaking off the lovely muse. "Do you know what your saying or what that means?" "Yes Matt, I do" she said flat and tonelessly. "In fact if you want to we can do it right here, right now" she said reaching for her blouse and beginning to unbutton the first button.

Matt was stunned and couldn't do much more than just stare as she moved in slow motion undoing the first button then the next. He couldn't grasp her logic or how anyone would be or could be so caught up into another person as to just let go of all morals and personal values and just resign to being a sex object to them. "Man! What it must be like to be a woman and feel that way, I don't get it!" No, Matt didn't get it at all, but what he was getting was an impressive ever growing hard-on that increased exponentially with each passing second. By now Cheryl had unfastened three buttons and was working on a third. Matt could clearly see her luscious full breast. They were threatening to burst from her lacy brassier and attack him. Cheryl never took her eyes off him. She figured that his lack of rejection or any attempts to stop her from undressing was him finally admitting to himself that he couldn't resist her anymore and had to have her as much as she wanted him . . . or so she thought.

Matt was however; captivated by her. Her long golden hair that playfully fell over her broad sensuous shoulders, her long tantalizing neck and butterscotch skin that would have been a vampires wet dream! Those delicate yet firm hands that he knew were soft when she had held his penis in her hand not long ago. Matt felt himself involuntarily jerk within his pants when he let his gaze fall to the lovely undiscovered depths between her full legs.

"DAMN! I wanna do this bitch bad!" his mind screamed at the thought of removing those panties. He was sure they would be either a thong or a G-string. They would reveal a most sensuous and full mound of the most inviting and irresistible hair in existence. Oh, how good it would feel to slowly part that forest and dive into the hot and wet depths that lay beneath. An unexpected gentle breeze worked it's way through the bus and across Matt's face chilling the sweat that had begun to form on his brow and bringing him back to reality.

"No! what are you doing Cher?" he said reaching out grabbing her hands and closing her blouse. "Sigh . . . But I thought you wanted me Matt?" she said feeling defeated yet again and feeling foolish once more for allowing herself to lose control and Matt to embarrass her again. "No! Cher, not like this!

Oh god please you shouldn't feel this way about me" he said doing his best to think of disgusting thoughts anything that would help his hard-on go away. "But Matt, I do and I can except it . . . why can't you?" "Because I can't alright?" he said clumsily and quickly trying to button up her blouse again. For a second Cheryl found amusement in this game of sexual dodge ball. She didn't stop him only sighed long and sat there sweetly with a little smile on her face and looking at him sidelong as if to say, "Matt you're a tough nut to crack and you do play hard to get but I know eventually I will have you mister . . . oh yes I will have you!"

Cher just sat quietly with her hands in her lap all the while offering herself unselfishly and completely to him without the slightest reservation. Matt's hands were shaky and he tried not to touch her breasts while buttoning her up, but she found his attempt at morality amusing and just leaned into him more and more as he tried to keep her at arms length. Her breasts were hot and very soft like large oversized yeast rolls fresh from the oven. "Cher! Behave dammit!" "Can't you see I'm trying to be a gentleman about this?" "And don't forget that

I'm only a man and can only take so much okay?" Cheryl just gave him a most cat-like smile and commented, "Oh yes . . . you definitely are a man Matt" she said looking at his crotch and visibly raising her eyebrows. "Oh you're just full of trouble ain't you Cher?" said Matt punching his leg to further decrease the motivation and growth of his penis but finding it hard to do being her crotch was still in front of him.

Cheryl just giggled at him and gave him a seductive pout. "Aw Matt, does it hurt much?" "You really shouldn't be so shy . . . are you shy? Here let me see if I can make it better" she said reaching for his crotch. "No! I'm not shy" he said batting her hand away. "I'm just not going to let you turn me into someone or something I'm not that's all!" "And what would that be . . . a man?" she taunted raising an eyebrow and crossing her legs for effect. "No a dog! That's what!" This made her laugh out loud and she covered her mouth trying not to be rude or making him feel insulted. Cheryl readjusted herself and finished dressing herself so as not to entice him anymore than he was.

"Cher you gotta know something babe, I respect you and I like you too, but don't do this, you're better than that!" "Look at you! You're beautiful, sexy, intelligent, and funny, hell you make me wish I was a dog, and to be perfectly honest with you, your beginning to get to me okay?" "Oh? How's that Matt?" she said faking innocence. "Oh, stop playing, you know what I'm talking about, let's just say it's hot in here and I need a cold shower." Cheryl lowered her gaze to Matt's crotch and a lusty smile crossed her lips. "Ooh Matt, why you're a real stud aren't you?" "No! just a little more aroused than I want to be right now." "Is there another time that you're more inclined to be aroused Matt?" she said coyly. "No! Cher there isn't, do you see that you have to stop this foolishness and forget about me in that way?" "No, I don't" she said tonelessly. Matt just shook his head and couldn't help but smile at her because of her audacious mind and refusal to agree to what he knew was the right way to be.

On the other hand Cheryl had it in her mind that he had a huge catfish on the hook and wasn't about to give it up without a fight! She looked at him with confidence and didn't speak but just smiled sweetly like she had done nothing wrong. Cheryl eased closer to him like a snake moving up on an unsuspecting rat in a bush. "And what will I get in return if I accept these terms?" "What do you mean get?" "You get to keep your virginity for one thing! . . . hell I don't know what, do you want? All I can offer is my friendship and support."

"Nah ah . . . not good enough" she said shaking her head and leaning against Matt pinning him against the window with her full torso on him. Matt could feel her heart beat and her warm soft breasts penetrating his shirt. "Then what do you want?" he said knowing full well what she was gonna say but felt he needed affirmation anyway. "I WANT YOU! YOU SEXY BASTARD THAT'S WHAT" she said then grabbed his shoulders and putting her full weight on him pinning him helplessly to the seat.

Matt couldn't move fast enough to dodge her and then again didn't expect her to be so aggressive. But then again she was from Texas and a ranch girl who was used to roping and wrestling calves. Matt wiggled and tried to be polite and lift her off of him but she had long since mastered the art of keeping down what she had caught. Cheryl had his arms pinned with her knees and her hands on his shoulders. Matt tried to move but could not. Cheryl was really enjoying this game now and the aggressive woman she really was had now begun to show it's head. "Okay Cher you got me . . . now let me up" Matt asked politely as he grunted under her weight. "No, not really but I will" she countered then attacked him with a blazing hot kiss full on his mouth. She stretched out and lay completely on him now and was grinding her hips into him as she devoured his lips.

"Aw shit! Here we go again" said Matt in his mind not able to speak and honestly getting closer to not wanting to. Matt could feel her crotch grinding away on his leg all hot an steamy as she adjusted herself to get in the best position to show her full intention and molest Matt into submission. Matt resisted where he could but was stuck in between a wall, a seat and hot blonde who wouldn't quit. "Damn! this girl is strong and she wants sex! And I mean now!" Matt managed to raise her up by the arms just enough to break her lip lock on him. "Cher really barking up the wrong tree girl" he said getting more tired by the moment and fighting the urge to let the dogs loose. He was getting more and more aroused by the moment. "Oh yeah Matt?" she said forcing herself back down on him thoroughly mashing her large breasts into him. Now her kiss was really fierce and her tongue probed deep into Matt's mouth like an oil drill almost choking him.

Matt had to admit that this felt damn good but was also bitter sweet as images of Retta kept dancing in and out of his mind. Matt was determined not to have anything to do with her and could probably do a better job at dismissing her but at the cost of being really cruel and mean to her. This is something he could not bring himself to do to her or anyone and she knew it and exploited it. Just when Matt thought it could get no raunchier he felt her hand work its way between them and jam itself down into his pants. "Damn! I should have worn jeans instead of kaki's." The semi loose material offered little resistance as Cheryl's delicate but powerful hand probed and found its target.

Matt squirmed and tried to pull it loose but her grip was doing a two fold job on him. It was definitely keeping him from pulling at her not wanting to castrate himself and also the shear warmth and feel of her hand around his penis was just the bomb! Every movement and twitch was retranslated into pleasure over and over again and she knew it because it grew in her hand with exceeding speed and excitement! Now feeling him grow in her hand Cheryl began sucking and biting his neck.

"Oh shit! Oh . . . shit! Cher you can't do this to me girl . . . your fucking up huge now!" "Oh yeah?" she taunted but never released her teeth from his neck.

She sucked harder and moaned even more. Her hips ground into him fiercely daring him to respond in kind. "So do something about studly" she breathed in his ear then went back to work on him. "Oh fuck! I don't believe this shit is happening" Matt protested doing his best to fight her and his own lust off but losing badly. "You're right sweetie I don't believe it either, I should have had you stripped by now but you're a lively one aren't you?" she taunted him further then increased her efforts by using her knee to pry his legs open further and get a better grip on his penis.

Matt struggled like a mouse in the grip of an alley cat's teeth. All he could think about was Retta, the shame he was going to subject himself to if he didn't get her off him soon and how much he wished that this was her on top of him instead. In Matt's heart he really did want to fuck the shit out of Cheryl but the knew it wouldn't be worth the backlash to follow. Then all of a sudden it came to him, "Hey stupid it was your charm that got you into this why not use it to get you out since your strength and moral won't help, Yeah that's it!" he thought now remembering Ant's advice.

"Hey Cher, hold up! Baby." "Nah ah, I got you where I want you now mister" she said getting his pants open and proceeding to jerk him off. "No really! I won't fight you baby, you got me real hot now and I'm just dying to get at this body of yours now" he said as convincingly as he could. "I don't believe you Matt, you're too sneaky and you've pulled that on me twice today, you're not getting away from me a third!" "I'm serious!" Matt protested grinding into her for emphasis and to be more convincing. It must have had some affect because Cheryl started slowing her movements and slowly loosened her grip on his penis but not pulling her hand away as yet.

She slowly raised her self up and looked down at him. Her hair was all tousled around her face and her chest was heaving from the effort. She looked at him with piercing and intense eyes that looked like a scene from the "Perfect Storm." "Do you really mean it this time Matt?" she said cautiously. Matt knew he had her now and went in for the kill. He didn't answer her in words but just let a really lustful smirk cross his lips. He then reached around her and grabbed half of her ass making sure he dug his fingers as deep between the crack of her ass as he could get then raised his hips to grind into her most aggressively. Cheryl sucked in hard at the feel of his hand in her ass and the added pressure from between her legs as he drove himself into her. It was so unexpected and exquisite her head snapped back and she swooned as she returned the grind back to him. Her chest flew out bold and strong and she rode him like a mechanical bull slowly and purposefully. Matt let this go on for a minute more to convince her of his intent and to trick her into believing there would be more if she but got off of him. "Sss oh, yes Matt" she said grinding harder and harder.

"Come on baby lets do this right" he said giving one of her breasts a vicious squeeze. Cheryl sucked in hard and squealed at the action with pleasure. "Okay

Matt okay" she said slowly removing her hand and getting off of him. She looked weak with desire and lust Matt thought and he wasn't too far away from sexual stupidity himself so he'd better move on this plan quick. At first he thought now that she is off of me I can just blow by her and get off the bus. But then again he thought better and figured no I better make sure she can't stop me or run after me. Cheryl saw the pause in Matt's face and set herself to jump back on top of him. "Matt . . . your telling the truth right . . . your not kidding me again are you?" she said beginning to unbutton her pants, zipping down her fly. "Naw girl!" "So why are you hesitating then?" "I'm just waiting on you to move and let me get up, Oh and I want to get on top too" he finished lying easily. "But Matt I want to get on top!" she protested pushing him back onto the bench seat and looking distraught like she would die if she couldn't be.

"Come on now . . . let me get it the way I want it now, I wanna hold that sweet round ass in may hands and drive deep into your sweet spot" he said making fuck motions with his hips and hands. This action stirred Cheryl something terrible and set her hormones wild! "Oh Matt you are an animal!" she said. Her eyes growing wide becoming truly motivated. She took a quick look around the windows to see if anyone was near or could see them, then jerked her pants and panties down to her ankles in one brisk shot!. "Oh shit!" said Matt completely flabbergasted at the sight of the thick and straight mound of golden hair that stood out to greet him. It was well coifed and covered an even more impressive plump and wet pussy. It was only inches from Matt's face and he could smell her essence and oh how sweet it was.

He noticed that her lips were quite swollen and pink with a light sheen of moistness working it's way from between them. He couldn't believe he had been doing his damndest to avoid this world class coochie! For a good minute, he had forgotten what he was going to do and his penis was quickly telling him what he should do! "Oh hell . . . I don't know if I can go through with this now" he said to himself still staring at Cheryl's ample display of womanhood. Cheryl noticed Matt's dumbfounded look and was inspired and felt well complimented on one of her best assets. It made her even hornier and she began to toy with the idea of him burying his face into it and using his mouth.

The thought made her tingle all over, but the desire to feel that shaft of his that she had been playing with was even greater and she wasn't going to blow that experience on a muff dive. "Get up silly!" she chirped jumping up and down a little to get his attention. She couldn't wait and wanted him now! "Don't make me wait Matt, I want it now!" she complained with a pouty mouth that made Matt's penis feel as if it had just grown 6ft.

Matt eased up off the bench. He moved slightly to the side and Cheryl quickly hoped on the bench on her knees to take his place. She got down on all fours jutting her ass out and up to him, exposing a most lustful and motivating sight! Cheryl wriggled her ass teasing Matt and exposing a hungry, wet and hairy taco that begged to be stuck!. Matt began to seriously wonder if he could resist her at this point. He was hungry for her and that pussy looked good! "Come on baby don't make me wait, get those pants off, I want you now!" she begged. "I want to feel that chocolate python deep inside me Matt" she teased further. "OH SHIT!"

Matt's mind screamed for the hundredth time. He saw himself in a fog slowly zipping down his pants as he moved closer and closer to Cheryl's awaiting ass. "Oh god oh god oh god" he kept saying over and over in his head as his hands reached for his pecker and bringing it out. Every thing was moving like a three way collision between a plane, a train and a diesel truck. The noise in his head was so deafening it was like a jumbo jet landing right next to him. He wanted to fuck Cheryl bad, really bad! And he was beginning to lose the battle with himself when just then a subtle but cool breeze came down the isle of the bus and cooled his sweaty forehead and throbbing tool just enough to get out of the fog.

Matt stopped just before pulling himself out of his shorts completely and was already touching Cheryl's ass with one hand preparing to mount her. He backed up on his heels or fell back on them and looked at Cheryl who was also aware of his return to sanity because he had not entered her as yet and should have long ago. She turned her head to look at him much like a cow when it's about to be milked.

"Matt?" she said in a distant voice. "What are you thinking? . . . why haven't you taken me yet?" she looked at him with passionate eyes that went from passion and lust to blazing and hell fire. Matt gave her a sheepish grin, leaned over and kissed her lightly on the top of her ass. She moaned with pleasure but still did not like what she felt was happening, yet for the third time. Her look quickly turned to one of horror as she saw Matt quickly pull up his pants and run down the isle and out the door shouting, "Sorry Cher, see ya next lifetime!" Cheryl was livid, "Mathis! I'll get you for this, just you wait!" she shouted pulling up her clothes and fixing her appearance.

Matt just ran all the way down the dirt road heading for where he thought Ant would be. "Damn! that was close" Matt muttered as he ran and trying to get himself together so no one could tell what he had been up to.

"Hey Matt, where you been man?" asked Ant coming over down the road to meet him. "Don't' ask man . . . don't ask" Ant quickly looked him over and saw how his clothes weren't quite the way they looked before he disappeared. Add that to the fact that Cheryl wasn't anywhere to be seen either and you could guess the rest. Ant burst out laughing when the revelation hit him. "You sneaky sonovabitch!"

Fifth period was about to end and Aretta was sitting quietly musing and rubbing her sore and bruised butt. "Damn! Mrs. Walker didn't have to hit me so hard!" Mrs. Walker was the assistant principal. She had called Aretta to the office after fourth period to discuss the fight that took place earlier that morning. It was later proven that she didn't have anything to do with starting the fight she still got five licks with the paddle for fighting anyway. The boys she fought of course got much worse. They each got 10 licks and three days suspension.

Retta was still wondering if she didn't go to far with Camille in gym class, though then decided "Nah! I got her ass good. That heifer has been at me all year and last year too in the ninth grade. I'm just sorry I took so long in getting even with that bitch!" "PSST! Retta" hissed a girl from behind her. "What?" "I heard about what happened to Camille in gym class." "Yeah, what about it?" "I wish it was me that did it that's all . . . way to go girl" she said patting her on the shoulder. Retta's behind felt a little better now and she felt a sense of pride like she had struck a blow for all who had suffered under Camille's hand's.

Soon the bell rang and she was heading for the door. Alfrieda was waiting for her as she came out. "Wus up girlfriend?" she said slapping her on the arm. "Ow! Freida, that's my sore arm!" "Oh, I'm sorry I didn't know." "Yeah, you know that's where that damn stupid boy stomped on it." "Excuuuse me then! I didn't mean to!" "Its alright it feels much better now than it did awhile ago." "Girl, you should hear the stories going around school!" "Oh like what?" "Like you, that's what!"

"Did you know that every girl who ever did something to you or ever thought about it has quickly changed they mind?" "Oh yeah?" "Yeah! Girl!" "Well that's good to know, now I won't have to worry about them trying to get revenge on me." "Naw, I don't think that's gonna be a problem." "What about Camille?" "What about her?" "Well you know she has three brothers" said Frieda with a definite note of concern in her voice. "So! I'm not worried." "Girl, I would be, you know they don't live far from us."

"So, you know how she is, she'll be too embarrassed to tell anyone what I did, and then again who would believe that lying cow anyway?" "Yeah, I guess your right, so where are you this period?" "Nowhere, this is my free period." "Oh yeah I forgot, I wish I could get that." "Well stop fooling around in class and do your work, then maybe you can get honor roll too." "Ha ha ha, very funny smart ass, you know I do my work." "Yeah, but obviously not good enough or you wouldn't have got held back in the ninth grade." "Oh no I didn't!" Frieda protested. "I went to summer school and got mine!" "Yeah but you shouldn't have had to." "What ever . . . Retta" she said waving her off.

"Well I gotta go girl, I got band practice this period." "Alright then, I'll see you later" said Retta heading for her locker to get her stuff. The hall was mostly empty now and she was glad. Retta had grown tired of the stares and snide remarks from just about everyone she passed not to mention people bumping against her sore arm. Retta turned the combination quickly and as she opened the locker an envelope fell out on her shoe. She put away her books and reached down to pick it up.

"That's funny . . . this wasn't in there last period." She noticed that the envelope didn't have any name on it, she did notice that the message scribbled on the back said, "For You Bitch!" in red block letters. She opened it slowly and took out the note. "You may have gotten the best of me this time you little yellow bitch but next time, and you won't know when or where, but when I see you I'm going to hurt you bad, so don't get too comfortable, and you better watch your back cause I'm gonna fuck you up!" Retta let the note fall from her fingers and she clutched her mouth to subdue a frightened sob that leaped suddenly to her throat.

"Who could have wrote it?" she wondered. "Them guys or was it Camille? what should I do about it? Do I take it to the principle? . . . Naw cause then they'll think I'm afraid and that won't change anything." "But I am afraid!" she sobbed into her hand. "Oh god why me!" Just then a hand touched her shoulder. Retta screamed loud enough to break glass and spun around frightened out of her wits! "Hey are you alright? I'm sorry I startled you" it was one of her teachers.

Seeing there was no threat Retta began to relax and calm down from her sudden shock. "Mr. Simpkins?" she whispered placing her hands over her heart. "I'm sorry Retta, I didn't mean to scare you sweetie, are you alright you look pale as a ghost?" "Here, come into my classroom and sit down a minute." He closed her locker and took her gently by the arm. As he began to walk her into the classroom he noticed the note on the floor.

"Is this yours?" he said picking it up. "Yes sir" she said quickly taking it from him. "You really are shaken, look at you your trembling." He took Retta into the class room and closed the door. This was her home room teacher. Mr. Simpkins was a tall, athletic, casually dressed black man with short curly hair and a nicely trimmed beard. He was very gentle Retta noticed and he always smiled. Retta thought he was quite handsome for his age and from time to time had played many mind games with herself about him and her in less than academic accommodations. Most of the other girls in class like him too and kept after him every chance they got. He sat her down in his big soft high back chair and grabbed a stool for himself.

"Now tell me honey what's wrong?" Retta didn't know if she should talk about it or not but then again thought better of it because it was Mr. Simpkins. He would understand and want to help so she sheepishly handed him the note. He took it slowly and giving her a smile of thanks, he began reading it to himself and Retta could see from his furrowed brow that he didn't like what he saw as much as she did. She sat quietly until he finished. Soon he was done, he slowly and methodically folded it and put it back into the envelope and gave it back to Retta. "Any idea who wrote it?" he asked her. "No sir . . . not exactly." "Any idea why they wrote it?" She didn't answer right away but just looked at her feet. "Look Retta I can't help you if I don't know what's going on sweetie."

Retta began teasing a lose thread on her skirt and mulling over how much she should tell him. "Here let me make it easy for you okay?" he said tossing her a bone to make it easier for her to talk. "I know about the fight this morning with those three boys and I must say I've never heard of anyone working over three boys their size at the same time in my life! and certainly not a young lady of your size" he said smiling at her and making her blush. "I didn't know I had a Ninja in my class" he said smiling trying to get her to relax.

"Look Retta, I can understand your fear, those boys are quite large and a little dangerous as well, I honestly doubt that either one of them will be able to live down the whipping you gave them today." "It's also very likely they may want to come after you for it for some get back." This made Retta fidget in her seat. She was sure he was only trying to be honest but knowing this didn't make her feel any better.

"But hey, don't sweat it none, myself and a few other teachers are aware of this and will be keeping an eye on them so you can relax, okay, unless there is something else you want to tell me" he prodded. Retta thought for a minute whether she should tell him and what could he do after she left school. "He won't be able to protect me all the time, I guess I'll just have to figure a way to find out who it is that wrote the note so I don't get blind sided" she said to herself. "No Mr. Simpkins, that's all I have to talk about, I'll be alright, it just caught me by surprise that's all, but I'm alright now." "Okay then if your sure." "Yes sir I'm sure."

"Don't be afraid to come to me and tell me if anything is wrong okay?" "You'd be surprised at just how much we teachers know and can find out about . . . okay?" "Okay" she said getting up to leave. She gave him a light peck on the cheek and a hug. "Thanks Mr. Simpkins, I'll see you tomorrow." "Alright honey you have a nice day okay?"

She just waved and nodded back to him. "Oh and by the way, tell Rodney I said hello." She froze in her step then turned to look at him. He just stood with his finger to his temple and his eyebrows arched with a smile on his face. "Damn! how did he know who I was seeing and what his name is . . . he don't even go to school here, I guess he was right, teachers do seem to know what's going on" she mumbled then headed down the hall to her locker to get her stuff then down and out the door.

Chapter 6

Weekend Madness

The warm sun and fresh air felt great on her chilled skin. The air conditioning in the school could be murder sometimes. Most of the time she wore a light sweater but didn't bring one today. Retta sat down on the brick wall outside the building near the bus stop. There were other students already there from the senior building on the hill. She found herself looking around at the other teens trying to see if any of the guys she had fought with were around waiting for her, none were.

Soon the bell rang ending her short solitude. It was quickly replaced with shouts and screams of hundreds of kids running wildly all over the place hopping and yelling, glad to be getting out. From her perch she could see everyone as they came out of the building, which was just how she wanted it. She saw Frieda rushing out of the building looking around for her. "Hey! Frieda" she yelled waving her arms. Frieda saw her and ran to her.

"Hey girl what's up?" "Hey yourself." "So how long you been out here?" "Not too long, I just came out here a little while ago." "Oh, so what you gonna do when you get home?" "Girl, I don't know I may go swimming, then again I may just take a nap."

"Doesn't Rodney live close by?" "NO girl he lives on Vineville Avenue across town." "Oh yeah, that's right, well why don't you go over there?" "I'd like to but you know I have to take care of Lori till mom gets home." "She could stay with me for awhile?" "Nah that's okay, mom don't like me to leave her . . . you know how she eats everything she sees."

"Yes honey! I remember one time she was over my house and asked for a piece of cake, I told her to help herself and do you know what that little butterball did?" "Naw." "She ate all but two pieces of a ten inch double layer cake!" "Ooh that greedy little monster! No wonder she didn't want to eat that time when she came home, she told momma she didn't feel good." "I'll bet she didn't!" Suddenly Frieda's eyes grew wide as hubcaps. "OOH! Chile, where did you get that ring! It's the bomb!" Retta blushed and felt herself swell with pride. "Oh this thing, you like it do you?" she said raising her hand for her to see.

"Yeah girl, is it real?" "Of course it's real!" "I betchu it ain't" said Frieda falling back on her hip and crossing her arms in a most defiant stance. Retta was about to jump on her friend when she implied that Matt's ring was a cheap fake. "I'm telling you it is!" "Then prove it!" "Okay smart ass, how?" "I don't know it's your ring" she said waggling her hand and empty ring finger for emphasis. "I know we can go ask Mrs. Fletcher in Chemistry." "Yeah, she always has on all kinds of gold rings and stuff, she'll know if it's real or not." "Yeah, come on lets go!" said Retta jumping off her perch and running towards the building with Frieda in tow. They ran through and around the crowds and back into the building. Mrs. Fletcher was still in her room packing to leave for the day.

She was one of the many Science or Chemistry teachers in school, but everyone knew her because she was kind of eccentric and funny. She like to wear lofty outfits from the 60's and 70's. Scarves around her head, psychedelic shirts and pants with really cool belts. The biggest thing people remembered was all the jewelry she like to where. Most teachers never wore more than a necklace or a bracelet or two.

Mrs. Fletcher wore rings on all her fingers and at least four gold chains around her neck with a half dozen bracelets made of Onyx, Jade and Topaz. When asked why she wore so much, she just said she was wearing her retirement early. Soon the girls rounded the corner and ran down the hall toward the science wing.

The door was still open so Mrs. Fletcher was still in. "Mrs. Fletcher! Mrs. Fletcher!" They shouted as they entered the room out of breath. "My goodness, is everything alright?" "Yes ma'am, we just wanted to ask you about some jewelry!" "Oh, is that all?" "Okay where is the trinket?" Retta jutted her hand up into the teachers face so fast she almost teetered backwards. "My goodness child you are eager to know aren't you?"

Retta smiled huge and nodded like a bubble head figurine in someone's rear window of their car. "Could you tell us if it's real or not?" "My what a lovely ring, I believe I can do that for you . . . would you take it off please?" "Oh no! I couldn't do that! My boyfriend put it on me . . . it wouldn't be right for me to take it off" she said retracting her hand most guardedly. "You want to see if it's a real diamond don't you?" said Frieda nudging her forward. "Yeah but . . ." "No buts, just take it off okay?"

Retta reluctantly took off the ring and gave it to her teacher. Her hand immediately began to feel naked and cold like it was a winter chill. "First we'll give it a laser scan and check if for carbon content" she said placing the ring in one of her ore sampling machines. The lights went on and the machine went to work. In about a minute or so a sheet of paper came out and Mrs. Fletcher read it. "Well it has a very high pure concentration of carbon atoms, that's good because real diamonds are compressed over thousands of years and put under great pressure to turn a carbon or a lump of coal into a diamond." "So that's good right?" said Retta feeling her stomach flutter with nervousness.

"Yes dear it is very good, but were not done yet, we still need to put it under a microscope and check it for it's "S" rating if it has one." "S" rating?" they both chimed. "Yes girls, an "S" rating is what is put on a diamond to establish it's purity, brilliance and cut." She took the ring from the machine and put it under the lens of a really fancy and powerful microscope. "Mmm . . . Hm . . . . mmm . . . hmm" she said wordlessly as she adjusted the lens. "What is it? what is it?" chirped Retta wringing her hand's like an expectant father. "What does it say?"

Mrs. Fletcher slowly pulled back from the microscope and held it up to the light. The ring twinkled like a star. "Well my dear after careful analysis I must conclude that your ring is . . . she paused for effect "WHAT, WHAT, WHAT IS IT!" said Retta jumping up and down about to blow a gasket. "The real McCoy, you have a ring that has a brilliance I would say around S1 or 2 which is really good and is damn near flawless from what the ore analyzer says."

"It's real?" said Retta sounding as if she didn't believe it herself. "Yes my dear, and probably around tow karats at a cost of $500 to $1000 dollars at today's prices, here you go" she said handing it back to her. Retta looked at the ring with renewed vigor and affection. She really did believe that Matt had gotten her a nice ring but the more she looked at it in private the more she entertained the thought of it being maybe a cubic Zirconium or something.

Not that it wouldn't have been nice too, but the fact that he did get her a real diamond ring and not a cheap one made her love for him sore! "Wow!" said Frieda with renewed respect for her friend's good fortune and her man for not being a cheapskate. "You have a special young man there Ms. Davis, he's definitely a keeper." "I think so too!" "Well let's go girl before we miss the bus." "Oh yeah I almost forgot, thank you Mrs. Fletcher!" they said running for the door. "Anytime girls, have a good day."

Retta and Frieda ran like they were going through hell with gasoline underwear on. They were deep into the bowels of the school and the buses had already began to depart. "Oh no the buses are leaving!" said Frieda. "Has ours gone yet?" "I don't know" she said starting to pout. "No there it is! Let's go" she said taking off in a sprint. The driver saw them coming and decided to have some fun with them. He slowed till they got near the door then hit the gas pulling away and leaving them to run after him. Everyone on the bus thought it was a hoot and picked at the girls as they ran to catch up.

"Hey wait!" said Retta huffing an puffing from the effort. "Now you see this fool?" "Yeah I see him, he think he being funny." Suddenly the bus stopped and the door flew open. "Come on Retta before he decides to pull off again." Frieda was a little ticked off now and decided she would give the driver a piece of her mind. "Hey you! let me tell you something!" She said climbing the stairs and trying to get her book bag, purse and gym bag in order. The driver was looking away from her just now at the other bus traffic that was going around him and Frieda hadn't looked at him yet. She got on the bus and slammed down her stuff in the nearest seat then turned to deal with the driver again.

"And what did you want to tell me little girl?" he said turning around, smiling and holding a little red box with a ribbon on it. Frieda's eyes popped! Her mouth flew open wide. "Oh my goodness!" The double shock of getting a present and it coming from her friend Curt made her lock up like an over-heated truck engine. "You be sure to give him a peace of my mind too . . ." said Retta finally getting on the bus and stopping at the bottom step when she saw who and what was going on. "Hey brown sugar . . . hello Retta" he said to Frieda then quickly acknowledging Retta. "I got you something." "Oh thank you Curt, but really you didn't have to" she said timidly reaching for the gift and blushing to beat all.

Ooh's and Ahh's could be heard all over the bus as the other girls put in their two cents about the little hallmark moment. "It's no problem, I wanted to, why don't you guys take a seat and we'll get going okay?" Frieda and Retta sat down in the seat across from the driver. "So how was school ladies?" he asked trying to remove the awkwardness of the moment. "It was okay" said Freida taking the lead. "The same old faces, subjects, and bull crap." "Yeah I know what you mean, college life ain't much different, just more people and more work." "How are you getting along on your subjects?" asked Retta "Not too bad, I just finished some midterms." "How well do you think you did?" "Not bad, in Calculus, I'll get a "B" in Chemistry I'll get an "A" in Biology I'll get an "A" and in History I'll probably get an "A." "That's good!" said Retta impressed with his efforts.

Frieda didn't say anything but just sat back looking at her new boyfriend and the gift he gave her with great pleasure. "Is this your first or second year?" "It's my second." "What kind of degree are you working on?" "Well, I'm kind of caught up between a Business Major and a Political Science Major, not quite settled on either one yet so I'm just doing the pre-requisite courses for now until I do." "You can do that?" "Yeah, you can do that, people do that all the time." "I didn't know that, I thought you had to pick a major right from the beginning." "Naw not really, you can go to college for years and not have committed to a major, just so long as you keep your grade point average up and make your classes you're okay."

"So Freida, what are you doing later on today?" he asked breaking her from her hypnosis. "Oh, I don't know, I haven't planned anything except maybe some home work and just hanging out with Retta." "Hmm . . . well tell me, how would you like to come help me pick out some furniture for my apartment?" Freida's eyes grew at the concept and she looked at Retta smiling huge. "Don't look at me girl . . . he didn't ask me, he asked you!" "Well what should I do?" "I can't tell you that, it's not my decision, that's for you to figure out, my choosing days are over" she said waving her ring around happily. "It's really not that big of a deal, we're just going to do a little window shopping."

"If I find something you can help me decide if it's right for me that's all." "I know Curt, I just ain't never done stuff like that with a guy before . . . it's kinda personal you know." "Oh . . . so you can go to Atlanta with me over night but you can't help me shop for furniture?" Retta cocked her eyes and turned her head towards the window grinning. "Yeah I see your point" she said giggling. "So you'll go with me then?" "Yes I'll go."

"Good, I'll come pick you up at 5:30 okay?" "That'll be fine" she said meeting his eyes in the rearview mirror. Soon they had come to the first stop and over half the load got off. There were only ten kids left on the bus now including Aretta and Freida. They would all get off on the next stop.

"So Retta, how's Rodney these days?" "Oh, he's fine I guess, I saw him yesterday when him and his father came over for dinner." "Sounds like you guys were double dating." "Yeah, something like that, it was nice and we had a good time." "I'll bet, he seems like a pretty good guy." "The BEST!" she chirped off more proud than she could remember being. "Have you seen her ring yet Curt?" said Frieda backing up her best friend. "You mean that rock on her left hand?" he said smiling in the mirror.

"Yeah, I saw it as soon as she got on the bus." "You don't miss much do you Curt?" said Retta blushing that he had noticed. "No, not much . . . especially when the glare of the sun bounces off something like that, you can't help but notice it, may I see it?" Retta got up carefully and stepped into the isle. She was careful to hold on because the bus was still moving. Once she got close to his seat she waited for him to see her in his mirror then she reached her hand down to him over his shoulder for him to see it. "Man! That's quite an expensive and beautiful ring!" "Thank you" she said withdrawing her hand and blushing a bright red. "I don't know much about diamonds, but that one looks like it's at least two carats."

"It is!, that's just what Mrs. Fletcher our science teacher said today when she tested it" said Retta surprised. "Man he must really love you or have a lot of money to throw around." "No, he's not rich, just thrifty and financially conscious that's all." "That's good, especially since he's in the tenth grade, learning how to manage your money early in life makes you much more solvent and stable when you get older."

"Yeah, you got a fine young man there Retta . . . hang on to him!" Retta was glowing now and blushed for all she was worth. "Thank you Curt, I'll do just that, you can bet on it!" "Retta, you never did tell me why he bought you that ring . . . what's the story?" asked Freida being her classic nosey self again. "Does there have to be a reason?" she said starting to get defensive. "No, not really . . . but was there any special reason behind why he got it though?" "Yeah, you could say that there was Freida since you asked, why don't you take a closer look at it again and see if you can figure out it's true nature" she said crossing her legs confidently an extending out her hand once more. "Okay, I will."

Freida looked at the ring a little closer and a little longer. She tried to remember when and where she had seen a ring like this and then it came to her. She had seen a jewelry commercial on television the other day and the lady in the commercial was getting married. Freida opened her mouth like a sea bass and her eyes opened to the point Retta thought they were going to pop! "Oh Shit!" she whispered over and over again.

Retta just sat with a cat that ate the canary smile. "You mean to say that this is an engagement ring?" "You got it!" "Ooh girl when?" "After we graduate." "Does Audrey know?" "Nope, and I'm not going to tell her either, at least not yet anyway, and you better not let it out to anyone outside of us!" "Hey, I won't tell, you know me." "Yeah, I do know you, that's why I'm telling you to keep quiet, because I don't want anything to get in the way of our future plans understand?" "Yeah, sure, sure I won't snitch on you." "Good" she said sitting back in her seat. "Now that's a committed woman" said Curt. "Your damn right I am! He's mine and no-one else's." "I wish I could have a lady like you Retta."

Frieda was numb at the sound of what she thought was her man, say he wanted someone like Retta. She didn't know whether to get mad or what because they really haven't become a couple yet, just kickin it and going out. Frieda just sat back in her seat numb, confused and just stared out the window. "I guess he only wants me as a friend, Oh well I guess it was just too much to hope for, I should have known he wouldn't want some silly old tenth grader when he can have his pick of any girl in college."

"I guess I'll just have to accept it for what it is . . . just a friendship." "Okay, you guys here's you stop." Curt pulled the school bus to the curb and pulled the safety switch so the sign out side his window would open stopping any cars from passing him. "I'll see you at the house Frieda" said Retta jumping off the bus. "Okay Retta" said Freida still sitting and waiting for that last person to get off the bus before speaking to Curt.

"So Curt, when are we gonna go out again?" "Oh, I don't know it's kind of hard to prearrange my time with the semester closing out and all, but hey, we got this afternoon right?" "Yeah I guess" she said slowly letting her eyes drop to her lap. "Is anything wrong?" "No not really." "Then why do you look so depressed?" Frieda didn't answer right away but just mulled over her feeling and whether she was making a fool of herself. "Oh it's nothing" she lied quickly getting up to leave. "I'll see you at 5:30 okay Curt?" she said giving him a fake smile and jumping off the bus also. "Okay Frieda, see ya soon" he said then closed the door and headed on his way.

"I wonder why she was so depressed, I don't think I said anything wrong did I?" "Oh! I know what it is! . . . it was that stupid crack I made about wanting a good woman like Aretta, way to go asshole!."

"You just messed up any chance of starting something with her" he said pounding the steering wheel. "I've got to make it up to her some how." "Hey Lori! get the phone for me will you?" "Alrighty" she said running off to get it. Aretta was taking a hot bath with lots of bubbles. "Ahh" the water felt luxurious on her tired stressed out body. She brought in her little radio to keep her company and to help sooth her frazzled nerves. "It's nobody Retta they just hung up" she yelled from the kitchen. "Okay, good cause I didn't really feel like talking to anyone right now anyway."

"Do you need anything else Retta?" asked Lori poking her head in the door. "No Lori, not right now sweetie . . . thanks" she noticed that Lori was wearing the locket Matt gave her the other day. "So how do your friends at school like you gift from Matt?" "Oh they think it's the neatest thing they ever saw!" she gushed with pride. "The girls wonder who he is and they say they wish they could meet him." "Over my dead body!" she said proudly.

"Retta he is special isn't he?" Retta sat up and looked at her little sister with renewed appreciation. As far as she knew her little sister had never had anything to say about anyone unless it was involving food. And now to hear her speak so affectionately about him made her take notice. "Come here pumpkin" she said opening her arms and beaconing Lori to her. "Here sit down beside me, you really like Rodney?" Lori just nodded. "Is it because he gave you the locket?" "Goodness no!" she said giggling. "I like him anyway." "Oh? since when?" Lori lowered her head and looked at the locket in her tiny little hand. "Do you member when you first started seeing him?" "Yes."

"Do you remember about a month later when you two went riding on his new scooter that day?" "Yes." "Well, when you got back he took me around the block once while you went over to Frieda's house." "He also talks to me like I'm older an not a little kid, he treats me nice too and do you know what else?" "What?" she said quite taken that Matt had spent so much quality time with her in such a short time and wondering what other experiences her little sister has been introduced to. "He gave me a kiss on my cheek" she said blushing uncontrollably and giggling till she fell off the stool. "Oh did he? and why did he do that?" "Because one day when he was here, just before you went to get the mail you yelled at me and made me cry."

"When you were gone he sat me next to him and talked to me." "What did he say?" "I don't remember all of it but he said not to feel upset and mad with you because you didn't mean it and that you really love me, so I shouldn't feel bad because I'm special too." "I see" said Retta feeling quite guilty at her sisters report. She raised her chin to look into Lori's eyes. "Then he kissed me Retta" she said eyes all aglow and full of tears of happiness. "He did pumpkin?" Lori nodded and pointed to her forehead. "It made me feel all squishy and good inside and afraid too." Retta was somewhere between confusion and frustration. She knew her man was solid and wouldn't stoop to playing mind games with a child. She also knew he could be very deep and affectionate with people and he pulled out the stops when it came to expressing himself. That's one of the reason's she fell in love with him, there were no games in him and he was genuine. "Do you know why you felt that way?" "I didn't then, but when I got to thinking about it I did." "What did you come up with?"

"I got to thinking that the reason I felt that way was it was love Retta." "Love?" she said taken aback and holding back the desire to faint. "Yeah! Love I didn't know it till I saw you an him staring at each other last night at dinner, now I know that's what I feel when I see him and that's what I felt when he kissed me and I was scared but not now." "And that's what I feel when I see him now too!" she said brightening then she let her smile fade into a soft scowl as she dropped her head. "Retta is that wrong?" she said beginning to pout.

"No baby!" she said pulling her off the stool and close to her squeezing her soft little body like she was a doll. "He seems to have that effect on a lot of people sweetie." Lori nodded, her little head resting on Retta's shoulder. "It's okay to love him Lori, I'm glad you do, I was afraid he and you wouldn't get along but now I see that you and him have long since gotten past that." "Really, you not mad at me for liking him like you do?"

"No pumpkin I'm not" she said squeezing her till she grunted. "Retta . . . will you marry him so we can be with him all the time?" she said pulling back from her sisters wet embrace, looking down and playing with the bubbles on her chest. Retta couldn't believe what she was hearing. Her little sisters words hit her solid like a wall and right before her eyes she saw her little sister awareness and emotions graduate from that of a grade schooler to that of a younger woman like herself. "You'd really like that if we did?"

"Yes! oh yes, yes" she clapped happily, her little face shining like gold and glowing with a joy Retta had never seen in her before. "Well you know I have to talk to him first okay?" Lori nodded briskly. Retta already knew the answer to that but thought it better to divert the child or defer the truth for now so as not to give it away.

Audrey, her mother was yet another problem she had to worry about. "So until then Lori you must keep it a secret between us okay?" "Okay" she said giving her big sister a hug. "OOMPH! Lori you're squishing me to death sweetie." "I'm sorry, I'm just so happy that's all, I've never been this happy before." "Me either kiddo . . . me either, now why don't you go and play with your friend Quita for awhile so I can finish my bath." "Okay" she said then ran off. "Don't forget to lock the door Lori!" "Okey-dokey" she said then slammed the door behind her.

"My goodness Matt you have a charm don't you old boy, I'm gonna have to stay on my toes from now on or some cow is gonna try to rope you right out from under me." Retta settled back into her bath relishing the sweet warmth and silkiness of the water. "I wish Matt was here right now" she thought to herself softly caressing herself with the bar of soap. "But then again if he was here there would be water all over the place . . . Haa! Ha ha." After awhile the music and the bath had gotten to her and she dozed off.

Dreams and sweet oblivion began to wash over her and she saw herself in a mystical place with unicorns and fairies playing tag amongst a sea of daisies. It was now 4:30 in the afternoon and Matt and Ant were at Ants house. The boys had decided to hang out awhile and do some homework together.

"Hey Ant do you think we'll get an "A" for that bull frog you found?" "I don't know, we might, what about that snake you came across?" "Man I didn't even know it was there until I stepped on him!" "Your just lucky he wasn't poisonous or you would have been through dealing." "Yeah today was a wild day wasn't it?" "Yeah it was, did you see how nasty Cheryl was staring at you on the bus? What did you do to her?" "It was more like what I *didn't* do that's more like it." "What do you mean? . . . you dissed her?" "Worse than that, she tried to give it to me and I ran out on her." "No you didn't!" "With drawers down and ass ready!" "Aw man, I don't believe you walked out on that, and it was right in your face too!" "What did it look like?" he asked with lust gushing from his excited voice.

Matt went over to Ant's night stand and came back with a playboy magazine. Ant watched intently with baited breath as Matt flipped through the pages. "Like this one" he said pointing at a center fold. "Oh shit!" said Ant clutching his crotch. "You're a fool to walk away from a piece of ass like that!"

"Hey wait a minute rover, remember Aretta? short, fair skin, beautiful, my girl?" "Yeah, but damn Matt you were face to face or ass with this, had it all to yourself and you still didn't get it!" "Yep" "Man, you're a better man than I am" he said nodding. "No, not really, because I did want it and if I couldn't have gotten her off of me when I did, I would have just given in and beat the brakes off that ass!" Ant just rolled over and laughed at him till his stomach hurt." "So do you think she'll get over it?" asked Matt not really caring if she did. "Hey man I don't know, she looked mighty pissed to me, I think she'll want some pay back." "You serious?" "Hey, I would be if it was me."

"Yeah, I guess your right, but she don't seem to be the type to hold a grudge though." "Hey man, it's always the one you least expect who gets you in the back." "Well I won't sweat it or lose any sleep over her." "So how's tricks with Brenda?" "Not bad, she wants me to come over to her house after school tomorrow." "Oh yeah?" "You think she's up to something?" Like what?" "Like finally getting the signal from her brain to her butt to get in the mood for some sex! that's what!"

"Hell, I don't know, I done told you I ain't sweating her." "If she wants to fine, if not that's cool too cause I got better fish to fry." "I hear ya, what about Melanie?" "I'm not counting on her either, she's okay and all, but she still talks about you and gets mad at me for not telling her anything about you."

"Well why don't you just kick her to the curb then?" "Cause she still likes me and I think she might give me some play after awhile." "Well go for it then, just don't blow too much on it okay?" "Yeah I gotcha." "Yawwwn!" "Well I'm getting tired, so I'm gonna go ahead and break." "Alright Matt, I'll catch you later okay?" "Okay "B" take it easy" said Matt and headed out the door. Matt sluggishly went out the door and down the steps. He was too tired to ease his bike down the steps to the side walk but did it anyway cause it was the nearest way to the street. "Damn Ant, how come you guys don't have a normal yard instead of this castle on a hill" he mumbled to himself.

He stopped and thought for a moment whether or not he should go through the back yard or not with all the broken pottery, boards and other stuff that had been dragged out from under the house by his Ant's uncle just the other day. "Naw I'll just muscle it down." The bike bumped down the stairs slowly as he held the brakes tight. Once on the side walk he started her up, put on his helmet and zoomed away.

Matt took a few short cuts and side streets to avoid the evening traffic. Soon he'd gotten to his street and stomped on the gas to sprint the last 50 yards to the drive way. Matt noticed that his dads car was gone so figured he wasn't home yet. He pulled the moped into the back yard, parked against the house remembering to turn the bike around for tomorrow.

It felt good to get home and he couldn't wait to get into bed. The neighborhood was quiet as usual with only a faint hint of children's play going on. It was always at this noise level and Matt loved it. This was one of the main charms about living in the Vineville area. You could always hear yourself *think*, peace always reigned and no one ever seemed to have a problem, at least not to his knowledge.

The lock clicked easily as Matt turned the key. The house had a cryptic silence about it and made him feel a little apprehensive sometimes, especially in the evenings. Most of the old big southern houses were built well but had a creepy air about themselves when you were alone in them. Matt dragged himself to his room glad that he was about to crash.

He stopped by the phone in the den to turn on the answering machine so he wouldn't have to answer it. "There, now I'll get some peace and quiet." Matt's room had a gentle breeze going through it and the soft rich golden glow of the setting sun bathing the room. Matt loved his room and thought it was perfect and just right.

Matt dropped his books on the chair, popped in one of his special tapes into the radio and turned it on. The tape was called "Tunes to Snooze by." He made it sometime ago and just for that reason. It was composed of classical music by Mozart, Tchycofsky and a few other great composers.

He plopped down face first down on his bed and lay that way with his arms beneath him. The music did its job and as soon as 'Midnight Sonata' started to play, Matt drifted off into sleep, another time, another place with musical wings to carry him. "The Oboes, Clarinet's and Flutes lifted my soul from my tired body and floated me higher and higher until I could see my body lying peaceful below me. A flute floated slowly into the room with a passionate gentle movement.

I was caught up in the sounds and sights of the world of beauty and sky. The resonating urgent bellow of a base cello trundled in and took the place of the flute in a most arcane yet harmonic way. It felt like it was guiding me and the other instruments to another place. This went on forever it seemed until the end of the song then the next one took over to complete the journey and carry me on in its movements. Listening to classical was my inner most favorite thing to do when I was alone. It gave me such peace of mind and clarity that I sometimes marveled at my own awareness of life and the things around me.

Things always smelled different, felt different and gave me a sense of contentment. The music challenged me, enslaved me, daring me to move and break its magical hold on me. I love classical music and was glad Aretta did too. This was one of the things I loved about her. She was so peaceful and mild. She was a wonder and a pleasure to be around. As Matt dreamed and allowed his mind to float endlessly through time and space, he found himself going back to the days when he first met Retta and began to get serious.

It started as a fog and then began to clear. I was seeing myself and her sitting at the lunch table eating and talking. From what I could tell by the scene it would have to have been 1982, sometime in May and school was getting ready to end soon for the summer.

"So Retta have you got any plans for the prom?" "No Matt, I didn't really think about it to tell you the truth." "How come?" "Cause I've never gone to any of them before and never thought much about them." "I see." It was quite awhile before I spoke again. I was trying to let her know how I felt about her and how much I wanted to take her to the prom and be with her but I didn't know how. "Are you going?" she asked. "I'm not sure, I don't have a date yet."

"Yes you do silly!" she screamed in her mind wishing he could hear it without her having to say it. *"I'm right here Rodney, I want to go with you, be with you . . . oh why won't you ask me . . . or are you as afraid to ask as I am."*

Soon we had finished our lunch and got up to leave. "Do you want to go outside for awhile?" I asked not wanting her to go away. "Yeah . . . sure Matt" she said putting away her tray and walking out beside me. We walked through the lunch room and headed for the door. A short skinny girl Aretta knew named Marcie came up to us. "Are you too going together?" she chirped with all the curiosity and tact of a woodpecker on a tree.

The question scorched us both like a steam bath and dared us to answer. Retta and I looked down embarrassed (for what I don't know) and shared a warm blush. We slowly turned and looked at each other and grinned bashfully at each other. Neither one of us knew what to say. We each thought one of us knew what to say. We each thought about it and wanted it to be so but never had the courage to approach each other about it.

Marcie didn't budge an inch and just stood there with her hands clasped behind her, swiveled happily from side to side like a child awaiting an ice cream cone. She just waited quietly and patiently with a huge smile for an answer. Finally the tension became too thick and I just had to speak up, hoping I wasn't making a fool of myself. "Uhh . . . nno Marcie . . . we don't." "Why?" she persisted.

"Oh god I want to die" thought Retta turning a lava like crimson red and feeling sick. "Why now Marcie . . . and why here!" thought Retta trying to figure a way to diffuse the situation before the little busy body asked were we sleeping together. Soon we began to notice many eyes and ears had tuned into our direction it was like an E.F Hutton commercial. "We just don't" said Retta finding her voice and sounding more cool and confident than she actually felt.

"Hmm, what a shame" she said shrugging and walking between us on her way. "You two look good together!" she tossed back as an afterthought without turning around. Me and Retta couldn't move or speak for a moment but just stared after the little girl in the yellow sundress and the sea of faces that were still oriented on us.

I couldn't take the heat so I grabbed her arm and quickly got out of the kitchen! There was a chorus of OOH's and AAH's as we rushed out of the lunch room. I wasn't sure where I was going, I just knew I had to get us both out of there. Finally when we got outside I looked left then right then headed to the left behind the school near the gym.

There was nobody around except for an old janitor who was busy cleaning the inside of his car out. We laughed for a minute and then got silent again. We didn't know what to say but the situation screamed for something. Suddenly out of the blue our silence was broken and no further questions needed asking.

The old guy had turned on his radio as if on cue. There was a song by a group called "Sky" playing and the tune was called "It's real love." As the music played and the words came out, so also did our feelings and it was powerful!" I felt a painful yet sweet tension building inside me as I turned to face her. I couldn't hold back my feelings anymore, and I grabbed her around the shoulders and pulled her to me and just held on like the world was ending. It was the first time I had ever touched her really and the feeling was explosive.

I relished in how sweet and sublime her warm soft body felt against me and I couldn't help myself but hungered for her more and more. I just wanted to pull her inside my body and keep her there forever. The clean sunny way her hair smelled was like an intoxicating drug that I breathed in deeper and deeper every second she was there. The music and having her in my arms was killing me and I loved it. We didn't speak at all but just squeezed each other tighter and tighter.

"Oh Rodney, how I've wanted you to hold me for so long, you don't know how wonderful you feel to me!" Retta cried within her heart. "I want you Rodney, I've wanted you from the first day we met!" "Oh how I prayed that you felt the same way, can you feel my heart beating your name? tell me you do, oh please say it!" As the moments ticked by, I had become overwhelmed by her closeness and the exquisite feel of her body. I began to swoon and fade as my arms ached to hold her, feel her and bathe in her warmth. She was an angel in my arms and I would worship this moment forever. I was no longer afraid but overcome with passion for her. I felt the sudden urge to tell her something, to . . . to talk to her . . . something I didn't know what. This was so new to me! I didn't feel them come from my lips but much further down inside me.

They build with the force of a canon blast then leaped from my mouth. "Aretta . . . I . . . I love you Aretta . . . please be my lady" I heard myself say. My mouth was dry and sticky as I said this and no sooner had I said it, wished I could recall it for fear of being rejected. "Oh *Rodney!*" she whispered, then seized me around the neck pulling me to her suddenly and planted a hot passionate kiss on me! Her mouth was salty sweet with tears. The softness of her lips was like corn silk. We kissed hungrily and wantonly for what seemed an eternity.

Suddenly the music gained volume and strength. It was as if the singer was right next to us singing her heart out just for us. Retta whimpered and the sound and feel of it on me turned me ravenous with desire for her. We sought each other more and more ferverently with each passing second. We lavished in an uncontrolled fire of each other's embrace.

"Oh Rodney, I love you too, I've always loved you . . . yes! I want to be yours always my love." Soon we had expended all our strength and our passion it seemed. It felt as though the world had stopped and everyone and everything was motionless. In the distance we heard a person chuckling and it startled us both. For a brief moment we parted to see who or what had intruded into our world. We turned to see the old janitor looking at us with old tired red eyes and chewing on an even older looking cigar while he slowly buffed the hood of his car.

"It never fails" he said laughing and sputtering at the look on our faces. He laughed and coughed and spat out bits of his unlit cigar. "That spot over dere don't never fail to get a hold of ya'll youngun's."

Me and Retta just looked at each other perplexed not sure what the old man was talking about, then back to him. "Look ova ya heads youngun's" he said pointing up above us. At first we didn't see it then we backed away from the wall. "Oh yeah, now we see it" it was a hand painted message written in red spray paint. "Lovers Roost" it said with a heart under it. We grinned at each other and told the man thanks for showing it to us.

Soon the bell rang and we headed back inside. "You two behave yourselves now . . . ya hear" the old man said as we walked away. "We will" we promised as we went back inside the building. We had big smiles on our faces and a light in our eyes that wouldn't go away. We held hands as we walked and for some reason everyone began to stare at us in surprise like they had never seen anyone holding hands before.

We didn't care, we were in love and nothing else mattered. Just then little Marcie came bopping down the hall. She saw us and stopped dead in her tracks, looked us over for a second then shouted loud enough for all to hear. "Now that's more like it!" This stunned the entire crowd. People were looking at us funny. Some were smiling, some smirking and some frowning. We looked back in silence not sure whether to move through the crowd or just stand there. We were never the type to draw attention to ourselves and didn't mind it when we were unnoticed. This was a new experience and it felt strange.

I began to feel a odd boost of courage and daring creep up my spine and into my gut. It felt kind of naughty but good. I couldn't think of anything that would tell them how much contempt I had for their looks but wanted to do something. Suddenly it came to me. I quickly spun Aretta around to face me and her books hit the floor. She looked at me with wide eyed curiosity and surprise but didn't say anything. I smiled a confident smile at her as if to say "I got this babe, just hang on" then I scooped her up in my arms in a bear hug and gave her the most passionate kiss I could muster.

To my surprise she joined in and the hallway was filled with OOHS and AAHS. It sounded like a ghost convention or wind blowing through and old house. Soon after we broke from each other smiling bashfully at each other. I put her down slowly and picked up her books. I held her hand and turned to walk down the hall. For a brief second I stopped and turned back to the mob and just shouted, "now you got something to talk about!" I grabbed Retta close again giving her a light kiss on the lips "I'll see you after class okay?" "Okay Matt" she said, her face a glow and smiling.

As she went to her class she could hear other girls talking about her and us in general. "Ain't that the new boy from Central?" "Yeah girl, you didn't know?" "He is fine honey, I wouldn't mind getting me a taste of *that!* Charger girl" "Mmm-hmm" they went on ogling and doting all kind of lustful concepts into Retta's more than attentive ears. She didn't mind it so much but just smiled to herself and feeling ten feet tall.

"Cackle all you want "chicken heads" cause he's all mine now" she said evenly with much pride and confidence. "You go on girl" said an unseen voice behind her just before the bell rang.

The sound of the phone brought Matt out of his wonderful dream and pissed him off. He didn't get up but just lay there hating the interruption. Either way the nap was sweet and he felt good and refreshed. All of a sudden the ringing stopped and he heard a strange woman's voice and it was calling for him.

Matt listened intently and didn't move, soon the voice had stopped and he grumbled and rolled over to try and regain his deep sleep. "I wonder what Melanie wants, I hope she don't want to hang out or anything cause I ain't having it." Just then Matt heard his dads truck rumble down the drive way. He got up and wobbled over to the stereo and turned it off. The sun was down now and twilight was just setting in. "Damn! I didn't know I had slept so long." Matt headed for the den "Rodney!" called his dad. Matt quickly picked up the pace and sped to his dads room. "Yes sir?" "Oh there you are, I didn't see any signs of life and wondered if you were home." "Yes sir, I was in my room asleep, I got home from Ant's house awhile ago." "That's good then" he said taking off his heavy walking boots.

"So what did you guy's do today?" "Oh, we just hung out and did some studying on a research project for Science Class." "Is that right?" "Yes sir, we went on a field trip to Central City Park and collected some frogs and lizards and other stuff." "Well it sounds like you had an interesting day." "You don't know the half of it" he said mumbling under his breath trying not to smile as he thought about the antics of Cheryl on the bus.

"So whatcha got planned for this evening?" "Oh nothing . . . I still got some other home work to do and then I'm just gonna hang around home tonight." "Well that's good, its' been awhile since you hung around home with the old man" he said grinning at him. It kind of made Matt feel guilty so he quickly changed the subject. "Hey dad are you hungry?" "Yeah, I could stand a bite . . . whatcha got?"

"Well I thought I might cook some chicken and some vegetables and maybe some corn bread." "Sounds good, think you can do it?" "Yes sir, I can manage it." "Okay then, go to it hot shot." Matt turned on his heals and went into the kitchen. It felt hollow and dark as he fumbled on the wall for the light switch. The old switch made a loud click as he flipped it on. Going into the freezer, Matt picked out a quartered chicken. He took the bird to the sink and peeled away the packaging and noticed that it was as hard as stone. "Well maybe I can defrost it in the oven, that way it won't take so long to cook" he thought to himself as he pulled a large pan from he cabinet under the sink. He ran some water in it then put the chicken into it. He got the lid to it to cover it then put it in the oven.

"Mom said to defrost a frozen chicken in 20 minutes you have to set the heat on 350 degrees" once he'd finished with this he started getting the pots for the vegetables and the bread. Matt took out two can's of green peas and corn and a bag of rice. "This ought to do it, and with some left over for dads lunch tomorrow." Once Matt had gotten that on the stove he grabbed some jiffy corn bread mix and started mixing it up in a bowl. Once he'd finished with that he stuck it in the stove with the chicken.

He quickly checked it to see how it was doing. It had no more ice but was still cold and a little stiff. He took the opportunity to make some punch and put it in the refrigerator then went in his dad's room and picked up his dirty work clothes and took them to the laundry. Matt put out some bed clothes and went back to check on the chicken's progress. It felt good enough to work with so he took it out and put it in the sink to clean it.

The chicken smelled like it was trying to cook a little. "It's a good thing I took it out when I did." Before he ran the water over it, he took the juice from it and poured it in a cup to make a gravy from it later. It didn't take long to clean an prep it. In just a few minutes he had it on the stove sizzling and cooking well in the frying pan. Matt sat down at the table to read a comic book he had found on top of the refrigerator.

"Rodney!" "Sir?" "How's it coming?" "It's going okay I just put the chicken on the fire so it shouldn't be long." "Okay . . . hey, thanks for putting me out some clothes." "Your welcome." Matt sat back down to read when he heard the phone ring.

"Hello" "Hello, may I speak to Rodney please?" said a girls voice. His dad picked up on his end. "You got it Rodney?" "Yes sir" "Okay, click" "It's me!" "Who's this?" "Your buddy silly" she said pertly. "I've got a lot of biddies but I can't figure out which one you are." "Rodney you mean to say you've forgotten me already?" "I don't know, it depends on who you are?" "This is Melanie" she said sounding a little crushed.

"Oh, hi shorty! . . . what's up?" "Oh, nothing much just hanging around the house doing this and that." "Yeah me too, I'm just cooking a little dinner." "You cook?" "Yeah, doesn't everybody?" "No . . . at least none of the guys I've ever met, and only a few girls, so what are you cooking?" "Oh, just some fried chicken, rice and vegetables with some cornbread." "Sounds good! what time should I be there?" she said happily and putting him squarely on the spot.

"Oh, you caught me on the wrong day Mel, were going to have to take a rain check on that" he said sputtering and back paddling a little. "I'm just kidding, but that would be nice though if you really want to get together." Matt thought for a minute, biting his lip. "I don't know, let me think on it awhile." "Okay" she said sounding a little deflated that he didn't want to go out with her as much as she did him. "So whatcha been doing all day?" "Sleeping mostly." "Since when?" "Since about 4:30."

"Did you get my message?" "Message? What message? I haven't had time to play back the answering machine yet, so what's up?" "Nothing . . . I just thought I'd call and see if you would like some company that's all" she said sounding more deflated by the moment that she had called. "I don't know Mel, I got some home work to do and I'm gonna stay in tonight." "Oh I see . . . well . . ." "Hold on Mel, I gotta check my food" said Matt running to check on the food. It was done on one side so he flipped it and added butter to the vegetables and rice. Then took out the corn bread and sat it on the stove to cool.

"Okay Mel I'm back." "So what kind of homework do you have?" "Some Science, Algebra and Trig, what about you?" "I'm taking Algebra, Trig and Biology this quarter." "Pretty good . . . sounds like you got a load on your hands." "Yeah a little" she said with her voice trailing off as she thought about her work load for a minute. "Hey Rodney, I'm not doing so good in math do you think I could get you to give me some help . . . I could really use it?" she urged trying anything she could think of to get to see him. "I'll try if I can, but I'm no rocket scientist either" he said offering her a little hope, not thinking for a minute that she meant tonight. "Well how about I come over and bring my books then!"

"You mean tonight?" "Yeah!" "I don't know Mel, it just isn't a good night for me okay?" "Oh please? I really need the help, if I fail math this quarter I may have to do summer school, and I don't want that." Matt paused and sighed long looking up at the ceiling and messaging his head. "Come on Rodney, I promise I'll behave" she added hoping to spark his male sense of adventure.

"Ahh! Okay you can come" he said finally giving in rolling his eyes and hoping he wasn't going to regret it. "Great!" she said bouncing on her bed full of glee. "What time should I come?" "What time? You don't even know how to get here yet." "Oh yes I do smarty" she said defiantly and quite matter of fact. "Oh yeah, how's that?" "I made Anthony show me." "Oh you did . . . did you?" "Sure did" she said giggling openly now. "And just how did you manage that trick?" "Hasn't he told you anything yet?" "Told me what?" "About what I did to him." "No, I can't say he did." "Ooh that little clam shell!"

"WHAT? . . . what did you do to him?" stressed Matt more than curious now. "When you see him again take a look at his neck on the right side." "Ooh Mel, why you little perpetrator!" She was laughing now and quite happy with herself. "Hey when I want something I know many ways to get it!" "Is that so?" thought Matt reliving the Cheryl incident and wondering if he had another one on his hands. "You better believe it bucko . . . wanna try me?" "Oh heck no! that's alright, I'll take your word for it." "So what time Rodney?" "Let's say about 7:00 o'clock okay?" "That sounds great!" "Well I need to go Mel before this food burns."

"Alright Rodney, I'll see you soon." "Matt" "What was that Rodney?" "Matt, my friends call me Matt" he said correcting her. "Am I your friend Matt?" she said almost solemn. "It looks like your heading that way."

Melanie felt a warm flush over come her and she had to hug herself. She knew it was gonna be a fight of some sort to get closer to Matt based on what Ant had told her. But now having been brought closer by him made her job all the easier. "Okay Matt, I'll see you soon." "Bye." Matt hung up the phone and just stared at it for a moment shaking his head. "Well now! It seems that ole Ant has been holding out on his ole pardner."

"Who was that Rodney?" "A girl named Melanie, me and Ant met at the mall some time ago, she wants to come over so I can help her with her home work." "So you do have something planned after all?" "No sir, not really, she just wants me to help her on some school work." "Well that's nice, what's her name again?" "Melanie." "And what grade is she in?" "You know dad . . . I don't have the foggiest idea, but she works at Annabelle's in the mall, so I figure she's at least in the tenth or eleventh grade or about 17."

"Do you think you can help her?" "I don't know, her Math is in the same area as mine and I've passed her Science level so who knows." "So how does this fit in with your girl Aretta?" "It doesn't, I'm not getting involved with her or any other chick for that matter." "You sure about that?" His dad said giving him that all knowing all seeing grin as he lit his cigarette. "Yes sir, I'm sure, but to be honest with you she is after me I can feel it."

"So do you still think it's a good idea inviting her over?" "Yeah I'm sure, if I remember anything you taught me about women I should be alright, you said once that the best way to control a situation is to keep it close to you." "I guess you was listening to me after all weren't you?" "I always try." "Okay son . . . you handle it your way, is dinner ready?" "Yes sir it's done."

"Well lets go and get greasy." "Okay, you go and get a seat and I'll bring the plates." After dishing out the food they began to eat. "Pretty good son" said his dad biting into the chicken. "Thanks!" Matt had learned to cook from both his parents. "So how was work today?" "Oh, not too bad, my boss is putting me on another route to break in some new guy."

"That helps to make your load lighter doesn't it?" "Yes, a little, but what do you mean *help* . . . he's going to carry the mail not me!" "Oh I get it, your gonna make him your pack mule." "You bet your allowance I am!" "No thanks, I'd rather not, is this a city route or a rural one?" "City." "So dad how do you like Retta's mom?" he said changing the subject. "Oh she's alright I guess, maybe a little forward sometimes, but still nice enough." "Do you think you two will be hanging out more often then?" "It's hard to say, I'm always busy and you know I never have much time for socializing." "Yeah that's true." "Why do you ask?"

"No real reason I guess, me and Retta was just doing some talking and she had some concerns about you two getting seriously involved." "Well you can tell her to relax, I don't see that happening anytime soon." "You sure?" "Yeah I'm pretty sure" he said cleaning his mouth with his napkin. "That was good son, I may have to let you cook all the time." "Oh no, I couldn't take advantage of your generosity dad!"

"No son . . . by all means feel free to do as much as you like, in fact if you like you can clean the yard, the car, the gutters, and heck if you really feel up to it you can do the house on the inside too!" he said laughing at Matt. "You know dad, all of a sudden I feel a hernia and severe back pains coming on . . . OOP! There it is, I gotta go dad, See ya!" then off Matt ran out of the kitchen and down the hall into the den with his dad laughing behind him. It was great the way they got along and it was even better that he trusted Matt so well.

It really made Matt feel good and gave him a sense of pride. Not too many boys could say they're dad was their best friend but He could. Matt looked at his watch and saw that it was 6:30. "Man I better get busy on those dishes before Melanie gets here." His dad had gone to lay down awhile before settling in on his income tax paperwork he was doing for some people. It didn't take Matt long because there weren't many dishes to do. Once he'd had this done he made his dads lunch for tomorrow. "Now that's got it" he said tossing the dish cloth on the rack and turning off the kitchen light. Matt then headed to the bathroom to get a shower.

Matt showered quickly and got dressed. He knew he wasn't going anywhere so he just put on an old pair of shorts and a shirt. He looked at the clock on the mantle and saw that it was 6:45, he went into the den and turned on the television to pass the time while he waited for Melanie to arrive. "Okay Mel, let's do this" he breathed loudly.

Just then the doorbell rang. "That's her" Matt thought confidently based on how eager she seemed to be to come over. "Who is it?" "It's Melanie." Matt opened the door and there she was. For a minute he couldn't speak but just stared at her from head to toe. As much as Matt hated to admit to himself he had to say she was *sexy as hell!* She wore her hair long with loose braids and a pink and white ribbon woven from the top of her head down the back. Matt noticed that it was shinny and looked soft to the touch.

She wore two, button down collar polo shirts, one pink and the other white. This was the "preppie" style of the time. She also wore a short, black and red plaid pleated cheerleader skirt that hit just above the knee. Matt looked her up and down slowly and deliberately, secretly enjoying the little game his mind was trying to play with him. He slowed on his second accent up and let his gaze rest on her eyes. *Oh!* How sultry and alluring they were. She followed his eyes all over her body and tingled from the feel of it.

Matt didn't speak for a minute or two but just stood glued in the spot he was in at the front door. He couldn't believe that the same girl he had talked to so cavalier and trite a week ago was standing here at his door looking good enough to eat! The eyes that he had not long ago thought were blue were actually an intense sea green color like a storm. Matt allowed a clumsy grin to cross his lips as he smiled in spite of himself. How really beautiful her eyes were, and the way the light reflected off of them. It made them look iridescent in the subdued evening light. "May I come in?" she asked finally.

"Oh! I'm sorry Mel, I . . . I was just . . ." "Yeah I know" she finished for him trying to squelch a giggle that was trying to come forth. "And thanks" she said turning to face him with a warm smile her hands crossed in front of her. "For what?" asked Matt not sure what he had said or done to warrant it. "For the look you gave me just now." Matt smiled openly and just nodded as if he'd been caught red handed at something he'd thought he'd gotten away with. "For a minute I thought I had lost some of my clothing the way you were looking at me." "Uh . . . yeah" he said scratching his head looking sheepish.

"You have a very nice home Matt" she said quickly changing the subject. Matt not used to getting compliments on his house just nodded agreeably "Thanks." "I just love the fireplace and mantle, is it very old?" "I think so . . . the house is early American or Victorian I think, and there's a fireplace in just about every room." "That must be exquisite, may I have a tour?" "Sure, if you really want to, just sit your book bag on the dining table and I'll give you the ten cent tour." "Okay" she said setting her bag and sweater on the table. "Well first of all this is the living room as you can see and this is the dining room . . ." In a short while the tour was over and they had returned to the dining room and sat down at the table. "Your house is really cool, it's like a museum of American History."

"Yeah, it does have that Alexander Graham Bell or Benjamin Franklin feel to it doesn't it?" Mel nodded in agreement. "So what's it like sleeping in that big bed of yours?" she said with animated curiosity. Matt couldn't help but get the feeling that she was more than just platonically interested in that bed. Especially the way she seemed to perk up when she said it and the way she touched his covers. He didn't let on though, but just played along.

"Oh, it's comfortable enough . . ." "So Mel, where would you like to start?" "How about Science" she said reaching for her bag and unzipping it. "We have some work in chapter 10 to do." "Okay then, let's get to it" said Matt adjusting his seat closer to the table and looking at the page she had opened to.

Mel was sitting beside him quite close and Matt could feel her soft skin against his arm. Her touch made him slow his reading and confused his thinking for a moment. He could feel her looking at him and it was very disturbing. Matt looked up to see if she understood what the book was talking about and found her looking at him with a most enchanting smile. "*Oh hell*" he thought as his mind was quickly jolted back to the park and the school bus incident with Cher earlier that day.

"Why the hell do I have to keep getting tagged with the dangerous ones" he thought to himself. Matt did have to admit she did have a really sweet smile and a pair of lips he could just drink from." He tapped his pencil anxiously on the table in monotone rhythm and just looked at her. Mel was a magnet and she knew it, so it didn't bother her a bit to let herself or intent drip all over him like sweat on a hot day.

"Melanie look, this is going to be challenging enough without you gawking at me like that all night." "I'm sorry Matt, do I make you nervous?" she said in buttery-innocent yet fake tone as she eased from him a little and giving him just a cat's hair of room to breath. "Yes you are as a matter of fact." This made Mel really happy and she smiled really big in spite of herself. "Well I'm glad to see this amuses you, shall I tell you a joke or two to finish the routine or will this do it for you?"

Mel just laughed openly at him now and thought the whole incident simply too delicious for words. "I may as well, seeing as how I can't think straight enough now to do you any good" said Matt tossing his pencil on the table in defeat and leaning back into his seat in resignation. "Oh I wouldn't say that Matt" she said quickly squelching her laughter and repositioning herself, resting her chin on her folded hands on the table and leaning toward him. "I think you're doing me a lot of good!" "And how's that?" said Matt now leaning on two legs of the chair with his hands behind his head and a most stern look on his face.

"Well your keeping me company aren't you?" "Yes, but I'm your tutor not your suitor!" She looked at him giving him a most alluring smile. She reached into her book bag and pulled out a small hand purse then opened it and pulled out a little red and gold plastic card. "Here" she said handing Matt the card. Matt looked at her like she was a spy or something then leaned forward in his chair resting it back on the floor with a thump. He took the card and read it out loud. "Name . . . Melanie Johnson . . . Northeast High Honor Society (PHI BETA KAPPA), Matt, I have to be honest with you . . . I didn't really need any tutoring."

"So what's the deal then?" he said handing her back the card. "The deal is I just wanted to spend some time with you Matt, that's all." "Well couldn't you have just said so?" "Would you have let me?"

"Probably not, seeing as how I planned to just hang out and do some home work of my own." "So then there wasn't anything wrong with what I did after all." "No, not really . . . but you did trick me though." "Sorry" she said shrugging and smiling sweetly. "So what do we do now?" she asked still hopeful. "Well I don't know about you, but I'm in no mood for school work now and I'd just as well watch TV than anything else." "Great! Let's do it." "Would you like something to drink?" asked Matt as they got up from the table. "Sure, what do you have?" "Soda, O.J, punch and water." "Orange juice is fine." "Okay then, if you'll just go in the den, I'll get the drinks and be there in a minute." "Okay Matt" she said walking towards the den.

Matt watched her go and quietly admired her nice heart shaped behind and the generous way the skirt revealed it's curves. "Dammit man!" he thought to himself as he grabbed his crotch and shook his head. Melanie could feel his eyes on her and just smiled.

Matt stopped by his dad's room and peeked in to see if he needed anything. His dad was surrounded by stacks of income tax forms and other documents. His typewriter and adding machine were humming and clicking up a storm. His dad stopped what he was doing and noticed Matt looking at him. "So how's it going with the school work?"

Matt gave him a defeated pout, rolled his eyes to the ceiling and gave him a thumbs down. His dad just chuckled, sat back in his chair and lit a cigarette.

Matt bowed his head and backed out of the room. "Sigh . . . this isn't going as planned, I should have the upper hand not her!" thought Matt shaking his head. "Seems like I've played right into her hands from the looks of it, but I got a surprise for her little butt" he said as a grin formed in the corner of his mouth.

Matt returned to the den. He saw that Mel had already turned on the television and taken off her shoes. She was sitting in the middle of the couch with her legs curled under her, arms spread across the top of the couch like she was waiting for him. She really looked inviting he thought with those long, sexy, cheer leader legs and breasts that Matt could only imagine were softer than goose down to touch.

Matt should have been more wary of her true intent when she told him of how she had seduced Ant into telling her where he lived, but instead just blew it off and ignored it as he came into the room and placing a tray with a small dish of fig cakes and drinks on the coffee table in front of her.

Mel watched his every move with delicious interest as she quietly smiled to herself. Matt looked at her as he sat down the items and suddenly felt like he was back on the bus earlier that day again. With a delicate but confident finger, Mel beaconed him to come sit next to her on the couch. Matt did so, but not as close to her as she had intended. "Nice and comfy?" he asked raising his eye brows and gesturing to her modified posture on the couch. Mel inhaled deeply and audibly and slid herself to the end of the couch, repositioning herself with one foot touching the floor, the other bent at the knee and arms open resting on the arm and back of the couch. "Not totally but I could be" she said teasing him by slowly bending her knee further to expose more of her leg.

Matt sighed within himself and just smiled, waving off the move like it had been done by an amateur. "So what's on TV?" he said sitting near the opposite end much in the same posture as she. Mel noticed the intended move but was not insulted but only spurred on. "*Ah! there's a game afoot*" she thought to herself as she lowered her head just a little and smiled at him. "I haven't checked yet, I just turned it on."

"Well let's see" Matt picked up the remote and clicked off several channels before she stopped him. "Wait, leave it there" she chirped sitting up for a moment. It was a cop drama. "So you like cop shows huh?" "No, not really, I just like the romantic scenes between the police captain and the DA." "So it's the love scenes you like, is it?" 'Yeah don't you?" Matt just shrugged at the question feeling she was baiting him. "I can take e'm or leave e'm." Mel pouted noticeably then curved it into a toothy smile. "You're a *meaney* Matt."

Matt shrugged, stretched and yawned then lay back with his hands behind his head to watch the show. Matt was doing his level best not to notice her, but it was getting hard with her musk oil cologne attacking his nose and mind. She was very tempting the way she was laying there all open and inviting. Just then Mel got up and repositioned herself across Matt's lap. She lay on her back with one arm behind her head, resting against Matt's torso and the other across her stomach. "Now that's more like it" she said looking up at him with a most confident and happy smile. Matt just shook his head and sighed quietly as his core temperature jumped 10 points. *Man just when you think things can't get any worse they do"* he thought to himself. It was bad enough for him with her sitting the way she was with her legs like that and the way the light from the television was playing peek-a-boo with her short skirt and shadow at the hem between her legs. And now to have her resting across his lap like that didn't help much either.

It amazed him how a woman could be so brazen and casual about her affections or contact boundaries and to whom she displayed it. But this was 1982 and women were aware of themselves, on the go, and nothing stopped them.

Mel looked so tempting laying across his lap all stretched out. Her young and voluptuous breast rose like over sized oranges against her shirt and blended nicely with her figure. Matt walked his eyes up and down her body in the dark and enjoyed every inch of her that he could see and not see. As he came back to the top for the umpteenth time he was surprised and embarrassed to see that she was quietly staring up at him as well. Her eyes unmoving and with a hint of passion locked into his holding him there like a prisoner.

Matt dumbstruck wasn't quite sure what to say or do cause he was cold busted! Mel lightly teased and bit her lower lip much the way an insect teases it's antennae as if to taste the air around it. The expression blended out into a cat that ate the canary smile. "Do you like it?" she asked evenly with a hint of suggestion in her tone.

"Like what?" said Matt biding for time to collect himself. "My body" she said flatly, raising the other hand slowly to join the other behind her head. This move gave maximum exposure to her breasts and raised them up a notch to expand into the most enticing orbs Matt had seen to date. And as impossible as it would have seemed he could swear that her nipples were breaching the two shirts she was wearing to make themselves known.

"Oh . . . um its nice . . . I guess" he said none to confidently. "Do you want it Matt?" she asked almost as clinically still staring at him. Matt's mind was a train wreck. He had thought he could handle this girl and toss back her intentions much the same he had done Cheryl. But for some reason this girl was getting to him. He was weakening and losing his hold on control by the second. He didn't think she or anyone would be as bold as Cheryl and to have it happen twice in one day was a bit more than any teenage boy could handle . . . hell he was just a man!

Matt's heart beat hard and his pulse moved fast. He felt his body going rigid and stiff in places he would rather them not be. Especially with her resting right on top of it. Mel could see him beginning to sweat and decided to turn up the heat a little more. She slowly and purposefully raised her knees causing her already dangerously short skirt rise to the occasion, then allowed them to fall apart revealing so much of her upper bare thighs that his imagination could fill in the rest as the light from the television teased him with brief shots of her crotch just barely covered by the skirt.

"*Damn!* *t*his shit is getting thick" he thought to himself. Try as he might Matt couldn't keep his third leg from growing and making it's presence known. Mel just looked at him as a surgeon would a limb he was about to sever. She felt his response to her question and was exquisitely enjoying the effect she was having on him. "I got him now!" she mused to herself and feeling a sweet tension of her own begin to build in her lower back and legs. "Matt?" she whispered to him. "Yeah?" "Do you?" "Do I what?" he said trying to side track her again. "Do you want me?" Matt sighed turning his head for a second to break the hypnotic trance. "Would you believe me if I said no?" "Not in a million years" she said still staring at Matt with total surety. "So what are you waiting for?" Matt grinned and looked away.

"*Oh shit!, this is Cheryl part two for sure, what is this, ground hog day?*" Matt mumbled just under his breath, hoping she didn't hear him. "No it isn't Matt, and just what does that have to do with what I asked you anyway?" "Well it seems to me that all day long women have been trying to jump me that's all." "Is that so?" she said sitting up and positioning her bottom directly on Matt's lap for emphasis. Mel raised her knees up to his chest and just sat there putting much pressure on Matt's lap and crotch. Now sitting face to face with him, she rested her back against the arm of the couch. He skirt slowly began to collapse into her lap revealing more and more of her bottom that Matt could already feel was bone bare but couldn't see.

Mel could tell that what she was doing was having the desired effect on him and just sat their smiling and watching him squirm. Matt was kind of wishing he was the television just now because it had a better vantage and view of her butt than he did. As Matt contemplated all that was happening to him at this moment, he just starred at the television. He wasn't really watching it but just used it to stall and try to extinguish the fire Mel was trying to build in him.

"Matt?" she said softly breaking his hypnotic stare. "Yeah?" "You still haven't answered my question yet." "I didn't?" "No." Matt stalled a little longer trying to play dumb as long as he could to discourage her without hurting her feelings. Unfortunately he began to feel within himself that he was losing this battle. He was deftly aware that he didn't like this game or the way it was beginning to feel. "Matt, if what I'm feeling underneath me is any indication of how you feel about me right now, then why don't you stop teasing me and take me to bed!" she stabbed at him with finality.

Matt was undone. His penis had sold him out and betrayed him once again. Mel had played her trump card and he had none to follow. Her words were like fire and ice on his face, blunt and damn sure of their intent.

"Because that's not our bed in there, Melanie" he heard himself say. "It belongs specifically to me and is only reserved for one other woman and you know who that is" he told her in a cool clipped tone looking as deep into her eyes as she was him. Mel was a little moved but not so much in the way he had intended.

In fact she was actually a little stimulated at his coldness and it turned her on even more! "You know Matt, good love and a good woman is where you find them and you would be foolish to pass me up, I realize that you are a committed man and I respect that." "In fact, it impresses me greatly because most guys would have taken me in a heartbeat by now if I let them, but no not you, you have been dilly dallying around dodging me for the last ten minutes, when we could have been spending that time doing some serious love making."

Matt was slightly impressed by her boldness and savvy but not enough to be moved by it more than he was. After all she was to him just another female trying to break his will. "But know this Matt" she said readjusting herself on his lap to add more pressure and reveal more that she was not wearing any panties.

"You must understand something about me, I'm not in the business of passing myself on to every man I see or who looks at me, in fact my standards are quite high, so far no man has even come close to touching me or having his way with me until now, and that exception is you!" The knowledge of this made Matt's eye twitch. "And when I decided long ago what kind of man I wanted and who I would give myself away to, I have never backed away from my course not even once" she said in a low voice leaning closer to him.

Matt allowed himself a bewildered stare at this comment and smiled meekly as if to say, "well I'm pleased as punch for the opportunity to deflower you." "Yes Matt, I'm still a virgin" she said with a coolness that sent a shiver to his spine. Mel looked into his eyes to see if any of what she had said moved him or not. "If you don't believe me I'll prove it!" she said reaching for his hand. Matt had no idea of her intent or next move of even if he should be trying to stop it. Mel had taken his hand and forced it between her legs and massaged her vagina with it.

Matt was shocked, surprised and mentally fucked up at the sudden act. He had thought for a moment that she may not have had on any panties but was completely sure now! The exquisitely soft wetness and furry feel of his hand rubbing up and down her crotch made him go rigid like a corps. Mel flattened his hand and manipulated two fingers between her vaginal lips and slid them back and forth to give him complete exposure to her most well kept and hidden secret.

Matt could feel only a firm yet moist heat greet him. Mel, though her intent was to prove her chastity to him was also getting a thrill from his firm hand touching her so closely and deeply. She sighed deep and the force of it all made her swoon and throw back her head. She quickly recovered herself as this was not what she was wanting, a cheap thrill, but instead the full attention of Matt and his swollen manhood upon her.

Matt was feeling like he wasn't going to win this battle as his penis spasmodically jerked savagely within his pants as if pulled by and unseen hand. Mel felt it too and moaned at the movement. She looked at him with a lusty smile as she gyrated upon his hand and lap. Matt forced himself to think of something nasty and awful to cool his own fire.

"Mel why are you doing this to me? don't you see I'm not going to play ball with you?" he whispered harshly not wanting his dad to hear. "Oh you are a strong man, aren't you Matt?" "Most guys wouldn't wait a New York minute taking what I'm offering, but no not you!" she said insipidly but still enjoying his handy work. Matt quickly removed his hand from her. He noticed that she was about to try and insert it into herself, two fingers at a time. "But that's okay Matt" she said sucking in hard at his retreat. "Because I love a challenge, and you are definitely up to the task mister" she said repositioning herself to straddle him. "And do you know what else?" she chirped putting her arms around him like a python holding a small animal. "I'm going to have you anyway whether you like it, want it or not, so just watch out lover I'm on to you now and Melanie always gets her way" she said before kissing him deeply in the mouth with full tongue.

Matt allowed her to satisfy herself at his lips expense but was in no way intending to let her have her way otherwise, no matter what she thought. Matt looked at her grinning when she pulled back from the suffocating kiss. He had to admit he felt a little nervous because he had never been threatened by a girl before in any capacity and certainly not that way.

Matt was a little exhilarated too because he had to admit that the feel of her on his hand felt so good that he was sure he would slam her on her back and drive his flesh stake between the waiting legs of this little vampires heart. Matt let his mind wonder a little longer than he should have under the circumstances.

"Hell why don't I nail her to the bed? She's willing and no one would know! . . . but then again I would and I ain't having it!" he concluded to himself feeling a most welcome chill run through him and kill his desire along with his erection.

"Nice try Mel but no cigar" he said lifting her off of him and laying her to his side on the couch. "You can work on me if you like, but I can't say that you'll be successful." "That's okay Matt" she said recovering herself and sliding to the far end of the couch like a cat planning to re-attack. "It gives me something to do anyway" she said smiling seductively at him. "Why don't you go after Ant, he's a nice guy and he's single too!" "I know but he's not you, and your responsible for lighting my fire and it's you who will have to put it out" she said looking at him with a most unnatural and intense stare as she rested her chin on her hands on the arm of the couch and retook up watching the television.

Matt just sighed deeply with some relief that at least for now the attack was over. He was just about overcome with mental and sexual exhaustion. Sometime this week he was gonna have to run down Aretta to relieve all this pent up stress, and he was looking forward to it. "Boy what a day" he sighed and relaxed to watch the show.

After awhile the show was over and it was time for Mel to go home. They had not spoken much for the remainder of the program but just looked at each other with sidelong glances and smiled cordially. Matt walked her to the front door and out to her truck. "Nice truck, a little big for someone your size isn't it?" "Mel just leaned against the door and folded her arms and giving him a smile as if to say, "You don't think I can handle it?" "Well for your information *"Mr. Man"* I like large things under me, I like to feel the power of something strong and solid around me" she said raising an eyebrow to drive home her implication.

Matt just shook his head and laughed. "Yeah right Mel, if you say so!" She just smiled timidly and shook her head slowly. "Matt if you only knew what it was that was in front of you . . . I doubt you would be so smug" she said to herself.

"You'll see Matt . . . you'll soon see just how much I can accomplish, so don't sell me short too soon okay?" "OOH! I'm sooo scared" taunted Matt putting his hands to his face and feigning being scared. "Did it ever occur to you Mel, that it's *me* you should be wary of?" Mel just smiled, shook her head in disbelief. Matt walked over to her and put his arm above her head on the door and leaned into her. "As I've told other women like yourself, I'm not having it and it's a good thing for you all that I'm not as weak as you would like me to be because you would quickly find out how much wolf there really is under this sheep like appearance" he said putting his face close enough to hers to feel her breath on him.

Matt didn't smile or blink, but just stared into her eyes as if looking into her soul. "Or in short Mel . . . I would *beat the brakes of that ass! of yours faster than you can drop your drawers.*" Mel, stimulated thoroughly but not intimidated just looked at him, arms folded and grinned. "If you say so Matt" she taunted breathing in deep enough for her ample breasts to touch him. Matt saw the gauntlet and picked it up quickly. He suddenly grabbed her by both arms and hoisted her up a good foot off the ground.

Mel was shocked at his power and looked down at her dangling feet with wide open eyes and gaping mouth. She was about to protest but Matt had in the next moment seized her lips savagely much in the same way she had done him. He pressed himself into her, pinning her against the door of her truck and kissed her with a primal ferocity that she had only dreamed of and seen in movies. Mel went weak in his grasp and felt like a rag doll to him.

Matt heard and felt her moans of pleasure and defeat at his unyielding control. He held on to this kiss for a good moment but only long enough to know that not only could he huff and puff but he could also blow her doors down too. Matt slowly released the powerful kiss and eased her back to the ground. Mel didn't speak but just looked at him with awe stricken and pleasured eyes at his control over her.

"Good night Red Riding Hood" he said simply as he opened her door, seated her in the truck by her hand and closed the door. "Don't be a stranger now . . . ya hear?" he said in a most southern drawl then walked away with his hands in his pockets whistling. It was a full minute or more before he heard the engine to her truck start. Mel was sitting there still radiating from the assault and her body wouldn't let go of it . . . of him! "Oh Matt you charmer you . . . why did you have to go and do that, now you really got me going." "No man takes me and gets away with it and now that I know what you are capable of and where you live, you've got some major problems lover boy . . . all five foot four inches of me, girlfriend or not."

Soon Matt was in his room quite happy with himself and horny to beat all but still good, and about to crash for the night. Matt plopped his head on the pillow, adjusted for comfort and was about to slip into oblivion when the phone rang. "RING!" "Aw nuts! Just when I was about to zonk out."

Matt reached over and picked up the phone from the night stand. "Hello?" "What's up man?" It was Ant. "Nothing man I was just about to crash." "Oh I'm sorry dude, I just called to see what you were up to." "Nothing man I just got rid of Melanie a few minutes ago." "Oh yeah? . . . what was she doing there?" "She said she wanted me to help her with some home work but it turned out to be a booty call." "You shittin me!" "Does a bear shit in the woods?" "Aw man you lucky dog . . . did you get it?" "No man, you know better than that." "Why not? Who would know?" "I would dog breath." Ant just laughed off the insult.

"You know Matt, I'm beginning to think you and Milton are related." "Don't even try it! I wouldn't be related to that clown if my life depended on it, besides where were all these chicks when I was a freshman and by myself, what about then?" "Yeah, I guess you right." "Besides, I get all I need from Retta!" "I gotcha Matt, but still you gotta admit you been turning down some real class "A" booty calls lately." "I mean look at Cheryl and now Mel . . . *BOOYA!* . . . you know what I'm saying?"

"Yeah I hear ya, the only way any woman is gonna get me without my permission is if I'm drunk, fucked up, and outta my mind!" Ant just cracked up hysterical at the comment. It never ceased to amaze Matt how little it took to get his best friend in stitches. "So what's up for tomorrow Matt?" "Man, I don't know, I'm still trying to recover from today." "I've been talking to coach Jones about the track team and he's going to be having tryouts tomorrow after school." "You gonna get on the team?" "I don't know my home room teacher has been asking me about it too." "What did you tell her?" "Nothing yet, just that I would think about it awhile." "You ought to do it man, you've got some good speed and

I'm sure you can do other events as well." "I might man, its just rough this year and I'm trying to stay low key . . . you know."

"Yeah, I guess but think about this, you can get some brownie points for it and its also a good way to get away from Cheryl." "Oh yeah" he said brightening. "And think about this too, if your on the team you get out on Fridays earlier and your classes are set where you have two P.E classes so you can train during school." "Which classes?" "4th and 5th period" "Hmm, that don't sound too bad Ant!" "So are you going to do it?" "I will if you will."

"Hey, wait a minute, you know I'm no road runner, I play "B"ball" "So, you can cross train until the season starts." "What if I get hurt . . . then what?" "Oh you won't, you could do a field event like the jumps or either the discus." "Can you really see me throwing the discus?" "Yeah with them spaghetti arms of yours you could be a good long distance thrower." "I don't know man, I'll have to think about it." "*Yawn,* okay then, well I'm gonna go ahead and crash dude." "Alright Matt, hey why don't you stop by and pick me up in the morning." "Okay doc, what time?" "How about 7:30?" "That'll work." "Okay Matt, check you later." "Later Ant . . . click."

A gentle breeze danced lightly through Matt's room lulling him to sleep. It was a good idea to join the track team he thought to himself as sleep began to set in. "Boy, I can't wait to get started!" he thought then drifted into oblivion.

Chapter 7

Quality Time

A retta woke up in bad spirits this morning. Her back ached and she felt cramps all over, not to mention the lack of sleep from an awful night mare she'd had. She groped her way to the bath room a and turned on the light. The glare stung her eyes closed again as she flipped on the switch. *"Oh god"* she mumbled sitting down on the cold toilet seat.

"Can this be Monday again or what?" she mused putting her face into her hands for relief. She slowly began to doze off again, her mind a dense fog, began to reanimate and scrawl together bits and pieces of her nightmare and yesterday's events.

It took on the perspective of a Picasso painting gone bad. Suddenly she was brought back to the present by a gut wrenching cramp. *"Ugh!"* the pain shot through her lower mid section and crushed her insides in a vicious grip. It was awful and made her wince and moan. *"Dear god, what's happening to me! could this be my period, or is it something else?"* she said to herself. Retta flushed the toilet and tried to ease herself up praying that the pain would not come back until she got to her room.

Unfortunately this was not to be. The next shock put her on her knees in agony. The bathroom took on a psychedelic mosaic appearance as the early morning light began to work it's way through the night. Tears were flowing freely as wave after wave of pain wracked her body. She tried to cry out for her mother but only managed a weak croak. This saddened her more and she just curled up into a fetal position and cried.

Once more the pain attacked her body with the sharpness of a javelin then crushed her insides like a building had fallen on her. The moan she let forth was more of reflex of being stomped on then and actual attempt to call her mother. *"MOM!"* she groaned holding her stomach in shear a pain.

Audrey had been half asleep when she first heard the sound. Because it was so early she discounted it as neighborhood noise and gone back to sleep. The second time she heard her daughters cry of pain it was purely from maternal instinct that made her jump from her bed and run through the house towards the sound she had heard. Her eyes had not yet acclimatized to the darkened apartment and she stubbed her foot against the leg of the coffee table. BANG! *"Dammit! SSSS"* she stumbled and regained her balance without stopping.

As she burst into the bathroom she screamed at the sight of Aretta lying on the floor in a growing pool of blood. *"Aretta!* what's wrong baby?" "Tell mama what's wrong." Retta was kind of in her own world of pain and sounds. Everything after she heard her mother shout was garbled and kind of blended like so much white noise.

"Mama!" she gasped not quite able to speak because of the severe cramps and violent contractions she was having. Lori was awakened by the excitement and noise. She got up and went to towards the sounds still rubbing her eyes. The first thing she saw was the blood and she screamed so loud that Aretta almost forgot her own suffering.

"Mama! Retta's dying! EEEE . . . EEE . . . EEE" She screamed in a sonic succession over and over again. *"Lori! . . . Lori . . . Retta's not dying honey, stop screaming!"* Lori was not hearing her, she was completely in a state of bedlam and stood there stamping her feet as if she were running in place and wailing like a newborn. Her little face was red with stress and slobber was slowly coming down her mouth.

Audrey was just about to lose it herself with the dual tragedies going on to her left and right. She almost didn't know what to do first calm Lori or treat Retta. *"Lori stop screaming honey, it's alright Retta is not dying honey, she just had an accident is all!"* she said trying to sound more calm than she actually felt.

Audrey picked up Retta in her arms and carried her to her bed. She had seen painful menstrual cramps before but never anything like this! *"Lori go get mama some towels baby okay?"* Lori just stood there in her footy pajama, whimpering with her hands in her mouth and staring at the huge blood stain that covered her sisters night gown.

"Come on baby, it's okay go get mama those towels okay?" she said with pleading eyes. Lori blinked twice and turned to go still looking at them, then ran into the bathroom. Audrey was trying to stay calm not knowing what was really wrong with Aretta and afraid it may take more than just some towels to fix.

She with trembling hands slowly raised Aretta's bloody gown. She saw that her face was pale and flushed from shock and pain. Her skin felt cold and clammy. Audrey tried to remember anything she could about first aid and what looked like what.

"Okay Audrey what do you see, what do you feel, what do you hear" she drilled herself trying to remember. She pulled back the gown to reveal a blood soaked little girl from the waist down. *"Oh sweet Jesus, my baby is losing so much blood but why?* "*Mama . . . I'm cold"* whispered Retta in a week voice. *"Lori where are those towels honey?!"*

Lori quickly returned and gave her mother the towels then stepped back in horror and fear at the site of all the blood on Retta. *"MMmmm! . . . Lori don't start again honey it's going to be alright okay?"* she said trying to stop her from relapsing before she started. Audrey then took one towel and doubled it length-wise.

"Retta let momma move your legs okay?" Retta didn't speak but just grunted and allowed her mother to spread her legs. It was quite a mess, Audrey noted. It looked like she had been shot or cut or something, anything but a monthly cycle. There was thick dark – coagulated blood around her crotch where as all other was bright red.

Lori whimpered and squirmed at the sight and ran from the room sobbing wildly. *"Well at least she's in her room and not here"* she mused as she blotted her gently until she'd gotten the majority of it and could see better, if what she was thinking was the immediate cause. She took another towel and pressed it up against her crotch and closed her legs.

"Retta, baby I know your in pain but I want you to squeeze your legs closed and keep that towel there okay baby? I'm going to call the doctor" Aretta was beginning to shiver some now even though her mother had taken one of the large towels and wrapped it around her to keep her warm till she could do better.

Retta couldn't figure why she was so cold and it felt like she was outside during late fall with an icy November wind blowing on her. Her teeth began to chatter some and all the while thinking about Matt. *"Oh Matt, I hope I'm alright, I couldn't stand to be without you . . . leaving you alone, Rodney can you hear me?"* She went on. Sweat beginning to bead on her forehead.

Audrey had just come back from calling 911 and heard her babbling with her eyes closed. She put her hand to her mouth to stifle a sob. *"It's gonna be okay baby"* she said laying down behind her, holding her and stroking her head. *"There's an ambulance on it's way baby so hang on for me . . . hang on!"*

Audrey pulled a blanket over her and rubbed her arms and legs for warmth. She put her hand to her forehead and noticed that it was wet with sweat but cold to the touch. A quick look at her hand and nails showed that they were turning blue and all the color had begun to drain from her cheeks leaving her a ghoulish pasty color.

Even though it was the last part of spring and the house was rather warm, she got up and turned on the heat to 80 degrees. *"Hang on baby, it won't be long, just hang on for momma baby"* she encouraged as she rubbed her vigorously and wrapped her body around her. Just then there was a knock at the door and the sounds of a walkie talkie squawking coded messages.

"Lori go get the door honey!" she shouted not knowing exactly where Lori might be at this moment. Lori had recovered her favorite stuffed animal and sat on the couch cuddling it for comfort. She sprang from the couch and ran to the door. When she opened it three paramedics in red and white jackets rushed in passed her. Two men and one woman.

"I'm in the bedroom!" she yelled in relief and panic when she heard them come in. Lori was stunned as they brushed by her carrying what looked like over sized fishing tackle boxes. They ran into the room and saw Retta curled up in bed and very bloody form the waist down.

"We have her now ma'am, if you would please stand over there we'll take care of her."

Audrey was reluctant to let go of Retta much less leave her side, but she knew that medics could do more for her than she could and for that she was grateful. She stood beside the bed away from them giving them room to work.

"Ma'am what's your daughters name?" "Aretta . . . Aretta Davis." "Okay, Aretta honey, can you open your eyes for me sweetie?" coaxed the female medic. "Come on honey, I need you to open your eyes for me." The other two medics were opening up bags and stringing plastic tube and popping open syringe bottles. Aretta felt like she was walking down a long tunnel filled with mud. She could see a light in the distance and barely hear her name being called but it was so far away. She heard her name being called once more and tried to speak. It came out little more than a croak.

"Ma'am, can you tell us when this happened?" "About a half hour ago . . . I think" said Audrey holding her arms. "I woke up and heard her calling me and I ran into the bathroom and she was on the floor like this covered in blood." "How old is she?" "15" "Has she started her period yet?" "Yes . . . about two months ago . . . I think . . . what's the matter with her is that the problem or is it something else?" she pleaded as they put Aretta on a stretcher that had just been brought up. The technicians worked quickly and methodically as they strapped her in and hooked up the I.V bag above her. "Were not certain yet, but she may be suffering from TSS." "What's that?" "Toxic Shock Syndrome." It happens when girls don't remember to remove their feminine napkins or tampons frequently enough or in some cases at all and they wind up subjecting themselves to situations of blood clots and toxicity due to failure of blood being properly excreted from the body.

"Oh my lord!" said Audrey covering her mouth. "We won't know for sure till we get her to the hospital and the doctor has a chance to give her a more thorough examination." Another paramedic checked her temperature and blood pressure. "She has a temp of 106, BP 150 over 90, pulse 110bpm." They lowered the gurney to the floor so the legs would not get in the way as they went down the stairs. "Northside one to base." "Go ahead Northside." "Were transporting a black female, 15 years old, approximately 115 lbs. she has severe vaginal hemorrhaging and fever, BP is 150 over 90, pupils dilated and pulse rate at 110 BPM, we've started an IV and are preparing to transport, ETA 10 minutes, Northside one out."

"Confirmed Northside, crash unit on standby, base out." Audrey was stricken with shock and was terrified. Her baby had never been this ill before and she felt completely helpless as the medics rolled Retta out the door and down the stairs.

Lori who had been forgotten during the drama was now standing in front of the picture window looking down at the ambulance and the flashing lights as they bounced relentlessly off the building across the parking lot. By now the glow of the early morning sun was cresting up over the trees in the distance. This added to the ambulance lights, giving the whole area a surrealistic crime scene appearance.

People who were going to work were surprised and a little dumbfounded at the early morning light show involving a little girl most of them had come to know. The lights and the indelible images Lori had seen had burned themselves into the cornea of her tear stained eyes and were permanently seared into her mind. She was locked into a long deep and dead-pan stare at nothing in particular. The lights seemed to move in slow motion as they stabbed, flashed, and bathed her little face in a Technicolor light show.

Lori was gone and unobtainably deep into her own little world. A world of preschool sing-songs and disembodied lullaby's long since forgotten. The medics had made it to the bottom of the stairs and were out the door without losing Retta in the process. The spiraling maze of stairs made for one hell of an obstacle if you were just walking empty handed. But one of profound challenge with anything larger than a laundry basket. As they made it to the ambulance, ghost-like onlookers stood by in house coats, pajamas and various other "I'm still in the bed" clothing. The large double doors of the ambulance opened and bathed them all in a crystalline white light that lit up most of the parking lot. The team was fast and knew what they were doing. In a flash Retta was placed in, locked down, and the doors closed.

The crowd instinctively parted like the red sea to move out of the business end of the ambulance so as not to be its next fare. "Wasn't that, that girl from upstairs in "D" building?" "I think so . . . where her momma at?" "Chile, I don't know, she be gone most of the time anyway leaving them girls by they self" said one woman with more rollers in her hair than a porcupine had quills. "*Lori!, where are you honey?*" called Audrey in a shrill voice from the bedroom. Lori broke from her trance and ran to her mother as she came out the bedroom with the bloody bed clothes. "Come on baby, we gotta put on something so we can go to the hospital."

Back in the ambulance the medics were working on Retta quite fiercely with injections and bags of liquid and oxygen masks. The female tech was taking her temperature again and checking her blood pressure while shining a pen light in her eyes.

"Guy! we need to step on it she's fading fast!" Retta was now completely unconscious from the loss of blood and couldn't feel herself anymore. She felt as if she was just floating out and above herself in a mosaic soup of light and garbled sound.

Audrey and Lori came running down the stairs half dressed and jumped into the car just as the ambulance was turning out of the parking lot heading to the hospital. "I hope she be alright Ms. Davis" shouted one onlooker. "She gonna be okay Audrey . . . you be strong" chirped another. But Audrey didn't see nor hear anyone except the beating of her own heart and the screaming in her mind. She stabbed the key into the ignition and prayed.

"Please start!" Audrey began to cry a little herself but maintained control anyway for all of them. The trip took only ten minutes and ended at the Northside Hospital emergency room. Audrey could see nurses and doctors standing on the dock waiting for the ambulance to back in. She pulled into the first spot available. She parked then got out and went around to the other side of the car to get Lori.

She had quieted some but still whimpered a little. "Come on Lori lets go baby" her legs felt heavy like lead and didn't want to move. Audrey ran up the stairs near the ramp and burst into the rear entrance of the hospital just as the paramedics cleared the door. "Doctor her blood pressure has lowered to 100 over 60, a fever of 105 and has lost a lot of blood, her pupils are dilated also" said the technician. "Get her into ICU and get me a crash cart on standby STAT!, god I hope this child doesn't go into cardiac arrest!" the doctor mumbled to himself.

The nurses and other staff scurried around to do the doctors bidding as quickly as they could. The nurses hustled Aretta into the intensive care unit and hooked her up to several machines and put tubes down her throat and in her arms.

Retta's eyes were closed and she had a ghoulish pale color. "Ooh! It's so warm and bright but I can't see anything . . . am I dead?" Wondered Retta as her mind and body separated from each other. "Where am I? . . . and where did this white robe come from?" Retta's mind was eons from reality and she was in a state of rapture.

She no longer felt pain or sickness just happiness and freedom. She walked along in bare feet on a glistening trail of silver. Her heart felt so full and light that she smiled. She didn't know where she was going, but felt as if she was being led by unseen forces who sang her name. "Where am I?" she asked again to no one in particular. "You are with us" said a soft gentle voice. "Where am I going?"

"You are going to see him that made you." Aretta gasped and put her hand to her chest as her pulse raced. "God!" "Yes!"

She was afraid now and a little saddened. "Why?" "Because he loves you!" "Come on nurse get that adrenaline into her, we're losing her!" yelled the doctor as he squeezed the air bag forcing air into her lungs. Another doctor was giving her CPR and ordering paddles to shock her heart. Aretta kept walking and finally the clouds opened up revealing a beautiful view of a gigantic castle with golden gates. They were so high that she couldn't see the top of them or the sides. There was a man standing near the gate and he wore a blinding white robe with a golden sash about his waist. His eyes were soft but intense and filled with love. His face was stern and strong but very beautiful to look upon. He smiled at her and waved her to him. "Come my child sit beside me."

Aretta came and reached out her hand to him. The man picked her up and placed her ever so gently on his lap. "Are you my Father . . . God?" she asked unsure. "I am the one sent by him, my child" he told her holding her hand. His voice was like a gentle babbling brook. It was warm and peaceful and made her feel good inside. "Is it my time?" she asked pouting as the enormity of where she was began to come clear to her. The man's brow furrowed a little and he placed a finger on his thoughtful chin. "Hmm let me see" he said producing a large book from out of thin air. He opened the book and scanned a page. "No my child, not yet."

Retta was happy and saddened at the same time but mostly confused. "Then why am I here?" "Because he sent me to talk to you my child." "Doctor I'm getting a flat line . . . she's in full cardiac arrest!" "Quick get me the paddles, everyone clear!" he said then pressed the trigger on the defribulator paddles sending a body wrenching shock through her small body.

"They are calling for you my child" he said cupping her cheek in his tender hands and kissing her on the forehead. Retta smiled and felt a most exquisite rush of satisfaction and love wash all over her. "Thank you . . . and I love you" she whispered as she hugged the man's neck fiercely. The angelic man put her at arm's length, smiled touching her cheek . . . ! "And I love you too my child" then picked her up and placed her on the path from which she had come.

Retta nuzzled her cheek against his gentle strong hands, kissed them as she smiled at him then released him. Retta could feel herself falling backwards away from the man but this time she wasn't afraid. She began to spin around quickly and fell through a timeless space towards a hole that seemed to get bigger as she went. A fear began to overcome her and almost as if he could feel her thoughts the voice of the man came to her and comforted her. "I will be with you until the end of time my daughter."

The castle was disappearing now and everything around her began to fade to black. She had stopped moving and suddenly began to feel cold and a shock of pain. "We've got her!" yelled a nurse. "Her pulse is getting stronger doctor."

"Come on Retta, hang in there for me!" he urged looking at the monitor. "Get on an IV drip, a culture and some antibiotics, we need to find out what the hell is going on in her body" said the doctor taking off his gloves and cleaning up to leave.

He left Retta in the care of the remaining nurses and interns who moved about like ants on a hill. Retta's mother sat in the waiting room praying silently and trying to console Lori as she rocked her back and forth on her lap. "Mrs. Davis?" said the doctor coming towards her, his hair tousled and tie loosened. He had been working relentlessly on Retta for the last half hour. "Yes! that's me . . . how's my baby? . . . is she alright? . . . can I see her?" she said getting up quickly still holding Lori.

"Aretta is going to be fine Mrs. Davis" he said giving her a reassuring smile and patting her on the shoulder. He could see that the trauma had reeked havoc on her and her younger daughter. Lori didn't respond but just looked off into space sucking her thumb.

The doctor gave her a quick glance and noted her demeanor and size. Lori looked to be around seven or eight as best as he could tell and felt that she may be under some form of mild shock by the discoloration in her skin and the sweat on her brow this early in the day.

"How are you doing sweetie?" he said placing a gently hand on Lori's back and lightly stroking her. Lori didn't respond but just sucked her thumb and lay her head on her mothers shoulder. The cold clammy feel of her made a hair on the back of his neck stand up and he wanted to say something but didn't want to send Audrey into a break down, being she already had one daughter in the hospital. He thought for a moment how to get her in a room to examine her and maybe get a sedative into her without alerting Audrey or scaring Lori further.

"Can you tell me what happened Mrs. Davis?" he said sitting her back down and resting beside her. "Well it all happened so fast that I didn't have a chance to find out!" "All I know is that she called me from the bathroom and I ran in to find her on the floor in a puddle of blood!" "Is she menstruating yet?" "Yes she is . . . for about three months now." "And how old is she?" "She'll be sixteen in June."

The doctor thought a moment still looking at Lori and stoking her back and neck ever so gently. He was getting some ideas now and really wanted to get her on a table for a complete examination. "Doctor what do you think is wrong?" "Well from what I can see she is hemorrhaging badly and it doesn't appear to be a hemophilia issue, does anyone in your family have a history of bleeding disorders?" "No, not to my knowledge." "Okay that's what I thought, which leads me to the second option, she may be suffering from Toxic Shock Syndrome." "Toxic shock what?" "Syndrome, Mrs. Davis, it's a condition caused by poor and improper use and management of feminine hygiene products, primarily tampons."

"Oh! Jesus" she said sitting down again shaking her head in disbelief. The doctor sat down beside her taking her hand and tried to console her. "Mrs. Davis, I understand how you feel but you can be at ease now because although she's not out of the woods, the worst is over and we have her condition stabilized." "Right now as we speak I'm having some blood work done and cultures taken to determine the cause, but given her age, the symptoms, and the fact that she is menstruating I would say her condition was caused by a blockage in the vaginal tract that caused clotting." "Once that occurred the coagulated blood began an infection of the uterus or there about, I'll know more soon as I get the cultures and lab work."

"Thank you doctor" she said smiling through tear stained eyes. "I just don't know what I would do if I lost any of my babies" she said cuddling Lori closer. The doctor had remembered his concerns about her from a few moments ago and tried to suggest a subtle way to ask Audrey to let him examine her.

Years of medical training and dealing with patients severed him in most cases but when It came to children he wasn't as confident. "Uh Mrs. Davis when was the last time Lori had a check up?" "Sometime last year I think . . . just before school let in . . . why?" "Oh no reason really, she just looks a little pale and I thought since we have her here, why not just go ahead and get her checked before summer gets here."

"It's good for a year, and she won't have to have one for the next school term" he said trying to appeal to her sense of practicality. Audrey was a little leery about it, thinking there was maybe more to this than general concern but conceded anyway and let the doctor examine her." "O . . . Okay if you think its best." "Great! . . . Ginny?" he waved to a nurse at the station behind him, "Yes doctor?" "Take Mrs. Davis and her daughter Lori to an exam room and prep her for a PTS physical and some vaccination shots" he said raising his eyebrows for effect.

The nurse having dealt with the doctor on many prior occasions knew what he meant by PTS, it was a code for Post Traumatic Shock. But he didn't want to say that in front of Audrey and scare her even more than she was already.

"You just go with Ginny and she'll take good care of you and Lori okay, I'll go and check on Retta and see how she's doing, I'll get back to you as soon as I know something." "Thank you doctor, I really appreciate all your doing for my little girl." "Your welcome . . . it's my pleasure . . . I'll see you soon" he said handing her off to the nurse and retreating in the direction of the emergency room where Aretta was located.

It was now 8 am and the sun was moving high into the morning sky. Matt sat in his home room and stared out the window. He didn't know why, but for some reason his heart hurt, his mind raced and his eyes jutted about erratically and he felt numb all over. He couldn't move or blink and just barely could he breathe. All he did was sit and stare blankly into space.

Just then the girl next to him reached out to touch and to get his attention because she had been watching him and was a little curious if not concerned at the change in his mood. Matt turned to her quickly when her hand touched him. He looked into her soft blue eyes not really seeing her. For a brief and fleeting moment he could swear he thought he saw Aretta's face instead of the girls. At that moment he suddenly knew why he felt the way he did.

Something was wrong with Retta! The revelation hit him hard and made him look the other way quickly as if he'd been slapped. Confusion and pain welled up in him as warm tears began to fill his eyes flowing silently down his cheek.

This he hated, cause he knew without looking up that they pretty blonde girl to his right wasn't the only person who was aware of him and his sudden mood change. The knowledge of this made him hurt all the more and more tears came and splattered on his desk. Everyone hurt sometime in high school and some people even got away with it . . . . mostly girls.

But there was a standing canon that you just didn't break and that was if you were a guy you just didn't cry in school . . . ever. The sight of this shook the young girl next to him and she wanted so badly to ask him what was wrong but didn't know how to go about it just now. She thought about the look he gave her and decided to swallow her fear and go for it.

But just then the bell rang and everyone bolted from their desks and the room, whispering and pointing at a tear faced Matt. Matt just sat there and wept in silence with his head down and his heart breaking more and more with each passing second. He felt it so strongly that the love of his life was in grave danger and needed him badly!

The girl who sat next to him didn't run off as the others had, but was filled with compassion and concern for the boy she only saw during this period. She eased to the front of the room to the teacher's desk and alerted her to what was going on in the back of the class. She rose from her desk, looked at Matt and the pool of tears that was forming on his desk and shook her head in sadness. She patted the young girl on her arm, smiled, thanked her, and sent her onto her next class.

Mrs. Pratt slowly walked to the back of the room where Matt was. She didn't know just how she was going to approach the crying young man and just put her hands in her skirt pockets and kind of crinkled her mouth in confusion. Matt for the most part had been somewhat of a pariah to her and wasn't the type of person to cry about anyone or anything. So it struck her as odd to see him in this seriously weakened condition. She knelt down beside him, then gently placed a hand on his arm.

Matt felt the gentle warm touch and thought it was the girl still standing by him. "Leave me alone Katy" he said snuffling and sniffling, thinking it was her. When she lightly stroked his arm he had a feeling it wasn't her and looked up

240

to see that it was Mrs. Pratt. She could see that he was in pain and it came as a shock to her to see him that way and made her feel bad for him.

Matt to her was always so vibrant, alive and maybe a little wild, but never this. "Rodney . . . . Are you alright?" she asked in a motherly tone. Matt just shook his head and kept his head down. "What's wrong sweetie, is there anything I can do to help?" "No . . . not really" he said sucking in hard and wiping his face with his sleeve. He sat up and braced his hands on the edges of his desk and just stared at them.

"She needs me" he said simply looking at her now. "Who needs you Rodney?" "Aretta" and with that he got up, picked up his things and left. Mrs. Pratt still kneeling by his vacant chair, silently watched him go and wondered what he meant by his statement. Then it slowly dawned on her. Her eyes widened and lit up some as she remembered from her own life a time when she had someone she cared for deeply and they went away.

"He feels her" she thought to herself and allowed a little smile of inner peace cross her lips. "And he's going to her as well . . . where ever she is" she finished getting to her feet and going to her desk to get some wipes to clean his desk for the next class. As she did this the revelation of this matter took her back to her college days when she was in love like that. She remembered what it felt like when she lost her love in a bicycle accident.

Matt had left behind his gym bag and she picked it up slowly as if it held fond memories from long ago. She lifted it and looked out the window and said what her heart had uttered more than it being something she felt encouraged to say.

"You go to her Rodney . . . you go to her." Matt didn't quite know what to do so he left school and headed to her school. He had a feeling he was going to get into trouble for ditching but didn't care he just wanted Retta. Matt got on his moped and sped off as fast as he could. He went up Holt Avenue the quickest way and least noticeable way so he wouldn't be seen. Ant saw him blast by from his perch on the bleachers across the street. He was going to hail him but when he saw the determined look on his face he though better of it and just kept his hand down. The trip across town was quick and once Matt got there he ran into the building to look for her.

Matt was frantic and didn't know where to go first. He had never been to this building before and didn't know where to look. His mind raced like a rat trapped in a maze. He knew that every minute he spent standing there and hovering in the long huge hallway was time he could get busted by some teacher or staff. He got an idea and started going down the hall looking into the narrow door windows into each classroom.

He had hoped he would get lucky and see her or at least Alfreida who could tell him where she would be right now. Suddenly a door opened behind him and a tall black man appeared. "Hey young man! What are you doing? you should be in class right now not running around in the hall" he said glaring at Matt with hands on his hips.

"Damn!" Matt thought to himself as his heart sank. "Please sir, you gotta help me, I'm trying to find Aretta Davis, do you know where I can find her?" he said with tear stained pleading eyes. "Who are you and why do you want her anyway?" he said getting defensive and posturing as if his next move was to grab Matt and hold him for security. Matt could feel the tension build and his plan spinning away like a dust cloud but he had no choice and pressed on.

"Sir My name is Rodney Mathis and I've just got to see her . . . I think she may be hurt or in trouble!" the teacher shifted his weight to rest on his heels and folded his arms across his large muscular chest. "And why do you think this? Are you psychic, do you know her? And just what do you think you could do if she was in trouble?" he chided on.

Matt had to admit the questions were valid and true but no less stung like bees on his heart and mind. He just bowed and shook his head in resignation not having anything to say that could refute the teachers questions. The man could tell that Matt had more than a casual concern for her and even felt a little bad for him but he couldn't just give up the location or even the existence of any student to some strange distraught kid.

He was about to tell Matt to leave the building and take his concerns to the office but then his name started to ring in his mind like a dinner bell in the distance. *"Rodney? . . . Rodney . . .* did you say your name was Rodney?" "Yes sir" said Matt under his breath but not looking up. "So your this Rodney Retta has been talking about?" Matt looked up slowly, kind of perplexed because he had never met the man before till now and wondered who he was. "Yes that's me, but I don't know you sir." "Oh, I'm Mr. Simpkins her supervision teacher" he said proudly like she was his daughter.

Matt's hopes rose exponentially and he straightened up immediately. "Please Mr. Simpkins can you tell me where she is?" he said quickly looking around behind the man through the window to see if she was there. All he saw was a sea of strange faces looking back at him, some smiling others reticent.

"She's not in there son" he said calmly and eased the door closed so they had privacy. "She hasn't made it to school as yet or at least missed role call and is in her next period class." *"Oh god!"* said Matt letting the words trail off his lips and out of him like air escaping a balloon. Mr. Simpkins could clearly see that this was devastating to Matt and tried to calm his fears. "Hey! Hold on sport, I'm sure she's alright, she may just have been late and missed the bus or something and had to get a ride to school, that does happen sometimes."

Just then Alfrieda seeing it was Matt at the door came forth and opened the door. "Mr. Simpkins." "Yes Frieda" he said turning around. "Aretta is in the hospital" she said clutching her chest and swallowing a lump in her throat. "WHAT! NO!" "Yes sir, she was taken by ambulance early this morning before 7:00."

Matt's mind screamed as he reached for Frieda grabbing her by the arms. "What's wrong with her? How come you didn't tell me?" "I don't know Matt, I couldn't, I didn't know what to do, so I didn't do anything!" she said sobbing and collapsing in his fierce grip. "They just came and rushed her out of the house into an ambulance and carried her off, Matt she wasn't conscious when I saw her and it scared me." She went on now holding onto Matt for support.

Mr. Simpkins was stunned into silence at what was unfolding in front of him and felt paralyzed to do anything but listen. "What about her mother, why didn't you ask her?" "I couldn't Matt, I was upstairs looking at everything from my window and didn't get a chance to ask her anything, she got into her car just after they put Aretta in the ambulance and took off after them!" "I was gonna go with her but she left too fast." By now the rest of the class had picked up on the drama and overheard what was going on.

There was much murmuring, chatter and pointing at the door. Matt took it all in and long since lost his sadness and replaced it with fear and devout concern. This steeled his resolve some and helped him to think.

"Which hospital is she in Frieda . . . did you get the name on the ambulance?" "It said Charter North Side on it." Matt didn't wait further for anything more. He squeezed Frieda to him. "Thanks Frieda" he said then kissed her cheek and turned to run down the hall. "Thanks Mr. Simpkins!" he tossed back before bursting out the double doors into the sunlight. "How did he know about it Frieda? I only just found out myself and you're the only one who knew" he asked incredulously. "I don't know Mr. Simpkins . . . I guess he loves her that much and just felt her."

After awhile Audrey and Lori had received some good news from the doctor. A nurse came to them and escorted them to the doctor's office. "Dr. Jessup, here is Mrs. Davis" she said opening the door and calling to his turned back. "Thanks Alice" he said putting down a journal he was thumbing through.

"Please sit down Mrs. Davis" he said pointing to a chair at the side of his desk. "We have the results of Aretta's tests and know now for certain what the problem is." "What is it?" she said sitting on the edge of her chair. "Retta suffered from a chronic case of endometrioses." "What's that?" "That's when the lining of the uterus has collapsed normally during a menstrual cycle but not have completely cleared the vaginal tract by normal hemorrhaging." "This was followed up by her second cycle coming on and not being able to clear due to coagulation caused by the first which created a sore or cyst which festered on the walls of her uterus."

"Once that burst or was torn loose by either rough physical activity, sexual contact or even a strong hot bath it released causing the infection to go toxic in her system, this is why she collapsed and had such bleeding."

"Oh my god, what could she have been into to have this happen?" "She's always been good about taking care of herself as a woman, I made sure of that long ago and I reinforced it, in fact I not too long ago had a discussion with her about sex and any activity she may have had with anyone."

"Mrs. Davis, do you have any knowledge of any of her activities as the last few weeks that may help?" "No I don't, I work late but I do know that she is always home from school on time because my neighbor keeps an eye on them for me till I get off work." "Hmm this may create a problem." "Why?" "Well you see Mrs. Davis, although we know what initially caused her symptoms and collapse we don't know what the originator other than poor management, that caused it all was, and without that knowledge she could have this happen again."

"Momma can I tell you something" whispered Lori as she tugged at her mothers collar. "Not now Lori, momma and the doctor are talking about Retta." "Wait Mrs. Davis, she may know something that can help, Lori do you have anything to tell us about your sister sweetie?" he asked gently.

Lori nodded yes, still looking at her mother's blouse and fussing with the buttons. "Would you like to tell us?" "Yep, but Retta said not to tell" she said crinkling her nose and pouting. Audrey looked at the doctor with a hint of a smile and sadness. She knew herself from experience that if Retta told Lori to do or not to do a thing she listened and you couldn't pry it from her with a crow bar. "Lori please tell us . . . mommy won't be angry I promise."

Lori just pouted more and played with her mother's buttons as she straddled her lap. "TATTLE TAILS EAT SNAILS" she chimed through pouty upturned lips. The doctor though concerned leaned back in his chair and allowed a grin to cross his lips. He had heard many things in his many years as a trauma doctor and always marveled at the comments from children. "Where do they get these things?" he said to himself. He drummed his fingers lightly on his desk thinking of a way to get around Retta's inbuilt safe guards on her little sister.

"You know Lori that's a good thing you're doing for your big sister, I wish I had a little sister like you when I was young." Lori slowed her fussing with her mother's buttons and turned to look at the doctor. "BIG GIRLS DON'T TELL TAILS" she chirped off proudly. "And your right not to do so . . . but I'll tell you a secret if you'll tell me one" he said leaning close and conspiratorially. For some reason this appealed to Lori and she began to brighten and turned to face the doctor. "You got's a secret?" "Yep! wanna hear it?" she nodded with enchanted interest.

The doctor leaned in close and whispered into Loris little ear. She cringed and giggled with delight. Audrey could not imagine what a grown man could say to a child like Lori that would set her off so quickly. Once done he retreated to his seat and let Lori giggle a little and bask in the what she felt was a singular privy to a great secret.

"Now will you tell me one?" he asked like a playmate in a tone Lori would respond to. She looked at her mother queerly then back to the doctor. "Aretta got into a big fight at school yesterday with some stinky boys." "Oh my lord!"

"Mrs. Davis" he said evenly halting her for fear she would silence Lori's tale. "How many boys was it Lori?" asked the doctor. She held up three chubby fingers. "Well that explains the physical activity" he said sighing long.

"Mrs. Davis, did you notice anything wrong or any bruises on her yesterday?" "No I didn't, she was fine as far as I can remember, she had taken a long hot bath before I came home and was in bed when I got home." "Well that explains how it ruptured, all things considered she'll be fine, she's just gonna need a week or so in bed and a lot of antibiotics to fight her infection."

"Can we see her now?" "Yes, but only for a few minutes, she's in ICU, come on I'll take you" he said getting up. "And Lori" he said leaning over to touch her shoulder. "Thank you for telling me your secret, you really did a big girl thing and it helped your sister a lot!" Lori just beamed and hid her face into her mother's chest.

As they went into the hall Audrey looked up to see Matt standing at the nurse's station asking questions about Retta and getting quite stressed because she wasn't giving him any. *"Rodney!"* cried Lori when she saw him and jumped from her mother to run to him. Matt bent down and cradled her little body like she was a life preserver in the middle of the ocean. Lori squealed and squeezed equally hard and filled with joy.

"Is this your son Mrs. Davis?" asked the nurse as they approached. Audrey smiled and blinked back a tear as she looked into Matt's loving eyes and knew what he was feeling. "Uh . . . yes in a way he is" she smiled bashfully covering her mouth and bowing her head slightly.

"He's actually my daughter's boyfriend." "Okay, I didn't know and couldn't give him any information on her if he wasn't family." "Thank you nurse, I appreciate that" she said coming over to give Matt a hug, very thankful that he was here but didn't quite know how or why. "Okay, since we're all together we can go see Retta" said the doctor leading them to her room.

"Oh Rodney, I'm so happy you're here!" she said squeezing his neck and kissing his cheek. *"Were going to see Retta she's sick"* she said pouting again. "Well let's go see her then okay cutie pie" he said cupping her chin making her giggle.

Audrey was amused at the dialogue between Lori and Matt but couldn't help feel a little curious and displaced at him being there. She didn't recall telling anyone about Retta being ill, much less him! And yet he was there. She was curious but at the same time glad that he had come.

"I came as soon as I found out about her Mrs. Davis" said Matt reading her mind based on the look she had given him earlier. She looked at him and could see that he had been crying. "Thank you Rodney, I glad you're here" she said hugging him to her as they walked down the hall. "How did you know and where to come to, I hadn't talked to anyone yet?"

"Frieda told me." "Oh I see." "Excuse me, but we must be very quiet now, Retta needs to rest." "Yes doctor" they all said together. As they stepped into the room the sight of Retta in a that bed tore Matt apart. She was laying there with tubes in her arms and wires connecting her to a heart monitor. She had an oxygen mask on and she looked so very pale.

"Oh! Retta" he said breathlessly, easing Lori to her feet. He looked at her from head to toe and back taking it all in like he was looking at the aftermath of a train wreck. Her beautiful hair that was so alive and vibrant just lay there matted to her face as if she had wax in it. He slowly caressed it and gently stroked her cheek with the back of his hand. Audrey looked on and just held her hand and wept quietly.

"Oh my little girl" she cried over and over, squeezing her hand and kissing it. Matt tried to hold it together but couldn't and just broke down and cried his eyes out kneeling beside her bed. He reached out a trembling hand to gather her frail and delicate little fingers in his and hold them. Audrey could see the deep love he had for Retta and it touched her so much so that she cried all the more.

Lori just pouted and buried her head in Matt's shoulder. She would cry too but the nurse had given her something to ease her sadness and it made her feel less sensitive but still sad. "What happened to her?" said Matt looking up at the doctor. "She had an internal infection son and a fight she'd had in school triggered it's movement through her system." "I'll tell you about it later Rodney" said Audrey drying her eyes.

Matt accepted this but deep inside was burning like a furnace to know who had hurt her so. He looked back to Retta and rested his head on her hand and prayed silently. "I love you Retta . . . I love you so much, please you have to get better, I can't live without you!" This brought another tear to Audrey's eyes and she just squeezed his hand from her side of the bed.

They stayed with her for only a short while because that's all the doctor would allow. As they got up to leave it dawned on Audrey again that she had told no one about Aretta being ill and Frieda doesn't go to the same school as Matt so how did he even know she was ill and to go looking for her in the first place!

"Rodney, how did you know she was ill? You don't go to Southwest anymore." Matt stopped and turned to look at her. They held each other's stare for quite a moment then he said simply. "I felt her calling me Mrs. Davis" Audrey blinked at this and had to readjust her thinking as she felt she misunderstood him.

"She called to you? Is that right?" "Yes ma'am, I can't explain it, but I could feel her calling me." Audrey just looked at the doctor in disbelief and he just shrugged and walked away to his next patient. "Love transcends all things Mrs. Davis" he said as he went on his way. "Sigh! . . . Rodney what am I gonna do with you?" she said squeezing his face in her hands and pressing her forehead to his.

"I don't know . . . make me a son-in-law I guess" he said smiling but serious. Audrey just laughed and they walked out of the hospital. "How did you get here anyway?" she said fishing for her keys in her purse. "I rode may scooter." "Aren't you supposed to be in school right now?" she said mock chastising him.

"Yes ma'am, but when I got Aretta's message I broke down crying in class then I got up and left." "You really do love my baby don't you Rodney?" she said placing her hand on his cheek and looking into his eyes with renewed appreciation and love for him. "More than life itself Mrs. Davis!"

"Don't you think that feeling that way is a little strong for a young man your age?" She said leaning against her car. "Maybe so, but it's how I feel." "What about other girls Rodney, don't you ever get approached by them? I mean let's face it you are a handsome young man and I can't believe that other young girls aren't trying to get to you, hell if it wasn't for your father who's just as handsome as you I don't think I would let you see Retta."

"How come?" "Because I couldn't trust myself around a young man like you." "Aww, come on Mrs. Davis . . . !" "It's Audrey, Rodney, and I'm not as old as you think, and don't take me so lightly because I do have a tendency to go after what I want even if it's somewhat borderline in nature . . . you feel me?" she said getting into his face to the point her ample bosom was pressing into Matt's youthful chest.

Matt's eyebrows went up and he blushed near the point of perspiration as the electricity of her touch scorched his inexperienced mind. Audrey feeling playful and seeing how what she had done took the opportunity to tease him further and make her point. She slowly reached up and squished his cheeks till he had a fish-lips expression then gave him a resounding pucker face kiss. *"Smooch!"* Matt's mind imploded.

"Ooh, I'm tell-lin" whispered Lori as she stood holding Matt's hand, swinging to and fro, watching the whole affair. The kiss wasn't long, nor passionate but served more as a period at the end of a most imputative statement. One that Matt thought was sure to condemn him to hell. Audrey released his face and eased away from him with a most satisfied smirk on her face. "You see Rodney, we Davis women are a determined, bold, and seditious breed, when we want something, we work at it till we get it . . . understand?" she said cupping his chin.

"Yes ma'am" he breathed, relieved that she was a comfortable distance from him now. "Good now, you don't worry about Aretta, she just had a mishap with a period, sometimes it happens, just not this critically." "Okay" he said nodding in acceptance. "What about this fight with three guys in school?" "I don't know, but I intend to find out!" "No Audrey, let me do that okay?" "Why . . . you don't need to go getting yourself into any trouble over this, I suspect you're up to your armpits in it already for skipping school to come here" she scolded not really meaning it.

"I know, but really it's no trouble and you could accidentally do her more damage than good." "How's that?" "Look at it this way, if you got into a fight with someone, that's bad enough, but if that person snitched on you to the principle or a parent and you got sent home for it, then that's something else and you'd want to get even for it wouldn't you?"

"Okay go on." "If you go to the school and get those guys into trouble they'll come back at her when she's not protected and really try to hurt her, I've seen it happen." "Okay, I see your point so what do you plan to do?"

"Don't worry, I got it under control and I'll fix it so she'll never have any more trouble out of them or anyone else, and I won't get into trouble either." Audrey folded her arms and shifted her stance. She looked at Matt somewhat incredulously but found she did believe that this may be a better way than her going up there and embarrassing Retta and putting her in more jeopardy later. She sighed long and decided.

"Okay Rodney, you do it your way but don't go getting yourself hurt or into trouble okay?" "I won't, I'm good at getting things done and dealing with problem children" he said smiling and nodding confidently. "Okay then, do you want to ride with us back to school?" "No ma'am I got my bike." "Oh yeah I forgot." "Besides I want to get some flowers for Retta and maybe try to hang around awhile and see if she wakes up."

Audrey smiled inwardly at this thought and secretly envied her daughters choice in a man. "Okay Rodney we'll see you later then." "Bye Rodney." "Bye bye Lori" he said giving her a big hug and kiss on the cheek.

Audrey put her in the car, got seated then started up the little import and drove away. Matt went back into the hospital and looked for the flower shop and got Retta a nice arrangement with daisies, carnations and roses in a cute little vase. He talked the nurse into letting him sit with her just a little longer if he promised not to go all mushy and weepy on her again. He agreed and smiled at her thinking he didn't realize that he was that distraught. It was now lunch time and change of shift in the hospital was about to take place so Matt had to leave. He kissed Aretta on her forehead and promised to come back later on today even though she was still asleep and couldn't hear him.

Matt walked out of her room and headed out of the building back to the parking lot where he had parked his bike. He felt better since seeing her and was glad she would be okay.

The ride home was quiet and subdued and Audrey was thinking about how this could have happened for the umpteenth time and why she hadn't noticed Retta hadn't had her menstrual cycle yet. She was just about to turn 16 in a month and should have by now.

Lori just sang quietly to herself and played with a doll she'd found in the back seat. She felt better now and was glad her big sister would be okay. "Lori, do you want to go to school today sweetie?" "Yes ma'am" she said not looking at her. "Okay sweetie, just give momma a few minutes to get you something to wear and I'll run you up there okay?" "Okey dokey." "Are you hungry, you haven't had breakfast yet?" "Yes ma'am" she said nodding her head and poking out her bottom lip.

It was now 10:00am and the city had come to life. People were driving or walking either to work or some other place of importance. The parking lot was empty now back at the apartment and everybody who had to be somewhere was already gone. Audrey backed the car in to her spot and killed the engine. The car sputtered two or three times then died letting out a long exhausted hiss as if it were glad to shut down.

Audrey and Lori got out and went up stairs. As they entered the main entrance Mrs. Johnson the lady downstairs poked her head out of the door. "Hi Mrs. Johnson" she said trying to smile. "How are you this morning?" "Oh I'm fine, I'm just sitting around watching TV, I don't get out as much as I used to you know with my rheumatism acting up and all." "Oh, I'm sorry to hear that, what are you taking for it?" "Oh . . . this, that and a little bit of everything else" they both laughed at this and it felt good to be happy once again even if for a moment thought Audrey. Mrs. Addie Mae Johnson was a sweet little old lady in her late 60's who moved into the complex about five years ago before Audrey and her girls.

She'd move there from a little town in Brunswick Georgia to be closer to her family. Mrs. Johnson was short and thin with long silver hair that ran down to her waist in which she always wore in two long girlish braids. She had kind soft brown eyes and a warm smile that she didn't show to too many people unless she knew you. To Audrey's amazement she still had all of her own teeth and kept them sparkling white. Mrs. Johnson walked with a cane and was slightly humped over from her condition that came from so many years of agricultural work in the fields of Georgia.

She had cream colored skin that reminded you of a perfect cup of coffee and from her high cheek bones and girlish figure that a hint of could still be seen, gave you the impression that she could have been quite striking in her younger years. Today she wore a pretty rose pastel dress with a knitted shawl she had made herself. Her stockings were tan brown and hung kind of baggy on her legs giving an elephant skin impression. "So tell me what happened to that little girl of yours, I saw all the ruckus this morning with all dem lights a flashing in my window?"

Audrey sighed and bowed her head some not wanting to retell the tail but knowing she would have to at least one more time to Mrs. Johnson. "She had a bad period caused by an infection she didn't know she had in her uterus, it caused her severe cramping, fever and a lot of blood loss, but the doctors are taking good care of her now and she should be fine with some bed rest and antibiotics." "Oh, the poor darling, bless her heart" she said shaking her head side to side and working her cane like a gear shifter in a truck.

"You know back in my day when a young girl had dat change of life it wasn't no doctor or stuff like you have now to help with the flow." Audrey nodded in agreement as she could remember her own mother telling her about how it was being a young girl in the early 1930's. "And dey say she gonna be fine?" "Yes ma'am, the doctors had some trouble in the beginning with her fever and the loss in blood pressure because of the severe bleeding." "Well I'm glad she gonna be fine, I woulda hated for that precious baby of yours to be hold up in da hospital like dat for something like that."

"Yes ma'am." "Well I'm gonna pray for her so she'll be fine." "Thank you Mrs. Johnson, I really appreciate it." The older woman waved off the gratitude as if praying for someone was the most common of things and she should not worry or concern herself none. Audrey looked at Lori who was sitting on the step holding herself and frowning because she was getting really hungry and ready to go to school to see her friends.

"Well I gotta go and feed my other baby Mrs. Johnson and get her off to school before she starts to fade out on me" she said smiling at her. Mrs. Johnson laughed and stabbed her cane into the floor working it some more like she did. She looked at Lori and waved her over to her side with a slight hand gesture. "Come here baby." Lori got up slowly but came to the older woman remembering what her mother had always told her about respecting and minding whatever Mrs. Johnson told her to do. "How you been sweetie?"

"Fine" said Lori looking up into the old woman's eyes and holding her about the waist. "You miss your big sista don'cha?" Lori just nodded. "I know baby I can see it in your eyes, but you gotta be strong okay? She gonna be home before you know it." "Yes ma'am" Lori mumbled. Mrs. Johnson gave her a big hug and kiss on the forehead. "Well I'm gonna letchu get on with your morning, I need to get on in here and take this god forsaken medicine for my back." "Okay Mrs. Johnson, I'll see you later then."

"Okay baby, you keep me posted ya hear." "Yes ma'am" she said as the little old lady shuffled into her house. Lori was at the top of the stairs waiting when Audrey finally got leave to go. "I'm sorry I took so long Lori you know how Mrs. Johnson goes on once you get her started." Lori just nodded. "Lord a mercy" she said getting to the top of the stairs and unlocking the door. "It has definitely been a day! Lori you sit down on the couch baby while I go clean your room okay?" she didn't want her to see the bloody towels because it may set her off again.

"Can I have an apple momma?" "Yes baby, go ahead then come back in here okay?" "Yes ma'am" she said running into the kitchen. As Audrey opened the door to the bedroom she noticed that it had a funny metallic odor to it. It was the dried blood. She surveyed the carnage that was the girls room and didn't quite know what to do first. The bloody towels still lay in a heap on the bed. The smell was repugnant and made her gag some. Not so much because of the smell but the fact that it was her babies blood.

She picked up one by the end and lay it on the floor, then dropped all the others onto it. She saw that the bed spread had gotten stained as well so she just rolled it all up in a big ball then gave one quick look around to see if she had missed anything. When she saw that she hadn't she took the bundles and went into the kitchen. As she got to the entrance she remembered that Lori was in there and stopped short.

"Lori I need you to close your eyes for momma, okay baby?" "Okay" she said with a notable whimper in her voice. "I'll just be a second okay, then you can go into the living room okay?" "Okay." Audrey peeked quickly to see if Lori's eyes closed. They were, she moved quickly to the machine and opened it. For a brief second she rethought her plan then decided to trash the whole lot. "I'll just have to buy more that's all" then stuffed it into the trash can and tied it closed. Lori sat with her eyes tightly shut eating her apple. "You can go now baby all the nasty stuff is gone." Lori ran out of the kitchen without further prompting. "It smells funny" she tossed back as she went.

Audrey just smiled and headed back into the bedroom to air it out. She sprayed and wiped down everything with bleach water. "Okay Lori, you can come in and get changed for school now, I'm gonna go ahead and fix your breakfast."

Lori got up and went into her room she cautiously stopped at the door and peeked around it to see if there might be something she didn't want to see. There wasn't, so she ran in and started rummaging through her drawers looking for something to wear. She selected a pair of jeans and a pink top and began peeling off her clothes tossing them on the bed. "Lori! Are you done yet?" "Almost, I gots to put my cloths on." "Okay, your breakfast is on the table, I'm going to call my job and let e'm know I won't be in today." Lori just continued stuffing herself into her jeans and blouse.

Matt was heading for school himself now that he had taken care of the situation with Aretta's assailants. A simple phone call was all it took and his cousins who went there knew all three and would deal with them when they returned to school. Now he could get back in the swing of things, mainly Retta.

He had wondered should he stay home or go back to school but decided he would go on to school. The semester was almost over and he needed to pull up a few "C's" he had picked up. More absentee's on his record wouldn't help his grades at all. "I wonder should I go back to homeroom or just go to 3rd period?" "I'll still got some stuff I left behind in there, not to mention I did miss first and second period and they are gonna have me down for AWOL for sure, Oh well no use sweating a load about now I've already made the bed so now I just have to lay in it."

Matt rolled in the back of the school near his home room and parked. Mrs. Pratt would be having class just about now but he needed to get his gym bag and couldn't avoid her forever. Just then the bell rang. "What period is this?" he wondered, not having wore his watch today.

"Hey dude!" he called to a white kid running from the building. "What period is this?" "It's 4th man." "Okay thanks . . . Damn! the day is almost over, that means it's well after 12 o'clock now and I'm late as hell!" Matt ran into the building, down the hall and around the corner into the classroom.

Mrs. Pratt was straightening some desks that had been upset by fleeing students. She looked up and saw him standing there half out of breath again. The sight made her smile some and she allowed herself that little pleasure but with her back turned.

Matt on the other hand had a different feeling. The kind of feeling you get the morning after sleeping with your best friend. Matt tried to clear his throat not quite sure what to say. "Uhmm! . . . umm Mrs. Pratt, can I talk to you a minute?" She stopped what she was doing and stood up. "Yes Rodney, come on in."

She walked over to the door and closed it as she didn't have a 4th period class and could take some time with him. As she closed the door Matt caught a whiff of her perfume. It was very seductive and almost made him forget what her wanted to talk about. He noticed that she was wearing a long 'Jordache' jean skirt with a split in the back and a yellow long sleeve satin blouse.

He didn't know why he hadn't noticed her earlier this morning but he hadn't. Her hair was hanging long with a dark blue rose ribbon tied in it over half way down her back. He noticed that her hair was wavy and looked very soft and wondered how it would feel to touch it. She also wore yellow stockings and blue pumps to complete her outfit. "It's funny how white girls always seem to dress in color coded sets" he thought to himself.

Either way he thought she looked very nice and youthful. In the time it had taken Matt to observe and obsess about Mrs. Pratt's cloths she had crossed the room, sat at her desk and been watching him quietly just stand there. She had made eye contact with him and broken his fixation.

Aware now that she had been watching him watch her made Matt burn with embarrassment. He looked away and blushed accordingly. He wondered now why his mind always analyzed everything and everyone no matter what his mood or the situation.

He really hated that about himself and even more so now as this line of thinking had nothing to do with what he was there for. "Please come and sit down Rodney" said Mrs. Pratt crossing her legs and folding her hands peacefully across her lap. This action made Matt's mind wonder again and he was currently deliberating how sexy she looked crossing her legs.

He quickly shook the idea and focused. "Mrs. Pratt, I wanted to apologize for this morning, I had an emergency come up that I wasn't quite sure existed in the first place, but was sure involved me! . . . or at least someone close to me" he said sitting down across from her.

Mrs. Pratt reflexively narrowed her vision unconsciously. "Is everything alright?" "Yes ma'am, it was my girl friend Aretta, she suffered a massive hemorrhage around 6am this morning and had to be rushed to the hospital." "Oh my word, what happened . . . is she alright?" she rattled on sitting forward in her seat. "The doc said it was because of an infection in her uterus by something called TSS."

"You mean Toxic Shock Syndrome?" "Yes! . . . that's what he said." "That's terrible, that kind of thing can kill a girl, she was very lucky Rodney!" "Yes ma'am, I know" he said dropping his head at the thought of losing her.

"You know Rodney, you could have talked to me before you left, I would have understood and maybe tried to help you in some way." "I'm sorry, I guess I just didn't think." "Well don't worry, I covered for you with your other teachers, we all know you're a good guy Rodney, and you work hard in class, so I knew you were in serious pain when you left without saying much, so what hospital is she in?"

"North Side." "Do you know how long she'll be there?" "No ma'am, the doc said she would need to rest at least a week or so." "Okay . . . so how do you feel now that she's okay?" "Oh, I'm fine I guess, I'm much better than I was earlier." "I bet you are, it's really hard on a person when someone they love is ill or has had a life threatening injury, it always helps to talk about it with someone so you don't have to carry the pain alone."

"Yes ma'am that's true." "So Rodney in the future, should anything major happen again and I pray it doesn't, please don't be afraid to come talk to me." "I think you'll find I can be a good friend as well as a teacher" she said placing a gentle hand on him, giving him a reassuring squeeze.

Matt felt himself flush warm inside with her closeness and concern. "What a joy it must be to be married to such a woman" he thought to himself. "Now, if you feel up to it you can still finish out the day or go home, because all you classes are covered for."

"Nah, I think I'll stay and finish, I need to get some points in my English and Math classes." "Alright then, you still have some time if you want to get some lunch with the last class, but you better run." "Okay Mrs. Pratt" he said getting up to leave. "Thank you for all you help and support, and I'll remember what you said about any future incidence." "Okay, you have a good day Rodney."

Matt turned to leave, then stopped at the door. "Oh by the way Mrs. Pratt, do you remember what you was telling me about the track team?" "Yes." "Well I'm going to sign up today." "Oh! That's wonderful Rodney, good for you, I just know you'll be glad you did!" she said gushing with delight. "I think so too" he said then walked out the door.

"Bye bye Mrs. Pratt . . . have a nice day!" "You too Rodney." Then he was gone and she leaned back in the chair and propped her feet up on an open drawer. "Sigh! Now there goes and original young man, I hope he gets all he strives for." Matt was running down the hall and felt 10ft tall! He couldn't be happier with himself and the world right now.

The hall was empty except for a few custodians and a student or two. Matt glanced at the clock on the wall as he raced past the boy's bathroom on his way to the chow hall. "Damn! I've only got ten minutes to eat, I hope they haven't started closing the lines." Matt rushed through the double doors and the distinctive smell known by everyone throughout all lunch rooms in America told him they were having sliders (hamburgers) today. A handful of people were still eating and no one in line.

"Aw shit" he spat disgusted at his luck. "They done stop serving!" Just then he saw a kitchen worker he knew so he ran up to him. "Yo Yo! Gumbo, what's up man?" "Nothing much just slanging hash and hauling trash" he said shaking Matt's hand in the usual "Brother-man/homeboy" way. "Hey G-man check this out, I'm running a little late on chow man how about a hook up?" Gumbo put down his serving tray and looked around the room as he dried his hands on his apron. "Okay . . . sure whatcha need homey?"

"Aw man, anything will be fine, a couple of sliders or something will do." "Alright Matt, gimme a second and I'll setcha straight." "Cool man" he said shaking Gumbo's hand in a one-potato-two-potato fashion all boy's during that time used to connect with each other. "I'll be down at the end getting some bug juice." "Bet" he said then shuffled back into the kitchen. "That's one cool brother" thought Matt as he walked away.

Gumbo was a stout, heavy set guy of about twenty years old with real dark skin and a muscular build. He had soft black eyes and semi crooked teeth. Matt had met him on the way to school some time back when his car had quit on him and Matt stopped to help him get it going again. He found out later that Marcus or Gumbo as he was used to being called, was heading to his school for a job interview as a cook, and by Matt stopping to help him he had saved him from losing out, so they had been friends every since. Matt got a cup and flipped the handle on the beverage urn. He scrounged up his face at the sight of the strange blue liquid. It smelled okay but had a funny tint to it.

He took a big swing *"SPWTHPPP!! YUCK!"* he said spitting it out all over the counter and drawing the attention of staff and students alike. "What the hell is this stuff?" he said to no one in particular. He stared bewildered into his cup. A young white woman with a hair net walked up to him and smiled notably trying hard not to laugh at him. She bent down in front of the urn and produced a gallon bottle of blue liquid and held it up for him to see.

"It's sanitizing cleaner." "What! . . . you guys could have poisoned me with that mess!" Matt protested trying not to get too loud and create a scene. "No, not really but if you like we do have it in three other flavors if you don't like "Aqua blue" said the young woman giggling openly now at Matt's failure to read the sign in front of the urn which clearly said, "Caution Do Not Drink, Unit is Being Cleaned."

"Aw that's damn cold man" he conceded accepting his mistake. Matt could hear laughing and giggling around him and felt the cold shoulder of embarrassment creep all over him. The young woman saw his shame and decided to rescue him by pointing him to an urn he could drink from. "Come on sweetie, you can have something from this one down here, we haven't begun cleaning it yet." "Thanks" he mumbled and walked to the other end of the serving line. "Don't mention it, just be more observant next time okay?" she said cutting him a an appraising look of interest before returning to her work.

Matt dumped out the cup and grabbed another. This time her poured just a little in the cup and touched it with the tip of his tongue and smacking it between his lips for confirmation. It was okay to drink. "This sucks too, but at least I won't die from it . . . . at least not right away" he mumbled.

Soon Gumbo was back and had a plate with two large homemade hamburgers with the works and a whole slew of French fries to boot. "Here ya go my man." "Alright! . . . thanks a lot "G!" "Don't mention it, it's cool." Matt took the plate happily and sat down near the windows and began eating. He took huge bites of the burger and it was good! He could tell Gumbo had made it himself because it had extra everything on it unlike the regular sliders with the one tomato slice and meager portions of lettuce and a lone pickle slice.

He soon finished the burger and started in quickly on the other one. He savored it as it began to fill the void in his stomach. Just then Ant came outta nowhere and plopped down in front of him. "Wuss up Matt!" "Damn! You're a sneaky bastard" he chirped almost losing his sandwich. "So where you been all day?" said Ant grabbing some fries from Matt's plate.

"The hospital." "For what?" "Aretta was sick this morning and almost bled to death." "Damn! Man I'm sorry to hear that . . . what was wrong?" "She had a problem with a period that went septic due to an infection." "I see, is she alright?" "Yeah, she just needs some rest and medication." "That's good, so why did you come back to school then?" "Cause I didn't have any reason to stay home butt wipe!" "Man shoot, I would have made one."

"I can't see it doc, I need to get my grades up some, otherwise I'll be in the 10th grade again next year." "Yeah, your right, you are kind of stupid" he said grinning facetiously at Matt and scarffing his fries. "Fuck youuu!" countered Matt and throwing some fries at him and laughing. Ant just caught what he threw and ate them with utter contempt and amusement. "So what are you doing here Butt face? You're not even in this building during this period!"

"Oh I was just chillin out looking at the cheerleaders practice." "How they looking?" "Man! They look real fine this year, do you remember Margery

Hawkins?" "Yeah" "Boy, you should see her *NOW!*" "Yeah, how's she looking?" "Man she got it going on and I mean bad too! When I was out there awhile ago she was doing them splits and I saw that big monkey print man! I almost jumped out of my pants man! and them legs . . . oh boy! Would I like to spend some time between them puppies!"

"What about that ass? I know you didn't miss that!" "OOH WEE! Man you talking . . . *BOOYA!* She got ass for days and booty for weeks!" "That good huh?" "Matt, man she is PHAT!" Ant always made up his own words to describe things that he considered too off the chain for normal words to describe properly. If a girl had big tits he would change it to "Tig Ole Biddies" or big ole titties. And to say Booya was to describe a girls extremely well rounded and luscious butt. "So who is she dating right now?"

"Nobody I know of, but you can bet it won't be long if she ain't and you can bet or that!" "Hey you know Cheryl has been looking for you?" "For what?" "I don't know, maybe she want's to give you some" he said smirking like the Grinch.

"Naw slick, I pass, you take my light weight." "I don't know man, I don't believe I could if I tried." "Why?" "You know why, you got her head all screwed up till where she can't see nobody but you, and to be perfectly honest with you she don't seem like she's gonna let up till you do one or two things." "And that is?"

"Well for one you could go ahead and knock them boots and put her out of her misery, and the other is transfer back to Southwest." "That's kind of crazy don't you think?" "Yeah, but it's either that or put up with her until she gets you and you bust that ass or runs you crazy trying to get you to do it."

"Well, you can bet she ain't gonna get any play here, and I don't plan on being chased all over the school system by a bunch of sex starved girls either." "Well old man, it's your problem and your decision all by yourself." "Yeah, I guess it is." "You done eating?" "Yeah I'm done" he said dropping the remnants of his burger on his plate. "Come on then, let's break." Both boys got up and headed for the door. They were the only two left in the lunch room.

"Hey did Mrs. Pratt write you up?" "Naw man she cut me some slack and actually gave me a hook up by contacting my other teachers and letting them know what the deal was." "That's dope!" "Yeah, she's a good lady." "She's a fine lady you mean!" "Yeah that too!" The last two classes of the day went by quickly and Matt was heading to the gym to meet up with Ant so they could dress out for track practice.

Several guys were already bunched into the locker room getting changed, some were football jocks and others were into baseball. Most of them still had fragments of old uniforms or unwashed jockey straps hanging from a hook inside their lockers.

Matt hadn't been assigned a locker yet and decided to wait till he was given one before undressing. Soon Ant came strolling in. "Matt where did you go man,

I was waiting for you?" "Hey as soon as the bell rang I split." "Didn't you hear me calling you?" "Nope" "Yeah, I was trying to catch up to you." "Well you knew where I was going."

"Yeah but Cheryl was with me and she wanted to talk to you." "Then it's a good thing I didn't stop, I ain't got no time for her shit today." "Well looks like you'll have to deal with it anyway." "How's that?" "She's on the girls team." "Aw fuck! When did this happen?" "Don't know, I just saw her running into the girls locker room." "Well she might not be on the team?" "Trust me dude, she is, in fact she has her shoes already." "Damn! Ain't that a bitch."

Just then coach Jones came in and he was wearing his usual orange shorts with dark blue strips on the side and an orange and white shirt. His whistle was polished to a high shine and he sported a healthy beer gut that only a Texan would love. However; his powerful arms, legs, and calves that you could break a bat on more than made up for it. "Okay, you little fart busters everyone gather round." Dressed or not everyone came to his call.

"Okay, I have a list of names and when I call your name go to the back of the room and stand in line. Jenkins, Marshall, Hopkins, Waters, Spalding, Fryer, Williams, Mathis . . ." Soon he'd called us all and we waited patiently in line in front of the gear locker. "Everybody listen up! There are two lists up here and two boxes on each list, you will put your name, shirt, and short pants size, on the other, put your shoe size."

"Now in each box there are tank tops and shorts, they are only temporary, so don't worry about what they look like, just get one of each that fits." "This will be your practice uniform, when you're done doing that file outside onto the track." Everyone moved fast and scrambled to get their gear and go.

Coach Jones wasn't one you wanted to keep waiting for anything. Apart from his large gut and appendages he also weighed in at a whopping 350 pounds and could put it to work on you severely if he chose to. He had sparse, bald to thinning grayish white hair which he kept trimmed around the edges of his melon sized head that most of us guys like to refer to as the moon going around the sun; his belly being the sun.

Coach Jones also sported a sinister like grin much like that of a skull grinning at you. It never seemed to leave his face. When he was pleased with you; which wasn't very often you could see the crows feet in the corners of his eyes. Other than that he had a voice that could melt lead bricks. Still, he was a good man and loved to see his boys and girls kick ass on the field and in the classroom.

To make sure they did, he trained them hard. Everyone filed outside on the track and waited. There were twelve boys in all. "Alright guy's, I want you all to pair off and begin stretching in the infield, take your time and stretch well because today we are gonna find out where you do your best at so you can get a spot on the team." Matt and Ant got together and did some butterfly stretches with their legs.

Matt commented that his legs were a little stiff but soon warmed up to the task. Ant was real limber already because of his length. He could easily bend his chest to his knees and would probably make a good hurdler. "What events are you going for Matt?" "I don't know, maybe some relay teams or something, what about you?" "I don't know, I shoot "B-ball" remember?" "Yeah, but you should try out for the hurdles or the long jump, I think you would be good at them." "You think so?" "Shoot yeah, all you need to do is get your technique down and you're in like flint."

"Okay, but I don't know what I'm doing so can you give me some pointers?" "Yeah, I can give you a few pointers I learned from my brother Jr." "That'll be cool . . . so you think you want to do relays huh?" "I don't know yet, I'll probably wait and see how I stack up against the rest of these guys on each one."

Soon everybody was good and loose and ready to get busy. "Okay guys, gather round, it's time to get it on! First of all were gonna do some field events then we'll move on to the track." "That way you'll still have some juice left to burn on the track, now the first event is the discus." "I've got Mark hear from the varsity team to show you the proper technique so you can get the max distance from your throw, also so you don't hit anyone in the area and avoid tearing your arm off!" he said chuckling and running his tongue around his teeth like he was checking his dentures. "Now don't try to throw it to the moon on the first try because it's got some weight and you'll pull a muscle, go ahead Mark."

Mark was a tall lean Adonis with manicured blonde hair and cable like muscles. He stood a good six feet six inches tall, powerfully build legs and steel blue eyes that gleamed when the sun hit them. He was smooth and methodical in his movements with no waste. He stepped into the cement circle and breathed deeply and rhythmically as he set up to throw the disc a good eight inches in diameter looked like a small flying saucer and Matt grinned to himself as he imagined little aliens inside of it screaming because he was about to put them back into outer space.

Mark set his feet apart a little more than shoulder width and one slightly further back than the other. He began his windup by slowly cranking the disc from behind his back in a wide arc to his front at a 45 degree angle in front of his face. He did this a few times gaining speed as he went, then made a powerful turn in one heel then released the disc with one a grunt, "Ugh!"

The disc spun cleanly and gracefully in a high straight arc. "Wow! What a throw" said Ant. "That thing ain't gonna land till it hits the river!" Coach Jones just grinned and nodded his approval of Marks world class effort. One reason why he was ranked number one in the state for two years running.

The disc flew long and far and finally leveled off and began its descent. It landed with a hard thud near the long jump pit. "Mathis, Williams, take this measuring tape and mark it from the edge of the pit to where it landed. "Okay coach" they said then hustled to get it done.

Matt took the loose end and ran all the way to where the disc had landed then touched it to that spot. Ant held the tape and watched the numbers tick off as he went. When Matt finally stopped he looked at the reading.

"Holy shit!" he heard himself say a little louder than he intended and quickly tried to right himself when the others began laughing at him. Coach Jones just grinned and played with his teeth. "Whatcha got Williams?" "110.8 feet coach." Mark just shrugged, "Guess I need to work on that some huh coach?" he muttered.

Coach Jones just crinkled his brow and shook his head. "Damn good shot son, damn good, now do all of you see how it's done?" They all nodded. "Good, now all you guys line up and practice your wind up and then we'll throw a few." "Mathis you and Williams stay put for a minute and measure that toss." "Yes sir" they chirped. Within the next half hour each of the boys took a turn and some had to go twice because they let the disc come off to soon and not straight enough. Matt and Ant went last. "Okay, Williams, throw that damn thing to the moon." He said grinning at the ungainly tall boy in the pit.

Ant was as tall as Mark but nowhere near the same build. He had the body of a potential Olympian and his movements were fluid and smooth enough, but he lacked a little muscle and definition. Ant did a few practice cranks trying to get his form right as he'd been shown. He spun himself hard and let go.

"Ughn!" he grunted and away the disc flew! The disc didn't go very high in fact it stayed at almost head level in a straight line. It went a good distance then landed. Hopkins and Thomas marked it. "100 feet even coach!" "That's good son, you got more juice in them arms then I thought you had, if you set your foot before you let go you'll get more range and height in your throw." "Thanks coach, I'll work on that" he said stepping from the pit. Everyone else had hit between 80 and 90 feet so Ant was in good standing. Mark looked at him and gave him a nod of approval and a smile.

A subtle kindness that Ant found meant something to him as he blushed from the acknowledgement of a proven athlete. "Okay Mathis, your on deck son, put it in the river if you can" he said chuckling trying to inspire him as he knew Matt was a competitive person by nature from watching him in gym class. Matt felt thick with ambition and his conviction to this task began to show on his face. His arms ached and his chest felt tight as his adrenalin level rose. He hadn't thought much about the event or that he would feel so intense about it when he got his chance. His stride to the pit was strong and confident much like that of a panther in the woods. His eyes began to burn as his focus drew sharp the closer he got to the disc.

Ant stood by the pit with his foot propped on the small brick barrier in the front of the pit with his arms folded. He gave Matt a conceited smirk as if to say, *"Do your worst ass wipe, you won't beat me!"* Matt walked up to him without looking at him and extended his arm. It shot out like a crane's boom and his hand planted in his chest. A glancing blow as he pushed him out of the circle. *"One side asshole"* he seemed to growl at him as the blow pushed the wind out of him and made him stumble. *"Ooph!"*

Coach Jones could feel the tension and competition in the air and the smell was sweet. He loved it when his athletes transformed into claw bearing, bold, lumbering timber wolves right before his eyes. He would often tell the other coaches that it was a thing of beauty. The other guys just snorted and shifted their stances much like nervous gazelles standing on an African plain and murmured their comments of challenge.

Things in Matt's mind seemed to move in slow motion as he reached down and picked up the disc. It had a cool smooth feel to it and felt powerful in his hands. He slowly wiped off some grass and dirt that had stuck to it and examined it as if checking for anything that would hamper his throw. He set himself in the pit and tried his best to mimic the stance and movements of Mark who had mastered his technique over the last two years. He watched Matt closely and marveled at his quick adaptation to the technique.

He thought that Matt looked powerful and full of conviction, a feeling he himself had experienced many times. It made his breathing shallow and he absent mindedly shifted his weight to the other leg, arms folded. A lonely bead of perspiration coalesced at the nape of his neck and slowly worked it's way down the center of his back. A soft breeze followed sending a chill down his spine making him involuntarily go erect. Matt wound up slow and smoothly. He went back low and came forward high. His movements were flawless and his concentration stoic. He saw no one and heard only the sound of his heart beat strong and constant. He did his wind up three times and on the last rotation, went into a mighty spin!, then stopped like a brick hitting a wall then let go. "Ugh!" he grunted giving the disk a powerful throw.

"Fuck me!" chirped Waters as Matt let go of the spinning disc. It launched like a missile, straight fast and true. The disc had a slight arc at about 30 degrees and flew almost perpendicular to the ground. The height had to be at least twenty feet as it flew like a clay pigeon. All eyes were on the disc as it flew like it didn't want to ever land. Matt still crouched, watched it as well with incredulous eyes as he wasn't thinking about the same things as everyone else but instead an invisible point in the sky way beyond the distance of the disc. After what seemed an eternity the disc began to waver a little and fall though its level flight path everyone saw where it was going and unconsciously voiced their thoughts.

"Hell no" "You got to be shittin me!" "No friggin way dude!" "Daaaamn!" "Sonofabitch!" uttered coach Jones as he shook his head at the amazing throw that everyone else was seeing. Mark's heart lapsed and he just bowed his head and shook it like he couldn't believe what he was seeing. The disc made a loud clank as it hit the goal post near the other end of the field. It deflected wildly and crashed to the ground with a thud. Marshall, one of the tape holders threw up his hands as the flat round bullet past him.

"TOUCHDOWN!" Coach Jones looked at Matt, then back at the goal posts several times, through squinting eyes, hands on his hips. He didn't say anything but just laughed to himself and shook his head. "Sonovabitch, I knew that boy was a jock" he mumbled. "Mark it!" he shouted without looking back, now facing away from the landing. Marshall and Hopkins gladly ran to their jobs as they were as curious as everyone else how far he had thrown the damn thing. Everyone had an idea it was well over 100 feet because the pit is located two thirds the distance of the field in the opposite direction. The football field was 100yards in length or 300 feet. Matt had hit a goal post on the far end well outside the range of the best throw. "Hey coach, It's 151 feet 3 inches!" shouted Marshall from the pit.

"Damn Matt, you need to get laid dude" said Hopkins holding the tape. All the guys started laughing at the comment thinking it would be rough for any female who would haplessly get in bed with a gorilla like Matt. Matt just pumped his fist like a golfer scoring a hole in one. "Yesss!" the guys weren't the only ones to see the throw and resultant impact with the goal post. Cheryl was standing off to the side with the girls team listening to the idle chatter around her about the same thing but with much more admiration.

"Oh yess, his ass is definitely mine!" she muttered to herself standing hands on hips trying to catch her breath after a hundred yard dash sortie. "Damn Matt, what have you been eating . . . monkey meat?" teased Ant as he walked up to shake his hand. "Maybe" he said smiling back. "Yeah, I believe you have, you fuckin animal" retorted Ant.

Coach Jones walked over and grasped Matt in a vicious head lock with his python sized arms. "You little fart buster, I knew you had some of your brother in you!" Mark looked on and just shook his head walking away towards the gym. "Damn glad he's not a senior yet, I'd be hell trying to beat him."

"Okay boys, we've got our two discus men so let's go on over to the shot put circle and get some time in there." "Mark had returned with a bottle of water and demonstrated this event as well as several other field events. He was an all around athlete and very good as all the guys came to realize. Even Matt had to admit the guy was good and he could never see himself doing a pole vault or high jump which Mark made look easy.

After all these events were demonstrated, tried, practiced and individuals chosen to take it. Everyone moved over to the track which needed no instruction except in the hurdles and that was just technique. By the end of practice, the line up was as follows; on the 220 meter individual medley was Hopkins and Marshall. On the 440 meter medley and relay team would be; Mathis, Jenkins, Ryeback, and Fisher with Jenkins doing the single 440 medley. On the 880 meter medley it was Williams and Thomas. Jones turned out to be a good sprinter so he took the 100 yard dash spot and the mile. On the mile relay team it was Mathis, Spalding, Fisher, and Williams. For the pole vault it was just Marshall. On shot put it was Jenkins. On hurdles Ant took that spot and finally in the high, long and triple jumps it was Marshall, Ryeback, Mathis and Williams.

Now the team was complete and all the spots were taken unless someone else decided to join the team. This wasn't very likely because of such a large turn out and the fact that the team sign up had been all over school for over two weeks now so anyone who wasn't there today lost out. It was now 5:00pm and practice was over. All the guys headed for the locker room to shower and get gone because they were beat.

"Man, that was one hellacious first practice" said Matt pushing Ant out of the way before he could sit and dropping down on a bench in the locker room. "Yeah, I didn't think it would be so rough." "Shoot yeah, you know how Coach Jones is." "No, not really, you played ball for him a couple of times and all I know about him is from gym class." "All I know is Coach Lightfoot and B-ball" said Ant dropping down on a bench opposite Matt's. "How is ole Lightfoot? I don't see him unless it's a game going on?" "Not to bad, he be running our ass like slaves though during basket ball season." "Well it's a good thing you're on the track team cause you'll get a chance to stay in shape in the off season, it will do you good and help you build your stamina because you do have some."

"You got some yourself" added Ant. "You ran that 440 relay like you was running through hell with gasoline drawers on!" Matt just laughed and shook his head. "Boy you nuts, I guess you could say it helps when I'm trying to stay out of reach of Cheryl" "Ain't that the truth!" said Ant giving him a high five. Once they had gotten showered and dressed they went outside and saw that some of the girls from the track team were still hanging around. They were talking and resting from practice.

"Hey Matt, why is it that when women sweat they look so sexy but when we sweat we just look beat?" "Hell, I don't know, you want me to get you a bra and panties so you can find out?" "Naw, Negro!" he said snatching his towel from his neck and popping Matt with it. *"Crack! Pow!"* "Oh you sonovabitch, that's your ass!" Said Matt rolling his own towel into a rat tail. *"Pow Pow!"* "Ow! Damn!" said Ant as Matt had caught him twice in the butt and lower leg. Ant started running with Matt quick on his heals and popping him all the way.

All of a sudden Matt heard a sharp crack and felt white hot pain on his own butt. He turned around quickly to see who had stolen him from behind. "Ow! Who the fu . . .?" he said turning around to find a laughing Cheryl standing there with her own rat tail and rolling it up again for a second attack. "Why you sneaky wench!" he grimaced rubbing his butt. Matt was hot but he couldn't be too mad at her especially when she was standing there in those tight shorts and top looking good enough to eat. Oh, she was gorgeous alright with her hair pressed against her head from sweating and her tank top revealing the little orb like nipples of her even sweatier breasts. The tight fitting shorts she had on left little to the imagination and she was looking hot!

Matt had to admit that the girl had skills and it was definitely a challenge to leave her alone especially now that he was seeing more of her than he was used to. Cheryl noted the long and lengthy walk Matt's eyes were taking all over her body. It felt good and she had to squeeze her legs together at the feeling he caused her to have.

"I told you I was gonna get even with you one day" she said getting back her control and tossing her towel over her shoulder. She stood there hands on her hips and propping on one hip. "So you did" Matt said coolly trying not to show his interest in her great assets. "Hey Ant" he said behind him without breaking his gaze on her. "Yeah" "What do we do with uninvited hot crossed buns who get in the way?" Ant looked at her vacetiously leaning against Matt's shoulder. "We eat um!" he shouted then they both started attacking her with towels. "Whack, crack, *Ow!* Snap, pop pow!" "*Quit it!*" Crack, crack. "Matt, wait I'm sorry!" she said trying to retreat but not doing very well. The onslaught went on and Cheryl ran from one direction to another like a stampeded calf. No matter where she went a towel was waiting for her.

Other onlookers just laughed and commented about how she was getting what she asked for. Finally she ran into the girl's locker room the minute the door opened. The boys stopped and Cheryl stuck her head out from the safety of the door and started taunting them. "Ah ha I beat you to losers you can't get me in here . . . Nah" she said sticking out a pink little tongue and did a little dance in the door. She then turned her rear end at them and patted it soundly then closed the door hard in their faces. She could be heard on the other side laughing wildly with several other girls.

Ant and Matt looked at each other incredulously still holding towels at the ready. "I know I ain't going out like that" said Matt. "Me neither" said Ant. They executed a series of over, under, hand clasp, hand shakes ending with two pats on the chest with their fists and a finger snap. Matt threw open the door and stomped in with Ant right behind him. After that, all that could be heard were screams and the sound of two towels going *SNAP, POP, CRACK!!*

After about a minute or two, two boys could be seen running out of the door. "We hooked that ass *UP!*" Said Matt giving Ant a high five. Behind them Cheryl with her hair a dismal mess and clothes all a mess and several other girls in like manner standing in the door hands on hips and sporting a most evil look on their faces.

Audrey was finishing the dinner dishes. She hadn't cooked very much today because her mind was on Aretta. As soon as she was done she and Lori would go up to visit her and see how she was doing. Lori was busy in her room cleaning and trying to be helpful so she wouldn't be sitting around and getting in her mother's way.

"Ring!" "I'll get it" said Audrey quickly drying her hands on her apron. "Hello?" "Hello . . . is this Audrey?" "Yes it is." "Well, Hello there stranger, this is Buford." The voice sang whimsically. "Oh hi, Buford how are you?" "Oh fine, I just got home awhile ago and decided to give you a call." "That was nice of you to think of me." "So how have you been?" "Not too good." "Oh what's going on?" "Aretta's in the hospital." "Oh my goodness, is she alright?" "Yes, but she'll be there for a little while . . . at least a few days." "What's wrong with her?" "Well this morning she had a massive hemorrhage because of an infection in her uterus." "My goodness!" he said concerned. "Do they know what caused it?" "Yes, it is caused by a blockage I think he said a clot that kept her from a normal flow, her last cycle didn't clear itself fully or she had something behind that contributed to the infection." "So when her next cycle came, it had trouble releasing." "Poor thing, when are you going to see her again?"

"Well, I was just getting ready to go as soon as I finished the dishes." "Well how about it I swoop by there and pick you guys up, then we can all go together." "That would be really nice if you don't mind." "No, of course not, I'd like to see how she' doing myself, does Rodney know yet?" "Yess! He got there only minutes after we did." "Who told him?" "Nobody, he said he felt her while he was in class, then just took off from school." "To where?" "To Retta's school I guess, that's where he found Retta's friend Frieda, the big girl that lives just across from us?"

"Yes, I seem to recall her." "She told him what hospital she was in." "You mean to say that boy rode all the way over to Southwest from school on a whim then out to the hospital?" "Well actually no . . . it wasn't a whim or a hunch, she was sick and he was right about what he was feeling, even if he didn't have any facts."

"I see" said Buford somewhat subdued and not liking to think of Rodney as running all over town when he should be in school. Especially when he didn't have any facts. He couldn't of course voice this because at best it would only serve to upset and alienate Audrey about her daughter and at worst would maybe get the phone hung up in his face along with a few choice words. Audrey sensed his hesitation and concerns in his long pause.

"Buford, I know all this is a lot to take in and smacks of a little recklessness on his part but there is one other concept you might want to consider." "What's that?" "The fact that our children are truly and deeply in love with each other." "Yes, I have seen some of their conviction and love for each other, but isn't that maybe putting to fine of a point on it to say they have become somewhat psychic with it?" "No, not really." "How so?" "Well I don't know how well you know your son, but I know my daughter very well, and her feelings are very strong when you tap into them." "Okay, but what about Rodney?"

"Yes I know my son, and he is equally as devoted, even passionate about things sometimes to a flaw but I don't see this evolving to the level you're putting it at." "Buford, your kidding me right?" she said delicately but sounding a little hurt at Buford's cold sense of or lack of insight. "Well . . . I don't mean to sound cold and insensitive, but I just don't see much in this and think it's just him wanting to get out of school early to go over there and meet up with her at school, this untimely condition seemed to just fit coincidentally."

"Buford Mathis! Our children have developed for lack of a better word a "spiritual bond" with each other and no time, place, or distance is gonna interrupt that . . . !" "Hold on Audrey . . ." "No! you wait, I have seen your son with my daughter and talked with him in and out of her presence, I have never in my life seen any man young or old with as much raw passion, conviction, and dedication to the one he loves than your son Buford."

"Hell, I wish that Retta's father had some of his qualities!" "If he had, maybe we would still be together, but since he doesn't, we aren't so, don't go trying to belittle him or my daughter for that matter . . . unless you think he's too good for her" she chimed before going quiet. "Audrey, I'm sorry I didn't mean to imply that our kids don't know what they feel for each other or the full magnitude of it, I was just thinking that it sounded a little far out for Rodney at least . . . I'm sure it could happen but do you believe that's what really happened?"

"I have to Buford, what if anything else explains it? I know I didn't tell him and he had to have learned it from someone because I left after the ambulance and Freida was in school sometime after we left, so there was no way she told him till he got to her school." "Yeah, I guess you're right, I know he loves her very much, but I wasn't sure just how much till now." "Do you think they've been intimate with each other yet?" he asked shyly. Audrey just laughed like it was the funniest thing she has ever heard. "Oh Buford, come on you mean you didn't know?" "Uh no . . . should I have?"

"Why yes, they have, but don't worry yourself I've long since given Aretta her pep talk and Rodney has proven his control and responsibility about the matter thus far." "So it doesn't bother you that our children are having sex then?" "Well I wouldn't necessarily say that, because all mothers worry about that particular day when their daughters start getting active, but I must commend you in this matter too." "Me, for what?"

"Well Buford, our children are reflections of ourselves." "True." "So in this perspective, you have raised him well up to this point and I think he is a perfect gentleman, all things considered." "And anything that he and Aretta do together I'm sure is of the utmost responsible and modest." "Well that's good to hear, I've always tried to guide him well, but as you know there comes a time we must let them go and do their own thing, make their mistakes and hope that some of our good advice and instruction has rubbed off."

"Like I said, he was taught well, so when will you be here?" "Give me twenty minutes, I'm still wearing my uniform." "Okay then, I'll see you shortly." "Okay . . . oh by the way is Rodney there?" "No, he hasn't come home from school yet." "Oh okay." "I'll leave him a message if he doesn't show up before I leave."

"Okay Buford, see you in a few." "Alright . . . bye now." Click, "Lori are you finished with you room yet?" "Yes ma'am" "Okay, Rodney's father is gonna come pick us up and take us to see Retta." "Is Rodney coming to?" "We hope so, his father said he wasn't home yet from school so we'll have to wait and see, so in the meantime why don't you run on over to Freida's and see if she would like to come." "Okay ma" she said running out the door. She couldn't wait to see her big sister and was sure that Freida would be glad to come too.

Audrey was putting away the last of the dishes and humming a happy tune. "That Buford is really nice to offer to take us up there, I wonder what he thinks of me? he'd make any woman a nice catch but then again he probably doesn't want to be tied down right now by someone with two daughters, still he's a nice distraction though, and I can't say I've had man lately since Butler split." "He said I was too possessive and came on too strong for him, I thought that's what all men wanted is to be pampered and sexed by a woman who loved them, Sigh . . . I guess some men don't adjust to such close attention and are quick to run when they feel trapped, Sigh . . . I guess I'll have to take it slower this time and not rush into anything." "Hell! What am I thinking about, Buford hasn't even said whether or not he's even really interested in me, I mean all we did was have a drink or two and talk a little bit . . . maybe a little cuddling but that doesn't mean he wants me, but still, he's a prize catch though." "Sigh . . . I wonder how he kisses?"

Buford was just finishing dressing. He put on a conservative blue sports coat and his tan slacks with the pleated pockets. He topped this off with a white short sleeve shirt. He was just now wondering where Rodney was and when he would be home. It's not like him to stay gone so long without calling home, or dropping by first.

"Oh well, I'll just leave a note for him so he'll know I went up to the hospital, it's a shame his girl is ill like this" he thought to himself. "But it's a good thing someone was around when it did happen, otherwise it could have been worse.

Matt and Ant were on their way to the hospital to see Retta in that same moment. "Hey, Matt do you think she'll be awake yet?" "I don't know, I hope so." "Yeah me too." "I hope those flowers I brought this morning will perk her up." "Do you remember which room she's in?" "Yeah, It's room 318 on the third floor."

Soon they had arrived and this time Matt parked near the front door in a bicycle rack. "Hey, you think they'll say anything about you parking here?" "Probably not, I mean it is a bike in some respects, so you can't really call it a motor vehicle totally, plus you don't need a license to ride it so we're safe enough." "The worst that can happen is they move it and that's no big deal either." "Okay Matt you know" said Ant shaking his head in disbelief at his friends logic. "Come on, let's go."

The hospital was cold and quiet when they passed through the electric doors. The only sounds were the nurses at the front desk in admissions and the low murmur of a few people to the right in a small waiting room. The lobby was pretty big, it had a gift shop to the left of the entrance and another large waiting area to the right. The waiting area had three large televisions and a magazine rack in the center surrounded by lots of comfortable looking couches and chairs. The floors, Matt noticed were highly polished and reflected like mirrors and had a brown and white checker board pattern in it. There were several offices along the wall behind the admissions desk and they ran from one end of the hall to the other and on the facing side were elevators and a small examination room. At the end of the hall to the left was a snack bar.

"Do we need to ask permission to go up?" said Ant. "Naw, it's time for visitation anyway and we already know the room so we can just go on up." "Alright, let's go." They took the elevator to the left side of the hall. It's amazing how fast elevators in hospitals work, if you had to get one someplace else you'd be there forever waiting for it. Suddenly the big steel doors opened and several staff and visitors stepped off. Matt hit two buttons and the door closed. "You ever notice how these elevators have a funny smell?" he said. "What do you expect knuckle head, this is a hospital" said Ant giving him a light smack up side the head.

"Ding" the ride was over and they were on the third floor. "Which way?" said Ant. "This way" said Matt pointing to the right. Retta's room was four doors down. "Let's try to be quiet" he said opening the door slowly. Retta still lay sleeping but with all the appliances removed accept a tube in her arm for fluids and a monitor. Matt choked a little as he looked at her. He also noticed that someone had brushed her hair, and washed her face.

She looked so delicate and so beautiful lying there that Matt could feel his heart pulling from him to be nearer to her. Her skin color also had returned and now she was a soft golden color as he was used to seeing. Matt slowly walked over to her and ever so gently picked up her hand and held it. Ant quietly found a chair and sat down beside her bed on the other side. His heart twitched a little inside him when he looked at his friend and saw the great love and care he had for her. It made him feel good inside and proud to know Matt. Matt gently sat on the edge of her bed and caressed her check with the back of his hand. Her face was turned away from him but he could still see that she was resting easy. Matt slowly walked his eyes all over her entire body from head to toe taking her all in.

She was wearing a white hospital gown with little pink dots and a red band on her wrist with her name and other information on it. He gently raised her hand to his face and caressed it with his cheek, inhaling and breathing every ounce of her essence as he did. He kissed it deeply and softly placed it back on the covers and held it there. Ant could see the intense love his friend had for Retta and wished he had someone to love like that. The thought and sight embarrassed him some and made him uncomfortable and he shuffled his feet and looked away out the window.

He wanted to leave but instead sat in silence not daring to speak but letting his friend have his private time and retrospect. Ant could imagine what Matt was feeling inside as he would have been feeling and thinking the same thing if he had a girl like her in a place like this.

Ant had, had a few girlfriends but none that gave him the true love he was looking for. Matt debated whether or not he should, but wanted to kiss her cheek so bad, but didn't want to wake her. He decided he would go for it and eased in close and kissed her cheek for a long second then recovered leaving a small tear on her cheek. He dried it with a tissue and marveled at how soft it was. Slowly Matt could see her eyes begin to flitter and movement in her fingers as he held it. Retta rolled her head to the side to see who was there and holding her hand. She blinked several times to clear the cloudiness in her vision. Her throat felt a little raspy and dry and she tried to clear her throat "*uh uh uh.*"

Matt saw what she was trying to do and quickly looked at Ant and pointed to the table with the cup of ice water on it. Ant was glad for the opportunity to do something . . . anything! Just something to get away from the feelings eating at him. Retta fluttered her eyes once more trying to adjust to the light. As her vision cleared, she saw who it was and was elated. She wanted so bad to sit up but felt so very weak. He saw her strain and shook his head no. "No baby, you don't need to get up, I'll come to you. She gave him her best smile as he hugged her and tried not to squeeze her as hard as his heart was telling him too.

Matt kissed her on her dry lips and a tear fell from her eye. Happiness was all over her face but she could not tell him as her voice had not come back yet, being they had tubes down her throat for a time. Ant stood holding the cup and hoping they would hold up for a second so he could give it to her. Not to mention the emotion in the room was so thick it was like being in a pool of molasses. Matt reached out for the cup and held it for her to take a few sips from the straw, all the while each never taking their eyes from one another. They beheld each other like life itself had been returned to them in a dead world. They didn't speak but just caressed each other's cheek lovingly and looked at each other with deep penetrating eyes of love.

The deep love and the fact that Matt was the first person she saw when she awoke made her love him more and feel very warm inside. "I love you baby" he whispered. "I love you too" she mouthed wordlessly. He gave her another kiss, but this time much deeper and held it longer before recovering. As he did he saw that Audrey, Lori and his dad were standing just inside the door quietly watching them.

Matt felt a little embarrassed but quickly put away the thought as she was the love of his life he was kissing and it didn't matter who saw. Audrey smiled at him and lightly elbowed his dad as afterthought to their recent discussion. Retta saw his eyes shift towards the door and slowly turned to see her mother, sister and Matt's dad.

"Hey sleepy head" said Audrey walking over to hug her. "*Hey ma*" she croaked reaching up to hug her neck. Lori ran over, grabbed Retta around the neck putting a crushing choke hold on her. "*Uh! Uh . . . Lori your choking me sweetie*" she croaked trying to loosen her little sisters grip. "I'm sorry" she said embarrassed and starting to pout as she eased herself back to the floor. Retta could see she was only excited to see her and just held onto her as long as she could to let her know she missed her too. "*It's okay pumpkin, you didn't do anything wrong.*" Matt could see the physical strain it was putting on Retta and he tried to lighten her load while not hurting Lori's feelings.

"Hey cutie pie how about a hug for me?" Lori was more than happy to oblige and her sweet smile returned as she let go of Retta and came around the bed to shower Matt with kisses and hugs. "Hey kiddo" said Buford leaning in to give her a hug. "*Hi Mr. Buford*" "How are you feeling?" "*I'm feeling much better, but still a little sore in my stomach.*" "It'll pass, your still recovering honey, it will probably take a while longer before the antibiotics really start to work" said Audrey. "*I didn't know you guys were coming, I really didn't expect anyone, I was asleep until Matt showed up.*"

"We were not expecting him to be here either, Buford and I had made plans to come and hoped he would be home from school before we left, but it looks like he got here before we did." "We had track practice Mrs. Davis, and we had just gotten finished about a half hour ago." "*Oh really?*" "Yeah, a few teachers of mine have been at me to join the team, I guess they figure that I would be as good as my brother Jr." "*So are you as good?*" "Don't really know yet, it's only been one day and we still have a ways to go in training, you have to ask Ant." "Yeah, he's got some juice." "*Well I guess I'm gonna have to hurry up and heal so I can come see you run sometime.*"

"That would be great, but don't be in too big of a hurry sweet pea, you're going to take your time and stay put until your well enough to leave, then when you get home you're going to rest some more." Retta just smiled sweetly at him and did not challenge his position. She knew full well that once Matt made up his mind about something it was futile to argue. Audrey and Buford just looked at each other out the corner of their eyes, sporting perplexed expressions of amusement. They were somewhat surprised at how Matt had pulled rank on Audrey and taken full responsibility and charge of Retta's rehabilitation.

"Oh by the way, I heard about what you had gotten into in school the other day" said Matt looking at her in mock anger. "Retta why didn't you tell me?" pressed Audrey. *"I'm sorry mom, I didn't get a chance to tell you."* "How did it happen?" *"I don't know, I was just trying to get in my locker and these boys started harassing me an pushing me around."* "Why didn't you tell a teacher or someone?" *"They wouldn't let me alone ma, and I couldn't get away to tell anyone, besides there was a crowd blocking the way."*

Her voice beginning to crack from rising stress of her mother's untimely interrogation. Buford didn't think that this was the time or place to be harassing Retta just now. He knew it wasn't his place to interfere but felt it his duty as a parent to at least try to put a halt to it for now so as not to make Retta's health any worse. "So what were you trying to prove by fighting them? you could have gotten seriously injured." "Mom, I had no choice, *they were trying to hurt me and no one would make them stop!*" she said croaking and tears welling in her pain stricken eyes. "Hey! Hold on Audrey" said Buford taking her arm firmly but gently.

He could see Retta had had enough and this wasn't doing her any good at all. "Sometimes boys can be really rotten and they seem to always get a kick out of harassing girls when they do, so let's not jump to any conclusions okay sweetie?" "I mean, she did the best she could with what she had and for the most part came out okay or better than most in the same situation." "Yeah that does happen every now and then Mrs. Davis" said Matt also coming to Retta's defense. "Sometimes we can be down-right belligerent and mean, so it's not Retta's fault, she fought back, in fact from what I've been told she put a serious hurting on all of them and they hardly laid a glove on her" he said squeezing her hand for support.

Audrey just stood there pensive and cutting her eyes at the three of them, not really believing Retta had no options. She knew her daughter and was well aware that Retta could be aggressive when she wanted to be and if the mood struck her she would open up a can of whoop-ass on anyone she felt was deserving or in her way.

"Well that's real convenient for both of you to say isn't?" she said somewhat frudroiantly and cocking her head to the side for emphasis. "Buford you don't have any daughters I'm aware of, so you don't know what It's like to have to protect and raise one" she said slowly stabbing a finger into his chest. "Hey, wait a min . . . !" "No you, wait Mr. Man!" She said squaring on him with one hand on her hip the other still pointing at his chest. *"Now I know where Retta gets it from"* said Matt whispering to Ant.

Retta caught the comment and squeezed Matt's hand viciously and gave him an angry pout. "I'm sorry boo, I was just poking at you." "And you, Rodney!" said Audrey squaring on him after sounding out his father. "Your not sitting to pretty either Mr., I have heard a little of the incident's you and this one have been engaged in." "Particularly an incident where Retta supposedly punched you in the gut in public and almost brought you to your knees . . . Hmm . . . sound familiar?" she said pointing at Retta and startling Matt.

Matt remembered the incident and then looked at Lori accusingly because he knew it had to have been she who played "song-bird" about the mall incident with the girl in the store. Matt had no come back so he just looked down at Retta's hand and played with her fingers. Audrey, now content that her point had been made, and her moral agitators silenced, stood with her arms folded and tapping her foot like a cat about to pounce on a rat. "Retta, who are these boys?" she asked. *"I really don't know mom, but I do know they have been suspended for 10 days each."* "Yes that's true, they have" said Matt backing her up again.

"How do you know so much about this Rodney?" said Audrey now getting a little perturbed at his constant up close and personal knowledge of all things *"Aretta."* "That's right Rodney, you don't even go to her school anymore" said his dad falling in with Audrey. Ant just looked back and forth from group to group enjoying the odd "tongue lashing" tennis match. "Well, I got connections over there and they keep me well informed of what goes on over there with Retta." *"You keeping tabs on me now Matt?"*

Retta easing her hand from his, sitting up in bed and folding her arms. *"Oh shit!, his nuts are in a vice now boy!"* mumbled Ant to himself snickering. "No sweet pea, I just have friends over there who I ask to look after you from time to time." *"Then how come they didn't help me when I was about to get my head kicked in then?"* she spat glaring at him with eyes going into slits. "Yeah!" followed his dad and Audrey.

"Oh hell" thought Matt wondering how this matter ever got to this point. *"Damn! I thought I was coming here to visit my baby, not get my nuts put in traction."* "Well from what I was told, two of my guys were in the gym that period and the other two told me that by the time they got wind of what was going on, you'd already made short work of them all." "And tell me . . . when did you learn Karate? I never knew you were into it."

"It's called TAI'CHI, and I've been doing it since I was eight years old, my father used to teach me, he was a Green Beret in the Army." "Ah ha!, so now I know what you two have been up to all those Saturday's you would take off into the woods all day!" Audrey said triumphantly. Retta just smiled bashfully. "Yes ma'am, dad didn't think you would like it too much so he taught me in a little clearing he made behind the house in the woods." "He said it was for self defense and I should never use it unless absolutely necessary." "Well I'd say it was necessary this time" said Buford lending a little support smiling at her.

"I used to teach that myself when I was teaching hand to hand combat maneuvers a long time ago when I was in Vietnam" he said proudly. *"Really? I didn't know that Mr. Buford"* she said animated and very interested in learning anything that would help her protect herself. "Maybe when your better I can show you some other techniques and how to put a man down with just your thumb."

"Now Buford, wait a minute! . . . she's bad enough as it is" said Audrey not wanting Retta to go out attacking everyone she saw. "I really appreciate your offering to teach her something new, but I really wouldn't feel comfortable knowing she could possibly learn more than she already does about this fighting stuff." *"Oh mom, don't worry, I've never used it before now and I've had plenty of situations in my life where I should have, so you can relax, I won't turn Kung Fu crazy on you"* she said laying back again in bed. "Retta when you coming home?" said Lori speaking up for the first time since they got there. "I don't know pumpkin, the doctor hasn't come to talk to me yet and I still feel a little weak and still hurt some in my stomach." Audrey went to hold her.

"My poor little girl, it'll be fine baby, you just need to stay in bed and take it easy like Rodney told you" she said flashing him a devious yet supportive smile. Matt blushed at this. *"Okay mama, I will."* "Have you eaten anything today?" *"No ma'am, they brought in some food a while ago but I couldn't eat."* "Why, is your stomach bothering you that much baby?" *"Yes ma'am."* "I'll ask the nurse if she can give you something for it, but in the meantime you must try to eat a little bit to get your strength up." *"I will, but for now I'm okay, just a little tired that's all."* "Okay baby, were gonna go ahead and leave and let you get some rest okay? I'll be back this evening okay?" *"Yes ma'am."*

She gave Retta one last hug and kiss, then Lori hugged her big sister. *"Lori you be good and don't worry okay? I'm getting better and I'll be home soon."* "Okey dokey" she said giving her another hug and kiss. Then Lori gave Retta her favorite stuffed animal for company. Retta's eyes got wet with the gesture her little sister made. *"Oh thank you Lori!"* Mr. Buford gave her a hug. "We'll see you soon okay sweetie? You get better now you hear?" "Yes sir, I will!" Then they left as quietly as they had arrived. Matt and Ant remained and for a brief second the room was completely silent. Retta sat in bed relaxed and looking at Matt with love swept eyes.

Matt thought she looked so beautiful and yet so sickly and frail. They just stared, looking at each other not saying anything, at least not with their mouths. Retta held out her arms for him and Matt came into them like a ship to a dock. He sat on the bed and held her close cradling her head in his hands and looking deeply into eyes. "I love you Retta" he whispered. "I love you too Matt!"

They gave each other Eskimo kisses and teased each others lips for a second or two, desire building with each passing moment. Matt lowered his mouth to hers and held her there feeling her breath in his mouth and luxuriating over every one she breathed into him. Retta was a little uncomfortable with her tummy still giving her shocks every now and then but it was minimal to the pain of wanting to have Matt in her arms and in her bed but couldn't.

"Can you possibly hold my heart any tighter that you do my love?" "I don't know Red bud I'm sure gonna try" he said, then kissed her passionately and deeply. Her lips were soft and warm. She kissed him with such conviction that

Matt could feel his spirit rising out of his body. He hadn't realized how much he had missed her and how much she truly meant till now. Matt heard himself whimper as he fell deeper and deeper into her embrace. Now there was no doubting that there would never be another woman but her. He would be hers and she would be his someday forever.

Retta felt him as much and tried her level best to pull Matt on top of her but he wouldn't let her. Not because Ant was in the room and not because he was in a hospital room and they could be discovered any minute. He didn't want to hurt her anymore than she already was. Ant got his cue and quietly excused himself. He started to say something but thought better of it and just quietly let himself out putting the do not disturb sign on the outside of the door. The two lovers kissed for what seemed forever. Retta could feel his love and devotion in every touch of his hand. She held him as tight as she could wanting so much to pull him in bed with her to lie beside her and hold her throughout the night.

"*Oh god thank you!*" she screamed in her mind. "*Thank you for sending me Matt, I could never have hoped for a more loving and compassionate man in my life. Oh how I want to be his wife someday and to be able to call him my husband. Just the thought makes me tingle all over. I want to have his children, I want to sleep beside him always and wake up to his loving arms every day.*" Just then a nurse came in, "Oops! I'm sorry, I didn't mean to break up such a loving scene" she said smiling devilishly and coming closer.

Matt and Retta parted quickly, surprised at the obvious intrusion. "Uh that's okay" said Matt getting off the bed and adjusting the covers. "I'm here to give Ms. Davis her sponge bath and medications, *are you Ms. Davis or Mrs. Davis by chance? . . . I forget which"* she asked being deliberately belligerent and rude. She knew we weren't married. "*No . . . I'm not Mrs. Davis!*" Hissed Retta sitting up with her arms folded.

She wanted to smack her for being persnickety, but decided to wait until she was better and on her way out of there. "She'll soon be Mrs. Mathis though, you got a problem with that . . . *nurse?*" Matt tossed back at her equally nasty. Retta had forgotten in all the hubbub about her ring he had given her. It was still on her hand and she proudly stuck it out for her to see. The sight of the diamond in the semi darkness made the nurse suck in and draw up short with surprise.

Aretta just smiled an looked at her as saucily as she could manage under the circumstances. "Well pardon me, maybe it's me that needs the medication" she said in mock exasperation trying to lighten the tension, seeing as how she had overstepped her bounds. "Anyway, since that hasn't happened yet, you must leave sir so I can bathe Ms. Davis." "Can I help? I'm good with my hands" said Matt smiling huge and reaching out with two very eager hands.

The nurse dipped her half cut glasses and looked at him like she was most annoyed. "Mr. *Mathis!*" she hissed. "Okay, okay! I'm just kidding" he said waving her off. "Baby, I'll see you tomorrow okay?" Retta pouted and bowed her head childishly. "You gonna go and leave me all alone Matt?" Those large piercing eyes, that pouty little lip.

"Now Red, you know I'm only a phone call away, but if you like I'll pull up a chair and sleep here tonight." "Naw, Matt I'm just playing baby, you know I wouldn't let you do that, I'll call you tonight okay sweet heart?" "Okay Retta" he gave her another hug and long kiss. *"HRRUMMPH!"* grunted the nurse tapping her foot, hands on hips and holding a sponge. "Okay, okay I'm going" he said getting up and heading for the door. "Bye love" he said as he opened the door. "Bye Matt . . . I love you." Then he was gone.

Chapter 8

The Mall

Retta felt much better now that he'd come and the nurse could see it. "That's quite a young man you have there!" "Yes ma'am, he is and he's all mine."

Ant was waiting outside the door when Matt came out. "Ready to go?" "Yeah lets break." "Are we going to your house or mine?" said Ant. "It don't matter, I'm just tired and want to eat something and crash for awhile." "Well, I'll tell you what, lets go to my house then we can order some pizza and crash in my room and watch TV." "That'll work" said Matt yawning.

Soon they were down stairs and heading out the door. The warm air felt and smelled good. "Ahh, fresh warm air, I don't think I could stand much more of that air conditioning." "Heck yeah, now I know why so many people stay sick in there." "Yeah, they be freezing to death!" Matt saw his bike as they rounded the corner. It was right where he left it but it had a small piece of paper on the handlebars.

"Rodney, I am taking Audrey and Lori home I'll see you soon . . . Dad." "It's from dad, he says he's taking Audrey and Lori home." "Anything else?" "Naw that's it." "Well, lets' jet man, I'm starved." "Get on then" Matt cranked the little scooter and they were on their way. It was dark now and the night traffic was really moving.

"I think we better take a short cut and try to avoid some of this traffic, otherwise were gonna end up somebody's hood ornament" said Matt looking for a way to change lanes. Matt drove on all the side streets and back roads he knew until he got to PioNono Avenue. Then he road on that for about five minutes, turned right on Napier Avenue, then pulled in front of Ant's house on Courtland Ave. He killed the engine and took out the key.

"Man, that was some ride!" said Ant getting off and rubbing his butt. "You're gonna have to get a bigger bike Matt, this moped ain't big enough for us both." "Then get your own damn bike . . . fool!" he spat smiling in a most obsequious manner. "Aw that's cold man, but that's okay I'm getting a car soon and you'll be watching me drive by! So think about that, "Evil Keneval!" "Yeah, but until then help me get it up the steps okay?" The two of them huffed and heaved the scooter up the long high steps from the sidewalk to the yard.

"Whew! . . . man who would'a thought this little thing could weigh so much?" complained Ant. "Well if you would clear that mess in the back yard I could cut through the banks parking lot and come in that way instead of humping up this hill all the time." "Maybe when I get time, but for now this is good enough, come on let's go inside, I'm so hungry my stomach thinks my throat is cut."

Matt just grinned at the sick metaphor and shook his head. He couldn't argue though because his own stomach was acting up something terrible too. Ant put his key in the door and opened it. "Hey gramma, I'm home!" "Alright Antney" she called back from somewhere in the house. "Me and my friend Matt are gonna hang out a while and get something to eat okay?" "You want me to fix you boys something?" "No ma'am, that's alright we'll just get a pizza." "Alright you enjoy." "Come on Matt let's go call em."

"You got a phone book?" "Yeah, it's over there somewhere by the door." Matt looked and found it sitting on an antique phone stand. "Who you want to order from?" "I don't know just pick somebody." Ant was busy undressing and putting on his favorite raggedy lounging sweats. He was in for the night and wasn't worried the least about how he looked.

"I'll call Little Ceasar's, they have a two for one deal and they don't cost a whole lot." "That'll work" said Ant flopping across his bed and turning on his TV set. "What do you want on it?" "Anything but onions and fish." "Yeah, me too, I don't see how people can eat fish on pizza." "That's gotta be real nasty."

"Well stop talking about it your making me lose my appetite. Matt picked up the phone and dialed. "Hello?" . . . "Little Ceaser's, may I help you?" "Yes I would like a medium pizza." "Get a large okay? . . . "Make that a large pizza with everything but onions and anchovies okay?" "Do you want anything to drink with that order?" "Ant, do you want anything to drink?" "Get me a Dr. Pepper and a Diet Pepsi."

"Okay sir, you order comes to $10.86 cents, will that be pick up or delivery?" "Delivery." "What's the address?" "2486 Courtland Ave." "Okay sir, it'll be 30 minutes on that order." "Okay, thanks." Click. "They said it would be about 30 minutes before they get here." "That's cool, cause there's a good movie coming on after this show so we can watch it when the pizza gets here" said Ant.

"Hey man, let me use your bathroom." "You know where it is." Matt had held his water long enough and had to go. It's amazing how long a person could wait when they had to. "Hey Ant, what time is it?" "It's 7:30 why?" "Nothing just checking, I need to give dad a call to let him know where I am." "I'll do it for you." "Okay thanks!" "Ring ... ring ... ring ... ring." "Hey Matt! There's nobody there." "Okay, he must be still over at Audrey's house or on his way home." "Why don't you give him a call and check him there." "What's the number?" "746-0202"

"Ring ring ... Hello?" "Hello, is Mr. Buford there?" "Yes he is, who's calling?" "Uh this is Anthony Mrs. Audrey, Matt's friend."

"Oh hi Anthony, just a second I'll get him." Buford was lounging on the couch having a drink. "Buford, Rodney's friend Anthony wants to speak to you." "Okay thanks" he said getting up to get the phone. "Hello?" "Hello Mr. Mathis" "Yes George, what can I do for you?" "Matt told me to call you and let you know he's over my house."

"Okay, where's he now?" "He's in the bathroom." "Alright, tell him I'll be home around about 9:00pm." "Yes sir." "What are you boys up to?" "Nothing much, just hanging around waiting for our pizza to get here." "That sounds good, you boys have fun now, and I'll see you all later." "Yes sir, bye." Click. "What did he say" asked Matt coming into the room zipping up his pants. "He said it's cool and he would be home about 8 or 9 o'clock" "Bet!"

"Hey, do you mind if I call some company?" "Hey, this is your crib dude, do what you like." "Well seeing as how it's Melanie, I was gonna call I thought I would check with you to see what you thought about it first." "Man, naw! go for it!" "Okay" he said then reached for his little back book. He found the number he wanted then dialed it. "Ring ring." "Hello?" "Hello, may I speak to Melanie please?" "Who's calling?" "Anthony." "Well Anthony, she's not here right now she left to go over to a friends house sometime ago."

"Oh, I see." "Would you like to leave a message and a number I can have her call when she get's in?" "Yes ma'am, could you tell her Anthony called? My number is ..." "I see it on the caller ID Anthony." "Thanks." "Bye bye now." Click. "Oh well, she's out of the question" he said sighing long and putting the phone back in its cradle.

"Knock knock knock!" "Someone's at the door man." "It must be the pizza guy" said Ant getting up to retrieve his wallet. "Can't be, it's only been ten minutes." "Well go and see then, you're closer to the door." "Matt got up and headed for the door but didn't get there quick enough, Ant's grandmother had been closer and answered it. "Who is it?" "It's Melanie Franklin, is Anthony at home?" she opened the door to see the bright eyed and perky smile of a pretty young white girl at the door.

"Yes sweetie, he's in, come on in." "Antney, you got company!" she said calling over her shoulder without taking her eyes off the young woman. Melanie felt a little awkward, but didn't quite know why. Maybe it had to do with not having had much contact with black people other than school or at work where she would see them in passing, but not up close and personal. The experience was kind of humbling and she found herself blushing.

"No need to feel shame face chile, I ain't gonna bite you." "Yes ma'am" she whispered blushing all the more and smiling at the older black woman. "I used to take care of a pretty little thing like you long time ago, when I worked for this nice family out of Mississippi when I was much younger . . . come to think of it you look a lot like her." "What's your name again sweetie?" "Melanie Franklin?" she said looking hopeful but didn't know why. She couldn't have been the girl Ant's granny was talking about.

All the while, Matt just stood there with his arms folded leaning against the wall just outside of her sight. "Damn, she's persistent!" he thought smiling to himself, then just went back into the room before she could see him. "Sheee's heerrre" said Matt singing it more than saying it much like the little girl on the movie Poltergeist. Ant sat up on the edge of the bed and tried to look cool. Melanie came into the room and she looked as beautiful as ever, Matt and Ant had to admit. She wore a blue and red plaid skirt and a blue short sleeve top with a white lace collar.

She looked like she went to a catholic school, but those gorgeous eyes told of more interesting things than what she went to school to learn. "Hi guys" she said smiling waving lightly at the two of them. "What's up Mel?" said Ant trying to be coy. "Here come and take a seat" he said getting her a chair. "Thank you."

"I just called you a minute ago but your mom said you went to a friends house." "Yeah, I did . . . Matt's house, I thought you guys might be there." "So what's up?" said Matt lounging on the floor. "Oh nothing much, I didn't have to work today so I thought I would look you guys up and see what you were up too." "Nothing much, just chilling out and waiting on a pizza." "Oh yeah, what kind?"

"Little Ceaser's with everything" said Matt from the floor. "Great!, I haven't eaten yet, do you mind if I chip in and join you guys?" she said quickly, now remembering herself and that she wasn't actually invited to this little eat in. Matt just looked at Ant with a broad grin as if to say, "*I know she didn't just play herself like that.*" Ant mirrored the same unspoken thought and just nodded. Mel felt that there was something in the air that she wasn't privy to or may like very much coming her way. She tensed reflexively. *"No! get your own damn pizza!"*

She jerked backwards suddenly and her mouth fell open in utter shock and surprise. For a second she thought she might just get up and leave but then saw the two of them rolling around on the floor near tears with laughter. After a second or two of high fives and hilarious laughing she got the message and she had been had. Mel smiled slowly and nodded in acknowledgement of being duped.

"Okay boys, I got you . . . so you want to play rough huh? . . . remember what they say about pay back guys . . . and don't forget I'm a woman so it counts twice as hard." "Yeah we know, we know" they said coming under control and waving off her threat that they knew she couldn't possibly make good on because they were not going to let her catch them with their pants down. "So how come you all dressed up?" asked Matt curious.

"Oh this? . . . no I'm not dressed up, my family and I took some pictures today and I wore this." "It's nice" chimed Ant also noticing how she looked really hot. "Thanks guys" she said blushing and self consciously adjusting her clothes. "So what have you too been up to today?" "We had track practice today." "Really? How did you do?" "We did okay" said Ant taking the lead on the conversation.

"Matt's got the discus sewed up and I'm in the hurdles." "How far can you throw it Matt?" she asked eagerly. "I'm not sure yet, this was just try-outs and I threw it about a hundred and fifty feet" he said cooley not too impressed. "You did what?" "Yeah, and that's only because it hit the goal post and was deflected" said Ant proudly backing up his friend. "If he hadn't hit it there's no telling how far it would have gone." Mel looked at Matt now with renewed interest and appreciation. She had been in sports herself and she knew something about that event.

"Oh hell why did he have to go and tell her that!" thought Matt seeing the light in her eye change from lucid to slow burn. *"Now I'll never get her off of me!"* "Matt" she said looking innocent yet attentive like she was going to spring on him, but didn't want him to know it till she did it. "Yeah?" "Did you know that current national college record is 195.6 feet." "Nope . . . is that so?" "It is and do you know what else?" *"Some how I just know I'm gonna regret this but what else"* he thought again in silence. "No, what else?" "He went on to the summer Olympics a year later." "No shit?" Matt chirped not realizing she was gonna drop that line. But instead something like he went on to the AA trials or something.

"Nope" she said grinning smugly now and not exactly for the reason's he thought just now. "You know Matt, you seem to have the touch and you should work on it, you could be the next track star to go Olympian" she closed with finality. "Hold on now Mel, I just threw it once and that was probably a lucky shot, I'm nowhere near college or Olympic material, the coach thinks I'm another black stallion like my brother Jr." "Was he your brother?" she asked surprised. "Yeah . . . why you know him?"

"Yes, I used to come see the meets with my Aunt Sharon, she and him used to go out together." "Naw! you joking?" "Nope, I'm not . . . tell me, do you remember him ever talking to a tall honey blond haired girl with green eyes and big boobs?" Matt gave it some thought, because his older brother used to date many girls; black and white and other, so it was a little hard to pin point that particular one.

"Did she drive a little red car?" "Yeah!, now I remember, she used to smile at me when I would get caught peeking in on them." "That's her." "Dude your dead" said Ant laughing at him falling on the bed. "Man I've seen some dumb luck but you're a legacy on this one and you can't get out of it." "Well I'll be damned" said Matt falling back on the floor and covering his eyes not able to believe what he was hearing.

"Small world ain't it?" he moaned to nobody in particular. "A lot smaller than you might think Matt" she countered. "Okay, so your family is familiar with at least one member of mine." "So what's that supposed to mean?" said Matt sitting up trying to defend himself for a potential future situation he wasn't even sure existed. "Well it seems Anthony, that your friend here is a member of a long line of young men that have lots of talents" she said pointing over her shoulder.

"Some of which are track and field, football, basketball, flirting, and leaving a girl unsatisfied when you have her on the ropes" she said leaning closer to Matt with her elbows on her knees and smiling a most cat that ate the canary look she could muster. "Oh, I know you're not going to tell him about the other night are you?" he grumbled under his breath only loud enough for her to hear. Mel saw Matt's discomfort and was encouraged by his attempt to keep things quiet. Mel sat up and crossed her legs slowly revealing to Matt a healthy pair of legs and a most luscious bottom that for a second he was sure didn't have on any panties! Ant of course couldn't see anything but was sure there was something to see because of the look he saw on Matt's face and his eyes told him volumes.

She gave Matt a naughty little smile and twinked her nose at him. "Oh, she's being really bitchy now" thought Matt adjusting his sitting position so he couldn't see what she had tried so hard to flash at him. He gave her a look that said, *"Not the other night and for damn sure not here! So put some ice on it sister."* "Do you guys know a girl named Cheryl . . . she goes to your school?" she said moving things along. "Yeah, so what?" "She's my first cousin." Ant fell on the floor with a resounding thud. "Ow! Damn your screwed Matt!" Then he laughed himself till the veins in his neck were bulging.

"Oh fuck . . . that's just perfect" said Matt shaking his head. "She's your cousin?" asked Ant getting up and whipping his eyes. "You betcha!" Ant just looked at Matt and burst out laughing again. "Man your through dealing for real dude!" Mel knew full well what Ant was referring to but kept quiet and just let Matt stew in his own sauce. It was just too delicious that she and Cheryl were going after him now and Cheryl had told Mel what kind of man Matt was, his tricks and what he was likely to do when trapped.

"Damn, a guy just can't win in this life can he?" Matt mumbled to himself. "That's right lover boy, you can't go around cooking up a girls bacon then not eat it baby." "So is she still mad at me?" "What do you think!" "Well I warned her, and I told her I already have a girl and she wasn't about to sway me." "Oh no?" she said pouting and shaking her head most lasciviously. "That's not what she told me." "Oh yeah? So what did she say to you?" "Well I can't say word for word but she did mention that either you had a fetish for keeping large cucumbers in your pocket or that you were very much interested in what she was offering."

"Hah! . . . offering you say? It was more like *give!* And take, I wasn't giving but she was going to do her best to take it anyway." "You're lucky Matt, she would have taken you if you hadn't tricked her, and who knows you may have even enjoyed it." "Oh, I don't know about that" he said getting up.

"I've been teased before, and it's gotten them nowhere so I'm not sweating it now." "I see, so your untouchable is that it?" "You bet you sweet ass I am" he said getting dangerously close to her face and causing her to lean away or fall into his arms which isn't what she wanted to do just now, at least not on his terms. "Well Matt" she said adjusting herself and moving a comfortable distance from him but not too comfortable. "You had your chance to find out how sweet but you chickened out on me" she said flashing him a most confident and vindictive look. "Naw you shitting me" said Ant looking from one to the other.

"Matt turned you down too?" "Like a six dollar bill in a bank!" Matt just eased back to the floor and propped his hands behind his head, crossed his legs and began whistling. He was very proud of himself and they knew it. Melanie looked at him and the smug expression he had on his face and had a strong urge to pounce on him and take him or at least shake him up into thinking she could.

It didn't matter that Ants granny was there, she had to protect her pride. Matt looked at her with baleful eyes of great satisfaction and zero concern for what she was thinking about doing. Mel felt herself slip a little closer to the edge of the bed and a sudden rush surge in her stomach. She was just about to jump him when the doorbell rang.

"I'll get it" said Ant leaving his perch and the show that was unfolding in front of him. He almost tumbled over Mel. He gathered up the money that they had put on the dresser for the bill and went to the door. The room was silent. Mel and Matt just smiled smugly and intrepidly at each other like a wolf and a cougar staring each other down and circling to get the best position. "Matt you know this isn't over don't you?" she whispered "It isn't?" "Not by a long shot bucko, we are going to get even with you studdly, so you better get your stuff together cause we are coming for you" she said easing back onto her elbows and slowly parting her legs to let him have the full effect of her intent and what he was truly missing out on.

"Have fun" he shot back un-phased at the move to shake him. He did admit to himself that is was a hot and delectable sight to see and he would have loved to have jumped her right there on the bed and beat the brakes of that ass! But higher morals and a greater love for Retta kept him from losing his cool.

"Oh we will, you can bet on it and do you know what's worse Matt?" "What?" "Your going to love every minute of it" she said raising one leg vertical letting her skirt fall and exposing her full package so Matt would have no doubt as to what was being aimed at him. Mel stoked her leg like a cat cleaning itself then let it fall slowly and crossed them. She then sat up and leaned forward close enough to kiss him, staring him dead in the eyes without blinking. For a minute Matt thought she was gonna kiss him, and tried to think of what his move would be, but then she spoke and by doing so granted him a reprieve.

"Bet on it" she hissed then eased back upon the bed much like she was before Ant had left the room. "Okay people the food is here let's eat!" said Ant returning with the two large pizza's and the two large drinks. He could sense that something had happened in his absence by the way they were smirking at each other and not speaking. "Okay, what did I miss?" he said looking back and forth. "Nothing that will make you lose any sleep Ant" said Matt smiling and getting up to get some pizza.

"Damn I missed a lot didn't I . . . *Shoot!*" he said moping off to the kitchen to get some cups so they could share the drinks with her. He returned and gave her one. "Thanks Anthony" said smiling brightly at him. She quickly flashed her eyes at Matt as if to say, "I'll just play with Anthony since you don't want to." Matt for some strange reason he couldn't fathom, was feeling a little jealous. He didn't know why cause he didn't want her, but as a man he felt slighted by her.

Mel reached for the bill then took out her purse. "No, no! that's not necessary, you keep that, this one's on me." "But I'll tell you what, seeing as how you girls are so stubborn and I'm not willing to give into you, if you and your cuz can either together or by yourselves catch me off guard and somehow lock me down, then you can take your revenge on me as you see fit and I won't do anything to stop you or trick you."

Mel's pizza fell to the tray like a sack of potatoes and her mouth stayed open like a recently caught bass on a hook. She couldn't believe what she had just heard. "Now there is one twist to this thing, you have only one week to do it, if either of you fail as a team or individuals, I win and you have to do what I say for one day on anything I ask." "You pose an interesting proposal Matt, one with an exceeding high price."

Ant wasn't sure what he was hearing either being he had missed what ever had transpired and related to this magilla. He couldn't wait to know what it was about but figured he had most of the data already. "Hey you girls play a mean game and I'm out numbered, so the ball is in my court." Mel sipped her soda slowly and bobbed her foot like a cat twitching it's tail. "So how do you propose we do this then Matt?" "Hey, that's your problem not mine, and you also must decide on this tonight by midnight."

"No fair, I have to talk to Cheryl first!" "Sorry, it's either decide for you both by night's end or lose all options forever, besides I'm the prize remember?" "I'm supposed to be your intended trophy not your advisor" he said cupping her chin lightly for emphasis. "But hey, if this is too much for you we can always keep it as it is with a flat no . . . !" "Hold on, I'm not backing out I'm just weighing the odds!" "Okay, go ahead." "Let me call Cheryl first and see what she thinks." "There's the phone over there."

Mel eagerly picked it up and dialed. "Hello? . . . Cher? . . ." "Yes" "This is Melanie, I'm over at Anthony's house with him and Matt . ." *"Your where? . . . with who! . . . why you selfish, sneaky little bitch!"* I knew I couldn't trust you to spit on you" she spat viciously. Matt and Ant could hear her clear across the room and just made faces and giggled. "How dare you go over there and not tell me!"

"Now hold on Cher, don't go getting your panties in a wad, I've got a proposition for you that you need to hear, I think you're going to like it." "Okay what's it about?" she said calming down some. "Well it seems that Matt is willing to give us our opportunity to get even and take full revenge in any way we choose." "You know Melanie . . . you shouldn't drink so much at your age, it's gonna stunt your growth one of these days, I can see it's already beginning to screw with your head." "Why are you talking crazy for? I just told you that we have a chance to get back at Matt for screwing us over all this time, and you say I've been drinking?" "You must be if you think Matt is gonna give you a chance at anything but a pair of hard nipples and a trip to a cold shower, and did you say *he* is going to let *us?*"

"Yes!" "Bitch please!" Matt was savoring the havoc he was creating between them and just rolled around on the floor holding his stomach from laughing so hard. Ant sounded like he was weeping and in pain, he had it so bad. Mel just shook her head. "Will you let me tell you what is on the table before your country ass get's the wrong idea?" "Okay shoot, let's hear this big deal you're getting us into."

"Well, he said he would give us a week to catch him off guard either alone or together, we can do with him whatever we like and he won't resist us!" Cheryl listened to her cousins so called proposal with disdain and much pity. She shook her head sadly and almost laughed at her for being so gullible. When she spoke again she sounded melancholy and somber. "Melanie?" "Uh huh?" "How long have you known Matt?"

"About two weeks." "And in all that time how many times have you been alone with him?" "Once." "Did you get any?" Mel blushed so fast and so red Matt was suddenly reminded of the little girl in the Willy Wonka movie who ate the blue berry gum. "Why you ask me that? . . ." "Did you?" "No, but what does that have to do with it?" "Melanie, I have know Matt for over a year now and I have been alone with him at least six times during that time and had him pinned, Hell! just recently I had him on the back of the school bus pant's down and my coochie all in his face and *I still couldn't get him to fuck me!"*

"So how in the hell do you think that just because you or I get him cornered he's gonna give it up to either of us? . . . He's got a girlfriend cousin." "And for the life of me I don't know what she has between her ears or her legs but this man ain't givin up *JACK!* So don't waste your time Mel, he ain't doing nothing but jerking your bra straps . . . give it up" she said going silent again. Melanie thought about what she had just heard while staring at Matt unblinking and bobbing her foot slowly. "I see." "What's his angle on this? . . . what does he get out of this anyway if we lose?" Mel thought a minute before answering. She almost gave up on the idea based on the logic.

Cheryl had put up. "Oh, he just gets to do with us whatever he wants and we have to do what ever he says for a whole day." "Your nuts" she said flatly. "Well that may be so, but don't worry because we won't lose, I've got some ideas in my head I'm thinking about, I'll tell you them later." "I don't know Mel, Matt can be pretty shrewd, I think were just jerking ourselves off and making fools of ourselves at his amusement." "You see how he outsmarted me the other day and I was on top of him and bare assed to boot!"

"Well cousin, not to insult your talents but you're not the sharpest tool in the shed, especially when you get horny." "Oh no you didn't?" "Come on girl, you don't really believe he can take us both at the same time do you?" "Tell me something Mel, is he sitting in front of you right now?" "Yes" "Betcha five bucks he's looking either between your legs and yawning or in your face and smiling." Mel looked at Matt and saw he was doing both." "He's doing both."

"Yes, he can take us both." Mel couldn't believe that anyone could be so catty and overbearing. Matt just sat leaning on his elbow eating pizza and chewing like a cow eating cud. He never took his eyes off Mel and even though he couldn't hear Cheryl anymore knew what she must have been saying to Mel. "But let's do it anyway!" "You sure?" "We could lose and be subject to god knows what." "I don't care, I want at least one chance to get even with that little cock teaser!" growled Cher rapidly twining her hair around her finger.

"Okay cuz, I'll call you later and we'll talk over the details." "Okay let me talk to him a second." "Matt . . . she wants you" said Mel smiling smugly now and handing him the phone. "Yeah babe?" "I'll baby you . . . you little prick!" Matt just chuckled tossing his head back. "You just wait lover, I'm going to have your tight little ass strung out and laid bare to the ankles on a bed sheet!" Oh, she was hot! "Alright" thought Matt as her voice dripped with intent and conquest. Matt just casually blew her off, "Promises, promises, you know Cher, when you talk like that you make me all warm and *squishy"* he said seductively stretching out the last word for affect. "OOH! Your through now mister . . . just you wait!"

He gave the phone back to Mel. "It's me Cher" "Oh, yes count me in, he's going to suffer now . . . I'm so hot now I can't think straight, I'm going to bruise his ego as well as his body!" "Now your talking, I'll holla at you later" she said then hung up.

"Well Matt, it seems you have a deal" she said reaching out to shake his hand. Matt moved slowly and purposeful. "Are you guys sure you want to go through with this? You know we can just call it even and stop the madness" he said finally reaching out and taking her hand. "I'm sure" she was about to say but Matt savagely jerked her off the bed and down on top of him in one swift movement. Mel was so shocked that the air was pushed out of her as she came to rest on top of him straddling his hips.

"Oh shit!" whispered Ant still eating. Their faces were centimeters apart and their lips painfully close. Matt could smell her essence and it was intoxicating and rich. Every time she breathed he found himself working to take it all in. Mel on the other hand felt as if a wild fire had run through her parted legs and she began to melt like candle wax. She could have gotten up, should have gotten up but found that she didn't want to.

Matt was in no real hurry for her to go either and just let her hover there a bit long while he prolonged the torture he was planning. Then it came. It was like a bug zapper going off. A most sinister and seductive smile began to form at the corners of Matt's mouth. It worked it's way to the front where pearly white teeth began to emerge like the rocks on a shoreline at low tide. Melanie wasn't sure what she was seeing, but it happened so smoothly and so quickly that she didn't have time to absorb it in her mind.

Matt flicked out the tip of his tongue and guided it up from the base of her chin to the tip of her nose in a teasing but most sensual way. *"You really don't think you'll win do you?"* he said in dry and dusty tone. The act and the sound of his voice made Mel sweat between her legs something awful and she just hung there wishing for more but not sure what.

"May the best man win?" she offered not sounding confident at all and offering her hand again. Matt sighed and lifted her by her arms up and off of him to her original sitting position. Mel didn't fail to notice the power in those arms and it made her want to feel the rest of him. All the drama being done, they all laid at the foot of the bed and got settled for the movie.

Aretta was busy just now trying to choke down her own meal they served her. It was a soft food diet and it didn't look or taste very good. They gave her mashed potatoes and beef broth with cream corn. "Yuck!" she grimaced and pushed the tray and the stand to the side. She then picked up the remote to the television and sipped her apple juice. "There's nothing on and Matt's not home yet, where can he be? He said he was going home. Knowing him he went over to Ant's house and I don't have the number."

"Man I can't wait to go home I hate this place!" Just then the phone rang, "Hello?" "Hey sweet pea!" "Hey Matt! I was just thinking about you baby, I miss you so much right now." "I miss you too baby, so how are you doing poo?" "I'm lonely Matt, and I don't like it here." "I know baby, I hate that you're there too, have you eaten yet?" "I tried to, but I don't like this food, it's terrible." "Yeah, I know, I remember being in the hospital when I was younger, it is nasty . . . no taste at all." "Yeah!" "So what can you have to eat?" "I don't know, they're keeping me on a soft food diet for awhile so I don't have a hard time in the bathroom."

"Yeah, I guess that's because your still raw inside and your stomach isn't ready for much yet." "So they starve me to death with this swill they keep bringing me?" "Well don't worry I took care of you." "How? You're not even here." "I ordered you some of your favorite food." "What? . . . Chinese?" "Yep" "Oh Matt, thank you! But I don't think I can eat it, and what about the nurses they're not going to let anyone bring that in." "I got that covered too." "Okay Mr. Man, how you gonna get me Chinese food in here, by way of a little oriental man and pass the nurses station without being caught?"

"Hey this is your man talking sugar bumps, if I say I can put a pig on the sun, you better look for it to rain pork rinds." "Matt, you're so crazy" she said laughing at him. Retta loved the way Matt could always come up with weird sayings and stuff to make her feel better. "Besides I got a buddy who works in the kitchen who will drop it off to you when he comes to pick up your tray." "Matt, you never cease to amaze me."

"Yeah I know, sometimes I even amaze myself" he said patting himself on the back and smirking. "What did you order?" "I ordered you some noodles, and a small order of Shrimp Fried Rice, that shouldn't bother you too much, should it?" "Nah, it shouldn't, where did you order it from?" "The Chinese Dragon on PioNono." "I know I'm gonna get rapped in the mouth for this but . . . how can you pay for it if he's supposed to deliver it here?" "Sigh . . . details, details . . . I told him I would give him a nice tip if he stopped by here first." "We're really just up the road from you on the same side of town, so he won't be going out of his way." "Oh, so he's already been paid then?" "Yep" "Thank you sweetie . . . but do you think he'll try to rip you off and keep the food?" she pressed on.

"Naw these people are usually pretty honest and besides I also told him that the person this food is for is a third degree black belt, tae chi instructor" he said grinning at the lie. "Ooh! Matt why did you tell him that?" "Well it's not like he's gonna see you, besides you can teach me anything baby" he said in a low seductive voice. Retta gushed inside and blushed a deep crimson red at the comment. "Matt, you're too good to me baby, you know that don't you?" "Yeah, but I won't tell if you don't." Retta laughed at the surly comment and was very happy Matt had called. On the other hand Melanie was less amused and did not like the sounds of fidelity and devotion going on just on the other side of the bed.

Ant took notice and could see her mounting dislike for Retta rising in her face. The soft glow of the television revealed a pair of vicious eyes hell bent on destruction. Mel looked about ready to snap with each passing moment and loving endearment. The more Matt said to her the hotter she got and the more she hated Retta even though she didn't even know her. But then again she didn't have to, Retta had something she wanted. And it was Matt! Matt was totally unaware of Mel's hostile change over. He was sitting with his back to her and Ant, trying to secure a little privacy. While Mel sat there stewing she was trying to figure a way to get back at Matt that would hurt. She looked around the darkened room for something . . . anything just so she could bash him with it!

She tried to do this discretely without alerting Ant to her intentions, but it didn't work and Ant was well aware of her intentions and was ready for her to act. After a minute or two she spied a pillow between her and the television. She stealthily picked it up and was about to launch it. Ant watched as she brought it around like a Frisbee and swung it fiercely towards Matt's turned back. Unfortunately the pillow never made its mark. Ant had smoothly intercepted her swing by catching her arm before she could complete her swing. In the same motion he spun her towards him and onto the floor flayed out with arms spread.

Mel was speechless at his speed and actions. She just lay there with her feet curled under her and breathing laboriously. Mel's face was the picture of shock and surprise at being caught and not much else. Ant held her there and just looked at her with a semi-serious furrow on his brow and a crooked smirk on his lips. "Anthony, what are you doing? Why did you stop me" she whispered. Ant smiled at her, "Now you know, that what you were about to do was just a little bit wrong don't you?" Mel rolled her head to the side and sighed heavily.

"A woman like you shouldn't harbor such feelings for other people. You're too special for that." Mel rolled her head back to face him, teeth clenched and tensing against his hold on her wrists. "How would you know? Anthony . . . you don't know anything about me . . . not like Matt does." Ant thought about her statement for a second, feeling her stare burn into him. He eased his face closer to hers, Mel's lips firm and unyielding. "Oh, but I do Mel . . . I do" he said then seized her lips in a hot and passionate kiss.

Mel was about to protest as she wriggled to free herself, unfortunately, she found that as much as she has initially did not want this from him, she was as quick to accept it when Ant's soft warm lips began to feed on hers. Mel thought he would just steal a kiss then retreat like an addled school boy. But now feeling the urgency in his kiss build and the feel of his tongue search out hers and control it, she couldn't make herself stop him . . . or even want to.

Mel's brain was awash with images of sensuality and passion as Ant gave her more and more with each passing moment. His breath was hot and consuming and she could feel herself wilting like a rain soaked rose petal. She didn't dislike Anthony, but wasn't exactly interested in him that way. Now that he had taken her so completely and masterfully she found herself enjoying his attentions. Ant felt that his point had been made and hadn't intended on prolonging his control of her but now that she was beginning to respond to him, even encourage him, he was elated and his kissing became more ardent as he slowly released her wrists and repositioned his hands on either side of her head.

Mel reached up and gently place her delicate fingers along Ant's sides and caressed him from his hips to his back. Ant followed suit now that she had found his *"ready button."* Ant lay on her full with one knee between her parted legs. The move made Mel sigh with pleasure. She eagerly met Ant's kiss for kiss as the pair began to gyrate mouths and hips in sync with their passion. *"Oh Anthony, why are you doing this to me?"* she gushed in her mind. *"You know I love Matt, but oh god how can I resist you when you feel so damn good to me! I never let myself even think that you were such a good kisser and . . . and . . . sssss OH! MY Goodness! Anthony!"* she swooned when Ant's hand found it's mark far up and into the velvety walls of her soft and supple legs.

He slowly caressed her from bottom to top not forgetting to add just a little pressure to that exquisitely sensitive and dangerously moist entrance into her ecstasy. Ant's mind exploded with silent rapture when the nerves of his hand transmitted what they had found at the end of it. In no language of this world, in no written text, song or poem has it ever been accurately explained or described, what takes place in the mind or body when you touch something as archaically sweet and foreboding as a woman's body or a man's organ while in the throws of passion.

"Oh my god, I can't stop myself! I just know I'm going to give myself to you Anthony! Please stop, I don't want to." Melanie's mind screamed on. Her movements were deliberate and torched. She gyrated to him with every turn and shamelessly opened herself to his graphic and hungry probing hand and fingers. She pushed a hand against his chest in a weak attempt to discourage him but it didn't quite have the impact she expected. In fact when she felt the hard and sculpted muscles of his chest an lower stomach, her eyes reflexively rolled over in her head and her mouth lost all coordination much like that of someone on Novocain.

Ant was definitely in the groove and his mind was telling him something else. He had wanted Mel and wanted her as bad as Cheryl wanted Matt. He felt from her movements that she was ready to go all the way when she pushed him causing him to slip firmly and comfortably between her legs. Mel tried to stop kissing Ant but the more she did the more she found she didn't really want to, but knew she had to.

Once more she pushed but this time turning her head at the same time. *"Anthony!"* she whispered harshly almost screaming. The sound of his name being called that way was like a cold shower and it made him kill all action. Ant eased himself up from her till he was on all fours an just looked at her. "What's the matter?" he said breathing heavily and hurting something terrible in his pants. "I'm so sorry Anthony, I'm so sorry, but I can't . . . we can't!" she whispered feeling the redness of shame and bashfulness over take her. Mel was still lying there on the floor her face stricken with a look of confusion and fear.

She looked at Ant's equally confused and painful expression not knowing what to say to him. She knew how much she had lead him on and how much he wanted her she could feel it! *"But is it teasing a person if you want it too as much as they?"* she puzzled to herself. Mel sat up and held her face shaking it as if she couldn't believe what had just happened, in Ant's house, with his grandmother a room away, and worse, Matt just on the other side of the bed. "Anthony I didn't mean for that to happen, and I'm sorry if I led you on" she said sitting on her knees in front of him. "Then why did you act like you did? . . . I mean you gave me all the signals and I thought that you wanted what I wanted?"

"Anthony, I didn't expect or know that you were going to try and kiss me! . . . not that I didn't want to kiss you or wanted you to kiss me, I was just caught by surprise!" "Then why didn't you stop me then? You could have just pushed me away or turned your head, I woulda got the message" he said looking more and more defeated by the minute. Mel could see that what she had allowed to occur was as bad for him or more than it was for her. "Anthony when you kissed me I wanted to stop you but then . . ." she paused swallowing a small lump that was trying to form there. "Then it felt good to me and I like it" she said almost whispering. "The truth is the more you kissed me the more I felt I wanted to be kissed! and then when you touched me like that . . . . " she turned her head suddenly, completely flushed and red from embarrassment. "Oh Anthony, I have never been touched like that before and I have to tell you I lost it! . . . I liked it so much, in fact I liked it so much I *almost wet myself!*" she whispered conspiratorially in his ear, blushing all the more.

She shied away from him and sat on her feet looking up and smiling childishly. Ant had to admit she was hot and he was hot for her. He wanted to take her for all she was worth, grandma nor Matt being there meant a damn!

"Can you forgive me Anthony?" "I really do like you . . . but . . . " she paused looking down and harassing a thumbnail. "But you like Matt more . . . right?" he said finishing for her. Mel just nodded bashfully and looked away. "I guess, I love him Anthony, every since that day we met in the mall, he touched me Anthony, he touched me deeper than any man ever has, I could feel him in my mind and my heart all at once." "When he held my hand and looked at me the way he did I was his, right then whether he wanted me or not . . . " she paused again, but this time turned to look into Ants eyes. She searched them for compassion, understanding . . . anything that would say, "I understand and I'm not angry with you." "I guess that doesn't make any sense does it Anthony?" "Naw, not really, I mean you feel how you feel, I can't fault you for that, I don't like it much but I can't fault you for it" he said sighing long and looking down shaking his head in disbelief.

He wasn't mad at Matt or jealous because he'd known Matt for years and he had seen many occasions where this was a re-occurring situation with Matt. "Anthony, I do like you a lot and if Matt wasn't in my heart and mind so deeply you would be the only other person who I could see filling that void" she said looking into his eyes then smiling and looking away. Ant had to look away also because they both were guilty of the same thought at the same time when she was talking about filling a void."

They both knew and wanted that done. "Okay . . . I understand Mel, and I don't hold no grudge" he said sighing sadly at his magnanimous gesture of charity and loss. *"By the way . . . I'm a virgin!"* said Melanie reaching up quickly to whisper it in his ear. Ant just looked at her with wide eyes and disbelief. Mel nodded, smiling huge. She reached up a second time and placed her delicate hands on Ants chest and kissed him tenderly for what they both felt was the last time. Ant savored the sweet gesture and held onto it even after she had retreated back to sitting. "Like I said, you're something special."

Mel blushed again and her stomach did flips. "Thank you Antony." "No problem . . . but remember . . . he's still untouchable, he doesn't want you, I do!" As Ant said this they both heard the phone click on the base. Signifying that Matt had finished his call. "So you guys, what's the game here? . . . can I watch or is this singles match?" Ant sat back and helped Melanie up from the floor. "No there's nothing going on Matt" she said still looking at Ant. "We were just talking." "Oh yeah? It must have been real important judging from the way he was trying to suck the words right out of your mouth" this made them both blush. "Oh! Yesss, I saw it all!" chimed Matt pointing his thumb to a mirror behind him and rocking back and forth on his heals.

"Hey but don't mind me, I'm glad to see that you two are finally getting along, it gives Mel something to do with her pent up hormones" he added making a face as he said it. Mel wasn't amused by this. She glared at him with hot pensive eyes. Ant said nothing but just lightly placed his arm around her shoulder for support. Mel followed suit by wrapping her arms around his waist and showing great contempt.

"You conceited son of a bitch! I'll show you that your not so hot!" She thought to herself then pushed Ant towards the bed and spun him around to face her. Ant fell in a semi laying position on his elbows a little shocked at her new attitude. Mel then dived on him like an Amazon. The pressure made him grunt, but he didn't say anything because she followed this up by covering his mouth with hers. "DAAAMN!" thought Ant. "What the hell brought this on?" This was of course just an act for Matt. She was trying to show him that she didn't want nor need him as much as he thought she did. Matt just peeked over her head and down into Ants wide shocked eyes and smiled as big and hilariously as he could muster. Ant would have laughed at this but couldn't due to having his mouth under reconstruction by Mel just now.

Matt gave him a salute, *"Ah young lust, tis truly the spice of life"* he said in his best Irish voice. He then grabbed up a slice of pizza, pinched Mel on her exposed bottom and dashed out the door. "See ya, and don't hurt yourselves now ya hear?" Mel screamed inside Ant's mouth at the shock and pleasure of the violation Matt dished out. She pulled up fast to look at him but he was gone.

Mel got up off of Ant then ran to the door only to see Matt puttering away down the street. "Ooh I hate him, when he does that!" she said stamping her foot and folding her arms about her. "Does what?" asked Ant joining her outside.

"Throw my game back in my face, that's what." "Is that what all that on the bed was? . . . a game?" Mel started to flush whiter and wished she hadn't been so mad and said that. "Well in a way it was . . . but I liked it anyway" she said trying to play up to Ant and cool his burned ego. "No! you didn't" he barked and stabbing his finger in her face. "Your just playing games!" "But Anthony wait . . . " she pleaded reaching for him. Ant brushed away her hands and glared at her trying not to lose his temper cause his grandma would know something was up and come out raising hell. "No you wait . . . look Mel, it's like this man, I like you and I want to get to know you better, but I'm not going to be a pawn in you and Matt's game understand?"

"Yes, I understand and I'm very sorry I didn't mean for this to happen, I just got so mad at him and then I lost my head . . . please forgive me Anthony, I really do like you and want to be friends but . . ." "But your still hung up on Matt right?" he finished. "Let's just say I have some unfinished business to attend to first." Ant just looked at her pitifully and shook his head sadly. "I think it's time for you to go Mel." She looked into his eyes and they were unforgiving and full of hurt. She bowed her head and walked back into the house to retrieve her purse. Ant followed her but stayed a good distance behind her. Mel really felt bad about using him, but just couldn't help it. She quickly got her purse and walked back to the door.

Ant was standing there looking out into the street. She wanted to say something but didn't know what or how to say it without sounding phony. "Anthony, I really am sorry" she said lightly touching his arm. Ant shook off her hand then turned to face her. Mel felt a cold chill run down her back as Ant impaled her with his eyes. For a second she didn't know if he was going to curse her out or throw her out but anything was better than the silence he was giving her. Ant slowly reached into his pocket and produced a quarter. He raised her hand up, opening it then placed the quarter purposefully in the center without breaking his gaze.

"Why don't you go and call somebody who gives as shit!" he then eased her out the door and closed it in her face. Melanie was in complete bedlam and shock. She stood there with her mouth open and couldn't move. A sob pushed it's way to her throat and into her mouth choking her. She looked at the coin in her hand as if it was a human heart placed there still throbbing. Her lips trembled closed and she with drew her hand closing the coin in it.

"Okay Anthony, if that's how you feel about me i . . . . " the words never came. She whispered a final revelation in the dark and alone then turned and left. Ant could hear her run down the steps and get into her truck slamming the door. The engine roared to life then she too was gone.

Way back across town at the hospital, a nightshift nurse was making her rounds. She had taken care of all the medications she was supposed to give and gotten all her patients set for the night. As she walked down the long hall on the third floor, she could hear the faint sounds of a television going. "Now who can this be up at this hour of the night?" she mumbled to herself. Soon she found the source of the noise and it was coming from room 318, Retta's room. She eased the door open and the heavy earthy smell of Chinese food assaulted her nose. She looked over and spotted three square containers on the night stand by Retta's bed.

The television station was just signing off the air so she quietly went over and turned the volume way down and went back to collect the containers. "I wonder how she got this stuff in here!" she thought picking them up and placing them lightly in the waist basket to take with her. But then again after some thought she didn't mind it so much cause Retta hadn't eaten all day. She had refused all her meals and needed to eat something so she was glad to see that she had.

The nurse looked at Retta and smiled with her heart in her eyes. She lay there so precious and innocent. "Oh how sweet and beautiful you are my child, if only I had had a daughter she would be as beautiful as you." The middle aged nurse had gone through a messy divorce ten years and had bore no children. She had not re-married and due to one too many beatings from her ex-husband, could not bare any children.

That's why whenever she got the chance to work pediatrics or the children's floor she did. She bent over Retta and lovingly pulled her covers up over her shoulders and brushed her bangs from her eyes. She couldn't help herself and allowed herself the great pleasure of giving Retta a kiss on her forehead. As she raised up to leave she noticed an object clutched in Retta's hand. She looked closer and discovered it was a long stem red rose. The nurse smiled warmly blinking back a tear and nodded with approval. "Like I said . . . you truly have a special young man" she picked up the waste basket, turned off the television and left.

Audrey was feeling pretty good and in a happy mood as she drove to work this morning. She hadn't felt this good in a long time and it showed. Even though she was a little tired from staying up so late doing paper work, it didn't bother her much. She looked at her watch as she sat up and saw that it was 7:15.

"Oh! My goodness I better step on it I've got to be at work in a half hour, it's a good thing I let Lori stay over her friend's house last night, she can go to school from there." Audrey showered quickly and got dressed then left the small apartment in a dash. The little brown Audi cranked and ran like it was happy too. The drive to work wasn't too long but took a few minutes. She felt like a school girl going on her first date, all giddy and tingly inside. Audrey after so long finally had a new man in her life again and it felt wonderful! As she came down Industrial Blvd. she past several other businesses, ranging from air conditioning plants to aircraft manufacturers. Audrey's plant was located in between them.

She drove into the large plant parking lot along with many others. It resembled a motorized chow line as each car passed a guarded checkpoint. The plant was huge and took up at least twenty acres or more, not to mention the five acre parking lot. She pulled into her normal spot near the far end so she could beat most of the traffic out at the end of the day. She turned off the car then started grabbing her work gear.

"Oh well . . . another day, another dollar, it's a good thing today is Friday, but then again I have to work a half day tomorrow to make up for missing yesterday but no sweat, I can hack it" she told herself. "At least I get to see Buford that evening." "Hey Audrey!" she looked around to see who was calling her. "Audrey!" she looked around the lot and saw that it was her friend Elizabeth or Liz for short. "Hey girl" she said finally reaching her. "Didn't you hear me calling you?" "Yeah, but I didn't know where it was from."

"So how's Retta doing?" "Oh, she's doing better, I talked to her last night before she went to bed, she said that she was feeling much better but hadn't been eating much at all, and that Rodney had some Chinese food sent to her room." "That's her boyfriend right?" "Yes" "How old is he?" "He's seventeen." "And you don't mind him seeing Retta?" "Well, at first I did because I didn't think she was old enough to date, and I had not met him yet." "And what about now?" "Well after I had a chance to meet him and talk to him some I decided that it would probably be okay." "Uh, huh." "He's actually quite smart, responsible, and very compassionate from what I can see and he seems to love Retta a great deal." "All that from a seventeen year old boy?" "Yeah! that's what's so surprising about it" she said laughing.

"He doesn't seem to be hell bent on sex like all other boys his age either." "How can you tell?" "Well he and Retta have been seeing each other now for close to three months behind my back and she hasn't turned up pregnant" she said raising an eyebrow. "I mean, I don't know if they're having sex or not but I haven't seen any evidence of it with her." "I see." "When I did talk to him at great length sometime ago, he seemed to me to have goals and things he wants to accomplish with his life after high school, and girl let me tell you the boy has *style!*" "And he seems to keep some money on him and I'm not talking pocket change either!"

"What do you mean?" "He's just a boy, what money could he have of any great amount?" "Girl he bought Aretta a two carat diamond ring." "No, he didn't!" "I'm telling you the truth." "Well what do you think he means by it? And better yet where did he get the money for it?" "Girl I don't even know, Retta said something about him doing odd jobs and yard work in his spare time, his father also works for the post office and he's retired military, he also does taxes for some local businesses from time to time, that's probably where he gets the bulk of it from." "He sounds like a serious young man."

"That's what worries me some, he's just too involved with Aretta and they're still very young." "You think he might run off with her and get married or something?" "Run off? Hell girl she would gladly go with him without protest!" "I'm pretty sure that the ring he bought her is an engagement ring." "Have you talked to her about it?" "No not yet, she tries to keep it hidden from me but forgets to take it off sometimes." "And what about his father, what does he think about all this?"

"I don't think he knows anything yet, no need to go rocking the cradle till it's something in it." "Yeah, I guess your right, I mean at least your on top of it and know what's going on." "True" "So what do you think of his father? Have you had a chance to meet him or talk to him?" "Oh yes girl, and let me tell you, I can see why Rodney is the way he is, his father is just like him or the other way around"

"MMM . . . now how you know that?" she said propping on one hip and going into her "gossip pose." "We been visiting with each other and spent a little time together." "MMM . . . go on girl!" "Now wait a minute Liz, we haven't gotten that serious yet, we're just friendly for now . . . you know . . . two interested parents, in mutual consent, enjoying each other's company while supervising our children." Liz just looked at her sidelong with a twisted up nose, "MMHMM . . . I see, so have you gave up the booty yet?" she chirped wide eyed and completely animated. "Lizabeth!

How could you think that?" "Well have you?" "Well no . . . not yet but I'm getting around to it" she said blushing a little. "I thought so . . . so when you gonna do it?" "Now hold on Ms. Hot pants!

Don't push, I've only known the man a week or so, don't you think we ought to take our time? . . . I mean damn you act like were two horny teenagers necking in the back seat at a drive in or something." "What? . . . do my ears hear this right? . . . is this Audrey Davis, the same Audrey who set half the boys in high school on fire? . . . the same girl who believed every man ought to be fitted with a saddle and a whip?" Audrey just blushed and covered her mouth. "Shh! You know that was back in the days, I don't think like that anymore." "Yeah I'll bet, in fact I'll put ten bucks on it that your wearing red underwear and bra because you used to always wear that when you was on the prowl." "I am not." "Yes you are . . . let me see" she said making a grab for Audrey's work shirt and pulling it forward.

"Liz! Stop that" she protested as the taller woman revealed the truth of her accusation. "See! There it is" she said triumphantly. Audrey was slightly horrified and could only laugh as she smacked her friends hand away and readjusted her clothes. Some of her co-workers looked on as they walked to the building and just grinned and shook their heads. "Now see what you done did, you got everybody thinking I'm loose . . . Liz you a real dog you know that?" "I may be, but your no saint yourself *FIFI!*"

The two friends got themselves under control and walked on towards the building. "He is nice though Liz." "Have you told him so?" "No not really, but I think he knows it already." "So how long has it been since you and Butler split up?" "Oh, about a year I guess" she admitted sighing deeply. "Have you been seeing anyone since then?" "No" "Then I think it's time you did." "Oh yeah?"

"Yes I do, Retta's a big girl now and seems to be holding her own, so you can relax a little bit and let your hair down some, Lori has a ways to go yet and is no real issue at present, so take this time and make the most of it." "At the very least you'll get a chance to quench that drout you been under for so long and at the most you may get a good father for your girls." Audrey thought about what she was saying and it made some sense. "Yeah, I'm a good looking healthy young woman, why shouldn't I start living again." "Yeah! girl you the best" she said giving her a hug. "I know, so when do I get to meet prince charming?"

"I'm not sure to be honest, we're planning to go out Saturday night." "Where to?" "Dinner, dancing maybe and then a drive up to Lake Juliette." "Sounds fine, tell you what, if you don't have a restaurant picked out already why don't we meet at say . . . the Red Lobster." "Let me check with him first, he may have a place in mind already." "Okay, then you do that, meanwhile I'll call my friend Buster so we can at least take dinner with you guys before you run off to play." "Okay Liz, you do that."

As they went into the huge entrance of the plant they stopped to punch in. Some of the others hung around the door near that smoke area for one last drag before heading to their work areas. Audrey and Liz were machine press operators and their stations where in the middle of the plant floor. They stopped at the lounge for a quick coffee fill up and a Danish to take with them to their stations. Company standards didn't really allow for it but since the company had maintained such a good safety record for that last two quarters, it relaxed restrictions a little and let the employees do it. So long as they had lids for the cups. They ran into a few other women they knew on the way.

"Hey Audrey, Liz" they waved and greeted as they went. One large black woman they knew waved at them as she passed by on a forklift. Her name was Claire. Claire was one of the many female section foreman on the plant and was a bit of a pain in the ass if not a nuisance all around. She was at least 5'9 and weighed in at least at two hundred pounds. She had dark mean eyes and an odd but soft voice, an oddity that nobody who spoke with her failed to notice. Liz nor Audrey liked her, and would just as well ignore her, but she was a section foreman and their supervisor. So it behooved either of them to be at least cordial to her at the very least. "Didn't see you at work yesterday Audrey, were you home ill?" she asked slowing down the truck and stopping. "No, it was my oldest daughter, she's in the hospital." "Oh my goodness, I'm sorry to hear that, is she okay?

I hope she feels better." "She is, thank you" she said trying to smile at least a little but not feeling good about divulging anything about her personal life except maybe her backside for her to kiss. "Okay, well I'll see you guys on the floor" she said releasing the brake and pulling off. "Nosey bitch!" hissed Liz as she drove off. Neither Liz nor Audrey like her and both had heard stories early on about her being a dike. They would sometimes in the past catch a glimpse of her talking real friendly to some of the younger women in the plant. She would always be touching them she spoke and laughing.

Liz and Audrey had avoided her because she had once gotten a little too friendly with Audrey one day during her first week on the job many years ago. It seems that Claire was showing her how to operate her machine. Claire stood behind Audrey and watched her as she attempted to duplicate the actions Claire had just done. When she would make a mistake Claire would reach in to make the adjustment and adjust her understanding of what to do and not to do and when. That wasn't bad, but what was bad is when she would constantly brush across Audrey's breasts while doing it!

Audrey tried to brush it off and let it slide thinking it to be accidental and not on purpose. However; this changed when Audrey noticed that just about every time she would instruct or monitor her performance she was always rubbing against her breasts or over extending herself to brush against her. This made Audrey a bit more than concerned, and one day during a training session the shit hit the fan. Claire was monitoring her as usual, standing behind her while Audrey sat at her station working the machine.

Everything was going smoothly and she had made no mistakes when all of a sudden she felt Claire's breast on her back! For a minute Audrey thought she was going to reach in to correct or adjust something on her machine but didn't. This made Audrey tense up and she leaned reflexively away to break the contact. Claire then began to whisper in to her that she thought she had a nice body and wanted to be friends. Audrey's mind snapped! And she couldn't believe what she'd just heard.

She reached over and flipped the switch, shutting down the big press and evacuated her chair. She was so mad that she felt trembling in her legs. The sound of the big machine powering down got the attention of a few on-lookers, as it was not normal or something you wouldn't hear until around quitting time. Audrey turned and squared off on the big woman and just let it happen. "Look Claire, let me get something straight, I'm not gay or bisexual and I don't fuck women! If my man can't do it for me just what the hell do you think you can do for me?" "So keep your fucking hands and tits off me or I swear I will thoroughly fuck you up! *Understand?*" she said one hand on her hip and one pointed dangerously close to Claire's oversized chest.

Audrey hadn't noticed the other women who had been observing from their stations when she got started. But upon hearing her set the wayward woman straight, they all chimed in and chirped out their support. They all knew from watching Claire over the years that it would be just a matter of time before she made a move on the new girl.

Audrey was just twenty five at the time and Retta and Lori just little girls. Claire stood with hands on her hips huffing and breathing heavily. She knew she could take the younger woman but couldn't do anything just then because of so many witnesses. She toyed in her mind with the idea of how she would get back at her and the thought made her smile. But because she was such a mean, twisted woman it came out as a sneer.

She looked at Audrey with eyes that could burn through lead. Audrey had half expected the woman to say something in retort but when she didn't Audrey started to become concerned and wondered could she take the big woman if she attacked her. Audrey thought all this with fear rising in her but still stood her ground and waited not knowing what else to do. Just then Tabitha Morgan, one of the other section supervisors and two other women walked up behind Audrey. Audrey quickly looked over and saw them and her heart began to sink. "Oh god . . . she has friends" then looked back at Claire not wanting to take her eyes off of her.

Tabitha was a large woman herself, just a little stouter, taller, and certainly prettier than Claire. She ran the maintenance department and was a heavy equipment/diesel mechanic for the plant. She had paid her dues many years ago like everyone else and although she would get an occasional ribbing from the guys in her section she still got respect. They liked her and gave her many props for her mechanical abilities as well as being able to lift as much or more weight than any of them.

"You heard the lady" she said in a firm even tone, standing also with hands on her full and curvaceous hips. She was wearing her coveralls and stood feet shoulder width apart like a football player. "She don't want nothing to do with you so haul ass slut!" Audrey felt a warm flush come to her face as the large stranger opened up on Claire. She had been thinking she was going to get a three way beat down and was bracing for whoever was going to swing first. When it didn't come, she was shocked and elated at the same time. Claire flashed hot stares at the four of them.

"Dis ain't none of your business you yellow bitch, why don't you go and play with your boy friends in the grease pit, I hear they like it slippery that way" she retorted talking between her teeth. Audrey began to feel like a child in a tug of war between parents. And just sighed keeping quiet. "Ha! That's the best you can do? Aw shit, I thought that a big pussy hog like you would at least have something better to throw at me than that, shit you wish you could play with some of my guys."

"Hell not one of em would fuck you with his dick and me pushing" Tabitha rebounded. The other two women with her laughed accordingly as did some of the other on-lookers at other nearby stations. "You best get the fuck on while you still can, otherwise I might have to see just how much pussy you got when I shove this pipe wrench up your ass" she said producing a three foot long red pipe wrench from her thigh pocket. Audrey had never seen a tool so intimidating or so large as this. And it must have weighed at least ten pounds. Tabitha handled the big piece of steel like it was a toilet bowl wand, clanking it in her hand like it was a ruler. Claire knew the big woman would use it, she'd seen her go to town on a man once in a night club with a pool cue. "This ain't over Morgan, I'll get you for this you nosey bitch, I'll get you both!" she said jutting a long fat finger at Audrey who flinched from the threat like a child.

She turned on her heals and stomped off fuming with clinched fists. "Go on you ole witch, before somebody drop a house on you!" said Tabitha not being moved by anything she had said. Audrey just sank onto her stool and sighed deeply, completely spent emotionally. Tabitha put away her wrench and stepped over to where Audrey was sitting. "Thank you . . . I don't really know what I would have done if you guys hadn't come along." "Don't sweat it girl, that whore has made a play fo all of us at one time or another." "She has?" "Yeah, some give in and some don't, you can pretty much tell who does and who won't" she said waving her hand in the general direction of the plant floor. The two that were with her nodded in agreement. "We had been watching you for some time now and wondering which way you was gonna go, so we had to wait for her to approach you first."

"Why? Couldn't you have just told me about her? I would have listened" she said sounding hurt but grateful. "Maybe, maybe not, anyway that's not how we do things around here, you had to face her on your own, only then could we tell if you were a straight shooter or not." "Straight shooter?" she queried "You know . . . this instead of this" she said making a loop with two fingers on one hand and poking a finger of the other through it.

Then repeating the same action but with both hands looping fingers and bumping them together like the ends of two pipes. "Oh I get it!" said Audrey flushing red more from ignorance than embarrassment. "So what . . . do you guys have some sort of club here or something?" "Yeah something like that, we're all good women and most of us have kids of our own too, so we tend to stick together, look out for each other and keep the dogs off, like her" she said Tabitha pointing in the direction Claire and gone.

"We also get promoted more regularly than most too." "Really?" "Yep, look around you, all of these women in this area are in charge of at least one other crew or shift and are making anywhere between five and ten dollars more per hour above standard pay." "Well I'll be dipped in butter!" the big women and her crew just laughed at Audrey's country ways. She began to like Audrey and knew they would be friends and a nice addition to their group.

As time went on, Tabitha had introduced Audrey to all the other women on her shift. Some were about Audrey's age, others a little older. It was now break time and they all went outside together for some fresh air or a smoke. "Do you think I'll get fired Tabitha?" asked Audrey really feeling the weight of Claire's threats.

"Girl no, all that pussy eating bitch can do is talk shit and play with herself." Audrey covered her mouth to hide her laughter. "Management don't really pay her no mind because they know what kind of person she is and what she is up to most of the time they know she be trying to exploit these young women so don't you worry none."

"I'll go talk to the shift manager on my lunch hour and let him know what's what, he's a nice guy and can't stand her ass no more than any one of us." "Okay, thank you Tabitha you're really a nice person and I'm glad I had the opportunity to meet you" she said smiling genuinely and shaking the big woman's hand.

"You too sweetie, and for the record don't call me Tabitha, that's what my momma call me, call me Tabby instead, that's what my friends call me." "Okay Tabby." Right about then Audrey thought she heard a familiar voice in the distance. She turned a ear to the direction of the conversation. She could see two women talking. One facing her and the other with her back to Audrey. It was this one that was doing all the animated talking, propped on one leg with her hands on her hips.

"Now you know there ain't but one person I know who could run on like that." "Do you know her?" "I kind of think I do Tabby." "Then go on over and holla at her, you just might, I gotta go back to the shop right quick anyway and check on this new boy in my pit, God I hope he ain't gone ahead and dropped an engine on himself" she said laughing and getting up to go. "I'll be seeing you around the plant Audrey and maybe me you and some of the others can have lunch or hang out sometime."

"I would like that Tabby." "Okay, then you be good." "Bye Tabby" she said waving and feeling like a school girl who had just made a new friend in a new school. Audrey turned and walked over towards the two women she'd been listening to. The one facing her, a young white girl of about twenty that she had seen around, and the other who now that she had heard her up close, knew she had known from long ago.

Audrey came up behind her and just stood smiling. The other girl noticed her and stopped talking. Aware of somebody behind her the other girl turned and gushed as she threw her arms around Audrey's neck. "Audrey Davis!, girl what are you doing here? I didn't know you worked here?" "Yep, it's me in the flesh."

"So what's been up you little man stealer?" she chirped. "Man stealer! now Liz it wasn't my fault that Jordan picked me to dance with instead of you . . . hell we were standing there together and he could have had anyone of us" said Audrey feigning indignation at an accusation predating high school and a junior prom. "Well that's okay, because I got the best one in the place anyway" said Liz preening and adjusting herself. "Oh yeah? Who?" "Willie Farrel." "Not Willie the feret Farrel?" "Yep!" "Girl you must have been horny as a bull or just felt like living dangerous for awhile."

"Why you say that? . . . Willie is nice . . . or was." "So you didn't know anything about his reputation then?" "What reputation? All I know is the boy was a good kisser and had hands that should have been bronzed girl . . . you hear me?" she said smacking her bottom soundly. "Did you ever wonder why all the girls called him "Ferret Ferral?" "Yea a little bit . . . why?" Audrey smiled and shook her head wondering if she should tell her friend after all these years. "Let me ask you this first, did you marry him?"

"No" "Are you dating him now?" "Audrey you better tell me . . . No I ain't seeing him!" "Okay I'll tell you." "You know what a Ferret is don't you?" "Sigh . . . yes I know what it is, it's a furry little animal who likes to get into things." "Well your buddy Willie has seen more coochie between the ninth grade and graduation then any OBGYN in Macon."

Liz's eyes grew wider than a hub cap. "Go on girl!" "Yep I heard he has had his nose up more pussies than a box of tampax." Audrey was grinning so wide that her cheeks hurt. "That's why they called him the Ferret." "Now I see why them bitches was grinning at me and Willie when we was leaving, I guess they figured I was gonna be next" "Were you?" Liz grinned and cut her eyes seductively and leaned over to whisper in Audrey's ear.

"They should have called him Willie the whip, cause that boy tongue went places in my coochie that I' ain't never been!" "OOH! You so nasty!" squealed Audrey covering her mouth and laughing wildly. "Girl you so crazy" said Liz slapping her on her arm. The crowd of employees were beginning to thin out and go back inside. This got to the two women's attention and they began to come back under control from their hilarious and naughty trip down memory lane. "Hey Liz, what part of the plant do you work in?"

"I'm in shipping and receiving." "Okay, I'm in manufacturing in the press operator section." "Oh, I know where you are, so I'll tell you what, on our lunch break we'll get together and talk some more okay?" "That would be nice Liz It's been a long time girl." "Yeah, I know and we have to stay in touch now that I know your just under my nose." The buzzer sounded and the remaining workers went back inside.

There was an awful and discomforting pressure between Retta's legs and for a second she thought she would be split in two as the doctor inserted the strange and cold device. She was in the examination room on a table with her feet in stirrups. Oh, how bare and totally open she felt as the strange white man probed around in her sacred of most places. She cringed every time he touched her and wondered what he was thinking as he looked up inside of her. The doctor was getting tissue samples and inspecting her uterus to see how well her infection was healing. She didn't care what it was doing right about now and just wanted to close her legs and run away. Retta tried to displace herself and leave her body so she wouldn't feel anything, but it was very difficult.

The last and first time anyone had done this was when she was twelve years old and was getting her first physical. Her mother was with her holding her hand and she could still remember the fear and degradation of the whole experience. Even then it was some strange man looking at and touching her private parts and the worst of it was when he inserted that large cold metal tool into her. She remembered that the thing was huge, shiny, cold and hard when he inserted it into her virginal body.

"Oww! It hurts mama" she whined squeezing her mothers hand for support. Audrey could feel her pain and could only offer mild support. Retta sucked in her breath hard and winced with pain as the doctor slowly inserted the tool. "It's okay baby, it only hurts for a second or two" Retta tried to bear it like a big girl but it just wasn't possible. The object as big as it was seemed to grow and expand within her, and Retta could literally feel her body being stretched outside it's normal size.

"Oww! Mama Oww! It hurts" she whined more and beginning to move and gyrate trying to get away from the evil thing inside her. She squeezed her mothers hand harder till the color went from it and bones began to hurt. The pain seemed to go on forever and just when Retta thought it couldn't get any worse she felt a tiny object snake into her and brush briefly but harshly against her insides. *"AAEEEE!!"* She screamed in a loud shrill tone that was so loud it not only froze the doctor in his tracks but also shook Retta as well as her mother. *"Stop it your hurting me, you mean man!"* she screamed.

"Mama he's hurting me please make him stop!" she began to cry. The doctor was notably shaken and very embarrassed as Retta and Audrey burned him with silent looks no harsh accusation could ever compare to. He slowly but urgently removed the long Q-tip probe, relaxed the expander and removed it. Retta began to feel better already but was definitely sore on her bottom. "I'm sorry sweetie I didn't mean to hurt you, sometimes these tools can be a bit harsh and not too accommodating, please forgive me" said the doctor in a shaky but gently voice. Retta just looked at him with her knees up to her chest and pouted angrily at him. She was scowling something terrible at the doctor and it left him somewhat odd and slightly deranged.

Retta didn't say anything but just silently hated the man for making her feel so barren and for causing the throbbing pain she was now feeling around her bottom. "It's alright doctor, I know you didn't mean to hurt her and you were only doing what needed to be done to ensure she is healthy" said Audrey trying to smooth things over seeing as how the older man looked near death and about to pass out from stress. Aretta was once again feeling this way and instead of having her mother there, she had nurse Sadie. It also hurt a lot less now and the pressure wasn't so bad as before. Soon she was through with her exam.

"Okay young lady, you can get dressed now, we're all done." Retta quickly got up and reclaimed her underwear, smock and robe. She turned her back to him and got dressed. The whole experience made her feel as though she had been molested. The only man to ever touch her there with complete permission and tenderness was Matt and he would be the last! "You're looking much better today Aretta and I don't see any reason why you can't go home tomorrow." "*OH really!*"

"That's right dear, your infection is under control and when I get the lab tests back on this sample I'll know for sure just how well you functioning, other than that your fever is gone and you show no more signs of pneumonia, so you can be ready to leave tomorrow sometime." "OH! Thank you, thank you!" she said running up to hug the man. Retta in her happiness to leave had forgotten herself and just realized that the man she was hugging had just seen her totally naked and it made her blush hard and recover herself.

"Oh I'm sorry I . . . !" "It's alright Retta, I'm a doctor, I see you as a perfectly made female specimen, don't feel embarrassed." Retta smiled bashfully and eased towards the door side stepping all the way so she wouldn't expose her backside to him again. Nurse Sadie had just stepped out to get her Wheel chair.

"Whew! I'm glad that's over" she said sitting down as Sadie wheeled up the chair. "Where to now?" "Well we could go back to your room, because your finished for today, or we could take a stroll through the maternity ward and see the new babies." "Ooh! Could we?" "We sure can." Since Retta had arrived there Sadie had become her own personal guardian angel of sorts. The large cherry face white woman had adopted her and given her nothing but love and attention. Down the hall past the nurse's station and around the corner they went. They passed several nurses and interns along the way. They were mostly standing around and looking over some clipboards or patients records.

When they saw Retta and Sadie coming they waved and said hello. "Hi cutie pie" said one of the young male interns. "Hello" she said flushing warm all over from the comment. "There are a lot of nice people here Sadie." "Yes there are, but sometimes people can get overworked and be a little cross, but for the most part they're very nice people." "So what do you want to be when you grow up Retta?"

"Oh, I don't know . . . maybe an artist or an architect." "Well now those are great careers to have, what made you decide on those?" "Well I like to draw and I like the way some buildings look with all the glass and shiny metal, it's really pretty when the sun shines on them." "Well my dear, I've never heard anyone put it quite like that before, that sounds like your buildings will be the prettiest in town!"

"Sadie did you always want to be a nurse?" "Well not exactly, I think it was more like a calling than anything else." "How so?" "Well you see Aretta, it's like this, a long time ago when I was much younger, about twenty one to be exact, I had a husband and a nice job as a secretary." "We had only been married for two years but life was great!" "What kind of work did he do?" "He was an accountant with a large banking firm in Atlanta, after awhile I became pregnant."

"We had worked really hard and planned for this day and everything was right, Charles and I would sit for hours and look through books of names and try to decide on one." "You see my husband wasn't what you would call a traditionalist or a person who believed in following old fashioned ways too much, that being his way he said the child if it was a boy would not be called Jr. or named after him."

"He wanted him to have his own identity, if it was a girl then it didn't matter." "Some days we would go shopping for baby toys and furniture for the nursery." "Finally the day came to deliver, it was a really bad day and the weather was awful, rain came down so hard you couldn't see the road hardly, it took a long time to get to the hospital and when we did I started experiencing pains and bleeding."

"The doctor gave me an ultrasound and found that the baby had some how shifted and turned upside down in my womb." "Oh my goodness! Did he get the baby straightened out?" "No dear, she was in too much of a bind and during her delivery she stuck her foot outside of my vagina and got wedged even further." "You mean her foot stuck *out!*" "Yes sweetie, and even though they tried to do an emergency C-section it was too late, she had suffocated and strangled on her own umbilical cord." "Oh my lord!" said Retta completely stricken with shock and horror.

"Once they got her out, they did all they could to revive her but it was just too late and she was gone." "My husband couldn't take it and went hysterical, when I had next heard anything they told me that he had become delirious and ran from the hospital into the rain and was hit by a car." "He died instantly, I couldn't fathom what had happened and went into shock then a coma for two weeks I'm told."

"After I came to, my family told me that my baby and my husband had been buried side by side." "It took many years for me to come out of my depression, but I did, and now I'm here with you precious."

"*Oh Sadie, i*t's so awful . . . just so awful." Retta covered her face and sobbed bitterly. She had never heard of a tragedy such as this in her life. And to have it happen to someone as loving an caring as Sadie McIntyre . . . well it was just too much to bare. Sadie blinked back a tear and quietly pushed Retta into a quiet spot out of the way then bent down to console the heart broken child. "Shh . . .

it's alright baby" she said holding her and stroking her head. "Don't cry my child, all is better now."

"When I saw and remembered all the love and care I was shown by the nurses and doctors while trying to save my baby, I just knew that this is what I wanted to do with the rest of my life, and in a big way God has blessed me richly because of it." "H . . .How? Sadie. Y . . .you lost everything you ever loved." Sadie held up Retta's tear soaked little face. Retta looked into Sadie's warm honey brown eye's and saw nothing but love. "Just look around pumpkin, I have more children now then I could ever have hoped for! And everyday I get to take care of all these wonderful children as if they were my own. And to be honest with you I think of you all as my own real children." "It is because if this, through all of you that my Sara lives on forever."

"Do you understand sweetie?" Retta just nodded then lay her head on Sadie's large chest and cried silent tears of love and admiration for her. She raised her head momentarily and kissed Sadie deeply on the cheek. "I love you Sadie!" "Aw my sweet child" she said tearing up. "I love you too!" Just around the corner several nurses stood all whipping tears from their eyes.

Matt was sitting in his desk busy day dreaming again. The class was slow and he wasn't that concerned about missing anything cause it was Social Studies and he had that course down pretty good. The sun was rising higher and higher into the sky by the minute and there were bees buzzing around outside of his window. Matt loved to sit by the window because it always gave him a quick means of escape when he got bored or just felt the urge to let his mind wander. Just now he was watching a spider spin it's web on one of the bushes.

The tiny insect left long shimmering lines of silk everywhere it went, creating an iridescent tapestry of rainbow and silver highlights. He hated spiders but found it fascinating how something so small and without a mind could create something so beautiful and strong. The warm sweet smell of the trees and flowers came to him as a gentle breeze whispered by. The world was so beautiful at times he thought but yet so painful and harsh too. Sometimes he wished he could step out of class and into his dreams and live there where it was always sunny and bright.

And the plants and animals weren't afraid of you. It was so sublime to lay upon a thick grassy knoll and listen to the soothing sounds of nature. There were very few people he would ever tell about his daydreams and aspirations. Ant and Retta we're so far, the only two, then of course maybe his dad. He could always see the softness and wonder in his son's eyes. He always knew the worlds that existed deep inside of him and where he could be found. Matt was a sensitive, compassionate person and never fought against his true nature as other boys have.

He was neither afraid to show it when it came upon him either. He loved the feeling of love and all its wondrous ways. He liked the way a smile from a girl would make him blush and how tender a silent moment could capture his soul when looking into the eyes of the only woman he ever loved.

He felt so full and alive at times and could hardly contain himself sometimes. He often wondered what others thought of his somewhat displaced demeanor. Still he didn't care. He felt that it was them that were losing out not him. Sometimes he would get engrossed in himself so deeply when he sat listening to his classical music that he would find himself in a 3-D world of sound and color, all warm and sweet.

It made him feel sensuous and gentle like Ferdinand the bull. This thought always made him laugh when they would tip toe into his mind. Matt wasn't bothered by this either. He believed that only when a person allowed him or herself to be truly in touch with their feelings and gentler emotions, could they really experience the splendor of life and it's essence.

"Oh how wonderful it felt!" "Matt are you alright?" said a soft female voice. Matt was suddenly brought back to reality. "Huh? . . . what's that?" "I said are you alright?" "Yeah, I was just thinking." "What about?" She asked.

It was Tonya Rodgers and OH! How she could make him swoon! And reminisce. He thought she was beautiful and love incarnate. Tonya was very light in complexion with light bronze colored short naturally curly hair. Her eyes were grey green and so very penetrating and alluring. She had a soft sensuous mouth that seemed to be always touched with a hint of red lipstick but she never wore any. Her teeth were perfect and she was generally shy and soft spoken. She was friendly but still very kept and private.

Tonya was of average height and had a very nice athletic but soft figure and was in Matt's homeroom class. "Oh god!" he thought as he felt his soul flow out of him and his breathing become labored. He would fall in love with her a thousand times with each passing second. Tonya was the only other woman other than Aretta who could make his heart beat outside his chest. He could feel himself rising and floating into her while staring deeply into her magnetic eyes. All the while screaming from within that he loved her.

Matt would have given anything just to kiss her tender lips and look into her eyes as she spoke his name telling him she loved him too. He could hear music playing in his head and wondered could she hear it too. She didn't. She just sat there and smiled at him sweetly, further scorching his heart with her loving eyes. She was so pure and angelic and Matt could do little to avoid his private worship of her.

Over and over he heard himself say, "I love you . . . I love you, you wonderfully made, breath taking creature, I love you!" By some strange happpenstance they had drawn closer across the narrow isle and her face was so close now that he could smell her sweet essence. He didn't know how this was happening and it felt like he was in a time warp! And being phased closer to her without moving. She was so close now that each breath she breathed flowed through his lips and down into his soul. Suddenly and without any warning his desk fell over sideways, "Crash!" he landed on his face spilling his books and himself all over the floor between them. The class just let out a roar as they laughed at him in this ridiculous position.

"Mr. Mathis, are you alright?" asked his teacher. Matt was embarrassed and trying to free himself from the almost too small desk and chair combo. "Yes ma'am, I just slipped that's all." "Sideway's?" she said incredulously. "You see I was trying to . . . " he never finished his sentence. He thought about what was happening just moments ago and decided not to say anything at all. "Trying to what, Mr. Mathis?" "Oh nothing . . . I just slipped." The teacher gave him a strange look.

The kind of look you give to a person who shows up for a funeral in a clown suit. She then walked back up the isle to the front of the classroom. "Class! It seems that in all my years of teaching high school, Mr. Mathis is the only student needing a seat belt to stay in his desk." The class erupted again looking and pointing at him as they laughed. Matt just sank into his chair and cursed himself for being a fool. Tonya was just staring at her nails and working on her lower lip. She felt sorry for Matt.

Tonya was embarrassed too even though it wasn't her they were laughing at. She too had felt something as they looked at each other. She had never known love and didn't have a boyfriend. She had always felt afraid and unsure when it came to love. Boys would look at her often, but she would not speak and just smiled at them timidly, bow her head and look away. That's why it shook her so much that Matt would bother to look at her with such unbridled love and fire in his eyes. A feeling she couldn't deny he felt for her.

It coursed through her like a wave and she liked it. Tonya never quite understood him, he never spoke to her much except to say "Hi" on occasion. Did he not like her? . . . no was he afraid of her? . . . maybe but still that didn't make sense either because she always thought of him as confident and cool with a bit of mystery. She didn't know why she was going to kiss him just then or why he wanted to kiss her but something inside told her, "Yes! it's alright do it!" but now she would never know what it would have felt like and this made her feel a little sad and unbalanced inside.

Matt had resumed looking out the window to recompose himself. He needed to regain his perspective. Matt never could figure why some women had such power over him and why he found it so hard to resist them. Finally he drew the conclusion that it was just the way he was and he couldn't change it. He knew he wouldn't give into his emotions but always wondered why he let them run away with him. He thanked god silently for intervening before he did something he would regret, but then again, "Why should I deny my feelings to reach out to love and allow it to return from someone who was willing to give it so freely" he thought.

"I mean as cold as the world has become, people should take advantage of every opportunity for love that comes along shouldn't they?" He knew the answer, but felt he needed to run the course of this private game of devils advocate and self rectification. Just then he felt something touch him on the arm. It was a small slip of paper folded up with a kiss print on it in red lipstick. He looked around to see where it could have come from. He spied Tonya quickly whipping her lips with a napkin and putting it in her bag. She didn't look at him, but just stared ahead innocently. Matt quietly put the note in his shirt pocket and looked toward the black board.

The teacher was writing some assignments for them to do over the weekend and said she wanted them done by Monday no excuses. Soon the bell rang and Matt was out the door and heading for his next class which was gym. He had to go across the street to the boys school to get there. He knew he'd see Ant and tell him about what had happened, but for now he was trying to wind his way through the crowded halls.

"Damn! Why is it that every time I have to go to gym I wind up getting caught up in this muck?" he said to himself. "It would be easier to just have it over here, but NNOO! some jerk in the office thinks it's cute to watch people kill themselves while trying to get across the street with out getting trampled or run over by a car." He finally made it out of the building. It always amazed him how so many people could ever get where they were going on time when over half of them just hung around talking and playing while he had to run and was almost, always late! "Oh well, shit happens." "Hey Matt what's up?" Said his friend Frog passing by with his arm around some girl. "Yo! What's up" he said without stopping. "I see ole Frog has a new tadpole on his Lilly pad, not bad!"

Matt didn't have too far to go now and was ducking in and out of the crowd. "Scuse me . . . scuse me . . . oops! I'm sorry . . . scuse me" as he turned the corner of the side walk at the end of the fence by the track and football field. He ran head long into a little white girl who was just a little too small to see over the crowd. "Wham!" her books went flying and she tumbled onto her bottom. "Oh shit!, I'm sorry I didn't mean to run you over, hear let me help you up" he said quickly dropping his book bag and reaching under the girls armpits to hoist her back onto her feet.

She looked like she weighed about as much as a six pack of sodas if she weighed a pound. She looked like a child of eight years old. Matt quickly began to dust her off brushing her all over from top to bottom, front to back. She was wearing a lovely pompom dress with red roses on it. "What are you doing!" she protested smacking Matt's hand away.

"Oh, I'm sorry I was just trying to clean you up a little, I really didn't see you." "Well thank you, but I can dust off my own self if you don't mind!" she barked at him with anger and contempt showing in her voice. She didn't much like being handled like a small child as was the case. "Well there's no reason to be nasty, a little girl like you is hard to see in a crowd like this, besides aren't you supposed to be over at the junior high? Or are you with a group on a field trip?" *"JUNIOR HIGH!...A CHILD!"* she shouted.

"Why you, Neanderthal! How dare you call me a child or mistake me for being one, I'll have you know I'm a senior buster! and I'm 17, if its' any of your business!" she shouted standing with her little hands on her little hips. Matt noted that she was 38 hot (mad as hell) and her pink little face was crimson red and blended nicely with her white and rose dress. Matt wondered who had dressed her this way and thought she looked much like Alice in wonderland more than a high school senior.

Matt decided that since she was gonna be rude so would he. "Well if you would take a *little* time to do a *little* looking around you, you might have a *little* less trouble in your *little* life" he said smiling at her. "Are you making fun of me?" she asked curtly leaning towards him. Matt leaning way over until he was almost face to face with her then slowly held up one hand with his thumb and fore finger close together. "Just a little bit" he said then burst out laughing and went to get his book bag on the ground.

The little princess stood there with fists clenched and face red. She looked like a tea pot about to boil over. "Why you overgrown, air brained, dime store hood! I'll stomp your filthy heart out!" she spat then ran after Matt. He looked at the little demon coming after him and couldn't believe what he was seeing. "You have got to be shitting me!" The hilariousness of the attack made Matt laugh out loud as he began to run. He easily glided away from her as the girls legs were just not long enough to get much out of.

Matt trotted away effortlessly and even slowed down to let her catch up some then he would burst away in a shot of speed leaving her all the more frustrated. Soon she gave up the chase, stamped her foot and turned around with clenched fists to recover her books. Several students had stopped to watch the freak show and found it just as hilarious as Matt had. Matt raced into the gym and stopped as soon as he got to the locker room. "Hey Matt what's up "B?" said Milton.

"Nothing much man just trying to stay alive" "Trying to stay alive?... who did you piss off now?" "Now how you know I pissed somebody off?" "Cause every time I see you out of breath and running, you've pissed somebody off and It's usually a girl." "Matt just grinned and flopped down on the bench. "Okay you got me, I was just trying to help up this cute little white girl who I bumped into at the corner of the fence." "Uh huh" "And while I was helping her up I tried to dust off her dress, then all of a sudden she got all mad and started to yell at me and talk shit." "So what did you?" "Nothing much, I just reminded her of her small size is all." "Wait a minute! Was she wearing a rosey white dress, curly blond hair and blue eyes?" "Yeah, that's her, you know her?" "Man, that's Annette Wilson!" "So who is she supposed to be?" "Only the daughter of a Bibb County Sheriff." "Oh fuck! Are you for real?" "Can a monkey pick peaches?" "Damn I'm screwed now, every time I see a Deputy he's gonna give my ass a ticket . . . with roses on it!" "Maybe not, I might be able to save your bacon." "Oh yeah, how?" "Well I know her real well." "How well?" "Let's just say she may be small on the street but she's fifty feet tall when you get her in bed!" he said laughing and pumping his hips in and out. "Naw, you got that?" "Yep" "When?" "Last weekend over to my house."

"Well, I'll be damned, I guess even a dog like you can get a poodle once in a while." "And you know it!" "Well let me get dressed out before I'm late, I don't feel like running anymore laps than I need to before track practice." "I heard that." "Hey Jr. how come you didn't join the track team?" "Naw man, that ain't my style, you know me, the only sweating I do is in bed and that's only when I've got more than one girl with me." "Yeah yeah, right studdly, where's Ant?" "Have you seen him?" "Yeah he's in the gym talking to Cheryl."

"Oh yeah? What about?" "I don't know, they've been there for a while, I just got here not too long ago myself, so what's up with you two?" "Nothing, why?" "Well I just hear that you and her have been getting busy that's all" he said giggling. "Not! Who ever told you that is as lost as she is for trying, and Jr. don't go spreading that shit man, you'll only screw up what's left of your useless reputation."

"Yeah right, so she's been after you a lot then?" "Man I can't even get her to quit following me in the halls, every since that day at the park she won't give up." "I keep telling her that I got a girl but she still keeps after me! did you know her and that chick Melanie are cousins?" "Naw, really" "Yep, they are and they've got some crazy plan cooking to trap me into submission so they can rape me I guess."

"Matt, I don't get you bro. most guys would kill for a free look between Cheryl's legs, *with!* Clothes on, and you've seen it and won't take what she's dying to give you, plus her cousin to boot?" "Well like I've said, I'm not like you man, I got a girl who pleases me just fine so why get greedy?" "It's not greed man! . . . hell that's gravy!" Matt just laughed at him and shook his head in sympathy. "What ever you say Jr." Just then Milton noticed the piece of paper sticking out of Matt's shirt pocket. It was out far enough to see that some one's lips were on it. "What's this?" he said grabbing it.

"Hey wait a minute, I haven't even read it yet" he said grabbing it back. "Well let's see it then!" "Hold your water, wait until we get into the gym then we all can see it." "Okay but who is it from?" "Tonya Rodgers." "Bullshit!" "Naw, that's word." "Let me see the name." Matt opened it and looked at the very bottom of the letter. "See?" "Well I'll be cooked in hog fat, it is her." "You see what I mean? . . . now you got her on your jock too!" "Now wait a minute, I don't know anything yet, all I have is a note I haven't read yet." "Well quit screwing around and let's see it" he said making another grab for it. "Hold up man, wait till we get in the gym then we'll see it! It ain't going no where."

"Well hurry up and get dressed then!" "Okay don't rush I'll see you out there." "Why don't you go and keep Cher busy or something." "Yeah I wish, Can't nobody get near that, she done willed that booty over to you!" "Well keep her busy anyway, I don't need her stalking me in here." "Alright I'll catch you outside" he said then walked off through the dressing room door and into the gym. Matt sat on a bench and quickly went about changing his clothes. He just knew he was going to be late for roll call cause Milton used up so much time running his mouth. Soon he was dressed in his orange and white gym clothes. He stuffed his things into his locker and ran into the gym.

Matt could see everyone was lined up in two rows. Girls on the right and boys on the left. "Damn! He's already started calling roll." Matt tried to sneak into the end of the line and almost made it but just as he got there Coach Jones busted him. "Mathis! Come here you little fart buster" the class tripped out hard and bodies were all over the floor laughing at him for all time to come. Matt just cursed himself and walked up two rows to where coach was. "Nice try Matt" said Ant grinning and slapping him on the back as he passed. He had just about got there when he felt a sharp slap on his butt. He turned around to see that it was Cheryl.

"Nice ass Matt" she said grinning devilishly and flexing her eyebrows at him. "None of that now" he said pointing and scowling at her playfully. "Mathis!" bellowed Coach Jones shaking the windows.

Matt ran to his side and stood to attention. "Yes sir" "Son why are you always late for roll call?" "I don't know coach, I don't try to be." "That's right Mathis you don't try!" he said leaning his big nose close to Matt's face emphasizing on the word, TRY! "Assume the position!" he said pointing down at the floor without looking at him. Matt just sighed long and set about doing his twenty pushups. "Do four count pushups Mathis." "What!" "Or would you prefer to do a self destruct instead?" he said smirking at him.

"Oh shit!" whispered Ant. "That shit is hell! He better get with the pushups." "You ain't lying" added Milton. "You have to do twenty pushups, thirty sit ups, seventy five side straddle hops, fifty eight count body builders, and when you get done with all that you have to start all over again without a break. Matt was already moving "1-2-3-1 1-2-3-2 1-2-3-3" soon he was done and quite worn out. As he got up he could see Cheryl sitting on the bleachers with her legs stretched out and propped up on her elbows.

"Having fun Matt?" "No, are you?" "Oh, I always have fun watching you go up and down like that, too bad we're not alone I could have given you some motivation" she said seductively spreading her legs a little to make her point and sharpen his. "OOH damn! You little cock teaser, now why you wanna get a man all stirred up out here?" Matt could see that she wasn't wearing underwear and her shorts cut deep into her crotch. Matt could feel his member expanding wildly so he quickly ran up the bleachers to the top and sat down so nobody would see. Cheryl just laughed and skipped away triumphantly and quite happy that she could still set him off. "I'm gonna get that heffa just wait!" he spat trying to think of something disgusting to make his erection go away. He looked over and saw Ant and Milton shooting ball on the far end. "Hey Ant, Jr. come here!"

"Hold up, this is game point!" said Ant. Milton took the ball out and passed it to Gary Slappy, he drove to the hoop for a lay up but it got slapped away by fat Freddie. Ant quickly recovered the ball. He drove it in did a pump fake to Milton then went up for a two handed slam dunk. "Slam! In your face!" he said coming down and pointing in there faces. He gave Milton a high five and they ran off the court. "Come on Jr. let's break, they ain't no competition." "Aw ya'll sucka's just got lucky that's all" spat Freddie.

"Yeah right, thirty to twelve, that sure sound's like luck to me" said Ant as they ran up the bleachers to where Matt was. "What's up?" asked Ant sitting down. Matt reached into his pocket and pulled out the note and waved it. "This is." "Oh yeah, that's the note I told you about that he got from Tonya." "Well let's see it." Matt opened it and began to read.

"Dear Rodney I'm not quite sure why I'm writing this note to you, I've known you for sometime now and we have never said much to each other except for hello. First of all I would like to say I do like you and think you are really cute and a nice guy. But when you don't talk to me I wonder why I even think of you at all! Anyway when you looked at me today the way you did I felt you all through me and it made me tremble all over. Your eyes were like an eclipse of the sun and could see my every thought. And when you got closer to me I was a little afraid. Not of you, but because I thought you wanted to kiss me and I didn't know what to do because I thought I wanted to kiss you as well. A girl could go crazy thinking of all the ways this could have turned out and Rodney I don't even know if I'm making any sense at all but I do know how you have made me feel like and I will never be the same. I've never been in love before or had a boyfriend and now that I have seen in you what I think you see in me I can't hide from it any longer. Please meet me after school in the Science Lab next to home room. We need to talk. Signed: Over-joyed and not sure it's love. Tonya R.

Matt just dropped the paper and slumped back against the bleachers. Ant picked it up and folded it. "Damn Matt" said Jr. "It's worse than I thought."

"NO shit! Sherlock." He spat not feeling well all of a sudden. "Well what are you going to do?" asked Ant handing him the note. "I don't know, I guess I have to meet her and get her straight. It's partially my fault she feels that way."

"I know how you are Matt" said Ant looking stern and I know you have some feelings for her too."

"The question is how much and what are you gonna do about it?" "Well I gotta be honest man, if I didn't have to transfer to Southwest when I was in the ninth I would be with her now!" "That's bad" he said shaking his head. "So . . . as to what am I gonna do, I plan to evaluate the situation further, try an establish more understanding about the outcome and give it a lot of time in order to properly discuss our true feelings and my position on this matter" he said pacing back and forth, hands behind his back.

"You're gonna run and hide aren't you" said Milton flatly. "Like a man running through hell with gasoline drawers on!" Ant just fell over laughing. "Boy you are through!" "Hey what do you expect me to do? You know what happens when women get alone with me." "Yeah you let em dog you" chirped Ant. "Right! . . . now that we've established that fact lets get busy on my other problem." "And what's that?" said Jr. Matt pointed to Cher who was doing splits and other gymnastics maneuvers with some other girls. "Yeah I can see how she'd be a problem" scoffed Milton. "If she ever got you in bed you would be fucked Man!" "Yeah, I know one of us would be, but that's besides the point, they have something planned for me and I need to know what it is." "So you want us to keep our eyes and ears open right?" "Yeah, that's the idea but we'll have to go one better, we'll have to get with all the girls we know and have them pump her for information . . . you know make her tell on herself so I'll know how to prepare for her and Mel." "What happens if you lose and they get you off guard?" asked Milton "Then I'm fucked . . . literally!"

Chapter 9

A Time of Change

"That's not so bad dude, I can think of worse fates." "Don't fuck it up meatball!" snapped Ant. "This is important!" "Okay, okay I was just talking, tell you what, I got a few girls over at Northeast High that I can put on Melanie and see what she has to say being she's the mastermind of all this." "Okay, now you're talking" said Matt clapping his hands. "So let's get on it and remember don't let them know were onto their plans." "So Matt have you found out anymore about Aretta?"

"Nope, not yet." "I'll bet you'll be glad when she gets out of the hospital." "You know it!" "Are you going to see her when we get out of practice?" "Oh yeah!, Got to, that's my baby." "I'll be back, I gotta go to the head" said Milton bouncing down the bleachers.

Melanie was sitting in the library talking to her friend Monica. The two girls were working on her plan to trap Matt. "Melanie, I don't know what else to tell you, I think he's got you guys over a barrel and your gonna wind up his "Do Girls" for a day." "OH, no I'm not! I'm not, I'm gonna get him good!" "Well we've gone through just about every plot and possibility we could find and they are all either too dangerous or he wouldn't fall for it."

Melanie thought for a minute trying to mix up some of the ideas and come up with something that would work. "Hey Monica your brother is still and EMT right?" "Yeah so what?" "Can he get his hands on some tranquilizers or say maybe some Muscle Relaxers?" "I don't know . . . maybe, what are you gonna do with those?" "I'm cooking up a scheme but I need one or the other of those pills to do it, can you get them for me?" "I don't know, let me see what he says about it."

"Just tell him that you've been having trouble sleeping lately, he'll understand." "Okay, I'll ask him but I can't promise anything okay?" "Great!" "So what's your plan?" "Well what I'm gonna do is wait until my folks go out of town this weekend then I'll throw a party." "How's that gonna get him?"

"Listen silly I'll invite some friends over, all girls and he can bring some of his friends." "Are they cute?" "Absolutely gorgeous, just look at this picture of Matt and his buddies, Milton and Anthony" she said digging in her purse and producing a 3x5 picture. "OOH! They are fine, which one is Matt?"

"This one" she said pointing. "Damn! He is good looking." "Told you so" "Now I see why you want him so bad, invite me, I want to meet Milton." "Okay" "Now Melanie just what are you gonna do at the party?" "We'll get them nice and relaxed and have a few drinks to take down their guard then I'll just pop one of these pills into his drink and knock his pretty ass out." "Ooh! Melanie, your going to drug him?"

"No, just incapacitate him for awhile." "That's the same thing professor." "Not really, I'm not going use all of them, I just need one and once he's out then we can claim victory." "What then, I mean what's the prize?" "He is!" "Melanie do you mean to say you guys are going to rape him?" "Yep, me and Cheryl!" "Ooh Mel" she said giggling and covering her mouth. "That's wicked and deceitful."

"Yeah but all's fair in love and war, and besides take a good look at this picture and try an imagine the size of his pecker, then tell me if you wouldn't do him yourself if given the chance." Monica took the picture and looked at it from head to toe then and let her mind wander. A delicious smile crossed her face and she shook her hair wildly for a second like she had a bug in it, then put the picture down and blushed crimson red. Mel just grinned. "I see you get the point." "Do I?"

"But guess what?" "What" "I've seen it and it's larger than that!" "Oh my, goodness, he let you see it?" "No, I saw it when I went over to his house last week, he was in the bedroom drying off after a shower, I saw him through the window." "Melanie that was rude and sneaky." "Yeah I know, it was also an accident . . . a very educational one at that, that's why me and my cousin Cheryl are gonna take him together, I couldn't possibly take him alone he'd probably kill me with that monster."

"I'll bet" "So you'll help me then?" "Sure as long as I can have Milton all to myself." "Sure, you can have him all you want, I want Matt." Soon school was out and Matt and Ant were on their way to track practice. It was a nice day and Matt felt like running. The coach hadn't gotten there yet because he was busy doing some paper work in his office. The guys decided to take the opportunity to get some stretching in and loosen up. Most of the guys were there already when they got there.

"Hey Matt wait up!" said Cher running to catch up. "Aw man! What does she want?" he said frowning. "I don't know, why don't you wait and find out." Finally she caught up and was breathing hard and out of breath. "What's up Cher?" Matt asked not trying to sound too welcoming. "Nothing I just wanted to work out with you guys till coach Miller comes." Coach Miller was the girls team coordinator. "Well me and Ant usually stretch out together." "That's okay, we can do a threesome" she said hopefully. "Oh boy! Now ya talking" said Ant walking up to her and adjusting his shorts.

"Hold on Rover, not that kind of threesome." "Well you didn't say which" he went on, still pulling her up close to him till he could feel her breasts against him. Matt was just shaking his head. "Anthony stop!" she said pushing him away. "You know better, besides you couldn't handle the pressure anyway." "Oh shit!" said Matt covering his mouth laughing. "She bust on you then old boy . . . !"

"Come on Cher before you make him sweat." Cher gave Ant a seductive smile and trotted down the stairs after Matt. "I hope you had the good graces to put back on your underwear" he said not looking back. "Now Matt what ever made you think I wasn't wearing any?" "Come on, Cher remember that stunt you pulled awhile ago in the gym?" "What stunt?" "Alright play dumb, but you forget I've seen it up close remember?" "Yes you did, didn't you, but not as close as you could have lover." "You can cancel that, hot stuff, it won't happen."

"Okay Matt if you say so, but be warned I know something you don't know." "Yeah right guy just keep on dreaming and while you're at it don't fall asleep with any stray vegetables in your bed, you never no where they may end up!" he said with emphasis. "Ooh! Matt you are kinky aren't you? Just you wait, I'm going to make you eat those words and a few other tasty tid bits" she said slowly running her hand down the inside of her thigh, and coming dangerously close to her crotch.

"Come on Cher! Let's get busy before you confuse yourself even more." Ant had joined them by now and was trying to avert his eyes from her as they began to stretch. Matt was doing toe touches while Cher was doing horizontal splits on the grass. "Damn! Cher" said Ant awed by her flexibility.

"Don't that hurt?" "Naw I do it all the time, look at this move" she redistributed her center of gravity and turned a normal split into a horizontal yoga move with her legs straight out on both sides and toes pointing up.

She inadvertently exposed all of her charms in the process. Matt couldn't help but notice the plump furry mound that bulged there. Ant immediately caught a hard on. "Why Anthony I didn't know you cared" she said teasing him and laughing at his unplanned genital salute at the sight of her womanhood. "Cheryl I thought you said you were fully dressed!" hissed Matt getting a little pissed at the sexual antics. He turned his own head so he wouldn't join Ant in his embarrassment.

"Matt I'm sorry, but a girl has to have some mystery about herself doesn't she?" "Bullshit that's no mystery" said Matt still looking away. "That's a full page cover story!" "Yeah Cher, are you really that hard up?" asked Ant. "No I just love to express myself and get my point across when the mood strikes me sugar!" "You play a mean game girl" said Ant putting on his warm up pants to hide his embarrassment. "One of these days you gonna get what your asking for Cher." "Oh really? I hope so" she said looking at Matt and licking her lips. "Come on Matt let's go run a few laps and cool off, this girl is dangerous."

"You didn't know" said Matt getting up and dusting himself off. "Bye Matt . . . see ya later." "Not if I see you first!" he tossed over his shoulder and trotted off. The two of them ran at a decent pace to get their blood flowing and to generate a breeze. "Didn't I tell you she was buck wild?" said Matt. "Yeah man she's got it bad and I tell ya, if we was someplace else I would have got that homeboy!"

"Well more power to you, but in the meantime we need to find out what they're cooking up, otherwise I may be up to my neck in the stuff!" "Well that's not so bad . . . !" "Boy what I done told you!" "Okay, okay! I was just thinking." "Yeah with your dick!" "Hey that's not true, I don't think with my dick . . . my dick thinks for me!" he declared proudly. They both started laughing and ran on.

Just then a whistle blew. "Time to take it in, coach is calling us" said Matt slowing down to cross the field. "Let's cut across the field." "Naw we're already half way around let's run it out." "Okay on two . . . READY, SET, GO! Their speed quickly picked up to a sprint. When they took off they were even but Matt quickly widened the gap. As soon as they broke into a sprint Coach Jones hit his stop watch.

He never failed to take the opportunity to test his boys or get some honest raw data on them whether they were clowning or not. That's how he always knew what players in a given sport were best at. Matt and Ant were nearing the far turn at the bottom of the field and Matt was leading by five yards. "Come on Ant!" he puffed. "Your making this look too easy!" "Oh yeah? Five bucks says I smoke your ass!" "Alright lead foot, your on!" Matt put on a scorching burst of speed in the turn.

His arms and legs were pumping like a jack hammer, and his feet were barely touching the ground. Ant was thinking "Damn what the hell did I do that for." The other team mates from both the girls and boys team cleared the track to watch the race!. They were jumping up and down screaming, "Go Matt . . . Go Anthony!" Coach Jones was practically drooling! as Matt turned the last curve. His stop watch was showing 8.65 seconds. "You little stallion, I knew you had some of your brother in you!" he grumbled under his breath.

Matt was really pouring it on now and was chopping down the track like a cheetah! His lungs were on fire and his heart was beating like a mad drum. All he could see was the white string in the distance that two people were holding across the track. Ant was doing his damndest to catch up but it just wasn't enough. Matt had left him on the far turn struggling to catch up. Matt gave his last burst of speed and blasted across the line with his head down and forward like a hood ornament.

Everyone was yelling *"Mathis!, Mathis!, Mathis! . . . whoop whoop!"* Matt felt great. His body was burning all over inside and out but he felt great. Ant soon crossed the line and crumpled in a tired heap on the ground near Matt. Matt looked at him and made a motion, rubbing his thumb against his fingers like he was feeling powder. "Yeah yeah I know, you'll get it super chicken" he chided then fell onto his back in a crumpled pile of tired bones. Matt didn't sit down just yet but decided to walk it off like his brother used to do after a run. He put his hands over his head and walked around.

Cheryl and a few others ran up to mob him grabbing his arms and hugging him. "Way to go Matt" "Didn't know you had it in you boy" "Hope you got some of that for later" "Thanks you guys it was just a light race, we was just fooling around" "Mathis! Called coach Jones waving him to come over. "Yeah coach?" "I thought you said you had no speed son?" "I don't really. We was just messing around." Coach Jones flashed him his patented grin of the skull look, and showing all thirty two of his perfect hand made false teeth. "Well from my stop watch and a little number crunching you ran a 220 meter race in just under a minute, ten seconds" "Is that good?"

"Damn son that's not just good, it's good enough for state time!" "Oh shit! Did you guys hear that?" said Alex the team's 100 yard dash man. "Mathis if you keep this up you may be disqualified from "B-team" track" "Why?" "Cause the other team's coaches would swear you was a damn ringer" "A ringer coach?, what's that" "Somebody of exceptional skill operating in an area way below their level. People do this to ensure wins" "So what do I do then? I can't run slower or throw shorter just to make the other team happy can I?" "Hell no son" he said grinning and working his tongue around his teeth like a cat flicking it's tail. "So what do we do then?" "We put you on the varsity team just like we did your other brothers" "Varsity!" Matt started to envision his little self in the midst of all those much bigger and powerful jocks.

He couldn't imagine going up against any of the guys on their team much less some of the monsters the other schools had waiting for him. His other team mates were listening in and were very impressed that Matt was going to get an upgrade to the senior team without having graduated to the 11th grade first.

"Yeah you didn't know that Matt is the little brother of Tony and Perry?" "No!" "Yeah man I remember seeing them together a couple of times at some of the foot ball games and pep rallies." "Damn! man that's three in a row, now ain't it?" Matt's team mates mumbled and stared as they stood around listening to coach tell Matt about how the transition would take place and what he could expect.

Tony, Matt's brother next to him in age was one of the school's best left-handed quarter back/first baseman/pitcher combination they had ever seen.

He was in the 11th grade just ahead of Matt and now living with their mother in South Carolina. Everyone hated it when he had to leave after school let out for the summer last year. His oldest brother Buford Jr. or Perry as everyone called him, was one of the best wide receiver/track men they ever had as well. He graduated a year before that and joined the Navy.

"Coach, I'm not sure I'm ready for a jump like this, I mean maybe it was a one time thing . . . you know a fluke like that toss I made the first day!" "Mathis, in all my years of coaching I've seen a lot of strange things, but I have yet to see a fluke that operates in three's the way you and your brothers seem to" he said wiping his sweating neck and trying to show some patience with his new prodigy. "But I'll tell you what, since you don't have any faith in what I'm saying we'll go ahead and have you practice with the varsity team, and at the end of the day we'll see if you still think you can handle the pressure or not or believe you belong there or not okay?" "Okay coach." "If after that you don't believe me then we'll keep you on the "B-team.""

"Cool" said Matt feeling the weight of the world lift off his shoulders. Cheryl also breathed a sigh of deep relief at this short reprieve. If Matt goes to the varsity team she can forget seeing him outside of gym class anymore.

"Hey coach, how was my time? . . . did you clock me too?" asked Ant curious, but not feeling to confident that he was good enough to make the cut to varsity level. "Williams . . ." he paused looking at his notes and times on the clip board. "You did good also, not as fast as Mathis here but still better than your team mates, you might squeak on by and earn a spot on the varsity as a good alternate."

"Sweet!" said Ant pumping his fists. "Just keep training with Mathis here and you'll be one hell of a runner by years end." "Thanks coach!" "Okay people, let's form it up on the field! . . . Mathis, you and Williams are already warmed up so take a short rest and begin stretching out in the infield okay?" "Yes sir!"

"And Cheryl!" "Yes coach!" she said jumping as he barked her name. "Leave my guys alone and behave yourself, you might break something on one of them" he said smiling and walking down the steps not looking at her. Cheryl sucked in her breath sharply, clearly caught off guard by the coaches observation.

She hadn't thought she was being that obvious in her flirting or schmoozing with Matt and Ant. "WELL I NEVER!" she protested jutting out her chin proudly and putting her hands on her hips. Coach Jones just walked on down the bleachers smiling to himself. "Yep and as long as I'm around you never will" he said looking back at Ant and Matt on the bleachers not far from her. Soon the boys break was over and they rejoined the team on the top end of the field.

The girls had the bottom half. Coach Williams had them doing calisthenics and stamina drills, then broke them off to work on their events. Since Ant was a hurdler he had to go to the bottom of the field at the starting area for the hundred yard dash. Each of the hurdles were waist high and looked more like a road block than sports equipment. As he got there he lay out a set number of steps between each hurdle like he'd been taught and tried to develop his stride.

Cheryl was standing by watching him as she was the girls team hurdler and long jumper. Matt was up field busy with the discus. "Okay Mathis, give it a toss!" said coach Jones. "But this time try not to hit the goal post!" Matt smiled to himself as he'd remembered that throw and the awful twang sound it made when it ricocheted off it. He concentrated and began his wind up slowly, cranking it to and frow. After his forth swing he gave a powerful spin and let loose. "Ughn!" The disc flew a little wobbly but went a good distance. *"Thump!"* it landed just shy of a hundred feet. "Come on Mathis, what's with this 98 feet crap, give me some of that horse power I saw the other day son!"

"Okay coach" he said, then shook it off and picked up another disk. "Hey Matt hold up dude" said Eric Jackson. Trotting up to him off the track. Eric was about average height around 5'8 and had huge thighs and a powerful upper body. Matt was sure he had armor plating in it. His arms never seemed to touch his sides and the girls could never get enough of holding onto them in the halls. Eric was black and was also on the varsity football team as a full back. "Hey dude, I been checking you out and I think you got some skills but you need to work on your technique if you want to do your best."

"Thanks Eric, what do I need to work on?" "Mostly your windup and rotation, you got power enough already" he said patting Matt on the arm to emphasis his point. Matt just blushed a little at the compliment from such a well built athlete. "I might be able to help you get a better release if you let me help you." "Yeah! Sure, anything you can give me will help" he said happily stepping back a little.

Coach Jones just shifted on his hip patiently watching his full back give some much needed advice. "First of all your stance has got to be solid and flexible, spread your legs apart, a little more than shoulder width like this" he said taking the position. "Now when you begin your rotation or crank it, roll from the ball of your left foot onto your right keeping it flat, as you swing it behind your back." "Be sure to bend low on the back swing and reach high and forward on the forward like this" he said taking the disk from Matt and showing him. Eric looked like the tan version of the Greek god Zeus, as he rotated through the motions he was telling Matt about. He was smooth and clean and looked like he could put it into the parking lot if he wanted to. "Then once you begin your spin, stay low and do a full turn making sure to skip from your right to your left foot before letting it fly, it's really like a sling shot when you get familiar with it." "Would you like me to show you one time?"

"Yeah!" said Matt backing up out of the way for him. Eric looked up at the coach down field. "Hey coach, I'm gonna show him the proper technique to use, it may help him!" "Okay Eric, send it on down son!" he said folding his massive arms across his even bigger chest. Eric got into the circle and set his stance.

He was focused and his face devoid of all expression. Matt looked at him and wished he had arms and legs like that. When Eric started his rotation it was just like he had told Matt only smoother and much tighter. He swung around and gave a mighty spin with a snap moving from his left foot to his right. He grunted loudly as he let the thing fly off into the air.

Oh what a throw! "Daaammn!" commented Matt as he watched the disc fly off like a clay pigeon on a skeet shooting range. It was clean, it was straight and it flew like a shot! The disc flew about twenty feet high at its highest point and flew straight on for what seemed like to Matt forever! The disc began to waver and wobble slightly as it began it's downward decent. It landed with a thud and at a distance of 120 feet! "That was dope! Eric" rooted Matt giving him a high five. "Thanks, but do you see how I rotated and made my hop?" "Yep, it was so tight I almost missed it." "Good, now you try it."

Matt took the next disc as it came back from down field by a runner. "Hey Mathis! See if you can hit coach Williams car with it" joked Coach Jones. Coach Williams snapped her head up from her clipboard and looked at him with the most evil of looks as if to say, "He hits my car you tub of guts and I'm gonna hit you!" She flipped him off with a birdie and went back to her girls. "Okay coach" said Matt winding up like a pitcher to loosen up his arms and shoulders. He didn't expect to get that far down field but unconsciously looked at coach Williams car which sat just before the track.

She always parked it there so it was easier to tow the mats and heavy padding back to the storage building on the lower field. Matt set up like Eric had told him then began his windup. He could feel the difference of the change as he went into his spinning launch. "Ugh!" the small 8 pound UFO took off like a shot! It was spinning perfectly like a skeet disc. "Son . . . of . . . a . . . *BIIIITTCHHH!*" said coach Williams as she watched in horror as the discus went flying straight for her little blue Toyota. It had height, it had speed, and unbelievably it had distance!

The thing moved like it was laser guided. *"Bish!"* right into the driver side window! The little car didn't have a chance as the disc bounced around in the front seat then finally coming to a dead stop on the dashboard. The window just disintegrated and fell apart like rice being thrown at a wedding. "Touch down!" yelled Ant. "Oh hell!" added Eric turning and trying not to be seen laughing but not finding it easy.

Matt was awe struck and in shock. He stood looking from the car to Eric mouth open like a caught fish. He looked at Eric as if he was saying, "What the hell did you just teach me!" "Good job Matt" he said then smacked him on the arm and beat a hasty retreat to the locker room. "See ya in the Olympics Matt!" he shouted over his shoulder as he went. By then coach Williams was over half way to him and mad as a wet hen!

"Mathiiiss! You're a dead man!" she shouted in the distance huffing and puffing from the effort. She finally stormed right up to him as he was still in

the pit stuck by fear. *"WHAT THE HECK DO YOU MEAN BY KNOCKING OUT MY WINDOW MR. MATHIS! HAVE YOU LOST YOUR MIND?"* she bellowed at him almost nose to nose.

Coach Williams was a healthy rather buxom white woman in her mid thirties about five foot six and a nice body. She also had a pair of modest double "D's" on her chest that could shield a small child from the rain if he got under them.

Most of the guys loved to watch her play volley ball because when she moved . . . she really moved! Matt however wasn't thinking much about her physical attributes even though she was pressing two of them into his chest with great zeal. Any other time Matt would have had a warm fuzzy going and thinking about cookies cause she certainly *GOT MILK!*

"No ma'am" he responded bashfully and trying to ease away from those two burning melons she kept planting into his chest. "I was just doing it the way Eric taught me to." "Is that right?" she said breathing a little less labored now. A thing Matt was very glad of because when she breathed her chest heaved.

"Then tell me this young man . . . how come you had to aim that thing at my car?" "It isn't even in range of where your supposed to be throwing, in fact it's almost on the track!" Matt just stood there grimacing and taking his verbal beat down. Suddenly as if a light had come on in her head, Coach Williams stopped chastising him and paused as if she was hearing something no one else was.

What had happened was she had an epiphany. She thought about where they were in relation to where her car was. She slowly backed off of Matt and turned to look at her car again. "Well I'll be dammed! you slung that rascal over a hundred and sixty yards!" "One hundred and sixty eight yards" said coach Jones walking up. "He threw it one hundred and sixty eight and a quarter feet to be exact, but who's counting?" He said grinning.

"What was that again you were saying about a fluke Mathis?" he said folding his massive arms. "You're off the team . . . You and Anthony report to coach Carr Monday, you're on the Varsity Team." "Don't be late!" "Yesss sir!" "Now both of you grab a disc and head on down to the lower field and work on your throws for an hour, then do a half hour's work on the long jump pit and another hour of track work on the hurdles."

"Okay coach" said Matt picking up a disc and spare tape measure. "Come on Ant, let's break!" Coach Jones stared after them as they went. "You know Williams, it's a shame I couldn't keep him on the Junior Team, we could have really done some damage this year to the other teams!" "Yeah, but don't let it bother you too much, you still got some pretty good guys and girls left and they aren't too shabby."

"Now since you've found your ace in the hole what about my car?" "Oh, don't worry about that Brenda, I got a brother who manages at the Auto Glass

Works, I'll give him a call after practice and you should be good by tomorrow or sooner." "Okay then, I'll see you after practice, I need to work on my own Ace in the hole!" she said walking away. "Who's that?" "Cheryl!" "Hey, keep an eye on her, she's really sweet on a couple of my boys and I don't want them distracted!" "What can I say Fred, she's aggressive and when she see's something she want's, she takes it, but I'll have a word with her anyway for the good it'll do."

Matt took the long tape and spread it out to it's full length of three hundred feet. "Hey Matt, why so much tape man?" "It gives me something to shoot for." "Hell, you pipe dreaming now, you'd need a canon to put it out there." "Well we're not trying to, it's just something to keep us from getting complacent and under shooting our best."

"Good idea, I didn't think of that." Slowly the sun began to fade and practice came to an end. Everyone picked up all the gear and equipment and assembled on the bleachers. "Okay people settle down, we have exactly one week from tomorrow before track seasons starts and our first meet is against Southwest High on their field." "So with the time we have were gonna be practicing quite a bit, I'll try to give you guys at least two days without practice before our first meet because I don't want you to burn yourselves out, but you must do some training on your own on the weekend, at least one hour a day!"

A girl raised her hand. "Yes Marci?" "If we need a piece of equipment to work with how do we get it on the weekend?" "If you need a shot put or discus, see me on Friday after school and I'll check it out to you, if you need to use the hurdles you'll have to come here and use them." "Hey coach what about uniforms . . . when do we get those?" asked Paula. "Didn't coach Williams tell you?" "No, tell us what?"

"You don't get any this year, you'll all be running in your underwear!" he said grinning an laughing at the looks of horror and disbelief. "Nuh uh" said Paula knitting her brows together and looking around for confirmation. "No girls, he's just pulling your leg, you'll all be given uniforms next week after practice, but only if you earn your spot by then." "Yes, people that's correct, we have 15 boys and 16 girls, we only need 12 of each to make a team and 3 alternates, that's 27 players in all, so with the exception of Mathis and Williams here, if you want a spot you'd better bust your asses and do your best come next week!" "You got anything else for these guys, Coach Williams?"

"No I'm done." "Okay, hit the showers and go on home and relax tonight, you want to be fresh in the morning when you do your individual training." "Also! don't forget you school work because if you slip in that you lose your spot anyway . . . get me!" added coach Williams. "Yes ma'am!"

"Now hit the showers and get outta hear!" "Mathis!" "Yeah coach?" "You still got that tape measure and discus?" "Yes sir."

"Hold on to them, I wan't you to develop a relationship with that thing, sleep with it if you have to." Matt looked at the funny little device like it was a woman, he held it, stoked it, rubbed it against his face like he was in a soap opera with it, then he kissed it flagrantly like a wild man. Ant fell apart on the bleachers. "Boy you stupid!" "See what your girls are doing to my guys Williams?"

"Don't blame my girls, you need to get this one a couch or a paid professional if that don't work" she said laughing at Matt's crazed antics. "Mathis behave yourself!" Matt came out of his somewhat twisted romantic Trist with his discus blushing from the experience. "How are you and Williams coming with the jumps?"

"Fine coach, I think." "How far did you get?" "On the long jump and triple jump, Ant did a 21.5 and a 32.6." "That's good Williams, keep it up, how about you Mathis?" "I did a 22.5 on the long jump and a 36 even on the triple jump." "You boy's are really making some head way and real early in the game, good job, keep it up because I want you two good and ready for our first meet against Southwest." "I'm counting on you two to help run them little fart busters in the ground!" "We gotcha coach, we'll be ready!" "That's what I wanna hear, now go on and hit them showers, you boys did real good today!"

"Thanks coach" they said then ran up the bleachers and into the locker room. "Man we both made the Varsity Team!" said Ant. "We'll be so shit hot they can't touch us!" "You know it!" said Matt giving Ant a high five. "Can you imagine the looks were gonna get from everybody when they see two tenth graders running with the big dogs?" "Man that's gonna be the bomb, and I can't wait!"

As they walked into the locker room the other guys were slapping their backs and shaking their hands congratulating them on making the jump to Varsity. It was quite an honor and very few could meet the challenge to get there, they were the exception. Soon they had showered, dressed and was about to leave. "Hey Matt, there are some chicks outside waiting for you and Ant" yelled Washington from the door.

"Oh yeah? Who are they?" "One of them is Cheryl, I don't know who the other one is." "Okay thanks man, let's go see what's up" said Ant. They walked out and saw Cheryl and Melanie leaning against her truck. "Hi guys" said Mel. "Hi yourself" said Matt. "What are you doing over here so far from home?" "Oh, just hanging out and come to get Cheryl." "Well you got her" he said nodding and walking like he was going to head on their way. "You guys wanna hang out awhile?" Mel asked quickly.

"I don't know, I'm kinda tired from practice" said Matt yawning. "Well we could go over to your place." "Naw, I don't think that would be a good idea." "What's the matter Matt, afraid you won't behave yourself?" said Cher being facetious. Matt just looked at Ant shaking his head. "She just keeps on digging don't she?" "You didn't know?" Matt just stood there looking at the two of them kind of like they were oddities that required more study. He reached into his gym back and pulled out a large cold bottle of Gatorade.

He popped the top and took a long swig then passed it to Ant. It was hot that day and the drink was cool and refreshing. "May I have some Matt?" asked Mel reaching for it. Almost on cue Ant took the bottle from his lips, "No! get your own damn drink" chimed he and Matt together. Cher just smiled and shook her head. "You haven't learned these two yet have you Mel?" "No I guess not" she said sullenly withdrawing her scorched hand and pride. "But I seem to be catching on though!" "Stick around long enough and you may!" Ant then passed the bottle to Cher. She turned it up then passed it to Mel. "So you guys wanna ride or what?" "Yeah, come on Ant, lets cruise." "What about your bike?" "We can go get it" said Mel. "Then lets break, it's over behind the girls school."

Matt jumped in back and Cher joined him. "Hey Mel, turn on some music" he said. Ant got in but didn't speak. He just closed his door and stared out the window blankly. The truck started with a roar. "Hey Mel, what do you have under the hood of this thing?" "A 450 with a four barrel carb and a hemi blower!" "Damn girl! . . . planning on drag racing anytime soon?" "Every chance I get." "How's it run?" "Hang on and you'll see" she said popping the skull and crossbones Hearst shifter into first gear. Mel revved the engine, popped the clutch and floored it!. "*SCURRRCH!*" the truck squealed away from the curb like a scalded cat.

Matt and Cheryl were immediately launched forward to the tail gate. "Hey slow down Mel, we get the point!" yelled Cheryl. She had landed on top of Matt and he reflexively held her to him about the waist. She looked at the compromised position that they had been violently thrown into and thought that maybe this truck wasn't such a bad idea. Matt just looked up at her almost no emotion except for the fact that she was between his legs this time and he was feeling more of her just now then he was comfortable with.

"She always does this when we ride . . . sorry" said Cher slowly easing herself from him but not too quickly. She got up and helped Matt up and into the two bucket seats up against the cab. "Well she needs to chill out a little, this ain't Hazard County and my name ain't Duke!" Cher laughed at the light joke and eased back into her seat. "Matt how does it feel to be a track star?" "I'm not a track star yet, I still have to prove myself on the field with real competition if you know what I mean." "Yeah, but I wouldn't worry about it too much, I think your gonna do just great!"

"Thanks Cher . . . you know . . . sometimes you can be really nice" he said turning to face her. "And just for the record, I do like you Cher just as I've always said I do but I can't be what you want me to be." Cher looked away and began chewing on her lower lip. "You know Matt, you can be anything you want to be, don't let some girl fuck up your life okay?" she said sounding very morose and withdrawn.

She turned to face him. Matt couldn't ever remember a time when he had seen her so sincere and trite. Her beautiful sea green eyes glistened with a light mist of fresh tears forming. He was a little surprised at her sudden change of character. As far as he knew her only motivation seemed to be seducing him. This didn't make any sense. He allowed himself a dangerous liaison and reached for her. He slowly cradled her face in his hands and held her there. Their eyes were locked and neither moved, at least not physically. Cher's heart and mind were racing and screaming so loud at his honest touch that she felt she may explode if he didn't either kiss her or release her.

Matt was aware of the affect he was having on her as it was the same for him but he wasn't going to give in . . . not yet anyway. He brought two fingers to his lips and kissed them, he then pressed them to Cher's waiting and grateful lips. She melted. She absorbed Matt's hands into being through her lips and relished every bit of the mild gesture. She didn't want to, but she let herself swoon and tried to pull Matt to her, pressing his hand against her face, her neck and down onto her full and hungry breasts.

Matt made his had go rigid and Cher knew that the ride was over. She recovered herself slowly and sat back in her chair, hair still covering her face. "Cheryl, why the change of heart all of a sudden?" he asked her, hoping she could respond and recover from where they had both been only moments ago. She pulled a lock of hair from her face around her ear and cleared her throat. "Well in light of what you might think of me Matt, I do truly love you and care about what happens to you, I know that I come on strong at times but that's just my way, I am tough and determined but also sweet and gentle."

"Kind of like a bulldozer in a bakery huh?" "Yeah, something like that" she said smiling at his metaphorical whit. "So don't judge me too harshly okay, Matt?" "I'm really a good person, I just work people over too roughly when they interest me." Matt pulled her closer and held her hand. "You are a good girl Cher, don't let anybody tell you different, you'll find the right guy one day so don't rush it okay?" "I wouldn't want to see you hurt." "So you do care about me don't you Matt?" "Didn't I tell you so?" "Yeah" "Okay then." She eased even closer and lightly kissed his cheek. "Thanks Matt" she said resting her head on his shoulder.

"Alright now, don't go getting mushy on me" he said lightly tossing his shoulder and smiling at her. "Oh I'm not, don't forget were still at war!" "Yeah, I almost forgot about that." "I told you I was determined!" "So you did" said Matt looking into her eyes and nodding. Up front in the cab Mel was looking at the rear view mirror and fuming at the face with the time Cheryl was getting with Matt. When she saw him cradle Cher's face and look at her that way she almost ran off the road. Apart from watching them, her and Ant were having their own drama of sorts. Ant hadn't spoken to her since they got into the truck and was just drumming his fingers on the door to the radio.

He was still angry about the other night at his house and had resigned himself to being ambivalent to her. "Anthony" she called but he wasn't hearing her. "*Anthony please talk to me, I really can't bear you not talking to me!*" she said in a shrill choked voice. "Why would you want me to do that? I'm no one special" he said wistfully. "I thought your main thang was Matt!" "That's not fair Anthony, I told you how I feel about him and that it's difficult for me right now." "Why should it be?"

"You don't owe him anything and he doesn't even want you, so when are you gonna get that through your thick skull Mel?" His words stung her like bees, she could fully see how things were looking and hated herself for being so driven. Right now it didn't matter, she was young and had desires that needed to be satisfied, fantasies that had to live and a deafening hunger from within that she swore would be quenched. How could she explain to him what it felt like to be a woman! It wasn't possible. Maybe what he was saying made sense, but just now she didn't want to hear it.

"Anthony I'm sorry, I never meant to hurt you, I really do like you, but there are things I need to do before I can be free of this." "Well Mel, you do what you gotta do, I'm not gonna get in your way, I'm also not gonna wait around until you make up your mind about what you want either, I've got feelings too and I can't let you or anyone else stomp on them." Melanie didn't know what to say, so she just let out a long sigh and tried to change the subject. "Anthony I'm having a party next Friday, I would really like it if you would come."

"You mean Matt don't you?" "No! I mean you!" she blasted at him, now mad that he would insinuate that she was a liar. "I came over hear to ask both of you and to bring some friends, it's going to be a bunch of us girls at my house so don't bring any dates." "Isn't that kind of strange?" "No, this is a Sadie Hawkins party." "A Sadie who? Party" "Sadie Hawkins." "What the hell is that?" "It's a party where the girls ask the guys out." "Oh I get it, so how many should I bring?"

"Bring about eight, plus you and Matt." "Do it matter what color they are?" Mel flashed him a look of shock and pure fire. She slammed on the brakes just inside the driveway to the girls school. She squealed the tires and pressed Cher and Matt against the cab so tight they bumped their heads. "Hey wild child!" shouted Cher rubbing her head. Mel wasn't seeing or hearing anyone except the sound in her heart and mind telling her, *"Show him!"* she dived on top of Ant like a wrestler.

He didn't know if he was going to be attacked or what! Mel pulled him back to her by the collar of his shirt and down into the seat facing her door. "Hey what the fu . . . " he protested. She was laying half on him and half in the seat. Ant marveled at Mel's strength and how easily she was able to move him around in the truck. Mel grabbed his face in her hands and covered him in a hot passionate kiss! *"Oh shit!"* thought Ant as Mel's tongue probed and searched his mouth, enslaving and controlling his to do whatever she wanted. Matt and Cher looked in the window to see the wrestling match of sorts.

Cher just shook her head and thought to herself, *"I guess the party starts a little earlier than planned."* "What is your cousin up to Cher?" "Whatever she want's to be." Just as quickly as she had begun she broke from him, returning to her side of the cab. "Is that answer enough for you Anthony?" she tossed at him somewhat sarcastically, and looking at him with a well kindled sexual fire in her eyes. Ant just lay there and stared at the ceiling for a bit. "Yeah, I guess it does." "Good! Don't you ever let me hear you question my integrity ever again Mr. or next time I'll pop you in the head so hard you'll have to use your teeth to unzip you pants!" "Alright" he said sliding back into his seat and readjusting his clothes. Matt and Cher turned back to their seats facing rearward.

"Your cousins a real fire cracker when she wants to be isn't she?" "You didn't know?" "No, not really but I got a hint of it sometime ago." "Then you'd better watch yourself well or you'll be in a spot much worse than when we was on the bus." Matt gave that incident some thought then shook his head not giving the matter any weight. Soon they had gotten to the rear of the school and they could see Matt's moped sitting in the bike rack locked up. Mel pulled up next to it and Matt jumped out.

"Hey do you need a hand loading it?" asked Ant. "Naw I got it" he said unlocking it and rolling it to the rear of the truck. He then grabbed it between the rear wheel and the motor. "Ugh!" he hoisted the bike in one heave onto the tailgate of the truck. "Darn! Matt, you have a little muscle don't you?" said Cher getting closer to look at his arms as he moved the heavy bike. "Maybe, but it's not that heavy if you grab it right." "How much does it weigh?" "I don't know, I never looked to see."

Cher spied a silver metal tag near the motor with some engraving on it. "It says gross WT and tare WT, what does that mean?" "Those are the weights of the bike with and without a rider." "So it weighs 250 pounds empty and 475 with a rider and fuel?" "Sounds about right, you're the one looking at the label" he said tossing his eyebrows as he looked at her. "Smart ass!" Matt jumped back in the truck and closed the tailgate. "Which way Matt?" asked Mel "Go out the way you came in, then go left up the hill, and watch your speed, this thing ain't strapped in okay?" "Okay" she said grinning.

Matt sat on the wheel hub and held onto the bike so it wouldn't' move around. "Why don't you just lay it down Matt?" asked Cher holding the other side. "Have you ever had one of these?" "No" "I didn't think so, can you imagine how hard it is to start one of these after you flood the engine?" "No, not really." "It's a real pain and it messes up the starter" he said pointing at the little foot pedal.

"I see, how come you picked yellow instead of some other color?" "It wasn't my choice, this was a surprise gift from my dad when he went on a business trip to Florida some years ago." "That was nice of him." "It came with a shield, but I took it off because it gave me so much trouble and wind drag." "Would you like to go for a ride on it sometime?" "Yes I would!" she said lighting up. "But it doesn't look like it will hold us both." "Oh yes it will, don't let ole buster's size fool you." "Buster?" "Yeah, I call him Buster." "Why, it's a yellow moped, wouldn't it be more natural to give it a girls name?" "Maybe, but if you could see what It does you'd know why."

Cher just grinned and shrugged her shoulders not wanting to press more and potentially insult Matt about his scooter. Boy's tended to get upset when you diss their bikes. "You see this engine?" "Yes." "Well it's been modified a little, it's no longer a 50CC engine like it came, it's more like a 150CC engine now." "How'd you get that much into it?" "Oh, I have a buddy who races bikes and owns his own cycle shop on Napier Avenue." "He bored it out a little and gave it a bigger carburetor for guts." "How does it sound?" she asked thinking it would be similar to Mel's truck with it's modifications.

"It sounds about the same." "Shouldn't it be louder like this truck?" "No, not really, it's the exhaust that has more to do with it than the engine." "Oh I see, I guess I will have to take you up on that ride sometime" she said nodding and looking at the little bike with more appreciation. "Hey Matt which way?" asked Mel out the window. "Ant tell her the way to go!" "Just turn right, then right again, and you should know where you are." "Okay."

The Maternity ward was quiet when Aretta and Sadie got there. Most of the babies were asleep. The only ones that were awake weren't interested in making any noise. They just liked their tiny tongues in and out and yawned a lot.

"They are so tiny" thought Retta as she went in to see them. "Okay honey you must be very quiet and try not to wake them" said Sadie. "This is the only time the other nurses can get a minute to catch up on their paper work and take a break from these little guys." "Okay" she said moving around slowly and trying not to bump into anything that might make noise. "Which one's do you have to check on?" "The two on the end there, Watson and Moran." "What do you have to do to them?"

"Oh not much, on Watson I need to measure him and weigh him again, and on Morn she needs to have a small rash looked at, she seems to like scratching herself for some reason." "Would you like to help me?" "Can I?" "Sure just roll that bed over here so we can measure Watson." Retta got out of her wheel chair and pushed it in the office out of the way then quietly went over and eased the babies bed away form the rows of others.

She tried hard not to disturb them. *"The baby is beautiful"* she thought as she looked down at the little boy. He wore a blue and white pajama top with little baby bears all over it. His hair was curly and black. His skin was a soft creamy vanilla color. She figured the baby's parents were either white or Latino. "Where do you want him?" she whispered. "Right over there next to the table." "This one?" "Yes." Sadie came over with a seamstress's tape measure. "Okay, place the bassinette on the scale."

Retta noticed that even with the little plastic bassinette, the baby hardly weighed anything at all. She placed it on the scale and Sadie hit the reset button on it. The little red digital numbers ran all over the screen then stopped at 9 pounds, 6 ounces. "Now let's measure the little tyke" said Sadie reaching into lay out her tape.

"Would you hold his little legs for me like this?" she asked Retta gently straightening his little legs. Retta held onto them and the baby stirred a little but didn't awaken. Sadie quickly placed the tape beside him from head to toe. "Okay, he's 10 inches long." "Is that good?" asked Retta not really knowing what was considered normal length for a newborn baby. "Oh yes, usually after the first few days they gain about an inch, some more, but they all grow." "He's so pretty" she said stroking his cheek gently.

"I hope when I have one it will be just as beautiful as he is." Sadie gave her a warm smile. "You will precious . . . you will . . . Would you like to hold him?" "Could I?" "Yes it's alright, we always hold them for awhile every day anyway when we feed them." Retta picked him up so gently and carefully. She cradled him close to her breast and smelled his sweet baby scented hair. He was so soft and cuddly that Retta had to work at it not to squeeze him too tightly. She kissed him on the forehead and the little boy made a funny smiley face without opening his eyes.

Retta looked up wide eyed and enraptured as she looked at Sadie to see if she saw him. Sadie just smiled and nodded. "They know when they are being loved on!" Retta blushed and felt her insides melt with pleasure as she held him. "Here you can sit down in this rocking chair." Retta sat in the comfortable granny rocker and gently rocked and hummed a tune.

The little boy responded to her warmth and the comforting, resonating sounds of her humming. He began to move his little tongue more frequently and made sucking sounds. Retta held him close to her breast as she couldn't get enough of the feel of him. As it were, the little guy was hungry and did what most babies do when hungry and in proximity of a soft warm breast . . . loaded or not.

The baby began nudging Retta's chest until he found what he was looking for and latched on. Retta had not been paying his movements much attention but instead was daydreaming and fantasizing about him being hers. She had also found herself thinking of Matt the orchestrate of such a little prize should it happen. She merely thought that it was Matt in her dream that was moving on her breasts until she felt a very real pair of tiny warm and hungry lips latch onto her right breast! Retta's eyes flew open and utter shock and confusion was all over her face as she looked down to see the little guy had eased into her smock and hit pay dirt.

"Uh . . . Sadie?" she whispered. Sadie was at her desk filling dosage bottles and making notes. *"Saaaddeee"* she whispered a little louder leaning forward and holding the little guy somewhat rigidly. The little boy was really working at it and Retta blushed with complete embarrassement. She wasn't sure if she was embarrassed at the baby mistaking her for its mother or the fact that she had nothing to give it . . . so far as she knew!

"Saaddee!" she said a little louder almost singing it. Sadie looked over and saw what was going on and almost burst out with laughter. "Oh my goodness!" she said laughing and hurrying to Retta's aid." "I'm so sorry sweetie, I should have remembered to tell you that sometimes they get hungry and if your in the right position they will try to suckle you" she said easing her finger between Retta's breast and the baby's mouth to break the seal slowly.

Retta was beginning to perspire from the shear surprise and lunacy of it all. Not to mention the embarrassement of having Sadie pull her tit out of a hungry babies mouth. The little guy didn't want to let go at first, then did so with a notable "Pop!" as he let go." Retta quickly closed her gown as Sadie took the baby from her. She looked in to see if he had gotten anything and sure enough she could see a little white droplet at the end of her nipple.

"Sadie! I'm leaking!" she whispered smiling and full of confusion. "It's alright sweetie, it happens automatically when you come in contact with a nursing infant." "But I thought you had to be pregnant to produce milk?" "No dear, its as natural as getting your period, and since you have been menstruating for some time now it makes even more sense." "But don't worry, it will stop on it's own after you leave here."

Retta just looked at her breast and how excited it was. "Wow!" after a few minutes some people walked up to the window and stood looking at all the babies. There was also one lady in a wheel chair. Retta noticed that she had long thick curly black hair and tan skin. For some strange reason Retta concluded that this must have been her little boy that she was holding. She smiled at the woman and pointed at him then mouthed, *"Is this one yours?"* she smiled back and nodded yes. "Retta, you can take him to her if you like" said Sadie after finishing a diaper change and wrapping him up tightly in his blanket.

"It's about time for the mothers to visit and feed them anyway" she said handing the baby to Retta. She slowly carried the baby around to the viewing area and out the side door. The lady and her family were waiting. "Hi" she said smiling brightly at them. "Hello, hello." "We just measured him and weighed him."

"Really, how much does he weigh?" "9 pounds and 6 ounces." "Well he is certainly picking up some weight, and how tall is he?" "He's 10 inches long." "My that's a full inch more than he was a few days ago!" she said looking up at her husband. "I guess I'll call the NBA and let them know Jason is on the way" he said giggling. Retta just looked down at him and smiled. "And what's your name sweet heart?" asked the lady "Aretta, Aretta Davis ma'am"

"Well hello Aretta, my name is Carrie and this is my husband Bill, my mother Katy and my dad Joseph" they all waved and said hello to her again. "Is your baby in there?" she asked awkwardly. "Oh my goodness no! I'm not a mother . . . I'm not even married yet, but I will be when I graduate from high school . . . see?" she said launching her hand out proudly to show them the ring Matt bought. "Oh my goodness!" said both women.

"It seems that you have a very serious and committed young man on your hands Aretta." "I know, and I can't wait till we do get married and have our own children!" she said beaming pride and joy. "Well don't rush it too fast dear, you have plenty of time and living to do first." "Yes ma'am" she said coming down a little but still jacked up at he whole concept. "So if your not here for that, how is it that such a beautiful and healthy young lady like yourself wound up here in the hospital? . . . if you don't mind my asking" asked the older woman.

Retta dropped her head and smiled bashfully. She then eased over to her and whispered in her ear. "Oh my goodness, you poor dear" she said giving her a hug and kissing her on the top of the head. "We have to be very careful as women my dear, much more so than the men or we can bring a lot of trouble on ourselves if we don't . . . do you understand honey?" "Yes ma'am" she said nodding and looking up into the old woman's kind eyes.

"Are you better now dear?" "Yes ma'am, much better, in fact the doctor said I can go home tomorrow!" "Well that's wonderful child, I'm so happy to hear that." "Yes that is good news Retta, hey I have an idea, if you're up to it and don't mind it we could certainly use a good baby sitter like you sometime, what do you think Carrie?" asked Bill. "Yes Bill, that would be nice to have her help me look after little Jason." "How about it sweetie, would you like to baby sit for us sometime?"

"Wow! I haven't done that in awhile, but it sounds like it would be great, and Jason is such a wonderful baby!" "Tell you what, here's my card, if you decide that you can do it give us a call next week sometime, by then my wife will be up and around and will need a little help when her mother goes home." "Okay Mr. Watson I'll do that, thank you" she said taking the business card. "You're welcome dear, and you remember to take care of yourself" said the older woman winking at her.

"Yes ma'am, I will." "Okay bye bye now" they said turning to leave. "Bye . . . it was nice to meet you" said Retta waving to them as they wheeled the baby and his mother away. Retta was feeling quite energized and grand just now. She had had an amazing day! "It's really cool how many nice people you can meet in a hospital" she said turning to go back into the nursery. "Retta are you ready to go sweetie?" "Yes Sadie."

"Okay, I'll bring your chair out, just let me wash up right quick." Soon they were on their way again. "Thank you Sadie for taking me on your rounds with you today, it was great, and I had fun!" "Well I'm glad you enjoyed yourself, you were quite a help to me today, and do you know what else?" "What?" Those people that you spoke to, do you know who they were?" "The Watson's right?" "Yes, but have you ever heard of the name Bill Watson anywhere?" "No, not really."

"Well he's the owner and general manager of Channel 13 Television Station!" "Really?" "Yes and Jason is his first child." "Well, what do you know about that" she said reappraising the implications. "This certainly seems to be your lucky day kiddo." "Yeah it might be, but I have to check with my mom first to see what she thinks." "Of course dear, you do that." Finally Aretta was back in her room and in bed. She was a little tired and decided to take a nap. "Dinner is at five Retta, I'll see if I can get you something a little better than your current diet that they bring, of course I don't think I can match that shrimp fried rice and noodles you had last night" she said smirking and cutting her eyes at her.

Retta just covered her mouth embarrassed that she had been caught. "It's okay dear, I'm just glad you ate something, you haven't been doing much of that and you need to keep your strength up." "Thanks Sadie." "Now you get some sleep and I'll check on you later okay?" she said bending down to kiss her forehead. Retta felt good and totally loved by everyone. She hoped when she and Matt had their baby Sadie would be there to take care of her. Soon she was fast asleep and dreaming wonderful dreams of life and love with Matt.

They would have a nice modest home with a big yard and a fence all around it. They would have two dogs and a cat named Max. She saw herself working in an architectural firm and Matt as an engineer. Their little boy would be in daycare playing and learning and it would be so nice and wonderful. Suddenly and for no reason her dream began to cloud and change. It took on a weird surrealistic Picasso-like texture. Place and faces she knew became blurry, unrecognizable blobs and she was alone.

At one point she saw herself standing there looking at three faceless figures. Two of them were women and the other a man. The larger of the two women was pulling the other from the man. She refused to let go and tried to resist. Retta's heart beat fast and hard as she watched this heart breaking scene. The larger female figure pulled harder and in the process pulled his arm completely off! As she jerked the other female away from him. Tears flowed from the eyes of the faceless girl and the man just stood with is head bowed with one arm torn off. The whole thing had the flavor a an Alfred Hitchcock master piece thought Retta and her mind was beginning to spin out of control. She found herself screaming in her sleep at this macabre scene but nothing came out. She tried to speak but her lips would not move. She hysterically reached up to her mouth to open it and found that it wasn't there . . . none of it.

Neither were the rest of her facial features either!. The shock of this was too much for her and she collapsed in a spinning soup of darkness. As she fell to the floor and lay still, a disembodied but still moving arm twitched its way towards her lifeless body and held her hand. Aretta awoke in a cold sweat and her gown was drenched. The room was flooded with light from the late afternoon sun.

The light reflected off the furniture and the window giving her a surrealistic and bleached view of her room. Retta was still very disoriented and confused at her surroundings which were faded edges of unclear things. She began to cry and call for Matt. *"Matt! . . . Matt! . . . Matt! where are you! I need you!"* Her cry's of despair reached the ears of Sadie who nearly upset a nearby crash cart getting up to go to her aid. She pushed into the room with a burst and switched on the light. Retta was a tear soaked, sweat drenched mess. Her face was awash in horrid pain and her hair was all over her face like she'd been fighting with herself.

She sat with her arms cradled around her knees and buried her face in them sobbing. *"I want Matt Sadie . . . I want Matt! . . . where is he?"* I don't know sweet heart" she said going to her and embracing her tightly. *"Oh sweet Jesus, what could have happened to this sweet child to make her go on so?"* she thought while rocking Retta and rubbing her back to soothe her. "I'm sure he'll be here today baby . . . tell me what's wrong honey? Did you have a bad dream?"

Retta raised her head and looked at Sadie with tear filled eyes. *"Sadie I'm scared!"* "Of what baby . . . of what?" *"My momma . . . she's gonna take Matt away from me . . . I just know it!"* she sniffled. "Why do you think that sweetie, did she say that?" *"No, but I just know it . . . I feel it!"* Sadie didn't quite understand. None of what she was saying made any sense! "Hold on sweetheart, maybe you better start from the beginning." *"Well I was sleeping and I dreamed this lady with no face was trying to pull this girl from this boy."* "Uh huh . . . go on." *"He wouldn't let her go so the lady wound up pulling his arm clean off!"*

"Oh Retta baby, you just had a nightmare that's all honey, it doesn't mean your mother is out to get Matt from you" she said in a scolding but soothing way. *"No wait! You don't understand, there's more!. I was standing by watching the whole thing and when the lady pulled his arm off I started screaming but nothing came out! when I reached up to my mouth I didn't have one. It scared me so much I fainted. But then as I fell I could see the boys arm reaching out to me to hold my hand. That's when I woke up!"*

"But Retta that still doesn't mean . . ." Retta stopped her by placing her fingers to her lips. *"Sadie"* she said, her voice all dry and strained with crying. *"My mom and his dad have started seeing each other recently and if they stay together how can me and Matt have a life together? . . . we can't cause we'll be brother and sister!"* She finished with fresh tears forming in the corners of her eyes.

Sadie took all this in, weighing Aretta's hysterical words carefully. At first it seemed no more than a very bad dream by a girl very much in love with the person it was about. But now having been told this other part she could see that the dream although gruesome and horrid, did have merit. "Sighh . . . I think I see your point Retta, but don't you think you may be jumping the gun just a little?" "I mean you're talking marriage and they haven't been together anywhere near long enough to even think about it." *"But Sadie, you don't know my mom! She can be real persuasive when she wants to be, I just know she'll turn him her way."* "Well think about this Retta, do you think Matt's father is as flakey or gullible as all that?" "No." "Okay then, do you think he is desperate or in a spot where he would need a wife just now?" "No" "Okay then, there you have it, he sounds like he's a responsible man and wouldn't just jump at the first woman who comes along and most certainly take it that far that soon." "I guess" Retta said not wanting to believe Sadie's logic but finding it hard not to.

"Tell me, what kind of person is Matt?" Retta straightened up considerably now. Just the thought of telling anyone about Matt was grounds to be happy. She sat up and wiped away her tears. "Matt is the best!" she said simply. "He's gentle, passionate, loving and sensitive, he makes me feel all warm inside when I'm with him and the way he makes me feel when he touches me makes me tremble." "He's strong willed, generous and loves to make me laugh, he's silly sometimes, but I love that about him too, cause he's not serious all the time." "He talks to me like I'm somebody and he tells me his inner thoughts and feelings like we're soul mates." "I love the feel of his strong arms when he's holding me and he makes me swoon when he looks into my eyes and just holds me."

Retta had in mere second gone from a girl in utter turmoil to a starry eyed, love struck young girl. Sadie noticed that Retta had eclipsed and molted so fast from what she was a minute ago, she swore she was looking at the text book example of a bi-polar personality. Then again she remembered when she was in love at that age and tossed it off. "Is he a good kisser?" she asked cutting her off smiling conspiratorially. Aretta's mouth just hung open and her eye rolled around. She bowed her head and nodded. "Yes Sadie . . . . oh yesss yesss yesss! He makes my toes curl and my body tingle all over . . ." "Then there you have it! He's all that and a good kisser too!" she said cutting her off and bringing her back to reality.

"But Sadie, what does that prove?" "Absolutely nothing, but you feel better now don't you?" "Yes, but what about my mom?" "You don't worry about her or Matt's dad, they I'm sure wouldn't do anything to hurt you two under any circumstances, so you go ahead and stop worrying and feel free to love your little heart out." "Be at peace sweetie, Matt will always be there for you so long as you desire." This made Retta feel a lot better and she didn't think about the dream anymore.

"Thanks Sadie, you're the best!" "That's alright dear, I'm glad to help and remember I said you reminded me of my own baby girl, so in all actuality I'm taking care of my own child." Retta gave her a big hug and laid her head on her shoulder. "You are so wonderful Sadie!" "And so are you sweetie . . . so are you!" They held each other for a bit till Retta was truly feeling better. "Why don't you give him a call and see what he's up to dear?" "Okay I'll do that" said Retta reaching for the phone. She dialed the number and it rang several times but no answer. Finally she hung up.

"He's not there" she said down hearted. "Well don't worry he's probably on his way here now or tied up doing something." "Yes your probably right, I'll give him a few minutes then call again." "That's the spirit!" she said pincher Retta's cheeks. "Are you gonna be okay now honey?" "Yes, I'll be fine, I'm okay now." "Okay then I'm going back to the front desk, if you need me again just call me okay?" "Okay"

Melanie pulled into the driveway and stopped. Matt jumped out of the back then lowered the tail gate so he could take off the bike. "Matt can I use your bath room?" asked Cheryl. "Uh . . . sure" he said scratching his chin thinking about something tickling the back of his mind. "Ant would you show her where it is?"

"Yeah I can do that." "Never mind Anthony! I'll show her, I need to use it myself." "Okay then" said Matt giving her the door key. "I'll put this away then we'll meet you two inside." "Alright" she said then ran to the door. "How does she know where it is?" "She came over the other night before she went to your house remember?" "What for?" "She said she wanted to study with me . . . said she needed the help."

"Is that all?" "Pretty much, other than that she made a play for me, but I cooled her heels for her." Ant didn't say anything he just looked at Matt in an odd disbelieving sort of way. "Matt are you sure you're not funny or something?" he asked tweaking his eyebrows and grinning at him. Matt spun on him like a cobra. "Your fucking kidding me right!" he said squaring off on him with his arms folded. Ant for the first time since he'd known Matt had never seen him so pensive with him and began to feel as if Matt was gonna swing on him or something!. "*I mean you didn't just ask me if I was gay Ant, did you?*"

Ant didn't quite know what to say next. He had never seen Matt look at him and address him so harshly. "Well, I didn't mean to say it like that man! I was just wondering . . . . you know?" "No Ant, I'm afraid I don't know, it's not everyday your best friend calls you a fucking queer!" he spat snarling at him. "Look Matt, I'm sorry dude, I didn't mean to offend you, it's just that you have been turning down a lot of free coochie lately and I'm talking good looking primo babes at that, if I did that wouldn't you be a little suspicious about me?" "Hell no!" "No?" "That's right, and I'll tell you why" he said rolling his bike under the steps then walking back to him.

"I know you better than that, I know how you feel about people, so I have no stray ideas what so ever about you and your sexuality." "Hell, my shit gets a hard on just like yours, I'm not superman! but I do have something most guys my age and older don't." "What's that?" "MORALS!" plain and simple . . . morals."

"And don't forget devotion and pride." "You know me." "Yeah, I guess I do Matt." "So it's not all that hard to blow them off when they come at me like that, and let me tell you something else, if I wasn't with Aretta oh yeah! you can bet I would be in there knocking boots with both of them right now!" "Would you share?" he injected lasciviously. "Sure, I'm not greedy . . . hold up, wait a minute!" Matt said recovering himself.

He'd seen that Ant had side tracked him from his initial point and position on the matter. "That's beside the point, I love Aretta and that's that! . . . get me?" Ant was laughing at him now seeing that his little deception trick had worked and he had Matt out on a chain. "Yeah man I getcha." "Good now, let's go in and get some ASS!" he said stomping off with clenched fists and a stern face. He looked as if he were in a prize fight and the other guy was gonna get beat down. "Get some what?" said Ant tripping over himself.

"Ha! Gotcha back sucker!" Matt turned around smiling at him wide eyed. "Sneaky bastard" he mumbled then followed Matt to the house. Once they'd gotten in the house they could see Mel sitting on the couch and Cheryl coming out of the bath room. "It's a very nice house you have Matt" she said sitting beside Mel on the couch. "Yeah it's okay, you guys want something to drink?"

"Yes . . . yes please" they said. "Okay I'll go get it, Ant why don't you turn on the TV for them." "I'd rather listen to some music if it's alright?" said Mel. "Yeah me too" offered Cheryl. "Okay then, let me go see what's in Matt's collection." Ant got up and left the room. Cheryl and Mel just looked at each other and grinned devilishly. "We may not need the party after all" said Mel whispering. "We might be able to take them both right here!" "Well if we do, I want Matt first!" said Cheryl frowning at her cousin. "Oh no you don't, I brought you along so I get him first!, you can have Anthony!" "Wait lets draw straws or something." "We don't have time for that! let's toss a coin instead." "Okay" Mel dug into her pocket and produced a quarter. "I got heads" she said grinning at her own pun.

"Quit messing around and flip it" urged Cheryl getting anxious, not wanting either of the boys to know what they were up to. The coin went up and landed on tails. "Yes . . . yes . . . yess!" rooted Cheryl pumping her fists in victory. "I win!" Mel just sunk down into the cushion of the couch and sighed. "Alright then you get him first but don't wear him out okay?" Cheryl just smirked at her and tossed her hair.

"I'm gonna try to break it off and bust his balls! I've been wanting that stud for a lot longer than you have dear cousin and besides I want my revenge for that day in the park!" "Well still don't wear him down too much, I won't be able to get my pound of flesh!" "What are you complaining about! You got Anthony all to yourself . . . you won't be able to do much when he's done with you!"

"Ha, that's what you think! . . . I'll wear him down like a crayon on a sidewalk" she said lustfully. "If you say so cuz, but we best plan this right or we'll blow it and neither one of us will get zip!" "Okay Cher, so what do we do then?" "Well, we could divide and conquer?" "No, that won't work, I already tried that and so have you." "Yeah your right" said Cher deflated. "Well what if we try to appeal to their male hormones?" "What?" said Cher pulling back. "How do we do that, I thought we were already doing that with all the stuff we have been doing already."

"Yeah, but this time we make it impossible for them to refuse us!" "How?" "Let's undress a little . . . you know take off our shirts or something!" "Okay when?" "Why not now?" said Cheryl pulling her shirttail out and looking quite eager. "No better time than the present" chirped Mel and started unbuttoning her's. Matt was in the hall and he had heard everything. He laughed to himself and almost caught a cramp from suppressing it. Just then he heard the phone ring. "I'll get it" he shouted.

"Hello?" "Hey baby!" said an ecstatic female voice on the other end. "Hi sweetie face" said Matt glad to hear the one voice he was longing to hear from. It was Retta. "How's my girl doing?" "Oh fine now . . . I miss you Matt." "I miss you too babe, when are you coming home?" "The doctor says I can leave tomorrow!" "Well he planned that one on time" said Matt scratching his head. "What do you mean?" "Tomorrow is Friday, so there's no need for you to go to school." "Yeah that's right, I've been so busy thinking about you I forgot that."

"Hey, I haven't forgotten you or that gorgeous body of yours either" said Matt getting low on the phone. "Ooh Matt, you behave yourself, you know I'm in no position or condition to play those kinds of games yet Mr." "Damn! . . . sucks to be me" he said playfully.

"I guess I'll have to go and do something else then." "And you'll never walk again if you do too!" she said sternly yet with a hint of playfulness. "Hey you know me babe, I'm not the type." "You'd better not be" she said pouting. "I love you Retta!" "I love you too baby, and I need you too, when are you coming to see me?"

"What time is it?" "4:30" "Okay, you eat dinner at six right?" "Uh huh" "Okay let me get rid of a few pests and I'll see you soon." "Pest's? who's over there Matt?" she said curiously as a paranoid nerve in her eye began to twitch urgently. Matt began to wonder why he even told her that and even more how she came up with the aspect that they were girls and nothing else. Well he'd never lied to her before so there was no reason to start now.

"Oh just two pains in the butt from school." "Who!" she said sitting up straight in bed and feeling a steam rise behind her neck. "A girl named Cheryl and one named Melanie her cousin." Matt felt a sudden fear and foreboding creep into his spirit and rattle around in his stomach like a mad golf ball. Retta all of a sudden got real cool and correct. "Matt why do you have two girls in your house . . . are you cheating on me already?" she said, her voice beginning to crack as she blinked back a tear that was threatening her right eye.

"Hey whoa! Now you can forget that stuff right now!" he protested trying to ease her mind. "They gave me and Ant a ride home from track practice and asked if they could use the bathroom." "I see" she said in a whisper trying to collect herself. There was a long pause. "Retta baby, I'm telling you the truth, there's no one for me but you! . . . don't you believe me?" He pleaded trying to keep his voice down.

Retta was stunned and almost immobilized by what she was hearing. Her heart was near exploding with this news and she didn't know how to deal with it. Matt has never lied to me before and I know sometimes girls do try to go after him just like some guys try to hit on me from time to time . . . but it's not right! I'm here in this place and he's out there doing I don't know what! . . . I gotta get my mind right cause if I doubt him and he's telling me the truth then I will have hurt him and then he probably will go and see other girls cause he thinks I don't have any faith in him.

A tear slid down her face as she pondered this dilemma. She nervously teased a nail on her left hand when the light through the window hit her ring and shot a beam of eldritch light into her eyes. She stopped and looked at her hand and the ring as if they were trying to tell her something. She looked at it turning it this way and that and feeling warmer inside with every passing second. She sighed deeply "Okay Matt" she said to herself in resignation.

Matt on the other hand was losing it waiting for her to respond. "Damn! why did I ever let them chicks in here! I should have let them use the bathroom then got em out of here! Now I could lose my girl for this shit!" he said eviscerating himself mentally for being stupid. He could imagine she was crying silently on the other end with her hand over the phone. Her beautiful tear stained face wracked with pain and her lovely dark hair matted to her head from tears soaking it. He wanted to say something so bad but didn't know what and how it would come back to him so silence although cowardly was the best action at least for now he thought. "Retta?" he whined as his stomach did back flips.

"Yes Matt, I believe you baby, but it just doesn't look right that's all" she said evenly and even sounded forgiving! Matt could have blasted through the roof he was so elated at the sound of her forgiving his stupidity. "Yesss!" his heart shouted at just the sound of her voice. "Your right baby, I'm so so sorry, I was stupid and I didn't think, please forgive me." "I forgive you Matt, but you have to understand how I feel right now, I mean you're there and I'm here." "I know you have needs and desires just like any man . . ." "And that's what your there for baby" he said cutting her off.

She smiled and paused a second to recover her thoughts. "Just like your there for me poo." "Look Retta, Ant thinks the same way about me, but I put him straight awhile ago." "Now look baby I'm not going to lie to you, I never have and

I never will, but when I'm at school people do try me sometimes." "They do?" "Yeah" "Who are they Matt?" "Mostly white girls, but they've already gotten the message long ago." "Okay" she mumbled, following him but still not liking the contact of activity he had been experiencing with other girls. "Then again Retta, you could look at it this way, if I was gonna hide something from you or cheat would I be telling you that there are two girls over here right now?"

"No, I guess not." "Okay then, so don't worry my love, I'm yours all the way." "Okay Matt, I see your points, I'm just jealous that's all." "Hey! Who is that wearing my engagement ring?" "I am" she said smiling. "I thought so, and let me tell you something else that I wasn't going to tell you about." "What's that Matt?" "Did you ever wonder if the ring was real or not, or how I paid for it?"

"Retta's stomach cringed with embarrassement at the question. She suddenly had the feeling she was being watched. She didn't want him to think she didn't believe he would give her something so beautiful and important that was fake. "Uh . . . yeah, kind of" she said giggling a little. "Well I bought it in the mall that same day we had dinner over at your house, I cashed in one of my savings bonds for college and bought it for you from Zales Jewelers."

"It cost $1200.00 dollars!" "OH Matt! How could you? It was too much to spend on just me!" she said rapidly waving her hand like the ring had caught fire suddenly and she was trying to put it out. "No it wasn't, I spent exactly what I wanted to spend and for you it was well worth it." Retta really began to feel bad now! "I love you Retta, don't you see that?" she couldn't speak. There was a large lump forming in her throat and tears were falling freely. "Baby there can never be another woman like you and I'm making sure I get you before someone else does!" *"Oh Matt!"* she whispered choking back tears, her throat getting tighter and tighter.

"I love you too boy . . . oh how I love you, no one can ever have me but you . . . no one!" "And you can best believe the same about me Retta." "You are something else, do you know that Mr. Mathis?" "Yeah, they tell me that, but I won't say anything if you don't" he said teasing her and lightening her mood some. "Tell you what babe, let me get out of here and get these people gone and I'll see you shortly okay?" "Okay Matt." "Hey what do you want for dinner?" "Oh Matt, you don't have to do that sweetie, I'll be fine with what they give me."

"No, now I don't want my baby's last meal in there to be some mushy old soup or something that no self respecting hog would eat." "Ooh Matt! that's not nice." "Yeah, but it's true though, so what can I bring you?" "I don't know, surprise me." "Okay then, I'll do that, so I'll see you in a little bit okay babe?" "Okay Matt, and be careful in traffic and I love you!" "I love you too baby girl . . . bye now."

Matt hung up the phone and collected the drinks. "I'm sorry I took so long you guys" he said coming down the hall. "It was my baby Retta." Matt wasn't sure what to expect when he got to the den, but he was ready for it anyway. As he walked in the sight before him was one of surprise and hilarity. It also made his loins stir just a bit. Melanie and Cheryl were both laid back on the couch in a most seductive pose completely naked from the waist up! They were smiling fiendishly at him and twirling their bra's around their fingers like keys on a ring. Matt wanted to burst out laughing but then again he wanted to fuck them too! They looked really hot! and inviting, sitting with one foot propped up on the couch and the other leg slung wide to expose their more inviting treasures.

He could see that neither of them were wearing any underwear as well and the sensuous dark furry mounds that smiled at him threatened to expand his penis beyond it's limit and explode it! But Matt forced an awful thought into his mind once again to override the signals his eyes were sending his penis. "Hey Ant! come here man, you have got to see this" he shouted not taking his eyes from them.

He smiled and was enjoying their little tryst. "Yeah wuss up?" he said coming into the room. Matt slowly sat down the drinks on the coffee table and stood placing his hands on his hips. "So finally we have him where he can't refuse us" thought Mel as she became more and more excited as he looked at her breasts. She was beginning to feel the urgency of her own desire build and pulse between her legs with each passing moment. She could feel his eyes go through her clothes and into her penetrating deeply and hard like he himself was there. A warm tingle filled her and she could feel herself getting moist between her legs.

Cheryl was already over the edge and her hand had made its way down to her crotch to expose it further to Matt's unblinking gaze. She teased her right nipple with her other hand and just glared back at him in the most passionate and lusty way she could. "Matt I'm gonna fuck your brains out and you'll never want another woman after me, I'll own your body to do with as I please forever . . . if you last that long." Ant had come into the room and the sight blew him away! "Oh shit, what the hell is this?" he said standing on the right side of Matt. He too could see what Matt saw, but not being bound by any relationship allowed his maleness to flower letting his manhood grow to full size in seconds.

Cheryl was closer to him and saw with great pleasure how she made him lose control. Ant gave Matt a confused stare as if to say, "What do we do now? Why aren't we attacking Matt!" He just remained cool and gave him a look that told Ant the jig was up! "Time to cool these girls off a bit" then he winked and Ant was sure what was up now and just awaited Matt's lead. "Hey Ant, it's been a long time since I've see a plump and hairy pussy like these, how bout you?" "Me too!" he chirped honestly.

"It would be a shame to pass up such a fine piece of ass like this . . . what do you say?" "Hey man I'm right with you!" he said barely able to contain himself and hoping Matt was gonna end this torcher soon cause he was burning his best friend as well as the chicks in front of him. He didn't have Matt's ice man ability and wanted to pile drive either one of them into oblivion just now! Melanie couldn't believe her ears! The sound of Matt talking about the possibility of having sex with them was more than she was expecting and the shock of it caused her to spontaneously combust between her legs! Warm wetness flowed from her vaginal lips to soak her panties. She had half expected him to maybe pull another trick on them, but now hearing that he was seriously interested in getting busy with them, was more than a joy!

Cheryl was now massaging her already wet coochie and churning her hips in rhythm as she burned with the thought of having Matt finally inside of her. She licked her lips sensuously trying to entice him even more to take her then and there. Matt just casually looked at his watch. "I think we have time Ant" he said matter of fact like. "Which one do you want Ant?" He asked *"WE ALREADY PICKED!"* said Cheryl about to fall off the couch with excitement and making sure she made it known her claim had been staked!

"I get you Matt" she swooned seductively and rubbed her already red nipples. "Okay then let's get busy!" Matt winked at Ant one last time then quickly grabbed Cheryl up in his arms! She was so excited and shaken by his familiarity and strength with her body she swore she had had an orgasm right there! Just as quick, Ant did the same with Mel.

Matt made a mad dash into the bathroom. Cheryl was totally confused. She didn't know whether Matt was up to something or just being kinky!. "Your gonna love this Cher baby and I can't wait!" he said giving her a most fiendish smile.

"O . . . okay Matt if you like it this way" she stuttered still not wanting to believe what her heart was telling her was actually about to happen. "Great! Were gonna screw in the shower!" said Mel holding onto Ant for dear life anticipating a wild and tight time. Matt went into the bathroom followed by Ant and Mel.

He placed Cher in the shower and she began to take off her track shorts. Ant placed Mel in beside her and she followed suit ignorantly by undoing her pants and wriggling out of them. Ant hadn't ever gotten a shot of Mel's package before but had felt it. It was in his definition a monkey to be dealt with! Now that he could see it, his shock was complete. "Sweet momma!" he burst out with joy.

Cher was completely naked now and hot to trot! Ant couldn't believe the luck he was having and doubted that any two guys in all of Central was witnessing or having this kind of experience. "Matt take your clothes off!" urged Cher. "I am baby, let me get you guys straight first." Mel had just finished taking off the last stitch of her clothes and stood up with fire in her eyes. "Come on you kinky bastards lets get it on! I'm on fire!" Matt looked at Ant slowly and then at the two naked nubile in the shower.

"Then allow me to *COOL YOU OFF SOME!"* He said then savagely hit the cold water button on the shower. "EEEEE!" they screamed. Matt and Ant ran out of the bathroom laughing their asses off.

"We fixed their hot little asses" said Matt. Ant was in mild shock and couldn't believe what they had just done, but if was funny as hell! "Come on we gotta go" said Matt. "Where to?" "I gotta go see Retta, that was her on the phone." "What about those two?" said Ant pointing at the bathroom door. "They'll get out fine, let's go!" They ran out the bedroom door to the outside and into the front yard.

Then around the side of the house and into the back yard to get his moped. By now Melanie and Cheryl had gotten out of the shower and stumbled into the den soaking wet. "OOH! That bastard!" spat Cheryl trying to dry off. "I'll kill him for that!" "Well so much for your master plan" said Mel drying her hair. "He must have been on to us from the start Mel." "No, he couldn't have, he was in the kitchen getting soda then he got on the phone remember?" "Well I don't know" said Cher tossing the towel on the couch. "I guess he's just too strong for us." "OH no, he isn't, did you see that pipe in his pants girl?" "OH yess, he wanted us bad, there's no doubt about that."

"It still doesn't mean anything if he blows us away like this every time" whined Mel. "Well he won't get away come next Friday, we'll have him just where we want him, did your friend get the tranquilizers?" "Yep she got them." "What did she want for them?" "Matt's friend Milton." "I guess that's a fair trade, Milton is a fox . . . mostly dog, but a fox non-the-less." "Hey, where are they anyway?" asked Mel putting her clothes back on and noticing that she and Cheryl were alone. "Hell, I don't know . . . probably in the bedroom laughing at us." Just then they heard a roar pass by the window.

They looked at each other with their mouths open. "Oh shit, they're leaving us!" said Mel. "Let's go, we need to catch them before they get to far!" She said running into the bedroom with Cheryl close behind. Matt stopped by the truck and placed a note on the windshield then sped away.

"Hey Matt take the short cut through the field at the bottom of the street, that way we can cut across the tracks and get a good head start on them." "That'll work, good idea" said Matt then aimed the bike in that direction and zoomed down the street. They rode through the knee high wheat grass, up the small hill to the railroad tracks then onto the street. "SSSlow down Matt, my ass is gonna fall off!" "Your ass? I think I shook off a nut coming through the field!" Matt steered the bike down the center of the tracks then both of them got off and walked it over the rails and onto the street. Once there they got back on and were gone again! Melanie and Cheryl were just coming out of the house, both still a little wet and a lot mad! "Come on, they couldn't have gotten far" said Cheryl jumping in the passenger side.

Melanie opened the door to jump in then noticed a yellow post it note on the windshield. "Hold on Cher, we got something here." She got out and plucked it from the windshield. "What does it say?" "Dear girls, sex was really great and we really enjoyed ourselves, we hope it was good for you too, let's do it again sometime real soon, be cool Love Matt and Ant." He wrote the word cool in large letters and underlined it. "P.S., don't forget to lock up, I went to drop Ant off at the house and then I'm going to see my girl in the hospital, Seeya!" "Is that so?" said Cheryl. "Well lets get over there before they do, they can't have gone that far that fast on that thing!" said Cher. Mel cranked up the truck and floored it in reverse. She made a spinning turn into the street leaving two feet of rubber in her wake. They were mad and their prides were bruised. Never in their lives had they been so savagely, rebuked. Their bodies still throbbed from the thoughts of hot passionate lovemaking.

Now that it was literally thrown in their faces, it became the ultimate insult! "Which way did we come in here Cher?" "Umm that way!" She said pointing to the right. "Yeah I remember it now, it won't take too long to get to Ants house now." All she needed to do was make a left onto PioNono then go straight. "What do you think we ought to do when we catch them?" Asked Cher.

Mel thought for a minute and the question was like cold water on her back. True enough they deserved restitution but they did bring it on themselves and Matt was only playing his cards well by goading them on like that. And the fact that they started this strange sexual war game days ago didn't help either. Melanie slowed down then stopped. She leaned over the wheel and laughed to herself. She started slow but when the facts of everything sunk in she broke out in pure delirium. Cheryl had to join her because she had some of the same thoughts too. "You know . . . that's really funny when you think about it" said Cher between breaths. *"Yeah I was so hot I would have rode a bed post if I could have found one"* squealed Mel turning red from laughing so hard. *"No wait! That water when it hit me was so damn cold I came anyway! HA HA HA!"* Screamed *Cher.* *"Stop it, you're making me sick! . . . I can't take it anymore!"* said Melanie sucking air and tears rolling down her face.

Finally they came under control again and their laughter had subsided to mild giggling. "That Matt, he's sure one sharp cookie isn't he?" Asked Cher whipping her eyes. "Yeah, I don't know how he does it, if I were a man I would have been balls deep into both of us in the first ten seconds and trying to bury the rest of myself even further! after that!" she declared proudly with a semi wild look in her eyes and smiling. "Melanie you're a real freak aren't you?" asked Cher staring at her as if seeing her for the first time. "Who are you to talk? I can smell your coochie smoking way over here, you still got the hot's for him *CORN FED!"* she said lambasting her cousin.

"Do you think were crazy Melanie?" "I mean there are a lot of really cute guys out there and there's really no need to chase after Matt at all, he's never going to give in you know." "Well I don't know about the crazy part, but I've seen what's at my school and some of what's at yours and they don't move me at all like he does!" "When I see him I get all hot and tingly and when he looks at me I want to just pull him on top of me and bury him inside me! . . . you know?" "Yeah I kinda get that throbbing ache myself, what do you think makes him so special Melanie?" "His attitude and character, his whole outlook on life and women is different."

"What do you mean?" Well he's seventeen girl! And he's not a dog! Do you think we're the only chicks after him?" "No" "And he's committed himself to just one girl . . . I gotta tell you Cher, to find a man like him in this day and age is rare! And I'd give up a year of my life to have a man who would love and cherish me like he does his girlfriend!" "Do you know her name?" "Yeah, it's Aretta Davis." "Strange first name." "She's supposed to be part Indian and African American."

"Oh I see, what school does she go to?" "Southwest" "Southwest? . . . hell that's clear across town!" "I know, now you see why I say he's special?" "Yeah, I guess I do, so what we're doing is just having fun and keeping him on his toes against others so he doesn't stray right?" "Yep" "Why are we doing this Mel?" she chewed on her lip for a second and thought about it. "Because we're in love with him." Cheryl looked straight ahead and pondered this. "Yeah, I guess your right, we do love him, so how does this fit into our plans to seduce him?" "It doesn't, we're women and we want him and it's just that simple, and we'll get him too!"

Ant and Matt shot across Napier Avenue and down the street to the bank then turned in the parking lot and went through his back yard. "We made it!" he said rolling to a stop. "Hey what do I do when they show up?"

"I don't know . . . give em a bowl of milk, that usually pleases a pissed off pair of felines." Ant just grinned "Yeah right, so are you gonna stop by on the way back?" "Naw, I'm just gonna go home and crash out awhile its been a busy day." "Okay my friend, I'll check you out later" he said giving Matt their hand shake. "Later Ant." Matt pulled out and went back the way he came turning east on PioNono Avenue.

The drive didn't take very long once he got passed Pierce Avenue. He stopped along the way and went to the House of Olives Italian restaurant to get her a nice lasagna. He paid for the meal and was on his way again. Matt pulled up to the front door as usual and parked. Then he ran in and up the stairs to the third floor. He didn't feel like waiting on the elevator and wanted to stretch his legs a little. Once he got up stairs he dashed through the door and by the nurses station. "Hello Matt" said a nurse behind the large desk. Matt looked back surprised and wondering who had called him. Then he saw the full figured white woman smiling at him as she shuffled some papers.

He waved, then went into Retta's room. Aretta was sitting up running through the local stations and feeling very bored. When she saw Matt come through the door you could have heard her scream all the way down the hall. "Matt!" she screamed then dropped the remote and jumped into his arms wrapping her legs around him. "Oh Matt, I'm so glad to see you!" she said covering his face with warm kisses. She felt all warm and made his pulse race to be holding her. Matt walked over to her bed still holding and kissing her hungrily then put the bag he had on the table and fell into bed with her.

His long standing and pent up emotions spilled from him as he greedily sought her lips again and again. Aretta was tingling all over and moaned and squealed as her tongue probed in and out of his mouth in a sensual game of tag. She began to unbutton his shirt and expose his chest to her hungry fingers.

"Oh how wonderful he feels!" His corded stomach muscles were tight and full and her fingers enjoyed rubbing up and down his smooth skin. "Oh Matt" she whispered breaking their kiss, just long enough to explore his neck and face. "I want you now!" she breathed in his ear. She reached down between them and wriggled out of her panties. Retta feeling the former pain or discomfort of her illness and wanted so much to share love with Matt as they once did. Matt could feel himself swelling enormously. It was so hard it hurt, and all he could think about was making mad love to her there and now!

Unfortunately a distant beep of a machine and an intercom message brought him crashing back to reality and he remembered where he was. Matt sighed within himself and began to slow his movements and lust filled intentions. Retta noticed his sudden change in rhythm and became disheartened and confused. "What's wrong Matt? . . . don't you want me?" she said searching his eyes and still trying to undo his pants. "Yes baby I do! I want you in the worst way!" "Well here I am, why won't you take me?. I mean don't you love me?" "Yes I want you, and yes I love you too . . . but look at where we are . . . we don't exactly have any privacy and I don't think the staff would like us getting busy in their hospital like this" he said looking down at her with deeply saddened eyes.

Oh he was really pushing his human limits on morals today and his body was paying for it! Matt had passed on every sexual escapade that had come his way in the space of a week. And now that he could actually satisfy his long building desires he still couldn't. Oh the pain of it! Retta just lay there prone, still holding onto his waist and only giving impulsive movements into him. She wasn't quite ready to give up this fight just yet and felt she needed a more valid reason than "We may get caught!" as a restraining device.

Tiny beads of perspiration had began to form on her brow and neck, lightly coating her bare chest with a glistening sheen of sweat. Matt was taking all this in and it was fucking up his mind something terrible. He even began to wonder if after all of these pressure tests on his libido and no action, would he be able to perform when he could get it! As he hovered above her contemplating all aspects and possibilities of successfully engaging into sex with her for even a moment with out getting busted, he could feel his arms begin to burn from the effort. He wanted to collapse on her while still planted firmly between her legs but knew that if he did it would be on and there would be no stopping from there.

"Damn I hate my luck!" he said grimacing inside his mind. Retta could see that there was some serious inner turmoil going on in the heart and mind of the man she loved and she didn't like to see him that way. She wanted him bad and knew he wanted her as much but decorum prohibited it just now.

She also knew that he would not be the one to break their present position as it would send her a bad signal and he really didn't want to do more than he'd already done. She would have to be 21 and do the right or at least fair thing and let him off the hook. "Okay Matt" she sighed and scooted up and away from him towards the headboard. But not before getting one more good earth shaking grind into his partially exposed member. Matt swooned and almost lost it. Retta saw the look of sweet pain on his face at her move and relished it. She recovered her stray underwear under the covers and put them back on but not too quickly.

She wanted to give him as much of a motivational tool as she could for when she did get out of there. "You understand don't you baby?" he asked with pleading eyes and a throbbing penis. He was really concerned about hurting her feelings and really wanted her to understand. "Yes Matt I understand . . . I understand that you've been with somebody else and don't want me anymore! That's what I understand!" she said suddenly flashing him a very mean look and folding her arms across her chest.

Women for the most part are a complex, system of interlocking, interconnected, variably synchronize, collection of feelings and emotions governed by a mind more calculating and dangerous than the world's deadliest nuclear weapon system. Retta, within the space of a New York minute, graduated from acceptance and understanding to accusation and inquisition! She hadn't really accepted this excuse but merely took it as a precursor to cover a lie. She in her own mind hadn't fully worked out the particulars of how or why she had suddenly arrived at that state of mind but did and with deadly precision and speed! Retta couldn't have hurt Matt more than if she had stabbed him in the jugular with a 50cc syringe and pumped air into him.

Matt's eyes grew to the size of pie pans as he slowly got off of the bed. He stepped back a bit then flashed her with a look so scorching that it made her cringe away from him. Matt stepped to her and leaned over her and slowly raised and pointed a finger into her face! *"Let me tell you something right now"* he said evenly almost monotone.

"Don't you ever!, As long as you live, accuse me of fucking anybody, not loving you, or wanting you ever again!" Retta began to feel like a child and retreated into herself for safety. She had never seen Matt this angry before and it scared her! "But Matt . . ." *"SNAPP!"* he viciously snapped his fingers cutting her off then put two fingers together near to her face like he was crushing a pebble, signifying she should shut up. "Shut . . . up! Retta" he breathed through his clenched teeth.

Matt was so mad with all he had been dealing with lately that his body was trembling with violent anger. *"Do you know what I have been going through out there since you got sick? . . . The morning you got ill I knew about it before anyone even told me because I FELT YOU! That's how I knew you were sick. Nobody told me JACK!"* Retta was really beginning to digress into a fetal position now as Matt towered above her and got into her face up close and very personal. He was mere inches from her face as he spoke harshly and forcefully to her.

She found she couldn't look directly at him but instead straight ahead and only glancing up at him side ways every second or two. She had felt as if he may hit her and that too was causing her to flinch and tuck her head somewhat in preparation for the blow. *"Did you know that since then people have been trying to throw themselves at me left and right? But I keep them flying because they don't have jack that I want!"* Retta was about to speak when he paused but thought better of it and just waited.

"Do I get tempted or hot flashes from it? . . . Yes!" "Have I acted on any of it? . . . No! and have I been waiting and yearning for you all week? . . . Hell yes!. Woman do you know how close I came to jerking off this week because of you? Too damn close!" He said easing back a little seeing how she was cringing from him. Retta thought about him holding her picture and jerking off on himself wildly and it almost made her laugh. But she squelched the desire for better judgement. "I love you girl and there is no one who can change that! . . . not anyone!" "So if you still think I don't want you or love you and need you, then take off that ring and put it on the table and I'll leave" he said sounding more calm and in control.

This change in tone and his words and the thought of what he was professing scared her. It shook her so badly that she involuntarily hid her hand when he said it. Retta couldn't gear the idea of Matt leaving her for any reason . . . she just couldn't fathom it. She eased herself from the bed slowly, painstakingly and stood up. Her long beautiful black hair flowed down around her small shoulders giving off a most innocent and alluring sight. Matt thought that she looked like an angel without wings. Retta didn't blink as she looked at him with pain and love in her eyes. She just walked up to him slowly, put her arms around his waist, buried her head against his chest and held him tightly.

This gave Matt his answer and the madness he once felt slipped from him like a silk gown from her body. He enclosed her in his arms and kissed the top of her head then rest his face atop it. "Oh Retta, my baby girl please believe in me and love me, I would never do anything to ever hurt you, I said before that one day you would be my wife and I meant it! Hell anyone can have sex, but we have love! . . . deep passionate abiding love." "So what do we do? . . . we make love." "When you have that burning within you, casual sex with others is a waste of time and of no interest to me at all, do you understand baby?"

Retta just nodded and squeezed him tighter. He raised her chin to look into her eyes. "Do you really?" he asked again. She nodded then whispered "Yes my love I do, I am sorry I ever doubted you or your love for me, I know that now, and I'll never do it again Matt." Her eyes were like looking into the intense richness of the setting sun, and he could see forever in them. The effect of them made him weak just looking into them. "God your beautiful!" he breathed as he gently caressed her cheek.

She raised his hand to her lips and kissed the palm of it. "Only because of you Matt" she whispered returning love for love as they stood beholding each other. Matt picked her up in his arms cradling her and still holding her gaze. She felt so wonderful and light that he could hold her forever.

Their lips slowly melted together in a soft and sensual kiss. The power they felt in their love for each other made them swoon and Matt began to turn and spin slowly to some unheard music in his heart. He spun her around and around losing himself in love. Retta was in heaven once again and didn't want to leave. Wave after wave of wonderful feelings of love flowed through her and over her and around her making her weaker yet stronger in his embrace. She could feel herself melting in Matt's touch and relished the sweet aroma of his breath and mouth as kissed her. Somehow me managed to spin them to the bed and lay her down ever so gently, not wanting to break the spell.

Quietly and unbeknownst to the to lovers, Sadie was easing the door closed having accidentally walking in and seen the love that had filled the room as Matt held her and spun her around. She kindly placed a do not disturb sign on the door and walked back to her station. "How special it must be to be in love and young" she thought, a smile crossing her lips. Soon the sun had gone down and the first stars of night were beginning to appear. They had long since recovered from their spell and taken time for Retta to eat her dinner before it got too cold. Now they just lay together with Retta asleep on his chest and completely content. Matt was gently stroking her head and back.

It felt luxurious and silky and became a tranquilizer to him. Soon he too was asleep. After awhile Matt was awakened by a soft voice. "Matt, time to wake up dear." He opened one eye then the other and saw that it was the nurse who had spoken to him earlier. She smiled at him sweetly. "It's time to go honey, visiting hours were over an hour ago."

"Oh shoot!" he said rubbing his eyes. "What time is it?" "It's 8:30." Matt tried to ease himself out from under Retta without waking her. Sadie saw his effort and tried to help him. They eased her over and placed her on a pillow then put the stuffed animal under her arm in his place. "I'm sorry I didn't mean to stay so long, but after she ate dinner we just laid down to relax and she fell asleep, then I went right after her."

"It's okay Matt, I know and I understand, so don't worry yourself okay?" Matt smiled and nodded, then began stretching and yawning. "I need to call home and let my dad know where I've been." "Oh was that your father who came in with her mother?" "I don't know, what did he look like?" "Like you only a little taller and distinguished." "Yep, that's him." "He and her mother came in a while ago while you two were asleep, they didn't want to wake you two because you looked so sweet and content lying there." Matt blushed. He had never thought of himself as a sweet infant to be ogled and cooed at.

"So you don't have to worry." "Thanks . . . well I guess I better go, I got school in the morning." "Okay, you drive safely now you hear?" "Okay I will" he said then leaning over and kissed Aretta's cheek softly. "I love you Red" he whispered calling her by her nickname he had for her. He then rose and turned to leave. "Goodnight ma'am." "Call me Sadie okay?" "Alright" "Goodnight Matt." He waved and headed for the stairs.

The next day was fast paced cause everyone was ready for the weekend and no one was much interested in being there. It was the third period and Matt was in Science class. "Class today's subject will be studying the internal organs of amphibians and the digestive tract!" "Sighh!, Oh boy, Aw man!" went the complaints from around the room. "Yeah! This ought to be fun" thought Matt.

Mr. Turner, the teacher was sitting in for Mr. Burke today and it was quite a change of venue. Mr. Turner was a short, rotund little fat black man with a jolly demeanor. He sported a 1970's goatee with a fluffy full blown afro. He was good at the subject of Physical Science and even made it interesting. Whereas Mr. Burke was about as exciting as mud and about as interesting of a person as a corps. Mr. Turner and Matt would sit around sometimes and hold debates on different aspects of the subject and it's theories. Mr. Turner enjoyed their interactions completely and so did Matt.

After awhile the class became animated by their talks as well. Partially because it was fun playing devils advocate on a given subject, be you for or against it's theories and secondly because it was always good for burning up at least two thirds of the class time. This ensured that they wouldn't have much to do in the way of in class assignments. Today, Mr. T as they called him, had sat on each desk a specimen tray with a frog in it. Each one was splayed out and staked down belly up with pins in its feet and hands. The awful part came when you had to slice open it's small flat belly. Most of the girls refused to do it and just sat there with disgusted looks on their faces.

They frowned at the putrid smelling amphibian in front of them. Mr. Turner was an ole smoothie though and could talk an Eskimo into buying beach front property on a glacier. Soon he would have the girls slicing into the animal with scientific zeal! It's amazing how fast he could talk them into it. Today Matt was feeling on the clownish side and would make the most of it in class. Ivory or Frog his other buddy was in this class as well. A definitive mix that no teacher in her right mind would have. He too was into getting into devilment today. Once everyone had begun to slice open there toads Matt looked around at the lowered heads to see who might be looking. He spied Frog looking his way with a mischievous grin on his face as if to say "Let the games begin!"

Mr. Turner had disappeared into the store room to check on supplies and to get some more latex gloves. This gave Matt and Frog just the opportunity they needed. Matt eased out of his seat and up to Mr. T's desk. He slowly slid open the heavy wooden drawer taking care not to make it squeak. By now other student's were looking at him and just grinned because they knew that what ever he was up to would be a trip! Matt fished out a roll of synthetic jell tape. It was what Mr. T and Mr. Burke used to hold various things and animals in place on the table. The tape was a transparent, jelly like sticky celluloid. It stuck really well and was easy to peel off your skin. He got a large piece of it and closed up the drawer. Stealthily he stole back to his seat. "Whatchu gonna do Matt?" whispered Frog already animated with devious glee. "Wait an see" he said then tore off a piece from the paper and gave it to Frog. "Hold onto this for a minute." "Okay!" Then he pulled the pins from his frogs limbs and stuck a piece to it's belly. "Watch this shit!' he whispered grinning then he stuck the frog to the side of his face with a disgusting splat sound and left it there.

The sight of the flat green animal on his face made Frog burst out laughing. It was disgusting and soon others caught a glimpse of this and went to pieces in a horrified humorous Malay! "Alright people, what's going on in there?" asked Mr. T from the storage room. Matt quickly pulled the frog from his face and lay it back in the tray. "Nothing Mr. T" said one girl. "We're just looking at the frogs" she said grinning and trying to maintain sincerity. "Alright now behave" he said not really stressing it cause he knew it was Friday and all hell usually breaks loose on that day. It's probably why Mr. Burke decided to be elsewhere that day. Soon he came out and announced he had to go to the main supply locker down the hall to restock and that they should just go on with their projects quietly.

As he left Matt and frog grew the most devilish of expressions ever seen and Frog immediately went to work. He took small pieces of his tape and stuck them to his frogs legs and arms from behind then placed them strategically on his fingers so he could control them like a marionette. The class was very much interested in what he was up to and bunched up to see. Frog then ran up to the front of the room behind the desk and lay his hand atop it. "Hey you guys check this out" he said then started moving the frogs legs and arms like a chorus girl kicking them up and down singing. *"Hello my baby, hello my darling, hello my rag time girl, send me a kiss by wire, honey my hearts on fire!"*

The class was in an uproar and people were laughing so hard at this morbid puppet show they were tumbling out of their seats! Not to be out done, Matt had fashioned a miniature pair of sunglasses from a small piece of his notebook cover and taken out a black magic marker to color them. He then glued them to the poor frogs head with a small dollop of tape. "Hold up! Hold up" he said running to the front next to Frog. "Frog quick! Turn out the lights!" Frog was laughing all the way to the door.

As soon as the lights were out he switched on the desk lamp and sat the frog under the make shift spot light. The class burst out laughing again even before he began his skit! Matt stood the frog up and began dancing him across the desk singing . . . *"I heard it through the grapevine . . . baby won't you be mine."* Frog joined in and the show was on! They went through at least a dozen skits before the class told them to stop because they couldn't take it anymore. "Okay okay . . . one more thing" he announced. "Everybody who hasn't cut into your toad give them to Frog." "Frog turn on the light and go get em . . . . hurry up before Mr. T comes back!" Frog ran to hit the lights then picked up the first tray he saw and began collecting the toads.

Soon he had collected all but four. "Okay Matt what now?" "Okay you take this black marker and start making block numbers on their backs and then give them to me!" "Alright" he said setting in on the first frog. The two of them moved with expert quickness and grace. A skill developed over many years of being mischievous. The class anxiously waited for what their grand finale would be. Matt took each frog and placed a good size piece of tape to it's belly and soon they were all done.

"Okay go give one to everybody on the right and I'll do the same on the left." The boys ran to pass them out and soon each student had one. Matt ran to the black board and drew a bulls eye target, then placed numbers in each section. By now the class had caught the gist of his plan and began laughing hysterically again. Matt dropped the chalk and ran to the side. "Okay everybody throw em!" she shouted then ran out of the way. The class was in utter chaos with laughter and the sickening splats.

Each frog found it's mark on the target and stayed there. It was a hilariously gross scene. Each frog tossed hit either within the circle or somewhere around it. Just about the time the last frog hit the black board Mr. Turner came in. Everyone quickly sat down in their seats and played innocent. A feat that was next to impossible being the evidence of their activities was grossly displayed on the wall behind them. Mr. Turner looked around at the sea of smiling suspicious faces.

"Okay let's have it . . . I heard you little monsters way down the hall." "Have what Mr. T? . . . we was just doing our assignments" offered one girl. Mr. T looked at the empty trays around the room. Then cut his eyes at everyone as if to say, "something in the lab ain't clean." "Where are all the frogs people?" he asked raising his eyebrows. The class just burst out laughing. Mr. T looked at them and followed their eyes behind him to the front of the room. The sight he saw was way more than his many years as a Science teacher had prepared him for. He just shook his head and bent over laughing his ass off.

This made the class go even wilder. Time had run out and class was over as signified by the bell ringing loudly on the wall. "Get out of my class you monster!" said Mr. T holding the door, still laughing. "And have a nice weekend" he said as they burst past him carrying the infectious hilarity into the hallway.

Chapter 10

Trifling Times

The day was great thought Matt and practice for today was out for him and Ant because they were on the Varsity Team now. Also Retta was getting out of the hospital today.

Matt decided he would call her and see when that would be. "Hey Matt! Wait up!" called a female voice. Matt turned around and searched the sea of faces around him but didn't zero in on anyone in particular. Just then someone poked him in the ribs "Ow!" he looked to his left and saw it was Tonya Rodgers. "Hey Tonya, what's up?" "You Matt" she said smiling at him. "Can we talk for a minute?" "Sure, but it'll have to be quick, I got gym over at the boys school this period." "Well lets go in here then" she said leading him into the library. She guided him down a long isle of books and into a dead end in the back of the room. "Why all the secrecy?" "Because I don't want any interruptions."

"This must be important." "I think so." "So tell me what's up?" "Well for starters, you stood me up yesterday Matt and that hurt me!" "I'm sorry Tonya, I really didn't mean to, I had track practice yesterday." "Yes I know, I saw you on the field." "Really? What did you think?" "I think you'd better stop knocking out peoples windows in their cars or you're gonna make a lot of enemies . . . that's what I think." Matt just leaned against a row of books and laughed. "But that's beside the point Matt, I want to know what you thought of my letter?" Now he knew what this was about.

He felt a little odd about it and didn't quite know what to say because he hadn't entertained it at all or had a chance to. Tonya was staring at him with those deep grey green eyes and oh! How they penetrated his soul!. "Tonya it's really difficult to tell you what I feel, there are other complicating things in place." "Well let me help you un-complicate them" she said putting down her book bag. "First of all, I know you're seeing someone right now and she doesn't go to school here." "How did you know that?" said Matt his ears pricking up like a hound dog. "Your friends Matt, they do quite well protecting you from other people, I also asked Milton sometime ago." "I see." "Second, I know you have feelings for me . . . how deep I'm not sure, but I do know this, that they aren't casual."

And finally she stopped and took a deep breath letting it out slow, "I'm also falling in love with you." The words were like a sonic blast! in Matt's ears. Matt just leaned back against the book case and stared. Tonya stood arms folded, she looked so beautiful with her bronze colored naturally curly hair and creamy colored skin. It gave the impression that she may have lineage in Spain or somewhere in the Mediterranean countries. She wore a conservative jean skirt and white Izod shirt.

Matt could feel the space closing in around him and the pressure inside him was building. "Why me?" he thought. "Who am I that you should love me? . . . Why do things like this always have to happen to me? . . . Damn!" He knew he had to be honest with himself and deal with this problem. If he didn't, he would always be false and he couldn't live with that. "Tonya" he said in a raspy voice. His words coming out like air from a balloon. "How do you think I feel about you?" "Like I said Matt, I don't really know, I see how you look at me and I feel you want me, but I can't really say with any certainty, that's what I'm here to find out." Matt mulled over her statement and questioned if he should really tell her what he feels or has felt for so very long. He chastised a spot on the floor with the tip of his shoe contemplating this. "Okay Tonya I'll tell you, but I probably shouldn't be" he said then paused to swallow. "Ever since I first saw you at Miller "B" in the 8th grade about two years ago, you have always been like a dream to me, a distant wonderful dream."

"You captured my heart and from that moment on I became yours, you didn't notice me, but I fell for you a thousand times each time I looked at you!" Tonya started to blink and she had to reposition herself and hold on to the book shelf. She couldn't believe that she was hearing this! "Your golden soft hair, your enchanting eyes, you enslaved me without knowing it." Tonya couldn't believe her ears!

The sweet endearments he was saying to her. It couldn't be possible! She couldn't entice a goat with a news paper let alone Matt! She thought. "How is it that this desirable wonderful man could be taken by me?" "There has been many a night I dreamt of you, holding you, kissing you, making love with you" she thought blushing at this particular part lowering her head so he wouldn't see.

"Tonya, you were always to me like an angel perched too high to reach and I didn't even try to have a chance with you, so I had to love you from afar."

Tonya's head popped up at this and intense eyes full of wonder and intrigue looked into his. Searching, hoping, praying that what he had just told her was the truth and more important . . . that it was still true! "Yes Tonya, I loved you too."

Matt went silent and solemn after saying this and just waited for her to respond. His words hit her like a shot to the gut and knocked the wind out of her. Tonya felt bare and naked before him, tingling all over with excitement! She didn't quite know what to do now that her greatest fears had been allayed and her greatest hopes had been proven. Suddenly and impulsively her body made up her mind for her in an instant. Her arms reached up to encircle his neck. Her hands were shaking and her mouth was dry. Her knees grew weaker as she drew him to her. Matt didn't want to do what he was about to do but only knew he was in no position to stop it. His own heart had betrayed him once more. He did love her. Not like Aretta, but love just the same. "Oh god! What am I doing! I can't do this, it's wrong!" his mind screamed as he closed his arms around her soft warm body and pulled her to him.

He had never touched her before and the feeling was magical! Matt could feel the soft contours of her supple and voluptuous body. The sweet smell of her warm breath mixed with the tantalizing scent of her musk oil cologne. Her lips felt like silk and her tongue was like a whisper as their mouths melted together in an earth shattering kiss. For a long moment he couldn't breathe or move. All his energy was focused and their mouths clung in limbo unmoving, savoring the warmth and softness of each other. Tonya began a slow motion of her head from side to side sucking his tongue with growing force and intensity. She had never been kissed and didn't quite know if what she was doing was right but it felt like it and Matt was responding to it. Matt inhaled deeply as he could feel a raw tension in his upper chest growing and straining his arms to do much more than hold her.

It had a sweet ache to it and he began running his fingers through her silky curls and down her tender back. She moaned in pleasure and returned his touch by grinding into him with her full and ample hips. "Oh Matt!" she thought. "Let me die now in your arms and don't let me wake from this feeling! . . . I can feel you inside me and all around me . . . why didn't you tell me you loved me before? . . . why does it have to be too late?" Suddenly their movements got hotter and more deliberate.

Matt was getting turned on now and his mind was mush. All he could feel was the intensity of her body and the love that sizzled within her for him. "Oh god help me" he screamed in his mind. "I can't do this . . . this aint right!" Just then they heard whispers in the distance and a long owl like report. "OOOOHHH . . . look at them two honey, they going at it!" said a female voice. Tonya slowed her kissing then slipped easily and painfully from Matt's lips. Her eyes still closed. She lay her head on his chest and looked at the small group that had dared to intrude on their solace. Matt didn't know why but he kept holding her and they just looked at the four girls and two boys that stood watching them. Finally one of them laughed and broke the silence. "Girl, now that's a man there!" she said flopping a limp wrist at them pointing and dropping onto her hip to exaggerate her point.

"He didn't even move or nothing and we're still standing here." "Girl friend you didn't know?" said another. "Hey, ain't that Tonya Rodgers? and Mathis?" "Yeah honey child." "OOHH . . . they too hot for me!" Matt just looked away from them, ignoring them then looked into Tonya's eyes. She returned his gaze with as much intensity and fire as he. Matt then placed his hand along side her cheek to let her know these guys don't matter. "Ooh girl look at this! . . . they just too damn hot for me."

"I wish I had a man like that" said another. Matt nor Tonya heard them, but just listened to the sound of their combined heartbeats. Matt eased his face close to hers and kissed her again lightly but intimately. "Oh girl I can't take any more of this!" said one girl. "I'm about to mess myself up!" she said smacking her knees together. By now Matt had heard enough and started to leave. "Come on, let's go Tonya" he said reaching down to pick up her book bag and taking her hand to leave. She just nodded deliriously enraptured at the whole affair and it showed on her face. The two walked out and the little crowd just parted on cue and let them pass. Soon they were in the hall heading for the doors.

As they stepped out they could feel the bright sunlight and smell of the sweet spring air. Matt lead Tonya over to a nearby bench away from the passing crowd. "Here take a seat" he said gently sitting her down. Tonya was still overwhelmed, happy and scared at the same time. She looked into his face as she sat trying to find some obvious evidence of how he was feeling. "Tonya what we just shared will never again be repeated, the love we expressed for our long suppressed desire will have no equal and I know now how much you truly love me and how much I care about you." Tonya's eyes went into rapid movements and began to sting. Her mind screamed "NO! STOP IT! DON'T SAY THIS!"

"If the circumstances and location were different I'm positive we would have been lovers long ago." She squeezed his hand but didn't speak. "You know how deeply I care for you now don't you Tonya?" she just nodded trying hard not to cry. "Then you must also know how much deeper it is for my girl Aretta" she nodded again. "Tonya I missed having you by two weeks baby, and I will always have to live with that!" "Does this mean we can never share love again Matt?" she asked pain and despair in her eyes. "I'm afraid so baby" he said looking down.

Tears began to fill her beautiful eyes and the storm of despair in her heart showed up in her face. She placed a trembling hand to her lips to suppress a sob. "Matt please don't take this from me, I've never known a love like this till now . . . don't send me back into the darkness of being alone . . . never to know true love or share it . . . stay with me! . . . I don't mind being second." "But I do Tonya!" he snapped at her. Not so much for trying, but for putting herself in the position of being an alternate to any man. "There's no possible way I could treat you as a stand by, you're more than that . . . you deserve more that that, you need one hundred percent of a man not half, some or a piece but all and I won't try to make you accept less!" "But you're not Matt!" She begged with tears flowing down her cheeks. "I want it this way, honest!"

By now some students had slowed down to see who was upset. Matt got up and grabbed her hand pulling her aside to the corner or cleft in the building wall, next to some tall hedges. Tonya just let herself be led.

"Look Tonya, I can't change the way I feel about you and I won't and just can't give into it either or return it to you." "But why Matt?" "Because I can't . . . I love Aretta too much and I'm sure you understand." She just buried her face in his chest and wept. He held her tightly as if the world was coming to an end. Tonya reached up and seized his neck and kissed him fiercely. Her mouth was sweet and salty with tears.

She moaned and cried with heart felt despair as she struggled to love him and to make him love her. Tonya took his hands and moved them lower on her body breathing heavily. Matt was apprehensive at this sudden change but just followed suit thinking it may help her get over him. After awhile she had managed to get his hand down and under her skirt and into her panties. The sudden feel of a foreign hand touching her there was a shock as well as an exquisite surprise. She squealed at the feel of it and her eyes rolled over with pleasure. Matt could feel her smooth pubic hairs and the moistness that had begun to form. She felt excruciatingly wonderful and Matt felt himself in that place that he'd been in several times this week. Tonya sucked in hard and froze as Matt glided a finger down and into her.

"SSS OH Mat!" She almost screamed with pleasure. She began kissing him wildly telling him to take her. Tonya was a virgin and had never experienced any of this, so it was all so very powerful for her to feel. This added to the anguish and pain she was mentally enduring at losing the very person who was opening up her world as well as her body and it made for one savagely intense moment.

"Take me Matt! Take me now I want you to be my first!" The words hit Matt like a brick to the chest. He had never for a moment thought he would be making love to her and most certainly not outside in a busy area like they were in! Now she was telling him that she was a virgin. Matt quickly pulled his hand from her leaving her scorched and very unsatisfied. "No!" he snapped coming to his senses for the fourth time this week and stepping away from her. "NO Tonya, I won't do this, not here, not anywhere . . . your not mine dammit! and you can't make me!" he said shaking his head wildly.

Tonya was stricken and wracked with pain. Her whole body burned for him and now it was suddenly cold and barren. Her face glowed with hurt and grief. "NO Tonya, I love you and I always will, but I won't take what isn't mine and please don't force me I'm only a man and I have a breaking point too!" She saw his expressed tension then looked down to see his manhood swelling. She started for him anew but Matt just bolted and ran from the bush. He grabbed his book bag and ran through the crowd then turned briefly to see her emerge from the bush. Tonya was still crying but trying to hide it. Matt ran all the way to the other building and into the gym across the street. "That's it!" he said yelling to no one in particular. "I'm outta here, just wait! I'm putting in a damn transfer, I can't take no more of this shit!" Tonya had recovered her books and walked back into the building. Her face and eyes were red from crying so she tried to get to the bathroom without being seen. She pushed through the door and ran for a sink to wash her face and hide her tears.

"Oh Matt, how could you leave me when I need you so, and why did I do that?" she thought still feeling his hand inside her. "I must have been crazy to think he would take me then an there! I know he must think I'm a real sleaze or even worse a whore!" "Oh Matt! I need you so much!" The tears would not quit, now they came in waves flowing and gushing forth completely blinding her. She didn't even try to hid them with water but just put her head down on her arm and sobbed on the sink.

The one or two girls that were there looked at her with remorse and pain. They didn't know what was the problem but figured it must be about a man cause only a man or a woman could make a person weep like that. They didn't know what to do, so they just quietly walked out and left her to herself.

Aretta was eating her lunch and for the first time in awhile she actually enjoyed it. She couldn't wait to get home so she could see her mother and Lori. She really missed them and wanted to be with them. She had been watching Perry Mason on television and learned to enjoy it these past few days, but still she was a devoted Young and the Restless fan. The doctor said she could leave anytime after 1:00 o'clock as long as someone came to get her.

Retta called her mother and told her she could leave today and Audrey said that she would come or send someone to get her. Just then the phone rang. "Hello?" "Hello . . . Retta?" "Yes this is she." "Well this is Mr. Mathis." "Oh, hi how are you?" "Fine and how about you kitten?" "Oh I'm good, I just got through eating lunch." "That's good, well the reason I'm calling is I have a few spare minutes and I can come get you if you like." "Oh thank you Mr. Mathis I'm ready!" she said excited. "Okay I'll be over there shortly." "Okay I'll be ready." Click!

"Well that takes care of that" she thought. "I wonder is he going to take me home or over to his house, I guess I ought to go home first but then again Matt would be so thrilled to see me when he get's home!" Ring! "Hello?" "Hello . . . Retta?" "Hi baby" "Hey . . . how's my girl?" "Fine! . . . I just got through talking to your dad." "Oh yeah? . . . what about?" "Oh nothing he was just checking up on me."

"Well that was nice . . . so you got a ride home?" "Yes, mom took care of it." "Okay then, . . . I was gonna come get you but that's cool, so when you leaving?" "In a little while." "I see" "Matt is anything wrong?" she asked detecting something amiss. "Uh no, nothing but the usual, and I've taken care of it." "Okay" "Well I gotta go Red, I'll see ya after school." "You don't have practice?" "Nope I'm off the team." "Oh Matt, why? . . . what happened?" "Didn't I tell you?" "No! . . . what?"

"Well me and Ant got advanced to the Varsity Team." "OH! Matt! I'm so proud of you!" "Thanks baby, it really wasn't much." "Oh yes it was!" she shot back. "My man is good at what he does and everybody else will soon find this out too!" "Well thanks poo, but we still gotta practice this weekend on our own and then on Monday with the team." "Well you'll do fine just be patient and believe in yourself." "Well as long as I got you baby it's no problem!" Retta blushed.

"Oh Matt, be careful of what you say dear, I'm not ill anymore and you and I have a date!" "Oh, I believe you alright and as your newly appointed doctor I have a prescription of my own for you!" "And that is?" "Large doses of love and affection for the rest of your life!" "What happens if I over dose?" "Well I guess we'll just have to pass it on to our children then." Retta started laughing. "Why Matt you old schemer you . . . I can't wait to get started!" "Me either." "Hey, it's the bell ringing babe, I gotta go, as soon as I go home and change I'll come see you okay?" "Okay Matt . . . I love you" "I love you too angel." Matt hung up the phone and ran back to gym class.

Everyone was engaged in some game or physical activity. He went to sit on the bleachers by himself to think. His mind was a mess and his soul was in pain. How would he make the transfer back to Southwest? Most of the time it had to be either up to the school of school board. If he went to them with his trivial problems they'd just laugh at him and get rid of him telling him to grow up and be a man. But he was a man and he was trying to deal with this like one. But seeing as he had never had this problem before he was ill advised as to what he should do about it! He'd already gotten rid of two problems but now had a third to contend with.

Most men would be flattered and boast about their many women and their sexual conquests but not Matt, he valued a woman's love and wouldn't dare trample on it to prove his manhood or how many he could sleep with. Sex just wasn't that important. Now that he had rejected and broken so many hearts his life began to unbalance and become a nightmare. He'd told them his true feelings and meant it. He never lied about love and ironically found himself not able to resist his heart when it found or was awakened by a love he never knew. The worst of it was he belonged to Retta and she to him but no-one seemed to be listening!

Oh why did he have to be such a late bloomer. Why did women reject him all his life, mock him, abuse him and even go so far as to call him ugly and taunt him, only to come back to him years later when he had matured and had grown into a fine young man. Then again he always was. And who should be the first to notice and take advantage of his love and devotion but Aretta. She was much the same social outcast as he, but when they found each other all those who had been so evil and conceited, cruel and hateful had to stop and see what they had all passed up. And now they regretted it!

No, Matt would not hurt or feel sorry for them. He had found his strength, his reason for living and the desire that burned hot in his soul for so long unquenched . . . it was and always will be Aretta. "Matt are you alright?" said a soft voice breaking him out of his mental journey. He saw that it was Paula Jenkins, a tall blonde with green eyes and breast too large for her frame. Still she was a nice girl.

"Yeah, I'm fine . . . Why do you ask?" "Oh, I just saw you sitting her alone and you looked troubled." "Yeah, well I had some things on my mind I needed to hash out . . . you know how it is." "Anything I can help with?" she offered sincerely. "Naw, that's okay sweet pea it's under control" he said raising her hands and placing a gentle kiss on them, thanking her for her concern.

She smiled flashing him her pearly whites. Paula had always thought of Matt as a gentleman. Someone she would be more than willing to go out with if she ever got the chance to. "Well you let me know if anything comes along that I can help with or that you could use a hand with okay? I'm here" "Thanks Paula . . . you're a peach." She smiled and turned to leave then stopped after remembering something she wanted to tell him.

"Oh by the way I was in the locker room before class and I heard some girls talking about you." "Oh what did they say?" "Well one of them was saying that her cousin got some stuff to use on you at some party and that she only needed to get one tablet to get the job done, does any of that mean anything to you, or make any sense Matt?" Matt thought for a quick second putting his face in his hands. Images of Cheryl and Melanie kept rolling around in his mind. "Only need one tablet . . . only need one . . . only . . . need . . . one, Snap!"

"I know what them heifers are up to now!" "What is who up to Mat?" "I'll tell you about it later Paula but thanks babe, you did me a real solid, I owe you a big one! Lunch anytime anywhere you want!" then he grabbed her by both arms and gave her a big resounding kiss on the lips SMOOCH! He then ran off to get Milton and Ant. "OOH Matt!" said Paula sitting down fanning herself. "You really know how to thank a girl don't you, I'll have to be sure to bring you more information from now on!"

Soon school was out for the week and Matt and Ant were on their way home. They didn't bother showering they just bagged up their clothes an split. Crowds of screaming yelling student flooded the side walk and the street between the two schools. Matt blew his little horn like crazy for them to clear the way. "Come on Matt take a short cut or something." "Where, there ain't no place to go, all these cars and people got this place more clogged up that a constipated duck with a cork in his butt!" "We'll just have to weed it out best we can." "Hey which way are we going anyway?" asked Ant. "My house or yours?" "Mine"

"Well then, go right and cut across the parking lot!" Matt steered his bike against the traffic and rode down the narrow strip between the sidewalk and the street. It was pretty shaky driving but a lot faster than the other way. Soon they were even with the driveway to the school. They let two cars pass then made a dash for it!

They drove up the driveway then up across the ball field to get to the parking lot in the rear of the school where they keep the buses. "Hey man you think we ought to push it up the hill?" "Why?" "Cause this ain't no jeep, besides look how steep it is!" "Aw quitter bitchin" said Matt then he reached down to flip the throttle control to max. The little bike picked up speed like a flash! They hit the hill at 30 miles an hour. "Whoa! Dude slow down!" protested Ant squeezing Matt tighter trying to hold on as best he could. Soon they popped over the blind hill and headed straight for a group of cheerleaders.

"EEEE!, LOOK OUT!" "Oh shit!" said Matt the girls screamed and scattered out of the way of the speeding scooter. Matt ran right through them and into the cement bay with the dumpster. This was usually overflowing with kitchen garbage. BAM! Matt crashed right into a tall pile of boxes that had bags of milk cartons, salad and a multitude of other kitchen trash from the day. It had sat in the sun all day and flies were all over it.

Ant had jumped from the bike just after he passed through the crowd of girls. He was tall enough to see what was ahead and knew Matt was going way too fast to stop in time. By now everyone had crowded around to see what had happened to him. "Hey Matt! . . . Matt!" he yelled looking in the trash bay but only seeing the rear wheel of his bike. The cheerleaders had eased closer to see also what had become of the mad biker. "OOH Yuck!" Said one girl holding her nose. "He's buried in there!" "Serves him right" said another. "He made me break a nail!" "Well ya'll get out the way so I can find him" said Ant.

At that same moment Matt's buddy from the kitchen showed up. He had also heard the crash but not the cause of it. "Look out Ant" he said going through the boxes, tossing them up on top of the dumpster. Soon he found a shoe then the rest of him materialized. "OH what a mess!" Said Gumbo. Matt was sitting sideways with his back against the side wall. "You alright Matt?" Matt eased himself upright and spit out a banana peel. "PTUI! . . . I will when you get this bike off me." He was covered in garbage from head to toe! There were stray vegetables in his hair and molded bread stuck to his shirt. His face was splattered with milk and something that looked like green slime! His buddy quickly got the moped up off of him and rolled it out to Ant then he reached in to get Matt.

"Whew! . . . damn Matt you stink!" he said smiling at him, glad he was not hurt. The crowd just laughed and held their noses. "Very funny, you want some of this salad?" he said pulling the goo from his hair. "Naw man I pass!" Ant was trying to suppress a giggle but couldn't. He burst out laughing at him. "Hey Matt you know what they say about people and food right?" He said between gasps for breath.

"You are what you eat!" Now everyone including his buddy Gumbo was tripping out on him now. Matt wasn't amused in the least but never was he without a rebuttal or a snappy come back either. "Your right Ant" he said smiling wide "Here have some!" he took a the gob of muck he had pulled from his hair and slung it hitting him square in the face and mouth. "Splat!" now the crowd was really beside themselves and were on the ground falling all over themselves, delirious with laughter.

They had never had a Friday quite like this and wouldn't soon forget. Matt walked off towards the garbage can area to use the hose on himself while Ant was busy wiping the muck form his face. "That dirty sonofabitch!" he growled then followed suit. Once they had gotten reasonably clean they set out for home again. "Man that was pretty fucked up what you did" said Ant. "Hey you shouldn't have been tripping on me so hard." "Well you was funny looking and you still stink!" "You want some more, I'm sure I can dig a little out of my shoe for you." "Naw! that's okay I'll pass." "I thought so!"

"So what you got planned tonight Matt?" "Man I'm going to my girls house, she's out of the hospital now?" "Yep and in perfect health!" "That's until you get a hold of her." "Hell you didn't know, man this week has been a nightmare!" "Every girl with a patch of hair on her crotch has been trying to bum rush me!" "Yeah I know . . . how do you fight back so easily?" "Who said it was easy?" "Man my dick gets hard when the wind blows!"

"So how you been handling it?" "With a lot of cold showers and awful thoughts." "Damn that gotta be rough . . . I couldn't have done it." "Oh I wouldn't say that." "Why?" "Have you had any sex this week?" "No" "Okay then, so how do you do it?" "That's my secret/" "Yeah I know, that's why you keep such a large stack of penthouse and hustler magazines under your bed right?" "So! I just look at them that's all." "Oh yeah, then how come the pages are stuck together in some of them?" "NO they're not!"

Ant protested aware he was losing the argument. Matt was laughing at him an Ant smacked him in the back of the head. Matt just laughed even more. "Don't' worry dude you'll be knee deep in it real soon." "Oh yeah . . . how you figure?" "Well now I know what Melanie and Cheryl got planned for me at the party." "So" "So the other part of the deal was if I beat them at their own game they gotta do what I say for a whole day!" "So what's that got to do with me?" "Don't you get it, I said "Anything!" I say" "Naw! they won't do that." "Oh won't they, have you forgotten about yesterday already?" "Oh, yeah your right!" "They was practically giving it up right then and there!"

"Hell I coulda got some yesterday you coochie pirate." "Why didn't you?" "Because, of you!" "Hey don't blame me, I got mine, you gotta get yours." "And what about when they came to your house, why didn't you get one of them then?" "They didn't want to, they said they had to go and couldn't stay." "Well there you have it in a nut shell." "Yeah I guess." Soon they were at the house and Matt drove down the driveway and parked. "Hey Matt did you leave your stereo on this morning?" "Not that I can remember." "Well there's somebody in your room." "Naw!" said Matt doubting it.

But as they got closer to the front he could hear some soft music playing. "Lets go look in the window" said Ant. They eased up beside the bushes and peeked into the window. "There's nobody in there." "I guess I did leave the stereo on after all, come on let's go in." They went around the front and into the house. Matt used his key to open his bedroom door. "Hey Ant hold up! There is somebody here . . . Look!" Matt said pointing at a pair of shoes buy the bed. "Those ain't yours?" he asked "Hell no! since when have you seen me in a size 6 . . . come on let's go see who it is."

They walked slowly through the house listening for any noises. Soon they heard some foot steps and some humming in the den. "Quick! Grab that plunger" he told Ant. He picked it up then slid beside the door. Matt grabbed his softball bat. Just then Aretta came through the door with a dish of cookies and some milk. Because the house was dimly lit and covered in late afternoon shadows of the trees, she couldn't see them nor them her until they were on top of each other. "Get em!" Yelled Ant "EEEE!" screamed Retta and dashed the milk in his eyes. She then instinctively kicked to her right catching Matt in the gut. "OOMPH!" he went down like the stock market, bat and all.

While Ant was trying to clear his eyes she turned and kicked him in the balls, sending him sprawling to the floor into the fetal position. Retta was about to deliver Matt another blow to the body when he rolled over and she caught a glimpse of his face as he rolled through the stream of sunlight.

"Matt! Oh my goodness! I didn't know it was you!" They just groaned and rolled around in a pool of milk and crushed cookies. "GROAN! No shit Retta, its good to see you too." She wanted to laugh at his comment but put it off till later. She reached down to help him up. Ant was still holding his crotch with milk all over his face. She reached down to help him up too. "Are you alright Ant?" she asked "What do you think!" "Nope."

"Come on, let me get you to the couch, I'm really sorry Ant" apologized Retta trying to help him up. "That's okay Retta, I always wanted to know what it felt like to have my balls pushed into my throat." Retta just giggled covering her mouth. Matt and Retta eased him onto the couch. "UGH! Easy!" "You'll be alright" said Matt laying him back on the couch then going to the bathroom to get a wet towel.

"Here put this on our stomach down low, it'll make it feel better." "Thanks" he said taking the towel and easing his pants down a little. "Ahh! That feels good." "So Retta what are you doing here?" asked Matt. "Your dad picked me up from the hospital on his break." "I thought you was going home from there?" "No, I asked could I come over here and wait till you got home and he said okay . . . I wanted to surprise you." "Well you did!" "Yeahhh, get em" groaned Ant mocking Matt's famous last words.

"Retta where in the world did you learn to be so quick and dangerous!" asked Ant. "Her pop was in special forces in the Army, she's been doing this for years now." "Oh yeah, shoot we got off easy man, you should've seen what she did to three guys at her school! a week ago!" "Oh Matt, come on" she said tugging his arm.

"You're a lucky man Matt, not only is your girl smart and beautiful, she's a ninja too!" "Aww I'm no ninja, but thanks for the compliment though." "So Matt, I guess you won't be going anywhere after all, seeing as how she's already here." Matt just looked at her and smiled. "No I guess not . . . come here shorty I wanna smooch" he said grabbing her by the waist and pulling her to him.

She came more than willingly and their lips melted together in a sweet and playful kiss. Retta reached for his hair to run her fingers through it. "Ugh! Matt, what is in your hair?" she said pulling back in disgust. "Oh I had a little accident on the way home from school." "Little accident my eye!" said Ant sarcastically. "Ole Evil Keneval here was riding up the hill behind the gym and as we got to the top he broke through a crowd of cheerleaders practicing and into a dumpster!" "Oh my goodness Matt were you hurt . . . are you alright Baby?" "Yeah I'm cool I just smell bad that's all." "I have to agree with you there sweetie, you are kinda ripe!" she said holding her nose.

"Okay I get the message, let me get some clothes out and I'll go take a shower." "Never mind that mister, I'll take care of that you just go get in the shower." "Okay babe." "Well I'm much better now" said Ant getting to his feet. "And I need to go get washed up myself." "Well you could wash up here and change into some of my stuff" offered Matt. "Naw that's okay, I'll wanna crash and get some sleep right after but I will us the sink though so I can wash off this messy milk and cookie crumbs."

"Alright then, tell you what, why don't you take the bike with you, I'll just pick it up later okay?" "Okay then." "And don't forget . . ." "I know, I know, put some gas in it" "You got it." "Well I'm gonna go clean up the mess in there while you two do whatever." "Alright Red" said Matt watching her walk off towards the kitchen. They both watched her walk off. She was so pristine and voluptuous with her long flowing black hair. "Man you got it going on! Matt!"

he said slapping his shoulder. "So I see, now to keep it that way." "What do you mean?" "Well I've been thinking about maybe getting a transfer next year to her school."

"Why . . . what's wrong with Central?" "Nothing really, I'm just sick of getting bum rushed by women all the time." "Well you have to control that my man." "Yeah I know, but just when you get rid of one, two more pop up and it get's more difficult each time." "Who's after you now?" "Tonya Rodgers" "Naw! . . . you bull shittin." "I wish I were, she pushed up on me today big time and I couldn't resist her Ant." "I'll bet, she's a hard one to forget, but why you and why now?" "Well it seems she and I have had a long standing slow burn for each other for quite some time, ever since I transferred back from Ballard Hudson, problem is that by then I had already started dating Aretta."

"Man talk about bad timing" said Ant shaking his head. "Yeah and that's not all, she also tried to get me to do her outside in front of the girls school in the bushes." "Naw man!" "Yes!, and I'll tell you what else, you know how soft and curly her hair looks?" "Yeah" "Well it's the same downstairs only shorter and straighter, and let me tell you she's plump and juicy too!" "Naw! you didn't?" "No I didn't, but she rammed my hand up her skirt, into her panties and up her crack." "So she's hot huh?" "No . . . a virgin."

"Damn Matt! I wish I had your problems" he said laughing. "You can have them, I'm tired of running from em, one day I may not be able to!" "Hell, even Paula is giving me the eye now." "Paula, the tall blonde chick in our gym class?" "Yep" "It's worse than I thought, hell Milton could take lessons from you studdly."

"Forget it man, one dog on campus is enough and I'm not out to get fleas or do any body sniffing." Ant just laughed at the thought of all that. Just then he heard some footsteps in the hall. "Shh! its you know who." "So Matt let me go wash up so I can go, I need to get some rest so I can prowl tonight myself." "Alright then." "Matt, why do you hang your mop so high on the roof?" asked Retta. "It's not high, you're just short" he said grinning at her. "Yeah but you like it though don't you lover boy?" "Hey you didn't know?" "Well let me get this mess up before it dries any further."

"Okay babe." Soon Ant was out of the bathroom. "Thanks Matt, ya'll be good and I'll see ya'll later." "Okay Ant, give me a call later and we'll work on our plan for our little problem children" he said winking. "Okay that'll work." With all that being said Matt jumped in the shower.

The water felt great! As it sprayed all over him and massaged his body all over. He stood leaning against the wall and let the water just bathe his head and flow down his face and back. He marveled at how no matter how warm the water was it was always a little warmer coming off his head. He didn't understand this but didn't really care either and just welcomed the difference. He began to hear the faint sound of music playing in the distance. It was a soft slow love song. One of his and Retta's favorites. He just closed his eyes and let the thick steam fill his nostrils and warm him from within.

The bathroom was filled with a thick white blanket of steam and Matt couldn't see anything. Just then he heard a tiny squeak of the door then a pronounced click of the door lock. He opened his eyes and saw Retta slowly pulling back the shower curtain. Oh how enchanting she looked standing there in the thick mist all nude and seductive. She had a serious but prim smile on her face and the look of passion in her eyes. She didn't speak but just stepped into the stall an closed the curtain.

The scene took on the visual aspects of a medieval forest in the morning. The sun reached down it's fingers of light into the dense dark green shire to bathe and illuminate the forest floor with it's eldritch glow and bring life and passion to all within it. Retta was a princess and Matt was her secret lover in knight's livery, who would always meet with her in the dense forest at dawn. The water flowed down her long black tresses turning them a deep ebony color and pressing them on her neck and shoulders. The miniscule beam of light that penetrated through the window was just enough to highlight the glistening droplets of water that played about her firm and soft breasts.

Matt looked at her for a long moment and didn't move. He just drank in her beauty and the sensuality of the moment. Slowly she reached out to cradle his face in her hands. He looked so strong and virile she thought as she slowly glided her hands down his chest and stomach. His body was a Greek sculpture of flowing muscles sinew. The steam of the shower gave his body a tantalizing and intoxicating aura. Matt's legs, she thought were powerful and firm. She could feel herself melt from within as she saw his arousal beginning to peak. He had the most perfect triangular upper body and his waist blended smoothly into his chest forming as perfect "V" shape.

Aretta could feel her own desire building with each second as the water teased and pricked at her blossoming nipples. A delicious tingle ran though her and made her whole body tremble. The thick steam was making her heady and lusty as her body began aching sweetly with the yearning and want of Matt's touch. She pulled him to her then took her tongue and encircled his lips, teasing them, penetrating them.

Their mouths were like two infernos as they hungrily fed on each other, sucking and pulling at each others tongues in a sensual game of tag. The taste of her mouth and the water mixed together to give a strange and wonderful taste Matt thought as he relished each and every kiss. A fire began to build between them as he wrapped her soft wet body in his arms and pulled her closer to him.

Retta moaned with pleasure at the feel of his hard ribbed stomach against hers. Matt worked his hands slowly all over her body from head to toe, searching, feeling and enjoying every inch of her. He allowed his finger tips to explore into the deep crevice of her sublime and shapely bottom. He could feel the soft and curly hairs that taunted him to explore further. Matt's hand began to tremble with excitement and eagerness to touch her. He slowly eased the tip of his middle finger into her sensuous folds and swooned as he relished the soft velvety warmth of her. Retta froze with excitement at this sudden but sweet intrusion of her secret most place. It was such a devastating feeling she moaned and pushed into it driving it even deeper into herself. Now Matt was thoroughly excited and encouraged!

The hot water pattered down his back rhythmically driving him, massaging him and aggravating his manhood as the water cascaded down his back, in between his buttocks and off his testicles. The mixture of the sound of the shower and the music in the distance did excruciating and wonderful things to his mind. His manhood grew with the speed and consistency of an electric car antennae, straining, pulling and reaching out from deep within him. Matt had to have her now!

All week he had been challenged, tested and harassed to complete soreness. Now he would be satisfied, now he had his love before him, open, ready and willing to bond with him spiritually and physically, without any interruptions or doubts! Retta felt the power and desire welling up in Matt and his body grew ever tense and hard against her. The feeling was erotic and filled with wanting. She could feel his manhood all long and hot pressing against her and it felt incredible. She thought as it seemed to grow longer with each passing second, reaching out to her, begging her to save it's life.

She reached down and gently cradled it in her hand. She cupped it and stroked it from end to end, feeling the firm but soft strength within it. As she caressed the end of if she was happily surprised to see it involuntarily jerk in reaction to her touch. This excited her something terrible and her eyes grew wide as her own body responded by getting even wetter where it was needed. Retta began to swoon and raised her leg slightly to allow the hungry intruder to pass between them unimpeded. As she did this it took on the sultry feel or familiarity of straddling a bicycle seat. She reveled in the pressure it created by pressing into her and dividing her there. Matt thought he was gonna pop as the feel of Retta straddling his manhood was like lightning and it went right through him and into his already sore penis.

He felt suffused with a rigid strength and power that was almost foreign to him. His body was his but not. He felt himself grow heavy in his chest as his muscles seemed to expand and take over. Matt power lifted Retta under her arms up to eye level in one move. The move was so exciting and unexpected she sighed almost screaming as she wrapped her legs hungrily around his waist and locking them.

Matt then painstakingly and slowly eased her down upon his enflamed manhood. At first contact Retta whimpered slightly at the pleasure of it as it sent waves though her and made her instantly greedy with want. She drove herself downward onto him and moaned with delight. Matt just held onto her squeezing her well rounded bottom as if he was trying to juice them like an orange. He felt spasm after spasm radiate from his shaft. He didn't want to go just like that and knew he was at the door. Retta sought his neck and face covering him in kisses, suckling and feeding on his neck and chest with great zeal!

Matt now under control began a long slow drive raising her up and sliding her down as smoothly as riding an elevator. Retta was so into the feel of him that she began to lose herself. She threw her head back, leaning slightly away from him and gave herself up to his strength, passion, and control. The spray of water cascaded all over her face and hair. Every droplet sending electric pleasure through her as Matt drove and rotated her body around his penis with machine like control.

He initially wanted to just pile drive into her with all the power and lust he felt. A hunger built up over the last seven days. But being who Matt was he was thinking of her and not wanting to bring discomfort or hurt to the woman he loved by being so arcane. Seeing now that she was so very into him and moved with total abandon, he began to increase his movements to keep up with his mounting desire. He drove into her deeper and with more energy than before. Retta moaned and tightened her legs around him, she was happily impressed at his strength and control of her, and how easily he could hold her and manipulate her body with such mastery. She lazily opened her eyes for a brief second to look at his face. She could see the passion and strained pleasure she was giving him on his face and it made her go carnal. She raised herself back into his embrace locking her arms around his neck again. Then to Matt's surprise she eased her heels behind his knees and began to drive against him and apply even more down pressure on his manhood. The new feeling and pressure was exquisite and Matt's eyes popped open as he moaned from the feel of it. "OH baby . . . what is that?" he whispered, straining to keep up. "I thought you might like that lover, I learned it in a book I read."

"SSSS damn! I need to read more!" he sighed with pleasure. Retta did this for a while feeling a vibration and tingle generate through her like electricity. Matt was getting there too and maneuvered her back into their former position for maximum penetration. Matt drove now like a mad man looking for oil. He suckled both of her breasts making her react wildly as she tried to bury his head in her chest.

Finally he could feel that old familiar feeling dragging slowly up from his toes through his legs, up his buttocks and into his crotch. His toes locked, his ass froze in a painful grip and his back and upper torso refused to move. The only thing that would was his arms which even though were painfully strained by now and hurt with a sweet fire, worked even faster. Pumping her faster and with a greater intensity. Retta knew this feeling and was gaining on him with her own pulsing contractions.

"AHHH! SSSS AAAHHH!" "Retta! . . . OOH . . . RET . . . TA! . . . I'm cumming baby . . . oooh! I'm cumming!" he cried squeezing her bottom so tight he could swear he had juiced her some. "Yes! Matt give it to me . . . give me all of it baby!" Burst after burst from Matt went into her and she luxuriated each one putting her fingers in her mouth sucking them as the searing pleasure continued.

Each crash and explosion left her warm all over and feeling every part of him. She could taste him, smell him and feel him everywhere in her body. Retta seized up during Matt's climax and began her own with ferocity. Matt felt her seize around his member and begin a crescendo of contractions over and over again. "OHHH MATT! OHH MATT! OHH . . . OHHH!" she went then finally spent, collapsed onto him. She lay slumped over his shoulder, legs totally rubber, sliding from his waist.

Matt just held her and slowly crumpled to the floor of the shower with her on top of him. "Wow!" was all he could manage and just lay there as the water continued to bathe them and give witness to the most exotic, wild and exciting love making session they had ever experienced to date.

By now the water had gotten luke warm, but they didn't notice it. Cause their bodies were still thrumming radiation with thousand degree heat. Matt could no longer feel his arms and his back had long since locked out. Retta just slumped in his arms with her legs barely around him. "Matt . . . we gotta go baby" she whispered, her arms dangling loosely with her face against his chest. "I know baby" he said weakly. "Can you stand?" "I don't know I'll try" she said, then unlocked her legs and eased away from him against the shower wall. They stood up and showered, washing each other slowly, totally satisfied. Matt toweled them both off and carried her to the bedroom to dress. "Matt I wish we didn't have to get dressed, I want to lie next to you naked and sleep baby."

"Me too poo, but this isn't the place and dad will be home shortly, it wouldn't look good for us to be caught this way." "Do you think they know about our lovemaking?" she asked. "I wouldn't doubt it, but still we can't openly let them see it . . . they'd kill us!" Retta grinned at the idea, but agreed it would be fatal to be caught this way. "Soon we'll have a place to ourselves and we won't need to worry or be afraid to express our love openly, run around the house totally naked and make love all day!"

"OOH Matt that sounds delicious, when do we start?" "Cool your burners Davis, we ain't got there yet." "That's Mathis to you mister" she said poking him in the stomach. Soon they were dressed and just lay out on the bed. Retta felt wonderful on top of him and soon they both were fast asleep in each others arms. After awhile Matt awoke to the rumbling sound of a truck going down the driveway.

He looked at his clock and saw that it was 5:00 o'clock. "Retta" he said speaking softly and kissing her lightly on the temple. "Mmmm, what Matt?"

she said purring and rolling over to face him. "It's time to get up baby, pops just came home." Retta just moaned but didn't move. "Come on poo, we gotta get up before he gets in the house." She lay a bit longer, then finally she raised up on her elbows with sleepy eyes. "I'll get you for this" she said tonelessly then kissed him.

"Come on then" she said getting up and pulling him along. They shuffled into the kitchen and met him at the door. "Hiddey hoe you two." "Hello Mr. Mathis . . ." "Hi pop." "So what have you two been up to?" "Oh nothing much just lounging around sleeping mostly" said Matt yawning. "Well that's good I guess" he said not pushing it more. "How was practice today?" "I'm . . ." "Let me tell him!" said Retta cutting him off covering his mouth. "He's not on the track team anymore." "He's not, how's that?" "He got promoted to the Varsity Team! Yesterday, him and Anthony." His dad let out a wide grin and laughed heartily.

"Well I'll be jiggered, I'm proud of you son! I knew you had it in you and now so do you!" Matt just bowed his head and smiled bashfully. "Yeah, but I still got work to do, the hard part is on Monday with the Varsity Team, they're a good bunch." "Well don't sell yourself short, you and your brothers have always been exceptional in sports and with hard work you can be as good as you want to be." "So tell me, what do you two have planned this evening?" he said changing the subject.

"I really hadn't planned anything." "What about you Retta?" "Huh uh" "Well that's good then, and since you two don't have anything to do this evening you won't mind looking after Lori for a few hours, me and Audrey want to go out for awhile." "Okay, where do you want us to watch her?" "It doesn't matter, either here or there if you wish."

"HERE!" chirped Aretta before Matt could answer. "Okay, then it's settled, when I go to pick them up I'll drop her by here on the way out." "Okay dad." Retta grabbed his hand and quickly moved out of the kitchen towards the den. "Matt! this is so perfect!" she said hugging him and jumping up and down. "Now we have all day and most of the night together!" "Yeah, but what about Lori, won't she get in the way?"

"Naw! one thing about her is if you feed her enough she just goes to sleep so don't worry, I can handle her." "Okay then." "Don't forget I still have to get even with you for the 4 times you made me orgasm today."

Matt just blushed and smiled. "Four times?" "That's right mister and I can't let you get away with that" she said pulling him into the bedroom and kissing him fiercely to show her conviction. "Well maybe you'll get your chance little rabbit" he said picking her up and placing her on the bed. "Oh no you don't Matt, I'm not that easy, and we're not alone, so you can just put it on ice mister."

"Okay, okay, I'll wait, lets' go down the street and play some games for awhile" he offered. "Naa, that's okay, I'd rather just sit outside and relax on the porch, come with me okay?" "Okay" he said then led her out the bedroom door to the front porch. Meanwhile, Buford was just getting settled in the shower, it had been a long day, he was tired but felt ready to go again anyway.

This would be his first date in many years and he wanted to make the most of it. He had made reservations for two at Cag's, a really nice two star restaurant down Vineville Avenue not far from the college. It was going to be nice but then Audrey had told him that her best friend who she hadn't seen since high school and her date would like to join them for dinner, so he had to make it for four. Of course they would go Dutch! He hummed as he soaped up and bathed vigorously.

The hot shower was a balm to his sore and tired muscles. He wished he could buy himself a hot tub or a Jacuzzi but just now he had neither the money nor the space to put one. One day he would though, it would just take some time.

Audrey was busy doing her own bathing and she had filled the tub with hot bubble bath and softener's, she wanted to be as soft and sexy as she could be. She'd had a feeling about tonight and wasn't about to take anything for granted. The hot and soothing bubble bath was so inviting. She covered herself up to her neck and just lay there slowly messaging herself under that water. Audrey caressed her skin and it was smooth and soft all over. It had been a long time since she pampered herself or allowed herself to be pampered.

As she lightly ran the sponge over her skin she couldn't help but remember how familiar and good it felt to be soft and be touched. She ran her hand all over massaging her arms, chest, legs, and neck. The velvety way her legs felt as she rubbed them together in the water had a sweet and naughty feel to it. She let her hand slide below the bubbles and caressed them sensually, raising each one up high and gliding her fingers down the length of each one all the way to her even softer ample bottom.

As he did this she noticed her hand getting closer and closer to much more delicate areas between them. When she got closer and touched herself with the palm of her hand it excited her, making her blush with embarrassment at the exquisite feel of touching herself there. For a brief second she felt a little ashamed and thought it something a young school girl would do but then again who was she to judge anyone.

And besides it was her body and she deserved to feel wonderful too, so she just closed her eyes and let the bubbles fall where they may. Audrey began her decent into ecstasy by slowly opening and closing her legs letting the water churn in and out between them. "Oh! My!" she whispered as the water jet between her legs, lightly tickling her feminine fancy. She did this over and over again driving herself wilder and wilder as she went. She added to the waters pressure a little help with her hands.

She eased them slowly but purposefully down between her legs and let her fingers do the walking. The shock was like lightning when she touched herself on the button and she bucked hard throwing her head back and splashing water out of the tube. "Oh god! Oh! Yesss!" she whispered, her breathing coming deeper and harder. She did it even harder the second time and the effect was even greater. Audrey was well on her way to an earth shattering personal intimate experience. The only problem was she forgot how very slippery the bath beads really were and the sides of the tube. She stroked herself one last time and immediately lost her footing and disappeared beneath the bubbles entirely. "OOH! MY Goodness! . . . PPPBBBLT! she came up sputtering water and face covered in soap bubbles. She looked like a pink Santa Clause. She sputtered trying to clear her throat of the small amount of water that had gotten in. "Serves you right Audrey for acting like a love sick school girl in heat!" she said chastising herself as she sputtered and spit out the soapy, oily water.

"My goodness Audrey you act like he was the last man on earth and you haven't had any for eons! Liz was right you are in heat and should be spayed." She wiped her face with a nearby towel and got on to the business of bathing. Soon she was done. She got out of the tub and went into her room to towel off. Since there was no one else there she didn't bother wrapping the towel around herself. She stood in front of her full length vanity mirror while drying off. As she did this she became acutely aware of herself and stopped toweling. She stood up slowly and admired every curve an crevice with renewed interest like she had not seen herself in years. Audrey's breasts were full and tight and were almost perfect orbs. Her nipples were small brown chocolate kisses and she had a very provocative "V" shaped torso which blended nicely with her flat stomach and shapely hips.

Her legs were slender and voluptuous. She placed a hand on her tummy and one on her lower back to straighten her posture. As she did this she simultaneously made a half turn to the side so she could look at her rear end. It had a nice gradual outward slope and rounded nicely as it blended with her legs. She turned all the way around to get a full view. Each cheek was nice and full with a rigid but soft firmness to it. She smiled to herself as she admired the way each tapered out to expose a little glimpse of her secret most place of pleasure. She gave herself a teasing smack on the rear and laughed as she did a girlish twist and spread her legs then bent over to see her rear in the mirror at an inverted view.

She didn't know why she was behaving so, but enjoyed the freedom of it all the same. She stood and faced the mirror to look upon herself one last time then saw that her nice neat little bundle of womanhood was untamed and could use a touch up. It looked to be a bit nappy and over grown by her inspection. She went into her closet and fished around in some shoe boxes. "Now where did

Butler put that mustache trimmer?" she said to herself. "Ah! here it is, I've got it" she said finding it in a box in the rear of the shelf.

She flipped the switch to see if it still worked. The little appliance hummed with restored life. "Now how should I do this?" she thought. "Do I want to taper it, trim it, style it, or just cut it all off?" "I know, I'll do them all!" She picked up a small brush from the table and sat on her bed and began to tame her shrew. She stopped then thought about it and decided to stand up placing a foot on a chair instead. Once she was done with the remake on her sensual mound she stood in front of the mirror once again, she had tapered the outer ends into a very neat oval shape then trimmed it down to just barely outside her vaginal lips. She thought it was a pretty neat job not ever having to do this before.

"Audrey you are HOT!" she said then blew herself a kiss and went over to her bed to get dressed. First she put on a sexy peach colored teddy with little tiny roses all over and lace. Then she took out her sheerest flesh tone silk stockings and waist strap. She placed one foot on the bed and slowly worked it all the way up her thigh to secure it in front and back, then she did the same for the other. Once she had done this she stopped and remembered that she hadn't put on her all over body spray. She sighed with impatience for her absent mindedness then quickly pulled down her teddy to her feet and applied the spray. She put on Malibu Musk. One of her favorite scents. Once done she quickly put back on her teddy because she still had much to do before she was ready and time was running.

Back at Matt's house, he and Aretta were walking around the block holding hands and holding each other as they walked. The evening air was nice and breezy with a warm tint to it. The trees swayed ever so slightly as the gentle wind played touch and go from top to top. By now the sun had gone down to where it looked like a half an orange in the sky. The scene from where they stood was a breath taking sight.

The sky was a shocking Caribbean blue with billowy cotton ball clouds drifting here and there. The horizon was a combination of tropical orange and red explosions of color that seemed to radiate from the ground somewhere at the end of the earth. They could see children playing in the field and older people on their porches talking. Matt nor Retta had spoken or said anything since beginning their walk. They had just been content to be in each other's company an holding the other close. If there was any speaking to be done it would be done by their hearts. "Have you ever thought about what our kids would look like Retta?" asked Matt breaking the silence. "Hmm . . . that's a thought" she said looking off into space as if the clouds would show her. "Well women have been dominant in my family and from what I can see men in yours, I guess it would be a test of genes and who's is stronger."

"We could have one of each if you like." "Twins?" "Why not?" "Cause it's not your butt that will be stretched like a balloon! that's why not" she said in mock anger. "So you don't want to have any at all then?" "Of course I do silly, I was just kidding you baby, you know how much I want to have your baby Matt" she said looking up at him with complete sincerity. "No not really, we never spoke on it before now."

"Well I do, in fact if you really want me to, I would have one with you right now . . . I mean get pregnant if you really wanted me to." Matt stopped her there and turned her to him. He looked deep into her eyes as he held her shoulders gently. "You would do that for me Retta?" She looked at him in the most solemn way Matt had ever seen her. "Yes Matt, I love you . . . and do you know what that means?" "Yes baby I know." "I don't really think so" she said searching his eyes and placing his hand on her heart. "Do you feel that Matt, can you feel my heart beating for you?"

Matt just nodded a little overwhelmed by her conviction. "Let me tell you what it means to me Matt, it means that you are the most important thing in my entire life, there is no one above you but God and nobody can say or do anything to take me from you." "It means giving up all I have so you can have, it means wanting to wake up every morning beside you, going to bed with you at night and loving you with all I got inside me!" "In short Matt, it means giving my life for you if necessary my love . . . . that's what true love means to me Matt, is it the same for you, is that how you feel?"

Matt just looked at her as if seeing her for the very first time. His mouth was dry and he swallowed hard to check a tear. He gently placed his hand on her cheek and nodded. "Yes I do Retta . . . I do and then some." She smiled at him brightly and reached up to hold his hand to her face. She drew him to her and whispered his name. "Rodney Wendell Mathis, I love you with all my heart and soul for the rest of my life, I want you to know that no matter where we are or whatever we do I will love you forever." "If you ask me at any time or place to have your child now or later I would bare myself to all and make love to you right then and there in the strongest most loving and devoted way I know how and give you your wish." He pulled her to him and kissed her passionately.

They held each other as though time had ended. Matt kissed her for all he was worth and it didn't matter that they were around others. They didn't care, they were the only people that mattered. Soon the sun had gone down and the first stars of evening had appeared so they started for home. For them this day would not be soon forgotten but instead relished and savored forever.

Audrey was just putting on the final touches of her makeup. "There! Now that looks fine" she stood back and looked herself over. She wore a long satin evening gown that had spaghetti strings on the shoulder with a low flowing back. The waist was well defined and the bottom flared slightly in a scarf like manner. It was bone white and she wore her matching heels to go with it. Audrey's hair was styled in a French fashion.

It was a simple yet elegant style with small tresses coming down her temples and a high mounted curled ponytail. She looked gorgeous the way the white dress was accented by her honey colored skin. "Lori are you ready yet sweetie?" "Yes ma'am." "Okay Buford will be here soon, and don't forget to pack you overnight bag and Aretta's just in case you guy's wind up staying over night, okay?" "Okay mama." "Lori, come here a second sweetie."

"Yes ma'am" she said dropping her bag on the bed and coming around the to her mothers room. "Yes momma?" Audrey turned around dramatically. "Tell me how does mamma look?" Lori grinned bashfully and swayed from side to side wringing her fingers. "You look pretty momma, like a princess." "Oh, thank you sweet heart!"

"That's the nicest thing anyone has ever said." She then reached down to give her a big hug. "OOOH! You're so precious!" Lori was filled with joy as she gave her mother a big hug and a kiss. "You are too momma!" Audrey just laughed, "Okay pumpkin lets go finish getting ready."

Lori skipped back to her room feeling light as a feather. She went through Aretta's drawers and pulled out a long pink night gown and a pair of footy pajamas. Then she grabbed her some socks, underwear and a bra.

"Now that takes care of that" she said stuffing the items in her bag. "Oh yeah . . . clothes! . . . she gotta have clothes for tomorrow if we stay silly" she said to herself. Lori went back to the closet and pulled out a red polo shirt off the hanger and pair of jeans. Then she grabbed Retta's blue Docksiders. She carefully rolled it all up and put it in Aretta's bag. "I'm done momma!" she called to her. "Okay baby just put them by the door." "Alrighty!"

Aretta and Matt were in the kitchen preparing dinner. Buford had gotten dressed long ago and was making calls to recheck his reservations. "Rodney, Retta?" "Yes dad?" "Could you two come in here for a minute please." "I wonder what's up" said Matt. "He sounds serious."

"I don't know, let's go find out" said Retta cleaning her hands on a towel. They took the shortcut, went through the pantry into his office, and opened the double French doors to his room. "Yes sir?"

He was standing near the fireplace with a hand in his pocket. He looked sharp and debonair. He was wearing his smoke grey double-breasted sport coat and white pleated slacks with a black short sleeve shirt buttoned at the collar. He also wore his white Stacy Adams shoes. "Sit down for a second will you, I want to have a chat with you." Matt and Retta eased down on the couch and sat up rigid as if awaiting a drill order.

"I've been meaning to have this talk with you two for quite sometime but I've been so busy and you guys have been elsewhere." "Now you two have been going together for quite some time and I can see that you are quite fond of each other, I'm glad to see that, it's always good for two people who feel that way to be together."

"My main concern is your level of self control and discretion." Matt was beginning to feel a little raw and exposed. He began to feel quite transparent and his ears began to ring for some unknown reason. Aretta was just as apprehensive given they had not too long ago literally burned down the very bathroom he had just taken a shower in.

"Audrey has informed me of some of your activities in public, she said she caught you two in a lip lock in the main deck of the mall, is that true?" "Yes sir" they both admitted. Wringing their hands and looking down and their feet somewhat ashamed. "Come on Rodney you can do better than that!" he chastised. Matt just shrugged. "I know you love Retta but you don't have to broadcast it so blatantly!"

"And you Retta, he said shifting the torch. Looking straight at her. She sprang up right in her seat. "Yes sir!" "Discretion and self control has always been the hallmark of a woman's character, you get me?" "Yes sir" she said nodding in agreement.

"When Rodney gets beside himself with you in public pop him in the chops, he'll get the message." Retta looked at Matt and smiled thinking of how that would look. Matt thought it was a little funny himself and gave up a weak smile. "My reasons for having this little chat isn't to chastise you two because I know you're being as discreet as your ages will allow."

"What I want you to do for me is watch yourselves around Lori, she's still a baby and doesn't quite understand what she sees at times, if she were to catch you two doing anything at all she may want to try it with some of her friends and that just wouldn't work out . . . do you understand?"

"Yes sir!" "Okay good, now me and Audrey will be out for a couple of hours and I know and trust you two to handle things while were out." "Retta you're in charge of the house and all that takes place in it, it's your responsibility, can you handle it?" "Yes sir!" "Rodney!" "Yes Sir" "You're in charge of security and handling all the emergencies, here is the number to where we will be if you need us, if anything really serious happens, which it shouldn't, I'm intrusting you two to use the truck but only in an emergency."

"Yes Sir" "Okay good, now how do I look?" "Very handsome" said Retta "Real slammin dad!" "Slammin?" he repeated with a twisted brow. "Okay I'll take that." He reached into his back coat pocket and pulled out his wallet. "Okay here's $50 dollars for you two, you can go and buy some junk food or whatever" he said giving the money to Matt. "Give five dollars of that to Lori, it's good for her to have some mad money of her own sometimes." "What are you two gonna do tonight?" "Well you know me, movies, ice cream, comic books and bed." "Okay, that sounds like a plan, by the way Retta, if you and your sister get sleepy you can come crash on my bed or on Rodney's, he can sleep on the couch" he said grinning at him.

"Aw dad!" "Aw nothing boy, be a gentleman, how do you expect Retta to appreciate you if you don't." "Yeah Matt!" she added hugging up next to his dad. "See what I mean?" He gave her a light squeeze and a kiss on the top of the head. "Well I gotta go, you two be good and I'll be back with Lori in a few shakes." "Okay dad" they said as he walked out. The pair exhaled loudly once the front door closed.

"Whew! Boy can your dad lay down the law! For a minute I thought I was seeing my own father." "Yep, that's dad . . . firm but fair, strict but flexible." "Yeah gone but not forgotten" she added laughing wildly. "Well what do we do now?" asked Matt. "Well since I'm in charge of the house, I say let's finish the dinner we started." "That'll work." Retta and Matt had begun a chicken dinner.

Aretta was making Chicken Parmesan with broccoli and cheese sauce and Au Gratin potatoes. So far they had the chicken set and ready to put in the oven. Now they just had to work on the vegetables. Matt was busy cutting up the potatoes in small round disks, while Retta was making her cheese sauce for them and the broccoli. "This is nice" he said looking over at her working with the large plastic bowl. "What's that Puddin?" "This, us, being together in the kitchen cooking." "You like this kind of thing Matt?" "Yeah, it's nice and cozy, I hope we get to do this more often when we're alone in our own place someday." "Oh Matt that's sweet, I didn't know you enjoyed being together this way." "I think it's mostly because of you baby . . . you make it fun."

"Matt your gonna make me cry if you keep on spoiling me like this" she said putting down her bowl and coming to hug him. "Well it's true baby, I mean look at us, here we are, me almost eighteen and you almost sixteen and were already responsible people!" "All we need is good jobs and our own place and we're set!" "Matt you make it sound so easy." "Well to a point it is, look at us were reasonably intelligent and are goal oriented, all we need is a skill and we're good to go!"

"Well I guess when you put it that way it does seem pretty simple." "You better believe it!" "Hey Matt, what are we gonna do for the summer, it's not so far away you know?" "Yeah, graduation is only a short time away." "Probably spend it here, I never go anywhere other than Lake Tobosofkee or Six Flags." "Well I guess we'll come up with something" she said letting go of him and returning to her bowl. "Are you done with those potatoes yet Matt?" "Yeah, here you go."

"Thank you" she said taking them from him and placing them in the Casserole dish. Retta put the food in the oven and set it on a medium setting to bake. "Come on Matt, let's go relax and watch some television till Lori gets here." "The food should be mostly done by then." "Okay lead the way." It's really nice being able to spend some quality time with Retta, thought Matt as he followed her to the den. The distance between them was difficult to deal with sometimes which made having his little scooter a God send. Retta really hated it when the city re-evaluated the zone change, forcing Matt to go back to Central or his dad would face some strange tax increase of some sort.

The change for Matt was no party either, but they managed to deal with it and keep their relationship strong. Matt sat on the couch laying towards one end and Retta laid between his legs with her head on his chest. Matt enjoyed having her there this way. It was really comfortable and cozy. He slowly rubbed her soft back and caressed her head, stroking it from top to bottom. Her hair felt like silk and he loved playing with it. Retta just sighed long enjoying the whole experience of being there with him this way and the wonderful feel of his hands on her body. She hungered so much for his touch and relished each and every one. She just lost her self in his caress and forgot all about the television.

"Matt how come when people get married they sometimes don't last long?" "I'm not sure Red, sometimes it's because they fight over money or their kids or something between the two." "Do you think we'll fight?" she asked nuzzling deeper into his chest. "We may . . . we have already, but we always manage to talk over our problems, so I don't see why we couldn't handle it on a larger scale." "That's nice, I like the way you put things" she said. Just then the phone rang. "Aw shoot!" she spat kicking the end of the couch. "Somebody always interrupts us when we're enjoying ourselves!"

"Yeah I know." "Don't answer it Matt" she said looking up at him with puppy dog eyes. "Just let it ring okay?" "Okay you're the house manager, but let me put this out, it could be dad or your mother, and being they both know we're here alone, wouldn't it piss them off if we didn't answer?" The logic made sense to her but still didn't make her any happier about it. "Oh okay Matt . . . go get it." Matt eased up from under her and ran to catch it in the kitchen. "Hello?" "Hello . . . Matt?" "Yeah" "This is Ant, what's up?" "Not much, me and Retta are just chillin out and watching TV." "She's still there?" "Yep, dad and her mom are gonna go out, so they'll be here for awhile." "Oh okay." "So what are you up to?" "About the same . . . nothing, Brenda might come up a little later." "That sounds good." "Maybe . . . hey why don't you tell me about your plan for next Friday."

"Well it's not all that special, they'll do most of the work and we'll just reap the benefits of their mistake." "Okay . . . sounds easy enough how will we do it?" "First of all, you already know they intend to use something to put me out." "Yeah" "It'll probably be a tranquilizer or something they put in my drink, now when I get tipsy or tired they'll want me to go lie down some place quiet and out of the way." "Yeah, that makes sense." "They'll be thinking that I won't expect anything strange would happen with all those people around." "Okay" "So when they get me alone, they'll wait for me to go to sleep, that's when they'll try to dog me out." "Slick plan! Do you know for sure that this is how it will go down?"

"Not really, I'm speculating on the larger part, but based on what I learned from Paula and how shrewd they are . . . I'd go with that assumption panning out."

"So what are we gonna do?" "Well, I'm thinking that they will wait until the party has been going on for awhile before they try it, you know, let me get a few drinks in me." "We'll have to keep an eye on them to see when they move on my drink, once you, Milton, or Frog see it or get a feeling that they're up to something, give me a signal by blowing your nose." "Then what?" "Then I'll have you go an hide in the room, they'll try to take me to ahead of time, make some excuse to go to the bathroom or something." "How will I know which room they'll use?" "You can bet it will be one out of the way, so no one is tipped off to what's going down." "So when we get there I'll have each of you ask to use the rest room at different times, while you're doing that take a minute to check out the room situation to see which one is easiest to get to and most out of the way."

"What if they have a two story house . . . what then?" "We can't go roaming all over the place, then they would get suspicious." "Yeah your right . . . let me think a minute." Matt was mulling over the many possibilities but all were too risky and would call for too much man power. His counter plan had to be simple and clean otherwise it would alert them to his knowledge of their intentions and they would just change to something else . . . no he had to find a way to play it out to the letter so it would be over once and for all!

"Okay, we'll do this, if they do have two stories, and they try to take me upstairs, I'll play like I'm a little dizzy and say I can't make it, they'll have to keep me on the first floor then!" "You guys just find that room okay?" "Alright, but I still don't see how I fit into all of this by getting to the room first." "Well, while you're in hiding waiting for them to leave I'll tell them to turn the light off, that way it will be dark and they can't see." "Then me and you will swap out, and since we're about the same height and build they won't know the difference until it's too late!" "That's good . . . so what if they try to talk to me?"

"Don't answer, play sleep, it'll just give them more courage thinking their drug worked, hell, all they want is some play time." "You sure about this are you?" "Have you forgotten about Thursday already?" "No!" "Okay then, think about that." "Alright, I believe you, but just one more thing . . . why me for the ginny pig?" "Who has more to gain from this than you?" "Better still, you want Mel anyway don't you?" "Hell to the yeah!" "Okay then, you're getting her and Cheryl to boot, you'll be the only man at Central to crack that virgin safe and you'll have access to them both anytime you want after that."

"You sure about his man?" "Hey, I know how virgins think, particularly these two!" "You've had that many have you?" "No, I haven't, except for Retta, but I do seem to be cornering the market on em lately." "Yeah, ain't that the truth!" "But hey, won't they get mad when they find out it wasn't you?" "Maybe, but at the same time they'll be too pleased getting boned by you, so however you sling that pipe will determine how mad they'll be."

"But in the end, we both still win, get me?" "Yeah I gotcha." "Good, now how about calling up all the guys on the track team plus Milton and Frog and give em the low down, if they don't want to come pass em up but let all of them know that they stand a good chance of knocking boots with some fine Northeast High babes." "And keep the number of guys down to twelve, you me, Frog and Milton included." "Okay Matt, I'll get on it . . . tell Retta I said hi." "Okay doc, call me tomorrow and let me know what you come up with." "Okay, Matt . . . check you later . . . "click" "Matt you done on the phone yet?" "Yeah babe, it was Ant."

"Okay, how about checking on the food for me while your in there." "Will do babe, do you want something to drink?" "Yes please." "Okay" Matt stuck his head in the oven to check. The food was cooking nicely and smelled great. It would need it's final prep soon. "Man can she cook!" He thought dabbing at the chicken with his finger to get a taste.

"Good looks, sexy body, and a brain to boot! . . . man I jut hit the jack pot!" Matt closed up the oven then went to the refrigerator for a couple of drinks. Just then there was a knock at the door. "I'll get it!" said Retta getting up. She ran to the door slipping and sliding all the way because of her stockings on the wood floor.

She slid down the hall, skidded through the dining room and finally ran through the carpeted living room to the door. "Who is it?" "It's me baby, your mother" said Audrey. Retta pulled open the door and saw the most beautiful woman she had seen in ages standing before her. "Hey Ma!" she said grabbing her and squeezing her.

"Ooph! girl your gonna choke me to death baby!" Retta let go smiling. "Hey Lori!" she said reaching down and giving her a big squeeze. "Hey Retta." "How you been doing you little butter ball?" she said still hugging her so hard she grunted.

"Retta your gonna squish out all my stuffing." They all laughed happily at the comment. "I'm sorry, I'm just so glad to see you guys!" she said. "And mom you're a knock out!" Audrey smiled in spite of herself. "So I've been told" she said looking in the direction of the driveway. "So are you feeling better baby?" "Yes ma'am, tons better, the doctor gave me some antibiotics and a couple of feminine wash items, he said I should be completely cured of it in about a week or so if I don't skip my medications."

"That's good Retta, I'm just so happy you're home, you gave mamma a terrible scare." "I know and I'm sorry, I wasn't more careful and watchful." Lori stood by swinging her bag from side to side and looking at the floor.

Audrey noticed the reaction the conversation was having on her younger daughter and quickly changed the subject, winking at Retta. "So where are you guys going?" "Me, Buford, Liz and her friend are going to have dinner at Cag's." "Oh, that's a nice place!" "I know, then were going to split off and go our own ways." "What are you gonna do after that?" "Buford made reservations at the Colinade Room at the Macon Hilton and were gonna do some dancing, prancing and maybe a little romancing" she said giggling.

"Ooh I'm telling" sang Lori and Retta covering their mouths. "Aw you two hush . . . can't a girl enjoy herself once in awhile with a terribly sexy man?" "And before I forget, you and Lori may wind up spending the night if things get a little warm, so I got you some over night things and some clothes for tomorrow." Retta's eyes got as big as oranges at hearing this.

"Now don't go on like that, I know that Buford already gave you the low down on how you and Rodney should behave, so I'm not worried the least bit that you will" she said flexing her eyebrows. "Where is he anyway?" "I wan't to say hello."

"Matt, there's some strange lady here to see you!" she said giggling "Oh yeah, who is it?" he said coming into the living room cleaning his hands on a dish towel. Audrey had bowed her head some so as not to give herself away to quickly. She had wanted to see really how good she looked. "Yes ma'am, may I help you?" he said sounding quite older and more mature. Audrey looked up and smiled at him. "Hi Rodney."

Matt's eyes flew up and his hormones did a double take. "Damn!" he blurted out before he could catch himself. "I mean, oops! . . . sorry Mrs. Davis." Retta, Lori and Audrey just laughed at him openly. "That's alright Rodney, I know just how good I look tonight."

Matt put his hands in his pockets and just shook his head and recklessly eyeballing Retta's Mom. "Mrs. Davis, you don't know the half of it!" he said still shaking his head. "You look BOOYA!" he said snapping his finger loudly to his side. Audrey blushed notably at the young man's audible assessment of her.

"He means you look really hot tonight ma" said Retta translating. "Well thank you Rodney, you are so sweet" she said reaching over and hugging him. Matt took full advantage of the body check and just buried himself in her embrace. He remembered the last time he had hugged her and what he discovered. This time he was ready and meant to return the gesture.

Audrey squeezed him modestly, pressing her breast against his youthful and strong chest. She mentally recorded the feel of his virile young body and the confidence he used holding her, unlike last time. "Damn, I hope his father is this good!" He then backed away from her smiling capriciously.

"Boy is dad in for a ride!" he thought to himself. "I was telling Retta that depending on how much we have to drink and what we get into, we may wind up staying overnight." "Oh . . . really?" Matt said trying not to show his true feelings about the possibility. Audrey of course knew the truth and wasn't fooled by his casual coolness. "Yeah, dad mentioned that should the girls get tired or sleepy they could take his bed." "Yes, but like I said, it's just a possibility, we may be back sooner than planned." "BEEP BEEP!" "Oh, I better get going, that's your father blowing, girls you be good and don't get into trouble okay?" "Okay mamma." "And Rodney, would you walk me out to the car please, I'm not too sure footed in these heels yet" she said playing delicate. "Yes ma'am."

"Bye my babies" she said hugging each one. "Have a good time." "We will." Audrey hooked her arm around Matt's as they left. "Rodney the reason I wanted you to come out with me is I wanted to talk to you about Retta." "Yes ma'am" "Now you know she loves you a great deal and would do anything you asked her to don't you?" "Yes ma'am" "She would also do anything her heart and body dictated to her to do as well, now I know you also love her a great deal and wouldn't want to harm her in anyway." "Yes ma'am" "I didn't doubt it for a second, what I'm asking you Rodney is to try and restrain from any physical activities with her for a while . . . you know what I mean?" "Yes ma'am" he said swallowing hard. He was completely disoriented having this conversation about having sex with Retta.

It was bad enough that he had already violated her trust and wishes earlier this afternoon, but now he was lying about it by trying to act as though it wouldn't happen . . . or didn't. Matt could feel a warm rush go all through him. He had never truly thought she knew anything and was positive Aretta hadn't spoken about it to her.

"Don't worry Rodney, Aretta doesn't know I know that you two have been intimate and I'm not angry about it, I was a little earlier on and a little afraid too, but since I got to know you a little better these past few months I feel I can relax a little and not worry, I know Aretta's nature and I'm comforted to know it's you who she has given herself to."

Matt looked in her eyes and couldn't begin to form anything to say. She had him dead to rights and she knew it. Audrey smiled a little at this, not because she had cornered him but because he had enough integrity not to attempt to lie about their sexual involvement or comment on it. This made her feel even more secure about him and her sense of judgment.

No parent wants to have to deal with their child's sexual development at any age. It's just not something parents feel comfortable with no matter what they say. And for Aretta to be sexually active, four months shy of her fifteenth birthday, was more than a shock and cause for concern. For it to have happened at the hands of a much older boy of seventeen, was a real challenge to Audrey as a woman and a mother. She either had to stomp on it and take a chance on destroying her daughter's perception of life as a young woman, and positive growth into sexuality by doing what she may have felt was just protecting her. Or she could teach her as best as she could, give her the best information available and guide her responsibly so she can make wise and informed decisions . . . She chose the latter.

"So being that this is going on between you two, I just want you to please be your utmost discreet and reserved about how often you indulge your desires and where, I have taught Aretta all I can about sex and responsibility as a young woman, but condoms do fail and girls forget their pills sometimes, do you understand what I'm saying Rodney?" "Yes ma'am" he said slowly. "I really hope you do son, because it would really frost my ass if you two were to get pregnant and have a child at this time, so give her some time to get back on her feet . . . say about a week or so, then you two can go back to being your normal selves okay?" "Yes ma'am, I will." "Okay then, I'm done" she said walking to the car.

Matt opened the door for her. "You guys be good okay, and have a good time, it's Friday night" she said winking at him. "Alright Mrs. Davis, we will." "That's Audrey . . . Rodney" she said flashing him a look that said, "I'm going to roast you for that one day." "Okay Audrey" he said smiling but feeling a little odd calling a grown woman by her first name, especially the mother of his girl friend. "See ya later son" Buford said starting up the car. "Bye dad."

His dad pulled away from the curb and drove down the street. The two couples turned the corner and were gone. Matt didn't go back inside right away but just stood there on the side walk pondering the discussion he had just had with Audrey. He had a lot to consider regarding how he was going to relate to Retta and Audrey from that point on.

Most would say, "chill out you have just been given the keys to the JAG, go out and drive your ass off!" but Matt didn't really see it that way. He felt that now that their sex life had been exposed and accepted, it seemed to have lost something or lacked in the hidden luster and secrecy that makes being a teenager and having sex all the more mysterious and fun. He had to reevaluate himself and this if things were going to stay normal between him and Retta. Just then a gentle hand touched him on the shoulder.

It was Retta, she had been watching and listening to the discussion unknown to her mother and felt it quite a bit for Matt to have experienced in such a short time. She was grateful for her mother's open minded and total disclosure method of dealing with the matter. It did matter to her a lot, and Retta didn't know what she would have done if her mother would have forbid her to have anything to do with sex. It's not that she was overly hot to trot for Matt and just had to have sex. It was much more than that, she was very, very much in love with him and it took almost a year before she was even comfortable with even the concept of sex much less doing it.

Matt had not been pushing the idea on her relentlessly or unnecessarily either. He was as timid about it as she and had given her every opportunity and excuse to stay away from it for as long as she wanted until she felt comfortable with it.

No, Retta gave herself to Matt not as a need to satisfy teenage lust and sexual frustration but instead as a way to fully express in the most heartfelt, honest, and dedicated way she knew how. She didn't just give her body, her chastity, her most prized personal identity, she gave every ounce of who she was and the most expression of her love for him.

Retta slowly came around to face him. She silently put her arms around his waist and embraced him. She looked up into his eyes and felt a wonder and passion for him that raged through her body and mind like a high speed trip through space. Matt held her face in his hands gently. He looked deep into her and marveled at the translucent glow in her eyes cast down by the street lamp at the end of the sidewalk. Her hair glistened and shown like hot black silk. Matt drew into her and inhaled her essence as he lost himself in her lips. It never ceased to amaze him how he would feel like his entire body was being drawn out from the inside every time he kissed her.

It was a painfully sublime and sweet feeling he ached to feel over and over again. Retta welcomed each and every kiss with the hunger and thankfulness of a person being fed. She felt as though she was starved for his kiss every time he kissed her and hungered even more for it each time she didn't have it. They held the kiss for an eternity. Finally and slowly Matt released her, still staring into her eyes.

"Is everything okay Matt?" she whispered. "Yeah, it's fine . . . everything is just fine." "What did she say to you?" "Let's just say there isn't anything under the sun that she doesn't know about us . . . and I mean anything." Retta searched his eyes for signs of discontent. "Matt, I never said anything to her about us baby . . . honest." "I know angel, she said so, she just wants us to chill for awhile till you're a little better that's all." "What did you tell her?" "Nothing . . . what was I supposed to say?" "She had me dead to rights, she knew everything." "Yeah, I guess your right are you gonna do what she asked you too?" "I don't know babe, it's not all my decision to make if you know what I mean, how do you feel about it?" "Well, we've already made love just hours ago and in the most ardent and passionate way we ever have and I feel wonderful, so I don't know" she said putting her face on his chest. "Sigh . . . but, I'll follow where ever you lead me Matt."

Matt held her close squeezing her ever tighter. She snuggled as close as she could get. "I guess we'll have to play it by ear baby, that's all I can say." "Okay Matt, what ever you say we'll do." "Hey you guy's, I'm hungry" whined Lori standing in the door pouting. "Come on Matt, lets go check dinner, it ought to be done by now." "Yeah, I'm kind of hungry myself." As they got into the house they could see Lori standing in the doorway of the kitchen tapping her foot impatiently. "Come on you guys the food is done and I'm hungry!" "Oh how would you know . . . you would eat a burnt doughnut and swear it was barbeque." Matt covered his mouth to squelch a laugh that was gushing forth. He took Lori's side and told her to come on with him. "Let's see what this bird looks like Lori." She happily grabbed his hand and went with him. "Yeah babe, it's done." "Go ahead and put your cheese sauce on the broccoli."

From what Buford and Audrey could see, the restaurant was top flight and well deserving of the two stars it had been given. The lobby was exquisitely and very tastefully designed. The carpet was royal red with gold and royal blue boarders around it. There was a huge chandelier that hung in the center of a roman sculpted ceiling in the main dining hall. There were beautiful paintings all around and the walls were done in a raised wallpaper with gold accents around blue squares. This was intermingled between walnut stained mahogany panels. The entire rendering looked like a copy from the Kremlin or some other Russian architecture.

The podium in the lobby where the concierge stood looked as though it came from courtroom in an old England. "Good evening and welcome to *Cag's*" he said as they walked up. "Do you have reservations sir?" "Yes . . . Mathis party of four." The concierge looked down the list and found him. "Yes Mr. Mathis we have your table ready" he said speaking somewhat loftily like and English butler.

"If you'll just follow me this way to the Endicott room, we'll get you and your party seated" he said extending a graceful arm directing them which way to go. They walked through many areas or what looked to be rooms that were partitioned into separate individual dining areas, each having their own personality. Their room was quite cozy and had sort of a Mediterranean feel to it with the subdued reds, browns an blue primary colors.

Audrey liked the surroundings and the intimate table setting they had made for them. It had flowers around a beautiful candle in a vase on the table as a centerpiece. Rustic pottery porticos and vases were on the wall beside them and accented the large paintings and tapestry around them. She felt like royalty. As soon as they were seated the gentleman raised his hand and made a gesture, kind of like the queen when she waves in a parade.

In the next moment a very well dressed and friendly waiter appeared at his side. He gave them menu's and greeted them warmly. "Good evening everyone, I am Paul you waiter for this evening, we have a wonderful menu for this evening and it's full of many exquisite dishes from around the world."

"Tonight's specials are from the Mediterranean countries like Madagascar, Portugal and Gibraltar." "We also have some very American favorites on the menu, many of them surf and turf . . ." "Surf and Turf?" asked Audrey not familiar with the term. "Yes ma'am, that's what we call seafood and steak."

"Any dog and pony on that menu?" said Buford joking with him. "No sir, not tonight, we had a little yak loin and chicken's lips last night and it went like hot cakes!" he said whispering conspiratorially and winking at him.

Audrey and the others just laughed at the light verbal jousting and food foolery between Buford and the waiter. Liz was casually eye balling Buford with modest appreciation and interest. He seemed to be quite a gentleman an a cultured person. Not to mention quite sexy for a man his age. "Damn . . . I need to go an find me a mailman!" she thought to herself. "May I suggest a pre-dinner drink or aperitif?" "Yes, I'll have a rum and coke and the lady here will have a white wine" said Buford looking at her for her approval. She just nodded and smiled her answer. "I'll have a gin and tonic and she'll have." I'll have a white wine too" said Liz speaking up. "Very good, I'll return shortly with your drinks while you decide on your dinner choices" said Paul giving them a prize winning smile and leaving.

"This is very nice Buford" said Audrey smiling at him. "Do you come here much?" asked Liz. "Goodness no, there's no way I could come to this place more than twice a month, I'd have to be promoted to Post Master General for that to happen" he said chuckling lightly. Butler nodded in agreement looking around and thinking about how big of a dent this evening was gonna put in his budget.

"So Buford, how did you and Audrey come to meet each other?" asked Liz still probing. Audrey wasn't quite agitated yet because of her questions, she knew Liz was always on the prowl for an upgrade and it didn't matter that she had one next to her when she started taking applications. She was waiting for her to get into the stalker mode first before she invited her to the ladies room for a verbal beat down. "Well I'd seen her before from time to time on my route, we never really spoke but, she would always smile at me and wave."

Liz just glanced over at Audrey who was already looking straight at her but with a most reticent yet dangerous smile on her red lips. She had an expression that said. *"I see you, you horny bitch and this ain't high school, so watch it."* Liz acknowledged he silent threat by blinking and returning her subtle smile as if to say.

"He's not taken yet sister girl, and until you pop the cork on that severely aged chardonnay between your legs . . . he's fair game." "One evening a couple of weeks ago my youngest son came home with her and her two daughters, that's how we met really for the first time" he said going on completely unaware of the war of the roses that was going on right in front of him. "That must have been quite a surprise for you . . . three women busting up in your house like that" said Butler chiming in.

"Yes, it did catch me off guard but it was okay, I was just doing some taxes for some clients, I do accounting sometimes." "It sounds tiring, working all those numbers and accounts then working all day at the post office as well" said Liz unfettered by Audrey's posturing. "Yeah, it's a bit, but it pays well." So Butler what are you up to these days old man?" He said rerouting the conversation in another direction. "I do cross country hauling for LJL trucking." "So you stay pretty busy yourself then?" "Yeah, I'm gone three weeks out of each month, this is one of the few times I get some time off, but it pays well so I'm not complaining." "Don't they have some sort of a buddy plan with that company?" "Yeah, they do and I've been trying to get ole Liz here to quit her job out at that plant she works at and travel with me, she could make a lot more doing that then what she probably makes now."

"Liz I didn't know you were considering doing some traveling, that would be exciting don't you think?" she said giving her a look that basically said, "hit the road bitch, it would be the best thing you could do right now." "Liz caught the hint." "Well maybe I will someday, but I haven't decided yet, I'm not too crazy about those big trucks, they're kind of scary and noisy." "Aw! Come on Liz, you know they're not that bad, you didn't seem to mind it so much last year when we went down to Florida for a week and we slept in the cab" he said pinching her on her hips goosing her and giving her a look filled with lust. "Butler! You know better" she said looking around to see if anyone had seen him being mannish. Audrey just grinned at her and made eye contact.

She sat back in her seat and lightly teased a lock of hair she felt was a little out of place by twirling in her fingers. To the untrained male eye it appeared that she was just doing a classic female thing. However to another woman it was a light slash across her wrists with a razor blade. Audrey and Liz had a lot of history and as black women go, not all of it was good. She knew Liz from high school and knew she had a reputation for boys and vehicles. She remembered the time she had left a dance early with her date and they both walked up on Liz and her date in the front seat of his truck doing their best to wear the covers off the seat. It was this that Liz knew Audrey had to be thinking about when she made her little move.

"What was that you called me at work the other day Liz?" she said nonchalantly. "Oh you hush too Audrey, you know how you were back then too!" she whispered across the table in full view of both men. Buford nor Butler had a clue of what was going on or had transpired to bring up this heat in their dates. He and Butler just looked at each other and laughed at this little family feud. "So what's everybody gonna order?" he said cutting in.

"I'm starved." "Yeah me too" said Audrey recovering to her original self so fast and so smoothly you couldn't tell there was ever a riff. She picked up her menu and looked at it. "Ooh this all looks so good . . . and fattening" she mumbled hoping Buford didn't hear it. "Good, I'm not trying to lose any weight" he said grinning at her. "I'm gonna have this Cajun Seafood Jamboree" said Butler closing his menu.

"How about you Liz?" he asked as the waiter returned with their drinks. "Here you are folks, two Chardonnay's, one rum and coke and one gin and tonic, has everyone decided what you would like for dinner?" "Yes, I'll have the grilled lamb." "That comes with scalloped potatoes and either rice almandine or stuffed mushrooms." "The rice will be fine." "And a salad?" "Caesar please, with ranch dressing." "Very good" he said scribbling quickly in his pad then looked over at Audrey. "I'll have the Spicy Red Snapper with Mango Salsa." "And what sides will you have?" "I'll have the chutney with a baked potato and a house salad." "Okay that sounds delicious, I may have to try that myself when they let us eat again" he said looking at them slyly with a small grin. "Most of the time they just let us have what falls on the floor and we have to fight for that." "But every now and then they actually feed us" he said joking. Audrey and Liz just erupted in laughter at the morbid joke. Buford and Butler were equally amused and chuckled as they turned up their drinks.

"And how about you two gentleman, what can we get you for dinner?" "I'll have . . . well you know I can't decide" said Buford looking at both sides of the menu. "I've got my mind on a dish I had in Germany many years ago." "Well sir, we do offer specialty orders if you don't see anything you like on the menu." "That's great because I don't remember the name of it but it had a nice large steak about a half in thick with a slab of liver on it of equal size, the whole thing was smothered in gravy, onions, and mushrooms with a side order of rice pilaf and small round red potatoes, do you guys have anything like that?" The waiter thought a minute pressing his pen against his chin.

"Yes sir we do, I know just the order your talking about, I had it myself not too long ago and it was great! A little filling for me, but still great" he said patting his stomach. "Will that be all for your order sir?" "Of course it will silly, he's gonna need a wheel chair to get out of here after eating that" he mumbled to himself being funny. The table just giggled at him once more. "That sounds delicious, I'll have that too!" said Butler putting up a finger. "That sounds like a lot of food to put down Buford" commented Audrey. "Well the German's believe a man should be full in order to do a full days work." "So is that what I am?" she said whispering and looking at him with bedroom eyes. Buford was unscathed by the comment and easily fielded it back to her. "I'm not sure yet, it's hard to tell from this position, but if you feel the need to explore that idea you're more than welcome to try later on tonight" he said. Then flashed his eyes at her. Audrey felt a tingle go down her spine as he held her in his gaze. She slowly looked away, reaching for her drink and saw Liz looking at her.

"Don't look at me . . . he called your hand, not mine!" Audrey got a little warm and sipped slowly to cool herself down some. "No, I think I'll call it quits, you win . . . . till later" she said flexing her own eyebrows like he had. "Oh Buford what a lascivious web you weave, I think you'll find this moth you've snared is a bit more than a light snack, so bring your appetite."

Back at the house Matt, Retta, and Lori had eaten and cleaned up the dishes. They also just finished polishing off a large bowl of cookies and ice cream. Now Lori was laying crashed out across Retta's lap and she was across Matt's. It was only 9:00 o'clock but everyone was getting sleepy. They had been watching a good movie on the TV, it was an adventure movie, one they had seen before but enjoyed anyway.

The house was pretty quiet then Matt jumped. "What was that!" "What Matt?" Retta said groggily raising up. "SNGXXX!" "THAT!" "That's just Lori baby . . . she does that all the time." "Your kidding me right?" he said quite rattled at the unearthly sound coming from Lori's head area. "How in the world do you sleep through that?" "I just tune her out." "You want me to put her in dad's bed?"

"Yeah, she's out of it and won't awaken unless you shake her up." "You think we ought to dress her for bed then?" "I don't think dad and your mom will be back tonight." "You think so?" "Yeah . . . I got a feeling." "Okay then, take her in there and I'll get her dressed."

Retta got up slowly not wanting to disturb her little sister. She helped Matt up and he picked up Lori and carried her in his dad's room. She just hung like a rag doll with her arms flopping loosely. "Don't forget her bag Retta." "Okay" she said reaching back for it.

He pushed the door open with his foot and carried her in placing her gently on the large captains bed. She stirred lightly and turned over on her side in a fetal position. Retta came behind him and put the bag on the bed then reached in for Lori's nightgown. Both of them worked together undressing Lori. Matt took off her shoes and socks, Retta slid off her pant's and her shirt. She sat up with eyes still closed like a corps in a horror movie then flopped back on the bed again.

Matt tried hard not to laugh but it was the funniest thing he'd ever seen a kid her age do while asleep. Retta pulled her gown over her large head, complete with a myriad of hair bows and barrettes. Matt marveled at how she had such a small foot for a girl her age and size. But then a again he thought it made sense.

For some reason he couldn't figure, girls around Macon seemed to be genetically upside down. They were pre-teen to teenager looking, short with a nice to well built body and as old as twenty or tall, with poorly formed, immature physical features and as young as twelve. Which made it quite a challenge for a man to find one who would tell the truth about their age and not get him locked up for statutory charge.

Finally they had her dressed for bed and pulled back the covers and tucked her in. "I'm going to take a shower Red" he said as they walked out of the room. "Okay Matt, I'm going to put on my gown" she said heading to the bedroom as they got into the den.

"Could you put me out some clothes for bed babe?" "Okay" she said going into the room. Matt walked into the bathroom and closed the door. Moments later you could hear that shower going and a long stretched out grunt of pleasure. He washed quickly because he wasn't really dirty but just like the fresh feel of a shower before bed.

Aretta was just slipping into her night gown and stopped to look at herself in Matt's vanity mirror. She stroked her hair with both hands and looked at herself speculatively. She turned sideway's and ran her hands down the length of her young body from her breasts to just below her tummy. She hovered there and studied herself a moment. "I wonder how I would look pregnant?" she thought to herself. "I'd probably be huge!" she thought giggling at herself then reaching over to Matt's bed for a small throw pillow.

She shoved it under her night gown all the way up to just under her breasts. She held it there a moment. "Not bad, I think I would look pretty good pregnant." "Yeah, if all you ever reached was your third month" said Matt leaning against the door. Retta was startled when she saw him because she thought she was alone.

"Matt you scared me!" "I'm sorry, I was just standing here looking at you play with yourself" he said smiling at her. "I wasn't playing with myself!" she said squaring on him and putting her hands on her hips. The pillow as if on cue slid easily down to her feet. Matt just started laughing hysterically. "I think you just lost something" he said pointing at her feet. "Oh well better luck next time" she said looking down.

"Yeah next time, get inseminated by a man instead of a bed, it might last longer" said Matt still giggling at her. She bent down picked up the pillow and threw it at his face, "Smart ass!" Then she ran and jumped on him hugging him and kissing him.

"Come on Matt let's go to bed, I'm tired Puddin." "Okay let me just go make sure the house is locked up." "Okay" Matt left the room still in his towel and walked through the house checking all the doors. When he returned to the bedroom he could hear music playing some of their favorite soft music and the lights were out. "Retta where are you sweet pea?" she didn't answer so he assumed she was already asleep and just tossed off the towel and went groping for the bed. He felt her under the covers and followed her torso upwards to her head. She slept with her head under the covers.

"That's an odd way to sleep" he thought as he eased them back and slid in himself. Matt had never slept in the buff before neither by himself or with her and the feeling was electric. As he slid under the covers next to her he was greeted by her warm silky smooth skin. She was naked also and it excited him, Retta was a living fantasy and a dream to be lying next to. As Matt slid all the way in and got comfortable, Retta instinctively threw her arm across his chest and her leg across his, pulling herself closer until they were almost one body.

Matt could feel her body heat beginning to burn him and her sensual mound was rubbing against his thigh teasing the hell out of him! Matt reached down and slowly tried to slid under her raised leg and putting her on top of him to set up for a hit. Retta's hand quickly changed his mind when she viscously grabbed a hand full of his package and gave it all a firm squeeze. "OOP!" "Don't . . . even . . . try it" she said in a level tone while increasing pressure. "Okay, okay!" he gasped praying she didn't use her Ninja skills.

Retta released them slowly, patted his bruised personal package, then gave Matt a quick peck on the lips." Go to sleep Puddin." "Sighh! . . . damn she's hot!"

Meanwhile, Audrey and Buford had long since finished dinner with her friends and both had left and went their separate ways. Liz and Butler to their play pen and Buford and Audrey to theirs. Fortunately their's was nearby at the Macon Renaissance Hotel. Audrey and Buford had been dancing to the tunes of Smokey Robinson, Etta James, Luther Vandross and a host of other greats all evening in the hotel ball room. She had had too much wine and he was long over his brandy limit as well. Audrey's head rest against his chest and she had her arms around his neck. They were doing a soft two step and basically holding each other up at this point.

She was falling in love with his strong hands that held her so tight and yet so delicately on the dance floor. He held her just right and quite close to her shapely bottom. She had wished he would caress it since he was already back there but she knew he was too much of a gentleman for that. It was midnight and only a few couples remained. Most had either retired to their hotel rooms or gone home. Some still remained and were dancing, others were sitting close together at their little romantic tables.

Soon the music died and they were still standing there holding each other. "Hey gorgeous" he whispered in her ear. "Are you ready to go?" "Go where?" "I don't think either of us should drive tonight" she said looking into his eyes smiling. "Well I didn't figure we were going to be able to awhile ago." "Oh?" "So are we going to take a cab?" she asked a little disillusioned at the thought of going home. "No, not exactly" he said grinning. Audrey thought she caught a hint of lust on his tone when he said that. Then she saw him dangling a hotel key on his finger. He looked at her with a sheepish grin hoping he didn't overstep himself. "Oh Buford, you are on time aren't you?" she whispered then took the key from him and pulled him into an embrace. Her lips were soft and sweet thought Buford as she hungrily sought his. Neither of them had had a sexual encounter in a long time and this was building into a pretty good one! Audrey pulled from him slowly and took his hand in hers.

She recovered her purse from the coat check and headed for the exit and into the main lobby where the elevators stood. They got on and rode it to the tenth floor. Their room was to the right as you get off. Buford took the key from her and opened the door. The room was spacious and beautiful with a huge king sized bed. Audrey kissed him again then headed for the bathroom. "I'll be right out sweet heart, you go ahead and make yourself comfortable. "Okay pretty lady, if you need anything just yell okay?" he said smiling seductively at her. She just smirked and went into the bathroom to undress.

"Oh yes lover" she mumbled to herself as she undressed. "I'll yell alright but it won't be for something I need, it'll be because I'm getting something I want!"

Soon she came out of the bathroom. She noticed that all the lights were out save for one and it was the soft glow of a small wall lamp over the bed. Buford was sitting up in bed with his hands behind his head and smiling appreciatavely as she came into view. The sight of her made his eyes grow wider. "Damn! she's gorgeous!" he thought. She was wearing a pink paisley teddy and it looked simply delicious on her. She stood at the foot of the bed in a most provocative pose with her hand on one hip.

Buford marveled at her long sexy legs and hour glass figure. She had full round medium breast that held their own and nipples that just wouldn't quit. They were putting enough pressure on her top to let him know that she was definitely getting warm. She slowly and seductively walked over to the bed and stood letting him see the full package up close.

"You like?" she asked sweetly and smiling innocently. Buford didn't speak but just nodded. His eyes did all the talking for him. "You want?" she said giggling at his school boy loss of words and awe stricken face. She was more than happy with her choice in undergarments at this point. Buford smoothly crossed the distance between them and took her hand. She came willingly and full of anticipation and desire.

He pulled her up close and embraced her, cradling her in his long powerful arms like a baby. Audrey was more than happy with the cradle of man she had found herself in and decided she was going to enjoy losing herself entirely. He drew her in and kissed her. It started slowly and somewhat clumsily but quickly became passionate and all to consuming to them both. Soon they had both shed their clothing. Their love making was fevered and lusty. They had traversed the entire expanse of the bed several times and experimented with one or two positions that Audrey remembered from an Indian book on love that she'd read.

Finally after having reached their sexual zenith they both climaxed powerfully and collapsed in each other's arms, exhausted and more than satisfied.

The next morning was glorious and the sun was a shimmering fire ball in the early morning sky. The clouds were like gossamer puffs of cotton in a blue Caribbean sky. The sweet smell of Cherry blossoms, Magnolias and a multitude of perennials showered Retta's nose and senses in a ballet of exotic scents and aromas. She lay in the bed still half asleep. Her thoughts were of wonderful places and enchanting emotions of love and beauty. She felt completely wonderful . . . inside and out.

As her young voluptuous body lay naked beneath the warm covers she let her mind wander aimlessly into the sweet oblivion of sensuous feelings and scant reminders of the previous day. Retta felt full and rich and her body still tingled from their love making yesterday. She rolled over and lay her hand on the place where Matt should have been. Now noticing that he was no longer in bed with her, she opened her eyes. The piercing sunlight made her squint and blink. She put up her hand to block it so she could orient her vision better. She sat up slowly and yawned stretching herself and looked about but didn't see him still.

She put her hands together in her lap and listlessly looked down at her feet, watching them as she tapped them together. She sat and slowly collected herself. Her hair was lying loosely about her shoulders and she was blankly meditating while starring at her feet. Retta wasn't sure as to what she wanted or should do today.

Matt was in the kitchen humming to himself as he went about the chore of preparing breakfast.

He had been up for an hour and thought he would get the jump on the girls by taking a quick shower and fixing breakfast. His mind was listlessly fading to black as he stood staring into the sizzling frying pan. The bacon and eggs began to take on 3-D proportions as his vision phased uncontrollably into a blur.

He could see Retta in his mind's eye lying sweetly in bed as he crept into the room to recover some clothes without waking her. She looked so gentle and beautiful as she lay there. He wanted so much to go to her and hold her. The feeling inside him radiated and surged but he just resigned himself to just admiring her from a distance.

Oh how he loved her and couldn't tell her enough. Even the words "I love you" weren't strong enough to express what he truly felt for her. She was his sun and his moon, his every breath and most heart felt pain. She had become to him his reason for existing and when she is gone he too would be no longer.

Just then a stray molecule of grease popped up and attacked his cheek bringing him abruptly back into the present. Matt began to turn and toss the sizzling breakfast so it wouldn't burn.

Just about then Lori wandered into the kitchen moving like a boneless mass. She rubbed her sleepy eyes with her fist's and half stumbled, half dragged into him not seeing where she was going. "I'm hungry" she moaned leaning against Matt still rubbing her eyes. She looked so sweet and baby like in her long night gown. "It won't be long sweet pea" he said hugging her with his free arm. She put her tiny arms around his waist and buried her face in his side.

Matt smiled as he looked at her small frame and the cute way her hair a shorter version of Retta's hung precariously in her face. All that was visible was her cute little nose and the tops of her rosy cheeks. "You wanna go change and get ready for breakfast sweetie?" he asked her gently. She shook her head. "No I wanna stay here with you" she said almost whispering then she readjusted her hold around his waist even tighter.

"Okay then you can stay if you want to, but will you help me set the table?" he asked her. She nodded yes. Matt reached up in the cabinet and took down three plates and glasses. He gave them to her and she slowly walked to the table with them.

Soon he was done cooking and he had all the items he cooked on the table. It was a nice breakfast. He made grits and toast, eggs and bacon with milk and juice. He made sure he had cooked enough before turning off the stove because he knew Lori would probably want seconds. "You go ahead and get started Lori I'll go get Retta." "Okay Rodney" she said digging out a huge scoop of grits.

Matt could hear the shower running as he walked into the den. He figured Retta had finally gotten up. He didn't bother disturbing her and decided he would go get her some clothes to wear. He grabbed the bag from the floor and threw it on the bed then opened it and took out her things and lay them out neatly on the dresser.

Aretta was soaping herself richly and singing to herself. the hot water felt great and she was in the best of moods she had been in for quite a long time. She couldn't wait to get the day started. Retta wondered where or what they would do or go today. She really didn't care as long as it was just them together. She was also thinking that if this was a brief into what it was like to be married then she couldn't wait! She mused all about this while rinsing herself off.

Matt was busy making the bed and cleaning the room. It wasn't much of a chore being that he wasn't the messy type and the music was a nice distraction that made it relaxing. He was listening to a song by the group Journey. He like d the lead singer Steve Perry. And though his voice was really soulful and expressive.

"Lying . . . beside you here in the dark . . . this empty house seems so cold . . . wanting to hold you . . . wanting you nearrr . . . how much I want to bring you home. Matt sounded pretty good he thought to himself as he kept singing. He could almost overlap the voice singing and mimic it perfectly.

He had sang in the choir when he was in Jr. High at Ballard Hudson. He managed to develop quite a rich and soulful singing voice. So also thought Aretta. She stood leaning against the door listening to him. She marveled at how his pitch and tone varied each time the original artist voice did, keeping perfect time and tempo with him. He looked quite handsome standing there in the sunlight swaying and making gestures and expressive movements with his hands. She didn't know he could sing! She had known he was in the chorus but never had the opportunity to sample his voice.

"We sailed on together . . . and drif-ted apart . . . now here you are by my side . . . . so now I've come . . . to you . . . with oopen arms . . . hoping you'll see . . . what your love means to meee . . . open arms."

Matt finished the song and stood quietly listening as the last of the melody played and ended the song.

This particular song never failed to inspire and capture his soul. It had always been one of deep meaning and feelings to him. It was also the song he and Retta first danced to and fell in love in the Jr. prom. Aretta had quietly crossed the room and placed her arms around his waist pressing her face into his back.

"That was beautiful Matt" she said squeezing him. "I didn't know you could sing so well!"

Matt placed his hands upon hers and smiled. "Oh its nothing, I just like that song and I just felt like singing." "Well I'm glad you did, it brought some wonderful memories, do you remember?" Matt gently pulled her around in front of him to face her. She was still wearing her towel around her. She smelled sweet and clean. Her hair was still wet and was slicked back as if it were combed while wet. He skin was soft and moist he noticed as he held her around the shoulders. "Remind me to sing you a love song sometime." "That would be nice Matt" she said folding her arms around him and kissing his cheek.

"Well I set you out some clothes and breakfast is on the table." "Thanks Matt, what are we having?" "Nothing special just eggs, bacon, grits, and toast . . . you know the usual." "Sounds good, is Lori up yet?" "Yeah she got up a little while after I did, she's eating now." "Well we'd better hurry and eat or there won't be anything left to eat." "Don't worry I made extra just in case she was still hungry for more, so you go ahead and get dressed and I'll go check on her."

Chapter II

Poor Choices

Retta was looking at Matt now like he was breakfast. She pulled the towel away without breaking her hold on him. "You sure you wouldn't like to help me dress?" she said grinding into him playfully. Matt could feel himself beginning to stir an how bad he felt last night when she shut him down. "No I better not, if I get one good look at this body of yours you won't have to worry about getting dressed!" "Aww Puddin!" she said taking his hand and rubbing it up and down her warm and very moist furry mound.

Matt pulled his hand away like it was burned and ran for the door. "Oh no you don't, you're not gonna get me started again hot stuff, so you can put it on ice." She just laughed at him coping a seductive smile and a very suggestive pose. "Chicken!" she yelled after him.

Audrey and Buford were enjoying a nice breakfast and a quiet conversation in the hotel restaurant down stairs. They had gotten up a while ago and decided it would be nice to have breakfast downstairs as opposed to in bed lest they wind up feeding on each other again instead. "Thank you" said Audrey taking a bite of her Belgian waffles. "For what honey?" "You know . . . . for last night." "Oh! Don't thank me, I should be thanking you, you really made my week Audrey." "I've never had so much fun in one night and I owe it all to you . . . so the pleasure is all mine."

Audrey was smiling. She had felt the she had received the best part of the deal. She had no idea that when she first met him he would turn out to be such an interesting and fun person to be with. Becoming intimately involved was definitely the last thing on her mind and now that they have been she was even more! Impressed with him.

"So Buford, I was wondering that now that we've gotten onto such a fast and interesting start, where do we go from here?" she said slowly feeling that the question may have been a bit premature or come at an odd time but still valid.

He stopped eating and touched the corners of his mouth with his napkin. "Well Audrey, I much like yourself, had wanted this to be a slow building friendship that could possibly turn into something even more satisfying between us." "But as you can see we've jumped the gun so to speak." "Yes I agree." "And now that we've done so I don't think we could really stagger our interest to what would be considered by most . . . normal relations." "So your saying?" . . . she urged him on. "I'm saying we play it by ear and try not to let our involvement with each other affect Rodney's and Aretta's relationship." "I agree . . . . so tell me . . . what are we then? . . . are we just friends, casual lovers or more?"

He sat back in his chair and blankly stared into his plate. "Well we've passed friendship don't you think?" "Yes" "And I don't think I could get used to you seeing me and other men as well, so casual lovers is out."

Audrey's ears began to warm as his words were taking her right down the path she wanted to go but didn't want to seem pushy and force his hand. Men don't like it too much when you push. "So your saying you want us to date exclusively, you being mine and me yours?" "If it's what you want" he said evenly smiling at her. "It is" she said softly, more happy than she could express in a lady like manner just now.

"Did you enjoy yourself last night" she asked blushing and giving him a sultry smile. "More than you can possibly imagine sweetie!" then he leaned over and kissed her lightly on the lips and getting some of her syrup on his lip. "MMM . . . smack smack . . . taste like chicken" she just laughed and whipped his mouth on her napkin.

"How about you?" he asked her as an after thought. "I'm still trembling" she said placing her hand on his letting him feel her light jitters. "You know . . . I have a cure for that" he said giving her a naughty look with his eyes and nodding towards the hotel. "I'm sure you do" she said placing his hand inside her blouse and caressing her swelling nipple.

Buford was contemplating what the bill would be for another nights stay and thought better of it. "Let's save some of this energy for next weekend." "Alright lover" she said demurely and eased his hand back to the table and just held it. "So tell me how did you get out of work today?" "Well that wasn't too hard, I normally wait for an emergency or a day when I'm not feeling well to take some sick leave." "So I just told my boss Friday that I needed this Saturday off for something important so he said go ahead." "Well that was nice of him" she said sipping her coffee.

"Most supervisors want you to give them at least a weeks notice before they give you any time off." "Well I've got some time in so he bends a little for that and let's me get away with it sometimes." Buford then looked at his watch; "Hey it's almost noon, you about done?" "Yes, I'm ready." "I wanted to do a little work on your car today while it's nice outside." "Okay, that would be nice" she said getting up.

Buford left a tip on the table and they walked out into the lobby. A small blonde woman at the front desk told them she hoped they enjoyed they're stay and to come back again soon.

Matt, Retta and Lori had been busy cleaning the entire house. They even did his dad's room. They went through the hose like a blaze and finished up in decent time. Now they all just sat on the couch and rested. "I'm pooped" said Lori drooping in the seat. "We must have been cleaning for days!" she said exaggerating. "Look at it this way Lori . . . you'll be in good practice for it when I'm gone to college and it's just you and mom" said Retta drooping a little herself. "Well you guys can rest awhile now cause were done!" said Matt. "If you guys want to in a little while, we can go for a walk or something." "I don't wanna" Lori whined. "I'm too tired . . . where's the playground?"

Matt gave Retta a most peculiar look. "Hey, don't ask me, I've know her all my life and I still don't understand her." "Well I'll tell you what Lori, you have a choice; there's a park around the corner a little ways and a playground behind the school up the street and you have a field down the street." "What's down there?" "Nothing really just a large grassy field next to an old cotton mill and a pond." "There's a pond?" she said perking up greatly. "Yeah but it's fenced off so you can't get to it." "Lori sank in her seat once more. "Aww gee! How come they did that? . . . now nobody can play with the duckees or see the fishees." "Well don't worry about it too much, there's not that much to see anyway." "I'll tell you what, why don't I take you to the store around the corner so you can play some video games for awhile?" "I don't got's no money" she said holding out her pudgy little hands pitifully. "Oh yes you do" said Matt reaching in his pocket and pulling out the five dollars he was given last night. "Gee thanks! Rodney" she said happily and giving him a hug.

"Come on Retta let's take her around there." Retta slipped on her shoes and soon they were out the door. The clean warm air was rich and filling. Matt drew in a deep breath "Ahh! Boy this smells good!" he announced, stretching and yawning. "This oughta be a good summer" said Retta. "Yeah it could be but you know how boring it is in this town, everything is set up for the whites and the only places available to us is the pool and the gyms in Unionville or Bloomfield."

"Well what about the one in freedom park?" asked Retta "They have a fishing pond and baseball leagues don't they?" "Yeah, but it cost's money and

I'm not too hot on the idea of spending it there." "You could always go to Six Flags in Atlanta?" "Yeah, that's about it though unless you got money to go traveling around."

"Sighh . . . yeah I guess your right Matt, this town just ain't got what it takes to live here" said Retta agreeing with his assessment.

Macon Georgia was about as interesting as a wet mop. The city itself was large but didn't offer very much in the way of physical activities and recreation centers. What was available to you or how much you could participate in was in direct proportion to what part of town you lived and your color as well as your financial standing.

Macon was during the 1980's a town most people grew up in, left after high school or came to for retirement. It was much like most of the medium size southern towns in Georgia. If you were young it wasn't so bad a place to grow up but once you were older and into your teens and early twenties it didn't offer much. Those who didn't have any or much ambition and a little money quickly became ingrained into the interior never to leave or grow. Basically disenchanted and impoverished.

The store around the corner was buzzing as usual with the neighborhood kids who would flock there on the weekends. The owner a testy and impatient white man with crooked teeth ran the place. He was ambivalent as usual and didn't much like all the kids hanging around in his store. He was partially afraid of one or more of them shoplifting but still he tolerated this because he was making money from them.

"I'll get some change for you Lori and you go see which game you wanna play okay?" "Okay" she said handing the money to him. Lori walked towards the games against the window and listened to the many cool sound effects. She heard zaps, buzzers and explosions. Somewhere in the distance Pac-Man could be heard running around his set.

As she got closer to the video games she couldn't see much more than the tops of them because the crowd of kids had them blocked in and surrounded. Lori stood behind the nearest boy and sheepishly craned her neck in and around to get a look at the video screen.

A boy of about 9 or 10 with cherry red hair and freckles was working over the machine. His little hands were flying madly about the many buttons and levers with a good bit of body English thrown in. The way he ducked and blanched at the screen you would think he was actually in the machine himself. "Come on Mark get him!" yelled the boy in front of her.

"I'm trying dill weed! he keeps getting away and blind siding me." The game looked pretty interesting she thought but decided to look at the other games first. Soon she decided on the first one and came back to stand beside it and wait her turn. "Is this the one you want to play Lori?" asked Matt returning with her change. She just nodded. Matt had gotten her two dollars in quarters and gave her the other three for a snack later. Just then the game ended when the last of the boys ships were destroyed in a fantastic explosion.

"May I play now?" she asked politely to the boy with the red hair. "Naa! No girls allowed, this is a boys game." "That's right!" said his shorter friend beside him. "Girls ain't good a nuff to play Space Invaders." "Yeah! they're too dumb!" Lori poked out her mouth and put her little hands on her hips. "That's not true!" she snapped back scowling at them.

"Girls are not dumb and I can beat anyone of you stupid ole boys!" Matt had been standing just off to the side and had seen the exchange. He didn't like it and moved to intercede. He didn't like bullies and the boys were being just that!

Aretta caught his expression and grabbed his arm just as he was about to step to the boys. "No Matt wait!" she whispered pulling him back. "Why?" said Matt confused and getting a little hot under the collar. "Don't you see how mean they're being and how much bigger they are?" Retta could see the fire in his eyes and was filled with pride at him taking exception on Lori's behalf. However she felt afraid for the boys as well and didn't want Matt to get a hold of them.

"I know Matt but she must start to be her own person and learn to handle situations like this herself or she will always need help as she gets older. that's how my daddy taught me" she said pulling him around so she could hug him and get his full attention.

Matt mused this over a bit. He would have just preferred to snatch up the lot of them and carry them outside. But he saw how Retta did have a point and saw it from a more logical perspective than he did. His way would have only been just fun.

"Okay we'll do it your way but if they start getting pushy then I'm clearing the road with em!" he said thrusting his finger towards the busy road outside. "Okay baby" she agreed hooking his arm and smiling at him.

The boys were laughing and making light of Lori and her statement She just stood her ground and looked at them still pouting. "She's nuts Mark, she thinks she can beat you!" Mark was leaning against the game with his elbows resting on the screen. He smiled in contempt at her challenge and her even smaller female body. "You ain't got a snowballs chance in summer of beating me girlie" he spat.

Right about then Matt and Retta saw Lori pull of the neatest hat trick they had ever seen anybody do! Much less a kid of her age and size. Without breaking her eye contact with him Lori pulled a quarter from her pocket, flipped it way up and over and behind her head and caught it effortlessly with out moving!

"Call it! . . . heads or tails" she said calmly The other boys oohed and ahhed at the neat slight of hand. Mark was no longer leaning but stood completely erect his face going white. "H . . . How did you do that?" "Call it" she said again this time more smugly now aware that she had gotten his full attention. "T . . . tails." Lori slapped the coin on her wrist with a resounding smack!. "If I win you pay . . . if you win I pay" she declared evenly. The other boys just stood back and looked at her with new eyes and a little respect like they were looking at a pit-bull that had just shown it's teeth. They knew that they had grossly misjudged the little girl in front of them and made a grave mistake. Even Retta and Matt were thrown off by her total eclipse in personality and the way she was controlling the situation with the older bigger boy.

"Okay it's a deal" said Mark sounding a little less confident then he did moments ago. Lori removed her hand still looking at him, she cut her eyes down for a second. "You lose! Turkey."

Matt and Retta just grinned at each other.

Now that they had seen that Lori had things under control and going her own way they left her to herself. "Let's go for a walk Red." "Okay" she said hugging him around the waist as they walked out the door.

"It's real nice over here Matt, how did you dad ever come to find this area?" "I don't know, he probably saw it on a route then decided to check into getting a house in it." "I wish our side of town was this nice" she said. "Your side of town ain't bad Retta, you guys have Crystal Lake and a nice wooded area to chill out in, all we got is a shady neighborhood with a lot of old folks." "It still ain't nothing to do around here." Retta just nodded and looked down watching their feet as they walked.

"Matt have your ever thought about what you want to do when you get out of school?" "No, not really . . . why?" "Oh no reason I just thought I'd ask." "I don't know, I guess I just never gave it much thought . . . Naw! that's not true" he said quickly reversing himself and shaking his head. "I did have one idea."

"What's that!" she said getting animated and looking at him. "Well I always wanted to fly airplanes, so maybe I'll go into the military or something." "That sounds good, maybe I'll go too, I could be your co-pilot or something." Matt just laughed "What's so funny" she said stopping in front of him, giving him a pensive stare with her arms folded. "Well nothing really, it's just not something you see a lot of in the military, especially in the Navy which is where I may go."

"Oh, so your saying men are better than women?" "No not like that, but there are just jobs men do better that's all" he said giving her a sheepish grin then shrugged.

"Why you chauvinistic pig!" she spat at him, "I can out do you in anything you can do!"

Retta was hot now and her cute little eyes flashed like sparks. She twisted her mouth into a mean pout and stared at him.

"Hey hold on babe you know you're the best" he said trying to calm her down. "And I'm sure there isn't anything you can't do if you put your mind to it."

She allowed him to pull her to him and cottle her. "It just won't be flying that's all" he said reversing himself. "Why you conceited, air headed, self-righteous asshole!" she shouted pushing him away harshly. "How dare you say that to me!"

Matt just smiled and backed away with his hands up in defense. "But Retta, wait baby." "Don't you dare wait baby me you pompous ass!" "Pompous ass?" he mimicked her. "Yes! that's the part I'm going to kick!" she said swinging at him and missing. "Hold still you wimp! I'm just a girl remember?" Matt tried to run but she was too close. She caught him square in the butt with her foot. "OW!" He ran up the street towards the house with her in hot pursuit.

"Isn't that Rodney and Retta" said Audrey as Buford made the turn onto their street. "Yes I do believe that is, but why is he running from her like his hair was on fire?" "Don't know, but he probably did or said something to tick her off."

Matt was laughing as he ran and was staying just out of her reach baiting her as he went because he figured she couldn't catch him. As he got to the steps in the yard he tripped and flew face first onto the yard. "OOMPH! Damn!" he landed hard and fast. "I got your ass now" said Retta jumping right on top of him without breaking her speed.

Buford and Audrey were laughing at this. They were moving slow so as not to interrupt the scene. Retta rolled him over and straddled him sting on his arms so he couldn't move.

"So smart ass!" she said breathing heavily with a gleam of victory in her eyes and a crooked smile. "What were you saying about women being too stupid to fly planes . . . huh?" Then she punched him in the chest. "Bam!" "Ow . . . wait . . .!" "BAM!" "Wait! I didn't mean it!" he said struggling. "Yeah? . . . I was just kidding too!" she said then gave him several more successive punches to the chest, pinched his nose and a few light slaps to the face.

"Give him a good one for me Retta!" said Buford as they got to the front door.

Retta wasn't aware of them till then. She was too busy correcting his bad manners.

"OH, hi Mr. Mathis, how are you guys doing?" "Fine just fine." "Retta why are you beating up on Rodney?" Asked Audrey beginning to feel sorry for him and the sight of Retta opening up a can of Whoopass on him. "Cause he' being a chauvinist pig!" she said grabbing his nose between two fingers then slapping down on it with her other hand. "SMACK! . . . OW!" "You just wait till I get up" he said wriggling his nose to realign it.

"And just what makes you think you will sport?" Buford just laughed at him. "It seems you have met your match son" then he motioned for Audrey to come inside and leave them to themselves.

"Okay Retta I think he's learned his lesson" she said before going in. "You can forgive him."

"You're lucky Matt, I was gonna womp you for at least another hour or so!" "Aww don't you just hate it, oh well better luck next time." Retta just shook her head smiling down at him. "Remember it was a woman that saved you sweetie" she said thumping him on the nose then jumping off and running into the house. Matt got up and dusted himself off. "Well you can't win them all."

Buford was inside changing into some old clothes while Audrey and Retta were chatting in the den. "So how was last night?" "It was wonderful, we had a great time! and Buford is such a gentleman." "Sounds good, where did you go when you left here last night?" "We went to a restaurant called Cags." "Retta you should have seen that place! It looked like a palace on the inside and the food was so good I didn't want to stop eating!" "What did you have?" "I had some fish and some rice dish I can't remember and Buford had some big ole dish of steak and liver . . . girl that man can eat!" "So after you guys got through eating what else did you do?" "Well Liz, and her friend went off to some place in Atlanta called the Purple Onion I think . . . anyway they went there and they asked us if we wanted to go but Buford said no and that we had our own after dinner plans." "Where did you go!" said Retta pumping her mother as if she was a girlfriend giving her the latest juicy gossip on a sleep over.

"We went to the Hilton and did some dancing." "Oh, you should have seen that place and the music was so romantic. Buford and I pretty much closed the place down." "Yeah?" "Yeah, we was one of the last two couples to leave." "We had a few drinks and did some talking then we went upstairs to bed."

"BED?" asked Retta in a sly sort of query. Audrey caught her intonation and repeated her answer but with as much inflection as she could without telling her outright. "Yes . . . BED!" "OOOHH! I'm tellinn!" chimed Retta as she bounced on the couch hysterically with laughter. "Now Retta I'm grown, so you can just save it!"

Retta gave her a sidelong stare grinning. "Okay Audrey, be that way It's none of my business if you want to run off and get all crazy about a man in a hotel room" she said sitting up straight and prim like a psychiatrist. "Why you little BRAT!" chirped Audrey, her mouth wide open, false indignation showing on her face as she smiled guiltily at her. "I'm YOUR mother, not the other way around" she announced putting emphasis on YOUR.

Retta was un-phased and pressed on. "Is he a good kisser? . . . is he as good as Matt?" Audrey sat back and folded her arms, giving Retta a most peculiar look. "Now Retta, how would I know that? I haven't kissed Rodney before . . . but if you like I can" she said moving like she was getting up. "OH no! that's okay mom we'll just call it even."

Audrey and Retta were used to having catlike conversations like this and teasing each other. It was one of the ways they bonded together and actually in its strangeness worked quite well. They were like sisters and Retta wouldn't have had it any other way. Audrey liked it too even though sometimes Retta would get a little obnoxious depending on the subject of discussion.

Matt had just come in and was thinking of ways of getting even with Retta for the beat down she gave him awhile ago. "There you are, you little minx" he said glaring at her hoping she would try to run. Retta remembering her mothers last statement and the fact that she still had on last nights evening gown, got up from the couch to leave. She took Matt's hand like he was her child and she was taking him away from the playground or something.

"Come on Matt, let's go listen to some music." Matt felt like he'd walked into a crime scene and missed the best part. He just let her take him back into the bedroom. Retta led him into the bedroom and jumped onto the bed. "Put on something nice babe, I want to relax a little."

Buford was in his room finishing up and told Audrey they would be leaving shortly. She just laid back on the couch putting her feet up and letting her mind wander. "Ahh this is nice" she thought. "It's nice to have a man around again to be close to and to share with." Buford is such a nice guy, I hope things will continue to go well between us. He's such a catch and what a lover WHOOO WEEE!, can he go! I'm surprised I didn't pass out on him last night. I must have climaxed at least three times before he did! Come to think of it, if there is anything to that old saying, "Like father like son" then I can see why Retta is so in love with Rodney.

"Hey sleepy head" said a voice startling her out of her sleepy day dream. "Oh, I'm sorry I was just relaxing and I guess I dropped off for a minute" she said sitting up and unconsciously adjusting her clothes. Buford was smiling down at her. "Ready to go?" "Yeah sure" she said slipping on her shoes. "Are we gonna take the kids with us?" she asked as an afterthought. "Yeah, sure if they want to go" he said standing up. "Let's go get them."

They walked to Matt's room and knocked on the door. They could hear classical music playing on the other side. They opened the door and went in. Matt was sitting in his favorite lounge chair with his feet up on the bed and Retta was curled up asleep on his lap like a tiny squirrel.

"They are a pair aren't they" whispered Audrey. "Yeah it's almost a shame to wake them." "Rodney" . . . Retta?" she said softly. "Wake up you two, we're going to the house."

Matt opened an eye and saw them standing there at the door. He just yawned and stretched letting his arms come to rest around Aretta. She cuddled deeper into him burying her face in his neck. "Retta" her mother said more firmly, "Lets go dear heart, vacation is over." "Aww shoot" she whispered getting up rubbing her eyes.

"Where's Lori? I didn't see her when we came up." "She's around the corner at the store playing video games." "Well you two go get her and then we'll leave."

Just then there was a slam of the porch screen door. Matt looked out his window and saw it was Lori. "Here she is now" he said opening the door. Lori was grinning when she came in.

"Hi Rodney, Hi momma, Hi Retta, Hi Mr. Buford." "Hi Lori" they said. "So how was your game?" Asked Matt closing the door behind her. "It was fine . . . I beat them all!" "That's good, you didn't spend all your money did you?" "Huh uh . . . see" she said reaching into her pocket and pulling out a large wad of bills.

"Lori I gave you five dollars, two dollars in quarters and three dollars in bills, where did you get all of that!" Matt asked surprised. "Those boys" she said innocently and beginning to feel like she had done something wrong.

"Lori sweetie" said Audrey coming over to her. "What else did you do while you were there honey?" "Nothing, just play video games." "So where did you get all that money pumpkin?" "Well they kept betting I wouldn't win and I said I bet them I could." "How much?" asked Matt "Five dollars each." "Five dollars!" chirped Retta now completely awake. "How many boys were there betting Lori?" asked Audrey.

"At first their was just three, then five more showed up and started betting to." "May I?" asked Matt reaching for the wad of bills. He straightened it out and counted it quickly.

"Holy smokes Lori you got fifty bucks here!" "Is that a lot?" she said standing with her thumbs in her belt loops and rocking nervously. "For you and anybody else too" he said smiling.

Buford just chuckled and stayed quiet. "Well it seems Lori has made herself a small fortune on someone else's ignorance."

"Lori when did you start gambling sweetie?" asked Audrey. "I didn't momma, they just bet me, I didn't think they were for real, but every time I beat one of them on the game they paid me . . . . did I do bad momma?" she said pouting and looking like she was about to cry.

Audrey scooped her up and held her close. "No, my baby you didn't do wrong" she said kissing her all over and making her smile again. "You just proved your point and made a little profit at the same time that's all."

"Here Lori" said Matt handing her back her winnings. "I don't wanna keep it" she said pushing it back to him. "Okay sweet heart, I'll hold it for you so when ever you want to buy something just let me know" said Audrey as Matt handed it to her. "Okey dokey" she said then gave her a hug.

Retta just looked at Matt loftily and said nothing. "What were you saying about women not being able to do things as good as men?" she said evenly. "Hey, what do I know! . . . my name is mud" he said then went out the door.

"Well if you guys are ready we can load up the truck and go." "Sure Buford, but you need to move the car first don't you?" said Audrey nodding towards the driveway just out the window. "Oh yeah, I almost forgot" he said walking through the room and out the same door as Matt.

Just up the road a bit Ant was busy playing on his Nintendo when he heard the door bell ring. "Just a minute!" he yelled then went back to his game. He was playing basketball with Dr. J. He twisted the little black joy stick wildly almost tearing it off the base. He was guiding the little digital superstar around and through other players, up and down the court. He did a half fake right then left and passed it to another player who took the ball and made a slam dunk. "Slam! Sucka" he yelled victoriously. "Rinnng!" "Damn who can that be?" he said annoyed and getting up to see.

As he got closer to the front door he looked out the window and saw a red pickup truck on the street. "Melanie!" He pulled the door open. "What's up Mel" he said flatly. "Hi Anthony, whatcha up to?" she said timidly not too sure how he was going to react to her being there. "Nothing much just chilling out and playing some video games." "Really? Which one?" "Basketball" he said still standing in the door. "May I come in?" Ant gave her a cursory look of disdain from head to toe while chewing on his lip. "Yeah sure . . . come on in" he said opening the door wider for her to pass between himself and the door. She cautiously walked into his room and stood looking around. "He's not here" he said coming up behind her, brushing against her as he walked by. "He who?" she said squinting at him. "Matt! That's who . . . wasn't that who you were looking for just now?" "No" she said lowering her head and looking at her nails. "Then why'd you come by then?" he said raising his voice a little more. "Can I sit down?" "Yeah go ahead" he said waving towards a seat nonchalantly.

Mel sat on the edge of his bed clearly frustrated by something on her mind. "Anthony, I didn't come to see him, I came to see you." "Oh really? . . . what for . . . I'm not your type remember?" he said being deliberately mean. Mel thought he was being unfairly hurtful but figured it wasn't totally uncalled for. "That's not fair Anthony" she said almost whispering. "OH it isn't?" his voice changing and going up an octave.

He was sitting in his lounge chair next to the door across from her with his hands behind his head. "Tell me Mel, what do you know about fairness? You go all out of you way for a man who has told you time and again that he doesn't want you." "Then you come over here stalking him in the weak hopes that you can catch him and maybe get him anyway, all the while pretending that you like me! now you tell me what's fair!" he snapped at her like a cobra, thrusting his finger at her face to emphasis his point.

Ant's words stung her like a thousand bee stings as she knew his words rang true. Ant had sounded her out fully with all the anger he had pent up within him. She was just lonely and needed a friend. Being that she was from the upper crust and long ago found her peer group to be superficial and fake, she wanted some real friends.

Friends who didn't put on airs and walk around like gaudy chickens on display. She had found this friendship with Matt, Ant and her cousin Cheryl, who was always glad to see her because she never saw her enough. As children they played together a lot but as they grew up her father got better at his skills in business than her uncle Cheryl's father, so he moved up and away taking her with him. Recently they returned to the area because her dad had been made Vice president of the company he worked for and was starting a new division in Macon.

Mel didn't like what was going on with her and Matt and was unsure as to how to handle it. She had other boyfriends in the past but they were all stuffed shirts who just wanted to get her in bed and brag to their friends. She fought them all off and maintained her virtue as well as her sanity but now that she has gotten a little older and met Matt she was really confused about who she was and what she wanted. Not to mention she was genuinely in love with him. No one had ever made her feel as special as he did the night they met and for several days afterward when he would call and talk to her.

It didn't matter that he was black and she was white either. All that mattered was he swept her off her feet. But how could she relate any of this to Anthony, he wouldn't understand it at all. Sure she liked him too and thought he was nice but he just didn't bring out the fire in her like Matt could! It was becoming too much for her and her mind was reeling and spinning. Her emotions were a turbulent wash of bitter sweet feelings and utter dismay.

Mel could feel a dry tightening in her throat and a gut wrenching sob rising from her stomach. It wouldn't stay so she let it come forth in full measure. Mel put a trembling hand to her mouth and turned her head so Ant wouldn't see her cry. Unfortunately the bitter tears that ran down her face told it all. "I'm sorry Anthony . . . I'm so sorry" she croaked then ran for the front door.

Ant was stunned. He hadn't meant to make her cry but only to let her know how he felt about her and what she was doing to herself and him by trying to hang on to this illusion of love for Matt! He quickly sprang up not quite sure what he was going to do or say once he reached her. He caught her as she reached the front door opening it. As she did, he stopped her and closed it.

"Anthony please let me go" she cried quietly her voice trembling. She didn't turn around to face him but just stood pressing against the door and weeping. Ant just held her by her shoulders gently and pressed himself against her. "Shhh" he said softly trying to quiet her some. He could feel the violent shudders and trembling that wracked her delicate body. He pressed his face into her soft luxurious hair. It had a rich fragrance that made him draw in his breath deep and caused his mind to wander. He squeezed her shoulders a little more, drinking in her heavenly essence and warmth.

She was so soft and wonderful to touch he thought wordlessly. "Oh Mel, how I want to hold you and feel you against me." "Melanie?" he whispered her name. "I'm sorry I hurt you, I didn't mean to, I was just upset and felt bad because I don't want to see you hurt and . . . ." He couldn't finish.

Mel's trembling stopped and she slowly turned from the door to face him. Tears streaked her lovely face and went tumbling down her cheeks as she blinked. Her blue sea green eyes were breathtaking, her lips were so supple and sensual that he could feel a strange and wonderful power emanate from them and penetrate him to the core. The feeling made him giddy and a little weak.

Ant's pulse ran high and his heart beat hard against his chest with each passing second. Mel's long flowing hair showed iridescent in the splinter of sunlight that pierced the window in the door. She was a goddess he thought as his hand slowly crept up to caress away a shimmering tear from her cheek. She didn't speak but just stared at him with the same powerful feelings of awareness and emotion. They drew closer and closer together. Melanie swallowed hard and slightly parted her lips to receive him. Their lips met in a soft hesitant embrace and it was incredible! She could feel his desire for her and just melted into him, giving him herself completely as their kiss grew stronger and stronger.

Mel had kissed him before but it was all in jest, never anything like this. It was pure fire and she floated like a feather as his soft firm lips commanded her and worked their will to enslaver her further. Ant's tongue probed sweetly around in her mouth giving her the sweetest sensation from head to toe. She could feel herself growing hotter and her desire for him becoming more urgent as his hands slowly caressed her entire body. Mel was tingling all over and getting weak. All she could do was droop listlessly in his arms like a rag doll, savoring him again and again.

Ant was as lost in her as she in him. His mind was awash with desires and confused thoughts of lovemaking and sensual discovery. She felt so soft and silky that he was sure he was going to leave bruises from caressing her so harshly and ferociously. Ant didn't know where he got the strength from but he slowly reached down and grasped her legs in the cleft of his arm and picked her up.

She willingly feel into them, accepting his will over her completely. He carried her gently to the bedroom and lay her on the center of the bed, never breaking their kiss once. As he joined her, there their movements became more intense and hurried. Mel could feel his strong virile muscles through his tank top shirt. She let her fingers and hands walk shamelessly all over him on his back and chest. Ant climbed on her completely covering her now and Mel just loved it. She shifted herself to accommodate by spreading her legs.

She could feel his muscular stomach pressing against her and the feeling was exquisite. She could feel her juices beginning to flow and a sense of urgency growing between her legs. She ground her hips into him and moaned because of the tawdry and decadent feel of it. Ant's body was on fire now and his manhood was growing harder and more erect with each second.

Mel pushed herself into him. He drove into her equally as diligent but was trying to hold himself back just in case she was teasing him again. He didn't want to commit himself on another wild goose chase. He could feel her womanhood underneath him and he focused his tool on that spot and pressed with verve and hunger to be inside of her. Mel swooned at the move and her breath was lost for a brief second as she looked into his desire filled eyes.

She pulled him back to her and kissed him with new diligence and hunger as she ground into him gyrating her hips in time with his movements. She moved shamelessly and with true abandon. Ant remembering what she looked like down there bore a wolfs lust on his back and he hiked up her legs grabbing her by her thighs and pulling her bottom up into a steep angle. He then proceeded to bear down hard and grind into her with a fierceness that mad Mel suck in hard and pause. He could feel her trembling as she wrapped her legs around him wantonly for the next assault. The move caused his penis to lurch in his pants sporadically. Oh! He had to have her now!

Ant raised his head from her slowly, breathing hard as if he'd been running. He looked longingly into her eyes as he held the pressure on. Mel's eyes had been reduced to sensual slits and her mouth was a dry wellspring of taste and warmth. She gave him a slow but solemn nod of acquiescence and submission, telling him, "I know you want me and it's okay . . . I won't reject you." Ant leaned into her to kiss her once more and lay beside her so he could undo her pants. He was so excited and eager that his hands trembled and were shaky. So shaky in fact that she eased her hand down on his and gently helped him unzip them. Once she had done that she guided his hand into the fold of her silky panties and down to the heaven that awaited just beneath.

"SSS OH! YES!" she sighed as he touched her and delicately parted her full and moist lips with his finger.

The silky wetness that Ant felt just about made his mind explode. He pressed his finger deeper and caressed her again. *"SSS . . . OOH . . . ANTHONY!* She swooned, pressing his hand down even more as she drove her hips up to meet it.

Mel slowly spread her legs to give him full access to the deepest recesses of her. Ant, taking his cue from her movements, pushed his hand down into her and pressed as deep as his finger would go. She gasped and moaned at this new feeling. Ant could feel her firm softness as if she surrounded his finger and clamped down on it, this told him that she was still a virgin.

Now aware of this new knowledge, Ant knew he would have to be especially gently or he would hurt her and ruin any pleasure he or she might feel today.

Mel sucked in hard and deep as Ant massaged and caressed her to the point of madness. He stroked her slowly and deeply, being sure to harass her clitoris with his thumb every now and then. When he introduced two fingers into her she froze and went rigid. The feeling of the new intrusion excited her so much she didn't know whether to let him go forth and take a chance on screaming like a banshee from the sheer pleasure of it, or holding him back and maybe losing out on what it would have felt like to have him do it . . . . she went for broke and released his hand letting him press on.

Mel bucked like a horse. She threw her head all the way back and arched her back, pressing into Ant's hand so harshly he had to reposition himself to keep up with her movement. She breathed heavily and gyrated like a spinning top. The feeling was so delicious and decadent that she began to suck her own fingers in time with his movement in and out of her. The feeling went all the way down to Mel's feet and up her bottom into her back.

Ant couldn't believe how wet she was getting and thinking a towel might have been beneficial here but he didn't know he was going to be doing anything so didn't have one on standby like he usually did. Mel ground herself against his hand with energy and complete lust.

Ant was really not doing much but just holding it in place she did all the work. Suddenly she went wild and was holding onto his hand with both of hers and driving it into herself as she gyrated up and down on it. She buck hard then froze in mid air and started trembling and vibrating with her head bridged all the way back.

Ant could feel a sporadic pinching of his fingers inside of her as she squeezed them in quick succession. She hardly made a sound except for a trembling *"Oh . . . oh . . . oh . . ."* that trailed off her lips like air escaping a balloon. Her face was sweaty and her beautiful tresses were stuck haphazardly around her face covering most of it. She lightly tapped his hand as if to say. *"Anthony we have to stop now . . . this is getting too intense."* "Anthony . . . wait" she whispered but not removing his hand.

Ant's mind released like steam as the sound of her voice dropped him from elation and lust to devastation and dejection. "Aww here it comes" he said to himself readying his mind for the rejection once again. "Damn! I was so close!" he lambasted. "Did I do something wrong Mel?" he asked not wanting to ask the obvious but feeling he had to at least know. Pain and anticipation were painted all over his face. Mel just wistfully and with semi-delirious lazy eyes smiled at him. "Oh no Anthony, I just need to remove my pants because you're making me so wet! I don't want to mess up my clothes sweetie."

Ant thought he'd died and gone to booty call heaven! He tried not to let his joy show but it was impossible and he smiled a huge toothy grin and eased his hand from her slowly to help her take them off. Ant pulled her pants and panties off with one smooth motion, "OH SHIT!" he thought as his mouth fell open at the full exposure of her sweet love mound.

Mel laid back and spread her legs exposing a most gorgeous site to the male eyes. Her mound was a smooth, plump grassy knoll of womanhood that screamed to be touched. Ant thought that if it was a golf course he'd play 36 holes without stopping, if it were a taco he would gain ten pounds from eating it. Either way she was a blissfully lovely specimen of a woman.

Ant resumed his foreplay wanting to work her into as much a frenzy as he could before taking her. This wasn't very easy because his own penis was a raging fire right now that was threatening to explode any minute.

Ant's hand moved quicker now and more deliberate in the areas she seemed partial to the most. Mel showed her approval of his attentiveness by grabbing hold of it again and grinding in to it as before. "SSS . . . OH ANTHONY THIS FEELS SO DAMN GOOD!" she cut lose not caring if anyone was around to hear. Ant had added another finger and it had gotten the expected response. Mel drove, ground, and bucked herself in to a frenzy and was shaking her head wildly in a convulsive fit.

"ANTHONY . . . NOW! . . . TAKE ME NOW! BABY PLEEESSSEE I WANT YOU INSIDE ME NOW BABY! She demanded almost yelling it. She looked at Ant with a lust that bordered on pain and he knew she was ready for him completely.

Ant removed his hand at the sound of her sucking air like a popped hot hair balloon. He began stripping off his clothes. He tore at them feverishly wishing he had on something less sturdy. As he climbed back into bed and between her waiting legs he reflexively looked out the window and saw a familiar shape walking slowly up the flight of steps. "OH DAMN . . . it's big momma and she's coming up the stairs now!" "She's home? . . . Oh my god Anthony" whispered Mel almost hysterical. "Quick, run into the bathroom and get dressed, I'll straighten up the bed!" he said scooting off the bed and getting into his own clothes a lot faster than he took them off.

Mel jumped off the bed then reached down for her own clothes and ran for the bathroom.

Ant couldn't pass up one last confirmation of the booty he'd just been denied. He smacked her lightly on the bottom as she passed him. "Anthony!" she said looking back smiling and pleasantly shocked by the more than pleasing encroachment.

She ran semi naked into the bathroom closing the door. Ant worked frantically trying to get the bed in order then reached for his can of air freshener under the book shelf. He blasted away like he was spraying roaches and trying to kill every one.

He wanted to make sure that there were no signs and scents of sex anywhere in the house. Soon the rattle of keys against the hard wooden door could be heard and his grandmother was opening it and coming in. Mel on cue had just finished dressing and fixing her face and hair and quickly came out of the bathroom. To Ants amazement she looked and smelled much like she did when she first got there.

Ant motioned her to sit on the floor near the video game system. She dropped down and began playing as if she had been doing it for the last hour. "Hey gramma" chirped Ant as he greeted her at the door. He tried not to sound too nervous or guilty knowing big momma had a bullshit detector built into her ears. "Hey Antney, how's my boy?" "Fine just sitting around playing video games with my buddy Mel" he said emphasizing her name in the masculine form and trying to disenfranchise her femininity by stressing the word *buddy*.

He did this to lend weight to the idea that she was not a girl friend so his grandmother wouldn't suspect anything. "I thought that truck out there was your friend Melanie's?" she said furrowing her brow and pointing over her shoulder. "Yes ma'am, that's just what we call her, she's kind of a tomboy if you know what I mean" he said in a low and conspiring voice, hoping the little distraction from the truth helped. "Is that right?" she said putting her hand to her mouth and shaking her head. "Lawd a mighty, such a pretty young thang and she thank herself a boy . . . tch tch tch . . . these younguns today" she said getting ready to go into the next room and put down her things.

Just then Mel poked her head around the corner, "Hello Mrs. Williams" she said in her normal sweet way. "Oh hey baby how you doing?" she said giving her a big hug. She grunted some as she was being crushed into the older woman's huge breasts. "Is you two hungry?" "Uh no ma'am" answered Ant quickly. "We was just about to leave and go meat up with Matt and get some pizza." "Now Antney, you can't go on eating that kind of junk food all the time boy! you'll just waste away to nothing, look atcha now . . . just skin and bones" she said grabbing his wrist and wriggling it like a bag of grapes.

Mel just laughed heartily. "I wan't you to have at least one sit down meal this week you hear?" "Yes ma'am" he said grinning bashfully. "Well let me let ya'll younguns go do ya business, I need to sit down and soak these hear fee o' mine, they hurts something terrible from standing all day." "Okay big ma" said Ant watching her hobble slowly into the next room then out of sight. "It was nice seeing you again Melanie, you come back soon okay?" "Yes ma'am" said Mel shouting in her direction.

"Whew! That was close" said Ant grinning. Just then, Mel reached up like lightning and soundly but lightly slapped him across the face. The shock of it was so sudden all Ant could do was stand there and look. Before he could get a chance to think anything Mel followed up by snatching him to her and giving him a blazing kiss. "That was for suggesting that I was a man!" she spat at him as she pushed him away with a smack as their lips parted.

Ant just stood rubbing his face and wondering what the hell just happened. "The next time you confuse me for a man Anthony Williams you better look between my legs!" she whispered harshly and standing with one hand on her hip and pointing the other at him like a poker. "Get me?" she said smiling at him and pulling him back to her to hold him.

Ant just nodded mindlessly, "Okay!" He didn't have a clue of how or what would make a woman wanna fuck you one minute and beat the shit out of you the next. "Ready to go?" he asked her easing her from him. She nodded and they went out the door. "That was too close Anthony" she whispered as they walked to the truck. "Yeah I know, if I hadn't looked when I did . . . our asses would be busted right now . . . well maybe not your ass, but mine sure as hell would have been!" Mel just giggled lightly at the thought of Ant getting run all around the house by his grandmother as she wielded a switch after him.

"So what do we do now Anthony?" "I don't know, that was just something to get her off of us for a minute." "Well we could do what you suggested and go meet up with Matt, maybe you, me him and Cheryl could go cruising or something?" she said looking most innocent and hoping he didn't detect any falseness or deception in blending the four of them together.

"Naw he's with his girl Retta this weekend." "Oh . . . I see" she said looking away a little disappointed. "Still hung up on him huh, Mel?" he said leaning against his door and lightly drumming his fingers on it.

Mel didn't want to lie to him and didn't think it would work anyway, so she just nodded without turning around. Ant just sighed long and loud, shaking his head as if he was dealing with a wayward two year old who wouldn't stop playing in the street. "Oh well, you'll learn one day I guess, but for now I won't push you Mel, cause I know you'll do what you think is best for you anyway."

She reached out and touched his hand squeezing it. "Thanks Anthony, I appreciate that." "So come on . . . . "love struck!" let's go to the mall and play some real games!" Mel smiled at him then started up the truck. "Okay then . . . better hold on your ass!" "Oh hell!" he said gripping the seat and dashboard. Mel peeled off the curb so fast, Ants head was jerked backwards bumping it against the head rest. "Ow! Crazy girl." Mel just giggled and left a skid mark in front of Ant's house.

The afternoon was turning out to be really nice and Matt and Retta were having a good time. It had been quite sometime since they last spent any quality time together without interruptions. It's really hard sometimes when you love someone who lives across town and goes to a different school than you do.

They managed to get by and keep the relationship alive and very much on fire! Their romance was a special kind, the type that could outlive all bound s and barriers of time. They loved each other with a fervor that would see no equal or ever be broken apart.

Living in the 80's and being a teenager in high school was a special time. It was a time of fast living and new discoveries. A time of great friendships, confused feelings and just trying to simply fit in. A time when romance and great first time loves blossomed and grew until the final day of graduation when we all say our heart felt goodbyes and make false promises to stay in touch.

It was all, so very wonderful and hurtful at the same time. It usually left you with feelings and thoughts of inadequacy and doubt about who you were or were going to be, what you wanted to do with yourself and life as a whole . . . . Still it was wonderful and magical and all that mattered was who was dating who and was this person playing any sports or not.

The boys chased the girls and the girls made sure that the prize sought after was well worth the catching and that everyone knew about it. It wasn't odd to see several girls or guys in competition for the same person, hell that was normal.

What wasn't normal was not being part of an in-crowd or someone that everyone recognized as popular and respected. Being in high school could be a trauma all it's own when it wanted to be. It was a totally insular, self contained, and manipulative environment of the worst kind. It was a secular and private class system so demanding and controlling that it weighed against some of societies best examples in history, it would out shine most of them as a hierarchy.

Parents, even though they themselves had experienced much of the same things as their children when they were teenagers, would still find it inconceivable the rate at which things in their children's lives have changed and become so controlling.

Just to have others speak kindly or supportive of you, especially when they just happened to be part of the social elite, could and has so profound an effect on a boy or girl till it could make you whole or make you kill yourself.

No . . . high school in the 80's was an institution all it's own. How you developed throughout the rest of your life could and usually did depend on how you lived or died in this concrete jungle called high school.

Aretta and Matt managed to get by without too much hazing and emotional bruises. They weren't really any more special than anyone else or even part of the "IN" crowd, but more or less members of their own sect, a branch in the tree of social acceptance.

They really didn't give a damn and thought of those who operated under the pressure of others opinions as "Air heads" and weak. So what if they didn't wear Jordache or Calvin Kline jeans every day of the week. Who cared? Whether or not they made a fashion statement every other week. Or hung around with the pretty people, that too was considered by them to be signs of a deteriorating sense of self worth and a lack of moral fiber.

Something they had no problems with. They simply loved each other for who they were to each other and without reservations of how others thought of them.

Ant and Melanie had just come into the mall at the arcade entrance. They were holding hands and seemed to be at ease with each other in light of their recent tryst and it's tragic death before it could completely blossom into the earth shaking experience they both knew it would be.

Their general appearance to others drew a collection of funny looks, interested glances and more whispering than you'll find in any kindergarten classroom during quiet time.

Melanie was of average height and Ant was tall. She was dressed in debutante casual, he was the perfect jock in pro league basketball shorts and matching tank top. This really didn't seem odd at first but then again she was white and the daughter of a successful well know business man and he was black and a blue collar workers son.

In a place like middle Georgia a couple like this was a little rare especially in broad day light and out in the open like they were and showing obvious affection for each other. Ant looked at the many faces that seemed to target and bore into him like a core drill. He felt a strange awareness and uneasiness that he had never felt before. This was compounded by the fact that Ant stood over six feet tall and really stood out.

He began to feel like some odd looking side show freak being led by his handler. His hand started to feel a little uncomfortable and tacky and he thought about releasing her hand to remove some of the heat he was drawing. Some of the people were old and some where their age but all noticed them and showed their uneasiness or dislike at him being her escort.

Melanie could feel the same odd disconcerting feeling of being observed herself and it was just too blatant to be called casual glancing but more along the lines of reckless eye balling. She also saw the growing concern in Ants eyes and noticed that his hand that held hers so tightly as they walked to the building had grown less as they went. She could feel his discomfort and rising pain and the feel of his now sweaty hand as he slowly tried to release it from hers.

This made Melanie mad. She had never in her life been exposed to this kind of rebuke from anyone much less a bunch of strangers in and over crowded mall, who really couldn't care less if she lived, died, or grew roses out of her ass. She had never been taught that it was right or lawful to dislike a person because of their color or nationality but instead to accept all people as individuals, with each having their own personality and habits.

Even her father had stood up against such bias at one time or another and she felt empowered by this pre-established moral code and strength of character her father had laid. She would not succumb to it either as she had seen so many of her former friends and some relatives do when the situation or mood struck them.

"Anthony" she said softly but firmly looking up into his furrowed eyes. "Don't let go of me baby . . . okay, I know how you feel right now and I feel it too but I don't care one bit about any of them so hold onto me and don't be ashamed or afraid of anything okay?" she said caressing his hand with the other. Ant looked down at her and smiled.

He didn't know what she was feeling and thought only to save himself and her from any further scrutiny from others. But what he forgot was that Mel was different and not to be corralled with other small minded people of bigots in this town.

"Thanks Mel, I really needed to hear you say that, I wasn't sure how you was feeling and I didn't like the feeling of exposing you to unnecessary attitudes." "Hey babe, don't sweat it!" she said lightly punching him in the arm. "I'm not that fragile and I'm for damn sure not! Screwed up like those assholes over there, so come on let's forget about them and go have some fun!"

Ant smiled wider and led her down the main concourse of the mall. "Let's get something to eat first" he said. "I got the munchies." "Me too, I didn't eat much for breakfast this morning." "How come?" asked Ant. "Oh I don't know, sometimes I just wake up in a certain mood and then I don't wanna eat much or anything at all." "Yeah, I know what you mean." "So where do you want to eat?" he asked her.

"We could go to Mickey D's if you want, or we could go to Annabelle's."

"I don't know about Annabelle's, they're a little outside my pocket range right now." "Don't worry Anthony, I get to eat there free once a month when I'm not working, it's part of the perks of working there." "Oh yeah?" "Yep!" "Well let's go then!" he said eagerly leading her on their way.

Matt and Retta had been leisurely browsing through several shoe stores and other shops trying to find a good pair of hiking boots or some that would go along with their outfits. They finally found some in a store called the "Bootery." "Okay Red, we've got everything we need, can you think of anything else we need to go with this stuff?" "No, not really, I think we got it covered." "Okay, so what do you want to do now?" "Well I am kind of hungry and tired from all this running around" she said drooping some. "Well I'll tell you what, let's go get a sandwich or something from someplace then maybe take in a movie." "Okay that sounds good" she said rubbing her tired and tense neck. "How about Mickey D's?" he offered. "Oh no Matt, their food sucks and the only thing worth eating is the fries."

Matt scratched his head and nodded in agreement. "Yeah, it does taste kind of synthetic when you think about it." "Yeah, you're right Matt, it does kind of leave an awful taste in your mouth awhile after you eat it, can we go back to Annabelle's?" Retta asked hugging him and looking at him with big cow eyes.

"Yeah, we can do that." "Do you have enough money left . . . I mean they are kind of high . . . maybe we should get something someplace else, I don't want you to spend all your money on me today, you might want something for yourself later" she said starting to pull him towards the food park. "It's okay babe, I got it covered, besides, when we ate there last it was dinner and we had drinks and stuff, they also have a good lunch menu that's pretty good and don't cost a lot." "Okay if your sure." "Yeah, I'm sure, let's go."

They walked a short way down the main concourse to the end and turned right. The restaurant was below them near the exit. As they came down the elevator, Retta saw Ant walking around the corner heading to the exit with some white girl.

"Matt there goes Ant!" "Where?" "Over there, going towards Annabelle's . . . see?" she said pointing at the tall young man in a red basket ball outfit. "Oh shit!" he thought seeing the couple. "He's got Mel with him! . . . what the hell do I do now?" "I can't let them meet, how do I know how they will react to each other, I can't just turn around and not go! Retta would get suspicious as hell or mad . . . maybe they won't see us and we can sit someplace else." "Matt are you alright?" "Huh?" "I said are you alright? You look like you've seen a ghost or something?" "Naw, I was just looking" he said not sounding to sincere.

Retta gave him a doubtful look and leaned against the door with her arms folded. "Matt are you keeping anything from me that I need to know about?" "No! babe I'm fine . . . I was just thinking about something" he said trying to laugh it off but it wasn't working. "Like what?" she asked imploringly and looking at him like he was as transparent as the windows around them. "Um, like what's he doing here, that's all." "Why wouldn't he be here Matt, it is a free country . . . why wouldn't he be here?" she said pressing him like a vice.

Retta was nobody's fool and when she smelled a rat or thought she was looking at one. She seldom let the little critter go if she thought he was guilty of something. "No reason . . . I just remembered that he told me he had some stuff to do today that's all" he said looking at her and trying his best to lie his way out of this growing situation. Retta looked at him and for a brief second felt that she may have been getting jealous again and that wasn't fair to Matt who was only trying to spend some quality time with her.

"Okay Matt" she said dropping her arms and hugging him again. But she could still feel it in her woman's heart that he knew more that he was letting on. Soon the elevator stopped and they got off heading to the restaurant. Matt looked around sheepishly to see if he could spot Ant but it was difficult. The restaurant was always kept in a dim light for privacy and atmosphere. "Let's go sit over there" said Matt pointing to the right side of the room. It took a second or two for their eyes to adjust to the change in the light, coming from bright light to almost no light.

He put their packages down beside the table and slide in beside Retta in the half moon type booth. Just then a waitress appeared from nowhere and almost scared him to death.

"Matt are you okay?" she asked when he squeezed her shoulder hard from sudden fright. "I'm sorry babe, I didn't see the lady and she spooked me." "I'm sorry sir I apologize, it is a little dark especially when you come in from the outside, anyway my name is Joanne and I'll be your server today, what can I get you today?" "Uh we haven't decided yet, we just got here." "Well I'll give you a few minutes to look over our lunch menu, in the meantime what can I get you to drink?" "I'll have an ice tea" said Matt. "Me too" said Retta starting to look at Matt strange again.

She noticed that he was still staring around the room blankly as if he were looking for someone. "Matt! Who are you looking for?" she asked getting a little hot and very suspicious.

"Uh nobody, I was just looking around trying to get my eyes adjusted." "Are you sure you weren't looking for Ant and his date?" "No . . . why would you say that?" "Because if you were, you're looking in the wrong place" she said pointing directly in front of them and slightly to the left of his vision. Matt looked around and saw Ant and Mel Sitting with their elbows on the table and looking straight at him smiling. "Oh hell! . . . I'm fucked now" he thought as a bead of sweat suddenly appeared at the base of his neck and slowly trickled it's way down his spine.

Aretta just sat quietly and watched him sweat, wondering what kind of tall tale he would try to use to get out of this one. "Aren't you going to say hello?" she asked almost sweetly.

"Uh yeah, I didn't see them, it's so dark in here" he said trying to smile his way through it, but all the while thinking how he could turn this seriously corrupted development around and take the heat off of him.

He was sure Retta was scrutinizing the hell out of everything he said and did. "Do you mind if I invite them over?" he asked softening and lilting his voice just enough to sound sincere he even smiled and tried to look genuinely eager. Retta studied the mask he was wearing and wasn't buying it, even in this dim light she could tell he was hiding something and trying to throw her a curve.

She volleyed the psychological ball with great dexterity and shot it back at him. "Sure! Go ahead . . . he is your best friend after all." You could have sliced lead with the look she was giving him, her eyes were like industrial grade lasers and they were calmly fixed on his face not to be moved. "No! you are" Matt corrected her sharply and returning her look gaze for gaze.

"Ant is my buddy." Retta shifted under the weight of his look and sat back in her seat unmoved by his rash comment. Matt got up and walked over to them. "Hi guys." "Hi Matt . . . What's up ole buddy" said Mel and Ant. "What are you guys doing here?" he asked. "Oh just cruising around doing this and that, we came to play some video games and maybe look around awhile."

"That's nice." "What about you and Retta?" "Oh, we just came to do some shopping and maybe catch a flick" he said looking at Mel.

She had been studying her nails trying to avoid his eyes for fear of letting her feelings show. Ant was trying to be diplomatic as well but finding it hard being he just wanted to burst out laughing at his friend, knowing full well the intense amount of pressure he was being subjected to.

Matt could see it in his face and partially hear it in his voice, the laughter he was trying hard to swallow. "So would you guys like to come join us?" he said trying to sound inviting and praying Mel didn't want to accept.

He knew Ant wouldn't but it was a gamble on Mel. Women can be quite fickle and in a situation like this one . . . down right mean. Ant raised an eyebrow and looked at him as if to say, "Matt are you fucking silly or what? . . . look who I have here and look who you have there, you can't possibly be thinking of putting them together?" Matt was fully aware of his unspoken concern and quickly winked at him to show he knew what he was doing.

"I don't know Matt . . . are you sure we wouldn't be intruding?" said Mel still looking at her nails. "Yes I'm sure" he said giving her a sunny smile that he hoped was as convincing as he thought it looked. Mel and Ant got up and went over to their table where Retta was busying herself in the menu.

"Retta?" he said getting her attention. "This is Melanie Johnson and you know Ant." Retta smiled at Mel sweetly and shook her hand. "Hi . . . how are you guys today?" "Oh fine" said Ant and Mel. "Sit down please" she said motioning them into the booth opposite them. Mel went in first and sat across from Retta and Ant to the outside.

The situation was odd and nerve wracking for them all but for completely different reasons. Melanie just casually glanced around trying to smile and be aloof to the impending anguish she was feeling at being so close to Matt in the presence of his girl. "God she's beautiful!" thought Mel as she looked up at Retta who was also looking at her through the intimate glow of the candle light on the table. "Now I see why he refuses me and Cher so easily . . . this girl is certainly a beauty alright." "So Melanie" said Retta breaking the silence. "How long have you and Ant been seeing each other?" "Oh I'd say, off and on about a month I guess." "Are you guys dating?" "Uh, not really" she said looking at Ant sheepishly. "Right now were just good friends." "That's nice."

The whole atmosphere was wrong thought Ant. It was charged with an electric tension thick enough to cut with a knife and it made him squirm in his seat. Here he was sitting in the midst of a union that should never have been and was completely out of place! By the transparency of it all. He felt sorry for Mel because of the way Retta was patiently and painstakingly picking her apart bit by bit. On the surface it seemed harmless enough but still made him sweat.

If Retta only knew that the girl just inches away from her was systematically trying to seduce, engage in a team rape and fuck her man. She would shove that candle, lit straight up her ass! Ant thanked god when the waitress returned with their drinks.

"Oh I'm sorry did you have a table over there?" she asked Mel and Ant. "Yes we did, but we decided to sit with our friends here" said Ant. "Well let me get your drinks from there, I thought you had gone to the bathroom." "Naw we just moved." "Okay" she said leaving to get their drinks from the other table. "Now . . . what would you like to order?" she said coming back to the table and looking at Matt and Retta. "We'll have two bacon cheese burgers." "And you guys?" she said looking at Mel. "We'll have two Monte Cristo's without horse radish sauce" she said looking at Ant smiling lightly and attempting some brevity. He and Matt just laughed themselves into a fit. "What's so funny Matt?" asked Retta completely clueless of the joke.

"Well babe it's like this . . . ." "Matt, let me tell her!" chirped Mel trying to find or use anything to get her in edgewise with Retta and to try to diffuse this potential situation and her feelings. "It's like this Aretta, he and Ant were here sometime ago and ordered the same sandwiches, but Ant not knowing what horse radish sauce was ordered it and put a heap of it on his sandwich then bit into it, you should have seen him go!" "He looked like a blow fish with his mouth sewn shut, and that horse radish sauce was killing him!"

Retta laughed at this and felt a little better about things now and felt less like dismantling the girl across from her.

Soon the two couples had gotten their orders and settled down to a nice amicable lunch and conversation.

Buford was up to his elbows in dirt and grease as he worked on Audrey's engine. He had long ago found the problem and was in process of removing the faulty part. Audrey just stood by with her arms around her looking. She noticed that his hair was tussled and his coverall were soiled and drooping from the heat. Still she thought he was quite handsome in a rustic – rugged sort of way.

Buford had his sleeves rolled up to expose his powerful and strong arms. Audrey noticed that the veins in his arms bulged like cables and gave him a weight lifters appearance. She didn't mind this because she knew from experience that those same arms were gentle and could hold her just right. She caught herself blushing as she thought about this and tried to tone it down before she was noticed.

Buford looked up and smiled at her. He got up and took a short break to wipe his sweaty brow. "Whew! It's warm today" he said dabbing his face with a nearby greasy rag. "Sure is but it's still a nice day though" she commented. "So how are you coming along on the car?" "Oh fine I'm almost done, I just need to clean up your carburetor a little then re-install it." "That's great, I didn't think you would be done so fast by the way it's been acting for so long." "Yeah, well I've been under a few hoods in my time and I've found that European cars tend to be built a little better than some American cars, they usually don't need nearly as much maintenance or repairs if you take care of them." "So since you're almost done, why don't I go in and rustle up some lunch." "Sounds great" he said wiping his hands and fishing around in his coverall for his cigarettes. "What are we having?" he asked as an afterthought, producing a crumpled pack and tamping one out on his wrist.

"Well we still have some of that roast and stuff from last week . . . I could heat that up" she offered. "Yes that would be nice. that was a pretty darn good roast you made" he commented lighting his cigarette. "Okay I'll get going on that then" she said smiling at him and giving him a light peck on the cheek and walking away.

Buford just stared after her grinning to himself as he leaned against the hood of the car. He took a long drag on his cigarette and blew it from his nose. "She seems to be a really nice girl" he mused. "She's really thoughtful and sweet, and I wonder why no one else has scooped her up before now, but then again she said she has just broken up with her last boyfriend only a year or so ago, so maybe she's just getting back into the swing of things." He took one more drag from the cigarette and flicked it into an empty parking space then went on to finish putting the engine back together.

Just across from him in the window on the top floor, Alfreida was looking down at him. She thought he looked just like Matt only older and more distinguished. She had just come out of the shower and was waiting for Curt to come by. She and he was planning to go out to the lake for the afternoon and have a picnic. She really liked him and he liked her. Just now as she went about the business of drying her feet, her mind was busy reliving the day she went to help him shop for furniture. At first everything was fine and they had gone to every store they could find from Rhodes furniture to Haverty's but didn't find much they liked and only a few they did. Since they had no luck on that side of town they went over to the east side of Macon and that's when the sparks got going!

Alfreida and Curt had gone into a rental store that sold furniture for half price. They figured it would be a good deal and certainly cheaper. While they were browsing and looking around, a girl behind the counter had been watching Curt with great interest. She tried to do it on the sly and not be noticed. She looked up from her paperwork from time to time and gave him a curious and inviting look. Frieda felt herself getting annoyed and irritated at her gawking at him that way. But then again she felt a little foolish too and decided that she couldn't really get too mad about it because Curt wasn't her man . . . at least not yet anyway.

"Hey Frieda!" he called to her from across the isle. "Come check out this couch, it looks pretty good." Frieda broke from her thoughts and walked over to him and trying to give a little smile to hide her discontent. "What do you think?" he asked as she got there. "Oh it's nice, I like it." "Yeah, I kinda thought you would but I wanted to see ask you anyway."

The couch was a modern throw back to the 70's design. It was long and rounded in a rectangular sort of way with black and tan stripes all over it. It had a semi glossy texture and felt really comfortable thought Freida as she plopped down on it, testing it's feel.

"So Curt, what style or color scheme are you gonna work around?" she asked "Well my apartment is painted in a creamy tan color with a darker tan carpet in the living room."

"Then this couch should go nicely" she commented. "What about chairs and other stuff?" "Well I thought you could help me out on that stuff since I'm really no good at this sort of thing." Freida just smiled as got up. She felt a warm goodness in her stomach that he would value her opinion about anything that would become a part of his life or house. "So you want me to pick it all then?" "If you don't mind" he asked sheepishly. "Okay then, how much do you want to get or which rooms do you want to satisfy first." "Well, I thought I'd do it all in one swoop and just knock it out." "I see, so you brought enough money then?" "Oh yeah" he said producing a check book from his rear pocket. "Okay, then let's see . . ."

Frieda placed a finger on her chin and folded her arm across her chest and looked around thoughtfully taking everything in, including the short black girl who had still been reckless eyeballing Curt since they came in. "Well since you've already decided on this couch let's get the two matching chairs over there" she pointed across the room. "Get this tripod black and gold lamp, this black and glass coffee table and matching end tables . . ." "Hey slow down . . . I'm trying to write down these tag numbers, but you're leaving me!" he said laughing.

Frieda giggled at his awkwardness. "Oh, I'm sorry Curt I guess I just get carried away when I go shopping!" "Hey, that's okay, it's why I asked you to come, because I knew you had taste and would be a big help to me."

Soon she had gone through the whole store and picked out three rooms of furniture. The only thing left to do was to pick the stuff for the bedroom and bath. A few times sales people would come up to them to help but Frieda just shooed them away telling them, "I got this, when we're done we'll call you."

Curt was taken aback at Frieda's confident command of the situation and the fact that she was not quite an adult yet and dealing with them as if she were. That took him by surprise. It must have been her full body-well filled out figure that made them think that she was probably a little older than they first thought.

Soon they came by a large queen size water bed with black and emerald trim. It had a very nice modern head board done up in a strange collection of triangles that spread out in a fan like form. It was also colored in emerald with black flecks in the rendering plus gold trim around and between each section. It had a storage bin on each end and a light in each one. The doors were crystallized stained glass with flowers of green and gold to accentuate the setting. There was a huge black and green comforter on the bed and matching pillows, covers, and sheets. Underneath it were drawers for storage.

Now that's bad!" said Curt running his hand along the outer padding. "I ain't never seen a bed like this one before." Frieda was also moved with appreciation of this "Art Deco" creation. She had never been on a water bed but heard they were nice. She slowly ran her hand along the soft and billowy covers then eased herself onto the edge. The water moved like something was living in it. It swished and swirled away from her to the other side then back, raising her up some as it went.

Frieda eased onto it further then lay down placing her hands across her stomach like a dead person. "Oh Curt this is nice! You should feel it" she said smiling at him nervously not quite accustomed to the new feel. Curt didn't wait to be asked a second time and just scooted onto the bed and lay next to her. The wave action moved them closer together and they both just rose and fell with each wavy movement. The added motion made them giggle as the bed seemed to be on some sinister plan to move them ever closer and closer together. Soon they were face to face and their bodies were rubbing against each other as they went.

Frieda began to feel a strange tingling within her as her mind began to coordinate the movements of their bodies with her imagination of being with him in this bed naked. The thought made her nervous and a little excited as well.

Curt didn't say anything, but was beginning to see what the closeness and this sensual ride was doing to him as well. Frieda quickly looked away and got up. "We better go see about the bath set Curt, it's getting late" she said standing beside the bed and blushing quite openly. "Are you okay Frieda?" he asked concerned. "Did I do something wrong?" "Uh . . . no I was just thinking it's getting late that's all" she said looking at a dresser nearby so as not to look at him. "Don't you like the bed?" "Yes, Curt I like it." "Oh, I wasn't sure, do you think I ought to get it?" he asked half heartedly "Well it's your bed Curt why ask me?" she said sounding a little abrasive and guarded. "Yeah, I guess you're right" he said downcast.

Curt had thought secretly that she would someday join him on it but then he figured from her response to it that he had presumed too much, and in doing so frightened her again. *"Damn Curt! You screwed the pooch again knucklehead!"* he said lambasting himself for being a fool. "Look Curt I like the bed okay" she said interrupting his thoughts. "It's really nice, I'm just tired that's all." "Okay, well let's just go ahead and get the bath room stuff and then we can leave." "Okay then" she said forcing a weak smile.

Soon they were done and paid the lady at the counter. The stuff would be brought out tomorrow morning at ten. The ride home was subdued and quiet. All that could be heard was the soft sounds of his radio. The time was now eight o'clock and it was quite dark out. Curt decided to take the interstate to get her home quicker. Frieda was in her own world as she looked away out her window.

"How can I ever tell him how much I like him without coming on too strong. He's such a great guy and I really want him! I've never felt this way about any other guy before and I hope I didn't make him think I don't like him when I jumped away from him at the store like that. He probably thinks I'm a tease or something . . . Damn! Frieda . . . why can't you ever do anything right! You're gonna wind up losing the best thing that's ever happened to you and all because your too chicken hearted to speak up." She turned slowly to look at him. Curt seemed to be in his own world as well. *"I'll bet he wishes I'd never come with him and will probably never take me out ever again!"* He looked so fine and handsome, she thought looking at his profile as the lights from other cars illuminated the windshield ever so often. She wanted to tell him how much she liked him and wanted to be more than friend's but didn't know how. In the past she had found it easy to talk other boys because that's all they were . . . just boy's! and none of them came close to making her feel like Curt did.

Curt didn't know it but he intimidated her and made her very self conscious about herself and her life up to this point. Not to mention he stirred up hidden desires in her that she only felt when watching soap opera's. The problem was this wasn't a soap and he was no boy! but a man in every sense of the word and this alone made her tingle. She slowly eased her hand over to his and touched it lightly, giving it a gently squeeze. The feeling of him gave her a sense of urgency like she was doing something not forbidden but naughty and the feeling made her breathing pick up some.

Curt turned to her slowly then looked down at her hand, then into her eyes. He could see the longing in her eyes and her emotions and the rising turmoil within. Now he knew how she really felt about him and he no longer had to wonder. He gave her a sweet smile of assurance then turned back to his driving. "Oh god, can he know?" she thought elated if it were so. "Is it possible my feeling got the best of me and I gave myself away?" she felt him squeeze her hand and that told her all she would need to know.

Soon they were at her house. He pulled in to the parking lot and drove to her apartment. He shut off the engine and just sat. "Curt can I tell you something?" she said timidly. "Yeah babe, what's up?" Frieda began to tease her fingers rubbing them together over and over in her lap in a nervous fit. "How do you feel about me? . . . I mean really?" "Well Frieda, I've often wondered that same question about you baby, but if it'll help any I like you . . . I like you a lot and always have wanted you to feel the same about me, but since I'm so much older, I just knew you wouldn't want me." "Curt you're not old, you're just 20 and I'm 17 going on 18 in four months, and as for me liking you, you don't know how long I've waited for you to say that you really liked me and wanted me." "I always thought you only wanted to be friends and that's all, but when you and I were on that water bed together I got to feeling funny and it scared me so I got up."

"What were you afraid of Frieda, we've spent the night together in Atlanta?" "Shouldn't that have made you afraid more than that?" "Yes, but it was different, I hardly knew you and I was drunk so it didn't bother me, hell I was so strung out you could have done anything you wanted to me and I doubt I would have stopped you" she said light heartedly.

Curt looked away and felt like he'd been slapped, "Frieda don't say that, I'm not that kind of guy okay, and you're not that kind of girl either!" "I know Curt, that's why I've grown so close to you and care for you like I do." "You like me for me, and not what I look like" she said going quiet as she looked down at herself. "Curt I haven't dated anyone in a long time, and when I did it was just for laughs never anything serious." "I know what I look like and yes I am a big girl for my age, I also know that it's because of this reason most or all of the boys I've ever dated have been interested in me, for just my body and nothing more." "I didn't give into that or them and because of it, I have a bad reputation that I don't deserve, yeah, I get wild and have fun but I haven't slept with anyone ever . . . Curt I'm still a virgin" she said her voice growing raspy as tears worked their way up her throat.

"This is also why I have been somewhat skittish and distant from you because I had to know if you wanted me the same as they did, now after seeing that you don't, but you respect me for me, that means a whole lot to me!" "That night that we went to Atlanta, most guys would have tried to have sex with me the minute we got into the room much less wait until we got into bed, but you didn't do that Curt you treated me like I was something special . . . which makes you special!"

"So what your telling me is of all the boys or men you've been with, you've never done anything at all with any of them?" he asked incredulously. "That's right Curt, I only just kissed them and maybe hug them but I've never let anyone get any closer than that, I could usually tell what they were after within the first ten minutes." "Well how do you know I didn't want you that way and think that way?" he said evenly looking into her soft brown eyes.

"Because Curt, you had the chance, I was almost naked and in bed beside you passed out, but you didn't touch me . . . that's how I know, you were honorable and decent Curt." "Do you know how hard that is to find in a man these days?"

Curt just turned away and started messing with his stick shifter. Frieda lightly touched his chin and turned his face to her. She kissed him ever so gently on the lips. His mouth was sweet she thought and his lips were full and soft. His mustache tickled her nose but it was nice. She felt his hands reach around her waist to pull her closer but it didn't quite work out because of the stick shift being in the way.

Soon they broke from the brief but sensual interlude. "I guess we can't finish this in here can we?" said Curt smiling at her. "No, I guess not, but that's okay because we've got this weekend coming don't we?" "And there's plenty of time for love" said Frieda leaning over to kiss him again.

Soon they broke from each other and Frieda got out of the car. "I'll see you tomorrow sweetie" she said waving at him. "Yeah, you gotta help me put that stuff in order, I don't know where it's supposed to go" he said laughing as he started the car.

Just then there was a knock on the door. Frieda hadn't been aware that she had been day dreaming all that time until the sound of the door brought her back to the present. Although she had been looking out the window at Buford, she didn't really see him when he suddenly left to go inside. "Who is it?" she called. "It's me, Lori" said a small voice on the other side. Frieda turned from the window and went to answer it, when she jerked open the door she could see an exhausted and sweaty little girl in a pink one piece bathing suit standing at the door.

"Hi" she said walking in un invited. "Whatcha doing?" "I just got out of the shower" she said still standing at the door. "What can I do for you Lori?"

Lori just flopped down on the couch with her limbs flayed out like a rag doll. "Nuthing . . . I'm just tired, I just came to see what you were doing." "Well I'm expecting some company shortly so if you don't mind I need to get dressed." Lori just bobbled her legs and stared at her blankly as if she were looking through a window.

"Who's coming?" she asked dryly. "None of you business you little twerp!" She snapped at her getting angry for being held incontinent by a toddler. Lori wasn't fazed but just sat grinning at her. "It's a boy ain't it?" Frieda was completely floored. She couldn't believe she was being interrogated by an eight year old and much worse she was actually arguing with her about it where as no conversation was even necessary.

"Goodbye Lori!" she spat trying to maintain control and pointing out the open door. Lori noticed that her bath robe had come undone and exposed her nakedness. Lori just grinned more as she began to blush. She got up slowly taking her time. "Can I have some cake?" she asked smiling brightly at a very hot and aggravated Alfrieda. Frieda gathered her robe around her now feeling a breeze. She stomped over to the table where a chocolate pound cake lay in a serving dish. She picked up the entire confection, tray and all and shoved it into her little hands. "Here! Take the whole thing . . . you're the only one who seems to like cake around here anyway!"

Lori took the dish and flashed her a surprised look of happiness and utter confusion. Frieda turned her around towards the door and escorted her out. "Bye Lori." "Gbye Frieda!" she sang "Thanks for the cake!" but it was too late her words were lost as the door closed in her face with a slam. Lori just shrugged and walked away down the stairs.

"What a total pest! She is" said Frieda going into her room to get dressed. She put on a pair of hot pink underwear and a pair of loose fitting shorts with her schools logo on them. Then she put on her favorite fraternity shirt from Morris Brown College. She threw her robe over the door and relaxed on her bed to wait. She wondered how long she would have to wait before Curt got there. She really couldn't' wait to see him.

Retta and Matt had long since left the restaurant and were now playing some video games to pass the time. They had said goodbye to Mel and Ant at the restaurant. She didn't think a lot about the little gathering but still felt that the girl liked Matt more than she let on. She couldn't really fault her though, it was hard not to like him. He was cute and all around desirable. Not to mention a really sweet guy. He was busy finishing a round of his favorite space game while she had long ago lost out and didn't want to play anymore. Instead she just watched him. "What time is it getting to be Red?" he asked without looking up. "It's 3:30 Matt . . . you about ready to go?" "Yeah, I'm getting kind of tired myself and it's been a long day." Matt looked over to his right and saw a small boy of about ten watching him play. "Hey dude, you want this game?" "Can I?" he said happily. "Sure, take over" he said moving aside for him. "Cool! . . . thanks!" he said appreciatively.

Matt an Retta just smiled at each other as he reached down to pick up the bags to leave. "Let's go give em a call" said Matt stepping out the door. The nearest phone is back in the center of the mall Matt!" said Retta showing her fatigue. "Damn! I forgot about that" he said thinking for a moment. "I know there's one in the Sears entrance by the courtesy desk." "Aw, Matt that's way over there!" she said pointing down the far side of the mall past the loading dock. "Well, I'll tell you what, you just take a seat on the bench and wait for me, I'll be right back okay?" "Okay Matt, hurry back!" "Okay" he said then kissed her and walked off quickly.

Retta just put her head down on her arms and leaned over to rest on her knees. After a few minutes she heard some feet walking in her direction. She raised up expecting to see Matt but was horror struck as she stood in the evil gaze of Camille Murcheson and two of her three brothers. She tried to compose herself and not let them see her fear but it was difficult. The two boys standing aside Camille were at least 6'2" inches tall and weighed at least 180 pounds each. Both were wearing Morris Brown fraternity shirts and athletic shorts with their socks bunched around the tops of their sneakers.

"So if it isn't miss BITCH!" She spat standing between the two giants and looking quite pleased with herself. "I been wondering where you were all this time." "This is that little bitch that cut my clothes off me and threw me out into the gym last week."

Retta began to flush red and shrink inside herself. She was deftly afraid and was quietly praying that Matt would come back soon. "Did you get my note that I left in your locker? . . ." "Yeah, that's right, I put it there you little scrawny yellow bitch!" "Look Camille, I told you before not to be calling me no bitch . . . or I'll fuck you up again" she said coolly trying to sound as bold and unshaken than she actually felt.

Just now Matt was heading out the store when his old buddy gumbo walked in. "Yo! Gumbo what's up?" he said giving him their traditional hand shake greeting. "What's up Matt?" "Nothing much man me and my girl Retta are just out here chilling doing a little shopping." "You mean that nice looking redbone with the long black hair she keeps tied up?" "Yeah, that's her, but now she wears it long and loose." "Really . . . that must be nice to see."

Gumbo had seen them together once at a foot ball game some time ago and thought she was fine! "Where is she now?" "Oh I left her around the front on a bench while I call my pop to come get us . . . she was feeling tired." "Around the front?" he asked concerned raising an eyebrow. "Hey man tell me . . . is she wearing a red Izod and some blue jeans?" "Yeah that's her." "Hey man it's two big dudes and some chick around there giving her shit!"

Matt didn't wait for more he ran around the corner with Gumbo close behind. As he got into view he could see the back of the two large boys but not the girl. Aretta was standing between them and the bench. Suddenly he heard a loud slap! Then one of the boys pusher her down on the bench hard. Matt lost it. He ran up behind the nearest boy and shoved a hand under and between his legs then took a savage hold of the boys testicals.

He screamed loud and Matt proceeded to pull him over backwards with his other hand, bridging him over his shoulder and slamming him on his fucking face! Gumbo had also caught hold of the other boy who had tried to go after Matt. He was pumping blows into his gut like a boxer then he grabbed his arm and spun him around, slamming him into the wall face first! The boy bounced off the wall and fell to the ground with his face covered in blood. Camille was beside herself with shock and hysteria.

The sudden attack had caught her entirely off guard. She had thought it was her who would be passing out the ass whipping but now seeing she was wrong and was watching her brothers get beat down by two strangers. She just stood with her mouth agape with her hands up to her mouth. She had screwed up quite a few times that day. The first being to solicit her brothers for a job she should have done herself, wine, lose, or draw. Her second mistake was going after Retta thinking her to be alone and defenseless. Her fatal mistake was slapping Retta in the face then turning her back on her. Retta after seeing Matt and Gumbo dish out the whoop ass got up and took a savage swing at the side of Camille's head. She connected squarely up side her head with her fist sending her spinning to the ground.

She tumbled over her fallen brother and landed on her ass. "Now who's a scrawny bitch!" cursed Retta coming after her for a second round. Gumbo caught her first. "Hey hold on sweetpea, she's done."

By now people had started to gather and watched the melee and a police unit was summoned. Camille's brothers were a hot mess laying on the ground. One still held his balls rolling around on the ground with blood coming from his mouth and several scrapes on his face. His nose was busted as well. The other boy was being helped up by Camille who was sporting a nasty bruise on her cheek. "Come on Matt let's beat feet man! I gotcha girl, you get your stuff." Gumbo scooped up Retta like she was a baby and ran toward the parking lot with her to his car. Retta was surprised but didn't protest. Matt was close behind with their bags. They ran down the parking lot in the direction he and Gumbo had come from. His car was close by and they all piled in with Matt in back and Retta being placed in the front. "Scoot over sweety!" he said to Retta smiling at her. She moved quickly and he got in and started the car.

They tore away from the scene and out of the lot before the mall cops could get outside. "Damn that was close! Man" said Gumbo grinning and looking in the rearview mirror. "Are you okay baby?" said Matt reaching up in front for Retta who happily came over the seat to him. "Yes Matt, I'm okay now and I'm so glad you were there." "I thought they were gonna kill me or something!" "Who were they?" he asked still pumped up and upset. "That was that girl Camille I told you about and her brothers from college, they walked up on me while you was in the store." "What for?" he demanded. "Matt please don't yell at me, I'm shaken up enough as it is." "I'm sorry baby, I didn't mean to, I'm just mad is all" he said holding her close and rubbing her back. Retta pulled from him and kissed him deeply.

Gumbo just happened to catch the move in the rearview mirror. "Damn! that's gotta taste good" he thought still driving off the mall property. "Matt I'm sorry if I got you guys into trouble." "Hey don't sweat it little mama" said Gumbo from the front. "Any body messes with Matt or his, he knows I got his back!" Matt just smiled and reached over to pat Gumbos shoulder.

"Matt all this started sometime ago when I got in that fight with those three boys." "What did they have to do with them back there?" "Well you see, after I had dealt with them, I walked on to my gym class." "Once I got there Camille was in the locker room trying to start some more trouble." "So what did you do?" "I beat her ass too and threw her out of the locker room into the gym butt naked." "Oh shit! . . . scuse me" said Gumbo sniggling to beat all.

"No you didn't?" "I sure did" said Retta proudly. "Then all the guys in the gym were chasing her all over the place whacking her on her ass with towels." Gumbo was stomping his foot on the floor board and laughing his ass off at the mere image of what that must have looked like.

Matt was laughing too and just shaking his head. It would have been funnier to him but the fact that if he had been just a minute or two late getting back to her or if Gumbo hadn't been there, there's no telling what might have happened to Retta.

"My Retta" he said hugging her. "What am I going to do with you?" Gumbo was still laughing. "Matt your lady has class! . . . I'm just loving that shit, I wish I could have been there to see it!" Retta just smiled and bathed in the warmth of their admiration and clung to Matt.

Matt gave Gumbo directions to Retta's house and soon they had arrived. His dad was just getting into the truck. Probably to come after them.

"Hey Gumbo, blow your horn! That's my dad." "Okay, BEEP BEEP!" Buford stopped and looked around to see who was blowing and why. He saw the little car coming at him, then stop. "Hey thanks again Gumbo, man I really appreciate you" he said giving him a solid grip and eye contact. "No sweat man, you know I gotcher back, just like you did for me my brother." "And Retta, you take it easy little mama, and don't you worry bout nothing either okay, Gumbo gotcha okay?" "Thanks Gumbo" she said then reached up and gave him a big hug and a kiss on the cheek from the back seat. Gumbo blushed a little. "Ya'll be cool Matt." "Alright G, I'll see you Monday." "Okay then."

Matt and Retta got out and Gumbo drove away tooting his horn as he left. "Who's that Rodney?" "That's one of my home boys." "I see, so tell me how come you didn't wait, I was on the way." "I'm sorry dad, we ran into a little trouble and had to leave in a hurry." "Oh yeah . . . what happened?" "Can I tell you about it later, I want to get her in the house first, she's still a little shaken." "Okay son, go ahead."

Matt took Retta and led her up the steps and into the apartment building. "Are you sure you're alright Retta?" he asked still holding her close. "I will be as long as you keep holding me." "Well I won't leave you then" he said as they reached the top of the steps. "No Matt, that's okay I know you love me and wouldn't leave if I asked you too, so don't worry I'll be fine, I just need a hot bath and some time to rest, it's been a busy day." She opened the door and went in. "Here let me set you stuff on the couch for you" he said walking in. "Retta is that you?" asked her mother. "Yes ma'am, it's me and Rodney." "Hi Rodney!" she yelled from the kitchen. "Hi Audrey!" he said then sat Retta on the couch. "What about Monday, will you be okay at school?" he whispered. "I don't know Matt" she said leaning on his shoulder with her face buried against his chest. "Well don't sweat it. you know I got people over there, I'll get word to them tonight and you won't have any trouble with Camille anymore, and as for her brothers, they just came home for the weekend and won't be bugging you either anymore." "Are you sure Matt?" she said looking into his eyes with all the hope and faith in the world brimming in her eyes. "Have I ever let you down yet?" "No Matt." "Okay then believe me, it'll be just fine."

With that he held her in his arms and kissed her passionately. "Oh how I love you so much" she whispered in her mind as they hungrily sought each other again and again.

"HONK HONK!" his dad was blowing the horn and getting impatient. "I better go sweetie" said Matt breaking from her. "I'll call you okay?" "Okay Matt . . . I love you." "And I love you too" he said then kissed her on the forehead and rose to leave. "I'll see you guys later Audrey, Lori." "Okay Rodney!" they said. Matt winked at Retta with a smile and dashed out the door and down the stairs.

"What kept you son?" asked his dad with a note of frustration in his voice. Matt climbed into the truck. "I was just talking over some things with Retta that was bothering her." "I see, so what's this about you having to leave the mall in a hurry?" "Well dad it's like this, when I went to call you I left Retta sitting on the bench outside because she was tired, when I came back I met a buddy of mine who told me Aretta was having some trouble with these two big college guys and some girl." "When I got there one of them had slapped her and one of the guys pushed her down on the bench hard, right about then I lost it." "Well what did you do?" he asked completely interested and wondering what his young son had done after getting pissed off. "Well dad to coin a phrase you know well . . . me and Gumbo Fragged their butts!" "I went up behind one and grabbed a hand full of his balls then I did a reverse fire mans carry on him and dumped him over my back and on his face." "Gumbo worked over the other one like Mike Tyson and Retta cold cocked the girl knocking her down over the one I put down." "The girl was the one who started it all from the get go." "Well son I don't understand why would someone just come up and try to hurt her for no reason, it just doesn't make any sense." "Well dad in a way it does." "How?" "Well from what Retta told me, the girl she hit is in her school and some of her classes, she's supposed to be a real witch and always trying to hurt people and down grade them to make herself look bigger." "Yeah so what?" "So the same day Retta took on those three guys she pushed up on her as well, shortly after the fight and wanted to fight Retta too! Retta gave her plenty of warning then wound up kicking her butt and throwing her out of the locker room and into a crowded gym butt naked." "NO she didn't?" he said smiling. "Yes sir, she did." "That girl of yours is really a fire cracker" he said shaking his head. "I know she don't take any crap from anybody and can take care of herself most of the time." "So I see . . . " he said lighting a cigarette. He blew out a long stream of smoke before he spoke again.

"High school has certainly changed a lot since I was in it." Matt just coughed and shook his head in agreement as he furiously rolled down his window for some air. "So what do you have in the bags?" "An outfit I bought and some shoes." "Did a little shopping eh?" "Yes sir, I thought I would get me another outfit for school."

Soon they were home, it had been a heck of a day and Matt was ready for bed. "So what are you doing after school tomorrow?" asked his dad. "I have track practice with the Varsity team." "Oh yeah, that's right you told me that, wasn't you supposed to be working out this weekend?" "Yes sir, but it kinda got side tracked when Retta came over." "Yeah, I know, so how do you feel about your ability to do well tomorrow?" "I feel okay about it I guess, I mean I feel strong enough and I've got good wind so I should be able to handle them without too much trouble." "I guess we'll see won't we?" he said pulling into the drive way.

He put the truck in park and they both got out. His dad unlocked the door and they went into the darkened house. "Are you hungry Dad?" "No not really I had something at Audrey's awhile ago, why were you gonna cook something?" "I thought I would warm up something from yesterday." "You can if you want to, but I'm fine, other than that you can put me together a spot of lunch for tomorrow if you would." "Yes sir."

Matt put his things on the table and went about putting together a lunch for his dad. He didn't warm up anything because it wouldn't be warm by the time he got to it tomorrow anyway. After a minute or two he was done and headed for his bedroom. He quickly undressed and took a quick shower. After a few minutes he finished and got out. Just as he was about to get into bed he remembered he was supposed to call Retta. "Oh shit! I almost forgot to call my boys to let em know what's up and to look out for Retta for me tomorrow." He quickly made three phone calls and all of them agreed that they would watch out for her being they knew the low down on Camille and couldn't stand that yellow bitch themselves. They would however need to stay out of sight or not let her know who they were. Once all that was done he fell asleep without hesitation. Morning came and brought with it the gentle whisper of the sound of rain. Sometime last night clouds had formed and given way to a light shower that would carry on to the morning and throughout most of the day. This was part of the charm about the sub-tropical climate some meteorologist had assigned to this region of Georgia. Matt only know it as the rainy season. Something which had no preset time or order for coming upon you. It came and went as it wanted to, bringing with it new life as well as a means to hate going to school. The damp dusty smell of the rain on the street filled Matt's nose and the warm dampness gave the room a cozy feeling. He knew he had to get up but fought against it anyway, rolling and curling up deeper in bed for a final dive into the cocoon of warmth he had formed within his blanket overnight.

Finally he threw the covers off with a flourish and jumped out of bed. He rubbed his face and looked at the clock on his dresser, it was 7:15. "Good!" he thought to himself. He would have some time to get there on time and because it was raining he would need it. Matt didn't waste any time. He ran into the bathroom to wash up. He had already taken a bath the night before so only needed to wash his face and brush his teeth. This saved him a few minutes that he could use to grab at least a sandwich for breakfast.

As he dressed he wondered whether or not he should ride his bike today. He wasn't worried about getting wet from the back wash of the tires, but knew long ago from experience that people seemed to forget how to drive when the ground was wet. He decided he would chance it and went to his closet in the den to get his rain suit.

Now it was 7:30 and he was making good time. He grabbed his book bag and ran into the kitchen. He pulled down a loaf of bread and pulled some cheese out of the refrigerator. He had hastily made a sandwich and was headed out the door. The rain had slowed some but that didn't mean a whole lot. This sort of rain came and went with as much consistency as a lightning strike. As he got down stairs Matt could see that his bike was soaked but it wouldn't matter because he was wearing his rain suit and mostly concerned about the engine being water logged. He grabbed it and shook free the excess water. "I hope this heifer starts" he said mumbling to himself.

Matt put the key into the ignition and kicked the starter on it. "PRR . . . PRRR" "Come on you ole yellow bitch!" he cursed it, still trying to hold onto his sandwich with his teeth.

Finally it started and he jumped on and floored it kicking up mud behind him as he went up the driveway. The bike skidded as he hit the street. The mud on his small tires was like a coating of grease and the abrupt skid made him lose his sandwich while he was wildly correcting for control. "Fuck! I was just beginning to enjoy that . . . damn I hate Mondays!"

Right about the same time on the other side of town, Retta and Frieda were getting off the bus at school. They ran into the building to avoid the torrent that had just begun from the light shower it had recently been. "Come on Retta!" yelled Frieda as she splashed into the building. A teacher was trying to get her to slow down as she came in but it was too late. Wet sneakers and waxed floors don't go together too well as she quickly found out.

Frieda's feet started sliding the minute she hit the floor. "EEEKKK!" she screamed in utter shock as all control went to hell in a New York minute. She flayed her arms wildly, slinging her purse and book bag to west hell somewhere. She grasped wildly at the air but the hall was so wide that their was nothing to grab onto. She slid like a bowler on a greased floor. She looked much like some crazed and epileptic stork landing on ice. Finally inertia had taken over and her feet took flight. Up she went, pure asshole and elbows as she landed on her backside with a resounding *SLAP!* Frieda sounded like a wet salmon being dropped on a pier.

"OWW!" she moaned whining and laughing at the same time. By the time she had stopped moving Retta had entered the building. She made sure to stop and wipe her feet before going further as she had seen Frieda's rapid and hilarious departure from controlled walking into uncontrolled flight.

Frieda was laying on her back and laughing at herself even though her ass, back, and pride were sore as hell. The teacher at the door, a smaller woman of about 40, ran over to her to check on her. "Oh my goodness child . . . are you alright?" Frieda raised herself slowly and looked at her hands that were red and stinging from hitting the floor. "Yes ma'am, I think so, I just hurt my hands and my butt a little."

Retta was hovering over her now and smiling trying not to laugh. "I knew that big behind of yours was good for something" she commented snickering. "Oh very funny smartass" she hissed at Retta through clenched teeth, not wanting the teacher to hear. "If you're still hurting later on, I want you to go to the nurse and let her check you out." "Okay Mrs. Crocker . . . thanks" she said gathering her stuff and walking down the hall. "Now you know better than to come in this building like that" she said as they got down the hall. "You know you can't come in here on a Monday like that running, especially if it's wet!, cause you know they wax on the weekends." "Yeah, I guess I forgot." Just then they heard someone else yelling, screeching and the sound of skidding feet just before going airborne and smacking into the floor. "*AWW NUTS!*" "Oh my goodness, this is starting out to be a very bad day" they heard Mrs. Crocker comment. They laughed and went onto to class.

This Monday was certainly collecting it's quota of victims and holding true to the nature of Monday's as all people knew it to be, which is SNAFU or Situation Normal . . . All Fucked Up! Soon the girls had reached their home rooms and as they went in they could see that almost everyone was there and huddled together in little groups talking.

Most of them were girls. At first Retta thought they were talking about her and the episodes of last week or maybe even yesterday. A pall of paranoia began to settle over her and make her uneasy and apprehensive. No one looked up at her really at all but just casually glanced at her nonchalantly and lightly acknowledged her presence and went back to their discussions.

Retta took her seat in the rear next to Frieda. "Hey short cake . . . what's up?" said a boy next to her. It was Marshal Jessup, on of her close associates. Marshal was a bit of a pariah of sorts as normalcy goes. He was a small little white boy who looked like he'd be more at home in a romper room than a high school. He had black curly hair and freckles with a gap in his front teeth that most say gave him an odd English look. He had soft hazel eyes and a confidence about him that intrigued some of his class mates and irked others.

He also had a crush on Retta. He had always like her since he first met her a year ago and would always call her short cake even though she stood a good foot taller than he. "Hi Marshal how are you?" she said less than happy. "Oh, I'm good and how about you?" "I missed you last week and nobody knew where you were." "I was out sick, I wasn't feeling too good and had to go into the hospital for awhile." "I'm sorry to hear that, I wish I could have known, I would have gotten you some flowers or something" he said sincerely and leaning towards her from his desk. "Oh that's so sweet of you Marshall, thank you for thinking of me" she said squeezing his hand and making him blush from the contact. "My boyfriend and mother got me some though, so I didn't go without" she said smiling at him. "Oh I see . . . " he said sounding a little deflated and disheartened by the news of existence of Matt.

Chapter 12

Needful Things

Retta could clearly see how the comment had hurt him and tried to ease his heart ache some. "But hey, you know you're always gonna be my best buddy right?" she said mussing his hair. This made him smile cause he always, much like a puppy, loved to be touched or petted by her. "Aww come on Retta, everybody's watching us" he complained appreciatively. And of course no one was looking but he liked to think they were.

Soon the bell rang signaling the start of the day. Their teacher was running a little late and looked a little out of sorts as he ran into the room, a thing he had forewarned his own students about many times.

"Good morning class!" he said putting his briefcase on his desk. "Good morning Mr. Simpkins" they all sang. "I'm sorry I'm a little late but as you can see we've got a little rain coming down and I got stuck in traffic because of an accident along the way." He quickly looked around the room to see if everyone was there before calling role. He spied Aretta in the rear of the room and their eyes met with a warm flash. He was so glad to see her there and gave her a warm smile and a nod not wanting to call attention to her and embarrass her by doting all over her. Retta smiled back and blushed at the eagerness she saw in his eyes at seeing her there. She would have to take some time during her day to come see him.

"Walker!" "Here!" "Micheals!" "Here" "Wilbert!" "Here!" "Preston . . . Preston!" he said repeating the name louder and looking around. No body answered to the name so he just shook his head and scribbled in his role book. "Man this class is becoming a carousel . . . one kid out today . . . another kid out tomorrow" he said to himself. Soon he was done and sat down at his desk to arrange his papers and class materials for his first class. Aretta, like everyone else was busy gossiping to Frieda and Marshall about her week of absence.

Matt was busying himself with his last minute homework he didn't get to finish over the weekend. Mrs. Pratt was putting out the announcements and told them that track practice would be postponed unless the rain stopped. Then said that the varsity would practice in the gym anyway, but minus all jumping and throwing events. She had laughed at him when he came in earlier than usual and dressed like a fisherman from Maine. The weather and the ride was hell and Matt was just glad he got there at all.

Tonya Rodgers had seen him come in to and tried not to look at him but found it impossible. Just now she was giving him the eye and trying to get his attention. Matt could feel her penetrating eyes on him and tried not to notice her. Finally fed up with this game and no longer afraid of anyone knowing what she felt for him, she wadded up a piece of paper and threw it at him hitting him in the head.

Now he had to acknowledge her. Matt looked up quickly and saw her staring at him in the most urgent and pensive way he'd ever seen. She looked right into him as if to say *I SEE YOU MATT . . . WHY ARE YOU AVOIDING ME?"* Matt felt butterflies in his stomach. He wanted to avoid her but found he couldn't cause she wouldn't let him. "What's up Tonya?" he whispered. "Matt haven't you noticed I've been trying to get your attention for the last ten minutes?" "No not really, I've been trying to finish some late home work for social studies." "Well I have!" "Oh, I'm sorry . . . so what's up?" "You know full well what's up . . . why didn't you meet me after school the other day, and how come you've been avoiding me?" "Don't deny it, you have because I know it's true." "Well, as for the meeting I already told you why I couldn't see you and as for avoiding you, I haven't really been trying to." "Matt you lying!" she hissed cutting him off.

Matt just sighed deeply and tried to think of a way out of this mess but the more he thought about it the harder it became.

Just then the bell rang for first period. Tonya tensed up sensing his intent to escape and she quickly placed her hand on his arm halting him. "Matt don't go anywhere, we need to talk about this" she said with all the hurt of the world showing on her face. He thought about protesting or just getting up and leaving but the look in her eyes forbade it. "Okay Tonya, but not here let's go outside somewhere so we can have some privacy." "Alright Matt, I'm for that."

They both got up and headed out the classroom and to the right into the old chemistry lab. It was just a storage area now for books and extra chemistry supplies. There was a side door that went outside in the rear of the room. It overlooked the cotton mill just behind the school. He led her out and they stood on the patio. "Okay Tonya" he said looking at his watch "We've got exactly ten minutes before we have to split so let's have it." Tonya's mouth flew open and her eyes widened as she was now confused as to what to say. She didn't expect him to be so clinical and cold being that he said he loved her as much as she him. "Matt how dare you treat me so cold and flat, what did I do to you to make you to treat me so bad, all I wanted was to love you . . . is that really so bad?" "Look Tonya, I'm sorry and I apologize for being so direct and harsh with you." "You haven't done anything so bad and that was wrong of me, but there is something you must understand and there really is no two ways about it . . . we can never be!"

Matt's words hung in her mind like a cobweb and weighted her heart down like lead boots. She wanted so badly not to have heard him clearly and was praying in her mind that she just imagined it. "Tonya baby girl, I love you like you can never know and in ways I can't explain, you've always been that bright star I could never find the courage to reach for and this is my fault!" "I blame myself for being weak and lord knows had I not been, we wouldn't be standing here talking but instead something closer to passion and love."

Tonya began to disintegrate right before his eyes. He held her by her arms and she began a slow painful twist much like that of worm that had had a fish hook thrust into it's body. She was hurting and her pain was profound and hard as her beautiful face contorted and twisted with a pain that bordered on holocaust proportions. Matt's words made her numb all over and her legs felt stiff with tension as well as the desire to wilt and buckle. She marveled at how easily her body responded when he suggested they could be lovers but not now. "Tonya, I love my girl Aretta and I won't give her up for anyone or anything . . . and I won't cheat on her either no matter how much you want me or I want you!" "*Matt*" she said almost whispering. "Baby I had no idea you felt so much for me and wanted me as much as I wanted you, I respect you even more for standing up for your love for her and I'm also hurt because of it, Matt I can only think of how proud I would be if it were me instead of her and that too makes me love you even more because you're devoted to her." "But you must also understand something about me Matt, I don't take love or my feelings for you lightly, a woman like me only gives her heart once and when I do it's for keeps, do you understand?" she asked searching his face.

Matt just nodded and was about to speak but she put a delicate and trembling finger to his lips making him pause. "Do you know what you did to me that day in the library when you kissed me Matt? . . . You literally blew my mind completely! Prior to that day all I had was a weak fantasy or a dream of what it would be like kissing you and holding you, and none of them came even close to what I felt then or feel for you now Matt." "Baby you are a special guy and I can see it if no one else does!" "It's those little things I know of you from watching you since the eighth grade, it made me adore you in the first place and love you the way I do now . . . can't you see that?"

Tonya had slowly closed the distance between them and was now lightly holding him about the waist. Matt just stood with his hands to his sides so as not to accidentally touch her and set anything in motion he did not want to.

"Matt I love you and always will, if you tell me you can't be with me, I have to understand, I don't like it, and won't pretend I do, but for you I will, and give you what you are asking, which is the unhindered freedom to love your girl completely" she said letting a tear fall as she held him and straining not to pull him into her.

"But Matt will you do me just one last favor before you go?" she asked almost begging him. Matt thought about the many things she could come up with, none of which he was interested in because knowing how she felt about him, she may ask him to make love to her right there. He was a little concerned but thought . . . maybe it will be alright.

"Okay Tonya what is it?" "Just hold me and kiss me the way you do her just this once" she asked, her whole body alive and straining for him and also the possible rejection he could deliver instead. Matt once again could not refuse her because he did truly love her and wanted her so badly that she would freak out to know the extent of the dreams he had lived with her.

"God she's so beautiful!" he thought as he contemplated this. "Lord help me, but I want to kiss her too, but I just can't and I won't do it!" Matt just shook his head. "No Tonya, I can't do that." She let her eyes drop along side her heart that had already hit the ground. She let her head fall and rest against his chest and trying to accept this final dismissal.

"I understand Matt" her voice sounding dry and cracking with tears. "But . . . I can kiss you like I would do if it was you" he said evenly. Tonya thought she was losing her mind cause she couldn't have heard what she thought she did just now. Especially being he just put her down. Tears were flowing openly now and she just hung there with her head on his chest. Matt slowly and so gently raised her chin, bringing her eyes up to meet his. Every tear was a thousand carat diamond being shed by two of the purest and most rare of all precious stones ever. Matt looked deeply into her eyes and for the first and last time he let her see and feel all the love and passion he had ever felt for her and would summarily never let her experience again.

Tonya trembled so badly at what she was seeing and feeling she couldn't help but let out an uncontrollable whimper. Her heart was exploding and she couldn't stop it. The intensity of him washed over her and through her like a storm. She could feel his love like a lightning bolt as he drew her into him. Matt cradled her face in his hands like he was holding corn silk. He descended down and upon her lips like a dove on a rose bush. He could smell her, taste her, feel her as he drew in each breath. Their lips melted together like the springtime sun on snow.

At first his body hesitated and became rigid with resistance but then changed to the all to empowering force of his deepest desires. Their mouths just hung there motionless, clinging together only with the power of anticipation. Their tongues lightly teased each other then he took her into his lungs and kissed her!

Matt kissed her powerfully and hungrily with a passion that exploded all over them like the sound of a thousand waterfalls. The desire he put into it was so strong she whimpered with shear delight and heart break. Matt's love for her resonated through his lips and into Tonya's body with each passing second. He held her and held her and held her again, exploring and taking from her as well as giving unselfishly. Tonya trembled and whimpered as tears of sadness and exquisite joy flowed together side by side down her beautiful cheeks. She dug her nails into his back and everywhere else they wanted to go! They loved on and fed on each other ravenously but with the abandon of pure love and fire.

Matt couldn't help himself he gave her all he felt for her and was ashamed as well as elated, because his heart and mind knew it wasn't Aretta, yet his love was true and honest because he loved Tonya with a passion unlike that of Retta, but passion no less.

A bell could be heard in the distance and the two lovers slowly tried to bring their passion to a close. It wasn't easy and it wasn't quick, but then again why should it be . . . . When you are on fire for someone you genuinely love and want, why should you have to stop.

Matt eased himself from her ever so slowly. They held each other and looked deeply into each others eyes just close enough for their breath to be felt but not for their lips to touch. They didn't speak but just looked at each other then slowly released their embrace.

"I'll always love you Matt . . . no matter where you go or what you do or who you see . . . I'll always love you with all my heart" she said letting a tear fall. "And you will never leave my heart Tonya, my thoughts or my eyes for as long as I live . . . I love you" he said, then gently caressed her cheek then reached down and picked up his book bag, slinging it over his shoulder, and walked away.

Matt could feel Tonya's eyes on him but he refused to turn around for fear that he would do something stupid . . . . like go back to her. Matt didn't say anything to anyone as he walked to class. He even refused to speak when the teacher asked him why he was late for class. He just shrugged and went to his seat and put his head down. The teacher started to approach him but then thought better of it and went on with the lesson.

Slowly but surely the day wore on with Matt going through the day pretty much like he began . . . disconnected and in a mental soup. It was not fourth period and he would be out soon. The rain hadn't let up much but just kind of hovered between a spring shower and an irritating mist. Either way, still too much to have track practice though. Matt tried to pick himself up a little and enjoy the rest of the day but he seriously needed a boost from something to get him on his way.

Just then a ball hit him in the side of the head totally rattling his brain and jerking his neck savagely. He quickly got up from where he had been sitting on the bleachers and began looking for the culprit. He was mad as hell at having his thoughts interrupted and even more at the attack. He looked around but saw no one who looked guilty.

Just then he saw Cheryl peeping at him from behind the bleachers at the end. He got moving and ran towards her and when she looked up again to see if he was still searching she met him face to face and it scared her so bad she screamed.

"Oh Matt! I'm so so sorry" she said cowering away from him. "I didn't mean to do it!" "Oh yes you did, do you see the mark you put on me?" he said pointing at the imprint of the basket ball on his face. Cheryl put on her best Scarlett O'hara act. "Oh Matt, please don't hurt me I just love you dawlin so so much!" she said grinning broadly. Matt grabbed her by the arms and forced her back under the bleachers out of sight. "Matt! What are you doing" she asked surprised and a little afraid she may have really pissed him off. "I said I was sorry! . . . what are you going to do to me?"

Matt had a most sinister look on his face and an even more wicked idea boiling in his mind. Oh she was in for it and never did Matt's mind work any faster and with the keenness of a needle than when he was pissed off and seeking revenge. "Oh I'm gonna getchu back my way and give you just what you've been begging for, for so long! That's what."

Cheryl didn't have a clue just now of what that could possibly be, but only knew her heart was pounding a mile a minute and getting more and more afraid by the minute. Now that he had her a quarter of the way under the long dark bleachers, far enough for nobody to see or hear them. He began to force her to the floor. "Get down Cher!" he hissed and staring at her pensively. "Oh Matt what do you want? . . . why did you bring me here?" Matt sat her on the floor still holding her arms, "Lay down Cheryl I want some sex!" he said giving her a crooked lusty smile. Cher was horror stricken ands shocked.

Matt had never treated her so harshly and to be asking, no taking something from her she had so many times before offered freely to him just blew her mind. She felt a strange urgency in her loins and began to perspire. She was thinking that in his present state of mind and the slightly above normal size of his manhood he could actually hurt her and do some damage to her virginal body.

Just to emphasize his want and intent Matt slid down his shorts exposing his jock strap wrapped tool. She could see now that he really did want to screw her and this made her hot. "Matt you can have me but be nice to me or I'll bite you" she said evenly giving a little but serious smile to him as she pulled down her own shorts. Matt could smell her juices beginning to flow from her building excitement. He could see it now and oh! She was fat! And juicy! She had a most perfect and luscious mound of womanhood, much like those you see in a penthouse magazine. It was smooth and nicely curved with healthy well coifed mat of blond hair on it. she lightly placed her shorts and panties beside her and lay back spreading her legs completely, resting on her elbows. "Come on Matt take me I'm yours . . . come feel how good it is to love me and be inside me. I knew you couldn't resist me for too long big boy . . . and now you'll see why" she said looking at his more than eager penis. Coaxing him to her with her long sensual finger. Matt looked at her in all her lustful sexy glory and he had to admit his tool was throbbing like his heart had changed places with it. He felt as if his penis had grown five feet long and he wanted to shove it all into her up to the hilt!

But then again he had another idea. Matt just smiled in a way she knew too well. "Oh no, Matt you wouldn't . . ." "Oh wouldn't I?" he said then reached out and gave her exposed clitoris a teasing pinch. "SSSS . . . . OH! Matt! . . . you bastard!" she swooned throwing her head back and reaching for him. He then grabbed her clothes and ran out the way he had come in.

Cher was dumb struck and getting pissed off. "Oh Matt, please baby don't do this to me again! . . . come on back here, I can make it real good baby." She begged him, probably a little louder than she wanted and was afraid she may have been heard by someone. "Damn!" she cursed closing her legs quickly and getting up. She groped around looking for her clothes and couldn't find them.

"Oh god . . . no he didn't!" she said in total bedlam. She headed out from under the bleachers after him, trying to be as quiet as possible. Matt was sitting comfortably on the other side of the gym looking at where she would come out. He had her under wear and shorts folded nicely in front of him on the floor where he sat resting with his elbows on his knees.

Cher finally poked her head out and looked around frantically for him. "Damn you Matt, where are you, you lying snake!" Just then she spied him across the room looking at her with the most satisfied shit eating grin she'd ever seen. She waved for him to bring them back to her while mouthing obscenities and scowling hatefully. He just smiled wide and shook his head. Cher was beside herself with anguish at possibly being discovered or called out by the coach which really would screw her up. Besides that her bottom was catching quite a chill!

Just then he got up and grabbed her stuff. She smiled in elation thinking he was bringing it back but he just walked off further away towards the far end of the gym near the coaches office. Now she was really pissed and completely mortified at what he looked like he was going to do! How would she get out now without being seen. And the bell was going to be ringing in just a few seconds.

Cher hit the wall with her hand. "Ow! . . . I'm going to kill that little bastard just wait!" Suddenly a girl poked her head around the end of the bleachers and it scared her so bad she screamed and tried to cover herself. People stopped what they were doing to look for the sound but couldn't locate it and went back to what they were doing.

Marcie Parker, a tall, slim, white girl with red hair, who was also one of Matt's buddies had noticed her bedlam and come to see what was up. "Missing something Cheryl?" she said smiling and dangling a pair of shorts on her finger. "Oh god thank you Marcie . . . I thought you were some guy!" she said taking the shorts and quickly putting them on. "No, not this time butter milk, but it could have been" she said grinning at her. "Hey where are my panties?" asked Cheryl as an afterthought. "Oh, Matt still has them, he said to tell you they are his trophy and to keep the home fires burning." "Why that little shit! I'll fix him just you wait!" "So Cher how was he?" asked Marcie sporting a crimson blush and more than interested to know. "Sorry Marcie, I never got the chance to find out, the little prick set me up again." "You're kidding? You mean he's done this to you before?" "Yes and no." "What do you mean?" "Well yes, he's had me in a compromising and ready position, all hot and bothered if you get my drift, but no, he's never taken my clothes before, he just gets me out of them then ditches me." Marcie gave her an odd look then looked in the direction where Matt was. "No Marcie he's not gay!" "Then why does he keep turning you on then off?" "Cause he's got a girl and I'm trying to seduce the little pecker, but he won't budge."

Marcie shrugged her shoulders and smiled to herself. "Strong man . . . you think he's any good?" "Have you seen that bulge in his pants?" asked Cher propping on her hip, arms folded. "Yes!" "What do you think of it?" Marcie thought for a second and blushed again with no comment. "I think that whoever she is that's getting him is one hell of a woman and one lucky girl!" "So do I" said Cher, "and come Friday I'm gonna know what she knows and bust his balls!"

Retta was at her desk busy doing some drawings for a teacher. This was her free period and she had time to kill. Retta was quite an artist and could really draw and just now she was working on a poster for a church gathering coming up.

It was an all day out-door event with bible studies, songs, games, food and sporting events. The poster was to show this. She had been working on it for quite some time and was just about done. Mrs. Calloway, the teacher she was doing it for was also busy doing some of them herself.

Retta was also thinking of Matt and what he was doing right now. She wished he was still at Southwest instead of way across town and Central. She began smiling to herself when she thought about how well he looked after her and took care of her.

Sometimes she thought of herself as a baby and he her guardian. She quickly dismissed it for she knew full well that Matt respected her and loved her and knew she could take care of herself. She also thought it was very irritating the way he would entertain other women instead of just quickly dispatching them when they would come on to him. He wasn't the mean type or even nasty and had told her it wasn't necessary to be cruel to a person when telling them something or trying to get your point across. Retta always did it with the tenacity of an executioner. No feelings no folly.

But even though he had this little misgiving she still believed in him and knew he wouldn't do anything to hurt her like mess around on her. "Hey sport, how are you coming with the poster?" asked her teacher. "Oh fine, I was just finishing up." "That looks very good Retta" she said holding up the drawing. "You really like it?" "Yes I do, you have quite a talent there, did you ever consider doing it as a career?" "No, not really but being an architect sounds nice though." "Well that's close enough" she said shrugging. "Who knows . . . maybe you'll design the next Trump Towers or something" she said smiling at her. Retta just nodded in agreement and said nothing more. "Well be better start putting things away, the bell is gonna sound shortly." "Okay Mrs. Patterson" she said putting her things in order and straightening her work area.

Time was really running by now she thought and school would be out soon. "I wonder is momma gonna want to go up to see gramma and grampa this weekend or not, I wish we could take Matt with us if we do, he'd like that." "Maybe I'll ask her today just to see what she says." Just then the bell rang. "Okay everyone slide your chairs under the tables before you leave and have a nice day."

Aretta was already out the door and heading for the wall outside in the courtyard. This was her favorite spot because the sun always hit that spot just right and she had a good clear view of the area. Right now she was aching to be rid of the chill in her bones from sitting in this ice berg called a building. Retta never did know why they kept the air on so high and since there were no windows on the building, none of the accumulated cold air could escape.

Soon she found her spot outside and it was already occupied by some fat white girl sitting there eating a Twinky.

Retta grinned when she imagined the image of a blimp eating an inner tube. And just how she managed to hoist that much bulk onto the 4 ft. wall she'll never know. As Retta looked at the girl and the situation she got an evil an devious idea. So rotten in fact it made her grin from ear to ear. She walked up to the girl and greeted her.

"Hi what's up?" she asked her in a cheerful tone. The girl just shook her head cautiously not able to speak due to the mouth full of pastry or sure why anyone as pretty as Retta would come near her much less talk to her. "Hey, it's really none of my business but I couldn't help over hearing some guys back there saying how far up your dress they could see and plump they thought "IT" was" she said using a lot of facial expression and nodding toward her lap conspiratorially. She made sure to emphasize "It" so as to get the max response from her. Boy did it work! The girl after hearing this turned beet red and her mouth fell open in complete shock and embarrassment, exposing the totally destroyed remnants of her Twinky.

She looked around bashfully then jumped down from the wall. To add insult to injury the thin table cloth material parachuted and fluffed out full as it caught air on the way down. This further embarrassed her and for a second Retta thought she was gonna explode from holding in her laughter.

"Nasty boys!" the girl hissed under her breath as she quickly smoothed down her dress. She quickly waddled away with her head down and her books clinched tightly to her chest. Retta was beside herself laughing now and had to lean against the wall for support from laughing so hard. "Girl now you know you should be ashamed of yourself." She hoisted herself up on the wall and lay down with her head on her book bag to enjoy the warmth and fresh air. Retta wasn't the least bit concerned about someone looking up her skirt because today she wasn't wearing one.

Oh how wonderful the wall felt with its stored up warmth on the sun baked bricks. She began to defrost almost immediately and shuddered as the ice fell from her bones. After a few minutes she fell asleep, completely content and without a care.

Of course the problem with that is much like in the jungles of the wild, you always have something watching you from somewhere, and it was usually something that wanted to eat you. Now asleep Retta was unaware of the that she was being watched. "Look at her laying up there like she owns the place!" scoffed Terry, one of the three boys who had fought with her over a week ago. "I oughta go knock her ass off that wall just for the hell of it!" "Naw not now, it's still some people around and we might get busted" said Earnest the tallest and obviously wiser of the bunch. "She's lucky she ain't wearing a skirt or something cause I'd dragged her ass off somewhere and showed her what for." "Aw you couldn't bust grape!" chirped Terry scowling at him. "She put your ass outta commission right behind me, so you can't say shit!" "Aw, what do you know, you ain't had a piece since you came out of one!" countered Ernest. "That ain't true, I had some from this big bitch last night" said Terry matter of fact like. "Oh yeah who?" "YO MOMMA!" he barked at him. Troy just laughed at him and tripped out. "You can shut the fuck up too fart face" barked Terry. "Your sister told me she saw you playing with it in the closet once." Hearing this he quickly stopped laughing. "That's not true!" "Yeah right, that's what your mouth says." "Aw fuck that shit man! . . . we here to see about getting even with that yellow bitch over there!" he said pointing at Retta.

"I heard her say to some girl in the gym that she was going to be at the varsity track meet this week, we could try her there?" said Ernest. "Okay then we'll wait till then" said Troy. "Come on let's go to the back of the school, I got some herb." "Alright let's break" said Terry digging into his pocket to get his tops rolling papers.

As they ran down the drive he saw a guy and a girl standing between two dumpsters talking and copping a smoke. He didn't pay them any attention but just went on his way. "Did you hear that Dexter?" said the girl. "Yeah, I heard." "Who were they talking about?" "My boy Matt's girl Aretta" he said thumbing over shoulder towards the wall up and just behind them. "Not her again, she's already had enough bad breaks this month, not to mention she already dusted their assess off last time she dealt with them." "Yeah, I know, but that was because they underestimated her, they won't make that mistake this time if they get their way" he said taking a long drag on his cigarette blowing streams of smoke from his nose. Dexter took another drag then thumped it away. "Hey baby, I'm gonna catch you later, I need to go do something" he said leaning over and kissing her lightly on the lips then walked away. "Okay Decks, I'll see you after school!" He just waved over his shoulder without looking back.

It was now sixth period and school would be out soon. Retta was still snoozing peacefully and was dreaming about Matt and everything that was good between them. She loved him so much and sometimes couldn't believe it was real and that she could be having so much fun and happiness with one person. Especially when all she ever heard from other girls was how many boys they had been with and the varying sizes of their packages.

She cared not for these things and thought more of her body than to use it like a wash cloth, letting every boy around wring it out then toss it aside. Retta's philosophy was this: "a man could sleep with a dozen women and he's a stud, but if a woman does that she's considered a slut!" And Retta was never going to be called that or live like one under any circumstances. No, she had the man she wanted and needed nothing else.

Soon the bell rang and woke her up from her sleep. Not to mention the hot dream that was beginning to form between her and Matt. "Aww nuts!" she mumbled at the interruption and sat up rubbing her eyes. "Just five more minutes is all I needed." She looked around and saw the hordes of screaming teenagers running from the building. Most were surprised that the sun had come out and that it was mostly dry out. Soon Frieda appeared all happy and bouncy. She saw Retta and ran in her direction.

"Hey chil'e what's up?" Retta just shook her head and yawned. "You been out here all period?" she asked. "Yeah I was taking advantage of the sun and getting a nice warm nap." Frieda looked at the bed she had chosen and just shrugged. "You slept on this Wall girl?" "You'd be surprised at how comfortable this wall can be, especially when you already frozen from being in there all day."

Soon the buses were arriving and everyone came at them in a rush to be first onboard. Usually the buses were there before the last bell but today they seemed a little late.

Curt's bus, number 234 was first to show up. "Hey there's Curt!" said Frieda waving wildly at him. She could see him smiling at her through the high window. "Come on Retta let's get a good seat before everyone else gets em."

Coach Jones was standing on the top bleacher overlooking the track field. It was a mottled landscape with tidal pools and small ponds all over it. The track in some areas was not better.

"I told them we should a had that sucker paved last year" he said under his breath. The track was a sand and pea gravel mix about six lanes wide. Some how it managed to turn a dark grey color over the years like a navy ship. Many years of athletes stomping and grinding it up had changed it from the sturdy field he knew it to be years ago into the patchy sodden mess of dirt he was now looking at. He couldn't train his team on this muck and their first meet was this week Friday. He tried to think about how he could drain it off but nothing came to mind. The sun helped a little but came out too late to be of any real help. He could train his runners in the gym but they only made up a little more than a third of the teams events he needed to train. He needed to train his in-field people but that couldn't be done in the confines of the gym.

Just then Coach Williams came up behind him. "Looks pretty bad don't it?" she said shaking her head. "Yeah it sucks, hell I'd piss on a spark plug if I thought It would do any good" he said spitting from between his teeth. Coach Williams just huffed in surprise and awe at his mannerism and smiled at him shaking her head. She though he was something of a beast at times but secretly liked him and thought his coaching style was very effective. Some of the team was now beginning to come out. "Damn!" said Jenkins "We can't do diddly squat on that mess." Coach Jones just gave him a casual glance over his shoulder then turned back to the field.

Matt, Cheryl and Ant came up next looking at the messy field. "Hey coach what are we gonna do about practice?" asked Ant. "I don't know just yet son . . . I'm thinking about that now" and so was Matt. "Hey coach I've got an idea if you wanna hear it" he said tweaking his eyebrow as he told him. Coach Jones just smiled a toothy grin at him with his arms folded and shook his head as if to say, "What is up with this kid . . . he's always got something going?"

"Sure Mathis let's hear it." "Well nobody around an indoor track that's big enough to do what we need to do today." "We know that Mathis, so what's you plan son?" he said getting a little irritated. "Well as I was saying no *high school*, but Macon college has one and they sometimes let people and special groups use it." "Is that right?" he said looking at Matt with renewed interest. "Just how big is this place?' "I don't know for sure but it's bigger than this field" he added

446

shrugging his shoulders. The two coaches looked at each other. "Well what do you think Bill?" "Hell, it's worth a try . . . I'm all outta ideas and options . . . go make the call and see who we need to talk to."

Coach Williams walked back towards the gym to use the phone. "Good job Matt" said some of the crew. "So Mathis how did you learn about this place?" asked coach Jones. "I get around a little and besides my dad is a postman so he tells me things that he thinks I will be able to use sometimes when he comes upon em."

Coach Jones just nodded. Soon coach Williams reappeared. "Okay people gather round, I got some good news and some bad news." "Good news is the field is available for us to use." "Yes!" they all chirped. "Bad news is, there is somebody already using it and we will have to wait till later on today before we can get on it say about 6:30." "That means we'll be doing night practice?" said Cher. "Yep" said coach Jones. "So how bout it guys we really need the time but if you all don't want to, then I don't know what your gonna do come Friday."

Everyone looked at each other and whispered their thoughts. "Let's do it!" said Matt chirping up. "Shoot most of you lame ducks can't see to run when its light out so doing it in the dark should hurt you none" he said smirking and folding his arms. "Aw screw you Matt, you're no night owl either" commented the others talking accepting to his comment. Matt just did that to goose them so they would want to practice. "Were in coach!" said Jenkins and some others nodding.

"Okay, I'll get us a bus and we'll meet here at say quarter after six then?" Everyone agreed. "Okay get out of here and don't get into anything that will wear you out or get you hurt before practice cause you'll do it anyway" said coach Jones looking at them with a steely grin like a skull.

Everyone ran back towards the locker room to change back into their street clothes. "Come on Ant let's go over to my crib and wait." "That'll work" he said tossing his book bag over his shoulder and walking away. "Hey Matt! Wait" said Cheryl running up to them. "What's up?" "Well I just wanted to know if I could come along" she asked with a basset hounds eyes. Matt knitted his eyebrows at her thinking of the concept. "Now why do you want to do that?" "Well my mom usually comes and gets me after practice when she gets off but since it's so early I don't have a ride." "What about Mel, can't you call her to pick you up?" "Well yeah . . . I guess I could but that's an awful long way for her to come and I don't think she's there anyway, she usually works on Mondays and goes in early so she can get off early." "I see" he said looking down and sanding his foot on the ground. "Well I rode my bike and it's only made for two so how will you get there?" "I don't know, I thought it wasn't far." "Well it isn't really, but I just ride my bike all the time." "Oh" she said looking down at her shoes and feeling more and more like an orphan each second.

"Okay Matt I just thought I'd ask . . . . I'll just wait here till time to go to practice or my mom gets here, whichever comes first" she said turning away dropping her head. Ant thought she looked quite defeated and felt for her. He quickly looked at Matt giving him a silent reprimand. He knew Cher was a freak and not to be trusted around Matt for too long. But he couldn't see abandoning the girl alone for the next 4 hours. Matt sighed deeply and just rolled his eyes toward the sky. He walked up behind her and grabbed her around the neck with his arm cuffing her.

"Come on Rabbit, lets walk!" Cher brightened exponentially. "Thanks Matt!" she said putting her arm around his waist and giving him a quick peck on the cheek. "Ant! Come get you're adopted sister!" he said then rolled his eyes at her pointing his finger at her. Cher just bathed in the light of his embrace and reprimand because it didn't matter. She was where she wanted to be doing what she wanted to be doing and that was sharing time with Matt. The trio walked on towards the back of the school. "So Matt what did you do with my under wear?" she asked sort of matter-of-factly smiling at him like she'd asked him how long he'd been going to Central. Ant's eyes sprang up like a frog on a griddle. "What!" he said looking at Matt in disbelief. "What's this about some underwear?" "She didn't tell you yet?" he said walking and cuffing her neck again. "No! tell me what?" "We was under the bleachers knocking boots" he said without looking at Ant and going for the shock factor.

Cher also blanched at his wild accusation, she wanted it to be so but found it hard to grasp why Matt would lie about something he could have had freely. Matt was just being devious again, he loved to operate in the moment and get something going.

"You bull shittin!" barked Ant almost dropping the moped. Matt just reached slowly into his book bag and pulled out a pair of peach colored cotton bikini panties then twirled them around his finger like a horseshoe. "Think I'm lying now?" he said looking at him side long.

Ant was speechless on so many levels he couldn't begin to ask the right question. Cher tried to take advantage of his distraction and make a grab for them. Matt felt her moving on him and quickly dropped his hand and clutching the underwear away from her. "OH come on Matt! You can't seriously want to keep them?" she said half flustered and turned on at the same time that he was holding something that had recently been all around her bottom.

"Oh no? . . . watch me" he said putting them away into his bag again zipping it closed. "Come on Matt! My ass is getting chafe from these shorts." "Hey I didn't tell you to take them off in the first place!" "No you didn't you lizard, you took them off for me and said we were gonna make out" she said narrowing her feisty blue eyes and getting in Matt's face even closer than she already was. "And you believed me?" "Oh Cher, you are one naïve chick" he said smiling and shaking his head.

"Well who could tell with you being all mad and stuff when I hit you with that ball, I thought you were going to rape me under there!" "Naw I just wanted to get even with you." "Well you did!" "Oh and by the way . . . . nice ass" he said pinching her on her bottom and whispering in her ear. Cher lost her breath and pulled up short with surprise and delight. "I didn't know you noticed or cared Matt" she said blushing. "Well really I don't, but you're a woman and I'm a man and I'd be lying if I said you don't turn me on or get to me sometimes."

Cher was really smoking now and completely off guard. Matt never spoke his true feelings about her to her or ever suggested he was even paying attention to her body accept in jest. She just looked at him with her mouth open in shock. "Why Matt . . . . you really do want me then?" "I didn't say that I just said you are a lot of woman and I appreciate a healthy well made woman." "So what would you say if I said you could have me anytime you wanted me?" "I would say you were blowing smoke and I'm not interested in it." "OH yeah? . . . so why do you have a hard on then?" she said smirking and raising and eyebrow as she pointed at his shorts and the notable rise in them.

Matt was embarrassed now caught in his own web. "So! That doesn't mean I don't have control" he said pushing her from him lightly only for her to return to his embrace. "What you don't get is I have control and morals, you don't." "Well I'm a woman as you said and we operate under an emotional basis so we usually are quite impulsive when the mood strikes us . . . . what's your excuse?" Matt just waved her off not feeling he could win the argument, then walked on.

"Just you wait until Friday studley . . . you going to be all mine and I'm going to enjoy watching you squirm and twist as I take you apart inch by inch" she whispered. "That's what you think" thought Matt looking at her smiling and shaking his head.

They decided it would be quicker to go across the tracks and through the field as opposed to going all the way around the road way. The field was still kinda wet and marshy in some places and the tall grass stuck to their legs. Ant was wondering how this grass could have gotten so tall so soon after being cut. The field belonged to the Cotton mill and it was up to them to cut it.

Soon they were at the house. Matt's dad hadn't gotten home yet, so he still had some time before he got home. The three of them went onto the front porch and into the foyer. They were all beginning to itch something terrible and rushed Matt to open the door so they could run to the bathroom to wash off. "Come on Matt!" Whined Cher scratching and rubbing her legs until they began to get red. "Yeah man, my legs are itching like crazy!" Soon he had the door open and the two of them burst pass him and dropped their books on the floor as they went in. "I'm first!" said Cher as they raced for the shower in the den. "Only if you beat me to it . . . chicken legs" he said darting around her as they came into the room. He beat her to the bathroom and slammed the door shut locking it. "AW! Nuts, come on Ant, what ever happened to letting a lady go first?" she whined as she scratched with a wild ferocity. "Sure soon as you get me one" he said laughing at her through the door. "Why you chauvinistic prick! I'll fix you Anthony" she said stomping her foot and folding her arms.

Matt saw her standing there looking completely fit to be tied from irritation. He grinned at her but felt her pain. "Come on girl, this house has more than one bathroom in it" he said waving her behind him as he went towards his dads room. "You can use this one in here" he said opening the door. "Thanks Matt" she said then shuffled into the bathroom and immediately taking off her shoes and socks so she could get into the tube. "You're not going to take a bath are you?" asked Matt in surprise at what she was doing. Cher after taking off her socks reached up and put her thumbs into the waist of her shorts and jerked them down with one quick movement. Matt was caught by surprise and the sudden appearance of her well made naked bottom made him look away reflexively. "No, but I'm gonna get damn close to it though!" she said smiling at his embarrassment. "You're not shy are you Matt? . . . I mean its not like you haven't seen it before" she said saucily and stepping into the tube slowly to fully expose her lovely features to his partially turned head. "No I ain't shy but I am outta here" he said closing the door and running to the bathroom in the den. He pushed open the bathroom door as it was not stable. Ant screamed at the sudden intrusion thinking it was Cher. "Move over asshole I'm fixing to bathe!" he said jumping in the shower fully dressed with Ant. "Boy you crazy!" he said laughing and moving over to share the shower.

Soon they were all done and went into Matt's room to chill out and listen to some tunes on the radio while they waited for 6:00 o'clock to roll around.

On the other side of town Retta was at her desk doing some home work and writing poetry for Matt. She would mail it to him later when she had finished her math home work. "Retta I'm hungry!" said Lori coming in the house with a loud clatter, dropping her book bag and things all over the floor. "Okay, wait a minute and I'll fix you something." "Okay" she said sitting down on the edge of the bed quietly still wearing her red rain coat and hat. Her silence alerted Retta and made her stop what she was doing. Normally Lori would whine until fed or just go grab something to eat on her own but not today. She just sat examining and biting at her nails with a pout on her little pink lips.

"Lori are you okay? . . . is there something wrong?" "No, not really . . . . I was just thinking." "About what?" "Having babies" she said like she was talking about dolls. "Having what!?" snapped Retta almost shouting. "Why are you concerned about that? . . . especially at your age." "Well Billy Thomas asked me to marry him today." "He what!" said Retta definitely shouting now and about to fall out of her chair. She was laughing hysterically but still alarmed at all this.

Lori just sat with her hands on her little rain coat covered hips pouting in defiance at Retta making so lightly her situation. She jutted out her little chin and scowled at her big sister and waiting for her to come back under control. "Yes, he wrote me a note and asked me would I marry him . . . Retta I don't wanna have no babies! I wanna be a doctor lady!" she said whining and sliding down the side of the bed, Indian style and pouting with her chin on her fists. Retta thought she looked simply precious in her little rain suit and the frustrated look on her little face. Retta slid her chair closer to her and leaning over her.

She gently took off her little hat and smoothed her angel soft hair. "Lori what does having babies got to do with getting married?" "I mean it does relate, but that's not really what he meant when he gave you the note, besides you're too young anyway." "Well that's what he said and people usually do have em after they get married . . . . look at us . . . we're here aint we?" she said looking up hands still on her chin.

Retta had to smile because Lori did have a point albeit a little abstract and lacking in a few things. It amazed her at how her little sister could flawlessly go between logic and lunacy with little or no understanding of the situation at all. "Look Lori, he just wants to be your boyfriend that's all pumpkin." "What's that?" "Well that's what Matt is to me . . . a boyfriend." "You mean I gotta do kissy face and touchy feely stuff like you do?" she said skewing her face uncomfortably. "Yuck! I don't wanna do stuff like that!" she declared shaking her arms and rubbing herself as if something was on her. "Well good! I'm glad, because at your age, all you should be thinking of is games, school, and dolls." "So what do I tell him Retta?" she said pouting again. "Tell him no, tell him you're already married but just tell him" she said getting up patting her on he cheek and heading to the kitchen. "So what do you want to eat?" "Anything, just something." "Okay, how about soup and sandwiches?" "Okey dokey."

Just then there was a knock at the door. "Go and get that Lori." "Okay" she said running to the door. "Who is it?" "It's Frieda squirt, open the door." Lori skewed her face, pushed her hat back on her head and snatched the door open. "I ain't no squirt! . . . hippo hips!" she said standing with one hand on her hip and pointing her finger at Frieda indignantly. Retta was laughing from the kitchen. "Damn Frieda, she bust one on you!" Frieda just smiled big looking at her and walked in.

"Yeah, I see she's been taking nasty lessons from you." "Not me! that's her personality." "So what's up?" "Oh nothing much, what are you doing?" she said coming in and sitting down. "Home work and fixing lunch for Lori." The big smile that had been Frieda's mask when she first came in was now a collapsed and flattened remnant. She sighed long and deep looking around at nothing in particular. Retta could see that something was bothering her. "Do you want to talk about it?" she asked trying to be cheery. "Huh?" said Frieda jerking back to reality. "I said do you want to talk about what's on your mind?" "Is it that obvious?" "As plain as those oversized jugs on your chest" said Retta pointing at them. "Well honey you can have these heffa's if you want em!" she said standing up and shaking her more than ample breasts till they jiggled like water balloons. She smacked them for affect. Retta just laughed and shook her head. "Girl these things give me a back ache and I can't seem to find a bra that helps at all!" "Well that's your problem, so tell me about what's eating you?" "Not here, lets' go in your room." The two of them got up and went towards the room, Retta looked in on Lori and saw she was into her cartoons. "Lori let me know when you start smelling the soup, by then it will be done okay?" "Okay" she said not turning around but locked into her program. Retta closed her door and flipped on the radio for privacy. Frieda just lay on her bed like she was a patient in a shrinks office.

"Retta I think something is wrong with me." "How do you mean?" "Well Curt came over the other day and we kinda got into something." "Really?" "Well kinda." "I don't understand" she said sitting back in her chair. "Well you see it's like this, we were kissing and touching and stuff and it was feeling really good!" "But when we started to undress and I saw him naked I got all nervous and scared so I couldn't do it!" "Why? Was he rough with you or something?" "No!" "Then why didn't you do it?" "Well, besides being afraid of him putting that huge thing of his in me I don't know" she said sitting up and looking quite disturbed.

Retta smiled and started giggling. "What's so funny? I can't help it if I'm frigid." "No dear heart your not frigid, a little afraid yes, but not frigid." "So what's the matter then?" "And what do I do, I really like him and if I keep putting him off he may go to some other girl and then I'd lose him!" she said with pain written on her face.

"You really like him don't you?" asked Retta more serious now. "Girl I love him and I'm sure he feels the same because he's so patient and gentle with me." "Well when do you plan to see him again?" "Tomorrow when he comes to get me to help him pick out some kitchen stuff and rearrange his furniture." Retta sat up and put her head in her hands in deep thought.

"How was it with you and Matt?" she asked timidly and teasing her nails feeling a little impromptu at asking Retta about her man's love making endeavors. "Was he . . . . you know . . . big or small?" she asked again smiling bashfully. Retta could see that the subject was foreign to her and bothered her too. She just grinned at Frieda and mentally blew it off taking it as an opportunity to brag on her man.

"Oh honey he definitely ain't small I can tell you that for sure!" Frieda clutched her stomach thinking about what she had seen of Curt's tool. "Then how did it go for you?" "Well when me and Matt first made love we were at his house." "We had played around a lot and teased each other over here several times but could never finish before being interrupted" she said pointing in Lori's direction. "He would start off by touching me slowly and caressing me all over then kiss me passionately." "What about the sex part!" complained Frieda getting a little warm from the conversation.

"Hold on freak, I'm getting to that!" "Now after we had done that awhile, he'd put my hand on it and let me feel it." "Girl let me tell you, I was a little scared too! It was like holding a polish sausage and it was long too!" Frieda was really becoming animated now and was bobbing her legs nervously and getting a little squishy between the thighs. "It had veins in it and felt like a pipe in a stocking!" Frieda began to perspire some now and she was becoming nervous and turned on at the same time.

"The head of it was like a warm hard boiled egg." "Now while I was rubbing and stroking him, he was doing the same to me, he had started just sliding one finger between my lips and rubbing me, massaging my G-spot." "What's that?" "It's what my book calls your most erogenous zone and is usually just inside and upwards, evidently mine isn't as far back as most because as soon as he touched it I felt like I was gonna wet myself!" she said laughing wildly.

Frieda just looked sown between her legs curiously and wondered had she ever noticed hers while having a time in the tub. Retta then reached under her bed for a large book that was titled; "The Joy's of Sex." She opened the book and flipped a few pages then stopped pointing at the page for her. "See that?" "Yeah I do, what's that thing?" she said pointing. "That's your clitoris or that little knob you've seen sticking out between the lips when you get a hard on."

"We don't get hard on's Retta, we're girls remember?" she said looking at her sidelong and putting her hands on her hips. "Yes we do to, when was the last time you were in the tub touching it?" "Who says I touch it? I'm not like you Ms. Davis!" she said getting proud and lying boldly.

Retta just looked at her straight faced and nodded slowly. "Yeah . . . . right . . . Okay so there's no reason to show you more then" she said closing the book with a loud slap. "This book is for people who are either having sex or thinking about it and have at least explored their own bodies." "Okay I play with it sometimes okay!" said Frieda grabbing the book. Retta just smiled cause she knew the big girl was lying.

"Wow! Look at the size of that guy!" chirped Frieda showing Retta. "That's nothing, he isn't even hard yet." "Look at this!" she said turning a few more pages. "Oh hell no! he could never get near me with that thing!" "What does he have sex with . . . . cows?" Retta just laughed at her. "Yeah I know that's how Matt is, but not as big and not white." "Damn girl, he's gotta be killing you with that thing of his." "Naw it doesn't hurt anymore, the only time it did was the first time and then only for a second or two." "Really?" she said getting quiet and turning her head to look at the wall behind Retta.

"Look Frieda, it's nothing to worry about, the pleasure that comes after is way more than you can imagine or the brief moment of discomfort." "Yeah, but how can you be sure?" "Well a woman's body is flexible so it stretches to accommodate." "Shoot a penis is nothing compared to a baby coming out of you" she said taking the book and putting it back under her bed. Frieda rubbed her stomach reflexively. "I see your point, so finish telling me about you and Matt" she said quickly recovering.

"Okay, anyway after he got me all hot and wet he slipped in one more finger until he finally had three in there." "Damn, was he trying to get his whole hand in you?" "No, just to make sure I was good and relaxed and loose enough." "Did it hurt?" "Girl no! it felt good! And I was so wet I was messing up the bed I'm sure! Finally I couldn't stand it anymore so I told him I wanted it and to make love to me now!"

Frieda was chewing on the pillow like it was a bit on a harness. She shook her head not believing what she was hearing from her little and once very chase and prudish little friend. "How could you be so bold and tell him to do that?" "Girl let me tell you, when you get that same feeling and your body is on fire and screaming to be satisfied you have no control over what you will say or do and you don't care, you just do it!" "Okay, then what happened?" "Well he got on top and started sliding the head of it up and down between my lips, bumping it against my clitoris and the entrance, it was exciting as hell!" "Girl, my nipples were so hard I thought they would pop off!" "My body was trembling and I was breathing hard and heavy and I couldn't wait to have that missile of his in me!" "Then he finally put it in, he did it slowly and only just the head of it at first then stopped so I could adjust." "Girl I was coming already and he didn't ever know it!" "My coochie was gripping like crazy, when he did slid it in further the pain was sharp and I had to catch my breath, it only lasted about two or three seconds then every thing really go hot!" "He pushed in the rest of it inch by inch until I had all of him honey!" "And let me tell you the cup was full! Okay" she said pointing at her crotch and raising an eyebrow.

Frieda just laughed wild with sexual excitement. "Girl I could feel that thing all the way up in my stomach when he finally stopped and it was so hot and juicy!" "I started moaning like a ghost girl when he started working that thing up and down." Retta's face was squishing and contorting with expressions of deep sexual pleasure and excruciating lust. Frieda was beside herself now and squirming wildly with pleasure. "He put his arms under my knees and raised my legs until my knees were touching my chest!" "Didn't that hurt?" asked Frieda grimacing.

"Girl no, it made me feel him even more and put more pressure on my G-spot." "It was wonderful!" "And when he started pumping it in and out I was gone girl . . . my body was going crazy with pleasure, I know I came at least four times before he did and another two after that!" "Wow! You climaxed six times? I didn't know a person could go that many." "Yep!" "What does it feel like when you have someone inside you and you orgasm?"

"It's really hard to describe" she said looking around and rubbing her chin in thought. "Its' a sweet cramping feeling that starts deep and squeezes really hard and fast, it takes your breath away and all you can do is give in to it as it crashes though you over and over again." "You wind up begging him to drive it in more and more deeper and deeper!"

"Girl how much deeper can he go? He's already done hit bottom ain't he?" "You just wait until you get to that day and you'll see what I mean!" Frieda just smiled devilishly and luxuriated in the sweet feeling that had been building between her legs and the thought that soon it would be here turn to feel this first hand. since.

She was all hot and moist now and felt that familiar urgency that she had felt when she and Curt were about to get busy a few days ago. "So basically what you want him to do is to tease you a little with it so you can get used to it and the feel of it." "Then you won't have any trouble at all when he puts it in." "You make it sound so easy Retta." "Well it isn't anything you could call hard, it's all in your mind so don't be afraid of it."

"Matt sounds like quite a man the way he takes so much time and is gently with you." "Girl you don't know the half of it, he gets better all the time!" "Really?" "Yep and I get hungrier for him every time we're apart longer than two days." "So when was the last time you two did it?" "Saturday." So how many times does that make since you started dating?"

Retta started counting on her fingers and looking off into space trying to figure the number. "DAMN! girl . . . has it been that many!" Retta grinned and nodded. "It would have been more but because of the interruptions and he being way over there it's been hard." "So when are you gonna get it on again?" she asked in a sultry voice.

"I don't know, it's when ever I can get to him or him to me, hell I wish it was now! You done got me all horny telling you about it." "Yeah me too!" said Frieda pressing her knees together and making a face.

Just then there was a knock on the door. "Yes Lori?" "The food is done Retta" she said through the door. "Okay I'm coming, so like I said don't sweat it you'll love it" she said getting up. "Oh by the way are you on the pill?" "Yeah girl! You think I'm stupid?" "No, just uninformed that's all, I was just checking cause I didn't know if you were a virgin or not."

Frieda just made a face as if to say . . . . *don't even trip, you know ain't nobody done got this yet.* Retta turned and went out the door towards the kitchen. As she got there she could see Lori sitting at the table bobbing her feet anxiously back and forth.

"Okay I'm here . . . I'm here" she said turning off the pot and pouring its contents into a medium size bowl then handing it to her. Lori sat the bowl down and then took the plate of sandwiches Retta had made earlier. She didn't wait further for the soup to cool but instead just plunged a sandwich into the hot steaming liquid and bit down huge on it. Retta shook her head in awe at how she had such a voracious appetite all the time. Sometimes she wondered did Lori have a tape worm or something. She decided not to comment and left her to her lunch, heading back to her room. As she got there and went in closing the door she could see Frieda hanging up the phone.

"So who were you talking to?" "Nobody . . . I just wanted to see if Curt was home yet." "Was he?" "Naw, he's probably still in class." "Well don't sweat it you'll see him soon." "Yeah I guess, I just don't want him to be mad at me and think I don't want him and I am just teasing him." "Well I'm sure he doesn't think that, so just stop worrying about it, meanwhile I'm gonna give my baby a call" she said reaching for the phone. Ring . . . Ring!

"Hey Matt it's the phone dude" said Ant. Matt didn't hear it, he had his walkman on listening to his classical music while doing his home work. Cher and Ant were hogging the stereo and listening to some Prince tapes while they did there's. "Hello?" "Hi baby!" "Hey what's up sweet pea?" Cher looked up suddenly like she had heard the sound of a car crash in progress. She put down her book and tuned in on Matt's conversation. She knew it was his girl and began to flush warm with jealousy as he sweet talked her and said things he should have been saying to her. She spied Ant looking at her out the corner of her eye. He was studying her with a clinical expression but didn't speak. He just tapped his pencil on the desk rhythmically.

Cher felt embarrassed and just went back to her book but still listening. Retta was laying on her back and unconsciously unbuttoning her pants and slid her hand in half way and into her panties. Frieda's mouth fell open as she watched the smooth and detached way she dropped into this intimate and comfortable posture. This was more or less a man's favorite posture not a girls! "So what's my baby doing?" "Nothing me and the crew are just doing some homework and waiting to go to track practice at 5:30." "But I thought you got off at that time, especially being that it rained today, I didn't think you guys would be doing anything . . . . Our guys didn't." "Well we wasn't, but we got the use of the track over at the college so we will be going over there to practice instead." "Oh that's nice that they let you have it, do you know how long your gonna be there?" "No not really, probably no more than two hours." "Aw Matt! I was hoping we could get together today and do something" she said speaking low and seductively.

"I want to do that too baby, but right now it's crunch time and we have a meet with you're guys Friday." "Yeah, I know but you know how I can't stand being away from you for too long, especially after this weekend." "Yeah that was good wasn't it baby?" he said grinning wide and reaching down into his own shorts. Retta winked at Frieda.

"Yeah Matt baby you know what I want to do to you now?" she said in lusty and low voice. "No what?" "I want to tear off all you clothes and tie you to the bed." "Oh yeah? then what?" he asked getting aroused. "I'm gonna lick you all over like a lollypop and make you squirm." "Damn that sounds good!" he whispered with a wide grin on his face. One that Cher was sure meant they were talking dirty. Now she was really getting aggravated and wanted to do something rash to bust it up.

Ant was watching her and was waiting for her to move as he felt she soon would. "Then what are you gonna do?" asked Matt pressing on. "I gonna fuck your brains out lover!" she said in a naughty-nasty aggressive tone "You sure you can handle it?" he taunted rubbing himself more aggressively. "Oh, I can handle it and much more than that!" she said giggling.

Frieda's jaw fell open as she was dumbstruck with Retta's display of sexual dominance. She had never heard her speak so raunchy and it was exciting to witness. Almost like Betty Crocker giving sex lessons in an apron.

Matt was sporting a good size bulge in his pants now and Cher could see it. She wanted to jump on him and rape him right then and there so Retta could hear it and be driven crazy with her sounds of pleasure as she listened to her take from him what was rightfully hers. She wanted to fuck him hard and long while Ant watched and Retta listened. Cher wanted to make him moan and beg as she grinded him down like a piece of chalk on a rough sidewalk. The more Cher thought about this the more appealing it became by the second. She knew she could do it! he was already in position and rock hard. All she would need to do was straddle him and pin his arms with her knees! then put him inside her. Once that was accomplished she knew he wouldn't resist her anymore and she could have her way with him.

The thought was so erotic and consuming that Cher began to perspire and a bead of sweat slowly worked its way down from just above the nap of her neck and winded ever so slowly down . . . down . . . down her long lovely neck and over her shoulder where gravity took over and sped its decent down her back. She suddenly sucked in as the cool bead of sweat ran down her spin hitting and exciting every nerve in her body like a pin ball hitting all the lights as it went. Her plan in motion she forgot all about Ant who had been silently watching the show.

Cher started to rise slowly like a panther. She moved as if she was going to stretch. Every nerve in her body was alive and alert. Her muscles where straining and tensed like cables. Every movement was calculated like a cat in the jungle moving on an unsuspecting prey. She slowly eased herself into position taking into account possible movements Matt might make and countering them in her mind as she adjusted for a pounce.

Ant too was reading himself as he slid to the edge of his seat behind her and watching her every move. She couldn't see his face cause her back was mostly to him. If she could, she would have forfeit the plan. Instead she was about to make her move. It was almost like being at the edge of a diving board and about to commit. Just then when she was at the brink she heard the chilling sound of a truck pulling into the driveway and rattling down the side of the house.

"Damn!" she spat under her breath and straightening herself. She turned to sit back down and saw Ant sitting with a most pleased and humorous look on his face. She sat down hard and folded her arms pouting, now aware that she had been under surveillance the whole time.

"Hey Retta, dad just pulled into the drive so let me call you back later okay?" "Aw Matt" she said disappointed. "Okay baby but were gonna finish this you get me?" "Oh yeah, I get you and boy how I'm gonna do that!" he said saucily Retta just laughed and balled up as she thought about what that would mean. "Okay baby, I'll call you later." "Bye Retta." "Bye Matt." Then they hung up. As he did this he got up and went back to his books. About then his dad walked in. "Hiddey ho!" "Hey dad" he said looking up.

"Hello Mr. Mathis" said Ant standing up respectfully. Cher rose slowly as well because she had not yet met Matt's dad and was suddenly intimidated by him. Buford nodded at Ant and stabbed Cher with easy but piercing eyes. "And who's this lovely young lady?" he asked toning down his stare as he could see she was a little nervous. He reached out to shake her hand gently. "This is my buddy Cheryl Walker dad, she's on the track team too." Cheryl smiled sweetly and said hello as she shook his hand. "Hello Cheryl, so what have you guys been up to?" he asked in a not so inquisitive manner. But Matt was familiar with his dads tones and mannerisms and knew it really meant, *"okay who's been getting busy in my house?"*

"Oh nothing much, we got a late track practice over to the college because our field is flooded out." "Yeah it did rain a lot today, so why don't you just have it tomorrow when it's drier?" "We can't, our first meet is this Friday against Southwest so we need all the practice we can get." Matt's dad just nodded. "So how are you guys gonna get there?" Coach said to meet him at the school at 5:30 and he'd have us a bus." "I see" he said rubbing his chin. "Okay then that sounds good, have you eaten yet?" "No sir, we didn't want to put too much on our stomachs and take a chance on maybe getting a cramp or something." "A sandwich wouldn't hurt you that much would it?" "Usually it wouldn't, but the way coach Jones trains sometimes he could make a lizard toss his guts." Matt's dad just raised his eyebrows and smiled.

"Sounds like an old drill sergeant I once knew back in Fort Jackson, but okay if you don't want to eat anything, I'll let you guys deal with that." "Are you hungry dad?" "No not really, one of the ladies on my route was nice enough to make me a lunch to go so I have eaten already." "Okay then, I guess we'll go and finish up some of this homework before we leave so I don't have to worry about it later." "That's a good idea, well I'm gonna shower and rest awhile, Cheryl it was nice meeting you" he said waving at her giving her a smile. "You too Mr. Mathis."

"So Ant what do you have left to do?" I got about two or three questions left to do then I'm done." "How about you Cher?" "I got a few math questions to do but they're easy enough." "Okay guys lets get it done so we can break, it's almost 5:00 o'clock and we got a little ways to walk to get back to the school." "Alright then" they agreed then set about finishing up.

Cheryl looked at Matt curiously like she was reflecting on something. She was musing about how much Matt and his dad looked alike. She also thought he was quite handsome for a man his age.

After awhile they got done and headed out the door to the school. The three of them ran down the street and across the field which had dried some and wasn't so irritating this time. As they got to the back of the school and rounded the parking lot they could see the big orange school bus sitting on the hill with its running lights on.

It was dusk now and the grey sky gave an eerie background to the bright orange bus. Coach Jones saw them coming and waved them on to hurry up. "Come on people its time to go!" Once everyone was on the bus he took roll call. Everyone was there and he told the driver to get going. The trip to the college took about twenty minutes and once they got there they could see that the campus was well lit. The driver took them around back by a huge lake near some woods and they all got out and walked up a long side walk that went between two buildings.

Once they cleared that they could see the track and field. It was huge! It had eight lanes and was colored a soft orange color with faded green lines around it. The infield was just as nice and it had a long jump pit that was trimmed in the same colors or at least the runway. This was shaping up to be one of the best tracks they had ever seen or been on.

Especially with all the bright lights lighting up the field like daylight. "Okay people, we don't have all night so get out there, team up and stretch out." "Mathis and Williams, stretch out that tape and set out those discs. Walker you and the other girls go set up by the pole vault and start stretching out."

Soon everybody was buzzing around doing something. To maximize the limited time they had there, the girls did their track work first while the boys worked in the infield. Once they had worked each event and gotten the details covered they changed out with the girls who were good and sweaty by now.

Coach Jones and Coach Williams were pushing them and trying to squeeze every ounce out of them that he and she could because they knew from experience that Southwest High always had a strong crew and usually won most of the meets every season and finishing in first.

Coach Jones wasn't too worried about the teams running ability and speed in general. Most of the team was doing better than expected and it was still early in the season and much room for improvement. No, his biggest concern was his field events and the fact that he didn't have a lot of muscle on his guys and would need to do something about it if he was going to make an impact on the other schools.

He had a plan though and it should help. "Come on Mathis! It's not a dinner plate son! . . . . throw it like your trying to hit something" he shouted as Matt's throw was less than spectacular and landed a mere 90 feet. Matt nodded and frowned at himself for such a piss poor showing.

"Come on Matt . . . aim for the trees dude" encouraged Eric. "You been slacking this weekend haven't you?" Matt just smiled and nodded. "I thought so."

Ant was doing pretty good on the long jump and clearing at least 22 feet with each jump and not scratching nearly as much as last time. Eric had taught him to count his steps and focus on one spot on the track as he made his last step before planting and launching. He felt good about his progress and was enjoying the feel of the collegiate level equipment.

The strip for the long jump was spongy but gave a level of traction Ant had never felt. It was almost as if it was pushing him faster and further with each step he took. When he got to the end of the strip and launched himself into the air, he flew like he had wings.

As the night practice drew on everyone had achieved various levels of improvement and satisfaction as well as failure from their efforts.

Coach Williams wasn't very happy with some of her girls and drilled them over and over again about their technique on the hurdles and jumps. Cheryl had tripped over one of the hurdles due to not paying attention. If it were not for the track being partially made of recycled rubber and other reflexive properties she would have definitely had a nasty bruise to show for her not paying attention. Instead she had to make due with the embarrassment of tumbling flat on her face in front of the rest of her teammates.

"Cheryl, you have to concentrate on your timing!, remember the sequence . . . step . . . step . . . reach! . . . . step . . . step . . . reach!.

"That's easy for you to say . . . you don't have these jugs on your chest to throw off your balance!" she said mumbling to herself as she adjusted her twisted top and dusted herself off. She wasn't the only one crashing and burning this night. Two of the girls on the relay team kept missing the baton hand off and this was critical and had to be fixed.

Soon the practice was over and the team had worked itself into a sweaty and exhausted mess. "Okay people lets gather round!" Said coach Jones walking to the to the center of the field. "We got a lot accomplished tonight and I have seen some improvements and some failures as well." He said looking at some of the runners without speaking.

"I'm not gonna lie to you people . . . . some of you have a hell of a way to go and I just don't know if you can pull it together by Friday." "Southwest has one hell of a track team and hasn't lost an opener in the last five years." "Their team is made up of some of the best athletes I have ever seen and quite a number of them have gone on to colleges around the state and made national standings, so you people are gonna have your work cut out for you" he said pausing and looking around at the tired and defeated faces of his track team.

Matt sighed long and hung his head. Ant was somewhat indifferent and stood with his arms folded with Matt hanging on his shoulder. Cheryl bit her lip nervously and quietly lambasted herself for not getting her timing down better.

Coach Williams didn't like having her girls spiritually destroyed and broken but also knew that Coach Jones was right to do so and couldn't have them accepting less of themselves than he knew they could produce.

Coach Jones ran his teeth over his bottom lip grimacing as he usually did and with his hands on his hips. He looked over his team to make sure that his point was well received before going on. "Now, on the brighter side, you guys got something that they don't have . . . . and its guts and raw talent!"

Heads perked up almost immediately and furrowed brows suddenly went straight. "That's right guys . . . and girls, you people are fresh and hot for a challenge and I just know you are gonna take them apart." "They don't have a clue about what you guys are capable of and the legacy they had before is no longer there, so they can't rest on them laurels and have to prove themselves just like anybody else." "You guys buck up and be proud of your efforts . . . . I know you are winners and come Friday we are gonna serve up them Patriots like lunch!"

The team cheered and rooted loudly at the vote of confidence by coach. "We still have some work to do and we're gonna use the next three days to tighten up the loose ends." "Tuesday and Wednesday, if the weather holds up we're gonna bust our ass working on technique and stamina." "Thursday were gonna hit the gym and do some much needed strength training on the weight pile."

"Yeah!" injected Eric flexing and posing his muscles to show his motivation. Several girls squealed and screamed their approval of his well made body.

"Eric stop goosing my girls, they got enough to worry about!" chirped Coach Williams playfully.

"Okay people, that's about it, let's pack up the gear and hit the road."

Everyone moved a little quicker and felt a little better about themselves and their efforts for the day. Matt didn't feel half so bad anymore and figured that even though his throws were off tonight he still felt pretty strong and knew that when the time came he would do his best. Everyone soon had piled all the equipment onto the bus and got back on for the trip back to school and home.

There was little talk as the team had worked pretty hard and was just plain tired. Some were asleep and others just rode quietly. This was one of the first times any of them had rode on the bus at night and Ant was looking around the darkened bus and thinking how strange it felt.

After a while the bus had made the trip across town and was pulling into the schools parking lot. There were several cars waiting to pick up their own little athletes. Ant was asleep in the rear and Cher was passed out and laying across

Matt's lap. "Hey Cher" he said shaking her lightly. "We're here already?" she said groggily and rubbing her face and sweeping back her long golden tresses from her face.

She looked so sweet in the dim light and Matt could see her sea green eyes twinkling as the car lights illuminated the interior of the bus. Those who weren't awakened when the bus stopped were jolted awake by the inside lights of the bus as they came on. "Okay everybody . . . pile out!" shouted coach Jones. Everybody got off and said their groggy goodbyes and went to their individual rides.

Ant didn't live far from the school but coach Jones said he would give him a ride since it was on his way.

"Hey Matt I'll catch you tomorrow at school yo." "Alright doc, I'll holla"

"Bye Matt!" waved Cher as she got in her moms car. Matt didn't look but just waved over his shoulder and went about walking down the parking lot towards the back of the school.

"Hey Matt! . . . come on dude you can ride with me" yelled Eric pulling up beside him. Eric had a real nice car, it was a 65 Mustang. His dad and he had restored it from a wreck several years ago when he was a freshman. It was painted candy apple red with black interior and bucket seats with black and red striping. His dad let him customize it a little by putting some hot mag wheels on it and a spoiler. He had a chrome license plate holder and a plate that read: "Chgrs Prd" on it. This was often true, Matt thought as he got in and closed the door. Central had many great athletes come and go over the years and although his brother Jr. was one of the latest to come and go, he was sure that Eric would be soon to join them on the wall.

Eric pulled away with a burst, squealing the tires and leaving a trail of smoke behind him. Matt was plastered in the seat and felt like he had just gotten into a fighter jet without wings. "DAAMNN! Eric! . . . this puppy hauls ass!" "Yeah she does have an attitude don't she?"

"So how many people have you smoked with this thing?" "A few, I don't get into too many races because for one ain't too many places around here to run, and my pops told me if I get another ticket for street rodding he was gonna take her from me."

"Man that's cold, well I guess you better chill then." Eric nodded and smiled at Matt as he got to the bridge. Matt had the feeling that something was about to jump off but didn't quite know what and put on his seat belt absent mindedly.

The bridge was a high arching one that was laid over the train tracks. If you came over it too fast you would be air borne before you knew it. Eric floored the mustang and the 350 horsepower monster left a trail of rubber behind as he sped up accelerated up from 20 mph to 70 in a about 5 seconds.

The sound of the engine was powerful and confident as heavy exhaust poured from the cherry bomb twin tail pipes Matt had thought Mel's truck was off the chain but was quickly convinced that compared to Eric's hot rod she was driving a shopping cart.

As they drew closer to the bridge Eric shifted the "T" handle gear shift again and the car dug in and lurched forward again gaining even more speed. Matt was looking at the speedometer and noticed they were edging pass 85 miles an hour and smoothly going towards 90 as they hit the base of the bridge.

"HERE IT COMES MATT . . . BETTER HOLD ON YOUR ASS DUDE!" "WHAT ASS . . . I LEFT IT BACK THERE WHEN YOU SHIFTED INTO THIRD!" The front end sub-marined a little as the wheels rode up and onto the bridge. The rear end quickly came up on them and launched the car into the air.

"OOOOOOHHHHHH . . . SSHHHIIIIIITTTTT!" they yelled as the car flew over the apex of the bridge and into the air about five feet off the ground. Matt didn't dare look out the window but had a feeling they were pretty high as the door was even with a stop sign.

Time seemed to go in slow motion as the car made its decent. The cars engine never faltered once and the heavy machine landed almost evenly like a plane with rear wheels hitting first. *"SCRRRRCCCHH! . . . SCRRCH!"* went the wheels as they found street again in a wild bounce and skid.

Eric masterfully down shifted the car and kept it under control as they approached English Avenue, which was only a hundred yards from the bridge. Matt's heart was in his mouth and his stomach in knots.

"DAMMN! DUDE THAT WAS THE SHIT!" he shouted as Eric made the turn in second gear and rode smoothly down the street. He must have done it before because he was so controlled and polished when he down shifted and made the turn flawlessly.

Eric just laughed at Matt who was sporting a wild look on his face of joy and shock. "He said I couldn't race . . . he didn't say anything about flying" said Eric laughing and smacking Matt on the shoulder.

"Damn Eric . . . how many times have you done that?" "About five including this one." "Yeah, I can see you know what you're doing . . . how are you at dry cleaning?" asked Matt in a semi serious tone.

"Dry cleaning?" "Yeah I think I just dropped one in your seat when we went airborne back there." Eric laughed harder as he made the turn on Matt's street. "Man you're crazy Matt."

Soon they pulled up at Matt's house ending the evening of hot rodding. "Hey, don't worry so much about tomorrow okay Matt? I'm sure it will be fine if you just give it your best and don't let them sweat you." "Alright Eric, you the man, so I'll take your word for it."

Eric smiled and chuckled off the inference. "Naw . . . you the man dude, just keep telling yourself that you are and you will own them tomorrow okay?" "Okay doc, I gotcha" he said getting out and closing the door.

A little butterfly found its way into his stomach and made him shudder just a little when he thought about going up against such larger and more competitive athletes. Matt let himself in through the front door instead of his bedroom as he normally did and went into the kitchen to grab something to eat. He quickly put together bologna and cheese sandwich, grabbed a can of coke and went towards his bedroom.

"So how was practice?" asked his dad as he passed his bedroom door. "Oh it was okay, we just tried to focus on the techniques and timing more than anything else, some of the guys and girls will probably do okay but others might get their heads handed to them on a platter."

"How about you? . . . how well do you think you did?" Matt shrugged and made a face. "I guess I'll do okay . . . my distance in the discus wasn't too good and I could use some more time to get my technique down a little better so my throws will be more consistent."

"Well I guess what you have now will have to do for tomorrow then." "Yes sir."

"Just do your best and you should do well." "I will" he said then pulled away from the door and went down the hall way towards his room.

Matt put down his food and stripped to take a shower. He muddled the coming event over in his mind a while longer then dropped it all together.

"If I do stink tomorrow I only have myself to blame . . . shoulda been working the disk instead of Retta's hips." He sighed long then put on his bath robe and headed for the shower.

Matt didn't take as long as usual and just wanted to get to bed and sleep. He washed up quickly, dried off and put on his PJ's. It had been a long day and there would be much to come in the morning and that afternoon. No need being half asleep as well.

Matt hit the rack and sleep came easily. He didn't even think about eating and left his sandwich on the dresser with his coke untouched.

Morning came with a vengeance as Matt was awakened by the phone ringing in his ear. He jumped up still half asleep and reached for it knocking it over and onto the floor.

"Damn! . . . who the heck is calling me this time of morning?" "Hey Matt you up yet man?" "I am now . . . what's up?" "You! dude.,it's 7:45 and you're still in the bed."

"Oh shit! . . . damn . . . thanks Ant I must have overslept! . . . hey I gotta go I'll holla later."

"Slow down speedy, look out your window." Matt cringed and blinked wildly trying to adjust his vision as he stumbled to the window. "I don't see nothing . . . wait . . . what the – ."

It was Eric and Cheryl pulling up out front in his car. "What are they doing here?"

"We figured that you would probably be late again getting to school and we didn't want to take a chance on you getting detention and screwing up the works for the rest of us." "I talked to Eric and he said he would go get you to make sure you were on time." "What about his seat covers?" "Seat covers?"

"Yeah Cheryl is with him." "Really? . . . damn that chick is fast."

"I don't know dude, I guess she copped a ride with him from school or something."

"Whatever, let me get dressed otherwise this will have been for nothing."

"Alright dude, see you at school." click!

Matt slowly put down the phone and rubbed his face and yawned. When he opened his eyes again Cher was bouncing up the side walk looking hot, eager and ready to go as usual. He didn't even bother to open the door but just unlocked it and grabbed some clothes and headed to the bathroom to wash up and get dressed.

Matt splashed water on his face several times to chase off the sleep from last night. Then he pulled off his PJ pants and jumped into his jeans and squirreled on his shirt and brushed his hair. He didn't bother brushing his teeth but instead just guzzled some mouth wash and spat it out hoping his breath wasn't as bad as he felt it was. He rinsed his mouth really quick with cold water then turned to leave. The shock he got nearly made him stumble into the shower.

Cher was standing there with her arms folded, sporting a most alluring look in her eye as she bobbed from side to side with a finger tip perched in her teeth as if she was assessing a well make horse she was about to ride.

"Damn Cher! Don't you ever knock or something?" he said falling against the sink. Cher just giggled and shrugged silently. "Come on before we're all late and put in detention" she said reaching out for his hand to pull him along.

Matt didn't know why, but he gave it to her and let the saucy large blonde lead tow him out of the house and a good clip. Matt scooped up his book bag near the door and turned the lock as he went out. Cher ran on ahead to open the door and get in the back seat.

"What's up Eric?" "What's up Matt, sleep good last night?"

"Yeah man like a rock." "Good, now let's beat feet to school so we can use some of that new juice later on today."

"Alright."

"So when did you get the new seat cover?" he said thumbing over his shoulder to the back seat. "Oh Cheryl . . . yeah we go way back, we've been buddies since last year when she hooked me up with her girl Jodie." Matt pulled down the visor and looked at Cher through the mirror on it. "You're just a little match maker ain'tcha?"

"Well I do what I can" she said smiling devilishly and looking good enough to eat raw thought Matt looking at her more than healthy full breasts and cleavage in those tight fitting Jordache jeans.

"What's that they say Eric . . . always a bridesmaid never a bride?" Eric grinned as he pulled away from the curb making a U-turn.

"Oh I don't know about that . . . seems to me she told me about some dude she was getting jiggy with not to long ago and expected to be getting even busier come this evening" he said looking at Matt out of the corner of his eye.

"Is that so?" said Matt turning to look at her dead on.

Cheryl was purposefully reaching down into her bra and adjusting it as if it didn't fit quite right. She hefted and tugged at the mountainous peaks as if it was the most normal thing to do in front of a guy. She didn't even look at Matt while she did it and just acted as if she were in the car all alone. All Matt could do was shake his head and stare, knowing full well what she was up to.

"A guy could get whiplash from staring like that for too long Matt" said Eric with much amusement in his voice. He too could see from the rear view mirror what she was doing and had already filled him in on what her and her cousins plans were for the evening.

Matt just turned around and looked straight ahead and got comfortable for the short ride to school. Once they had gotten to school Matt jumped out by his building and told Eric thanks for the ride and looking out for him and to make sure he disinfected his rear seat against any potential diseases.

Cher caught the hint and gave him the finger as he ran away. Eric just laughed and pulled off heading to the opposite side of the road to his and Cheryl's building.

Matt ran into the building and down the hall towards his home room, dodging and ducking around people as he went. For some reason he began to get a de ja vu' and subconsciously slowed down a little as he got to the intersection of the main hall. As he did this, the large frame of Sammy Thomas loomed from around the corner as if on cue. Matt looked him straight in the eye and moved on down the hall but this time with plenty of room between them and no collision. Sam just looked back and smirked at him as if to say, "Yeah sucka! You better walk the line." Matt shirked it off and turned back to the direction he was originally going.

But this time he smacked into Tonya and both fell to the floor as he stumbled into her and fell. Some how he had managed to step into her path and bounced off of her twisting and falling side ways still holding onto her as if to lighten her fall by pulling her on top of him. They must have looked pretty Laurel and Hardy because not only did Sam see the hilarious collision but so did the crowd and they all burst out laughing when the pair crashed to the floor with Tonya on top of him all sprawled out!.

"OOF! . . . Slap! Ow!" . . ." You know Matt if you really wanted to get me on top of you all you had to do was ask" she said almost flatly but deadly seriously as she pierced his soul with her blinding grey green eyes.

Matt couldn't speak for a second because his back was sore from taking the weight of them both on the hard floor. He had to admit the situation was a little embarrassing and compromising. Especially with jeers from the crowd suggesting that she get some better glasses and they get a room or go into a broom closet to do their business.

"I'm sorry Tonya, I didn't see you." "Yeah I know . . . you've been doing that a lot lately."

Matt felt the soft stab into his heart and it was potent. He slowly eased himself from under her and moved to get up helping her along as he went.

"Are you okay Tonya?" "Yeah, its nothing that a few hours in your arms won't fix" she said still penetrating him with her love swept but hurtful eyes.

Matt tried to shrug it off but it was just too difficult so he just did the oddest and seemingly most sensible thing he could think of and leaned forward and kissed her gently on her forehead then slowly backed away from her going down the hall.

The kiss may as well have been a shot to her stomach because the painful look of love and hurt was written on her face like a clowns mask. She stood their holding her books tightly to her breasts and watching Matt leave her once again. Matt walked into the class with five minutes to spare and sat down at his seat.

Mrs. Pratt was reading something at her desk and had to do a double take looking at Matt and the clock on the wall. "Mathis?" she said almost in a question. He just looked at her nodded and found his seat. She just shrugged and skewed her mouth in surprise. "I guess miracles do happen."

Soon the bell rang and the last of the students ran into the room as she got up to close the door. Tonya was the last to come into the room and didn't look up as she found her seat behind Matt's. There was almost an electricity in the air as Matt could feel her eyes burning into his neck from behind him. He wanted to turn and say something to her but decided against it and just maintained his attention forward like he was looking into another world.

He put his head down and prayed the clock was faster than the beat of his heart or the racing of his mind.

"God why did I do that?" "I know I shouldn't have let myself go like that especially with her but I just couldn't help myself and she was so damn beautiful and looked like she could use it as much as I wanted it." "Man I must be the biggest louse in the world."

After a short report and message to her class Mrs. Pratt passed out some documents to them and then told them to have a good weekend. The bell rang shortly after.

Matt was considering getting up and beating feet for the door but then again decided he would not and instead stand and face the music feeling that he was responsible for whatever Tonya was going through right now and the outcome of the rest of her day and weekend.

"Tonya?" he said turning around slowly. "I'm sorry I have been avoiding you and not talking to you like you asked me to, I'm even sorry about what I did in the hall way a few minutes ago because I know that wasn't the right thing to do being I just told you that we couldn't be what you wanted us to be because I already have someone."

"Then why did you do that to me Matt?" "Why do you pressure me and lead me on so when you know how I feel about you and how much I want you?"

"I don't know Tonya, it's hard sometimes to understand it myself, I know how I feel about you but I also know that I can't do anything about it and be true to my girl Retta."

"I told you before I don't care about her and that you have her . . . you can keep her and still have me too . . . don't you understand that?" "Yes, I heard you and I understand what you said, but I still can't do it because it won't be fair to you or anyone else."

"Why won't it!" she said reaching out with her heart and hand as he drew close to him. She felt herself about to fall into his arms but stopped herself when she caught the curious eyes of Mrs. Pratt and a few other students zeroing in on their conversation.

"Matt can we go someplace else and talk . . . . please?" she begged in a whisper.

Matt just sighed and grabbed up his bag and headed out the door with Tonya close behind.

Matt subconsciously checked his watch and went left down the hall instead of right and into the old chemistry classroom as they were used to. Tonya followed but looked back wondering why the change. Matt was heading down the hall towards the storage room where old equipment and books were kept. Nobody ever went in there accept to take stuff out and take it to the warehouse but that was always after school. Matt did a quick look around and saw that no-one was paying any attention to them particularly but just chatting about the weekend and their plans.

He went inside the oversized closet and pulled Tonya into it as soon as he saw her reach the door. He closed the door and locked it from the inside and stepped away from her a few feet.

Tonya was speechless and excited at the same time. She was glad to be alone with him once again but sad too because her thoughts wasn't his thoughts.

"Tonya I'm going to put it out there and after I do you can say what ever you feel or think you need to but after its been said that's it and we are not going to do this again okay?"

She sighed heavily feeling the impending doom of his words and weight of his rejection reaffirmed.

"First let me clear the air" he said approaching her slowly but purposefully. She looked into his eyes and for some reason held her books to her chest tighter as if he was going to hurt her or something. Matt drew closer with a most stern and focused look on his face and gently took her books from her and dropped them on the floor.

Tonya felt as though she could hardly breath as she looked up and into his deep and penetrating eyes. She breathed harder now as he took her in his arms and burned her to the core with his most intense kiss ever.

Tonya felt the air leave her body like a party balloon with a hole in it. She fell into his arms like a drunk and relished in it all. Their kiss was more of a pause than anything else and they just held it there not moving or advancing. Matt slowly as he came separated from her to arms reach. She looked at him with fire and longing in her eyes but didn't question the short engagement. She was only too happy it happened at all.

"Tonya, I'm sorry and I'm not sorry that I did that, I'm sorry I did it because every time I do I know that I have cheated on the woman I love most in this world." "It hurts me more than you know to do that and go on doing it when I know its wrong!"

"So does that mean you love me . . . . more?" she said hopefully tilting he head sideways as if it would help her to hear better. "Sigh . . . no Tonya it don't . . . . it means I'm weak and probably don't deserve her or you for that matter, it means I have some devotion issues I have to work on and quick before I really do something stupid!"

"Like loving me?" she said quietly almost as an afterthought. Matt just leaned against a book case and folded his arms. He looked at Tonya almost as if he couldn't believe why she was trying so hard to get him but at the same time he knew and felt the same way so he couldn't fault her too much.

"Would it really mean that much to you Tonya if I did let go and just gave into you and made love to you? . . . would it really mean that much to you?"

Tonya turned her head and bit her lower lip in deep thought. "I mean can all this love and passion I'm reading in you be only about going to bed with me? cause if that's the case and all you want is that from me then get in line because there are two white girls out there now trying to do just that! but I won't let them" he said pushing himself off the wall and stepping to her slowly. Tonya just looked away and wouldn't face him, his words hurt and were somewhat cruel but made sense too.

She really did love him more than she had thought possible but now to put her love in terms so binary as to rubber stamp it a lustful feeling . . . well that was just about as bad as him ignoring her. "No Matt . . . it's not" she said in a whisper. "It's just the only way I could think of to show you how much I am in love with you and wanted you." "I wanted so badly to make you feel how much my heart felt for you and since I couldn't tell you enough or scream it to the world as I felt it . . . I could only show you by giving you all of me, body and soul" she said looking up at him now eyes glistening with new tears.

"I don't want to fuck you Matt . . . I want to love you and have you love me . . . that's all."

He put his arms around her shoulders and rested his chin on her head and just sighed deeply. Tonya felt herself swooning as he took such a familiar hold of her like she was always his.

She reached out slowly and placed her hands on his hips wanting to do more but feeling the moment was just too fragile and that Matt might break his heavenly hold on her before she could live and die a thousand lives in his arms before he let go of her.

The sweet clean and floral smell of sunshine in her hair made Matt's mind wander. He went out the door, down the hall and out of the building. His spirit flew high and wide over the entire expanse of the school and the town.

Each breath of her was like a boost from a powerful but gentle gust of wind. He let himself luxuriate in the soft flowing curls of her hair and just lived there for a moment. The urge to enfold her in his arms was getting to be too much and he knew if he did he wouldn't let her go. "Damn!" he said simply and just put her away from him and grabbed his bag from the floor.

He looked at her downcast face and beheld her soul tearing beautiful eyes and just said, "No Tonya . . . no" then walked out into the bustling hallway leaving her there in the room.

A large tear fell from her eye and landed on her shoe. "He loves me" she said to herself then wiped her face as she knelt down to pick up her books.

"Sniff! . . . and I will never give him up no matter what" she said as she rose to leave. As she closed the door behind her and looked about to see if anyone had seen her come out she caught the eye of the three girls she had seen the other day in the library when her and Matt first kissed. They didn't say anything or even smile but just looked at her as if they could feel her pain and just remained silent.

Tonya took this as a sign of girl solidarity and turned slowly with her head raised just a little higher and walked away down the hall. "Girl did you see how she looked?" "Yeah chil'e she got it bad!"

"Wouldn't you if you had somebody like Matt walk away from you?"

"I guess, but still you gotta be strong and keep going girl." "She will I'm sure . . . but not right now, she still got him in her blood too deep." "That's not where she wants him though" said one girl grinning devilishly.

"Yeah I know! did you hear about them last week behind the building?" "Chil'e no! . . . what happened?" "Well I don't know if it was true but this girl told me that he had her up against the wall and was digging for brown sugar! If you know what I mean" she said making a face and gesturing towards her own crotch with her two fingers.

"OOH! I'm scared of her." The girls raked the two of them over the coals for a bit longer then broke off to get to their classes.

Retta was just settling down in her first class, Science, when she felt the sharp end of something stick her in her bottom. "OW! What the . . ." she said as she got up and noticed a well placed tack in her seat. She quickly looked around to see who the guilty party was and caught a glimpse of her little white friend Marshall trying to look innocent.

She didn't say anything but just made a mental note of it and acted like she couldn't figure out who had done it. *That's okay Marshall . . . payback is a mutha."*

Soon the bell rang and class was in session. Retta wasn't very fond of Earth Science but found it had it's good points at times and could be interesting. In fact she discovered through learning about different kinds of rock formations, stones, celestial bodies like asteroids and comets, that she had a valuable stone in her possession.

A long time ago when she was in the 7th grade, her class went on a field trip to the Rock Quarry to learn about different formations and stones. While they were there Retta found a rock that she thought was really odd because it was covered in a brown rusty color. It felt like a rock and apart from it being brown like an old rusty pipe, it was also magnetic.

She being the tom boy most said she was used to keeping odd things in her pockets much like a little boy. She had a little plastic horse, an magnet she got from an old transistor radio speaker and a clear marble. She was supposed to be collecting samples for the classes collage but decided to keep that one for herself because it was so unusual. She put it in the pocket of her coveralls and immediately she heard and felt a click! Or a snap as something in her pocket moved.

At first it alarmed her because she knew she didn't have any bugs or lizards in there today, just some of her little do/dads and what nots. Retta reached into her pocket slowly and felt her horse and her magnet and her rock but nothing else.

She pulled out the entire contents and was shocked to discover that the rock and the magnet had taken a liking to each other and were stuck. Retta looked at the weird pair and couldn't figure out how this was happening. She knew that a magnet would stick to just about any metal but didn't know it would stick to rocks too!

The rock was about the size of a golf ball and had many little tiny holes in it like worm holes. She pulled them apart but it took a little effort. Once she had them free she held the stone in one hand and the magnet in the other and drew them close to each other slowly. The pair vibrated a little and rolled slowly toward each other then flew with a shot into each other with a click! Retta's eyes lit up and she was elated.

"Mrs. Jenkins! Mrs. Jenkins!" she said running to her and showing her the odd couple. "Look! Look! my rock stuck to my magnet." Mrs. Jenkins turned from the boulder she was telling the other kids about to look at the oddity Retta was chirping about.

"Hmm . . . it seems you have made a rare find Aretta . . . there aren't many of these in this part of the country let alone in this area" she said taking the pair from Retta's eager hand.

"What is it Mrs. Jenkins . . . why does it look like a rock but act like metal?" "That's because it is part metal sweetie, what you have here is a Meteorite stone or part of a meteor."

"What's that?" "It's a rock from outer space." "OOHHH!" sounded her classmates as they heard the comment. As soon as they heard Retta running up to Mrs. Jenkins they all turned and came too to see what she had found. Now seeing that she had found something Mrs. Jenkins called special . . . well that was all the celebrity she needed to get their attention.

"Gather round closer class! Aretta has found a very special and maybe quite expensive little rock."

"REALLY?" they all crooned in unison. "Yes children, sit down and let me tell you a little about this special rock from outer space!" she said emphasizing her point by making wide gestures with her hands and making google eyes.

"You see Meteors are very big rocks that fly around in space kind of like ships or boats do on our rivers and seas." "They travel millions and billions of miles around the galaxy and sometimes . . . just sometimes they crash! into each other and splatter into smaller pieces."

"Wowww!"

"Sometimes they are pretty big pieces that manage to make it to earth . . . ."

"OOH . . . OOH! I know Mrs. Jenkins . . . I know!" shouted an eager red headed little boy with freckles as he waved his arm wildly. Okay Jonah what do you have to offer?"

"I seen't one in a movie one time at my grampa Joes one summer!" "The word is Seen or Saw Jonah, not "Seent" go on.

"Well I was watching this moving with these space guys in it and they was blasting it out with this monster who had three heads and big claws and stuff! . . ." *"Jonah"* she said calling his name in such a way to let him know he was getting long winded again. Which was his nature when talking about something that inspired him.

"Oh okay Mrs. "J" I'm sorry." "Anyway, the monster got melted to goo and the space men had to haul butt outta there because more were coming, they set up this bomb and took off and the planet blew up into a million pieces and some of the rocks flew through space and looked kinda like that one only bigger!" he finished quite winded and elated with himself.

"Thank you Jonah for that elaborate space man's view of what a Meteor looks like" she said smiling at him but cocking her eyebrows to show she was glad he was done.

"Yes class Jonah is correct in a way . . . a meteor is nothing more than a particle of a planet or a moon from another galaxy that just wound up landing here."

"You said it was Spensive" chirped a little girl with missing front teeth.

"*Expensive"* Margret, yes it could be quite expensive, but I will have to check with some colleagues of mine who are scientist in the field of Astrology and Archeology, that is if Aretta wishes me to?" she said looking at Retta with raised eyebrows and smiling hopefully.

"Yes ma'am, you can let em see it."

"And when we get back to school I'm going to show you guys some pictures and films on the subject that I think you will enjoy."

Retta now well into her studies was trying to figure out one of the questions about the tectonic plates and what caused them to change over the years. Just then a piece of paper landed on her book from nowhere. It was wadded up in to a ball and she picked it up and looked around to see who had tossed it.

It was Frieda from two desks away. She opened the wad and smoothed it out so she could read it. *"Retta, are you going to the track meet after school? Curt said he would take us if we wanted to go."*

Retta looked up and nodded yes to her with a big smile on her face. *"Yesss I get to see Matt do his stuff!"* she thought to herself. She wadded up the paper and put it in her pocket to throw away later. She sighed and went back to work on her assignment thinking of what the answer could be and just couldn't get it.

She let her mind and eyes wander around the room aimlessly hoping to get some inspiration. All of a sudden she spied Ethel Carter across the room. Ethel was a really big dark skinned girl of about 300 pounds and looked like a half deflated beach ball. She was nice enough and could probably look pretty appealing if she decided to drop some of that grotesque weight she was carrying. Retta zeroed in on the blouse she was wearing. It looked like a rainbow anthem to gay pride or some circus clowns worst nightmare.

It had large multi-colored horizontal stripes and semi puffy short sleeves with spaghetti string straps connected to a hood that flopped over her back. Her torso just slumped into a stack of pancakes and looked similar to the way a cutout of the earth would look minus the colors. "Pressure!" said Retta to herself as the visual aid Ethel provided did the trick.

Classes wore on much like they usually did from there and Retta, before she knew it was in her fifth period class but only not like everyone else. Instead she was gladly perched on her wall much like she always was at that time of the day.

Matt on the other hand was not exactly enjoying his day at all and wanted it to be over as soon as possible. He had managed to avoid Tonya the rest of the day and Cher for the most part. He was in his science class trying to focus on his work with the frog he was using as a minstrel only a week ago. He found slicing into the amphibian to be more of a moral challenge than a surgical one. He wasn't squeamish or afraid to cut into the thing but just didn't want to.

He sighed long and deep and set his mind to making a slow straight incision from the throat to the naval (if it had one).

The rubbery skin opened to reveal a pale kaleidoscopic view of the animals organs. He did the same thing again from side to side making a cross on its belly. Once he'd done that he took the pins that were sticking in the pad next to it and pulled back each fold and pinned it to the pad. "Yuck!" Mr. Turner glanced up briefly from his desk and saw the sour look on his prodigy's face "Problem Dr. Mathis?" he said without looking up.

"No . . . no problem Mr. T . . . just don't really like gutting lizards is all." "A frog Mr. Mathis not a toad, a knute nor a lizard sir . . . a frog." "Now if you're having trouble identifying these creatures I can set some time aside and have you dissect each one and do a complete organ analysis and catalogue of each one."

"OH! No thank you Mr. T, I think I got it" he said quickly whipping out his pen and pad to catalogue the frogs innards and draw diagrams of each one.

"I understand you're on the varsity track team this year?" he said still working on a large chart on his desk.

"Yes sir . . . coach Jones felt I would make a good addition to the team and maybe I was a little bit beyond the "B" team level."

"Then you must be pretty good then if coach Jones promoted you the first week of the season." "How did you know that Mr. Turner?" said Matt looking perplexed because he didn't figure anyone outside the team knew that.

Mr. Turner stopped what he was doing and looked up in a mad scientist sort of way and pulled down on the lower eyelid of his right eye.

"Look into my eye boy, I know things about you that your momma don't know."

The class started giggling at the antics. Mr. T was quite an actor and dramatist when it came to expressing his points sometimes.

The class loved him and everyone else in school. He was a great man and love what he taught and being around the students. Matt just twirled his scalpel around his fingers and smiled. For the most part he had forgotten about the track meet that was to start just an hour or two from now. He had allowed himself the luxury of daydreaming and engaging into some much needed school work.

Now it was fresh in his mind again and he was nervous all over again. He wondered about how it would all go as he slowly sliced into the frog before him.

"I wonder what it's gonna be like when I get on the blocks with these guys. I remember watching Jr. run his heart out not too many years ago against these animals. I wonder did I bite off more than I can chew letting coach Jones talk me into getting on this team. Yeah, I have some speed and I have some strength too but so does a dog and it don't mean he's any more fit to run with cheetahs than I am." Sighhh! *"What the hell. I'll just do what I can and let that be it. besides ain't nobody I know other than the other team mates gonna be there . . . it's gonna be on their turf not ours so losing won't be so bad."*

Then it hit him, the thought unfurled in his mind like a just washed sheet blowing in a spring breeze. *"Ohh shit! . . . Retta is gonna be there!"* his mind screamed as he involuntarily cut the frog in half. "Damn! now look at this mess" he mumbled under his breath.

Mr. Turner, not slow to catch anything within his hearing, looked up and into Matt's direction. His thick eyebrow furrowed together and his full puffy lips twisted into a snarl that looked more like a smirk but his large 1970's mustache prevented that from being confirmed. He spied Matt attempting to hide his unplanned amputation of the animals lower half by spreading it's innards over and around so it could not be seen.

He'd done a pretty decent job as far as he knew and you couldn't really tell that there was now TWO! projects instead of the one.

Mr. T just eased to his full five foot nothing stature and slowly sauntered his way around the tables an workbenches to come up behind Matt quietly. This was relatively easy since Mr. T was so short and everything else served as an effective blind in which he could use to his advantage to creep up on gossiping girls or unsuspecting students engaged in non-academic activities with notes and walk-man radios.

Matt was quickly touching up his handy work as the bell would be sounding soon and he didn't want to get a failing grade for not completing his class assignment. That which he couldn't get to look right and had mutilated with his scalpel he just scooped up and stuffed into the creatures mouth to hide it.

Mr. "T" stood just behind him and off to his left so he couldn't see him should he turn to leave when the bell rang. He had seen what Matt had done to the frog being his many years as a science teacher taught him that a given animals liver should never be found below the stomach cavity atop the large intestine but above it just under the lungs and rib cage.

"NICE WORK! Mr. Mathis" he bellowed leaning close to Matt's unsuspecting ear. Matt jumped from his seat throwing his hands up as he did. Following this reaction he and Mr. "T" looked at each other as the notable "THUCK" of a sharp object seated itself in the ceiling tile just above them. The class went into bedlam.

Mr. "T" just stood there scowling at Matt with his chubby little arms and hands behind his back and rocking slowly back and forth on his heels. Matt just kinda froze, looking off into the distance and wondering just how much Mr. "T" had actually seen. Mr. "T" looked down at Matt's specimen tray slowly then shook his head as he looked back at him out of the corner of his eye. "Soo Professor Mathis . . . . I see you have decided to move on to amputation techniques instead of simple dissection and observation.

Slicing and dicing get too boring for you Mr. Mathis?" he asked in a most sinister and je'june sort of way, raising his eyebrow and leaning conspiratorially towards Matt.

"Uhh . . . no sir" said Matt swallowing hard. "I accidentally cut into it too deep with my knife and cut him in half."

"You mean your scalpel?" he said still scowling and ogling at him with constant input from his heavy eyebrows. "Yes sir." "You mean *this* scalpel?" he said nodding towards his tray with the frog.

"Yes sir Mr. Turner." Mr. T looked up without moving his head then reached out with a chubby little hand and nudged Matt back about a foot. Just as he had done this the scalpel that had recently been launched into the great unknown found its way back home as it fell like a star landing or rather sticking into the table right between them with the handle up.

"Or do you mean *THIS* scalpel Mr. Mathis?" Matt just looked at the cutting tool and remained quiet. The class however was not. They hooted to beat all.

"RINGGGG!" and away they ran for the door. Squealing laughing and looking back occasionally to see Matt and Mr. T still facing each other silently with half smirks and grins on their faces. "Well Mr. Mathis it seems that once again you are saved by the bell, however, I have one stipulation."

"Name it!"

"Southwest doesn't win today, if they do and you come in anything that's not 1st place you my man will be cleaning Petri dishes, catching frogs, nutes and sanitizing experimentation trays like this one for the rest of the semester . . . are we clear Mr. Mathis?"

"Yes sir Mr. T . . . no failure!"

"Now get out of my morgue so I can dispose of these corpses you monsters have left laying all over my room."

"Color me gone!" he said scooping up his materials and jamming them into his book bag as he headed for the door.

"Mathis! do your best son, I know you're a winner already" he said smiling at Matt as he turned at the door.

"Thanks Mr. Turner, I will" then he was gone and down the hall like a scalded cat.

Time after that seemed to go by quickly and the end of the day and the week was herald in by the sounding of the school bell at 2:15.

Matt and the his other team mates came into the dressing room just after the bell rang. Everyone was pumped up and ready to go! Matt sat down on the bench and commenced undressing and putting on his uniform. He moved slowly and marveled at the energy and anticipation that seemed to fill the room. It was almost a military air like they were going to war or something. Matt felt himself stand a little straighter and felt powerful!

"You feel that?" asked Eric slapping him on the back as he came in.

"Yeah . . . I do!" "Enjoy it my man its called self actualized power! It's a feeling you get and an awareness that makes everything around you seem electric, bathe in it! enjoy it! infuse your mind with it Matt because you're going to be using it all day to win!"

"Yeah!" said Matt giving him a resounding high five that was so loud and solid others turned from what they were doing to see.

Coach Jones just stood in the door way of his office with his massive arms folded and playing with a tooth pick in his teeth. He grinned his classic dead skull grin and just nodded.

"We're gonna kick their asses, HURRY UP AND MOUNT UP BOYS . . . MEAT IS ON THE TABLE AND I'M HUNGRY!" shouted coach Jones as he banged on the metal door for emphasis. The team picked up on the energy and motivation and shouted, rooted and hooted various bold declarations of success, defeat and war. They were pumped up and hot to trot.

"I want you guys to run hard!" "YES SIR!" run fast! "YES SIR!" run long! "YES SIR!" run mean! "YES SIR!" then run em into the ground! . . . "YES SIR!" "THEN LET ME HEAR IT!" "CHARRRGERS, ROCK-ROCK(badoobadoom!) CHARRRGERS, ROLL-ROLL(badoobadoom!) CHARGERS ROCK!(badoobadoom) CHARGERS ROLL!(badoobadoom) CHARGERS ROCK AND ROLL! (BOOM BOOM BOOM BOOM BOOM!) They beat and shouted the schools battle cry as they drummed the tune on the steel lockers. The sound was so loud and engaging the girls in the next room over were screaming and dancing to the sound of their male team mates. They also felt all charged and powerful with energy and victory.

"HEAR THAT LADIES!" shouted coach Williams standing on a bench prancing and grimacing. "THAT'S POWER AND CONFIDENCE IN THE NEXT ROOM!" "YES MA'AM!" "EITHER COME HARD OR STAY AT HOME! . . . GOT ME?" "YES MA'AM!" "THEN LETS HIT THE BUS AND GO GIVE SOUTHWEST SOME "ORANGE CRUSH!" "YEAHH! . . . WHOO! WHOO!" The two teams rushed out of the locker room and into the parking lot where the buses were waiting for them. There were other students standing around watching and rooting for them as they got on board. You could feel the energy in the air as they nosily got onboard and banged the sides of the bus and the seats.

Ant and Matt ran to the back to get a good seat in the rear. Eric and a few others sat up front wanting to get off the bus and get busy with the ass whipping.

"Okay every body lets count heads and make sure everybody is here!" "Mathis start the count." One, Two, Three . . . . and on it went until 30 heads were counted girls included.

All the equipment was put on board before the bus got to the gym to pick them up.

"Okay people this is the day we trained for and winning is what we are going to do, can I get an hell yes?" "HELL YESS!" "Okay, lets role this thing Billy" he said tapping the old bus driver on the shoulder and taking a seat across from Coach Williams.

The bus lurched and rolled away from the curb with all thirty of the rabble rousers full of gusto and anxious energy. Cheryl was looking at Matt from the front and smiling at him proudly and eagerly. She was so full of pride and nervousness that she hoped he couldn't see it. She really hoped she would do good job today and not stink. Matt was thinking much the same thing and hoping the sweat that was rolling down his armpits couldn't be seen.

He felt Ants comforting and warm hand on his shoulder. "Don't sweat it man . . . it'll be fine, if not then we go home losers and get drunk" he said grinning broadly.

Chapter 13

The Final Insult

"**B**oy your sick" said Matt punching him in the arm and laughing lightly as he felt a little better. The trip didn't take too long to get there being it was only about five miles from their school. As their bus pulled into the parking lot around the back of the gym and up to the track field from the opposite side of the field as the home team, everyone got a little quiet.

No one had anything to say as they looked at all the strange faces that stood along the trail beside the bus. Some sneered and others were diffident and reticent with no concern at all for the odd looking intruders in orange and white who had come to invade their sacred campus.

"PSST! Hey Matt, I'll race ya back to school?" whispered Cheryl looking at him and posturing like she was going to break the minute the bus doors opened.

"ALL RIGHT CHARGERS LETS GET WITH IT!" shouted coach Jones as he stood up blocking the isle.

"Too late" said Matt leaning over to tighten his shoe laces.

Coach Jones told everyone to rally at the back of the bus and pick up a bag or a piece of equipment and wait beside the bus. Everyone did as they were told and got off getting the gear they would need to compete. Everyone looked around with curiosity and nervousness. The campus wasn't much to look at but was a collection of brick buildings spread out around a large area much like a college campus.

Matt was already familiar with the school and the layout as he had been there before looking for Retta. Speaking of which, she was on the home team side looking around to see if Matt and his team had arrived yet.

She'd heard they did and was looking for the bus but didn't see it. Curt pointed to the rear of the school by the gym. She could see some people but couldn't make out Matt just yet. Matt's team started moving toward the field and away from the parking lot.

She could see them now and was impressed at the size and physique of the track team. "There he is!" she shouted jumping up pointing and almost knocking over Frieda in the process. "I see him girl! Dang . . . you almost knocked me out of the bleachers."

"Oh I'm sorry I was just so excited!" "We know you can't wait to see your boo" said Frieda taunting her and making kissy faces.

Retta just smirked and sat down folding her arms but secretly feeling very proud of him and wanting to go to him.

The air crackled with excitement and anticipation as hundreds of students, friends and parents sat in the stands awaiting the start of the first event. The Chargers had gotten settled on their side of the field and was stretching and warming up to get ready.

It was Southwest and Central the ancient and classic rivalry. They were once again about to lock horns in a combat like competition of skills and athletic ability. The warriors were dressed in there finest native battle colors. Red, white and blue for Southwest and sunshine orange and white with a trace of royal blue for Central.

The two teams were powerful and strong looking as they stood in the eldritch light of the Friday afternoon sun. Each team was equal in numbers, but that's where the similarity ended. Southwest being well known for its four "A" basketball team, was always producing taller, faster and more capable athletes each year.

They were unusually long, tall and sported Amazonian-like builds. The Patriots, because of their training and natural skill could jump higher, make longer strides run and throw great distances.

But not to be outdone, Central also sported its combat colors and banners of quad "A" championships. Central boasted and laid claim to a domination of the football, baseball and track field on occasion.

Their athletes were hulking, powerful boys and girls who looked more like gladiators than students. It was going to be a good match today!

Southwest's track was a little like Central's with a sand gravel surface. But it lacked the high spanning cement bleachers they did. Southwest's field also seemed short by comparison or at least it appeared that way. The fiercest competition would be between the two junior varsity teams and then a cap off with the varsity.

Matt was glad of this because it gave him more time to stretch and scope out the track for its good and bad points, and also a good look at who his rival might be. He felt good and nervous at the same time.

He and Ant hadn't spoken very much since they got there and was trying hard not to let each other see the chaotic conflict that was selling within. It gave them both a vicious case of butterflies. All athletes go through this and with varying degrees of intensity. Some experience a light jittery feeling, others like Matt were getting cramps and felt like they needed to go take a dump or at least throw up.

Eric on the other hand was the picture of calm contentment. He was sitting near Ant stretching out long and slow with his walkman headphones on. Matt wondered how he could be so relaxed at a time like this. Ant caught a glimpse of him as well. Soon the starter announced the first event and it was the girls 100 meter hurdles.

"That's Cheryl's event" thought Matt as he got up slowly to go watch and offer support. Matt saw six girls lining up on the blocks at the far end of the field. Three were black one looked Spanish and the other two were white. The three Southwest girls were looking good he thought letting his eyes wander up and down their long shapely legs and curvaceous bottoms. They were strong and muscular and wore intense mask of concentration on their faces.

Cheryl on the other hand was a nervous wreck and she was turning pale. She also had sized up the girls next to her on either side. "Just remember your training and technique . . . these bitches can't do anymore than you let them and they are actually kind of scrawny to tell the truth. I'll just knuckle down and run my ass off!"

"*RUNNERS ON YOU*R MARKS!" Blared the starter. "*GET READY . . . SET! . . . POW POW!*"

It was a false start. One of the Southwest girls had jumped the gun. Cheryl left the line just after her and it made her even more anxious but a little confident to, cause now at least she had an idea of who to watch out for.

The girls walked around to shake off the tension and to get ready to start again. Matt could see Cheryl was a bundle of nerves and was holding her stomach like she was going to be ill. Matt walked over to her quickly to talk to her and try to give her some moral support.

How he was going to do this, he thought was as much a surprise to him as it would be to her, being that both were virgin competitors. "Hey Cher! Hold up a sec."

She stopped pacing and smiled when he approached. "How's it going kiddo?"

"I don't know Matt, I fell so nervous I feel like I'm going to puke!" she whispered.

"Yeah me too" he said patting her shoulder.

"Matt you're scared?" she asked disbelieving.

"What because I'm a guy I can't be nervous? . . . what are you nuts?" he said cutting his eyes as her and smirking. She grinned at him and began to fell much better.

"Look Cher, these girls don't have anything on you . . . . *Look at e'm . . . they skinny, ain't got no meat on em, legs look like baseball bats . . . and I heard they got that nasty women's disease"* he said in a gruff voice quoting Caesar Romero from the movie the Color Purple.

Cheryl couldn't stop laughing and was now holding her stomach for a different reason. The other girls turned to see what all the laughter was about and looked at the two of them with less than friendly eyes.

"Matt! Stop your killing me" she laughed doubling over.

"These girls don't have anything on you! Just look at how you're put together . . . he said holding out her arm and turning her slightly."

Ant and Eric were looking on and wondering what in the world he could be talking about. "Man I'd hate to be running against you!"

"Aw Matt you're just teasing me."

"No, I'm not . . . think about it, you damn near out ran me last night after practice getting on the bus, so I know you can beat these chicks with no problem, just concentrate and believe you're the best and you'll win!"

"Matt I'll try" she said holding his hands for strength.

"If you believe I can do it, then I can."

"That's my little country girl! . . . now go get e'm"

"RUNNERS TAKE YOUR MARKS!"

"Okay, Matt I better go, they're calling us away, thanks okay?" she said giving him a quick peck on the cheek.

"GET READY"

Cheryl ran over and dropped down into her starting block. New confidence and purpose all over her face now. The other girls noticed the quick change as she jogged up to them.

"Don't think that little pep talk you just got gonna help you ass none!" spat one girl from Southwest's team. "Dis here our house an we say what go on here!" . . .

"GET SET!"

Cheryl just grinned at them saucily, "I'm about to own you and your house!"

They also as black women go, didn't like the close contact between her and Matt anymore than they liked having Central on their campus. The plan was to humiliate them and send them home broken and bruised.

"White bitches always thankin they can go anywhere and take your shit!"

"Yeah!" chirped another girl as they got down into the blocks.

"Just where the fuck do you thank you goin anyway . . . bitch!"

Cher just looked over at the two on her right without blinking, smiled in a most arrogant way. *"About a hundred meters bitch . . . and you can be smellin my ass as I go!"*

"POW!"

The girl on Cheryl's right was out of the blocks first, catching her completely by surprise. Cheryl felt the adrenaline flowing through her as she blasted off behind her.

All the girls moved like Gazelles as they left the line almost even. The order went like this . . . Southwest in 1st 3rd and 6th place. Central followed in 2nd 4th and 5th.

Southwest cleared the first hurdle with Cher gaining on her fast! She had gotten back her spirit now and was slowly overtaking her competition. The crowd was in an uproar with excitement as they shouted and screamed the names of the runners urging them to run faster.

Each time Cher cleared a hurdle she got closer and closer to the other girl. Her chest was heaving hard and she was chopping fast trying to maintain her rhythm and coordination as she was taught. She glanced quickly to her right to look at the girl just ahead of her and could see her over size jugs beating her literally to death . . . she smiled and thanked god that she had remembered to wear a sports bra like Coach Williams had told them.

As they neared the last two hurdles Cher took careful steps and closing the distance between them. First by a foot then two feet . . . then more! down the straights towards the finish line they went. Cheryl by now had closed the gap between her and the Southwest girl and was now passing her with only twenty yards to go!

"Stride Cheryl, Stride!" yelled Eric cheering her on. "Stick out those legs and stride girl!"

Cher did as she was told and extended her reach with those long and curvy legs of hers. The change in running style felt a little odd but was doing the trick. She soon passed the girl and out distanced her making a lunge for the tape and beating her by a half length!

"Yes, yes, yes . . . alright Cheryl!" cheered Matt and the rest of the team as she broke the tape with her forehead. She was exhausted but totally elated that she had won. She slowed and staggered to a stop then bent over putting her hands on her knees trying to catch her breath.

She stood up and walked into the infield toward her team mates who were running to congratulate her on winning.

Just then she caught the eye of the girl she had just beaten, who had so much to say earlier. She smiled at her, flicked her nose with a finger and sniffled. The girl just smirked and rolled her eyes walking away with her hands on her hips. By now the rest of the team had gotten to her and was jumping all over her congratulating her.

"See I told you, you could do it!, all you needed was some confidence in yourself" said Matt cuffing her around the neck and giving her a squeeze. Cher smiled brightly hugging him and giving him a light peck on the cheek.

"WITH A TIME OF 10.68 . . . CHERYL WALKER" said the announcer.

"I knew those legs were good for something" said Matt cuffing her chin.

"If only you knew mister!"

Soon the next event was setting up and about to begin. It went on like that the whole day with very little time in between each event.

Retta finally found Matt in the heard but could not get his attention even though she waved wildly and yelled to him as he got within earshot.

"Shoot! He ain't even gonna know I was here" she said frowning.

"He'll know" said Frieda smiling at her trying hard not to laugh at her friends hysteria.

After about and hour more had passed, the last event of the junior varsity was up. It was the long jump and Patrick Walters was to take it. Patrick was new on the team and was Matt's replacement. He was a good jumper and would go on to take second in the event. And first in the triple jump.

Now it was time for the varsity team to compete. Matt had looked around for the other team but couldn't find them, so he still didn't know who his competition would be.

All of a sudden he found out why. There were a lot of people on the field and it was difficult to tell just who was who unless they were in an event. The reason he couldn't tell or see who might be his potential competition was because the varsity team for Southwest hadn't arrived on the field and were just now coming onto the track.

"Damn!" said Ant justifiably concerned when he saw them.

"Those mothers are huge man!" Matt had to agree but didn't comment but instead just looked at the twelve well formed athletes as they cruised out onto the field.

They looked like college football players and exuded and air of power and confidence. Matt was beginning to feel a little ill again and needed to sit down. Eric had seen this kind of psyche trick before and wasn't phased by it one bit.

"Hey guys gather round!" he said calling to them calmly. "Look, I know some of you have never run before and seeing these monsters don't help your confidence much, just remember one thing while your making out your "Mental Wills" before you even compete . . . a big man can't run long or very fast because he's carrying most of his weight in muscle." "Yeah, he's got the ability to do the job but it's like carrying the cannon balls your gonna use to shoot at somebody . . . after you get to where your gonna do it, you're too tired to do it." "So don't sweat it okay?"

Ant and Matt just nodded and mulled over what he was saying as it did make a little sense.

"Hey Matt!" said Eric calling him over. "Look man, I didn't want to worry you none but you're event and Ants count for at least two thirds of our point spread and you'll need to come in at least second place for us to win, now I know you're nervous and so am I a little, but it'll pass cause I know these guys from last year and some of them ain't shit." "Just a lot of hot air!"

"So what do you want me to do?" asked Matt not exactly sure how this information is helping him. "I know how your mind works pretty much, from watching you operate these past few weeks, you think a lot like your brother when it comes to competition, you can hump it out all right but you need to light that fire inside you to win!" "Your big brother used music, maybe it's what works for you too?"

Matt looked at him strangely and with little faith in the concept but listened anyway. Eric could see the disbelief in his younger team mate but just smiled knowing something he didn't.

"Yeah, I know it sounds crazy, but hear me out first" he went on. "Everyone has something inside them that is stimulated by something else and makes them invincible and gives them that psychological edge, sometimes it's all you need to win in anything."

"So how will you know what will fit me . . . I mean I have some music at home that I listen to and like but nothing I would say gives me any juice?"

"I don't know, cause I don't know you all that well yet as an athlete or a person, but I'm betting the farm that you and your brother like the same things."

"Yeah some things" he said reluctantly.

"Okay good then! Here take my walkman over to the infield and listen to the tape I put in it, your brother used to play this just before a meet and it seemed to make a big difference in his game, it must be true otherwise he wouldn't have gotten the nick name "Black Stallion." "Hey, it worked for me too."

Matt just looked at the tape player oddly then back at Eric.

"You really think it'll help me huh?"

"Who knows . . . at any rate it will at least relax you some and get rid of them damn butterflies" he said punching him lightly in the stomach.

Matt doubled over dodging the weak punch and smiled at him. "So go on over there and listen to the tape, you still have a little while before your first event."

Matt just nodded and walked off with the tape player. He put on the head phones and sat in a nice sunny spot up against some padding equipment to let the sun help bathe away his nervousness and listen to the tape.

Retta was sitting in the bleachers still trying to get his attention.

"WILL THE PARTICIPANTS IN THE MENS 100 METER DASH REPORT TO THE STARTING BLOCKS!" said the announcer. This was Eric's event and he was the best. A tall boy from Southwest stepped up to him as he got in position.

"Hey Eric, long time no see dude" he said smirking and eyeing him from head to toe.

"I hope you don't think your ass is gonna win today slick" he spat arrogantly.

Eric just glanced up at him from his stretching then turned back to look down the track.

"You remember that word *ASS!* Butt head, cause it's the last part of me you going to ever see!" "RUNNERS TAKE YOUR MARKS . . . GET SET . . . POW!" they were off! And moving with blinding speed down the track! Eric moved like a Greek Olympian as his legs flicked out strong and straight and coming down so lightly on his toes it looked like he was flying!

His powerful arms pumped like pistons on an engine. The loud mouth next to him quickly began to fall behind. The two Central runners and the three Southwest guys looked like race horses as they stomped down the track. Neither runner had more than a half arms length over the next and the race was extremely close.

Just then Charles Hawkins or "Chappy" as the guys on Central's team called him, yelled out in pain. "Aw shit!" he cursed grabbing his right thigh and skip stomping to a stop and out of the race. He had pulled a muscle and the pain was excruciating. He hopped off the track and onto the infield where he eased himself to the ground and laid back in pain. The trainers and Coach Jones was on him almost from the moment he fell out of the race.

"You okay son?" he asked dropping to a knee beside him and putting a towel under his head. "It's that damn muscle cramp again!" he grimaced. His face a picture of pain.

"Gimmie that hot stuff Will" he said to the trainer. The man reached into a gym bag and pulled out a white plastic jar with a red label. It had a little devil on the lid smiling.

"Aw shoot coach . . . not the hot stuff!" he complained some.

"It's either this or you can ride it out in pain and maybe blow this meet."

"Okay then, I'll deal with it" he grumbled letting Coach Jones put a generous portion of the neon red greasy substance on his thigh. As he rubbed it in, Chappy clenched his teeth preparing for the burn.

"OW that stuff burns like hell Coach!"

"Yeah feels good don't it?" he smiled and chuckling lightly as he rubbed it vigorously into his runners leg.

Meanwhile Eric was feeling his own heat as the loss of his team mate was immediately noted and acted upon like a wounded animal in the jungle. The other competitors grew really aggressive almost immediately and the pace increased two fold. Eric felt the breath of the other three boys on his neck like a bull in a ring. He tried to will himself to focus and concentrate. The finish line was coming up fast and Eric had only thirty or so yards to make his move. He clenched his teeth hard and leaned forward digging in like greyhound.

He began to pull away from the pack at the last ten yards and broke the tape with a head lunge. The runner to his right lunged also but missed the tape by a foot or so and just stumbled to the ground as his over compensation threw him off balance. He hit hard and rolled on the ground creating a cloud of grey dust. Eric smiled to himself and just kept going till he slowed down naturally then began walking with his hands over his head.

"WITH A TIME OF 9.63 . . . ERIC REID!" the sound of his name being called as the winner gave him a sweet taste in his mind as the salty taste of sweat entered his mouth and made him spit.

He walked off the field and into the infield where he was attacked by his team mates and a few females he didn't know.

Things were really hot now and Southwest was beside themselves and couldn't understand how there best runners were being walked on. They just knew they were going to have the home team advantage but the outcome didn't ring any truth to that end. Eric walked over to see about Chappy. He was sitting or leaning against some equipment with his leg wrapped up and sweating like he'd just stopped running.

"How you doing man?" he asked kneeling beside him. "Not too bad, this leg of mine is acting up again, Coach gave me the fire grease to chill it out."

"Not the hot stuff?" "Yep" he said smiling weakly.

"Damnnn! That stuff will light your ass up like a bonfire!"

"Why the heck you think I'm sitting here sweating like a choir boy in a whore house."

Eric just laughed at him shaking his head. "You gonna be alright for the 220?"

"I hope so . . . I got some time before that comes up."

"I hope so cause that's when we really need you."

"Tell me something I don't know, how's Matt doing?"

"Don't know, I sent him off to chill and get his mind right."

"Think he'll hold up?"

"I'm counting on it, Coach has got us doing the hardest events first to break them down some mentally, truth is these guys could take us on the distance and field events cause we lost a lot of our team from last year."

"Yeah, we sure could use some of those guys now."

"Oh well we'll just have to kick ass and hope they don't figure out we are limited in numbers." After awhile it was Ant's turn on the hurdles. He made a good showing and came in a respectable second place. By now most of the races and events were over and the last to go was the discus, long jump and the 440 relay.

Retta was really getting anxious now and began to look around for Matt on the field. She hadn't seen him after that last time when they walked onto the field.

"Damn Matt where are you?" she said out loud to herself. "The meets almost over and you haven't even run or anything yet!" Just then she saw Ant.

"Ant! Hey Ant!" she said waving wildly.

Ant was getting in a few warm up steps on the long jump before he had to go. "Hey what's up shorty?" he said giving her a hug.

"Ant I can't find Matt anywhere, have you seen him?" she said obviously distressed and happy at the same time.

"Yeah he's someplace on the infield . . . probably meditating or something, you know getting pumped up for his events."

"Well I can understand that but where?"

"I don't know, go and try over near the gear pile next to the pole vault area."

"Thanks Ant" she said running off with renewed hope.

Matt had just finished the tape and felt quite pumped up inside. "Man that was some tape" he thought to himself bobbing his head to the memory of it as he took off the head phones. "No wonder Jr. was always so pumped when he ran."

The tape was a collection of upbeat pop tunes and instrumentals. He got up and started walking towards the middle of the field where most of the team was gathered. Retta met him head on coming from around the large pad of the pole vault. She crashed right into him flinging her arms around him and kissed him feverishly. The shock surprise and pleasure of this unexpected attack threw him off balance and he fell to the ground with her on top of him. He landed with an OOMPH!

"Hello sweetpea" he said breaking from her imprisoning kiss. "What's the rush red?"

"Matt! I saw you when you got here and I was waving to you and calling you but you didn't see me or hear me, after awhile you disappeared and I didn't see you anymore so I came looking for you!" she said panting and breathing hard from the effort.

"Well you certainly found me didn't you?" he said getting up pulling her behind him.

"Come on lets go" he said hugging her as they walked. It was now the final three events and Matt was ready to go! Retta stayed on the infield and tried not to be noticed by the coaches and other staff as she was not supposed to be there. Unfortunately Coach Jones and Eric had noticed her long ago and stood commenting on who she was.

"So that's Mathis's little flame huh?" said coach playing with his teeth again.

"Yep"

"I thought Cheryl Walker was his girl?"

"She want's to be, but Matt ain't giving her the time of day."

"I can see why, well he better keep it in check either way, otherwise we're gonna have a lot more Mathis boys running around than we can keep up with" he said grinning and rubbing his chin. Eric nodded in agreement.

Back at the meet the scores were beginning to rack up and balance out. Southwest had managed to make a come back and was doing some serious damage to Central's point spread. Non-the-less, Matt was in rare form and he came in first place on the last two events scoring a 160 feet on the discuss (a new state record) and jumping twenty two and a half feet on the long jump. Ant took a solid second place making sure Southwest had some catching up to do.

Now it was time for the last event and everyone was waiting for it. It was the 440 relay. Southwest needed first to win hands down. The team for Central was Rick Parker on start, Michael Woodard on second leg, Matt on third leg, and Eric Reid on anchor.

"Hey Matt, come here a minute dude!" said Eric waving him over.

"What's up E?"

"How do you feel?"

"I feel good man . . . real good, that tape really helped out, I can't get some of those tunes out of my Head!"

"That's great . . . just great, I was hoping that was the case, that's also why I want to swap places with you on the next heat."

"Swap places? You mean me run anchor leg?"

"Yeah"

"Oh hell to the no dude, I couldn't do that!"

"Why not?"

"Man you know you're the flame thrower on this team! How the heck can I take your spot! I don't run as fast as you!"

"Sure you can, you just think you can't that's all, and besides you don't have to run as fast as me, you only have to run faster than the next guy, so how about it?"

Matt was really off balance now and couldn't fathom why Eric would want him to do such a thing especially when they were on the brink of winning or losing. He knew he wasn't nearly as fast as Eric with a time in the hundred of 10.5 and Eric a recent 9.6. and what would the coach say about the change . . . he'd go nuts for sure.

"Come on Matt we gotta go line up . . . what do you say?" Matt sighed long and deep.

"Okay Eric I'll do it but I ain't promising anything"

"Good, now lets go give e'm hell and show e'm who owns this track!"

Matt waved to Retta as she headed back into the bleachers to sit with Frieda and Curt. Matt headed for his place on the track as she sat down. She saw where he was going and wondered what was up. She remembered that he told her he would be third leg not anchor. She had a lot of faith in him but also knew that Eric would probably have made a better choice for that position given that Southwest had and ace in the hole for this race and his name was Alex Strong.

He was a six foot 180 pound racing engine with legs. He had made state AA trials since he was in the tenth grade and was being primed for a college scholarship in track and football.

Eric had faced him before and had mixed success. He won one time when Alex pulled a hamstring on a hundred yard dash one year. He lost every event after that against him for the next year.

"Do you see that?" asked Frieda pointing in his direction.

"Yeah I do" said Retta looking on curiously. She had seen the switch and wondered what was up. She had faith in him and his abilities but the much stronger runner on anchor he was facing made him look a little undersized and not quite up to the task.

"Girl he can't out run Alex, that boy is on his way to the Olympics!" she said louder than necessary.

"Aw you just shut up Frieda, you don't know what he can or can't do!" she said getting up and squaring on her friend. Curt instinctively moved over so as not to get caught up if there is a cat fight between them.

"Hey I'm sorry, I was just saying what I know okay?" Soon the race was about to begin. RUNNERS TAKE YOUR MARKS . . . GET SET . . . POW! The first leg runners left the line so fast that dust was flowing behind them. They pumped and sped there way to the first exchange on the turn. All the while edging and trying to out run each other to the next leg. Matt's pulse was running wild and his mouth was dirt dry as he watched the race get closer and closer to him. In seconds the switch took place and second leg was on its way with Southwest in a comfortable lead of ten feet. The runner moved smoothly and like a well oiled machine as he churned his way around the track heeling like a fine race car to the inside lane. Eric was waiting for the baton and hoping he didn't get it too late to be of any help to Matt who was probably suffering from potential heart failure the closer the race got to him. Matt looked up at his competition and felt a little heartsick. "So this is my David and Goliath moment huh?" he thought to himself as he eyed the powerfully build runner next to him from the corner of his eye. He tried not to think of him but only the music and his own rhythm.

"Don't sweat it little man . . . it only hurts for a little while" said Alex glaring at Matt with ice blue eyes and a fence post perfect teeth. He was mixed; part black, part white and part Polynesian. He was known to some as the sphinx because he was stone cold when it came to concentration and running his game. Some say it was because of his varied lineage. Matt was thinking that it probably had more to do with his physique and stoic appearance right about now. Either way he was going to have to deal with him.

"Thanks a lot Eric" he mumbled under his breath.

"Eric? Did you say Eric as in Eric Ried?" he ask almost comically. Matt just rolled his eyes to look at him.

"Yeah, what about him?" said Matt a little defensively.

"Is he the one who got you into this? Man I knew the dude was afraid of me but I didn't think he would sacrifice one of his own just to save me embarrassing him again."

"What are you talking about?" asked Matt getting angry.

"Ask him to tell you about me sometime." Matt didn't know what the deal was but he wasn't afraid of the Amazonian runner anymore but instead pissed off. He didn't like anyone putting down his friends and he definitely didn't like them underestimating him at the same time. Matt got real cool real quick and a calm overcame him like a warm shower. He turned from him and set himself for the oncoming runner.

"Actually he told me to give you a message."

"What?"

"Kiss mine and his ass . . . . loser" then he was of. Matt didn't even look to see where Eric was but just instinctively took off and reached behind him after a few steps and was greeted by the solid slap of the cold aluminum baton.

"Go Matt Go!" Yelled Eric. And Matt went. He was running like he was possessed or at least running through hell with gasoline drawers on. He felt strong and he felt full in his chest like he had grown an extra lung. Alex soon began to catch up to him but Matt wasn't phased or startled by the sound of the bigger boys feet chopping their way up from behind him.

"Go Alex! Go Matt!" Screamed everyone. Retta was out of her seat cheering him on jumping up and down. She was looked upon oddly by those around her because she was wearing Southwest colors but cheering for Centrals runner to win. Alex felt equally as powerful as he slowly closed the gap between him and Matt. He was thinking a little upstart that was about to be put in his place . . . . last he grimaced and churned on getting closer and closer as they made the turn around the bend. He knew he was gonna take Matt in the home stretch and smiled to himself as he thought about passing him and making some comment. The crowd and both teams were in bedlam as some ran along the track behind the runners and others stomped in the stands to the point of shaking them. Matt could hear it all and it sounded like a huge waterfall of sound. He heard his heart beating, he tasted his own breath as is rushed in and out of his mouth and burned his throat and lungs. He also heard the music he had listened to earlier and it was coming into his mind slowly but building with force!

At first he heard a repetitive base note that came in counts of four then repeated itself. Then a piano followed and kept time with it in a snappy little

4-4 beat. Designer Music was the name of it and it gave him a chill as it raced through him with equal ferocity. Matt felt like a dog that had just shaken himself and he was powerful! He began to run in time with the music and sped up. His legs burned anew! His heart pumped harder and his lungs fired like a hot air balloon. He sped up like he was being pushed and much to the surprise and shock of Alex who was just about to pass him. He watched in horror as Matt pulled away from him like he was on a motorcycle and just sped away from him. There was only fifty yards to go and Alex gave it all the power he had and produced a very impressive burst of speed and closing the distance once again. Unfortunately Matt was running on renewed inspiration and unseen forces only the gods of Olympus could see or understand. Matt pulled away from Alex leaving him by no less than ten yards and broke the tape in first. The crowed was hysterical! They couldn't believe it! Retta couldn't believe it! Matt had beat the one person that Southwest knew would not be defeated by anyone!

Retta jumped down the bleachers and ran across the field to catch him. She was elated and completely overjoyed. She ran partially up the track and on the field to where he had slowed down and stopped. Matt was now walking with his hands on his head as Eric had told him to do so he wouldn't get a vapor lock or something from coming down to fast. Little did Eric know it but Matt was still running around the track even though his body had stopped. The music was still going in his head and he was on fire with energy! It really took something to come down and he finally did when he felt the hard contact of a hand on his back and arms around him hugging him jumping up and down.

"Way to go Matt! . . ."

"Damn that was hot man!"

"You smoked his ass dude!" was the sounds that surrounded him.

Soon the crowed parted and he was assaulted by hugs and kisses from Retta who was just about to climb on top of him.

"Matt . . . Matt I knew you could do it I just knew it!" she yelled between kisses that covered his face and neck

. "Whoa! . . . whoa people give the man some air!" said Eric wading in and pulling people off him. "Hey pretty girl . . . save some of that for later okay?" he said to Retta grabbing her around the waist and easing her to the ground. She looked at him and just smiled.

"Way to go Matt, I knew you could do it" he said shaking Matt's free hand.

"That's good to know doc . . . cause I didn't" he said cracking everyone up.

Coach Jones and Coach Williams waded into the crowed smiling and playing with his teeth as usual.

"Damn good job son! Damn good! I had a feeling that there was some of the Stallion in your blood and now I see its true, Good job."

"Thanks coach" he said shaking his massive hand vigorously.

Retta was basking in the glow of him and the light that everyone had cast about him.

"Okay people lets go and shake hands with your hosts for having us here and wish em a good game."

Everyone in the Southwest camp was upset. They just knew they were going to take Central apart with no trouble at all! Unfortunately the score board read differently. The final score was Central 47 points and Southwest 38. The last event was worth ten points which would have put Southwest over by one point if they had one. Instead they were handed the first of many loss of the season. As everyone turned to go and shake hands with Southwest's team they found it a little hard to do seeing as how most of the team had left the field and the remaining members were on their way to joining them.

Coach saw this too and just recalled everyone saying, "I guess they don't practice sportsman ship here either" he said smiling to himself and a little put out at the rudeness of the home team actions.

Coach Williams just shrugged and started herding her team up to get on the bus.

"Let's ride Chargers!" said Matt pulling Retta close to him and walking towards the bus in the parking lot. Retta stopped short frowning a little.

"Matt I can't go with you guys."

"Why . . . you're safe?"

"I know that silly, I just mean that I rode with Curt and Frieda."

"Well go tell them you're going with me over to my house and they can come too if they want." "Okay" she said running back over to the bleachers where they stood then coming back quickly. Matt was helping to put away some of the gear in the back of the bus and putting on his warm up suit because it was getting a little chilly. The sun had gone down and the day was just about over. He stopped a moment to look at the deep red setting sun on the horizon, and it was beautiful. Remnants of banners and signs flitted and flapped in the gentle fall breeze. He saw one that read "*SOUTHWEST PATRIOTS GONNA TAKE CHARGE!*" and depicted and colonial soldier unhorsing Centrals knight from his horse with his own lance.

Matt just laughed to himself "Yeah right guys" he said under his breath. "You just got charged". Soon Retta was back.

"Okay Matt we can go, they said they would catch us later and Curt said to tell you that you did a good job and reminded him of the Black Stallion!"

Matt just gawked in disbelief.

"Damn! is there anybody that don't know Jr.?" he thought.

"Matt who is the Black Stallion?" she asked hugging up to him.

"My oldest brother Jr. come on lets ride" he said cuffing her neck and walking to the bus.

As they got on he could see Coach Jones sitting in front with his foot propped up on the safety bar across from the driver.

"What's this Mathis . . . a little souvenir?" he said pointing at Retta with his thumb.

Matt blushed and was the sole attention of everyone on the bus . . . including a not too happy Cher who was burning holes into Retta's skull with her eyes.

"Naw coach this is the prize!" he said giving her a big squeeze and kissing her in the top of her head. Retta blushed crimson and tried to hide under his arm but couldn't escape the hoots and shouts of the bus load of athletes shouting their approval.

"Come on son lets break camp, we've already outlived our welcome" he said pointing at the driver indicating he could close the doors and all was on board ready to go. They went all the way to the back of the bus to sit and on the way passed Cheryl who didn't share the rest of the teams enthusiasm for his little trophy. She sat with her arms folded across her chest and a detestable frown on her face. Matt just slumped in the rear seat with Retta on his lap.

"Matt behave!" she said smacking his hand when he pinched her bottom.

"You know you can't finish what you start so don't even try it!"

"Yeah maybe not now, but just you wait till I get you home little red riding hood" he said in a gruff low voice. *"I'm gonna huff and puff and blow your clothes off!"*

Retta just squealed happily and grabbed his face kissing him sweetly.

"We'll see about that you old wind bag . . . . we'll see" she said then kissed him again but this time a little more passionate and tenderly with intent.

Cheryl on the other hand was listening to the soft drama that was going on behind her and was burning up like a brush fire with jealousy. She was getting fit to be tied with each passing second as Retta was taking up her spot with her love interest and giving him the kisses and affection that was hers to give.

"OOH! that little red hefer!, who does she think she is sitting back there with Matt getting all cozy and stuff! Just look at how she's sitting on his lap and kissing him. She's not even the least bit shy or considerate that others are looking at her and watching them! I hope she gets a fatal disease and her tits fall off!" she grumbled under her breath to Ant's amusement who was sitting across from her watching quietly as Cheryl turned several shades of red and frowned so hard that her face was turning into a pink prune. He just shook his head and chuckled to himself and turned around to face the front of the bus. He had seen all he wanted and didn't want to invite any hostility his way should Cher notice him looking at her.

Soon the bus rolled into the schools parking lot back at school. The scene was much like the night before when they used the college track to practice. There were many cars sitting and waiting for the track stars to arrive home. No sooner did the bus come to a complete stop then the team got up and start heading for the door in a mad rush. They couldn't wait to tell their parents and friends about the double victory that they had over Southwest. Unfortunatly Coach Jones had other ideas.

"Hold up people!" he said standing up and blocking the isle.

"I've got a few things to pass out before you go" he said bellowing over the frantic noise of the group.

"You guys did one hell of a job today and you should be proud of yourselves, but we still need to work on some things and a lot more practice, some of you need to really work harder and focus" he said looking at the junior varsity team and scowling a little.

"Others of you are improving and need to work on your techniques, on the whole you all did well and we kicked their butts but don't think it can't happen to you because as sure as a bear can crap in the woods . . . Southwest and the other schools you go up against can and will get some get back!" "The only way to make sure they don't is to work harder, smarter and do your level best all the time and not cheat yourself, now next week we have it with Northeast over here and Northside on their field so get ready for some long practices and intensive workouts all week." "People we're starting on the downside of things being that the weather screwed up our routine, but we made a good showing anyway and I'm proud of each and every one of you, take it easy this weekend and rest well cause next week we bust ass!"

"Now get off my bus . . . you guys stink!" he said pinching his nose and skewing his face smiling at them. Everyone laughed and attacked him at the door hugging on him trying to leave some sweat or scent on him as they went by as revenge. Some just patted his rotund belly as they went out. Matt and Retta were the last to get off the bus.

"Hey Mathis hold on" he said placing his huge hand on his shoulder.

"Yeah coach?"

"You did a great job today son . . . really good job!"

Matt blushed a little and felt a little squirm in his stomach.

"Thanks coach, I just remembered all you and Eric taught me and told me to do."

"Well you did it really well son and I'm proud of you, I'm sure if your brother Buford could be here he would say the same, how is he these days anyway?"

"Oh, he's doing good, he's just about to complete boot camp up in Illinois . . . Great Lakes I think its called"

"Yeah, I know the place I did some time there myself when I was a young man."

"You were in the Navy coach?"

"Yeah back in the day many, many years ago during Vietnam"

"Cool! what kind of work or job did you have? Jr. is going to be a hospital tech or something" "Well my job wasn't quite so neat and controlled as your brothers . . . I was what you call an Operator"

"Operator? You mean you where in some kind of communications job?" he asked thinking that coach didn't look like the type to sit at a desk and answer phones all day. And his physique definitely spoke adverse volumes of something much more physical and direct. Coach just grinned at the question thinking of all the missions he had been on and scrapes he'd been into. "Yeah I guess you could say that I did a little communicating but not with any phones"

"Oh" Matt said kind of feeling like he understood what coach meant with out him saying it. It made Matt feel a little small but yet proud and kind of full inside too because of who and what coach was to all of the students at Central.

"You just keep cranking like you did today and you'll be the best at anything you do son" he said patting him on the shoulder and looking intently into Matt's eyes smiling.

Matt nodded proudly and Retta clinched his arm tighter getting closer to him as she was proud of him too.

"Alright coach I will"

"Good now you have a nice weekend and don't do anything straining or physically exhausting okay?" he said winking at him. Matt just smiled and walked off the bus.

"What did he say Matt?" asked Retta who didn't quite catch the last comment.

"Oh nothing just a little pep talk that's all"

"Hey Matt, Ant you guys want a lift to the crib?" asked Eric waving to them from his car. "Yeah, dude if it ain't too much trouble"

"Naw man come on" he said waving them over.

"Eric this is my lady Aretta" he said introducing her as she got in.

"Hi Eric"

"Hey pretty lady" he said shaking her hand lightly and smiling.

Retta couldn't help feeling pampered a little and blushed with all the attention she was getting that day. Matt opened up the front seat and he and Ant got in back.

"So what are you and Retta gonna do tonight?" asked Ant

"I don't know probably just chill out or got to a movie"

"How about you Eric?"

"I got this date with this chick over at the college"

"When did you meet her?"

"I met her one day while I was at a seminar checking out the different colleges I might want to go to"

"Sounds like you've already started networking some" he said smiling at him in the mirror. "Well it never hurts to develop contacts early, you never know."

"Yeah your right."

The trip to the house from the school was fairly short and they soon pulled up in front of Matt's house. Retta got out then Matt and Ant.

"Hey dude I'll check you guys out later okay?"

"Alright Ant ya'll be cool" he said waving them on as Eric pulled away from the curb.

"He seems like a nice guy" said Retta hooking Matt's arm as they walked up the sidewalk to the porch. Matt opened the door and let them in.

"Are you guys hungry?" he asked tossing the key on the dresser.

"Yeah sure, watcha got?" asked Ant raising a hungry eyebrow.

"I don't know, go and see."

Retta reached up and kissed him lightly on the cheek.

"I'll be back I need to go to the little girls room"

"Okay babe" he said then sat down hard in his lounge chair, air escaping like a stuck balloon. The days events began to roll over in his mind and he found himself toying with various concepts of how he was going to attend the party tonight with Retta here. He knew that she would want to stay late or go out someplace being that it was the weekend. He got up and paced the floor thinking, "Damn! this shit ain't gonna work, I know I should have let her go home and then hook up with her afterwards but now she's here and I just can't leave or take her with me . . . fuck! How do I get into these messes." "I should learn to be more strict and firm with women, most of them are like children sometimes and all they know is they want and that's it, but then again I can't be too much better than them if I let em get to me like they do so it's really all my fault." Still I gotta clear this crap up and get it over with or it will get even worse if you can imagine anything over and above what has already happened."

Retta had come back into the room unnoticed as Matt was deep in thought. She slipped her arms around his waist from behind and just cuddled him to her.

"What's wrong puddin?" she asked looking up at him as he turned in her embrace to face her. She was so damn beautiful he thought as he looked into those deep penetrating brown eyes.

"I was just day dreaming that's all" he lied.

"What about? You look so distraught"

"Naw, it's nothing much, just floating some of today's activities through my head . . . you know just musing"

Retta looked into his eyes intently and felt that there was more to it than that, but had nothing to support it with. She breathed in and sighed long letting the matter go from her as it wouldn't serve any purpose to hold on to it. Just then the phone rang. Matt picked it up quickly, thankful for the brief interruption.

"Hello?"

"Hi . . . Rodney? This is Audrey, is Aretta over there with you?" she asked a little nervously.

"She didn't come home from school yet."

"Yes ma'am ,she's here . . . Retta" he said handing her the phone.

"Hello?" "How come you didn't say you were going over there or let me know something in advance?" she said more than concerned and a little pissed.

"But I did momma, I told Frieda to tell you I was going to be over here after the track meet, she said she would tell you when she got to the house."

"Well she didn't and Lori had to stay with Mrs. Johnson till I got home! You know better than to do something like this without checking with me first, you don't just take it on your own to just do a thing and pass it on to someone who is also as irresponsible as you . . . what are you thinking! I had no idea of anything. I thought something had happened to you. Do you know how worried I was?"

Retta's heart sank and her stature digressed smaller with each word her mother spoke. Matt couldn't really hear her but could see the effect on Retta's face as beads of sweat began to form at the nape of her neck.

"I'm sorry momma I didn't mean to" she said looking guilt stricken and fiddling nervously with the phone cord around her finger.

Matt just stood there quietly feeling her pain and hoping she wasn't in any kind of trouble. "Look girl, your gonna have to stop this craziness with Rodney and I mean now! Your beginning to get on my nerves with this mess!"

"Yes ma'am" she said almost whispering and down cast.

"I'm sorry mamma I won't do it again"

"You can bet you won't! cause if you do you can count yourself single because I'm not gonna put up with this kind of mess! Lord honey no! I'm too old for this kind of shit!"

"Do you want me to come home now?" she whispered terrified at the answer.

"No! you stay right where you are. You are going to your grandmothers for the weekend."

Retta twisted around like she was in pain and stamped her foot holding the phone away from her. The painful frown on her face told Matt that it wasn't good.

"Okay . . . bye" she said signing off and hanging up the phone.

"What's up babe?" asked Matt desperate to know what was up.

"Momma's mad cause I came over here and said I shoulda told her first." "She also said if I keep it up she's gonna stop me from seeing you!" She said almost in tears.

Matt was a little death stricken himself at the sound of this declaration and it sent a cool chill through him.

"All because of that?" Retta nodded with her arms folded around herself as if she was cold.

"I don't know what's wrong with her, she's never been that mad at me before."

"Well maybe once a long time ago but she never went off on me like that"

"Well let me get you home then, I don't want you getting into any more trouble because of me" he said reaching in his drawer for a pair of pants.

"No Matt, you don't have to, she's gonna come and get me cause we're going over to my grandma's house for the weekend. Matt stopped in his tracks and looked at her. "Really . . . where?"

"In Gray"

Matt tossed the pants onto the bed a little disgusted. He felt a little robbed but didn't quite know why. I mean it was the best thing that could have ever happened. Now he didn't have to worry about how he was gonna get rid of her for the party and better still not have to worry about staying out too late. Still he didn't like it.

"Well I'll be dammed, now we won't have any kind of a weekend now!" he said kicking his gym bag across the room, and standing with his hands on his hips.

Retta felt a rush of warmth and sadness at his outburst. She knew he really loved her and didn't want to be without her this weekend but also knew he was powerless to do anything about it which made her feel his pain also. Matt looked over and saw Ant leaning against the doorway munching on a hot dog or something with ketchup dripping from between his fingers.

"Ant what time is it?" he asked suddenly changing course. He didn't think to look behind him at the clock on the dresser that was nearer to him than Ant's wrist watch. Ant just looked at him incredulously and chewing like a cow. He slowly lifted and hotdog loaded hand and pointed in the direction of the dresser behind him as if to say "Look behind you stupid." Retta wasn't slow to get that either and it crossed her as funny that he had switched gears so suddenly.

"What's up Matt . . . do you have to go somewhere?" she said cocking her eyes at him curiously like something was amiss.

"No I was just wondering where dad was, he's running late and should have been here by now." "Is it bad that he isn't ?" she asked.

"No, not really but it's not normal either."

"Well shouldn't you be taking this time to get him something to eat for dinner when he does get home?" she asked readjusting herself and trying to forget about the imminent out of towner she was going to be pulling shortly with her mother and sister.

"Yeah I guess I'd better" he said sighing deeply looking at Retta somewhat sadly at their combined dilemma.

"Well I guess we'll just have to wait until next weekend babe" he said dryly without compassion. Retta was likewise and just nodded with her head down looking at her shoes.

"You wanna come help me fix dinner" he asked. Retta didn't speak but just leaned over and hugged him hard.

"It's gonna be a long boring weekend without you" she breathed then broke from him and taking his hand leading him out of the bedroom towards the kitchen. A little while later and a good combined effort they had finished his dad's dinner and not a moment too soon. Just as they put the last dish on the table they heard the strained sound of a pickup truck rattling down the driveway. The truck came to a quick stop then shut down. Seconds later they could hear the hurried sounds of his dads boots running up the back steps into the kitchen. He came through the door in a hurried gate looking quite dirty and with smudges on his uniform and face.

"Hiddey ho!" he said as he came in.

"Hi dad"

"Hello Mr. Buford"

"Hello Aretta . . . George"

"So dad what took you so long, it's 6:00 o'clock?"

"Well I had a little trouble with the jeep and had to wait for a tow truck and another jeep"

"What happened to it?"

"It was the transmission, it started slipping and finally quit altogether on me, I tried to do what I could to get it going thinking it was maybe a loose line or leaky hose."

"I thought they usually kept those vehicles in pretty good shape at the post office"

"Well they do but sometimes they miss one every now an then on an inspection cause they got so many, I just happened to get the bad one this time."

"I see" said Matt nodding.

"So you fixed something to eat?" he asked taking off his hat and putting down his cooler and lunch container on the counter.

"Yes sir, we made a meat loaf some macaroni and cheese, green beans and jiffy cornbread"

His dad gave them an appraising look and nodded.

"Sounds good" he said then walked off towards his bedroom to get out of his uniform and into a shower.

"How'd you guys do on the track meet!" he shouted from the next room.

"We did good! Both teams won and . . . ."

"No! let me tell him" chirped Retta as she went after him.

"You should have seen him Mr. Buford he was so fast I couldn't believe it was him out there running!"

"Do tell" he said pulling his shirt out of his pants and sitting down to take off his shoes.

"Yes! Matt was in the relay and instead of running the third leg of the race he ran the last leg" "Wouldn't that make his job a little easier?"

"No sir, harder! The last guy is the anchor leg and has to actually finish the race to win."

"Matt was going up against one of our schools best track runners and he beat him by two lengths!"

"That's about ten feet Mr. Mathis" added Ant seeing the peculiar looks he was going through trying to grasp an image of what Retta was describing.

"And on the discuss."

"That's that flying saucer looking thing isn't it?" he offered

"Yes sir, Matt through that thing so far everybody thought it had rockets strapped on it!" he chuckled at the image Retta was painting and her enthusiastic report on his youngest sons performance today. Matt just stood in the door bashful with his head down.

"He came in first place on the relay and first on the discuss, they won the meet!" she finished giving Matt a big hug and kiss on the cheek. She was so proud of him that it made him feel like dirt thinking of what he was going to be doing later on that night with someone else.

He tried to ease the sting of it by telling himself that it was for the best and he was actually doing it to ensure no more activity of that kind anymore in the future. It was kind of a weak excuse but it would have to do.

"Anthony did good too! and he came in second on the long jump and first on the triple jump!" she added as an afterthought hugging Ant around the waist with her free arm. Ant blushed a little and felt a little proud of himself also. Just then they all heard the door bell ring. It was Retta's mom coming to get her. Retta ran to answer the door. She came back with her mother and Lori in tow.

"Hello Rodney" she said smiling lightly.

"Ms. Audrey" he nodded and moved aside so she could enter his dads room.

Lori tugged at his shirt tail to get his attention.

"Hi Rodney!" she said all happy and gave him a big hug.

"Hey! you little tatter tot, how have you been?" Lori gushed in his acknowledgement of her. "Good!"

"Hey Buford" she said giving him a hug.

"Hi sweetie, and how are you doing?"

"I'm fine, I just came by to pick up little miss wayward there to go to my mother-in-laws for the weekend."

"Oh that sounds nice" he said but not really meaning it, he absent mindedly looked away as if he were alerted to something that wasn't there just so she wouldn't see his disappointment. Audrey however was no young girl and was very experienced in how she affected men and when they were lying to her.

"We can get together next week sometime though" she said holding up his face and looking at him smiling meekly.

"No problem" he said walking her to the couch to sit. Retta took this cue to leave and let them have their time alone. She also wanted to have some time with Matt before she would be snatched from him and taken to the country. Ant was aware that there was no room for him there and told Matt he was gonna go. Matt let him borrow the scooter and Ant took the keys and was off. Retta had taken Matt back to the bedroom and closed the door. But not before setting up Lori with something to eat and the television. She didn't waste any time and went right to work kissing and embracing Matt like he was going off to war. The two lovers hugged kissed and massaged one another to the point of frenzy but could do no more than this being her mother was just a room or two away and could be leaving anytime.

The two of them relished and ravished each other for a bit longer and was harshly brought back to the present by the sound of Retta's mothers voice calling to her.

"Yes ma'am!"

"It's time to go sweetie we have a drive ahead of us and I don't want to get caught up in the weekend traffic"

"Okay!" she yelled back still holding onto Matt resting her forehead on his chest.

"Sigh . . . well I guess it's that time"

"Yeah, come on walk me to the car, I wish I didn't have to leave"

"Yeah I know, but you can call me right?"

"Yeah, she's got a phone"

"Okay that's good then, why don't you give me the number to your grandmothers and then you call me when you get there." Retta quickly jotted down the number and gave it to him.

"What are you gonna do tonight while I'm gone?" she asked curiously with big doe eyes.

"I don't know . . . probably hang out here or go to Ant's house, if I do I'll call you first okay?" She didn't like this idea and wanted to have a more assurance of him being accessible to her later. "Okay Matt" she said reaching up to embrace him once more. Her kiss was warm and deep and he could feel it down through to his toes. It filled his mind with warm and fuzzy ideas and thoughts of the weekend gone by.

"Damn! its gonna be a long weekend" he thought. Lori was waiting impatiently at the car as she saw Retta and her mom come out with Mr. Buford and Matt.

"Momma I'm tired and ready to go to gramma's house" she said pouting as they walked up. "Well we're leaving now baby, you go ahead and get in the car and buckle up."

"So Buford I'll give you a call when I get there okay?"

"Okay then, you guys have a nice weekend and drive safe" he said reaching out and pulling her to him for a light kiss and hug. Lori thought it was hilarious and hid her eyes giggling. Audrey smiled at him warmly and caressed his chin as she eased away from him and walked around the car to get in. Matt was just opening the door to let Retta in and she gave him a last quick hug through the window.

"I love you Matt" she whispered. He just smiled and gave her a hand signal holding up his thumb and for finger to make a "U" then reversed it holding up two fingers and patting his heart. She got the message and it made her feel warm and loved inside. At least enough to get her through the weekend without him. Matt and his dad stood back from the curb as she started the engine and pulled away from the curb. They watched until the car was out of sight then sighed long putting his arm around Matt's shoulder.

"Well looks like it's just us guys again"

"Yep looks that way" he said nodding.

"Come on let's go find something to get into" said his dad flashing mischievous eyes at him and grinning as the returned inside.

"Hey Cheryl get me that roll of party paper so I can hang it!"

"Which one, there's a bunch of them" she said looking at the box of multicolored rolls of paper. "The red one!"

Cher picked up one and tossed it to her up on the ladder. The girls had been busy working on getting the house ready for the long awaited "Sadie Hawkins" party and were in a real festive mood.

Mel had decided to use red and gold color streamers with orange and blue mixed in to inaugurate Northeast's and Central's colors. They used this scheme because they were hosting the party and since Central was victorious today over Southwest they thought they would honor them by showing a splash of their battle colors as well. So far only Mel and Cher were there at the house. Her parents had left hours ago and were well on their way out of town and wouldn't be back till Sunday, leaving the house in the of both girls.

"So Mel are the other girls sure about the time of the party?"

"Yeah they know and I contacted each of them today to make sure"

"Do they know who's coming?"

"Yeah they know that too and most of e'm can't wait to get here!" she said flashing an excited smile from the top of the ladder.

"Hey did you bring your records and tapes with you like I asked?"

"*Yes!*" she said impatiently. "I brung them and Matt gave me a few of his special tapes he made too"

"Oh yeah . . . what's on them?"

"It would be easier to say what's not on them!" she said proudly.

"They're that good huh?"

"Girl yeah! he's got just about every slow jam you have ever heard since 1970 and all of em are bad if you know what I mean!"

"Well this ought to be a real bump and grind night then" said Mel coming down off the ladder. "Hey why don't you give Matt a call and see what he's up to."

"Okay!" she said flopping down on the couch and grabbing the phone on the coffee table. She dialed quickly and waited. There was no answer so she hung up sadly.

"This line is busy Mel I'll have to try again later"

"Alright we still have some other stuff to do anyway" she said walking over to her rolling up the spare steamer ribbon she had been hanging.

"So tell me what do you think of his girl?" she asked setting down the roll on the table and sitting down beside her. Cher just laid back on the couch and stared blankly at the ceiling as her mind buzzed with opinions, perspectives, admonitions and various levels of dislikes about Retta. She rolled her head slowly to the side and looked at Mel clinically while chewing her bottom lip. "What do you think I think of her?" she asked tonelessly. Mel just smiled and crossed her legs "You hate her right?" she pressed on.

"Yes in a way I do but in another way I don't" said Mel knitting her eyebrows as she thought about her statement.

"How so?"

"Well I think it's more jealousy than anything else, I mean look at her she's gorgeous! . . . what's not to like and she's a nice person too once you get to know her and talk to her for awhile"

"Well I've seen and heard more of her than I care too!" said Cher sitting up and rubbing her dainty nose vigorously. Mel just sat back and observed her like she was a small creature in the wild.

"How come you hate her so much Cher? . . . Isn't that a bit unnatural and psychotic?"

"No! I don't think so" she said with finality.

"She's got the man I've been after and wanting since the eighth grade and I won't share him!" "Well so do I but I'm not gonna die over it, there's just too many more good looking guys around, I mean sure he's cute and special and all that but I'm sure he's not extinct either, you just have to look around and not give into the first hard penis that waggles at you like most girls tend to do"

"Well I still don't care, you know how I get when I really want something"

"Yeah I do" she said skewing her eyebrows.

"You become driven and obsessed"

"Until I get what I want!" she cut in.

Mel just grinned and shook her head.

"Well I think you'd better prepare yourself for disappointment, he may not show up since she's there with him now."

"Oh he'll show up" said Cher folding her arms confidently and smirking to herself.

"He knows that if he forfeits then we win and you know what that means" she said cutting her eyes at Mel. Mel just grinned to herself and started bobbing her foot like a cat swishing it's tail. "So I know he will show up, besides he's not the type to give up easy"

"Well you better try and call him again just to make sure."

"So Matt what are you gonna wear tonight?" asked Ant.

"Oh I don't know, I'll probably go preppie or something, how about you?"

"Yeah I'll probably do the same." Matt repositioned the phone on his shoulder and reached into his top drawer to pull out some dark blue trousers with pleats. He closed the drawer and opened another and pulled out two button down collar shirts. One peach and one red.

"Hey wait a minute" said Ant.

"Won't we have to dress alike to be able to fool them once we get in the room?"

"No not really, but maybe we should at least keep the shirts the same shade so as not to alert them too soon."

"So what color then?" Matt looked over his selection again and changed the trousers from blue to khaki and a black button down collar shirt.

"Hey I'm going with Khaki pants and a black button down"

"Cool I'll wear my black and grey shirt and some Jeans." Just then there was a beep on the phone signaling an incoming call.

"Hold on Matt someone is calling, Click . . . "Hello?"

"Hello may I speak to Anthony please?" said a soft female voice.

"What's up Cheryl?"

"Oh hi Anthony what's up dude?"

"Nothing much, just talking to Matt on the phone and getting ready for tonight, how about you guys?"

"Oh me and Melanie are just about ready also, we were finishing some last minute decorations and stuff"

"That's good, so whatcha got to drink over there for tonight?"

"We got some soda and some punch"

"Is that all?" he said despondently.

"Now Anthony, you know better than that, of course we got some brews and coolers too." *"Alright!* Do you think you'll have enough?"

"Well I got a case of coolers and a case of beer"

"What kind?"

"California Coolers and Old English 800"

"My girlie!" said Ant. Cher was also exuberant that they had chosen something the boys would like and just smiled with satisfaction.

"But there is one thing you forgot though" added Ant bursting her bubble some.

"What's that?"

"Well you've got 24 people showing up and if my math is correct you didn't get nearly enough to drink."

"Oh I didn't did I, I'm sorry, I didn't think about that" she said a little deflated.

"Hey but don't sweat, we'll pick up the slack and bring some more okay?"

"Hey great! Thanks a lot Anthony"

"No sweat babe its' the least we can do since ya'll supplied the house and all the food and stuff" "Yeah I guess your right" she said.

"So you say you were talking to Matt?"

"Yeah he's on the other line . . . let me switch over to three-way."

"Click"

"Hey Matt you still there?"

"Yeah meat head whatchu up to?"

"It's Cher man she wants to holla at you"

"Okay"

Click-click

"Hey Matt it's Cher"

"What's up Cher?"

"Were just getting ready for the party"

"Ya'll just about done over there?"

"Yeah we just hung some last minute trimming and was trying to call you earlier but your line was busy"

"Yeah I was talking to Ant and getting our stuff together too" he paused for a second.

"Hey you know tonight's you guys last night right?"

"Yeah we know Matt and we decided that since we couldn't get you earlier we'll just chill and just have a nice victory party for you guys with no strings attached." Mel was watching and listening to her and shot her a vicious open mouth glare at hearing this. She was reaching for the phone to take it from her to correct the matter when put her foot in her stomach and held her back scowling and winking at her. Matt on the other hand was just as surprised as Mel but didn't really believe her and just went along with her.

"So you've finally come to your senses huh?"

"Yeah you're just too foxy for us gals so were just gonna chill"

"Okay" said Matt almost reticent.

"But it was fun though wasn't it Matt?" she said twirling the phone cord around her finger and feeling sexy.

"I mean all those times that you could have had me and saw me naked, tell me, did you like looking at my pussy Matt? . . . did you like it when I sat on your lap and put my tits in your face?" she said in a most demur way and tingling all over from the conversation at large. Matt leaned against the dresser and smiled to himself thinking about all the times that he had gotten a birds eye view of all of Cheryl's most abundant and enticing assets. He had to admit that he had worn many a vicious hard on looking at her healthy and hairy sensuous mound of fur and world class tits. Even now he was beginning to get a hard on and cursed himself for not taking advantage of what was so freely and often offered to him on a platter.

"Mat?" she queried softly thinking he had either left the phone or maybe she had said something uncouth.

"Sighhh, yeah Cher it was that and more sweetie . . . that and more."

Cher thought she was going crazy when she heard Matt acknowledge that he had actually enjoyed her little expose's and sexual assaults.

"To be quite honest with you Cher I wanted to fuck the shit out of both you and Mel many times, and that day that you guys took off your panties and sat on the couch with your legs open like that . . . . well I gotta tell you all I could think about was running up in you to the hilt and burying this nine inch python in that sweet little wet spot of yours!"

Mel watched in excited confusion and amazed as Cher's eyes grew wide as a pie pan and her face turned a crimson red right before her eyes.

"What did he say! What did he say? Cheryl" she chirped on trying to get the phone from her. Cher just held her off with her powerful and well built legs and began to touch herself. Ant on the other hand who was listening to the whole thing was fit to be tied as he covered the phone with his hand and laughed his ass off. He knew Matt was telling the truth but at the same time messing with her head as well cause he knew Cher couldn't resist him talking dirty to her. Ant also knew that she was bullshitting about canceling the attack on him so it was all good that Matt was playing dodge ball or in this case "Dodge Booty" the way he was.

As Matt spoke more and more lustful intentions into her reddening and perspiration tainted ear, Cher turned into an animal of seething lust as she gyrated and touched herself between her legs and breast.

Melanie was getting fit to be tied as she knew there was only one thing that would make her wayward cousin go out like that would be if Matt was talking trash to her and goosing her like a drag bike on a race track.

"Why you sneaky little bastard" she hissed through clenched teeth and narrowing eyes. Secretly she wished it were here he was talking to cause she could use a little goosing right about now. "Give me that phone!" she said snatching it from Cher who was nearing a comatose form of ecstasy and just let her take the phone from her. By now she had begun licking her lips and undulating and moaning as her mind was awash in all the wonderfully tawdry and sexual things Matt was telling her he would like to have done to her when he had the chance. Mel tried to compose her self as she took the phone and listened in on what Matt was saying, not knowing that Cher wasn't on the line anymore.

"Yeah you like that baby? Huh is that good for you? yeah me too . . . and then when I slide them silky panties off with my teeth I'm gonna drive my face deep into your fur patch and lick it like a wet popsicle."

Mel gasped with shock and delight as the sound of Matt's voice all gruff and sultry was like instant lightning to her mind and she responded almost immediately to his suggestion. She reached up and touched her forehead and slowly descended down her shirt to her breasts which were sporting two very excited nipples as they bulged and became more sensitive with each passing second. Ant couldn't take the mind fuck anymore and just let out a whoop! after letting go of the phone. The sudden shock of hearing someone else on the phone cooled Mel's heels suddenly and she felt embarrassed and exposed. She cleared her throat and tried to straighten herself remembering that all this was a ruse and Matt was just having fun giving them both a mind fuck.

"Uh Matt" she said almost clinically.

Matt was stunned back to the present also but still laughed to himself when he discovered that he'd gotten two for the price of one.

"All that sounds really good Matt but I don't think you'll be doing any of that with Cher tonight or me for that matter okay?"

"Okay but I might" he said further goosing Ant into delirium with laughter. Mel was not as easy as Cher to overcome and she stood her ground although the concept was getting the best of her and the truth that they were gonna try to seduce him before nights end to do just that.

"That's okay Matt I'll let you have your way and enjoy your little mind trick but you know what they say about pay back don't you?"

"Yeah I know . . . I know" he said waving her off.

"So Mel let me go so I can finish getting ready okay?"

"What's the hurry you still got some time till the party begins. Have you forgotten that its starts at 8:00 o'clock?"

"No I ain't forgot but I need to round up the guys and some of them I don't have phone numbers for"

"Okay Matt I'll let you go . . . I need to go tend to Cheryl who seems to be trying to take a shower in the sink thanks to the little steam bath you just gave her."

Matt just grinned.

"Oh by the way Mel, what time is the party gonna end?"

"Why? Does it matter?"

"No, not really I just thought your neighbors would complain about the noise and lateness of it that's all."

"Baby you don't even have to worry about that, our house is at the end of a cul-de-sac and the nearest house is over a hundred yards away so we won't be disturbing anyone, besides most of the people in my neighborhood go off on the weekends so it's cool"

"Okay Mel just checking, Oh yeah and how about food, what did you guys put out?"

"We got chips, dips, dogs, doughnuts, and pizza's on order and KFC"

"Damn! you did it up didn't you Mel?"

"Hey it's a party isn't it?"

"Yeah, but give me a break down on the cost and I'll split the bill with you"

"No need Matt it's all free food"

"What do you mean free?"

"Well the pizza and the beer came from one of my dad's associates, he owns a liquor store and the chicken I got from my cousin who's the manager at KFC, as far as the other stuff goes we keep stuff like that around in stock for when we go on tail gate parties during foot ball season." "Well I'll be soaked in mustard" said Matt rubbing his head.

"Looks like you have everything under control, so tell me how come you're not at least assistant manager at our job yet?"

"Because I'm still in school and can't put in the hours that a manager does, but this summer I'll be getting a promotion from what my boss says"

"Well I guess there isn't anything you can't accomplish is it Mel?"

"Not really . . . but there is one little thing I can't seem to accomplish"

"And what's that?" he paused for a second.

"I can't get you to make love to me."

Matt just froze and his mind seized up. He went dead silent and all the bravado and sexual mastery he had been spewing before seemed to run away from him like water down a drain. He was all powerful when he was dishing out the stuff but when it was a woman doing the dishing he couldn't handle it.

Matt never could get used to a woman being so formal and open about what she wanted. He knew he could never be so brazen if he was face to face with one and say that. And if he were to be born a girl instead of a boy he just knew he'd be the oldest living virgin on record.

"Well Mel" he said clearing his throat.

"We can't have everything now can we?"

"Oh can't we?" she countered in a most confident and sensual tone.

"Well I'm not old or dead yet so I've still got time to find out, see ya later Matt . . ."

"click!"

Matt stood holding the phone away from his ear and looking at it strangely. He smiled to himself then put it down on the receiver. It rang almost immediately as he had forgotten that Ant was still on the line.

"So what did she have to say?"

"Didn't you hear?"

"No man! I went to get a sandwich after Mel got on the phone"

"Well nothing much she just let e'm know what they got to eat on and stuff"

"What kind of stuff?"

"Let me put it this way, you won't have to eat much at home and you can bet you won't go home hungry either!"

Retta didn't say much the entire trip and just stared out the window looking at the lush green countryside. The setting sun was beautiful this time of day the thought as she craned her neck lightly upwards and closing her eyes to embrace its dying warmth. She was quietly amazed at how during this time of day the foliage just seemed to burst with color in the setting sun. Everything was bathed in a crimson red glow and the horizon was a creamy neon orange. Even the grasses of the many fields and farms they passed glowed with tall emerald stalks and blended nicely with the browning of the trees.

She opened her eyes slowly but just in time to see a dodge back into the underbrush. The sight and the thought of what it was thinking made her laugh to herself. She fought against going to her grandmothers in her heart but in her mind she couldn't help but relish and enjoy the tranquil and serene country road and its surroundings. There was no noise at all like in the city except for and occasional car or 18 wheeler that would blow by shaking the little car like a leaf on a tree. The air smelled wonderful and rich with all the smells of the country. Even the repugnant odor of cow dung and hay was an exquisite aroma to her nose and it made her mind remember the people and the heritage of the state and how long ago the thick smooth black top road they were on had been little more than a dusty ole dirt trail.

Retta allowed her pensive feelings to melt from her and dissolve as she relished the feel of the country. She had forgotten how long it had been since she had been out this way and began to realize how much she truly missed it. Soon she was asleep with thoughts of hay bales and rows of beans in a back yard garden and Matt holding her hand as they lay amongst the tall stalks of corn and stare up at the blue sky.

After awhile of driving Audrey pulled off the main road an went down an undeveloped country road. Dust and tiny rocks rattled against the underside of the car and the tires made a sound like they were driving over a combination of unpacked snow and corn flakes. The sudden change and subtle vibrations shook Retta awake again. She opened her eyes weakly and blanched from the occasional beam of orange sunlight that came in patches though the tree tops.

She no longer felt the warm glow of the sun on her face as when they were on the open road, but instead a slow cooling effect from being in the insulating denseness of the woods on the country road.

"Hello sleepy head" said Audrey smiling at her.

"Did you have a nice nap?" Retta just yawned and nodded stretching her legs and arms out like a house cat. In a way she felt somewhat drained and tired and didn't quite know why, not to mention the soreness in her neck and shoulder from leaning against the door for so long.

"We're almost there girls! Its only about a mile or so further." Retta didn't respond but just nodded and rubbed her shoulder and craned her neck from left to right.

Soon they were coming up on a small covered bridge. It looked more like a small shed or garage with no back wall than a bridge. Underneath bubbled a stream with a small water fall a little further upstream. Down the road a little further was their grandmothers house.

"We're here!" chirped Audrey happily and trying to be infectious so the girls would feel better about being there. Lori was no real problem. She would mold to whatever her mother decided to do and without complaint. Retta on the other hand was an entirely different matter. She knew that her daughter would have given her right foot to stay at home with Matt if she could have. She would make it up to her later. Meanwhile in the back seat Lori was scrunching up her nose as a light breeze brought her the scent of hogs and cows.

"It's stinky!" she whined in an nasal voice.

"Oh its not so bad, your just not used to it yet" said Audrey looking in the rear view mirror and trying to ease her youngest daughters concerns. Retta also was fighting the gag reflex at the pungent animal smells that covered every ounce of fresh air around. The house she noticed as she sought it out absent-mindedly hoping to get in and out of this foul air, was very nice looking and a bit surprising being that it was situated well into the woods and off the beaten path. The house was a 1970's ranch style house made of brick and wood treatments. It sat on the ground instead of on cement blocks instead of like others in this area. The house was painted a soft peach and green color and had a large display window in front on the left and a bay window on the right.

The driveway was covered in pea sized grey gravel that crunched as they rode down the drive. In the front of the house was a large deck porch with flowery patio furniture. There were willow and cherry blossom trees here and there and a wooden wheel barrow with flowering plants in it. Along the right side of the house and past the carport was a neatly landscaped planting bed about twenty feet long and half as wide. It had rows of bean stalks, tomatoes, collard greens and several other plants Retta couldn't figure out.

The yard in the back or just to the left of the house was much bigger but this was all they used to grow their staple of vegetables. As Audrey slowed down and came to a stop. A big black dog came bounding up and placed his huge paws on her door then huffed a loud jowl flapping bark. "Woof!" Audrey quickly ducked towards Retta. Lori dived onto the floor and screamed her head off. Right about then an elderly lady in her late 60's with silver grey hair and a short stout body looked out the window to see what was the commotion.

"Land-o-goshen! What in the world is going on our dere!" she put down her wash cloth and leaned towards the window to see out into the yard.

"OH my lord!" she breathed then dashed for the door. As she came outside she could see the big dog was literally shaking the little car as he pushed against it barking again and again. "Jobob! . . . you git away from dat car you hear . . . git!" the big dog looked at the old woman respectively and wagged his tail. He let his huge tongue roll to the side of his mouth and out like a rope, which Audrey noticed hung down a good four inches from his mouth. The dog looked back into the car at his recent capture then barked one last woof as if to say "you got away this time but I'll get you later" he did this then pushed his

Himself away from the car and lumbered back up onto the porch and lay down with his huge head on his paws looking at them. Audrey raised up slowly when she heard the dog go away. She looked around to see who had called him off and saw that it was granny. It actually wasn't her granny but instead her ex-husbands mother.

"Audrey . . . izzatchew in dere child?" she asked getting closer still wringing her hands dry on her apron. Audrey opened the door slowly and got out.

"Yes ma'am" she said sheepishly still looking at the big dog and hoping it didn't return.

"Lord as I live and breathe" she said coming over to give her a big hug and kiss.

"How you been child?" she asked holding her at arms length looking at her.

"Okay mother Davis . . . just fine" the old woman pushed her spectacles up on her nose precariously and looked at Audrey sideways.

"Now you know I done tole ya ta call me Annie Mae" she said with a rich southern drawl.

"Has it been dat long where you done f'got?"

"No ma'am" she said smiling and feeling bashful.

"Now whey's dem babies at?" she said looking over her shoulder and around her into the car. She could see Retta and Lori sitting up now and smiling bashfully at her.

"Come on outta dat car and give yo' granny some good". Retta was the first to get out. She felt a flush of bashfulness and amusement wash over her and she fought to hold back a giggle. She looked the elderly woman over clinically and noticed the classic prairie dress and apron with a slightly more up to date pair of house slippers. The dress was a caliclo floral print with daisies and dandy lions on it. It had a lave shawl around the collar that was so white she thought it was painted on. Annie Mae Davis, was about five foot five and looked to be over 175 pounds with humungous breasts and a huge pair of hips to go with it. She sported the prettiest white dimpled smile that Retta had ever seen and eyes that were as soft as a babies bottom and as brown as chocolate. She was a sweet as country butter.

"Don't worry nun bout dat crazy ole dog he won'e bitecha, come on give Annie some o' dat good" she said opening her arms to embrace her. Retta couldn't hold back her amusement and grabbed the woman tightly in a bear hug. She blushed when she felt the woman's huge breasts dwarf and collapse her own pristine debutant chest.

She noticed that her grandmothers hair smelled wonderfully fresh and sweet. Not like shampoo but just really clean and sunny like clothes that had been dried on a line outside in the sun.

"Lord how you done grow'd chile" said Annie Mae pulling Retta to arms length to look at her. "Da last time I saw you chile you wadn't no bigger'n a good size watamelon. How you been doin chile?"

"Oh fine granny just fine" said Retta smiling at her and looking at her mother who was just standing back looking on proudly.

"Now whey's my baby Lori?" She had gotten out and slowly worked her way around the car caustiously. Hoping that she didn't run into the dog again. She stood with her finger in her mouth just idling and looking on.

"Comere chile granny ain't gonna bitcha none" she said gesturing to her to come into her arms. Lori slowly walked over to her. For a minute she had the strange déjà vu of alice in wonderland and her granny was the queen of hearts. No real body to speak of but instead just a really large dress , arms, feet and a head. Lori hugged her and she could feel herself sinking into the fluffy softness of her and it made Lori giggle.

"What's so funny Lori?" Asked Retta. Lori held her head up to look at her and announced to everyone's surprise and embarrassment . . . "She's all warm and squishy!"

"Lori!" chastised Audrey feeling the warm of embarrassment cover her face.

"Aw now don'e go bothin the chile. She can say dat if she wanna" she said looking at Lori and smiling a wide toothy smile.

"Gramma Annie is all warm and squishy ain't she?" Lori just nodded and held on for another squeeze.

"Now ya'll come on new and lets get ya'll somethine a drank. I knows the dust don'e got in ya mout and dried it all out . . . Jo bob! . . . git yo mangy hide out'n front of da doe. A body cain't even move with out you gittin in da way!

It was now a quarter after seven and all the guys were there. Matt had personally gone out and picked up Frog and Milton in his dads truck. Earlier that evening he had told him he could use it for awhile since he had his license now.

Sitting around the living room and dining room was the entire posse. Most of which came from the Jr. track team minus Frog and Milton. There of the other boys had cars or the use of one and just now Matt was going over the game plan with them one last time and making damn sure everyone knew what to do in the event they saw Mel or Cher do something strange.

Matt, Milton, Ant and Frog would go in the truck and Hopkins, Walters, Marshall and Jenkins in one car and Ryeback, Fisher, Thomas and Waters in the other.

"Okay guys lets suit up!" said Matt heading out the door.

"Hey who's got the beer?"

"I do" said Jenkins.

"I got the wine cooler" said Frog.

"Good don't drink it before we get to the party." Soon they were on their way.

"Hey Ant you sure you know how to get there?"

"Yeah man I know . . . I used to live in east Macon"

"Okay just checking . . . and Frog try to behave yourself, you know how you get when you get a buzz" said Matt giving him a cursory scowl.

Frog just flashed him a manic wild eyed look with a ridiculous toothy grin. Matt knew what that meant.

"Look out world here comes Frog." Frog then growled at him in his throat like a rabid dog. Ant just laughed at him and Milton shook his head.

"I can see it's gonna be a tripping night tonight boy" said Frog rubbing his hands together.

Matt just ignored him and headed for the door and onto the Vineville avenue then the expressway. Once he there it would be a quick drive.

"Turn on some jams man!" said Frog. Milton flipped it on and there was a lot of static.

"Flip it to FM" Matt told him.

"My dad likes to keep it on the am oldies channel." Finally they found a suitable station to listen to.

"Yeah! Leave it there!" said Ant grabbing his arm.

"That's my song boy!" he said happily. It was the SOS band playing "weekend love" They all sang along and was having a good time. Soon they had gotten to there destination on the other side of town. They got off the highway at spring street then made a left turn up gray highway once Matt went through the light

Ant had him turn left again. Matt checked his rear view to see if the other guys were still with him.

"Okay Ant where to now?"

"Just follow this road all the way out till you see a two way then go right, Mel said the house was in a cul-de-sac on the left . . . 3241 Ceder lane." Matt followed the directions through the neighborhood and could see that this was definitely one of the best areas in town. Just about every other house had a Lincoln or a Porche 911 in the drive way and a multitude of BMW's to boot. The houses were no less grand and expensive looking either. Most were two story or small estates. He figured that the cost of them had to be somewhere over $200k or better.

Soon they arrived at the house. There were several cars along the curb and in the driveway. Matt pulled around the loop to the end to give the other guys room to pull in.

"Well guys this is it" said Ant in a reverent tone.

"Let's go then!" said Matt getting out and adjusting his shirt tail. The others got out of their cars and followed suit.

Chapter 14

Running Out the Clock

"Hey Matt, where did you bring us to dude? I feel like I need to have on a suit just to stand in the driveway man" said Hopkins smiling and tossing back his cow-lick of blond hair.

"Hey I don't know myself partner but you can bet it ain't Kansas Toto"

"You ain't bullshittin" chimed in Jenkins. Mel's house was quite grand and ornate and two stories tall. It had a big front yard that even looked good in the dark. You could see it was well kept. On one side of the house there was a sun porch and a wooden privacy fence that Matt was sure concealed a pool. On the other end of the house was a three car garage but all the doors were closed.

The house itself was white with red brick and something of an early American design. It had huge white pillars in the front of it like most of the plantation houses of this type. The windows were huge and covered a large part of the front of the house from the patio to the ceiling. All the guys were getting a little apprehensive and just a little out of sorts. These were simple inner city boys with little to no experience with the finer things of life. Neither of them had ever been on this side of town before and weren't accustomed to such grandness. Six of the boys were white, Hopkins, Marshall, Jenkins, Waters, Fisher and Ryeback. The other two were Latin and that was Thomas and Walters.

Matt had wondered about their names long ago and asked them how they could have such last names with Latin decent. Thomas told him that his family name was really pronounced "Tomas" and not Thomas as it was spelled in his school records. They had come to America during the Cuban crisis and the Boat lift or time when Castro let people leave the country during the early 1980's.

The immigration people misspelled his family name so they just kept it because it made blending in and getting services easier. Walters had a similar story but he was from Dominica and his family name was Alteras. His family opted for an additional letter instead of a complete change in their name. The rest of the guys were black and home grown except for Matt who was from South Carolina. As they got up to the door someone poked their head out the window.

"Hey you guy's there here!" shouted one of the girls.

The guys smiled big listening at the erratic and nervous activity. They were chattering away like mice and they guys had to admit although it sounded a little silly and made them laugh, it also made them feel good inside to be so honored by girls of this class. Just then Mel opened the door. "Hi Matt" she said smiling wide and waving at him.

"Hi guys come on in!" she said grabbing his hand and pulling him inside.

"Nice place you got here Mel" he said looking around in awe and wonder but trying not to let it show too much.

"You guys did a real nice job on the decorations, I didn't know you was gonna go through all this fuss" he said beginning to blush with embarrassment.

"Hey no sweat Matt, this was easy you should have seen the gym I helped to put together last year for the prom."

"I can imagine" he said nodding his approval of her work.

"So where's all your friends? We heard some chattering going on a minute ago"

"Oh you won't see e'm yet, as part of the ritual we have to blind fold you guys first"

"Blind fold us?" said Hopkins raising an eyebrow and looking at the others.

"I thought this was a party not an execution." Mel just laughed at the comment but quietly mused the it would be true for one of them then looked sweetly at Matt.

"No silly, didn't Matt tell you what kind of party this was?"

"No!" he said scowling at Matt some but none too seriously because either way he was here to party and get jiggy with the girls.

"It's a Sadie Hawkins Day party"

"A WHAT?" said the rest of the guys in unison.

"It's a party where the girls ask the guys out and they get to pick who they want out of the group" she explained sweetly.

"Oh . . . okay then, that's different but its cool" said Jenkins.

"God I hope I don't get some homely fat chick" mumbled Frog to Walters. He snorted at the comment and turned his head so Mel wouldn't see him giggling.

"So if you guy's would please go ahead an put on one of these blind folds and get in line, I'll bring in the rest of the girls" Matt was a little more relieved than the others as he already knew who was likely to get him if no one else. He played along and put one on and just stood beside his crew.

"Okay Mel it's your gig." Soon they could hear the sounds of female voices OOHing and AHHing and giving and audible response to their appreciation of what the choices were in their dates. Matt's mind and senses were assaulted with the fragrant smells of many different female scents. Ant was noticing the same thing and it made his heart flutter some with the mystique and all.

"Aw man! Somebody smells good!" chirped Hopkins.

"That one's mine! Said a female then grabbed his hand jerking him out of the line and into her arms.

"Whoa! Pretty lady, I might need that arm again sometime" he commented then let himself be handled.

"Who is Milton?" asked another girl getting into the spirit of the games. The sound of her sultry voice made Milton jump with excitement. He raised his hand like he was in school.

"Here ma'am!" the others laughed at his comment and his prospective date squealed with joy as if she had hit the jack pot. She launched herself at him and grabbed him around the neck pressing her more than ample breasts into him. Milton could only imagine what he had a hold of or better yet what had a hold on him. I quick run of his hands over her back and down her bottom quickly told him he had struck gold or at least bumped into it.

"You don't waste time do you Milton?"

"What for? I mean to live and love as long and as often as I can while I can baby girl"

"OOH you so nasty" she chirped with glee hugging him closer. She pressed into him hard and Milton was sure she had the biggest, softest titties in middle Georgia. Soon all the guys were chosen by an eager female and taken to the side.

"Okay boys you can take off you blind folds now" said Cher. They all snatched them off quickly to see who or what they had been chosen by. All the while praying they didn't get a dog or something worse in the process.

"So guys . . . you like?" asked Mel as they all had taken off their blindfolds. Each boy looked over his smiling date and quickly acknowledged in some way or sound that they were more than satisfied. Frog let out a whoop of joy at the look of his date then stamped his foot like a horse and shook his head,

"Whoa nelly! It's gonna be a boot knockin, body rockin night tonight boy!" his date just smiled broadly and hugged him.

"Oh hell, Frog done hopped out of his cage" said Ant.

"Hey you guys lets crank this place up already!" said Cher turning on the music and adjusting the lights a little. All of a sudden lights of different colors reflected off a huge mirror ball in the ceiling and strobe lights lit up the room. It was a bad jam thought Matt as Mel pulled him up to the dance area and started gyrating in front of him. The song was "When Doves Cry" oh it was a jam alright and everybody was getting off!

"So Matt how do you like it so far?" she asked putting her arms around his neck and letting him control their movements.

"It's dope Mel, you and your crew really out did yourselves." Mel smiled at the comment and used it as an opportunity to get in a quick huggy feely.

"Thanks Matt, that means a lot coming from you" she said looking into his eyes deeply and feeling a slight rush overcome her.

"Damn I can't wait to get him alone and in my control, I'm gonna wear his ass OUT!" she thought to herself as she smiled at him innocently. Everyone was having a good time and as the party heated up, Mel changed the music to something a little slower and put on a tune called "It's real love". The music had an enchanting effect as it began to play and all around the room bodies began to melt together in a passionate and seductive embrace, filled with sensuous movements and gyrations. Some would say this was "Slow Draggin" others; boning with your clothes on. Matt looked over and saw Ant in front of him dancing with Cher and he was working her WELL! He saw how thorough Ant was controlling and commanding her body and hips to keep time with his. He occasionally made a low sweeping dip with his leg between her ample thighs. Cher was more than lost in his control and his familiarity with her body and what made her tick. She was just about drunk with him and just held on to him with a death grip and buried her face in his chest.

The scene kind of made him feel a little awkward and shy with Mel who was staring at him and monitoring his every movement. She knew he was preoccupied and maybe even a little apprehensive about tonight being it was supposed to be their get even night even though they lied about putting it off and calling it quits. Matt was no fool and she knew this and it only helped to spur her on more in her and Cher's plan to seduce him. She also was aware that she needed to be on her guard mentally as well. She was beginning to fall in love with him with each passing moment and the drumming of the music in her ears.

Matt was trying not to go too far with his handling of her while dancing but it was next to impossible. How do you under handle a snake and it not bite you? How do you decrease your grip on a pole and not slid. This was his situation with Mel. She was erotic as hell! And she was using it against him. Every chime of the music brought her closer to ecstasy as Matt's muscular thigh wedged itself deeper and deeper between her legs making her sweaty and moist. She drove on him each time he turned her body in time with the music pushing herself into his leg even more and relishing the feel of its hardness against her pleasure zone. Matt didn't want to encourage her but it was next to impossible to avoid driving on her like she was doing to him. He tried to think gross thoughts but it didn't work. He sighed deep and long and just gave into it and allowed her to push him where he was dying to go anyway. The effect was akin to exhaling while in the grips of a python.

"Are you alright Matt?" she whispered after hearing him sigh.

"Yeah babe I'm cool, what's up?" he said being coy.

"Oh nothing I guess, you just seem so far away and lost is all, are you thinking about Aretta?" she asked meekly.

Matt thought for a minute wondering how he could use this situation to work in his favor and maybe get a break from her serpents arms and legs. The thought of what he would do and how made him smirk to himself devilishly. He pierced her with his eyes and looked away,

"No . . . not really until you brought her up." Mel was taken back at this as she was sure he was somewhere between her legs and Aretta's arms. This new realization gave her an unexpected surprise and elation. She smiled and readjusted her grip around his neck to get closer still to him if that was even possible. Matt . . . I know you belong to someone else she said softly and resting her head on his chest.

"And I know you won't make love to me no matter what I do to entice you" she said then swallowed hard.

"But do you think you could be mine tonight anyway? . . . I mean just let me love you okay . . . you don't have to love me back or anything but just let me enjoy you as if you were mine okay?" she said looking up and staring deeply into his eyes.

"God how beautiful she is" he thought looking at what he felt was the most sensuous and turbulent sea green eyes he had ever looked upon. They alone could enslave him if he let them. Matt could see her deepening love and desire for him was real and he could feel a small fire building in himself as well. He wasn't quite sure if it was the alcohol or not but it felt good and dangerous at the same time. She was about to speak again but Matt gently put a finger to her lips and shook his head slowly. His next move surprised even him. He pulled her into him further until she exhaled. Mel was shocked and excited because it was a new tact and one she had not experienced with him as yet. Her heart began to race and sore as she felt his hands slowly cradle her face and gently caress her temples enflaming them something terrible.

"Could I be dreaming this! . . . is this really happening to me right now right this minute or is it the alcohol" she thought, more or less screamed in her mind.

"Oh lord don't let this be a dream or the wine" she thought as a whimper escaped her slightly parted lips.

Matt pulled her ever closer and closer as her pierced her with his eyes. He could smell her essence and taste her even before he took her. He felt powerful and huge within himself and it felt sublime. Then he kissed her full and deeply on the lips. Mel felt lightning run through her and over her as his lips devoured hers. No fantasy that she had ever had about him could match the sheer ecstasy of what she was feeling just now. She felt her legs give and she just fell into his masterful embrace and control of her. Mel felt like a rag doll in a hurricane. She shamefully and wantonly bathed in passionate kiss with every inch of her being.

"OH! Matt I love you! . . . Oh god please don't end this" she screamed and begged in her mind as her breath left her and she began to swoon.

"I love you Matt . . . I love you!" They stayed that way forever it seemed and Matt was really feeling her now too. His desires were rising and falling with the speed and force of Niagra falls. Mel freely gave up more and more of herself to his hungry and intense gyrations and fed like a babe on his lusty and suggestive caressing of her back and enflamed bottom. Matt's hands covered every inch of her burning flesh from top to bottom and in between.

Mel sighed sharply and painfully as every touch of his hand, set afire everywhere he touched. She found she couldn't breathe and was panting harder and louder with each passing second. She just knew she was gonna pass out in his arms and only wanted for him not to stop if she did. Matt was a cannibal on her lips and body and literally began to feed on her and couldn't or wanted to stop.

Mel couldn't with all her pent up desires keep up with him and just gave up and did her best to stand because she could do little else. He mouth was like dough loose and supple. Her legs were like spaghetti all soft and weak. Even her arms were failing to hold her up and they were slowly falling to her side as Matt was the only force now that held her up. Finally the music died but they continued to move to their own silent beat unaware of the scene they were making from the others around them, Matt slowly began to return to the present from the world of pleasure and consuming pleasure in which he'd been willingly led.

"Hey baby" he whispered to her.

"I think we could us a drink or something, don't you think?"

She just nodded but still held onto him not wanting to release the delicious warmth and fire that had built between them only moments ago.

"Hey you guys" said Cher.

"Let's take a break and get something to eat, it's gonna be a long night and at this rate were either gonna pass out from exhaustion or die for lack of other needs" said Cher giving a suggestive glance at the guys who quickly understood her meaning.

And all at once dropped into the dog position and started a resounding meley of hoots and barks to emphasize and illustrate that they were ready to get busy anytime the girls were. Matt just laughed at them and shook his head then went back to filling his plate with any and everything he could find on the large table. Soon everyone had gotten under control and was sitting or standing around with their plates eating and talking.

"You dance pretty good" said Cheryl sitting on Ants lap in a large chair and blushing a little. "Well you got me started when you started grinding on me" he said grinning at her.

"Well I wouldn't have gotten so motivated if you'd kept your hands off my ass and your knee out of my crotch" she said blushing even deeper than before. Milton on the other hand was busy in a corner love seat with his date. They both were locked in a passionate and animated embrace kissing each other hungrily.

"Man, does he ever miss one" said Frog who was across from Ant.

"Hell naw, not if he can help it" said Ant.

Just then Mel got up and walked toward the kitchen giving Cher and another girl the eye as she went so they would follow her.

"Hey, where you guys going" said Matt.

"Oh we're going to get some more brews from the fridge" said Mel giving him a disarming smile.

Matt's mind though in slight haze from the wine coolers and beer he had already had was in motion and quickly deduced that Mel and Cher's plan was about to take hold, if it was to take at all. Matt saw Frog look over at the 10 gallon wash tub under the table that was still half filled with beverages. He was about to comment about it, but Matt cleared his throat loudly to get his attention. Once he did he shot him a warning stare and lightly shook his head as if to say let it ride, the gig is up.

Having caught this expression and remembered all Matt told him about what would possibly take place this night he quickly eased himself back into his chair and began shaking and rubbing his leg as to make it look like he was shaking off a cramp so no one would notice or get wise to their unspoken conversation. Ant and Milton as well caught his expression and were just waiting for this.

"Hey" Mel shouted.

"Ant, can I use your restroom?"

"Yeah, me too" said Milton getting up.

"Yeah, sure guys, there's one down the hall on your right and one back here in the den below the kitchen." Ant quickly headed for the one in the hall and Milton went towards the kitchen.

Matt just sat quietly slowly sipping his beer and flashing small undetected warnings to the other guys letting them know to be on guard for anything funny.

"Where did you put it?" said Mel getting a little tense and irritated at her friend.

"I had it in my shirt pocket in a handkerchief" she said stricken and excited.

"Well look in all your pockets" said Cher whispering harshly.

The girl ran through all her pockets in her shirt and on her skirt. Suddenly she looked up in surprise with a stark look of revelation on her face.

"I know where it is" she announced happily.

"Where" said Cher.

"I put it in my bra so it wouldn't get messed up if I spilled a drink or something."

Mel just sighed deep with relief and leaned back against the counter rubbing her temples. The girl quickly reached into her shirt and produced a little red handkerchief with four little orange pills inside.

"Here they are" she said giving them to Mel.

"Good, Okay, how many do I give him?" she said.

"Well my brother said it depends on the person's size and weight."

Mel thought for a minute trying to grasp how much he weighs. She bit her lip and looked casually over at Cher.

"Hey Cher, you've had him on top of you before, right?"

"Well yeah, but not completely though."

"Well that's more than I can say, so how much you figure he weighs?"

Cher just screwed her face and shrugged.

"I don't know, bout 180 I guess."

"Okay" said Mel accepting the estimate.

"I'll give him two then."

"Shouldn't you crush em up a little first so they'll dissolve?" asked Cher.

"That's what I'm gonna do so gimmie a spoon out of the drawer."

Cher reached over and pulled open a drawer behind her. She rummaged in a minute then produced a big stainless steel spoon.

"Will this do?"

"Yeah, give it to me" said Mel shooting out an eager hand.

Aretta was sitting in front of the television rubbing on Joe Bob's head. She had called Matt several times but he wasn't home and now she was wondering where he might be but nothing came to mind.

"Damn, I can't believe Matt would do me like this, he said he would call me if he went anywhere and now he's not home and I don't have George's phone number."

She hadn't noticed it but during her reflection she began to rub Joe Bobs head more vigorously keeping pace with her anger as she fussed. The dog began to get irritable and whine a little as she began twisting and bending his ear. Finally the big dog had had enough. He snorted irritably and got up then trotted away across the room where he resumed his lounging with his head on his large paws.

"Oh great" spat Retta said under her breath.

"Now even the dog has run out on me." She mused and fussed awhile longer then got up and headed outside to sit in the bleary night air. As she stepped out onto the porch she saw her mother, grandmother and Lori lounging nearby chatting.

"Hey baby" said her grandmother.

"Hi granny" she moaned.

"What's ailin ya child? Ya done sound so good."

"Oh I'm alright, it's just that I wanted to talk to Matt but he's not home and he said he would call me here if he went anywhere but he didn't."

"I see" she said nodding. "Well child I wouldn't worry ma self to much about it cause you knows a man is gone do what dey's a gonna do anyhow."

This logic didn't make Retta feel any better and she could more than well enough irritate herself with the ideas she was entertaining already, not to mention she was just as jealous as he was. "Give it sometime child, he a call ya soon-a-lata. so come on sit down by Annie Mae and tell me how nice looking dis young man a yourn is."

Retta blushed a little and reluctantly went over to plop down next to her granny on the large patio couch. As her granny put her arms about her she experienced a warm soft sinking feeling as she began to melt into the cottony folds of her hulking mass.

"Now iont dat betta." She soothed now lightly caressing Aretta's long tresses as she lay with her head atop her granny's large breasts. Retta just nodded.

"He's really a special guy" she said. "He's the kind of person who would go out of his way to help you and never ask anything in return, he's warm, loving and sweet, and he has the deepest most wonderful dark brown eyes you ever saw." Her granny just smiled and nodded.

"Oh granny he's just the best a girl could have and I love him with all my heart."

"My stars, alt guess you do have a deep luv fo' him and how duz he feel about you" she asked. "About the same or more" injected Audrey.

"Iz dat right?"

"You should see them in action sometimes and they make the hottest soap opera I've ever seen."

Retta tried to bury herself deeper to hide from the mounting shyness she felt and embarrassment.

"Tell her about the time I caught you two in the mall, Retta."

"Uh, that's okay mom. I'd rather not" she said getting up.

"Where you goin child?"

"I'm going for a little walk down the road for some fresh air and exercise, I'll be back." "Alright sugar, you be careful on dat doit road now ya hear, it gets a might dark down dere a ways on down."

"Yes ma'am I will" she said stepping out the door of the screened porch and onto the sidewalk. "Joe Bob, you get on up an gone wit'er" she ordered.

The big dog sighed and shook himself as he got up then trotted off the porch. He gave the old woman a curious look then headed on down the road after Retta.

"That's quite some dog you got there Ann" said Audrey.

"He seems to be well trained, did you send him to obedience school?"

"Honey no, dat dere dawg no betta den to not do what ah tole em, he aint nuttin but a big ole baby anyhow."

"What do you feed him? I'm sure he eats a lot."

"Oh I just give em taba scraps e're now n-den, he mostly just gone out dere in da woods n git his own food."

"My goodness" said Audrey "he is some dog."

"Yeah, he be alright."

Retta was to deep in thought to notice the dog who had slowly come up on her right side and with the black coat he had she wouldn't have seen him anyway until the moon peeked out from behind an occasional cloud that floated by. Retta was busy playing devil's advocate and really didn't like some of the ideas she was getting. She had thought everything from him going out on the town with his friends to being hold up with some girl somewhere.

She nervously fingered her ring in her pocket spinning it slowly around her finger. She didn't like the thoughts she imagined but felt ill at ease not to at least deduce them for her own benefit true or not.

"Oh Retta, your just being paranoid" she hissed at herself.

"You know Matt wouldn't be out running around on you, I mean for Christ sake you just said so yourself that he loves you more than anything and you already know your gonna marry him someday, so what's up with this wild thinking and what if he was out with George, so what?" "He's a man and can do whatever he wants, I mean I don't own him yet, do I?" she said unsure. Just then she heard a noise in a nearby bush and froze in her tracks completely.

Still she didn't dare move or even ask what it was, not that it would answer anyway, but she didn't want to alert whatever it could be to her presence and hoped it would go away. "Oh lord what is that" she thought.

Her mind stricken with fright all the while playing back pictures of everything awful she had ever seen on or off the TV. The creature made another noise rustling the dry underbrush and making crinkly snapping noises as it slowly shuffled in the bush. Now Retta was really afraid. The moon in its fullness gave an eerie incandescent glow and the night sky showed blue-black in its forbidding presence.

Puffy white clouds with thick grey black centers floated ominously by creating evil shapeless specters on the ground in their wake as they moved by in the breezeless night sky. Her mouth was ultra dry and her heart beat out a crescendo or silent S.O.S signals for anyone to answer and come to her aid.

Second by second she could feel her legs growing tenser, her stomach churning in sickening knots and her ears strained to their limit to here that which didn't want to be heard or seen. She began to notice an acute ringing almost whistling in her head as she fought hard to listen and locate the unseen specter. Her lungs strained inside her chest as every breath fluttered past her mouth trying hard not to make even the slightest sound.

"Oh god please save me" she whispered in her mind. "I don't know what this is but I don't want to die." Just then when she thought it couldn't get any worse the creature moved again but this time with definite and purposeful movement in her direction. Her legs felt like lead and began to buckle like wet noodles. Her mind had created in itself the perfect horror and now brought it to life with full antagonistic ferocity and coming to get her.

She was trembling violently as the noise grew louder and more pronounced then all of a sudden nothing, not even a light crinkle of leaves or dry bush. The next thing she felt made her loose her bladder. She felt something large and hairy rub against her bare legs. She screamed and ran back the way she had come with blind speed. Nothing so pure as the terror she felt. Surrounding her could make her move as fast as she was running then Audrey was the first to notice and jumped up.

"Retta what's wrong baby?" she said as she tore through the door and held her fiercely.

"Baby what's wrong?" she said more concerned now and confused at what could have frightened her so.

Retta was incoherent and sobbed and ranted on wildly about some thing or monster touching her and trying to get her. By now her grandmother and grandfather had retrieved a shot gun from inside the house and was standing just outside the door looking into the blackness of the night. "Do ya see anything Versy?" said Annie Mae.

Grandpa Versy just spat out a mouth full of tobacco juice with an audible splat on the sidewalk. "Naw, a kin see da moon light on everythin but das all, now wait a minute" he said raising his shot gun.

"What is it?" said Audrey. Just then Joe Bob trotted into the light with a good sized fur ball in his mouth.

"Joe Bob, you come hyea" he said slapping his leg.

"What's dat he got dere Versy?"

The old man bent down and wrangled the animal from the dogs grasp much to his dislike.

"Oh he done caught hisself a coon dats what."

Retta now calming down some pulled her teary face from her mother to look at what her grandfather was holding.

"Hear it is dawlin, it's just a ole coon, das all."

"But I heard it, it was big and I couldn't see what it was" she cried still a little hysterical.

"Well honey pot" soothe her grandmother.

"What you probably hurd was ole Joe Bob flushing dat coon, tell me, did you see him come up behine ya while you was walking?"

"No ma'am" she said shaking her head.

"Then dere you has it twas din nuttin but ole Joe Bob."

"Honey aint no munster in dem woods."

Retta just looked at the dog and the hug raccoon then shook her head.

"I think I'm gonna go to bed early momma" she said croaking.

"Okay Aretta, you do that and I'll join you later okay?"

"Yes ma'am" she said then headed inside for a hot bath and warm bed.

The party was in its upswing again and everyone had eaten and drank plenty. No one was in any condition to do much more than party and most of that was being done to slow music. Just now Matt was checking out the situation with his buddies looking to see how many were still capable of leaving or aware of anything curious. None gave him a hint of notice so he went back to dancing with Mel who was really working herself into a heat of passion with every sultry twist and grind of her hips against Matt.

She had long since put the tranquilizer in his beer but Matt didn't drink it and only appeared to. Milton had been hiding just behind the door of the kitchen on the other side and over heard the girls plot and told him about it. Now all was needed was for him to signal Ant to let him know it was time to put their plan in motion. It had been at least an hour since she fixed his drink and she kept giving him light glances to check his face for any signs of drowsiness. Matt saw Ant nearby and reached over to tap his shoulder.

Ant looked up and Mat gave him a thumbs up sign and nodded and kept dancing. Soon he kissed his date and retreated to the bathroom or in that general direction. Right behind the bathroom was a large bedroom with a canopy bed. It was covered with thick billowy covers and a heavy soft comforter. Ant slid under the bed quickly and waited.

"Hey babe" whispered Matt. "I'm feeling kind of groggy, I think I had too much to drink."

"Oh Matt, I'm sorry, would you like to rest awhile?" said Mel completely elated by this announcement.

"Yeah, do you mind?"

"No, come on, you can come back here to the guest room" she said smiling so hard it hurt. "Boy, I cant believe it. It worked!" she cheered to herself leading him down the hall.

Ant had recently taken Matt wobbled a little for effect wanting her to feel as confident as possible and uninhibited when she made her move. Mel led him to the large bed and sat him down on it.

"Why don't you remove your shoes so you can crawl on in and lay down awhile."

"Yeah, thanks Mel." Matt made quite a show of getting into bed and Mel began wondering had she given him too much but then thought not when she saw how strong he seemed to move as he turned over on his back.

Ant was grinning to himself and beginning to get excited with the anticipation he was feeling. "Matt, I'll close the door so you won't be disturbed and don't worry if you fall asleep, I've made arrangements for all your guys to sleep over if you want and my folks won't be home till Sunday."

"Okay Mel, thanks" he moaned and then let an arm flop over his face for added effect. Mel got up and left. Her blood was beginning to boil and her sexual juices were beginning to peak. "Damn, what luck" she said as she closed the door. "I'll give him about ten minutes then go back."

Hey Ant, you in here?" Matt whispered.

"Yeah, I'm under here."

"Well come on lets switch."

Ant scrambled out from under the bed.

"Here, change shirts with me just to be on the safe side" said Matt.

The two boys worked quickly and soon were swapped out.

"Cher are you ready?" said Mel meeting up with her in the kitchen.

"Yeah, is he asleep?"

"Yeah, I figured we should give him a few more minutes to be sure."

"Great" said Cher.

"So Cher how you feel?" she asked.

"What do you mean how do I feel? I feel hot and horny and I want to screw, that's how I feel." "Yeah, me too, Matt's been grinding on me so hard tonight I thought I was gonna come several times."

"Shoot, you thought you had problems" said Cher.

Ant had his hands in my shorts so long I thought they were made there and I almost said to hell with it and started to fuck him instead."

"So why didn't you?" asked Mel

"No way sweet pea, you're not cheating me out of my ride, so you can forget it."

"Well I wasn't, I was just saying."

"Well enough said, let's go get laid" said Cher then stalked off towards the bedroom.

"Shh, don't wake him till we get him undressed" said Mel.

"Then we got him."

"Yeah and I'm first" said Cher.

"Oh no you're not" hissed Mel.

"Its my plan and my bed so I get the first shot."

"Okay, Okay, just don't wear him out to much" complained Cher who was more than wet with anticipation.

Ant was lying the way Matt was before they switched and could hear everything they said. He had to fight hard not to laugh and his erection was little on the firm side now.

Mel and Cher slowly and quietly began to undress. Both stripped naked and stood at the foot of the bed. Matt couldn't see anything but the essence of a horny female was heavy in the air. "Okay lets take off his pants" said Mel.

Reaching for his zipper she painstakingly pulled it down slowly without a sound and Cher unbuckled his belt and pants. Now they both slowly eased Ants pants off him and placed them on the floor then went after his shorts. The light warm touches of their hands got Ant more than aroused and now he was fully erect and hard as a rock, ready to roll.

As Mel and Cher removed his shorts, they became aware that he was fully erect.

"Oh Damn, he's long and already hard to" said Cher.

"You think he knows what's going on?"

"Naw, its probably the beer, you know how it gets you" said Mel.

"Yeah, I guess your right."

"You ready" asked Mel crawling onto the bed.

"Yeah, hurry, I'm so wet I'm beginning to drool all over myself."

Mel eased herself onto the bed then straddled Ant's torso. Her heart was racing and her pulse throbbed in her swollen vaginal lips. She began to breath heavily and deeply as she reached between her legs for his throbbing penis. Ant thought he was gonna bust if she didn't put it in soon and finally she did. At first she rubbed the tip of his bulbous head up and down the entire length of her vagina. The fire and sweetness of its feel made her gasp as her virginal body responded by contracting wildly.

"Is he in?" whispered Cher who was just about beside herself with anxiousness.

"No, not yet" moaned Mel still gasping.

"Well hurry, I want some too."

"Just relax, I don't want it to hurt too much, you know I'm still a virgin" she hissed.

Cher just sucked her teeth hard and sat on her knees with her arms crossed. Finally she put him into her a little ways. Oh how hot and juicy he was she thought as fire and ice tore threw her. It would take a second to get used to his wide penis just inside her and the pain was beginning to subside. All of a sudden Cher pushed her down all the way completely filling her all at once. Ant locked up fiercely for he hadn't expected this any more than Mel did. She sucked in so hard she couldn't move. All she could do was sit still atop the huge penis that filled her completely. The feeling was intense and wonderful as well as painful.

She could feel every inch of herself stretched to the max.

"Now your getting it" said Cher through clenched teeth. Ant was now beside himself and began to work his rod into her with smooth synchronized strokes. All Mel could do was sigh with each retraction and whine with every deep penetration that followed.

"Ssss, oh Matt, ssss oh Matt" she moaned.

"He's fucking me, he's fucking me" she whined.

"Well fuck him back" said Cher who was now so wet her thighs and buttocks began to get slippery. Mel began working herself to his rhythm and soon became over whelmed with passion she started stroking and riding him more fiercely. Sucking and moaning with all the lust and passion that she had long waited for. Ant was in 7th heaven as he continued to drive deep into her tight wetness.

"Oh Damn" he moaned.

"Damn its good." He held onto her hips for control and began to crank himself into her. Fully roaming her insides with total abandon and hunger.

"Oh Matt. Oh baby. Oh fuck me. Yes, yes, I knew you were good, yes baby, yes" she cried as she bucked and slapped against him to drive him deeper within.

Cher couldn't take it. The smell of sex and the lust hanging heavy in her loins made her crazy. She quickly got up to straddle Ants face. To Ants surprise a very wet and hungry vagina had poised itself over his face and was now gliding up and down his chin.

"Come on Matt, eat me baby, eat me please."

Ant had never done this before but didn't think too much about it in his current state. He let his tongue flick out and glide into her wetness. Cher sucked hard and moaned with pleasure.

"Oh shit that's good, come on baby, eat my stuff, eat me now!"

Matt on the other hand was totally unaware of the wild ride that was taking place above him. He was tired and sleep had overcome him shortly after getting under the bed. All he could see in his intoxicating mind was him and Retta making mad passionate love.

Mel was well on her way to having her first orgasam and when it finally came she locked up savagely and reached out for Cher.

"Are you coming?" she said still grinding against Ants face with a ferocious fever. All Mel could do was pant.

"Ah, Ah, SSAH, SSAH." The powerful feeling that held her was excruciatingly sweet as she was being roamed savagely as wave upon wave of pleasure began to rack her body. She could feel a sweet cramping, a sudden tightening and contracting. Then all of a sudden it hit the earthshaking feeling that went through her made her head snap back and her body jerk up right. Oh this was good, to good and she gave herself up to it and whined and moaned loudly as her body vibrated and trembled.

Soon the feeling subsided and she just drooped over towards Cher. Cher seeing this though enjoying Ants flicking tongue quickly dismounted. She eased her cousin over on her side and watched her slide off his still hard but very wet penis.

"Great, he didn't come yet" she thought.

Cheryl quickly mounted Ant and slid him inside her without the slightest hesitation and by now was well beyond worrying about chastross and just sat on him full. Relishing the thick expanse inside her. She was on fire all over again and Ant couldn't hold back any longer. He grabbed onto Cher's hips and drove himself into her like a mad man making slapping sounds as they connected. Cher was elated and more than welcomed his deep penetrating thrust as she bounded up and down and pushed her ass rearward grinding hard to penetrate herself to the max.

"SSS, oh Matt, damn your good, sss oh baby, sss oh baby, ss yes, yes" she moaned getting louder each second and not really caring.

Just outside the door several ears were listening intently to the sounds of hot passion on the other side and a nervous grinning took hold.

Soon the couples began to branch off one by one to find their own little love nests so they could get their mounting hunger as well. By now the bed was a bucking mollen of plateau of sex. Cheryl was riding Ant like something wild wiping her hair wildly and bearing down with tremendous force. The slurping sounds of their juices created a decadent effect as their bodies slapped together.

All to quickly Ant began to feel a powerful cramping tingle creep up his legs. Curling his toes into blunted objects, it slowly worked its way up his thighs and through his anus causing him to tighten up and hold his breath.

Cher could tell that something was going to happen when she felt him swell inside her. This felt delicious and made her hold on tighter pivoting harder. Ant felt a surge of fluid gush through him as each orgasm burst from him to fill Cher with scorching rockets of semen.

"Oh shit" he moaned.

"Sss ooh damn this some good stuff." Hearing Ants voice for the first time and the exploding orgasms he released inside her excited her so much she let forth her own violent climax gushing all over him. Once this had happened she just collapsed on his chest in an exhausted but well satisfied leap. Before sleep finally overcame them both he whispered his final eulogy,

"gotcha sweetpea" then he kissed her and held her sweaty brow.

"Sneaky bastard" moaned Cher, then fell happily to sleep.

A slight chill and the not so comfortable floor brought Matt out of his drunken sleep and at first he was a little disoriented and unsure as to where he was. After raising his head it told him all he needed to know.

"OW!" He had hit his head on the bottom of the bed and all of the nights events came tumbling back.

"Oh shit" he moaned rubbing his sore head.

"What time is it?" he wondered, then worried his way from under the bed trying to be quiet. The house was completely dark and silent as he stood and listened for any signs or life and there was none. Only just the bleak outline of three naked bodies curled up together in bed.

Cher was on the left and Mel on the right. A thin smile crossed Matt's lips and a strange euphoria began to wash through him waking him further by hovering his awareness. The room was heavy with the smell of sex and it made Matt's loins stir a little. He shook it off and headed for the door quietly.

He creaked it open ever so slowly not wanting to make any noise and just before stepping out he looked at them once more, "Happy Birthday ole buddy" he whispered "you deserve it" then he was gone.

The inpiglo clock on the kitchen wall told him that it was 2 a.m. Matt reached his hand into the wash tub to put some of the chilling water on his face.

"Damn that's cold" he thought as it trickled down his neck onto his chest. There was no one around so Matt figured he and Ant were the only ones there but after he opened the door he saw that no one had left and was still here but hidden. Matt closed the door and headed for the truck. "The guys will just have to sleep it off and leave in the morning" he thought then got in and drove off.

On his way across town Matt rolled down his window to take advantage of the breeze. There wasn't many cars on the road at this hour and it gave him a sort of quiet peace. He began to think about Retta and how much he wished he could be with her now but it would have to wait. Besides, he still had to figure out how he was gonna get out of this mess with his dad and not calling Retta all night.

"Retta wouldn't be too much trouble" he thought but his dad was something else. He hadn't told him he was going to be out all night and he would surely be pissed when he got home. "Damn" he cursed to himself hitting the wheel. "I can count on not getting this baby anymore, sigh". "Oh well, aint nothing I can do about it now."

Suddenly without effort his mind wandered back to Mels house and the scene he had just left when he thought of how they would look when they realized it was Ant they had been riding. They would be pissed. The thought of this made Matt laugh out loud, "oh it was so sweet" and he was enjoying every bit of the plot he put together and how it materialized the way he wanted.

Soon Mat was pulling in the drive way.

He eased the truck into the back yard and stopped just behind the Mercedes. He thought this would give his dad a quicker retreat in the morning instead of pulling way down into the lower basin of the yard. He got out and closed the door quietly then headed up the back stairs. He was glad the door didn't squeak as he opened it cause he didn't really want to confront his dad just now and would rather wait till morning. Once inside Matt put the keys on the stove so he would see them then eased on down the hall toward his room.

He didn't bother taking a shower but just undressed and crashed on his bed. Sleep came almost immediately and once again he was dreaming of Retta.

It was 10 a.m. when Retta finally awoke. She had had a long peaceful rest and felt great. She no longer remembered the scare from the night before and just lay in bed relishing the sweet smells of early morning dew on the sun drenched grass. Sunlight filtered into her room and bathed her in a soft warm beam of light, the bed though huge felt great. It was like a huge beam bag but was soft and rich like a thick comforter.

Aretta always wondered why old peoples beds were like this instead of hard or mushy like newer beds. She prodded the bed curiously to see if she could determine what was in it but could not. It didn't matter and she just cuddled into the thick heavy covers more to feel the warmth and security they gave throughout the night.

Soon she got up and headed into the bathroom to get cleaned up and dressed. The bathroom was charming she thought with the classic black and white checkered tile floor and a bear's foot bathtub. The sink was also from a time long gone and sported spoke wheel hot and cold knobs with a short tube like spout that pointed straight down.

The toilet was an old water closet style with the tank positioned well above her head and a pull chain with a pine wood handle. She hadn't paid it much attention yesterday and only gave it a cursory glance. But now it had a charm all its own and made her giggle when she thought about using it and what happen if the water tank ever sprung a leak. Soon she had washed up and brushed her teeth. She noticed the water had a funny taste but then chalked it off to being well water.

After awhile she had gotten dressed and went looking for everyone else. The smell of fresh baked biscuits, bacon, eggs and fresh butter assaulted her nose and made her stomach growl. Retta went into the kitchen to find a plate on the table and her name on a piece of paper. Oh the sinful sweetness of it she thought as she looked down at the blue and white china plate completely covered with grits, scrambled eggs, four big strips of the most mouth watering bacon she'd ever seen not to mention the two big homemade biscuits and preserves. It all looked and smelled wonderful and she quickly said grace and dug in. Retta made a complete pig of herself as she ate. She stuffed her mouth with grits then packed in a healthy bite of eggs.

Then as if possessed, she bit off a healthy portion of biscuits to pack it all in. She laughed to herself with wild eyed pleasure as she had never enjoyed anything this much and her taste buds were a circus of taste and delight. After a brief moment to chew and swallow she began to search the table for something to drink. When she didn't find it she got up to look in the fridge. She saw an old fashion pitcher that was the same pattern as the plate with blue grapes, apples corn and a myriad of other fruits and vegetables on it.

Inside was milk but it didn't quite smell or look like normal milk but a deeper richer texture. She poured a big glass and sat back down to gorge herself again before anything got the least bit cold. She took a bite of her bacon then a swig of milk. Oh how sweet and rich it was. This wasn't store bought milk at all and she loved it and the way it mixed with her food to give it a unique blend of tastes.

Soon she was done eating and put her plate in the sink to wash it. Soon as she had dried her dish and glass and put them away she went outside. She could see her grandmother bent over in a row of bean stalks and cucumbers picking the ripe ones and inspecting the plants for bugs.

Audrey and Lori were just ahead picking tomatoes and rich fat okra. She could see Lori was enjoying herself as she hopped to the next plant and carefully swapped off the ripe vegetable. She was about to go help when she heard a loud puttering of a tractor starting up. It was her grandfather.

"Hey granddaddy" she waved from the porch. He looked over to her and smiled brightly while tipping his hat and spitting out a long dark stream of tobacco juice.

"Good morning sleepy head" he said as he drove up next to the porch.

"Did ya sleep well lais night?"

"Yes sir, it was great, I've never felt so good in all my life" she said happily. He just nodded and grinned at her.

"Yep, I kin tell by da way you was snoring loud."

"Uh uh granddaddy, that was Lori" she said dejected and happy. He just laughed to himself at her defense.

"Aw now your ole grand pappy was jus chawin on ya." She leaped over and gave him a hug and a kiss. She felt his rough scratchy beard against her cheek and the healthy outdoor smell of him. It wasn't really soap or anything she could figure but just a nice healthy outdoorsy smell.

"Well I'm a goin ta do a lil plowin on the lower twena acas, you won'e go wit me" he asked. "Yes sir , can I?"

"Gone over an ais your maw kin ya go." She leaped off the porch and ran to where Audrey was saying hello and thank you for breakfast to her granny on the way. Shortly she was back and climbed up next to her grandfather on the seat. He smiled at her showing off his brown and slightly crooked teeth then he plopped a straw hat down on her head like his and she squealed and laughed with pure delight.

"That's so you don't get sun boin. Hang on now" he said putting the big green tractor in gear and lurching away from the porch and turned to go into the road in front of the house.

"So granddaddy, how long you and gramma been living here in Gray?" she asked sitting closer to him as the tractor bounced down the road.

"Oh I guess about 30 or 40 years I spect."

"Wow that's a long time. But the house looks so new."

"Well your paw an his brothers hep me rebuild it about twena years ago fo' you's even bon'e. In fact he ain even met yo' maw yet."

"Well it's really nice and I like it" she said.

"Yep it's a cozy lil house."

"So tell me when you in dat young man a yourn gon'e tie dat knot" he asked. Retta was surprised that he could be so perceptive as to assume this fact.

"Well we were gonna wait til we graduate from high school then maybe after we got good jobs we would."

"Oh fiddle sticks, you mean you gon't make dat man wait all dat time fo ya."

"Well were not old enough yet, I'm almost 16 and he's 17 going on 18."

"Aw horse pukie. Me n' your granny got hitched when she wuz thirtheen an I was fifteen." Retta's mouth fell open wide with surprise as she of a little mental math.

"Wow granddaddy, you've been married a long time."

"Yep and still got a ways to go" he said chuckling and patting her knee. Soon they were in the field. It was a large corn field that looked like it was at least three football fields long and two and a half wide.

"Wow this is big" said Retta. "Are we gonna work all this?"

"Naw child. We's just gonna turn over some dirt. Winter go's I kin put down some winter seeds for the next crop."

"Where do you keep all your supplies and stuff?"

"Oh I keep it in a wood shed just around dis hyea bend" he said pointing. Back at the house Lori was busy having run with the chickens and the pigs. Her granny had showed her how to feed them and was now preparing some slop for the hogs.

"Lori honey".

"Yes ma'am".

"Come on and help me tote dis hea slop to dem hawgs." Lori ran over to her scattering the chickens. She saw that her granny had two 5 gallon buckets full of old bread pieces, corn husks, breakfast bits and several other things she couldn't and didn't care to identify.

"Yucky" she said scowling at the odd looking soup.

"Their gonna eat that?"

"Yep, dey loves it. See how deys a looking at us. Dey know we's fixin to feeds em. Lori lifted the bucket and waddled over to the fence with it.

"Okay now child, you be careful goin in dat dere pen. It's a sloppy mess and dey a knock you down to get to dat dere slop."

"Okay granny" she said sitting down the bucket. She shooed them away by yelling at them and spraying them with the garden hose the way her granny showed her. The pigs squealed in surprise and confusion then ran to the far corner of the pen for safety. Lori quickly waddled into the pen and leaned the bucket into the trough then tipped it spilling the disgusting mixture into it. The hogs, some of them not much bigger than the bucket and others who were as large as she stood back grunting and squealing as they observed her. No sooner had she done this did they all come rushing at her.

"Look out child! Deys a comin attcha" said her granny. Lori turned to see the stampede she tried to get out of the way but was a little stuck in the thick gooey mud. Suddenly a small pig ran between her legs shoving her over while at the same moment a bigger hog shoved by her on the other side sending her face first into the mud "splat".

"Oh my word" said her grandmother who was standing by in case she was needed. She stepped into the pen and jerked her up by her shoulders and hauled her out to safety.

"Are you alright honey?" she said whipping some of the mud from her face and cloths. Lori just nodded and flicked more of the goo from her hands. She was a complete mess from head to toe. "You know grandma" she said weakly with an almost calm and resigned tone.

"I like eating them better than feeding them."

"Aw my little dawlin" she said giving Lori a hug and walking her to the house to clean her up. "What happened?" Ann said. Audrey, who had heard the ruckus and came around the back to see.

"Oh nothing, the child just got her first lesson on sloppin hawgs."

"And what's that?" said Lori, completely unaware that she'd learned anything other than how to irritate a herd of hogs and get dirty.

"Never turn your back on a hungry hog while your feeding him" said Audrey smiling at her own little piglet.

It was a little after 12 noon now and Matt had long since gotten up, showered and had breakfast. He slept later than usual but was well refreshed when he did get up. He was now watching television and reminiscing about last nights bedroom follies.

The thought made him smile when he imagined the distraught and angry looks on Mel and Cher faces when they awoke to find a very naked and very satisfied Ant stretched out between them. "Oh it was gonna be fun!" he thought and wished he could have gotten pictures of them for posterity.

"Oh well you can't have everything" he thought. Soon the show was over and Matt dragged himself to his feet. He went into his dad room to recover the yard long laundry list of things he knew his dad would have for him to do. Surely enough there it was on the fireplace mantle.

It was a long yellow sheet of paper from a legal pad that had big letters on the front that simply read "for your eyes only" and a little smiley face on the end.

Matt grinned to himself slightly amused at his dad strange sense of humor and learned long ago when he started a work list like that it was bound to be a doozey. And surely enough it was. Matt mouth fell open wide like an oven door and when he turned the paper over, he saw at least a page full of jobs that needed doing and some of which he had never had to do.

The jobs ranged from cleaning the house to washing the outside windows around the entire house, most of which would require a ladder and a gallon of water. The most devious job was cleaning out from under the house near the back door steps. This was the worst because long ago someone had built a small room under there but never finished it. All that was done was a partial wall with a cement floor.

Leaves, dirt, garbage and tons of other nasty things that made their way into it and it was a mess. "This must be payback for last night." he said to himself shaking his head.

Also there was an envelope on the mantle. He picked it up and opened it. Inside was a 20 dollar bill and a note that read "seeing as how you forgot what time to come home last night and didn't bother to call to say you'd be late, I forgot also how much your allowance was and didn't bother to check either so have fun with your chores and don't plan on going anywhere, you're on house arrest for the remainder of the day and maybe tomorrow too, it depends on how well you do your chores and how I feel when I get home, cook up something for dinner and I'll see you later, Love Dad".

"Aw fuck" he said aloud looking at the note disbelieving and distraught.

"I knew I shouldn't have drink so much." He folded the bill and the list and put it in his pocket and set out to doing the jobs. Most were easy and didn't take much and he was soon finished with over half the list, now he had to tackle the outside jobs starting with mowing the lawn.

Matt had just finished cutting the grass and was about to put the mower away when a big orange truck pulled into the drive and stopped. Matt allowed a smile to cross his lips as he looked over his shoulder then strolled on down the drive way humming conceitedly and full of pride.

Ant, Mel and Cher were waiting on him on the porch when he got back to the front and their faces at Mel's and Cher's were the picture of revenge and contempt.

"Hi guys" he said loftily. Unfazed by their angry and displaced expressions.

"Hi yourself you little prick" hissed Mel who was leaning against the doorway with her arms crossed and sporting a nice little short set with white shorts and a Hawaiian shirt. Matt just grinned more and tried not to laugh out loud.

"So how did you guys enjoy yourselves last night?" he tainted.

"Was I as good as you expected?"

Ant just sat grinning quietly and shaking his head at his best friend. Show of all gall and complete immunity of the devious trick he played on the two horny virgins.

"You're a sneaky bastard you know that?" spat Cher who was sitting next to Ant on the deck couch.

"You knew all along what we had planned and you let us think you knew nothing."

"Well all fair in love and war" he said smiling.

"So tell me, when did you notice that it wasn't me you were riding?"

"Who said we did?" said Mel working on a nail as if it were most important. "You weren't even there."

"Oh come on now Mel you can quit lying, it's all over your face, look at you, hell, both of you are glowing and besides I was under the bed the whole time."

"Why you sonofabitch!" spat Cher.

"See, I told you he didn't leave this morning" hissed Mel pointing at him. "He left late last night." Mat just leaned against the wall and looked at them with a shit eating grin on his face. "So tell me, did you guys like it? I mean from what I was hearing you both enjoyed it quite well." Both girls looked away blushing and not wanting to admit to anything.

"Yes it was good" said Cher loftily giving Matt a proud look.

"Ant was a real stud and twice the man you could never be so there."

Matt just screwed his face and walked toward his open bedroom door.

"Well good! I'm glad you guys finally got that nut off your chest but I still win" he said not even looking at them as he spoke walking away. Cher was the first to bolt. She just couldn't stand the way he was so aloof and cool when they chastised him.

She ran behind him and tackled him to the floor from behind.

"I'm gonna kick your ass Matt." Matt was to quick and agile for her. He quickly rolled over taking her with him then scooted back onto her pinning her arms with his knees. Mel and Ant just stood in the door and watch to see what would happen.

"Get off me you prick!" she shouted trying to arch and buck him off.

"Sorry sweet pea" he said dryly with lust in his voice.

"My girl ain't in town this weekend and just now I could use a shot of this hot not so virgin pussy of yours."

Mel's mouth fell open like a barn door. She couldn't believe what she was hearing and didn't know whether to be angry or excited. Cher was totally speechless with the look of total shock on her face which blossomed 100% when Matt used his knees to spread her legs and arch them up. He was positioned perfectly between her legs and she was wearing a mini skirt.

A hot flash burst through her mind and body to quickly ignite her internal fire and send her juices gushing forth to moisten her excited vagina. Matt gave her a most lusty smirk and held her arms down but Cher didn't really believe him and that he would do anything and was just teasing her again.

But still without much effort, she didn't think she would move if she could and wanted to feel his closeness anyway. Suddenly she felt the delicious sensation of Matt's hips grinding into her to press and bruise her already wet vagina. She sucked in hard at the pleasure of it and swallowed hard.

"Could Matt really be planning to take me, I mean now, like this in front of Mel and Ant?" "Oh god let it be so, I don't care, I just want it."

Mel was holding herself and had placed a hand over her mouth to suppress a sigh of exasperation and utter surprise. Ant was a little off kilter himself but then figured his buddy was just pulling her chain again in the one truly creative way he knew how and it always worked. Matt leaned over to kiss her lightly on her slightly parted lips and could feel her dry breath flow into his mouth and the desire that was swelling in her. She was gasping now and pulled her legs up to put them around his back.

Oh how she hungered to have him enter her fast and deep and Matt was getting a little excited himself now and wondered could he stop himself this time but then pushed the idea from his mind figuring, "I've done it before."

Just then he seized her neck with hot viscous lips and bore down on her grinding like a wild thing. Cher just sucked in hared throwing her head back and moaned aloud. "Ohh Mat!" Just then he got up leaving her totally scathed and bereft with total shock and sudden awareness in her eyes. "Oh no, not again" she thought. "He can't do this to me again."

Mel had remembered this little trick of his too and even though she was unsettled because it wasn't her she got angry at him teasing Cher so. "So how was I?" he said curtly standing with his hands on his hips and a serious bulge in his shorts.

The next thing that happened took Matt totally by surprise. Mel ran at him and jumped square on his chest with her legs wrapping around his waist. The momentum and unawareness of her sudden attack took him to the floor with a thud.

"Matt you've played your last trick you sly bastard and this time you're gonna pay" growled Mel holding him down. "Cher, strip his ass" she barked over her shoulder. Then turning back to put a scathing stare into his eyes. Matt tried to move her but his shorts prohibited his movements when Cher pulled them down to his ankles and left them.

"Hey Ant get these girls up man" he said not sounding as confident about his strength as he did before. Ant thought for a second then just closed the door and flipped on the stereo. Then dived on the bed to watch.

"Oh its like that is it?" he said to Ant.

"Hey this is your party, I'm just a spectator."

With that Cher tore off his underwear with one viscous jerk downward exposing a fully erect 9 inch shaft. "Oh shit Mel, he's gonna be something else" she said looking at his powerfully veined penis with it bulbous head. She remember Ants was nice but not as long or threatening as this and she was still chaise.

"No matter" she thought, "I'm gonna get mine." Then peeled off her own underwear to expose a super moist and hungry vagina. Matt just stared blankly into Mel's eyes who was unblinking and beheld a scorching intent behind them.

"Okay Mel you guys want to play?" he said calmly. His voice dripping with lust again. "Have a ball, have two if you can." And just then he felt the sweet burning wetness of a tight vagina enshroud his now throbbing shaft in sweet wetness.

"Oh god" moaned Cher. "Ss he's so big and fat."

"Well he's ours now cuz and were gonna bust his balls" said Mel. Then got up to give Cher room to work him over.

"Come on Ant let's leave these two alone for awhile, he's not going anywhere" said Mel looking at the expression of total pleasure on Matt's face.

Soon they were out of the room and Cher was in seventh heaven riding slowly up and down the long thick expanse of Matt's tool.

"Oh yes Matt, oh yes! Oh you feel good baby" she moaned. Matt was lost too. He finally pushed all his guilt behind and resigned himself to his fate. It was bound to happen sooner or later he thought as he gripped her bottom fiercely to drive himself all the way into the roots and Cher moaned louder.

"Oh Matt please, oh gosh you're so big."

"You like that huh?" he said getting into it.

"Yes baby, yessss" she moaned giving herself up to his will and relishing the hot firey ride.

Matt slammed into her relentlessly making a slapping sound as her juices soaked them both. Suddenly Matt rolled her over and put his arms just behind her knees bringing them up to her chest. Cher just shook her head pleadingly with passion stricken on her face.

"No Matt, please, please." But Matt was already beginning his downward stroke. Cher squeezed him tightly and bit into his shoulder as he put all his force into the drive. She let a mild scream escape her lips and Mel and Ant heard it.

"He's got her now" said Ant folding his hands behind his head closing his eyes as they sat on the couch. Matt fucked her viscously and deeply putting her body at such an acute angle her bottom was pointing almost upward. He was pumping her hard and fast and she could feel every inch of his huge penis spreading and filling her to the max much more than Ant had previously. She shook her head wildly as the excruciating pain and pleasure washed threw her thrust after thrust. Her head was shaking wildly and she moaned more freely now with delicious abandon. "Fuck-me, fuck-me" she gasped hanging onto him for dear life. She was a molten mass of sweet tension and juices thought Matt as he pumped like a jack hammer going in from all angles now. She was good, damn good and he would fuck her till she burst with orgasm after orgasm.

Finally she could hold no more. Her body shudder violently and she felt a tingling tremble that came from her feet to her chest.

It was a resonating feeling that vibrated her very being and her mind was a mesh with colors, sounds, and strange light. Her first contraction made her howl "Ohhh! ssss,oooo!" with excitement.

"Ohh Mat!" she moaned. "I'm cumming, I'm cumming" over and over till the final burst, she froze solid and tossed her head side to side. Sweat and perspiration all over her brow and small tresses of golden blond hair were plastered to her forehead. The tightening contraction of her orgasm were like a vice around Matt's still swollen tool. He fought hard not to come and held on till she collapsed in his arms. They just laid there breathing hard and she was radiating all over with pleasure and satisfaction.

"Are we even now?" Matt whispered. She just nodded weakly then hungrily sought his lips. After a few minutes more he got up. Oh was she wet he thought as he looked down at her and helped her up.

"That was incredible Matt" she whispered her eyes a glow.

"But how come you didn't come?"

I'm saving it for the grand finale on your cousin."

"Oh, okay maybe I will get it the next time" she said shyly putting her arms around him.

"Now sweet pea this makes us even."

"Oh, okay, so how was I?" she asked.

"Everything I thought and more baby." She grinned and kissed him lightly.

"I'll go get Mel" she said then left.

"Mel your next" she said smiling broadly heading for the bathroom.

"You mean he's not out yet?"

"Huh uh, not in the least, he said he's saving the best for you."

Mel got up and hurried into the room. Now Matt was on the bed and completely naked.

Mel gasped when she saw his still rock hard penis pointing to the ceiling and still glistening with the moisture of recent sex.

"Are you ready?" he asked softly. She just nodded and undressed not taking her eyes off his long shaft.

"Oh god can I handle him, he's so big?" Soon she was in bed and the love making resumed but this time Matt didn't turn her on her back but on her knees to give her the ride of her life.

After a while when they had finished and gotten back under control, Matt, Cher, Ant and Mel hung out watching TV and relaxing on the couch.

"Hey Matt, what time is it?" asked Mel who was laying on him.

"Its 2:30 by my watch, why, you gotta go somewhere?"

"Yeah, me and Cher were gonna go to the mall and pick up something's.

"You guys wanna go?"

"Not me" said Matt.

"I got put on house arrest for coming in late last night."

"Aw Matt" she moaned.

"I'm sorry I got you in trouble."

"Don't sweat it, It was my fault, besides dad gonna lift it tomorrow."

"Oh good then we can hang out tomorrow then."

"I don't know Mel, we better chill, I mean today was great but I'm still taken."

She lowered her head.

"I know Matt" she whispered "but I still love you."

"Me too Matt" said Cher "and we love you too, Ant" they said.

"You guys are our first lovers and you're the best and we will always be yours whenever you need us and want us" said Mel looking at Matt.

Matt just pulled her to him and hugged her. "You're a nut, you know that don't you?" he scolded.

"Yes, but I'm your nut and nobody else's."

Soon the two girls were on their way to the mall. They kissed the boys goodbye and left.

"Man what a day" said Matt letting out a deep sigh.

Ant was standing by grinning at him.

"So what are you smiling at traitor?" Matt hissed punching his arm.

"Ow man, I ain't no traitor, you just got caught with your pants down one time to many and got screwed "literally."

"Yeah, and you helped them do it."

"Aw quit cha bitchin you know you liked it."

Matt just blushed and grinned.

"Yeah, that was sure sweet stuff boy, but now what do I tell Retta? I've really fucked up now and she'll never forgive me."

"So don't tell her nothing and she won't know nothing."

"I don't know Ant man, I ain't never lied to her about anything."

"Well you do what you want but you better know this first, once you tell her you lose her, you don't and only you, me and them will know about it, so think about it."

Matt was not really happy about this whole matter and he felt like a real shit for betraying her and knew he would never do it again but he knew he must come to grips with it.

"Come on man help me finish some yard work" he said finally.

"I'll work this out later." "Bet" said Ant walking along with him to the back yard. Soon the boys were up to their knees in dirt and muck under the house and were glad to be finished. They dumped it all on the street in several garbage bags then went about attacking the windows. Ant sprayed them with a hose and Matt washed them with a sponge mope on an extra extension.

It's a good thing the windows wasn't dustier than they were or it would have taken them the rest of the day to clean them"

"Whew, I'm glad this shit is done" said Matt.

"Yeah me too, look at us, we look like hell."

"So take a bath butt head or do you still run and hide when you hear the words soap and water?" "No fart face" said Ant. "I ain't got no problem with it but you might" he said then reached down quickly for Matt's soap bucket.

Matt tried to turn and run but it was too late.

"SPLASH".

"Oh shit, you sonofabitch" he sputtered as dirty soapy water splashed down his face and all over his body.

"Now we gotta rinse your nasty butt off" he said laughing then blasted Matt with the hose at short range stinging him viscously with the cold water.

"Ant I'm gonna kick your ass" he glugged fighting away the water trying to take the hose but Ant kept out of his reach and kept blasting him till he was a complete mess.

All wet and soggy, Ant dropped the hose and ran out of range before Matt could recover. He stopped at the end of the driveway and laughed his tail off at his carnage. Matt wiped himself down and shook the water from his ears and his bare feet. He slipped inside his leather shoes as he walked, making a squishy noise.

"That's alright Ant you know about payback, don't cha?"

"Yeah but you gotta get me first and I'm not that stupid." Matt just glared at him then pointed at him and nodded as if to say "okay asshole it's on."

Awhile later they had gotten cleaned up and were sitting around watching movies and pigging out on sandwich.

"So dude" said Ant.

"Have you tried to call Aretta yet?"

"Yeah but she's out in the fields plowing with her granddad and won't be back till late about 3 or 4 o'clock."

"So what do you want to do till then?"

"Hell I don't know" he said tossing his half eaten sandwich on his plate.

"But I don't want to sit around here all day that's for sure."

"Well do you wanna go to the store down the street?" "We could play some games for awhile." "Yeah, we can do that, let's go"

"Hey! You remember last time Retta and Lori was here for the weekend?"

"Yeah."

"Well Lori was playing against a hand full of older boys for money."

"Say what?"

"Yeah and she beat them all, man she walked off with $55 dollars of their money."

"Damn" said Ant. "What does she know about gambling?"

"That's just it, nothing."

"Well I'll be"

Chapter 15

Alone Again

"**N**ow you be careful" said Retta's grandfather as he let her drive the big tractor.

He had showed her how and was done with the work earlier than expected so he took some time to teach Aretta a few things about farming. Now all was left was for her to drive the tractor back to the house. Retta adjusted the seat and tried to remember how to work the gas gears and the clutch without screwing it up. Just the feeling of being in the driver's seat with the powerful tractor running gave her a cold sweat.

"Now don'e be nuvous Aretta" said her grandfather.

"Taint nothing but a tracta, it ain't gone bite lessen ya in front of it."

She smiled weakly and pushed down hard on the clutch then put it in first.

"Dats right honey now you's doin it, now jus easin off da clutch and give it some gas."

Retta's foot was shaking and trembling as she eased up on the clutch and applied the gas. The tractor lurched and bucked as it began to move. She was both ecstatic and terrified at the jerky response from the tractor and hoped she was doing it right.

"Das good honey" he yelled over the noise of the highly revved tractor.

"Now let go da clutch and give it sum mo gas."

Aretta did so and soon the tractor was on its way. It no longer jerked but just bounced a little from the big tires.

"Now member what I done told ya bout shifin dem gears" he said shouting.

"Its bout dat time." Retta listened to the rpms reeve up on the engine then jammed down on the clutch and pulled the long stick shift down. Then let up the clutch and poured on the gas. She was really moving now and steered a little wildly.

"Das good honey but jus slow down a bit so we un's don't turn over." Retta nodded and eased up on the gas pedal. She was ecstatic now and smiled so wide her jaws began to ache.

"Okay honey its all your'n" he said leaning back and propping up his foot. Aretta was enjoying this completely and began to laugh out loud with glee as the big tractor responded to her every whims.

She drove up and down the field changing gears. As she went after about a half hour of this her grandpa told her to take them in.

"You really want me too granddaddy!?" she gushed in surprise.

"Yep, you ain't no different den I was when my paw told me how ta drive so's you might as well do it too."

"Okay" she said happy then headed for the main road. As she got to it she slowed and stopped. Looking both ways then pulled out easily with a slight jerking, lurching as she eased off the clutch. She noticed that the road was much smoother than the fields and required less tension on the wheel to keep it steady.

Trucks passed by and she smiled brightly and waved as they waved at her. She felt proud and happy to be Vern's granddaughter and so was he.

Soon they got to the house and saw Audrey, Lori and granny sitting on the porch drinking lemonade.

"Oh my goodness" said Audrey getting up.

"Retta driving a tractor!"

Annie Mae just laughed out loud slapping her knee.

"I knowed dat youngun had some a her paw in her." Lori just clapped her hands with glee and waved at her wildly.

Retta was beside herself now and almost drove past the house but seeing this, her grandfather had her ease down on the gas and head into the backyard. Once they had gotten there she stopped just shy of the porch and killed the engine then hugged and kissed her grandfathers dusty face.

"Oh thank you granddaddy, thank you." He just laughed.

"Now, now honey you knows your grandpa don't mind an was glad to do it, now run on along and tells your grammaw how good you did."

She hugged him once more and jumped down then ran to the front yard.

"Did you see, did you see?" she ranted on running to her mother arms.

"Yes we saw you and you did good Retta."

"Granddaddy taught me how."

"Well ain't that nice" said her granny coming over to get her share of hugs and give the dusty girl a glass of lemonade.

"Thanks gramma." Retta hadn't realized how thirsty she was until she downed the first glass effortlessly without stopping.

"My stars child" said Annie Mae.

"You's musta been mighty thirsty, hyea, has some mo" she said pouring her another glass full. This time she drank it slower to savor the sweet lemony taste.

"So what did you do today Lori?" she asked looking down at her little sister who was beaming with pride at her big sisters new talent.

"I picked some vegetables and tried feeding the hogs but when I turned my back they ran over me and knocked me down in the mud."

Retta tried to picture what this looked like then burst out laughing as she imagined Lori face down with hoof prints all over her back.

"That's not funny" scowled Lori putting her hands on her hips.

"Oh, I'm not laughing at you Lori, I'm just laughing." Lori didn't quite understand but fumed about it anyway.

"Okay now you too" said Annie Mae. "Yall go 'n' get washed up for supper and me and your maw will set the table" she said getting up.

Retta washed up quickly because wanted to try to call Mat before eating. She had been thinking about him all day and couldn't wait to talk to him.

"Oh Matt please be home" she thought as she headed out of the bath room. She picked up the phone and dialed vigorously.

"Hello, Matt?"

"Yeah it's me baby" he said happy to hear from her.

"Oh baby where you been, I've been calling you and calling you but you wasn't there?" she said relieved and distraught.

"And tell me why didn't you call me last night and tell me you were going out?"

Matt cringed at the thought and held the phone just off his ear.

"Well baby I didn't know I was going to be going any place and when it came up I was caught off guard."

"Matt you still could have called me though, you had me worrying about you."

"I'm sorry baby, I didn't mean too, I just didn't think that's all."

Retta was still fuming but allowed his excuse to penetrate her defensive mood.

"So where did you guys go?"

"We just went over to Ants friend house with some of the guys from the team and had a few drinks and listened to some music, nothing special."

"Were there any girls there?" she asked sarcastically.

Matt bit his lip wondering if he should say or not.

"Yeah, there was a few."

"Were you with somebody Matt?"

"Uh, not really, I just sat and danced a few times but that's all, nothing else" he blurted, feeling totally afraid and off balance.

"Matt, how could you?" she said weakly her voice cracking with hurt.

"How could you lie to me and do me wrong? I thought you loved me! Why Matt?"

"No Retta, wait, you got it all wrong baby, I didn't do anything wrong last night, I just had some drinks then left by myself and I didn't do anything, honest, baby you gotta believe me."

Retta was trying to blink back some tears that were beginning to burn forth from behind her cloudy pain filled eyes. Her cheeks felt hot and her mouth sticky and dry. She didn't know why she didn't believe him and hurt even more when she couldn't make the thoughts go away but something in her told her that the man she loved had not told her everything and being that Matt was a creature of habit this sudden and abrupt change made her curiosity and doubt in him increase but she loved him and love him deeply so she forced herself to believe until she was sure otherwise.

"Retta please talk to me baby, please I miss you so much I can't stand this distance and the possibility that you don't believe me."

This brought the stalking tears forth with a steady stream and she didn't even try to stop them, all she could do was look longingly at her ring with diffused eyes and relish the thought of the man who had put it there as well as what it meant.

Okay, so he'd gone out no; no big deal. He had gone out before and this didn't bother her then so why now. Maybe she just missed him so and the fact that he may have been in another woman arms where she should have been.

Matt was feeling badly now and royally hated himself for hurting her like he did. She had always been there for him and never once did she ever stray but now he had and he felt so fucking dirty about it and now he was going to pay for it dearly. All he could see was Retta turning her teary eyes from him and walking away just after dropping his ring in his lonely hand.

"Matt" she whispered.

"Look baby, I'm sorry for getting so upset with you, you know how much I love you and how much you mean to me."

"Yes baby, I do and I'm sorry I did that . . . ."

"Wait Matt, let me finish" she said cutting him off.

His heart pumping wildly with anticipation and hope at a possible reprieve from her.

"Like I said Matt, you're my man and no one else's, I know this in my heart and I just got jealous and scared, that's all, but I want you to know something Matt and I really mean this."

"Don't hurt me Matt, please don't ever hurt me because as god is my witness I'll leave you no matter how much it hurts me, I'll leave you."

Her words were like crushed ice in a glass full of novacain.

They were chilling and yet mind numbing at the same time. Matt couldn't speak but only became fully aware of what she had said and meant.

"Matt, are you there?" she said calmly sounding almost normal.

"Yeah I heard" he said finally.

"Thank you Retta, thank you for letting me know how you feel about me" he said feeling totally lost and misguided by this. His room had an almost medical feel to it like it wasn't his and just a cold bleak examination room.

"I'll call you later" he said then slowly eased the phone from his ear.

"Matt! Matt!" she yelled but he was gone.

All that remained was a lonely dial tone. She slammed the phone down harshly then ran to her room and wept.

"What's wrong with Retta?" said Audrey who had heard the shouting and the phone slam down in its cradle. Lori just sat down quietly at the table and didn't speak.

"Dat poor baby" said Annie Mae. "She done got herself a touch of the blues."

"Hey Matt, where you at man?" said Ant who went wildly looking through the house for him. He didn't find him so he ran out the door and searched the back then the front of the house. He saw a figure just disappearing over the hill towards the cotton mill so he set out after him in full stride trying to catch him.

Ant knew Matt wouldn't just leave like that unless something really hurt him.

"Hey Matt!" he said huffing from the effort.

"Wait up!"

But Matt just kept walking with his head down and his hands in his pockets.

"Hey Matt, wait up man" he said again finally catching him. Ant stopped in front of him and put his hands on Matt's shoulders to get him to look at him and what he saw made him wish he hadn't stopped him.

Matt's eyes were brimming over with hot tears and his face was the picture of abandon hope and pain. He just put his arm around his shoulder and walked with him in silence. Ant knew Matt never cried about anyone he didn't truly love or something that didn't hurt a lot.

The last time he saw Matt cry was long ago when he had ran over to his house and threatened to beat Matt up if he ran away and left him. Matt and his father was going through a really bad time and he was really getting dogged. He had told Ant long ago that if he ever called and said he would see him around that would mean he had reached his limit and was going away.

Matt had just finished packing his small duffle bag and was about to leave when Ant burst into the house completely out of breath and upset. He had run the 6 ½ blocks from his house to Matt's in about 10 minutes which shocked Matt completely. Ant just threw down his bag and backed him up against the wall fiercely then held him there.

"Man you ain't going nowhere!" he shouted still huffing hard with pain all over his face.

"You're not gonna leave me you hear me, I'll kick your ass before I let that happen."

Matt just shook his head as tears began to fall.

"I can't take it no more man" he sobbed. "I've had enough of the man, he just keeps on dogging me."

"No Matt, you can't leave" said Ant. Tears filling his own eyes as his own pain became too much for him at seeing his best friend crying.

"You all I got man and if you leave I'll be all alone, you gotta stay! you gotta!"

Matt just shook his head no, and tried to reach for his bag on the floor.

"No goddamit!" shouted Ant batting it away.

Matt could see the intense love and devotion in his eyes and it made him feel worse. Not even his own brothers had cared so much for him. Matt's mind and soul were on fire with the combination of pain and love that was brewing in him. He had never felt this way about anyone and to now feel it for another man not his kin was over whelming.

He just lunged at Ant and they held each other in the doorway on this balmy spring afternoon and cried. They cried for all they had and didn't have. For the words they had once spoken and those never said.

Now this same fire was brewing again as he and Matt walked along in silence.

"She said she was gonna leave me Ant" whispered Matt finally.

"No she won't" he said not looking at him.

"But she said so man! She said if I ever let her down again or do her wrong she'll leave me." "Then don't do her wrong Matt" he said sympathetic.

"But I already did and I just know she'll find out."

"No she won't, not unless you tell her and you better not."

"But Ant!"

"No Matt! Shut up and listen" he snapped firmly.

"Aretta is the best thing that has ever come into your sorry life and mine" he said.

Finally Matt just looked at him.

"Yes, that's right, I love her too, I love her because she loves you and we already know how we feel about each other." "Since you met her man, both our lives have been richer and you can't say it hasn't, hell I have more fun with you guys than I ever have on my own.

"Except for last night" Matt said interrupting giving him a slight smile.

"Yeah, right butthead, that was good too, but then again it was because of you and Retta." "How Ant?"

"Don't you see that if you hadn't been already seeing Retta they wouldn't have gone through all this bullshit to get you and I would never have been in bed with either of them, so you see how it all fits?"

"Yeah, I guess I do."

"Good, so now you must see that you can never tell her at least not now, wait till you marry her then it won't matter."

Matt thought about it for a minute then nodded in agreement.

"Look Mat, I won't let Mel and Cher get to you again, I'll explain it to them and then it'll be cool, okay?"

"Okay Ant."

"So come on, lets go back before your dad comes home and busts you."

"Thanks Ant" he said squeezing his neck.

"For what?"

"For just being you." Ant started to blush and understood how he felt.

Aretta of course was not doing so good. Her grandmother had come to her after awhile and tried to console her and find out what was wrong and Aretta blurted out the whole sorted argument between her and Matt much to Annie Mae's amusement which only confused and upset Retta more. But Annie Mae, for all her years and experience was no slouch in the affairs of the heart and young men.

She had told her in the simplest way she knew how that boys are that way and would take a little molding from the woman he loved to correct that, and for the most part they were dogs, some good doggies but dogs none the less. Being such as they were needing house training so they always knew to stay in their own yards. She even used the dog Joe Bob as an example to Matt. She told Retta that they're a lot alike in a lot of ways and if she could see how to handle Joe Bob she could handle Matt.

Now that she was girded with this information she felt better and wasn't upset anymore.

"Why don't you go an give your young man a call an tells him how you feel honey, I'm shore he'll listen if you put chore foot down."

"You really think so?" she said hopeful.

"He didn't seem to want to talk to me anymore the way he hung up on me."

"Aw fiddle sticks, he's a probably hurtin too and just didn't know how to deal with you when you's tole him you's gonna leave em, so go on honey, call your man and make it right."

"Annie Mae done give you her best know how so you go an use it, okay?"

"Okay granny" she said squeezing her tightly. She broke away and ran to get the phone.

Retta dialed the number with renewed vigor and determination hoping all would be right again with the man she loved.

Matt was sitting at the table eating when the phone rang and his dad got it first.

"Hel-lo" he sang in his usual way.

"Hello, Mr. Mathis?" she said.

"Oh hi Retta, how are you?"

"Oh fine, fine."

Matt perked up when he heard him speak her name.

"So how are you enjoying the country?" he asked.

"Oh it's great, I'm enjoying myself completely."

"That's good, so how's your mom doing?"

"Oh she's fine, her and gramma are on the back porch relaxing."

"Well let me holler at her for a few minutes before you and Rodney get going."

Matt's heart sank and he bit down hard on his pork chop and chewed veltenerantly trying not to let his father see his eager aggravation at muscling in on his phone call.

Retta was no less distraught and stamped her foot when she put down the phone.

Just now she was thinking that she shouldn't have told him Audrey was there but since she already had she dragged out through the kitchen to get her.

"Mom, Buford wants to talk to you."

"Oh, is he on the phone?" she said hopping up eagerly to go talk to him.

Annie Mae just shook her head and chuckled to herself.

"Dems two got dey selfs a whole pack a man trouble" she said to her husband who nodded and kept on whittling.

"Hello, Buford?"

"Hi sweetheart!"

"Hello honey" she gushed like a school girl.

"So what are you up to?" he asked.

"Oh nothing, just sitting on the porch talking to my mother and father-in-law, how about you?" "Oh, me and Rodney are having a bite to eat."

"That's nice, so do you miss me?" she sang.

Buford just snorted a laugh and whispered something into the phone. Matt didn't quite catch but was sure sounded like sex talk and this made him a little uneasy and embarrassed so he excused himself to go in the den until they were through.

"Oh, Buford you old sly fox you, you know you shouldn't say things like that especially when I'm not there to indulge those desires with you, but tell me more anyway" she urged eagerly as she dropped into a chair to get comfortable.

Retta could hear a lot of giggling and wild laughing from the living room where her mother was. She had stayed on the porch and just fumed.

"Retta child" said her grandmother.

"Yes ma'am?"

"Have you ate yet?"

"No ma'am, I was waiting to use the phone when momma decided to hog it" she spat thumbing over her shoulder in Audrey's direction.

"Well child go eat fo your dinner gets cold, you know Annie Mae don't like to serve no cold food, so you aint gone eat no cold food."

"Yes ma'am" she said going into the kitchen.

Retta sat down and put her head in her hands then stared at her plate. She hadn't intended to touch a bite but the heavenly smell of the roast pork, macaroni and cheese, sweet potatoes, green beans and crackling cornbread was too much. She grudgingly chanced a nibble on her meat , not wanting to give up her stubborn slow burn but no sooner had she put the tender shard of meat in her mouth did her taste buds scream out and she found herself gorging herself again without pause.

"Oh man this is good., I wish momma could cook like this, but then again I'd look like Lori if she did and Matt probably wouldn't like me then all fat and ballooned out from eating so much." Still as Audrey yacked it up on the phone, Retta got down to the business of eating and she coordinated each item into her mouth like a ballerina in practice. She would pile her fork to her macaroni, stuffing a huge amount into her mouth then pivoted it over to the sweet yams for a gulping chomp. She laughed at herself when she imagined how she must have looked eating so wild and hungrily. Not in a million years would she have thought she could enjoy a meal so simply made so much, but then again this was her grandmother. A national born country cook born and bred in the Georgia country side.

Soon she had finished and sat back patting her stomach.

"Retta, you can have the phone now" yelled Audrey from the living room.

Retta got up slowly and left the kitchen and as she passed her mother she noticed that her hair wasn't as neat as before and her clothes were a little disturbed like she had been wrestling herself. As she picked up the phone she noticed it felt really warm.

"Hello, Matt?"

"Yeah, it's me baby" he said happily. She just smiled contently and melted into her chair.

"Oh Matt, I'm sorry about what I said earlier, I didn't mean it, I was just hurt and jealous" she blurted out.

"Hey, it's okay baby, I should be apologizing to you because I was wrong, not you, can you ever forgive me baby?"

"Oh yes, Matt, I love you, you know that and I meant it when I said I don't ever want to be without you!"

"Me too" said Matt eager and elated to be at peace with her once again.

"Oh Matt, I miss you baby, I can't wait till we get home."

"Me either baby, this week has been hell and I need you so bad I could burst."

Retta smiled bashfully to herself thinking of how he probably meant that but then again she felt the same.

"Matt I need you too baby."

"When you coming home Retta?"

"Tomorrow, but I don't know what time."

"Can you find out?"

"Yeah, hold on a minute." She put the phone down and scampered out the door.

"Hey mom can I speak to you a minute?"

Audrey looked at her curiously over her newspaper and grinned when she saw the eagerness written all over Retta face.

"Sometime after breakfast Retta" then she went back to her paper. Retta was caught off guard by her mother's apprehension and anticipation of her question. She just shrugged and went back into the house without further questions. Audrey was grinning to herself when she thought about the perplexed look on Retta's face and she too wanted to see Matt's father and get some things off her chest as well.

"She said tomorrow before lunch Matt."

"Okay, good then we can have at least most of the day together" he said.

"Yeah and I can't wait to get there baby, I'm gonna love you so good your gonna faint" she said laughing.

Matt just crossed his legs and squeezed himself in sweet agony.

"Okay Red, I'll see you soon then."

"Okay baby you be good and I love you."

"Not as much as I love you though."

"Well I guess we'll have to find out then, won't we lover?" she said seductively.

"Yep, I guess so." Retta threw herself on the couch and hugged herself after she hung up. She was back to normal and it felt great.

Life with Matt was a never ending roller coaster of passion and emotion. He was never the same twice nor did she really want him to be and the best part he was all hers for always and forever or she thought.

Matt was finishing the last of the dinner dishes and whistling a happy tune while Ant was on the phone talking to Mel and from what he could tell it was a good conversation meaning there was definitely a booty call in progress.

"Rodney, could you come in here a minute when you're done" yelled his dad.

"Yes sir, I'm just finishing now." Mat slipped off the apron he had on and dried his hands with it then tossed it on the sink and headed to his dad's room.

"Yes sir, you wanted to see me?"

"Yes, have a seat, would you."

Matt could see his dad was preoccupied with something and he gathered it was probably something to do with last night.

"Son, do you remember the agreement we made a long time ago about staying out late and drinking?"

Matt squirmed in his seat and felt a warm clammy rush course through him that made him unconsciously scratch himself. His dad could always bring this out of him with his cool machine like demeanor. Buford always had the cool monotone like voice of a surgeon about to cut into you.

"Yes sir." Matt mumbled with his head down.

"And tell me what did I say about it?"

"You said if I was gonna be out late I should call you and let you know first."

"Right, and what about drinking?"

"You said zero tolerance and that if I did do it, it would have to be at home and then only with your permission."

"And why did I say that?" he pressed, his voice becoming more stern and clipped.

"Because I'm not old enough to drink yet."

"That's right, you're not" he hissed.

"So just what the hell do you think you were doing out till 3:00 a.m. and drinking, not to mention driving!"

"But dad" Matt pleaded but he never got to finish. His father pointed a viscous finger at him and unequally evil look which Matt was sure meant, "shut the fuck up."

"All day I've been trying to think of just what your punishment should be but too many things that would boarder on child abuse come to mind" he said. His voice harsh and his face mere inches from Matt. Matt flinched because he thought he was gonna get hit and when it didn't come he felt relieved and foolish for having done it. Buford backed off and folded his arms. "Look son, I don't mean to lose my temper but you screwed up huge and this isn't like you, now you know I'm a patient man and understanding, so tell me why did you slip up on me?"

Matt started to speak but a croak came out. He quickly cleared his throat.

"Ugh, well dad it's like this, some of the guys and me went over to a party and we didn't know how late it was gonna be, I know I was wrong for drinking but I only had two wine coolers and I fell asleep afterwards, that's why I came home so late. I didn't even try to drive dad until I woke up and then I just came on home by myself. The other guys slept over. You can ask Ant because he went with me to the party."

Buford didn't speak but just listened intently and mused it over in his mind.

"Okay son, so you did use a little caution and responsibility but you still drank without my permission and away from home."

Matt just bowed his head.

"So I'll tell you what; I'll let you choose your punishment" he said with finality.

Matt's head popped up in disbelief and he looked at him as if he hadn't heard him clearly. "That's right son, you decide what I should do, that way you can't say I wasn't fair to you."

Matt thought about this and the more the mulled it over the crazier it sounded. I mean, how can you pass judgment on yourself or break off the switch that gonna beat your own ass? And better still if I come to lightly he may upgrade it worse. Damn! How come he had to ask me to do that. "Can I think about it for a while" he asked sheepishly, almost afraid.

"Yeah, I'll give you that much, I need to go to the store to get a few things, I should be back in about an hour, let me know what you decided then."

Matt just nodded and watched him leave.

"Hey Matt, what was all that about?" said Ant who had been listening.

"I got busted, that's what, dads mad cause I got blitzed at the party and came home late, now he wants me to choose my own punishment."

"Damn, that's fucked up man" said Ant shaking his head.

"So what you gonna do?"

"Hell I don't know but I got an hour to do it."

"I feel for you my man, it sounds like a raw deal."

"Yeah I know, so what do you and Mel have planned for tonight?"

"Oh we might chill at my house, hang out, you know, nothing special."

"So you guys dating now or what?"

"I don't know, I guess, I mean we already done had sex, so it ain't like we don't know each other."

"So you haven't asked her yet then?"

"No, not yet" he said finally.

"Well come on, let me give you a ride to the crib, ain't no tellin how the rest of the day is gonna go so I better take advantage of it now while dads gone."

"Yeah, you're probably right" said Ant.

"It's just a shame this weekend ain't been so good for you, maybe next week will be better, huh?"

"Who knows, let's boogie."

The trip didn't take very long and Matt was back home shortly. He was still sitting around pondering what he should do, but wasn't coming up with anything. When he finally did he just resigned himself to it and relaxed.

"What the fuck, it can't last forever."

Soon the weekend was over and Matt was well into his weekly routine again. He didn't get to see Retta and was hoping he would this week but lately Audrey had been showing up a great deal and he had seen her over at the house at least four times this week. He could see that his dad was beginning to get annoyed by all her attention and it began to weaken his productivity at work as well as his output on his home projects.

Buford didn't say much but just groaned every now and then when Matt told him she had called or was on the phone. He could see that things were beginning to go downhill with them and it was only a matter of time before the shit hit the fan, and then what?

Would this get in his and Aretta's way or would it just blow over and pass them by. Who knows? Just now Matt was busy in math class and suffering badly with his Algebra. He could never really understand the real difference between an integer and any other rational number and it was giving him hell.

Every so often he would look up to see Tonya staring blankly at him with her head on her hand and toying with her pencil. She had finished her board work long ago and just day dreamed awhile.

"Oh great, that's all I need, her staring at me, I got it bad enough without her screwing with my head, but then again I'm safe cause we put that baby to bed long ago so I ain't worried."

Just then Matt had an idea.

"Psst, hey Tonya" he whispered.

She came out of her daze in slow motion and reoriented on him. She gave him a warm smile when he called her.

"Yes Matt."

"Hey sweet pea, I'm having a fit with this math, can you give me any hints on this stuff."

"Sure, I'd be glad to" she said looking around to see if the teacher was looking.

She wasn't, so she eased out of her chair and crouched as she crept over to him.

"What are you having trouble with?"

"This stuff" Matt said pointing at his paper.

She took a minute to look over his method of solving it.

"Okay Matt, you're on the right track by finding the unknown signed numbers and working out those in parentheses first, now you have to do the same for the other signed numbers and reiterate your prior answers into the last."

Matt was listening closely but found it hard. Her fresh smelling perfume was intoxicating and made his heart thump. She looked so damn beautiful squatting down like that. She had her hair done in a reversed mushroom and curled all around and each golden strand glistened in the glowing sunlight.

She wore a modest silk blouse of gold and plaid skirt with gold, red and green squares. She was the perfect debutante he thought and would someday be the perfect teacher if she decided to be. But for now he just lost himself in her sinfully sweet essence and began daydreaming.

"So do you understand now how to do it Matt?" she said looking up at him with those piercing smoke grey eyes.

Matt felt like he was slipping and falling into a sweet oblivion as her glowing eyes and heady scent absorbed him like a sponge. He wanted to kiss her and she knew it. She wanted it too but something wouldn't let her. She slowly lowered her gaze and blushed, then quietly went back to her seat. Once there she looked down at her book not really reading it but using it to avoid Matt's magnetic stare that she knew would draw her back to him with hungry arms and that wouldn't work.

When the bell finally rang signaling the end of the period, Tonya bolted from her seat and out the door and several students were surprised at this because they knew her to be a quiet and controlled person, never loud or brash like other around her.

Matt basically went through the rest of the day in a fog and couldn't wait to get home. He was glad there was no practice today and would use it to get some much needed home work done as well as rap with Retta on the phone for awhile.

On the other side of town Retta was having her own troubles and was just about fed up with everyone. She had been picked by the principle along with several others to form a student tutor group. It would help a lot of students during school hours pull up their grades and was comprised of honor roll students like her. She was helping a guy with his English and the boy was more interested in her legs than her aid.

"Will you pay attention!" she said for the third time and crossing her legs.

Retta was wearing the outfit Matt bought her and everyone liked it. It showed off her legs nicely and she got many whistles from the guys. Some made her blush, others just became a nuisance. "Look Carlos, if you keep on acting up I'm going to let you hack it out by yourself."

"Okay, okay baby, chill, I was just messing around a little, lighten up."

"My name ain't baby, its Aretta and for your information I'm already spoken for so you can just chill out Rover."

The boy just laughed and slid down in his seat more slouching like a bag of laundry.

"Okay teach, I getcha."

"Good, now let's get back to your math work, you only have another ten minutes then I have to go."

Taking her advice he sat up more attentive now and got back to work with no more comments about her legs.

Soon the bell rang and the last period of the day had begun. All through the halls people went running and screaming down the corridors to their lockers or other places unknown. Retta just collected her books and set out for her spot outside on the wall but then as she got to the door she felt dry and thirsty and went down the hall towards the snack machines by the teachers lounge. She saw several people collected around the huge trophy case at the end of the hall and wondered what was up because all of them had a sad subdued look about their faces.

She spotted her little friend from Jr. High and walked over to her.

"Hey girl, what's up?" she said smiling.

"Oh, hey Retta, how's that man of yours?"

"Oh he's fine I guess, I haven't had much time with him this past week."

"Oh I'm sorry to hear that, is he sick or something?"

"No he's just into a lot these days and being on the Varsity Track Team takes up a lot of his time too."

"Varsity track team?" the girl repeated curiously.

"Hey wait a minute, I thought you two were both freshman?"

"We are."

"So how'd he get on the senior team then?"

Retta smiled proudly.

"Talent dear heart, pure talent."

The girl just frowned in surprise and nodded her approval.

"So he's fast on his feet, how's he do in bed?" she asked with a seductive grin.

"Ooh Shawn, you know better than that" protested Aretta.

"Aw girl come on, now you know everybody's been curious about him since day one, the least you could do is give a little gossip to your old girlfriend."

Retta just smiled disbelieving and shook her head.

"Girl I don't believe you, and since when did you ever get interested in other people's sex lives?" "You're still a virgin."

Shawn drew back and pivoted on her hips saucily and gave Retta one of those "girl please" looks.

"Hey, I may be small but it don't mean I don't get the itch and let me tell you something else" she said moving her neck side to side and snapping her fingers in Retta's face.

"You know Mark Watkins on the basketball team?"

"Yeah the junior point guard, right?"

"Yeah that's him." Then she smiled.

Retta just put her hand to her mouth in mock surprise.

"Yeah honey, that's right, he's just the right size to scratch my itch."

Retta just laughed.

"You go on girl" she said.

"So Shawn, what's up with all these people, they look mad?"

"Oh, you didn't know?"

"No. what's up?"

"Well they was caught smoking pot behind the lunchroom by a teacher and now they're waiting to see the principle."

"They'll never learn" said Retta.

"Hey, well it's been good seeing you again Retta, but I gotta go before I get busted by the bell." "Oh okay, I'll holler at you later on, okay."

"Okay and tell Rodney I said hi."

"Will do" she said then reached into her purse for some change for a Sprite. Once she got her drink she headed out the door. She was thinking about how she could get over to see Matt but couldn't come up with anything.

"I guess he'll have to come over to see me or call" she thought and eased herself up on the wall to roost. While she sat nursing her drink she allowed her mind to wander in a sweet day dream. The iridescent shimmer off her drink can served as a hypnotizing medium that opened up a hidden world of colors and patterns, shapes and sounds and sitting in the middle of it was her and Matt. She could see herself and him in a Greek statuesque position holding each other in a warm embrace. They were nude and sat upon a tiny grassy island in the middle of nothingness. It was like all time and space had fallen away to leave the two lovers alone and together in this mysterious and tranquil oblivion of silence.

Oh, how good it felt to be there like that with him and it made her stir inside.

"Oh Matt, is it possible that love could be any better than this" she heard her pseudo self say and then as if on cue she began to orient on herself drawing closer to her and seeing all the fine curves and lines of both their Grecian bodies.

Matt moved his hand from her waist to reveal a small but noticeable bulge in her tummy. At first she didn't believe it but then it grew and became more pronounced and Aretta saw herself reaching out to touch her semblance who hadn't shown the least concern but only stared completely enraptured into Matt eyes. Just as she came within finger tip distance the loud ring of the school bell brought her back to present. She shook her head to clear her mind and recover herself then looked down and noticed she was resting her hand on her own tummy. She quickly removed it bashful and surprised at herself for losing herself like that again.

"Damn, I gotta see my baby."

Matt didn't waste any time heading home. He made sure to park his bike over at the boys school by the gym during lunch so he could make a hasty retreat after school. Ant was hanging out talking to Cher when he whizzed by and they yelled after him but was not heard.

"I need to get this house done before pop gets home" he thought "cause he said Audrey and him was gonna hang out tonight, maybe she'll bring Retta. God knows I miss her and I ain't had no time with her in a long time. Man I'll be glad when dad takes me off this punishment.

I ain't getting any younger and sitting home all week is burning me out not to mention my sex life. Dam! I can't wait to see my baby."

Matt pulled on the throttle and zipped past the bustling mass of students and cars. He wasn't slowing down for anyone and just blew his tiny horn waving people out of the way. Soon he was out of the area and on his way to the house.

Chapter 16

Love and Happiness

"Hey Cher, how's about letting me get a ride home with you and Mel since Matt done hauled ass on me."

"Sure Ant, do you wanna go to his house or home?"

"I need to get home, I got some things to do, I'll run by his place later."

"Okay then, Mel should be here soon" said Cher.

"Bump, Bump, there she is now" she said pointing.

Ant and Cher ran down the drive to meet her. Instead of letting her get caught up in the traffic on campus.

"Yo, what's up Mel?" said Ant jumping in.

"You lover" she said then gave him a kiss.

"Where's Matt?"

"Oh, he jet a little while ago."

"Oh, I see" she said backing up.

"Well maybe he had something important to do and couldn't wait."

"Yeah, and I'll bet her name is Aretta" said Cher sarcastically.

"Well wouldn't you be if the last time you had sex was over a week ago" said Ant defending him.

"Hell he's been on punishment since last weekend."

"Well he can always hang with me" offered Cher.

"Me too" thought Mel.

"Well you guys had your shot, now you have to chill, you guys don't know how much you've compromised him that day and he really didn't have to do you guys."

"Oh, come on Ant" shot Mel. "He wanted it as much as we did."

"Yeah, but how many times has he fought you guys off?" Neither girl spoke but just nodded.

"I thought so" said Ant proudly. "So you girls gotta chill on that and give the man room, you know he loves both of you but he can't diss his girl like that anymore than he would you if he was dating one of you guys."

"What do you mean he loves us?" said Cher surprised and off guard.

"Yeah he does, he told me so, why, does that surprise you?"

Neither spoke.

"Well it shouldn't, cause Matt don't just jump on any girl who comes his way, if he did both of you woulda been laid several times long ago, so consider yourselves special, cause to him you are."

Mel bashfully looked over at Cher to see what she thought about this. Cher just worked on a nail looking away out her window.

"Okay Ant" said Mel finally.

"We'll be cool."

"Good, now let's head to my crib."

Audrey was busy pressing out a grid of zipper patterns on her machine and thinking about getting off soon. She had been buzzing all day in anticipation of seeing Buford tonight. She had seen him 3 times that week already but was still driven to see him again. She was a woman unchained and her desires and passions for him would not be denied one bit.

Oh sure, Buford had tactfully tried to put some space between them and slow down the number of visits she made but Audrey would just blithely laugh it off, saying, "Oh Buford you're such a tease" and then ignore it.

Buford on the other hand was not amused and it began to irk him that she would not respect his wishes and give him some room to breathe. He was long ago over taxed by her sexual appetite and sensual attentions. It was beginning to draw on his nerves mentally and physically. In fact just last week she interrupted an important meeting he was having with a local small business man.

They were discussing Buford becoming his permanent accountant, when all of a sudden Audrey showed up unannounced. She didn't try to be a nuisance but she didn't allow them much privacy and consideration either. She would sit between them and do little feminine things to distract Buford like occasionally crossing her legs which she exposed to the thigh or a casual teasing of his leg with an aggressive stroke to let him know that the business at hand wasn't nearly as attractive as the proposition she proposed.

Both men were not blind to her innuendos or very impressed. The gentleman was getting annoyed with her constant interruptions and suggestive intentions. He decided that this wasn't in his best interest and cut the meeting short in order to give Buford a chance to take care of his other business. Buford didn't like this very much but didn't let it show. He had yet to finish his pitch to the man and was more than vexed at this interruption. He tried to get the man to stay but he was already on his feet and preparing to leave.

Buford offered his apologies and the man shook his hand and said he would contact him again in the near future to finish their business. Buford didn't want him to go but couldn't deny that he couldn't wait for him to leave so he could fix his little problem. He walked the man to his car and hurried to return to the little fly in his ointment. He was rehearsing what he was going to say to her in his mind. But when he got back in the house he found her standing in the dim light of his room in the most revealing and seductive teddy he had ever seen!

The sight of her standing there and the look on her face quickly made him forget what he was going to say and he completely forwent his reprimand. He had tried to show his disdain and displeasure in her blatant interruption through his love making but it was misinterpreted as being lust and only worked to fuel Audrey's unquenchable desire. Now she was really on him and her body tingled all over and the mere thought of him made her sweat!

Her juices were flowing freely as the vision took hold and the living fantasy gained ground. It didn't help at all that she was currently at work and trying to do her job. She was beginning to perspire and kept shifting in her seat even though the plant was a comfortable 72 degrees. Her mind and body was in torment as she felt more than envisioned every thrust and drive of him on her enflamed body. She began to lose her focus more and more with each passing second. Her friend Pat had noticed her odd behavior and her pale moist skin. She worked right behind her at the next station and could see the perspiration at the nap of her neck and the way her hair was beginning to stick to it. She looked at her watch and saw that a break was due in about five minutes so she decided to shut down her machine early and go take Audrey out for some fresh air. Audrey on the other hand was in the throes of the most mind blowing fantasy she had ever had in her adult life so far.

She and Buford were on the tip of a sun baked, outcropping of a mountainous rock formation in the middle of nowhere. They were making mad passionate love under and scorching desert sun. She could see and feel the hot sweat trickling off their bodies in her mind's eye. The scene was hot and sultry as hell! The sound and feel of his hips slamming into her and punishing her body was lurid-sweet torture. Her legs were spread as wide as she could get them and Buford drove into them with a fierce machine-like force that shook her to the core. She bit him and sucked his ears, neck and lips hungrily with each impact. The blinding rays of light flashed in her eyes and made for an eerie but erotic experience, soon his movements became even stronger and wilder and she could tell he was reaching his climax and so was she.

Audrey clinched down hard on him and his member as she felt him expand inside her. Oh, how decadent she felt and started licking his chest and neck lasciviously as he worked her like a well oiled machine.

Pat watched her closely now because she had put down her work and grabbed the corners of her table and squeezed like she was experiencing a labor pain. She drew closer and more concerned about her friend who was exhibiting the oddest and most alarming behavior she had ever seen it a person who wasn't sick or about to die. Audrey was really feeling it now and the rapid clenching of her body around Buford's rapid moving hips. Her breathing grew labored and she half moaned half screamed with each passing sweet second.

"Oh, how I feel you inside me baby . . . don't stop . . . don't ever stop!" she begged.

Just then Pat reached out and touched Audrey on the shoulder. The contact was so sudden and unexpected that it crossed the boundary of fantasy and her dream. Audrey whipped her head back savagely and moaned aloud as wave upon wave of orgasm wracked her body.

"Ahh! SSSS ahhhhh!" she half screamed in a low strained voice.

"Audrey are you alright?" asked Pat starting to panic.

"OOHH! SSSS OH! SSS damn!" she moaned doubling over and starting to laugh.

She crossed her legs quickly and guarded like she was trying to hide herself from the eyes of someone.

Pat was really concerned now and held onto her arm which was for some reason very warm to the touch.

"Audrey are you okay? what's the matter girl?"

Audrey just kept laughing and turned a deep red from the neck up. Finally the bell for noon break had sounded and everyone started milling outside for a smoke. Some of the women in Audrey's area passed her and gave perplexed looks as they passed. They couldn't figure why she was laughing so hard and figured whatever it was had to be a doozey!

Pat just shrugged at them and returned their concerns. Finally she came under control and playfully smacked Pats hand away.

"Girl have you done gone crazy or something?"

Audrey just whipped the tears from her eyes still smiling.

"It's your fault if I am" she said finally catching her breath.

"What do you mean my fault? I ain't done nothing to your ass."

"Yes you did" she said looking up at her, eyes still wet from laughing to tears.

"You made me mess myself up."

"How! I ain't been near you till now."

"Well you did."

Pat scratched her head.

"Maybe you better explain yourself Audrey, you got me all confused now!"

"Okay but not here, let's go to the bathroom." Both women shuffled to the bathroom quickly. "Okay talk girl" demanded Pat leaning against the door, her arms folded.

"Well you see, I was having this day dream about Buford and me making out in the desert." "Mmm hmm . . . go on."

"Girl it was powerful! I could feel it for real and it was so hot too!"

"Mmm hmm" she said beginning to smile from ear to ear.

"Well just about the time we were gonna climax, you touched me and I just went all over myself right then and there!"

Pat's mouth fell open and a wild spark of surprise came in her eyes as she studied Audrey up and down.

"OOH Audrey . . . you ought to be ashamed of yourself!"

Audrey just smiled and shrugged innocently.

"Girl, how can you be getting off like that at work when the rest of us can't?"

"Hey get your own dream lover, mine is on Vineville Avenue and I'm gonna relive it again as soon as I can, but this time for *REAL!*"

"He's that good is he?" asked Pat interested, and sounding a little doubtful and jealous at the same time.

"Girl, NO! he's better than that, and I'm talking a *PIPE* dream honey!" She said then drew her hands apart to show how he measured up.

"Damn! Audrey, he's all that?"

"You better believe it and honey that mailman can deliver!"

Pat just laughed at her.

"Okay, Audrey just so long as you don't over *extend* yourself, cause even a man gets tired and worn out if you work him too much."

Audrey just lightly waved her off and went into a stall.

"Aw girl please, the man's insatiable and he loves it, you should see how he is when we're together . . . it's a wonder I can walk afterwards!"

"Okay, fifi, just remember what I said cause I'd hate to see you lose a good man because you were greedy" she said then turned and left.

Audrey thought about this for a minute trying to figure if she ever noticed any displeasure in him at her constant unplanned visits.

"Nah! Buford loves me and he knows I love him, he couldn't possibly be tiring of me I just know it."

Soon the day had ended and the crowd headed for the parking lot in a hasty retreat. Everyone wanted to be the first out of the parking lot and ever since Buford fixed Audrey's car she had no problems getting off with a quick start. This alone was worth the long trips across town to see him. Every time she had the urge she would show him her gratitude as well as her fiery affection.

Retta was busy doing some home work and trying not to think about Matt but it was difficult. She had just gotten off the phone with him awhile ago and discussed his dads and her moms plan to get together tonight. She wanted to see him but wouldn't try to push her mother to let her because she knew how Audrey was always harping on their relationship and how much time they spent together. It wasn't fair and she had no right getting between her and Matt and then running off to see his dad like some love starved teeny-bopper.

"Just what the heck does she think she's trying to prove? She wouldn't even know his dad if it wasn't for us being together, it's just not fair!" Soon Retta was jarred from her angry retrospect by a knock on the door.

"Who is it!" she yelled.

"It's me Frieda, open up"

"Oh great, I don't feel like being bugged today, I wonder what she wants." Lori go get the door please."

Lori got up from playing with her dolls and shuffled to the door.

"Hi Frieda" she said opening the door.

"What's up kiddo, where's Retta?"

"In the bedroom" she said pointing.

"Hey Retta you busy?"

"Well yeah in a way . . . why what's on your mind?"

"Oh, nothing I just thought you might wanna rap awhile" she said plopping down on her bed. Retta just sighed aloud and gave up on her home work, tossing her pen on the desk.

"So what's been up with you and Curt?"

"Oh not much be been just hanging around a little"

Retta noticed that she fidgeted with her hands a little more than normal and didn't look at all at ease with herself.

"Is there something you wanna tell me?"

Frieda didn't say anything but just gave her a look of relief that said she was glad Retta thought to ask.

"Lori how's about going outside awhile and let me and Frieda rap okay?"

"Aww! Retta I don't wanna, I can stay if I want to" she said pouting and folding her arms.

Retta didn't speak but gave her an evil piercing look that made Lori think . . . "Maybe I'd better go after all" and just got up angrily and went.

"Your mean!" she spat before heading out the door.

"Okay, what done crawled up your butt now?" asked Retta getting comfortable.

Frieda just bowed her head.

"You know it's funny that you would say that cause I think I may be pregnant."

"YOU'RE WHAT? . . . how? when? . . . have you been tested yet?"

"NO, but I'm late"

"How late?"

"About three days"

"Oh god, Frieda! What happened? Didn't you have your pills? . . . and what about Curt? . . . did he wear a condom?"

"Yes!"

"Then how did it happen?"

"Don't yell at me Retta! I'm scared enough as it is"

"Okay, I'm sorry but what happened?"

"It broke somehow I guess" she said looking down and picking at her shirt tail.

"You mean it sprung a leak!"

"No, I mean it broke"

"How Frieda, condoms don't break they leak unless he used an old one?"

"No, I was with him when he bought them"

"So how did it break?"

"I told you Retta, I don't know, all I know is I was so nervous when he got between my legs I started to cum even before he put it in and once he started to do that I got so excited at the way it felt that I just lost it and threw myself on him!"

"Damn! Frieda, you couldn't have waited a minute to get adjusted to it?"

"No! I was just so hot and wanted it!"

Retta just sat back smiling at her. She wanted to laugh but it wasn't quite that kind of matter even though the situation could have called for it.

"And let me tell you something, when I felt that big thang of his rip into me I wanted to die!" "Felt that good huh?" she said grinning now and thinking about her and Matt's first time.

"No! it hurt like hell!"

"Frieda are you still a virgin?" she asked surprised.

"Not anymore, I ain't but I was" she said laughing and crossing her legs guardedly.

"I thought you gave up that booty long ago."

"No! girl, I kept telling you I wasn't screwing around . . . why you didn't believe me?" she said kind of hurt.

"Well would you believe me if I flirted all the time and jumped at every guy I saw?"

"No, I guess not"

"Okay then!"

There was a long silence between them now and neither knew quite what to say or do. This was definitely a new experience and a definite surprise to say the least.

"So . . . um did you like it? I mean was it what you expected it to be?" she asked sheepishly.

"Well kinda" said Frieda awkwardly.

"Once the pain went away it felt okay, but damn! I didn't think he would be so big!"

"Well girl, one of these days you'll be glad he is, because let me tell you, there's nothing like the feeling you get from a well hung man!" said Retta more than animated and fanning herself. "Yeah maybe you're right, but there's no embarrassment so great as a well rounded belly too." Retta had to nod at this and her merriment quickly died. Frieda shook her head and buried her face in her hands and sobbed.

"Oh, Retta what am I gonna do?" she cried as warm tears ran down her face. Retta was as confused as she was and could only sit silent and hurt right along with her. She eased over and placed a gentle hand on her back and stroked her softly while she wept.

"Come on Frieda it'll be alright . . . maybe your just late for some other reason"

"Okay what?" she said between sobs.

"I've never been late before"

"Well you've also always been a virgin before too" she countered trying to offer her some solace. "So then I am pregnant then?" she sobbed louder.

"Now hold on, we don't know for sure . . . it could be anything like when I was in the hospital . . . remember that?"

"Yes, sniff, sniff"

"Okay then, so don't give up yet, you might not be" she said trying hard to console her but then again not feeling too sure herself.

"Let's give it some time Frieda, I'm sure it's going to turn out to be nothing, besides no body I ever heard of ever got pregnant the first time around."

"Is that true?" she said looking up with tear stained eyes and all the hope in the world that this was true.

"Yes, that's what I been hearing from all the girls."

"Yeah like who?"

Retta thought for a minute and feeling the sharp sting of her best friends eyes on her.

"Okay how about Jessica Taylor!"

"Who?"

"You know, *Jiggling Jessie*" that girl in Gym who came up from Alabama last year."

"Yeah what about her?"

"Well she got it on with Fredrick Jackson for a long time and didn't get pregnant till about two months after they started dating."

"How does that prove when she started having sex?" "She could have just started right before getting pregnant just like me!"

"No, I'm sure cause she used to brag about how big he was and how he used to eat her out and stuff."

Frieda didn't quite know what to say to that and hoped that what she was hearing was true but still felt in her gut that there was just no way that her luck was gonna fair the same way. Retta could see the cloudiness in her friends mind and heart and only wanted to ease her fears if but for a moment.

"Let's give it some time Frieda okay? I'm sure it's going to turn out to be nothing"

"Okay . . . if you say so" she said nodding slowly and whipping her face.

"But I'm not so sure and I'm still scared" she injected.

"Well what about Curt . . . does he know?"

"No, I haven't had the chance to tell him yet"

"Well, I think you ought to just to see what he says."

"Oh Retta, what if he gets mad and don't want me no more!" she said almost in a whisper tears flowing again freely.

"Well then fuck him, and to hell with him, if any man gets a woman pregnant and don't help to take care his child and his responsibilities then he's a no good dog and you don't need him anyway!" spat Retta in a most heated and venomous tirade.

Frieda couldn't believe what she had just heard and her mouth fell open like a trap door. She had never heard Retta speak so in all the years she has ever known her. And to be spewing such poison about the man she loved and may be pregnant by was earth shaking.

Problem was Retta was right, so she really couldn't fault her for saying what was right.

"Do I have a choice?" she heard herself whisper.

"No"

"So I guess I'll tell him then" she said wringing her hands nervously.

BAM BAM BAM!

"Now who could that be? . . . *Who is it?*"

"It's me momma, open the door my hands are full!"

Retta jumped off the bed and ran to the door.

Frieda dashed into the bathroom to wash her face.

"Good lord momma, what's with all these bags?"

"Oh, I stopped at the store and the cleaners on my way home, I got a new outfit for tonight when we go over to Buford's house."

"WE?" chirped Retta elated hoping it wasn't a slip of the tongue.

"Yes, we!" darling daughter. I know you haven't seen Rodney in awhile cause he's been on house restriction for awhile, so I thought it would be nice to surprise him, since me and Buford are going to the movies tonight. Retta just hugged her mother wildly.

"Hey hey! Your mushing up my chiffon dress, relax dear heart!"

"Oh, I'm sorry I was just so glad you said, "WE" were going out!"

"Well you can relax because it's not an over-nighter like last time, no tonight is a school night and we're just gonna have a nice time out at the movies . . . nothing more."

"Okay" she said a little deflated.

"So who's in the bath room?"

"Frieda"

"Hello Frieda!"

"Hi Audrey" she said coming out toweling her face and hands.

"How's your mom doing?"

"Oh, she's fine, she's at home talking to my dad on the phone."

"That's nice, tell her I said hello okay?"

"Okay" she said kind of subdued and trying to hide it.

Retta looked at her and could still see the pain she was feeling and tried to smile and nodded to her. Frieda dropped the towel on the chair and headed out the door. She turned her head and quickly nodded to Retta to follow. Retta got the signal and quickly helped her mother put her bags in her room then ran back to the door.

"What?"

"Retta you gotta help me through this mess okay?"

"Alright, just keep quiet and don't tell anyone else about it."

"Are you crazy!" who would I tell but you and Curt?"

"Nobody I hope, but you have a big mouth so I don't know"

"Well I ain't talking" said Frieda adamant and staunch.

"Good! Now go home and call him and tell him and I'll get with you later okay?" "Okay . . . thanks Retta, you really are my best and only friend you know that don't you?"

Retta let a small disarming grin cross her lips as he knew this but liked to hear it anyway. She reached out to her and hugged her neck and lightly pecked her on the temple.

"Yeah and your mine too . . . now go on home, it's gonna be okay!"

Frieda smiled weakly at her as she slowly descended the stairs.

On the other side of town Buford was in his room at his desk finishing some final touches on some late income tax forms for one of his clients. This one was an amended form and had lots of itemizations on it. He worked on the many figures effortlessly and barely touched his adding machine as he whizzed through the numerical soup.

Matt stood behind him holding a cup of hot coffee for him. He marveled at his father's mental control of the vast number sets and endless figures and personal information that could quickly change a four digit figure into a six in a New York minute. He was surrounded by piles of pink forms, blue forms and booklets that he referred to frequently to get the spin on the law about this or that.

Matt just shook his head and wondered if he would ever have to do any of this stuff for himself when he got older.

"Here you go dad" he said breaking his own silence and handing him the cup.

"Oh thanks son . . . preciate it" he said reaching for it and taking a healthy sip.

"So what's all this for dad?" he asked gesturing towards the mountain of papers, computer printouts and spreadsheets.

"Well this is an assets and liabilities breakdown of that guy I had that meeting with earlier this week, he owns and operates several 7-11's and that dry cleaner's over on Ingleside"

"Wow! he's got it going on don't he?" said Matt impressed.

"Yes, I guess you could say that, in fact he's got a couple of accountants that he has work on all this stuff for him." "Right about now he needs a replacement because he's been noticing some odd figures and things not adding up on some of his ledgers, he has been noticing a loss of money from time to time."

"Somebody's stealing from him?"

"Yes, that's the way it looks and since he's so busy and doesn't want to shake the tree until he's sure he asked me would I go over the books for him."

Matt just nodded in agreement and was even more impressed now.

"So how'd he get wind of you and that you could do this for him?" "I mean you don't actually do any advertising and a guy like him I'm sure can have his pick of any CPA in town."

"Well that's true, but like I tried to teach you and your brothers . . . if you build a better mouse trap . . . people will beat a path to your door."

Matt thought about the analogy and nodded.

"Yeah that's true"

"And my prices are more reasonable than most and that alone helps to boost my notoriety and word of mouth."

"So how much you plan on pulling down from this little project?"

"Oh around $20 bucks and hour."

"What? Man you could clean up!"

"Yep it's not too shabby when you consider most CPA's make about thirty or forty dollars an hour."

"Couldn't you charge more and still not be as high as the others?"

"Yeah, I could but my plan is to secure him as a client." "By that I mean I won't charge him nearly as much as the others, so I will be sure to get his business."

"So this is more like a favor or you baiting him?"

"Now you got it."

"So have you found anything yet that looks out of place or odd?"

"Yeah I have, hand me that printout over there" he said pointing to a stack on his couch.

Matt handed him a long thick computer printout full of figures.

"You see this figure here for $36,000 dollars?"

"Yes sir"

"Well is should be $52,000, you see this is his Net Expenditures column or what his average spending per quarter for supplies is and this is his gross expenditures for the year." "You follow so far?"

"Yes sir"

"Okay this is broken down to show how much was spent and how much he actually bought." "From what I can see he's spent more than he should have for what he actually has in inventory." Matt was a little confused and his dad could see it was probably getting over his head.

"Wait a minute, you say he bought this much with this much money right?"

"Yes"

"Well wouldn't there be some kind of difference if his people was using the stuff?"

"You're on the right track, but the problem isn't in what was used, it's in what was actually ordered as opposed to what was spent." "Somewhere his managers reported having bought a certain amount of goods for a certain amount of money, the trick is they over quoted on the amount because they didn't buy it but wanted to reflect that they did" he said looking at Matt to see if he got the concept.

Matt's eyes rolled around for a second then he smiled.

"Okay I get it . . . it's like a foot ball play where the quarter back pretends to draw back to throw so it will make the other team draw back but actually it's a deception and hands it off to a runner." "Yep you got it . . . that is what is known as Embezzlement and you can go to jail for a long time for that."

"So how much more do you gotta do before your done?"

"Oh, not much I just need to go over his reports for a ten year period to see just how much and when it started to slide into the negative." "I could be finished by tomorrow but with Audrey constantly bugging me all the time I can't get much work done."

"Yeah I noticed that."

"In fact I almost lost this guys business because of her arrogant interruption the other day."

"Matt nodded in agreement and frowned as he looked down shuffling his foot nervously."

"I don't know son, your friends mom is becoming much more than I can deal with now and frankly I'm just not cut out for all her attentions sometimes."

Matt grinned to himself and felt his face flush warm with embarrassment at his dad's description of Audrey's animalistic behavior. He'd noticed her increase in visits too and his dad's growing irritation of it. Even though he never said anything about it till now.

"So what are you gonna do dad?"

"Well we're supposed to get together for a movie tonight, I'll try to talk to her then, if I can't get through to her and she doesn't listen then I'll have to call it all off and just let her go."

"I see" said Matt looking away and sounding a little deflated.

Buford noticed his son's displeasure at the thought of their breaking up and the ramifications it may hold for him and his girl.

"Look son I know how you feel about your girl and I'm sure if it came to that nothing would happen to you two, I mean that would be childish for her to pull you guys apart or hinder your relationship because we can't make it so don't worry okay?"

"Okay" he said less than reassured.

"Hey I better get diner on, I'll be leaving in an hour or so" he said looking at his watch.

"So what do you feel like eating?" he asked.

"Don't worry bout diner dad I'm not that hungry and I can just grab a sandwich of something." "Are you sure?"

"Yeah I'm sure."

"Okay then I'll tell you what . . . how about I just whip up some French bread and spaghetti, that way if you do get hungry you'll have something to stick to your ribs, plus I'll have something for lunch tomorrow."

"Okay dad that sounds fine" said Matt agreeing to it.

An hour or so later Audrey, Retta and Lori were piling in the car getting ready to leave. It was now 7:30 and they had a date for 8:00 o'clock. Audrey looked luscious in her Jordache jeans and a red silk blouse with two large pockets in front. Retta thought she looked quite girlish and fresh out of college.

"So you gonna be back late or what?" asked Retta sheepishly trying to gauge her mothers evening. Seeing this Audrey just cut her eyes at her sharply.

"Well if I do! You can bet I'll call but don't count on it . . . it's just a movie and a light dinner then maybe a few drinks after."

Retta opened her mouth to speak but thought better of it and remained silent. Audrey was bad about changing things in mid flight but this was defintelney a change. All she was aware of hours ago was a movie. Now it's a full blown evening with drinks and dinner. If she knew anything about her mother and she did, sex wasn't too far behind.

"Now while we're out I want you two to behave and not get into anything" she said pointing at the two of them. Lori just pouted and looked at Retta like it was always her fault.

"That means no arguing, fighting, or gambling" she said cuffing Lori's chin lightly and smiling at her. She just grinned and dropped her head blushing.

"We won't momma" said Retta trying to look innocent and virtuous.

"Good! Cause you too have been at each other all week and it's time to stop and as for you Aretta!" she said stabbing her finger into her nose so quickly it made Retta take a deep breath and cross her eyes.

"Keep your shirt on . . . get me?" she said scowling at her.

Retta caught the hint and just turned away to stare out the window.

"Yes ma'am" she said softly and dejected.

Soon Audrey was pulling into Buford's drive way and the anticipation both women felt was getting the best of them and they couldn't wait to get out of the car and into the arms of the men they loved.

Inside the house Buford was just finishing some last minute primping in the mirror. He was patting and combing his slightly receded crew-cut hair style. He had worn it this way for years even before he joined the army over 30 years ago. He primped one last time and headed for his closet to get his coat.

"Knock, knock, knock!"

"Rodney could you get that?" he shouted from his room.

"Yes sir I got it!" he said running to the living room from the den in his sock feet. He slid across the floor purposefully for the hell of it then trotted across the living room floor to open the door. "Hello Rodney" said Audrey as he jerked it open. Matt's eyes quickly scanned her voluptuous girlish body as he tried to suppress a haughty, *"DAMMNNN! BABY!"* that was building deep in his throat. The bulge in his crotch quickly told Audrey what he thought of her jeans and how nice she filled them. She just grinned and walked on by tapping him lightly on the head as if to say "Good boy . . . now sit!" She headed for his dad's room to see what rise she could get out of him. Retta was not as amused at her mother and also had seen his rise to her mother's occasion. He tried to hide it but it more than showed in his loose gym shorts. He paled considerably and tried to smile it off hoping she was glad to see him and wouldn't chastise for his little indiscretion. Retta just stood there in the door with her arms folded and a look that could freeze lava.

Lori was standing there also, just looking on and grinning big waiting for her chance to say hello to Matt.

Matt slowly lowered his head knowing what was to come.

"SMACK!" right up side the head, she wacked him sharply but not too harshly.

"Ow! What was that for?" he said raising his head and acting dumb.

"You know damn well what for!" she hissed trying not to be over heard.

"Next time you lose control and go reckless eyeballing my mom or anybody else for that matter, I'm gonna knock your eyes out then cut it off and stuff it in your damn ear understand?"

"Yeah babe . . . uh sure I understand" he said rubbing his sore head.

Retta then reached up as swiftly and kissed him then walked on in. Lori waved at him smiling innocently as she came in. She stopped at the door and motioned him with her little finger to come down so she could whisper to him.

"Can you do that trick again?" she asked innocently and eagerly.

"What trick?" asked Matt wondering what he could have done that looked anything like a trick besides keep his head while Retta attempted to knock it off.

"That trick where you made you pants jump" she said pointing at his crotch aggressively. Matt flashed white hot with embarrassment and doubled over almost slipping on the slick wooden floor and crashing to the floor.

"Uh Lori, did I tell you that we bought some new ice cream this week?" he said trying to side step and distract her.

"Why don't you go into the kitchen and look in the freezer it's just inside the door."

"Okey dokey!" she said happily and skipped off to the kitchen.

Soon as she was gone Matt dashed across the hall into his room. His only thought was to take off those damn shorts before they got him into even more trouble.

After awhile Buford and Audrey left and Lori, Matt and Retta were huddled on the couch watching television or at least Lori was. Matt was busy snaking his hands into Retta's shirt and trying to move as slowly as possible. He didn't want to draw Lori's attention and blow his chance to cop a feel of Retta's soft spongy breasts. She just sighed with anticipation and pleasure as he found his mark and began slowly rolling her eager little nipple between his thumb and forefinger. She squirmed a little as the fie in her breast was ignited. She breathed harder and churned her hips the more he did it.

Soon the sweet urgency of her loins began to kick in and she was slipping away with each passing second. She tried keeping an eye on Lori as well but it was hard with the splendid torch Matt was putting on her budding nipple. She could hardly keep her eyes open. She finally just gave up and languished in the sensuality of his touch. If Lori asked any questions she would lie and say she asked Matt to scratch her.

Matt was beginning to get a little warm himself and moved his other hand slowly around her waist to make a stab at getting into her zipper.

Oh! The sweet anguish of it all. Matt was on fire now as he imagined the velvety feel of her soft silky pubic hairs and even silkier moistness further down. Retta tried to accommodate him and help his efforts by inching upward to shorten the distance between her crotch and his hand once she became aware of his intentions. All this was taking place right under Lori's nose who as usual was oblivious to all once placed in front of a television and given something to eat.

Retta finally had had enough and couldn't hold her desire anymore. She could feel Matt's manhood bulging against her back as she leaned across his lap to give him as much access as she could without giving away their activity. She just had to have him!.

"Lori, me and Matt are going to listen to some music for a while" she said tapping his arm to remove it so she could get up.

"Okay" she said not even turning to see them go.

"Just help yourself to what ever you want Lori" said Matt just before Retta jerked him around the corner and into his room.

"Lock the door Matt and hurry up and get over here!" "You done got me started now and it's been way too long since I had steak." Matt grinned to himself and almost laughed at her comment but he was also on a starvation diet from her for some time and couldn't wait to gorge himself on her smorgasborge of a body also. Matt was way ahead of her, he quickly dashed over to the stereo to put in his favorite love tape. All the while never taking his eyes from her.

She quickly undressed and tossed each piece of clothing to the floor.

"Oh shit! Baby" he said staring at her radiant body. She left her socks for last then turned from him and bent over to remove them knowing full well the view she was giving him would drive him crazy. Matt thought he would bust when he saw the beautiful oval of her hairy vagina peek back at him. He felt the lust of a lion roar up in his throat.

Retta could see he would be insatiable by the way his penis multiplied it's size right before her eyes.

"Come on baby" she beckoned to him holding out her arms sitting on the bed.

Matt was so hungry for her that he tore at his clothes with a vengeance.

"Damn! How come girls can undress faster than boys?" soon he was out of his clothes. He hit the light and leapt on her with pure lust and intent. Her body was like warm wine, all hot and silky to the touch and her intoxicating perfume made him drunk as he inhaled her heavenly essence. She filled his mouth with her hungry tongue and probed his mouth vicisously sucking and pulling his tongue from its roots. Their bodies inter-twinded like two molten snakes trying to eat each other. Retta could feel each throbbing pulse of his penis as it rested against her thigh. Oh! How she wanted it in her deeply and penetrating like before.

But Matt wanted to wait and prolong their pleasure as he began working two fingers between her swollen lips and began a torching rhapsody of give and take, in and out, up and down.

"Oh god it feel's good!" she moaned twisting wildly and holding his arm as if to help him to drive herself mad.

"Oh Matt baby please! Baby now! . . . now! . . . now! I can't take it anymore baby give it to me please!"

But Matt was not to be denied his sweet torches. Oh how he also wanted to drive into her like a jack hammer then blast his orgasm into her. But he wanted more, he wanted to give her more as well as receive. Not only because it had been a long time since their last time together and that it may be one of the last, but because she was his woman. The love of his heart, the only woman he would ever truly love and ever want so he couldn't let her go out like that in owe blaze of orgasmic firery juices. Matt eased from her and started working on her neck kissing and biting all the way down until he came to her perfect breasts. He sucked on them hungrily making Retta tremble and beg.

It made her so crazy she felt tears roll down her face as he pleasured her and made her suffer to the point of madness and desire. Retta moaned and whined as Matt touched, teased and nibbled his way down her severely enflamed breasts. He left a silvery trail of saliva from nipple to nipple. Retta was white hot now and could no long moan as her voice was lost. Now all she could do was whimper and writhe in ecstacy. Matt let his tongue tickle and tittle an electric trail down Retta's chest, to the center and down her trembling stomach.

She grabbed his head his neck his shoulders, patting them tepidly as if to say,

"Okay baby that's enough . . . that's enough . . . I can't take it!"

Just when she thought he was going to kill her with passion he dashed back up quickly and blew a soft breeze across her enflamed nipples. Retta screamed.

"Matt! . . . Matt! (whine) Oh Matt!" she cried almost sobbing.

"Oh baby I love you . . . please, please, take me now I can't stand it anymore" she reached for his shoulders and in a mad despearate move tried to pull him up and between her yearning legs.

"Not yet baby . . . not yet" he breathed wanting so bad to give it to her. It was hard and it was excruciating to force himself to wait. His penis was so hard it was limp with lumbering building pressure. Several times he felt himself dribble onto his own leg because his hard on was beyond hard . . . it was heavy!

"I just want to give you more baby . . . just a little more" he breathed. Retta was beyond passion. She shook her head rapidly with tear filled eyes. Matt had never taken her so far before and she was overwhelmed with feelings and stirrings within her that she had never felt. Closer and closer he got her to urinating on herself as he teased and made her orgasms grow higher and higher but not letting her have one. Matt eased his tongue down her belly making her wince every inch of the way. Every where his tongue touched lit a fire in her like pouring alcohol on a barbecue. Matt did this all the way down and between her legs.

Retta grabbed a pillow and bit down on it and moaned rhythmically as he went. "mmm . . . mmm . . . mmm" she went trembling and gyrating as he went. Sweat poured from her body like she had a fever. Matt could see what he was doing to her and he became lascivious with pleasure that he was causing her so much pleasure and pain. He wanted to fuck her! . . . hard and now! But he had to wait. His tongue flicked out and touched her pubic mound and she screamed. Retta covered her face and screamed each time his tongue went between her vaginal lips. Her mind was soaring and blazing with thought and feelings beyond her grasp or memory. Matt teased her clitoris till she started kicking like a toddler having a tantrum.

He held her legs apart and buried his face deeply between them. Retta hit and struck the bed and him more and more as the feeling was beyond comprehension and she no longer could tell where he started and she ended. Retta was a red hot dripping mess under him. Her sweat and love juices flowed freely as they destroyed the bed. Matt stabbed his tongue deep into her vagina and she bucked and froze in mid air like she was hit by lightning. Matt felt her convulse and strain so hard he thought she was going to break her own back. She held this for a good two minutes then crashed back to the bed with the pillow still covering her face. She trembled from time to time but stopped moving all together. Matt grew concerned and stopped his oral attack.

He slowly eased up beside her his penis still hard as a pepperoni. He removed the pillow slowly and looked at her in the dimly lit room. Retta was staring off into space like she was on a drug. Her eyes were wildly seeking something intangible.

"Retta?" he whispered gently. She slowly came back and grew catatonic for a second then a flash of clarity came upon her and she looked right at him with no expression. Matt was getting a little scared thinking he had done something wrong or went too far with her this time. He had only wanted to please her. She slowly put a hand to the side of his face and looked at him with deep abiding love. She held that look for a minute or so then went into what Matt could only call a smoldering fit.

Her eyes went serious and she eased herself up and rolled Matt onto his back where she just looked at him and caressed his face. A most sinister grin crossed her soft lips and put a chill down Matt's spine.

"My turn" she said simply with a most far away voice like she was in a tunnel. Retta climbed on top of him still looking deeply into his eyes. She professionally wrapped her legs around and behind his and straddled his still swollen penis. Matt was smiling but she was smirking and making him wonder what he had released in her.

She grabbed his penis and eased herself onto it. She teased him a second with her wet sopping love patch. Matt was trying to get into her rythm but she wouldn't let him.

"I'm going to fuck your brains out Matt" she said flatly. Matt couldn't wait or so he thought. Retta jammed his penis up and into her to the hilt! She used a bob-sled-like push to launch herself onto him. Matt felt it down to his toes.

"Oh! Shit"

"Not yet you won't . . . but your gonna want to" she whispered then began a machine like motion moving up and down and winding her hips around as she went. Retta was wringing him out like he did her and he had no idea how to handle it. She pushed hard and strong and fast. Matt tried to roll her but she had locked into his legs and he couldn't move them. She used her hips her lips her hair and even her ass to grind him to a pulp. Matt had never been inside her like this and the feeling was excruciating and sweet. She was literally beating the brakes off of him! Her pussy slammed and smacked into and onto him like a jack hammer and she ground down on him like a mad man. She grimaced and smirked at him as she fucked him hard, deep and long.

Matt wanted to drive up into her and control her but she had him locked down. He couldn't do anything but be ridden like a horse. Every time she felt him grow rigid inside her and try to lock up for and orgasm, she would freeze and pull back causing him to go cold. Retta's pussy was wetter than she ever remembered it ever being. The thought of it sent a tingle though her that made her shudder as she drove on him again and again. Matt moaned and his balls were getting sore as Retta did her damndest to ride him like a horse. She bridged, arched her back and ground down with a vengeance like she was trying to tear it off. Matt held onto her hips but she was in control. Matt could feel the pressure building in him strong. His toes curled and he squeezed her butt until she sighed in response. Retta gave a bit too much extension while lunging onto him and Matt looking for an opportunity, exploited it. He rolled her over onto her back, still deep inside her and pulled her knees up to her chest with his arms locked firmly behind her knees.

She sighed deep and held on to him as he drove and pounded her till the bed shook. They were beyond caring if Lori could hear them or was in anyway aware of what they were doing. They were making love, screwing and fucking their collective brains out for love of each other and some unknown perceived yet possible end to it all.

Matt reared up one last time and froze. Retta could feel him growing inside of her like someone blowing up a hot air balloon. The feel was exquisite and she pulled her legs up and over his shoulders for max penetration and feel.

"Come on baby! . . . make love to me and give me all you got!" she breathed almost out of breath. Matt plunged deep and hard and gave up every ounce of liquid passion in him. He shook and shuddered as each hot blast launched itself into Retta like a missel. She threw back her head and received each and every one with delicious pleasure.

She licked her lips again and again as he emptied himself into her again and again.

"I love you Matt . . . I taste you . . . I feel you . . . god I want your baby inside me" she whispered as she clasped her legs around his waist and held on. She began her own orgasm just after his and it was powerful. With each blast from Matt she returned one in a sensual tug of war. They both moaned and grunted as the feeling subsided.

Once Matt had shot his last rocket he collapsed on top of Retta and stayed there. They both breathed and panted for minutes after then slowly began to soothe one another with kisses and gentle touches.

Retta just laid back and relished the feeling of his penis still swollen and resting inside of her. Now she was lost, completely lost in his ardent kissing and love making. Matt had waited as long as he could and now had to satisfy his own desires. He drove into her tight wetness without restraint and he could feel her tightness round his rock hard penis like a vice. Retta sighed heartily and gave into his onslaught as he drove deeper and deeper into her with each bone crushing stroke.

"Ooh! SSS, she's so wet and juicy" he thought while fighting hard not to come to soon but it was out of his hands and he soon felt that old familiar fire building in his loins and traveling up his anus into his back. Retta felt this build up too and pulled him as far into her as she could by placing her knees on her chest and holding onto him.

"Y-yess, yess, yess oh yes baby, give me all of it, all of you baby." Their bodies were a wet mass of flesh writhing and sluicing about finally like two worms in a baby oil bath. Matt blasted off and oh what a surge it was. He moaned so loud he was sure Lori would hear not to mention the way his legs cramped and his toes curled. Retta just threw her head back and accepted each hot surge of his firey muscles coming back with her own mind numbing orgasms. What had started only twenty minutes ago was now over and done and both lay panting and sweating in each other's arms. They kissed and gave to each other all the heartfelt endearments in the world and unbeknownst to them would be their last time.

Buford didn't eat much at dinner but just sat there picking at it occasionally and sampling his wine. He was trying to figure a way to let Audrey down easy but just how couldn't think of to save his life.

"Buford is there something wrong?" she asked.

"Oh, not really, I just had something on my mind that's all."

"Do you want to tell me about it, cause you know I'm here for you whenever you need me?" Buford just tapped his glass nervously and stared at her.

"Well Audrey, to tell you the truth, it's about you" he said finally.

"Me, what's wrong with me?"

"Well Audrey, I really don't want to talk about this sort of thing here, could we wait till later?" "Why, is it so bad you're afraid to talk in public?" she said getting a little touchy and apprehensive. Buford was afraid of this very thing and really didn't want to tell her he didn't think they should see so much of each other anymore for fear of an embarrassing reprisal.

"No, not really but I just want more privacy than this that's all."

Audrey looked around the small intimate little restaurant. She could see only four other couples and they were spread out quite far apart.

"Well I think this is pretty good, so tell me what's eating you about me, is it that I don't come over enough?"

"No."

"Or how about my phone calls, am I not calling you enough?"

"Goodness no."

"Then What?"

He could see he wasn't going to be able to do this easy so he just sighed and resigned himself to the awful task.

"Look Audrey, I don't know how else to say this other than to say it, I care for you a lot and think you're a great girl."

"But?"

"But I think we're spending too much time together that's all and I think we need to put some space between us for awhile."

Audrey's mouth fell open like a trap door and she couldn't believe her ears.

"Did you say that you don't want to see me anymore Buford?" she said almost in a whisper now glaring at him.

"Well yes and no."

"Well make up your mind, which is it?"

"Okay, Yes I think we do see too much of one another to often and just now I've got a lot of things going on and I can't get them done with all these unannounced visits and phone calls Audrey." "Once in a while is okay, but not every other day."

"I see" she said shrinking back into her seat still staring.

Now it was out. He had said what needed to be said. He should've felt better but he didn't. All he could feel was the nervous tension rumbling in his gut as he sat looking at a mortally destroyed Audrey.

"So that's what's been bothering you all night, isn't it?" she said calmly.

Buford just turned his head.

"How long have you felt this way?"

"For quite some time now."

"Then how come you didn't tell me, I would have understood."

He just shrugged.

"So you didn't really care about me in the first place did you, but was just using me?"

"That's not true" he shot back now animated.

"Oh no, well you tell me if I'm wrong but didn't you say long ago that we would let things develop as they may?"

"Yes, I did but I didn't think it would be like this."

"Then what the hell did you think it would be like?" "This is how love is, or is it you never loved me at all and just wanted a quick fuck every now and then?"

"You don't have to be so belligerent Audrey, and that kind of language isn't necessary."

She leaned forward on her elbows.

"Why you selfish sanctamoneous bastard, how dare you tell me how to behave, you love a girl then leave her flat and expect her to be amiable about it?" "Well you can think again Buford cause I won't be."

"Now see here Audrey!"

"No! you see here, you tell me you want a relationship then you back away, you say you want me for yourself and I give you that, but then you tell me you don't want to see me anymore, just what the hell do you want Buford?" "Is it the heat getting to hot and you can't stay in the kitchen?"

"Audrey, will you please calm down you're drawing attention to us!"

She looked about slowly and noticed they had picked up a few onlookers.

"So what" she said flatly turning around.

"It's your fault!"

"Well if you'd have let me explain, I'm sure you would have seen that there was no reason to be upset, I mean for Christ sake Audrey we're adults here so let's act like it."

She raised an obstinate eyebrow and crossed her legs.

"Well at least one of us is."

"Look, I'm not trying to hurt you or us, I'm just saying we need some space that's all, it's not like we're separating."

"Oh isn't it?"

"No."

"Then tell me what's the difference?"

"Well when you separate you don't see that person at all and when you give each some space you don't see them as much or as often."

Audrey sat bobbing her foot like a cat about to pounce then folded her arms and rested a figurative finger under her chin staring at him queryly.

"Just tell me one thing Buford" she said flatly. "If I work from 6 to 6, Monday through Friday and you work from 5:30 a.m. to 4:30 p.m. Monday through Saturday, then spend the rest of your time doing paperwork at home, just how do you think we're gonna see each other at all?"

"Well there's Sunday" he offered hopefully.

"That's only half a day, I go to church till 2:00."

"Well then I don't know Audrey, things are just out of hand right now and until I can get some of this locked down I need to have some room to breathe for a while."

Audrey reached for her glass and took a sip then firmly sat it back down.

"Alright Buford, I've tried to understand you and please you the best I could, I have never denied you anything you ever asked of me or refused you any affection, but now I see it was I who was wrong in thinking you would be right for me in the first place."

"Audrey wait!"

She just turned her head and held up her hand cutting him off.

"Like I was saying, I cared for you more than you deserved Buford and now I see that all you are and will ever be is a miserly old asshole who's solely bent on being a spinster for the rest of his life, and you will never truly find happiness because you don't have a snowballs chance in hell of an idea of what a good thing looks like even when its staring you in your sorry ass face, so you go ahead and hide behind your pitiful paperwork cause that's all your ever gonna have and with that you can go straight to hell, now take me home please, I've had enough!"

Then she got up and walked towards the door. Buford felt somewhat stupid and like a child for the way he handled this matter. He had lost control of the whole situation and never regained it. Now she hated him and didn't want anything more to do with him and now he began to feel the loss.

He laid a tip on the table and went up front to pay the bill. Audrey just stood looking away from him at a painting, waiting for him to finish up with the cashier. He tried to clutch her arm disarmingly as they walked out but she jerked it away.

Retta and Matt had long since recovered themselves and were now laying in bed holding each other.

"Matt, I wish it could be like this all the time baby."

"Yeah me too, but don't worry, as soon as we're out of school we'll never have to be apart again."

"Yeah" she said smiling and snuggling even closer to him.

"You know we could always sneak away and do it and no one would be wiser."

"Do what poo?" he said groggily almost asleep.

"You know? Get married silly."

"Oh! Okay, I'm sorry I didn't quite catch what you meant but now I see."

"So what do you think about it?" she asked running her fingers along the gentle sloping contours of his mouth and chin.

"Well it's not a bad idea but where would we live? We're still in school."

"At home of course, where did you think?"

"I don't know" he shrugged.

"Yeah we'd stay at home till we got out of school and then we can tell everybody that we're married, no need rocking the boat till then love."

"Sounds good, so when do you think we ought to do it?"

"I thought I'd let you decide that."

"Okay, let's go over all we need to do then that'll let us know when."

"Well there's the blood test" she said counting off, then the license fee."

"Why do we need blood test?"

"Well it's the law, everyone who gets married in Georgia must get one."

"But why?" he asked again unsatisfied with her answer.

"I don't know pudding, I guess so two people who might have blood problems will be aware before they marry."

"Oh okay."

Just then a pair of bright lights flashed through his window illuminating the room then a crunching of pebbles under tires loomed in as the car went quickly down the drive and stopped. It was Buford and Audrey.

"Oh shit Matt their back early."

"No shit, hurry up and run to the den before they get on the porch."

Lori turned with a start as she saw the two teens running into the den shuffling and straightening their clothes.

"Wass a matter Retta?" she cooed curiously.

"Momma's back early, that's what."

"Oh." Then she turned back to her program. Matt and Retta plopped on the couch quickly and tried to assure a stoic appearance so as not to draw attention to themselves.

"Retta – Lori" yelled Audrey from behind them.

Matt just looked at Retta with his eyes wide and his mouth open.

"Oh shit she came through my room, you think she noticed anything?" he asked.

"I hope not, she's got an eye like an eagle and a nose like a blood hound."

"Come on girls it's time to go" she called.

Matt scrambled up to help them gather their things and then hustled them towards his room and out the door. Audrey stood just inside his room with the most milk curdling look he'd ever seen. He could feel her eyes burning right through him and it made his stomach flutter.

"Your back early" said Retta chancing an off-beat comment.

"Did everything go okay?"

"Come on lets go" she hissed.

"Guess not" thought Retta who quickly dropped her head and squeezed around her heading to the porch. Matt followed cautiously not sure he should but being compelled by forces unknown to him. He noticed his dad wasn't saying much but just leaned against the door and smoked a cigarette with his hand in his pocket.

"What's wrong with them?" he said as he reached the car and opened the door for Retta.

"I don't know Matt, I got a bad feeling about this and I don't think it will blow over soon." "You'd think someone pissed in their cish'e or something" he said attempting to ease the tension.

Retta just smiled weakly. They stood silent trying to hear what was being said between Audrey and Buford but could not.

"Now you just remember what I told you Buford cause I mean it" she said poking an angry finger at him then forcefully reaching up to kiss him heartily then broke from him and slapping his face.

"That's for ruining my night" then she was gone.

Matt gave Retta a quick peck then closed her door.

"I'll see you later Retta."

"I hope so Matt, I hope so."

"Um, good night Audrey" he croaked as she got near.

Audrey just flashed him a hot stare.

"That's Ms. Davis to you, understand!"

"Yes ma'am" he said with a snap backing away from the car.

She cranked up and blasted off down the street. Retta held on and gave Lori a nervous look in the back seat. Audrey was grumbling something under her breath and Retta thought hard whether or not she should say anything to her just now.

"Momma is there something wrong?"

"Just shut up! Just shut the hell up and don't say anything to me right now, ya'll make me sick" she snapped viscously.

"But mom we didn't do anything" she pleaded.

But Audrey was in her own world. A world filled with hate and confusion and she hated everyone.

"Ain't no damn good!" she muttered. "All they do is take all you got and then throw it in your face and leave, just a bunch of no good goddamn men! And you!" she barked thunderously then slapped Retta's face soundly. The blow was so strong it sent her crashing against her door.

Lori jolted upright the minute she saw it.

"Momma what did I do?" she sobbed holding her face, terror and dismay evident in her tear filled eyes. Lori just blinked wildly and pulled her stuffed animal close then curled up on the seat with her thumb in her mouth and wept.

"You little hussy" spat Audrey. "Just who the hell do you think you are laying up in that mans house like some cheap 2 dollar whore? Do you think you're grown? Do you think you're something special?" Then she reached out and grabbed a hand full of Retta's hair snatching it viscously.

"Ow momma" she cried. Shocked and totally traumatized as Audrey viscously shoved her against the door again. Retta's mind was a tidal wave of utter chaos and confusion. She had never in her life been treated so badly and for the life of her couldn't figure out what she did to deserve such abuse. Lori was beside herself now and just howled. She was on the floor board with her knees up crying her heart out. She had never witnessed anything so evil and mean in her young life and felt all the hatred and bile in the world for her mother.

"What did I do that was so wrong?" sobbed Retta now losing her voice.

"You know damn well what and if you deny it again I'll knock your damn head off, you and that boy laying up in there like your married or something." "Yeah, I saw you when you ran into the den you little whore" then she slapped her again and again getting more viscous with each swing and causing the car to swerve.

All Retta could do was cover herself as best as possible and sob bitterly.

"I'M SICK OF YOU! SICK OF YOU" she ranted on. "And I better not catch you no where near him ever again, you hear me!" "And if I catch him over my house again I'll blow his damn head off."

Now Retta really let loose and she moaned loudly as her heart shattered. She had a feeling her mother would do this but now she was assured and only wanted to die.

"Momma please!" she begged, mucus and blood running from her nose.

"I love him, please don't take him away please! Ohh!" she cried throwing herself into her seat and against the door hysterically. Now Audrey sported a sinister smirk on her face. Now she was glad. Now she was happy. She had struck back at Buford with the same ferocity and detachment that she felt he'd shown her.

"Yes! This was fair, if I can't have you, your son can't have Retta and that's that." Soon they were home and Retta didn't wait for her to put the car in park. She bolted from the car as soon as she stopped and ran up the stairs. She unlocked the door and ran inside then threw herself on her bed and wept some more.

Matt just sat in his room on the floor and numbly stared out the window. He was feeling awful inside like he was dying and couldn't feel anything. His stomach had a nervous tension and his body rang with numbness. Even his breathing was almost none existent. All he could do was stare blankly into the cool night. His father was no less disturbed and stood in the hall nursing a cup of coffee and a smoke. He too could feel his sons torment and could only guess at its source. He would be okay but what about Matt. He remembered long ago about his concern for his and Audrey relationship and what repercussions would come of it.

"Naw, she wouldn't do that to them" he thought. They don't have anything to do with this or would she? God I hope not.

Rodney would give up on life if he couldn't have Retta and I'm sure she would too. He smoked and drank in silence a while longer then put out his butt in the remainder of his coffee and went to bed. Matt sat there on the floor until he could sit no more. His back was acching and his bottom was sore not to mention his legs had cramped badly. It was now 3 a.m. and he had sat there like that since 10 p.m. and now he slowly and painfully dragged himself into bed and just lay there not sleeping but only staring blankly at the ceiling listening to his heart beat and the hollow sounds of his breathing. Soon he too fell into a fitful sleep.

The next day the sun came up quite nicely on this warm Saturday morning and showered the sky with rich warmth and crisp blue color. All this would have made a wonderful day had it not been for the pain that still crept in Matt's heart and soul. He never really slept and got up shortly after 6 a.m. something he never did on a weekend. He dragged himself from bed and slogged into the bathroom to shower.

Aretta was up too but just laid in bed staring blankly out the window, too devastated to move. She didn't care. What reason did she have to move any way. Her lip and nose still bore the ghostly pain and residue of blood from last night. She heard Audrey screaming something about taking her back over there to give him his ring back but she wasn't really sure because she was so delirious with anguish and crying.

"Did she really mean all of that or was she just drunk? But no, she couldn't have been could she, because they hadn't been gone but a few hours at the most, and why did she treat me like that beating on me and pulling my hair, she's never done that to me before." Retta felt a thickness coagulate in her throat as she thought this and then a hot pain scorched her nose as warm tears ebbed forth burning her eyes.

She couldn't really let go, she felt like because her throat was sore and she'd just about cried herself dry. Still one by one huge drops fell onto her cheeks, down to her trembling lips and onto her bed.

Lori awoke to the gentle sound of her sisters weeping. She too had wept bitterly at her mother relentless attack on Retta and hated her for it. She quietly eased out of bed and walked over to her. Her cute little face screwing and frowning because of the hurt and pain she felt seeing her sister cry. She whimpered a dry sob and reached over to hug her. Retta felt tiny soft hands touch her and looked up to see Lori with tears flowing and all the love in the world for her and this made her even sadder.

She scooped up her little frame and cuddled her close like a child with a doll.

"It's okay Retta, I still love you" she whimpered.

"And I love you too" sobbed Retta burring her face into the softness of Lori's body. After a few minutes Audrey came into the room. She startled the two girls and they quickly broke apart looking at her. She had gotten dressed and didn't appear to have slept much either. Her hair was haphazardly bound up in a scarf of maroon and green and she wore a conservative blue blouse and tan skirt with buttons in front. She looked at the girls strangely as if seeing them for the first time.

"Don't forget what I told you Retta" she said finally in a somewhat mean whisper.

"This afternoon when I get back we are going over to Mr. Mathis house so you can give Rodney back his ring because like I said it's over and I mean it" then she eased out closing the door.

All Retta could do was sit and rock herself with Lori cuddled in her arms. It had not been a dream but a nightmare in all its hideous omnipotence. It had reached out and ripped her heart out bleeding and still throbbing with nothing left but a ragged gaping hole in her chest. What would she do now? How would she live without her meaning for living?

"Lori you want some breakfast before I go?" shouted Audrey through the door.

"No! I don't wanna eat, I hate you, go away" she shouted back in the proudest voice Retta and Audrey ever heard then she rolled back over to cuddle with Retta.

Audrey put a trembling hand to her lips. She had never been sounded out like that before and never by her baby daughter; a child so sweet and full of life that just watching her baby talk to her dolls made you feel warm inside. And now listen at her, totally indignant and bereft.

Could she have made a mistake last night? But she felt justified and was right in lashing out, wasn't she? She turned on her heels and walked away then out the door.

After awhile Retta got a hold of herself and mustard the strength to get out of bed. She went into the bathroom to get a shower. The water felt warm but that's all. It couldn't lift her spirits anymore than a gerbil could lift a brick. She stood under the water and turned her face to it to wash away the old tears as well as hide the new ones that came when she thought of the times she and Matt had shared a shower and made sweet love. Slowly she sank to the floor of the tub, too overwhelmed to stand. Oh how she wanted to die and just be buried.

"Matt! Matt!" she cried. "I need you! Please God, don't let her take him from me."

Matt was sitting around listless. He had tried to call Retta but the operator said the phone was off or out of service. Now what could he do? He wanted to talk to her so bad and couldn't. He thought about going over there but something about the way Audrey looked at him made him stay put.

"Damn! What the hell is going on? Why is this shit happening? What did dad do to her mother last night? Fuck!" Matt was in rare form and ready for war. His mind reeled and his heart hurt. He had a feeling something awful was amiss but couldn't put his finger on it. The only thing that did come to mind was his worst nightmare and that he would not let take hold of him lest he would go over there and probably raise hell. Finally he went to his room to turn on the radio maybe that would help. He switched it on and went out the door and sat on the stoop in the sun. "Good morning you're on the WDDO request line, what can I play for you to get your morning right."

"Um . . . Um could you play um "let me be your angel?" by Stacy Lattisaw."

"Sure and who do you want to dedicate this to?"

"Um my boyfriend Charles in East Macon."

"You got it and we'll get that on for you shortly okay."

"Thank you."

(Click)

"This is WDDO and I'm Big George on your radio, if you want to make a request, call the request line at 777-WDDO."

Matt just laid back and let the music and warmth of the sun wash over him. He knew the tune and only wished Retta was there with him to listen and fall in love all over again. The song was soft and richly soulful with a compelling melody. The artist had a voice like cream and honey and it immediately cast him into a tumult of reflection and yearning for Aretta.

"Let me be you're an-gel-let me be the one you been needing-let me you're an-gelll-let me be you're an-gelll-let me be the one for you-uu."

As the song ended Matt found himself deeply sadden. All through the song he was lifted and tossed through clouds of love and emotion. His ears hungered and labored over every note and his body yearned and vibrated as each glorious melody moved him. He was animated from within and without his mind's eye was a grand scene of love. Beauty and light all which expanded and coalescent around one lone person who stood alone in the midst of it all and that was Aretta his only angel.

After awhile Matt got up and went into the house. He turned off the stereo and came out shutting the door behind him. He dug is hands deep into his pockets and walked away no direction no plan and no destination other than just to walk. Cars passed him whizzing by and children noisily ran and rode their bikes or scooters by him. Although he perceived them, he neither heard them nor saw them. For him there was only the song and Retta. He walked along head down with no volition as to where he was going but just turned as a curve became evident. He stared at the ground and was slowly becoming acutely aware of pebbles, cigarette butts and chewing gum wrappers as each step reduced his perception of himself in relation to his surrounding to smaller and smaller proportions until he could see the minute trash on a plane equal to it.

Matt walked along like this for quite some time until the blast of a huge truck horn brought him back to the present reality. He looked around and was amazed for he had made his way all the way to the far end of Vineville Avenue next to the I-75 overpass and all this all this way by dead blind reckoning. He stood looking down at the traffic below and wondered what it would be like to be someone else other than himself right now. He sat down on a nearby bus stop bench and wondered. His mouth dry and the sun beginning to get hotter as the day wore on. He hadn't eaten anything all morning and was now quite hungry. He got up and walked toward home. The trip back seemed much longer than the trip out but then again he wasn't hungry or thirsty when he left either.

Soon he'd made it home and saw that it was a little after 1:00. He went into the kitchen to get a sandwich then switched on his stereo to relax and eat. He didn't get in his first bite before he heard a faint knocking at the door. He opened it and immediately knew why he was feeling so bad.

For there in all despair was Aretta standing in the hall tear stained cheeks and the most heartbroken look he'd ever wanted to see. She just lunged at him and wept in his strong embrace. "Baby what's wrong?"

"Oh Matt, it's so awful" she sobbed.

"Tell me what's wrong?" he said afraid and concerned.

"Momma beat me up on the way home last night and said we can't be together anymore."

"Oh god, No! No Retta, it's not true" he cried wilting.

Retta just nodded and cried some more.

"It's true Matt and she even said if you called or came over she would shoot you!"

"No."

"Yes Matt."

"But why, we ain't done nothing to her, why?"

"It's your father, I figured it out, he broke up with her last night and now she wants to get even." "But why us?"

"I don't know baby."

"Well I won't let her, she can't do this, this is wrong, where is she? I want to talk to her."

"Matt it won't help, I begged all the way here and last night too, she just hates your dad and wants revenge."

"Well we won't let her, we'll still be together."

"How Mat?" "You're over here and I'm over there and she won't let me see you or talk to you." "I tried to call this morning but she took the phone with her and Frieda wasn't home."

"Well we'll fix that come on." He took her hand and walked out to the car. Audrey was leaning against the door looking at them like they were aliens.

"Ms. Davis, Retta just told me you don't want her to see me anymore."

"That's right and I meant it too."

"Why?"

"That's my business and you're in no position to question me."

"How can you do this? It's not right. What did we ever do to you that was so wrong?"

"Let me tell you something boy!" she said pointing and getting meaner.

Retta just stood beside Matt head down and squeezing his hand fiercely.

"My daughter is barely 16 and you are almost 18, now that alone is reason enough for you to stay away from her or didn't you know this state has a statutory rape law and from my understanding you have probably violated it several times, so if you don't leave her alone I'll have you locked up, get me?" she said in his face now.

All Matt could see was someone he hated and wanted to destroy. His muscles tightened and his fists clenched tightly. He was about to go after her but Retta sensing this in him squeezed his hand letting him know this was not the way.

"What did my dad do to you and why would you do this? Can't you see we love each other deeply! I have always loved Retta. How can you selfishly separate us?"

"Look, don't call my house, don't come near my house, if I hear of you even trying to get near her not only will I punish her but I'll have you locked up."

"Now Retta get in the car, No wait, give him his ring back."

"Momma no! Please! Not that, I'll do whatever you say but please not that."

"Do it now or I'll break it off" she threatened.

Aretta was mortified and Matt was no less awe struck. Aretta cried frantically as she worked the ring from her finger and Matt was in tears now.

"I won't take it" he said defiantly.

"I don't care what you do, so long as she doesn't have it anymore, now get it off, Retta now!" Matt just put his hands behind him avoiding Retta's out stretched hand.

"No, I won't take it."

"Matt please baby, please take it" she sobbed.

"Retta I gave that to you, you know this is our engagement ring."

"Oh Matt" she moaned, her eyes red with tears. She placed her hand on his cheek.

"Please for me my love."

Matt allowed her to pull his hand from behind him, tears running from the both.

"I'll never let you go Retta, you know that, never." She reached up and kissed him long and deeply. Her mouth salty sweet with tears and all the love in the world. Audrey in livid anger viscously pulled her from him.

"Get in the damn car now" she shouted forcing her in. Then she stood abreast Matt causing him to back away.

"You remember what I've told you" then went around her side and got in.

"I love you Retta" he said as she rolled away.

"I love you too Matt" then she was gone in a puff of smoke.

Matt stood there numb and cold as he looked at the ring in his hand. He wasn't aware of the person behind the huge oak just up the sidewalk. It was Ant and he had been on his way there and seen everything.

Matt let it all sink in and then it hit him. He was all alone and would never see her again and a deep sob wracked his body as he crumbled to the ground and he cried for all eternity. He didn't care and couldn't move, all he could see was Retta's face as she drove away. Ant came up beside him then reached down and put his arm around him and they both cried together.

"Why Ant? Why did it have to be her, why?"

Ant just held him and cried with him for he had no answer but none the less felt his pain. He managed to get Matt into the house and sat on his bed with him.

"Don't worry Matt, you'll see her again and you'll be together again."

Aretta sat looking out the window and wept quietly as her mother drove home. She had made a few comments about her and Matt then left her alone. What she didn't know was something inside Retta had snapped and she would never again be the same or look upon her with the love and admiration she once knew. All she was now was a spectra, a ghost, something she considered to be as insubstantial as dust. Oh she would speak to her and respect her but never again would she feel unconditional love for her. She had fiendishly raped her of that which she cared most about and would never see again.

The weekend soon passed and gave way to a new week, nothing which Retta wanted anything to do with. She sat in her classes like an empty husk. She saw nothing, heard nothing and responded to nothing, all this to the pleasure of Camille Murchison who'd been aptly watching her and completely enjoyed it.

Oh she didn't know for sure what was wrong but deduced that only one thing could make her withdraw so badly.

"Well I guess the carpenter found a new board to grind on" she said loudly so anyone near enough would hear. Retta just ignored her and kept silent.

"Shh. What are you doing Camille?" said her friend.

"Are you trying to start something. You know how she feels about her man."

"So! I don't care, I'm glad she lost him and he's probably got another one lined up already" she said aiming her words as she projected them.

Aretta was trying to be cool but Camille was slowly getting to her and just now she didn't want a confrontation.

"You know something Paula, I wouldn't mind a ride on that horse myself" she taunted on.

"Hell after being with her I'd be like a dream compared to that nightmare." That did it. Retta was up and on her in New York minute and didn't even fell rage when she planted her first punch dead center of Camille's face. Her nose exploded in a read burst then Aretta snatched her from her seat, threw her on the floor and commenced to whopping her ass. She grabbed hand full of Camille's hair and drove her head against the floor with a vengeance.

"Aretta. Aretta, you stop that this instant" said her teacher running over to intervene.

But Retta was livid with anger and her every fiber burned with rage. All the class was a maley of shouts and blood lust as chairs were over turned and desks thrown to the side. Now others who had heard the ruckus came running into the room. It was two male teachers and several students. "Move, move get out of the way" shouted one of them.

"Aretta stop it" he said grabbing her by the shoulders and pulling her away from a semiconscious Camille. She still had her hair in her hands and fought to keep her grip but the strength of the man holding her and the one pulling

Camille was too much. She finally let go. "Let me go, let me go goddamit, I'll kill the bitch, let me go you bastard."

And that's the way it went as they carried her physically kicking and screaming down the hall. Camille on the other hand would need medical attention because Retta managed to draw blood pounding her head against the cement floor.

"Retta calm down" shouted Mr. Simpkins, her supervision teacher. He had been the one to carry her away kicking and screaming but she didn't know it or care.

"What's gotten into you? You almost killed that girl!" Retta was a blank slate. She just sat there breathing and looking at her hands which trembled from the flow of adrenaline in her system. They had brought her to the office and took her in back to wait away from the other teachers and students. They would soon find out about the incident so there was no need to let her sit amongst their prying eyes of curiosity.

Finally the principal came in. It was Mr. Dickenson, a tall slender white man with a goatee beard, steely grey eyes and a reputation like a French inquisitor for dispensing punishment. In fact everyone called him as Dick the Destroyer but not to his face.

"So what's the problem here Mr. Simpkins?" he asked firmly staring down at Retta.

"Well you see Mr. Dickenson Aretta and Ms. Murchinson got into a fight, I don't know how it started but I and Mr. Philmore broke it up."

"Where's Murchinson?"

"I assume she's still in the class, she didn't appear to be conscious when we broke them apart or should I say broke Aretta from her."

"Find out Mr. Philmore" he ordered flatly waving towards the door.

"So Ms. Davis, what do you have to say about this?" She didn't speak or even acknowledge him, she just stared blankly at her hands wringing them and twisting them.

"I asked you a question young lady!" he said towering over her. Now Mr. Simpkins felt a little squeamish. He knew how Dick could be and had seen him in action many times before. He didn't want to see Aretta, one of prized students crushed under his interrogation.

"Ms. Davis, I'm talking to you."

"Uh Mr. Dickenson" he said mildly.

"If I may sir, let me try talking to her in private, maybe I can find out what's up?"

"Alright Mr. Simpkins, I'll give you ten minutes but if nothing chirps out of her by then I'll have to do it my way, do we understand each other?"

"Yes sir, completely."

"Good, I'll be outside checking on the other girl" then he turned and left.

Mr. Simpkins didn't waste any time. For he knew the man was true to his word.

"Aretta, honey talk to me, please" he said soothing her.

"I know she's been at you for some time now and I'm sure this couldn't have been your fault but you gotta talk to me okay."

Still nothing and she retreated within all the more. He put an arm around her shoulder and cuddled her tightly in an attempt to break her frigidness. But she just shook him off not wanting any man other than Matt to touch her.

"You know this isn't like you Retta, what would Matt say if he knew you were raising hell like this. Don't you think he'd be angry, you know how much he loves you, so come on sweetie tell me what's wrong?"

This did the trick. No sooner did he mention Matt did she turn into him and sob on his chest. Her small body trembled as he held her close.

"Matt-Matt" she wailed. "She took him away! She took him away!"

"Who sweet heart, Camille?"

"No" she motioned shaking her head.

"Then who Retta?"

"It was momma" she gushed sobbing harder now.

Mr. Simpkins was confused. He couldn't believe what he had just heard but knew Retta was no liar. Just then Mr. Dickerson came back and Mr. Simpkins quickly motioned for him to leave and that he would deal with her. Seeing the crest fallen girl in his arms he acquiesced and left.

"Hey, Hey it's alright honey now, why don't you tell me all about it, maybe I can help."

"No! Nobody can!" she went on her sobbing, rising and falling like a wave on the sea.

"Well, try me honey maybe I can but I can't if you don't tell me anything, okay." She nodded and began to talk sniffling and snuffling in between each word.

After awhile and a box of Kleenex, Mr. Simpkins came out of the office. Mr. Dickerson was standing at the counter talking with an ambulance driver about Camille. He looked over and saw him coming.

"So how's Camille?" he asked.

"She'll be fine, she's just got a nasty bump on her head and needed a few stitches to close it, the parents have been notified and should be here in awhile."

"What did you find out from Davis?"

"Well sir its pretty sorted but seems justified in a strange sort of way."

"How?" he asked purely sarcastic and disbelieving.

"Well sir it could take a bit to explain if you have a minute."

Mr. Dickerson held up his hand signaling him to stand by.

"Do you need me for anything further?" he asked the technician.

"No sir, we've got all we need."

"We'll just go on and take her down for x-rays and go from there."

"Okay, thank you for coming" he said shaking his hand then turned to Mr. Simpkins.

"Let's go in the assistant's office" he said stepping by him. Mr. Simpkins followed him in and sat down.

After a half hour he had given Mr. Dickerson the full story as it happened and as he understood it, he also threw in his own comments and recollections of Retta and Camille past involvement for the last year since he had Jr. high. The principle listened objectively but said nothing. Finally the two men came out.

"I'm sorry things got to this point with your best student Mr. Simpkins and it's truly a tragedy how all this came to be, I don't know what I may decide as yet but I will take all you've said into consideration, as I'm sure you'll agree this is a unique and grave matter."

"Yes sir I do and I want to thank you for listening and being so understanding."

"No problem, I care about my students too, that's why I'm so hard on them at times, so you go on back and sit with Ms. Davis until we can get her mother or someone here because I want to talk to her myself."

"Uh, excuse me Mr. Dickerson" said a secretary.

"Yes Miss Walsh, what is it?"

"Uh sir both parents are here now sir and they don't at all appear too happy with each other, maybe you ought to come intervene."

"Good, very good, thank you Miss Walsh, send them in, both of them."

"Yes sir." She went up front and escorted them back to the office. It was Audrey and Pat and Mrs. Murchinson.

"Come in ladies, please take a seat, how are you today? My name is Mr. Dickerson."

"Hi, I'm Camille's mom and I'm Aretta's mother" said Audrey shaking his hand.

"Well ladies it seems our children have had a little confrontation this morning."

"Little, Mr. Dickerson" said Mrs. Murchinson sarcastically.

"I'd hardly call a half-dozen stitches, little."

"Well ma'am I don't pretend to belittle the situation or your daughter injuries, I'm merely stating it in relation to all the other minor wars I've had to deal with here."

"So what happened, and where's my daughter?" asked Audrey.

"Well she's fine, she's in the other room with Mr. Simpkins and as far as what happened it appears your daughter, Mrs. Murchinson provoked this fight."

"My Camille?! You must be mistaken. My Camille is a wonderful child. She's bright, intelligent and a member of several school clubs as well as other civic organizations, she wouldn't have anything to do with the likes of that uncultured hoodlum" she said pointing at the door.

"Now you wait one damn minute, just who do you think you're calling a hoodlum?" spat Audrey standing up.

"Now wait ladies, this is childish, let's not repeat what's already been done, we're adults here." Audrey eased back down fully vexed at the arrogant and phony looking woman beside her.

"I'm sure you feel that way ma'am but the facts remain, your daughter initiated this."

"HA! I don't believe it" she said snobbishly.

"Okay I'll prove it then" he picked up the phone.

"Hello, yes send them in please" then hung up. He sat back in his high back leather chair and folded his arms across his chest and exuded the air of a chest master playing a novice. He had nothing but confidence in his dominance of the situation.

Soon in walked several students, 3 boys and two girls.

"Okay students if you would all just sit over there" he said motioning to his right.

"Now I understand you all were in very close range of the two girls prior to the fight."

"Yes sir" they nodded.

"And all of you heard the same things that caused Aretta to come unglued?"

"Yes sir."

"Okay good, then only one of you need speak."

"Paula Jenkins, why don't you tell us what happened seeing as how you're Camille's best friend."

"Yes!"

"Tell me what happened Paula?" interrupted Camille's mother.

"Mrs. Murchinson I'll handle this please" he warned.

"Well it's like this-Retta was sitting at her desk being quiet when Camille started teasing her about her boyfriend."

"Uh huh, then what?"

"Well I told her she should stop because it wasn't right but she just kept on, then she made a remark about wanting to have something to do with him intimately but I can't say it."

"Why not?" asked Mrs. Murchenson.

"It's too embarrassing."

"Here Paula write it down" he said giving her a pad and pen. She did so then gave it back to him as he read it the ladies saw his eyebrows pitch up querily then he pass it to the students.

"Tell me if this is what each of you heard?" he said looking at Camille's mother disdainfully like she had just broke wind.

"Yes sir that's what we heard."

"Okay pass it to Ms. Davis would you please." She did so and Audrey's and Pat's eyes lit up and scowled as they read it, then gave it to Mrs. Murchinson who by now was beside herself with anxious curiosity at what they all had seen.

"Oh you must be joking!" she protested throwing the pad on his desk.

"No ma'am" said Mr. Dickerson.

"She said it if these five students said she did and I must point out that Paula here hangs out with your daughter all the time and knows her quite well, she said it, do you deny their association?" "No! But still . . ."

"No butts, your daughter is the culprit here and from what I understand she's always provoked Miss Davis every since Jr. high, so you see even though fighting is not allowed or condoned in my school I can certainly see why it took place, so in that respect I cannot truly punish Miss Davis too harshly."

Audrey sat looking at her with a smug grin on her face.

"Sweet and innocent Camille huh, hmph, you better go check her pill supply, I'm sure she's been eating them like M&Ms."

"Well I never!" spat Mrs. Murchinson.

"You mean to say that you're going to let her get away with this!"

"Children you can go now" he said smiling at them, "and thank you for your help.

Once the last one went out and closed the door he turned his full attention on her, only now without the niceties and charm.

"Look Mrs. Murchinson, it seems to me that your daughter is what she is because you've raised her on 18 century southern girl school ethics, you have brought her up to believe she is better than anyone else and that others are nothing more than peasants to be trampled or tolerated and the fact that her father is a well known businessman in the community helps fuel her disgust and antisocial behavior."

"How dare you speak to me that way! I never!"

"And you probably never will" he said finishing for her.

Audrey was smiling openly now and sported a proud shit eating grin on her face. She was enjoying watching this airhead, hair-do-well get her just deserts from a somewhat common principle.

"It seems to me that if you had given her values instead of a credit card she may have turned out to be a more responsible and half decent child instead of the airhead aristocrat she's becoming." Mrs. Murchinson was as red as the evening sun. Her nostrils flared and her makeup cracked as she scowled at the principle for his abrasive assessment of her child and how she was raised. "And you, Ms. Davis" he snapped breaking her out of her smugness.

"You are also at fault here."

"Me? How?"

"Well the reason your daughter snapped was based on some things you said and did to her recently that involved another person whom I won't speak about but I'm sure you know."

"Yes I do know!" she shot back "and let me tell you this Mr. Dickerson, I raise my child how I raise my child." "If I deem something or someone unfit to associate with her then it's my business not yours."

"No that's where you're wrong, it's is my business!" he boomed getting up.

Audrey shrugged away from him in shock at his declaration of partial guardianship to her child. "When your child crosses that threshold in the morning they become mine, every last one of them, no matter what color or background and if something or someone hurts them or is hurting them be it here or home, it's my business." "You Ms. Davis, failed when you decided to make your daughter a pawn in your own personal life and when it went sour you sought to destroy her life by getting revenge on your ex associate, now to me that's not only petty but damn childish and irresponsible on your behalf as an adult and parent."

Audrey blanched away at this and looked down at her hands.

"Aretta is one of my best students in fact she's in the top 5 in the entire school and the top 10 in the school system." "Not too long ago my staff and I were discussing voiding her Jr. year and placing her in the 12th grade because we know she'd be one hell of a college student, but now that you have selfishly upset her life and destroyed her will and inspiration I fear it may affect her grades for the rest of the year causing her to lose out." "Now you do as you like Mrs. Davis because as you have stated you will raise her as you see fit, but I can tell you this, it's a sad day when a parent puts their own selfish gains above that of their child's education and happiness." "So having said that I think you both need to go home and re-evaluate yourselves and your parenting techniques Mrs. Davis before you truly screw up two beautiful and inspiring children." "Now good day to you both, I have other children to attend to and a school to run" he said sitting down.

"What about my Camile?" said Mrs. Murchison.

"Yes what about this incident?" asked Audrey chiming in almost whispering.

"Well as for Camille I'm giving her three days suspension and Aretta too."

"Why are you giving my daughter more time than her's?"

"Well Mrs. Murchison as I've pointed out your daughter brought this upon herself and you need some time at home with her, not to mention it'll give her time to heal from her injury which I'm sure you would want for her wouldn't you?" he asked leaning towards her and raising an eyebrow.

Camille's mom could see the logic and fought with the issue no more. She just looked away then back to Camille.

"Umm . . . yes I would. I see your point Mr. Dickerson and thank you for being so generous about all this. I apologize for my rudeness and closed mindedness."

"No problem Mrs. Murchison" he said waving her off and sitting back in his chair.

"I deal with parents like you every day and worse, so it's no problem"

"Oh . . . is that so?" she said readjusting in her seat preparing to defend herself.

"Yes it is,' he said staring at her and jutting his thumb over his shoulder at the wall behind him. Mrs. Murchison looked at the huge framed document that simply read; **Bob Dickerson, Dr. of Psychology, Harvard University**.

"Mrs. Davis, Aretta is next door, I suggest you say nothing to her today about this incident or anything else in light of a reprimand, given the trauma she's undergone and her high strung nature, she could explode and do worse than she's already done which makes your daughter a lucky girl Mrs. Murchison." "Now if you please ladies I have much work to do. Thank you for coming in and have a good day" he said rising from his seat and shaking their hands. The two women thanked him and left each feeling thoroughly chastised.

Audrey told Retta to get some lunch and rest for the remainder of the day and that she would be home from work soon.

Matt was sitting in his science class day dreaming and generally feeling bad. He was feeling the loss of Retta greatly even though it had only been a few days. Nothing Ant or his other friends did or said could bring any light into his life and they weren't sure there would ever be again. Just over to his right Frog was sitting watching him with curious concern. Matt hadn't said or done anything at all since he sat down at the start of class.

Even Mr. Turner was wondering why his favorite prodigy was so quiet and subdued. He would have even welcomed some of his morbid class room antics just to know he was still alive, anything at all just not this dead pan catatonic look of despair.

Unfortunately, Matt wasn't really there. His body was planted in his seat alright but his heart and mind was on the other side of town with Retta.

"PSST! . . . hey Matt" whispered Frog trying to get his attention.

"PSST! . . . Matt!, check this out dude" Matt briefly broke his muse and looked lazily over at Frog to see him making an ass of himself with a small octopus cadaver he had on his table. He had picked it up and splayed it over his face like it was alive and acted like it was alive, replaying a scene from Alien. It was quite funny in a sick morbid way and normally Matt would have burst out laughing and added to the anarchy with something as gross or worse. But instead Matt just gave him a faint smile and turned back to staring off into space. He was in a world of motionless retrospect and mental isolation.

"Oh Retta why did this have to happen to us . . . why didn't I listen to you when you tried to tell me this before. And now what can I do . . . I know what you said and how your mother threatened but I'll be damned! If I'll let it stop me from seeing you! there must be a way I know there is I just have to think of it."

The next few weeks saw Matt through a kaleidoscope of haphazard and failed attempts to reach Retta. He'd tried everything from getting others to call her on the phone to even writing her letters using phony names and addesses, all of which failed miserably and only succeeded in getting Retta put on stricter and more confining punishments.

In fact it had become so bad that Audrey resorted to having Retta watched by friends and driving her to school so as to eliminate any chances Matt might get to her. Retta on the other hand was no less miserable and began fading and withdrawing into herself even deeper. She knew of Matt's attempts to see and communicate with her and even tried to do some herself.

Unfortunatly her attempts didn't meet with any success either. There was the one time that she had managed to get a letter out to him but wasn't sure because there was never a reply to that address that she had prearranged it be sent to.

The thing is it never got to him in the first place but was intercepted by a cousin of her mothers that worked in the post office. This kind of cloak and dagger went on until school was out and summer had begun. Audrey had been thinking of a way to completely destroy any further contact between them and once school was out for summer would implement it.

Unknown to Matt, Audrey had made arrangements to move as soon as school let out. Now the two devastated lovers were totally at a loss and all hope for any contact now was a fart in a hurricane. A move meant a new address and new unknown location in a part of town not known of or known to by either until the unloading of the truck began. For Matt it meant a new location that he would never find or even know about and it would certainly seal their fate of permanent separation. As time came and went and summer had arrived, Matt spent most of it doing what he had been doing before then . . . looking for Aretta. He would get up early do his chores and leave the house only to return late in the evening.

He had burned many gallons of gas in his moped and traveled from one end of town to the other criss-crossing it from all sides. He had gotten the nerve to go up to Retta's apartment to confront or beg more or less her mother to let him see her and talk to her. But to his horror he found the blank uncovered windows of her upstairs apartment staring down at him much like the soulless eye sockets of a dead skull. He stood there feeling cold even though it was a balmy 85 degrees. His mind would not accept what his eyes were telling him and the remnants of household furnishings that you tended to find near a dumpster that told you someone had moved.

His breathing became shallow and his mind raced as a lump came into his throat. Matt's eyes slowly and painfully wandered over the remnants of discarded personal effects and household artifacts that he'd become familiar with and seen many times before in Retta's house. He hadn't realized that he'd been aware of those objects until now when he stood looking at them through tear clouded eyes.

Hair bows that were Lori's lay scattered amidst bits and pieces of outdated and crumpled Christmas wrapping paper and broken or out grown toys. He could almost hear her sweet tiny little voice as she engaged in one of her infantile sing-songs while playing with her dolls and tea sets. These also lay strewn amongst the many used magazines, no longer wanted shoes and clothes. He felt a warm tear blaze his cheek as he spotted one to the many string art mosaics and drawings Retta used to hang on her wall.

It might as well have been her because he walked over to it and picked it up gently cradling it as he dusted it off and removed little bits of confetti from it. He felt her hands when he touched it. He saw her face and the serious but gentle expression she had when creating something. He felt her presence and touch in everything she did and it hit him like a ton of bricks. He stood and turned to go back to his moped while slowly tucking the items into his shirt. For some reason that he couldn't figure he turned and looked up towards Frieda's apartment.

There was no one there or so he felt without really knowing and just wiped his eyes and walked back to his bike. Just inside the window and sitting on the floor with her back to it was Frieda. She covered her mouth with a trembling had and wept openly and alone. She had seen Matt when he first got their but couldn't muster the strength to go to him, not even to say hello. She also had been kept in the dark about Retta's moving and she was not at home when the move occurred. She knew about all the hard ship that she and Matt were being put though by her mother and even tried to help out when she could but it was over her head and her efforts to help them also failed badly.

She saw him reach for the discarded object and embrace it to his heart. She couldn't take it anymore and turned from the window just as he looked up at her. God she hurt for them. Matt got on his bike and took in the empty apartment window one last time. He gripped the object in his shirt as pain and hurt filled his face. He started his bike then slowly rode away. He didn't know exactly where he was going but just let gravity and the moped dictate.

Frieda as it happens wasn't the only one watching the lonely boy. Mrs. Johnson, who had seen the young man many times from the perspective of a silent pair of footsteps that tamped lightly on the steel grated stair case in back of her apartment at night. She had seen him during the daytime hours as well and actually waved at him once or twice when he and his dad would come by to call on what she considered; "Her girls".

She had been the only person Audrey had told about their leaving and she knew that Mrs. Johnson wouldn't tell anyone. Still her heart broke to see the young man she had come to consider and maybe even like, suffer so much and be in so much pain.

"That poor young man, He really loved that child" she said to herself then closed her curtain and walked back into the quiet interior of her own little house. As it were time moved on and it was now the middle of summer and Matt's condition or situation hadn't changed much. He was now closer to clinical depression than he'd ever been.

By his dad's observation if something didn't give soon he would be there shortly. Buford noticed that in the last three months since school let out till now, his son had digressed and deteriorated from the energetic life force that he once was, into this hollowed out lifeless shell. Matt's eyes that used to have a gleam of life in them, had been reduced to the sunken and dismal sockets of a skull. He hardly ever went anywhere anymore and just stayed in his room. He didn't watch television, he didn't play video games and the mall was no longer of interest to him. His dad and his friends had tried like hell to bring him around but nothing worked.

Ant would come by every day and sit with him quietly and try to engage him and get him to at least go for a walk with him but it was no use he just sat sullen and sad listening to he and Retta's favorite songs and looking at her picture. Once Ant tried to get the help of Mel and all their friends and take him up to the lake. She had gotten all the girls from the party and Ant had gotten all the guys and they were gonna go out on Mel's dad's pontoon boat and have a great beach party.

Matt however was not home the day the excursion was planned and was out looking for Retta on his scooter. The troupe was disappointed but went on in his honor anyway. Matt's dad even bought him a little blue sports car hoping it would lift his spirits and at least get him to go out and begin living again. He knew how devastated his son was about having his girl taken from him and he felt bad that it was in part due to ending his relationship with her mother. At first Matt didn't take to the car and just smiled a strained smile and thanked his dad for it.

The car sat untouched for two weeks and when Matt did finally come around to taking an interest in it, he just sat in it and would only drive it up and down the drive way seeing as how it had a manual shift and he wasn't familiar with operating it.

When he did start to drive the little car, he only used it to go to the store on one of his dad's made up bogus trips to get him out of the house.

As time wore on he came to the conclusion that he could go farther and much faster around town as he looked for Retta. And being he was in a car instead of his yellow moped he might just luck out and see her somewhere before he was seen if that was how he was being watched by her mother.

This thought lifted his spirits enormously and he felt renewed. Unfortunately all his efforts with the new car failed and his attempts to run into her by accident never happened.

One particular day it was hot and sunny and Ant was hanging out at Matt's hoping to talk him into doing to the lake for a swim and some chill time. Matt just said no and just wanted to stay at home and mope.

"Oh come on Matt! It's hot out there man, you can't just hang around the house all day. It ain't natural man."

"Can't I?" he said evenly as he just lay there arms behind his head and staring up at the ceiling. "No! you can't and why the hell would you want to anyway?"

Matt thought for a moment his argument. He knew Ant knew everything about everything that happened up till now so he would be hard pressed to offer anything tangible or relevant that would sway him. He couldn't think of anything and just sighed deeply.

"I don't , I just don't feel like doing anything today that's all"

"Man you ain't felt like doing nothing all summer! No six flags, no cruizin, no nothing! Matt you gotta get out of this mood man it ain't right! I know you love Retta and miss her like crazy . . . hell I miss her too" he said drooping his head a little.

Matt looked over at him and saw that this was true. Odd but true. Matt thought about what he was saying and although he knew in his head it was true, his heart was a different matter and it didn't want anything to do with anything that didn't have something to do with Retta. He just lay there further and sulked. The day was quite hot and getting hotter. If it weren't for the screened in porch, the trees around the house shading it, it would be unbearable. Just now a nice breeze was blowing through the house and it kept them reasonably comfortable.

"Why don't you go instead" said Matt quietly and tossing the keys to him.

"What! . . . are you nuts?" he said with mixed emotions.

"I can't drive that car! And besides your dad would have my nuts in a sling and you too for giving it to me. Other than that I can't drive a stick, so it's got to be you"

Matt rolled his eyes skyward and sighed. Ant could see that he was beginning to give in and was exilerated but didn't push. He wanted him to come by pure self motivation otherwise it wouldn't be worth the trip and nobody would have any fun.

"You know I'm right so why don't you just come on and let's go. Hell I could even call Cheryl and Mel if you want, I'm sure they'd come along" right up until then he had Matt at least entertaining the idea. But once he mentioned those two Matt mentally dived back into his hole like a ground hog in January. Matt flashed him an icy look that Ant knew had to say: "Your're crazier than a shit house rat!" then got up and walked out of the room.

"Hey Matt, I'm sorry man I didn't mean it that way dude, I just thought we could have some fun and hang out that's all!" he shouted to his retreating back. It was too late, Matt was gone. "Damn! I knew I shouldn't have said that shit knowing how he still feels about Retta. Now he probably won't even speak to me anymore . . . Damn! Ant you done screwed up huge now"

Just up the road and not far from Ant's grandmothers house on Brentwood Avenue, Retta was sitting on the back patio of their new house. The house was a one story brick house with wood trim here and there. The house was situated back a little ways from the street with a raised yard. It had a basement in the back of the house. All around it was pecan trees, pines and a few cherry blossom trees around the area. The house was In a quiet and cool area. Retta had found out that she was on the same side of town as Matt and not very far away. This could work to her advantage if she could manage it. One reason her mother moved to this potentially dangerous and accessible area was because it was across the street from one of her cousins and closer to Audrey's job. This was for Audrey a double blessing and for now she knew Retta would be watched while she was away. A fact that burned Retta all the more.

"Hi Retta" said her cousin Tiffany a girl about her age with short curly hair and a well formed six foot tall body. She lived across the street and was always entertaining two or more boys at a time. She could see why the boys liked her but other than that she didn't take to her very well. Today she was wearing a mid-thigh blue jean mini skirt with a peach colored tank top. She was giving away more than enough to feed any boys imagination and Tiffany knew it and didn't mind it. Come to think of it neither did her mother Casandra, who seemed to dress not to far different from her teenage daughter.

"Hi Tiff" she mumbled not turning to look at her.

"So what's up?" she asked Retta and leaning against the wall her arms folded.

"Nothing"

"You planning on going anywhere today?"

"Nope"

"Why?"

"Don't want to"

"Sigh . . . durn girl you just gonna sit around like an old maid all summer?"

"Yep"

"But why it's so nice out and the boys are even hotter!" she said smiling big and adjusting her top. "So"

"So get off your ass and let's go flirt with some of them!"

Retta just looked at her like she was from mars or something and shook her head.

"Aw c'mon, I know this boy named Greg who you'd really like!" Retta just sat rocking in the old chair much like Norman Bates mother just before she was to kill someone. She looked at her cousin with the most dead pan expression you have ever seen.

"Tiff, do you wanna stay my cousin?" she asked her in a monotone. Tiffany thought this a most peculiar question and skewed up her face wondering why she would ask such a question.

"Yeah why?"

"Then as long as you know me don't you ever come back in my face telling me about any boy you know or don't know do you understand?"

"Yeah . . . but . . ."

"*DO YOU UNDERSTAND!*" she snapped angrily getting up and into her face. A feat that even Tiffany marveled at but respected even though she stood a good head high over Retta.

"Okay okay! I understand . . . no need to get your panties in a wad"

"Good! Because the only man there will ever be in my life or who can touch *this!*" she said swirling around on one hip and hoisting her breasts to interject her point. "Is my man Matt and no one else! Now please leave I don't feel like being bothered just now"

"Alright! . . . gee whiz, I didn't know you had it so bad! . . . jeez! . . . try to give a girl a boost and what do you get . . . cussed out!"

Tiffany made a disgruntled retreat into the house and out the front door. Audrey had been sitting in the kitchen and heard the whole thing and just shook her head smiling to herself and continued on with her potato peeling. Retta was trying to imagine what Matt was doing and where he would be on a day like this. It's true it was nice outside today but with out him it was just another ordinary day.

Retta finally eased herself up and walked down the stairs to the driveway.

"Where are you going Aretta!" Yelled Audrey spying her walk down the drive.

"No place just walking!"

"Well don't go anywhere unless I know where!"

"Yes ma'am! . . . old witch!" she grumbled under her breath.

"We ain't been her a good month yet and already she thinks I'm gonna run off someplace. Well maybe I ought to do just that to show her ass a lesson. I mean who does she think she is anyway? . . . guarding me and having people watch me to tell her if I see Matt or try to call him or anything." "Lord knows I would if I could get the chance, but she keeps the phone in her room and takes it out when she goes to work and I don't know anybody so I can't use their phone!" She walked up the drive to the front of the house and down the sidewalk. A car zoomed passed making all kinds of noise with it's radio blaring at her but she didn't notice all she thought about was her love Matt and the great loss she was feeling.

"Oh how great it would be to see him again, to hold him and feel his strong loving arms around me squeezing me tight as he pressed his warm soft lips to mine in an endless kiss . . . oh Matt! How I need you now" she whispered then a tear fell from her troubled eyes.

The summer days dragged on as the weeks went by painfully slow. Finally just as quickly as it begun summer was over and a new semester was beginning. There had been a question to where Retta would attend school being she was closer to Central then Southwest.

Unfortunatly for her, her mother had arranged for her to make the bus and remain in Southwest. Retta's grades, although suffering some this past school year, was still more than enough to boost her into the 11th grade.

Matt also had managed to get his work in and squeak by but only because he quit the track team and put his energy in school and looking for Retta. At present neither of them cared much for school anymore or anything else for that matter. All their hopes and dreams lay with each other and because of her mother . . . never to be fulfilled or lived again . . . . or would they.

Matt was trying hard to throw himself into his work but was finding it difficult. This new grade brought with its own set of challenges and night mares. None of which he felt mentally or emotionally ready to deal with.

"Hey Matt" whispered Ant who this year would share half of his classes.

"Yeah?"

"Have you seen Milton yet?"

"No why?"

"I heard during the summer he went to Virginia and got into some shit with some guys and almost got shot!"

"Who told you that?"

"You remember that girl he's been dating from Mel's party last year?"

"Yeah"

"Well she told me"

"How would she know? Did she go with him up there?"

"I don't know but they been kinda close since the party so she might be on the up and up"

Matt just rolled his eyes and shook his head.

"Was there a girl involved in that mess?"

"I don't remember but I think she mentioned something about these two sisters he had met while at some club."

"Well there's you answer! You know anytime that cock hound gets with in sniffing range of a girls butt he's on it. And it don't matter if it's sisters, cousins or what . . . he's gonna screw em all if he can!"

"Yeah your right about that. Lord knows that boy would screw a wart hog if you put a dress on it and held it's head"

Matt just laughed at the joke mildly and tried not to be noticed by the teacher. This was one of the few times he had smiled or even attempted to laugh about anything since he lost Retta.

He still wore the scars and wouldn't give any girl the time of day not even Tonya Rodgers who seemed to be just about everywhere he was this year. Matt reassured himself that one day he would see her again and Macon wasn't that big and they would be one again come hell or high water.

"Hey Matt what you gonna do after school?" asked Ant thinking about cruising and doing a little skirt chasing with all the new females that were around. Not to mention the fact that his buddy had a car now.

"I don't know I'll probably just go home and try to get some of this stuff in my head . . . why?" "Oh nuthin" he said fiddling with his book bag on his desk.

"I just thought you might want to chill awhile . . . maybe go cruising and see what's up"

"I don't know man I might . . . we'll see"

"Okay! Bet"

Soon the bell for the last period rang and once again the street and side walk between Lanier "A and B" were flooded with gangs of students. All were running to get to their cars or whatever bus was going their way.

"Hey Matt, Ant! Wait up fella's" shouted Milton running to catch up.

"What's up fella's where ya'll heading to?"

"No place really" said Ant amazed at how Milton had the archaic ability to show up when anything good was about to happen.

Matt had yet to say whether they would be cruising or not. He was still very silent.

"Well ya'll wanna hang out?"

"I don't know you have to check with Matt it's his ride"

"Come on let's roll" said Matt getting a little irritable at their constant coercions.

"I need to get some gas first though" Ant and Milton began immediately fishing around in their pockets and wallets to chip in.

"Where is the nearest station from here?" he asked.

"There's one over on Montpilier up the street" offered Milton.

"We can shoot down Napier and Brentwood to get to it. That way is much quicker"

"Okay let's go. You know how hard it is to get out of this area after school and I don't want to run out of gas sitting in a line"

"BET!" the two sounded almost in unison.

Retta's bus had just pulled up to the curb and stopped up the street from her house and let her off. The bus picked up and dropped off at the intersection of

Montpilier and Courtland, or just up the street from her house. She like the smell of the bakery as she walked down the street and the fresh bread made her feel good somehow. Kind of like being at her grandma's house. She didn't really like or dislike the area and just accepted the change but missed their old apartment. Audrey had moved them into that area and told know one and because of this she wasn't worried about Retta and Matt hooking up again.

She separated them out of meanness and her loss and tried to justify it by saying Retta was too young for Matt and that they were out of hand and didn't need to be together. She broke them apart and meant for them to stay that way. She allowed Retta to ride the school bus instead of taking her to school like before.

Since Matt had no clue of their whereabouts, there was no chance in him seeing her. Retta walked alone slowly with her books huddled to her chest and her head down. This was pretty much her normal posture these days as she had no real interest in looking at anyone or talking to them. She didn't cry about Matt so much anymore but was still along way from getting over him and didn't intend to as far as she was concerned.

She still ached deep inside when she heard their song or saw something that reminded her of him and this was the worst part because just about everything did! Matt's essence could be found everywhere she looked. In the tree's on the sidewalk or even in some of the faces of many of the children she past occasionally. Matt lived in everything and nothing at the same time. She could still smell him in her clothes or at least she imagined she could. It didn't really matter because he still lived in her soul and would die only when she herself past away, and not until then.

Even then she would continue to burn his eternal flame forever.

Retta decided to make a turn down a side street to shorten the walk. Luckily enough it ran right in front of her house as it intersected with Brentwood avenue.

Matt had also made this turn in order to take a short cut to the same street. He drove slowly and methodically not really in any hurry or even sight seeing but just doing what the term implied . . . cruising. Ant rode shotgun and Milton was in back behind Matt. The two of them had fought for the position but Ant being so tall blocked Milton from getting in so he had to accept back seat.

While Matt drove Ant and Milton were ogling at wolfing at just about anything that looked female. They called out or barked their approval or dislike at each one as they went. As Matt made his turn down a side street Milton saw a girl just ahead of them about twenty yards away. He noticed her hair was bound up in braids and she wore a black and red plaid skirt with a red polo shirt. He thought she looked really sexy and had planned to yell out to her once they got closer to her. As they got closer to her something about her struck a cord and Milton went silent. She looked strangely familiar the closer they got.

It wasn't so much the hair but the way she walked and her complexion. Matt wasn't paying her any attention and she was just another girl to him. The only woman he could see was Retta and she wasn't around at present or so he thought. He just kept on driving blindly his mind on other things.

Soon they passed the girl and Milton looked back at her with increased interest. Mostly because she had her head down and he couldn't really see her face clearly. For just a brief moment Retta raised her head just a little as the little car went by, and what Milton saw struck him like a blow to the chest.

"HEY MATT!... IT'S RETTA!" He shouted. Milton known to be a jokester was ignored by Matt as he kept his eyes on the road. Ant taking his cue from Matt chastised Milton and his poor taste in jokes. He looked in the rear view himself for his own verification and was shocked to find that it was her.

"MATT! THAT IS RETTA!" he yelled also. Matt was drawn to check his mirror and his heart was going a million miles a second as he squinted to see the girls face. A gentle breeze made her raise her head again and Matt heard his heart scream.

"OH MY GOD IT IS RETTA!" he jammed on the brakes, opened the door and got out.

Matt was totally animated now and nothing like either of his friends had ever seen before. In fact in Matt's haste he didn't even put on the brake or shut off the car but instead just got out leaving the car to roll slowly down hill. Matt stood there looking at his hearts love standing less than ten feet away. His heart was in his eyes, his stomach was in his throat and the car with no driver was rolling down hill increasing speed into a brick wall on Brentwood. Ant and Milton screamed and yelled as they fought to get control of the car as it picked up speed. Matt didn't hear their screams or yells nor did he care. He only saw Retta and the light of the heaven's on her face.

For a long moment Matt could not hear, he could not feel, all he saw was the most beautiful woman in the world standing there looking back at him and with all the love he felt himself. Retta was dumbstruck with surprise, happiness and despair all at the same time!

"My god it's Matt! Oh Jesus please don't let me be dreaming this!" She breathed warm tears beginning to roll down her cheeks. But she was not. It was the man of her dreams in the flesh and standing right before her. She felt a thick knot come into her throat and her nose twitched as more tears burned their way forth.

It seemed like an eternity had passed and the world had disappeared. All that remained was him and her. Matt's feet were like lead as he ran towards her. His heart pumped a mile a minute and his chest heaved heavily like he'd just ran a marathon. He was driven on by a power he had never felt before. It was akin to a deep hunger a need or a mortal desire to live and breathe.

Retta dropped her books and melted into him as his aching arms, arms that had not felt her or held her for months, had not tasted her flesh or relished in the warmth of her body seized her fiercely. The contact was like an electric explosion and they were fused together. Retta wilted in his embrace and cried her heart out as she clung to him for dear life.

Matt had no shame as well in the tears he let bathe her gentle head. He called her name over and over and begged, pleaded cried how much he loved her. He squeezed her tighter and tighter with each passing second. Retta pulled her head from his chest and fused her lips to his. There was a carnal hunger and deep seated need in the way the fed on each other's lips. They both whined and cried into each other's mouths but never broke the kiss.

Matt relished with intense pleasure of her mouth. She was hungry for him and her salty sweet tears mixed with his to flow down and into their mouths Matt felt as if his heart had exploded and the world was spinning around in his mind like a merry-go-round.

People had been looking out their doors at them, shaking their heads and marveling at the scene. Other kids who had gotten off the bus only moments ago had stopped along the street to ogle and be awed by the expression of great sadness and even greater love. Some could understand and some couldn't but none commented as they in their own time past or present had or would experience and endure a similar tragedy.

Retta and Matt didn't care because outside their embrace no one lived or existed. They at this time were each other's light in this dark world and the only life preserver in which to save the other from drowning.

Little did they know that Audrey as well was standing in her door also. She didn't see the scene as everyone else looking on. She saw the passionate infusion of her daughter and Matt as a blatant violation of her authority and she was livid with anger. She had been watching since Matt recklessly abandoned his car and placed into forfeit his friend's lives. She cursed him viciously under her breath and wanted to run out and slap them both. But for some reason she did not. She just stood there hating their love and blaming them as the ultimate cause of her loss.

No she figured that she would deal with Retta later and call the police on Matt with a bogus statutory rape charge, thus killing this disease of a love between them once and for all.

Retta finally broke from Matt, tears still flowing down her beautiful face. She hadn't seen but felt that she knew her mother must have seen them by now and there would be hell to pay for this. She didn't care for herself but only for him and didn't want him to be hurt or worse. As far as she was concerned there was no greater punishment than being denied the man in her arms. "Matt" she croaked not having he voice yet and strained from crying.

She held him tightly looking deeply into his tear filled eyes.

"You better go my love; Momma is probably watching us right this minute."

"How? She's not here, how can that be!" he begged tightening his grip not wanting to release her.

"Because we live just down the street behind you baby" she said sobbing softly.

"NO! Retta please! I can't leave you again, I love you!" he shouted in despair and at the surprise of those watching.

"I can't live without you! I can't breathe when you're not near me. My soul hurts when I want to touch you and your not there. I can't see myself being without you Retta . . . please don't let this happen" he begged.

Retta pulled his forehead down to hers.

"Neither can I my love, but she's become someone I don't even know, something evil and mean and it grows every day, she'll never give us any peace or let us be together Matt . . . I know this now."

Matt looked into her sweet face, eyes burning with anger and tears at the same time. He was hurting on a level beyond natural and he was not afraid to act on it.

"I don't care baby . . . we can run away or something . . . anything just don't leave me again I can't bear it . . . I just can't bear it!"

"Oh Matt" she whispered, tears filling her eyes as she held his face.

"I'll never love anyone but you no matter where I am or where I go, and no one can or will ever take me away from you because our love is forever."

"Retta I need you baby please don't go!" he begged again but understanding all she had said to him. Retta just kissed him once more in the best and most love and passionate filled way that she knew how. She felt if not knew that it would be the last time. Maybe for a while . . . maybe forever. She eased herself from him. Matt's mind was awash in confusion and madness. He didn't know what to do and was grasping wildly in his heart and mind for anything that would hold her, keep her there! But he could only grasp air.

He felt the weight of the ring he'd given her around his neck and reached up and broke the chain holding it.

"Please take this, as long as you have this you have me and our love will never die" he said pushing it into her hand and closing his hand around it.

"As long as you have this I can live on in your heart and know that I'm still with you as you will always be with me Retta" she shook her head sadly.

"Oh Matt I can't"

"You must! Now please take it before I do something crazy" Matt had never said anything so rash before and she had never heard him say anything so finite. She believed he would and took the ring and necklace and put them into the pocket of her skirt. She held him one last time.

"I'll love you till I die Matt" then pushed from him, gathered her books and ran crying from him towards her house.

Matt didn't turn to see her go; he just stood with his head down, tears falling like rain onto the dry pavement. He could hear murmuring from people who still watched and shuddered as he heard an old woman's voice say,

"Lordy lord look at that young man standing there crying his heart out like that. What kin dem youngun's know bout luv?"

Matt stood there until he felt the firm touch of a familiar hand on his shoulder. It was Ant. He and Milton had gotten control of the car before it crashed into the wall below, driven it around the corner and parked just up from them and saw everything that everyone else saw . . . maybe more.

"Come on Matt, let's go home" he said guiding him around the car and into the back seat.

No one spoke but just rode in silence until the street was only a memory . . . . or so it seems . . . .

Endnote

The love of a boy and a girl is a powerful and fragile thing. No one has the right or authority outside of God to say who has the right to feel or enter into it based on their age or anything else. Love is love and lasts eternal. For Aretta and Matt theirs was a unique romance of fire and ice. She loved him with a fever and he loved her as the sun loves the earth. Never again would either see their like another person as long as they lived . . . . or maybe longer. If you have a great and real love for someone don't abandon it, don't cheat it and don't sacrifice it for no one and no reason.

If you're young and in love relish it! Bask in it and endure it! Because the day you give it up or forsake it you will have lost so great a prize as no man can replace. Don't let anyone tell you that you don't know what love is when the feelings you have for that person go beyond sex, beyond reason and beyond time. If you don't know if the love you have or feel is real then there is one sure way to find out. Look at them from a distance, from a secret place and in quiet privacy without them seeing.

Do they make you feel as your seeing them for the first time? Are you falling in love just looking at them? When you hold them do you inhale deeply as if coming up for air? And finally is there any difference in how you feel about them from when they are dressed or nude? If your answer to any of these is yes . . . then you're in love and you love them no matter how old or young you are. Peace and much love to you all.